But if the cause be not good, the king himself hath a heavy reckoning to make. . . .
William Shakespeare, *Henry V*

"A hard-hitting saga of the Tet Offensive, it has an enormous cast of characters and a compelling plot enhanced by intimate knowledge of the land and people of Vietnam . . . an old-fashioned story that brings the horror as well as the nobility of war to life."
The Chattanooga Times

"An authentic action story that will appeal to a lot of people . . . a calm, close-up look at war the way fighting men from both sides saw it . . . accomplished with an authenticity that is informative as well as entertaining . . . doesn't lack for action . . . excellent reading and a very realistic, believable story."
The San Diego Tribune

"Sturdy . . . tells graphically and straightforwardly how the Vietnam war was fought on the ground . . . rings with authenticity."
Austin American-Statesman

Also by Chris Bunch and Allan Cole:

STEN

WOLF WORLDS

THE COURT OF A THOUSAND SUNS

FLEET OF THE DAMNED

A
RECKONING
FOR KINGS

Chris Bunch and Allan Cole

BALLANTINE BOOKS • NEW YORK

The poem "Eighth Air Force" by Randall Jarrell that appears on page 87 is used with the kind permission of Mary Jarrell.

Library of Congress Catalog Card Number: 85-48147

ISBN 0-345-34668-8

This edition published by arrangement with Atheneum Publishers, a division of the Scribner Book Companies, Inc.

Manufactured in the United States of America

First Ballantine Books Edition: January 1988

for
the late Norman and Margaret Dorn
Leo L. Bunch
Elizabeth Rice Bunch
the late Helen Frances Guinan
and
the names of the Black Wedge

*But if the cause be not good, the king
himself hath a heavy reckoning to make,
when all those legs and arms and heads,
chopped off in a battle, shall join
together at the latter day and cry all,
"We died at such a place"; some
swearing, some crying for a surgeon,
some upon their wives left poor behind
them, some upon the debts they owe, some
upon their children rawly left. I am
afeard there are few die well that die
in a battle; for how can they charitably
dispose of any thing, when blood is
their argument? Now, if these men do not
die well, it will be a black matter for
the king that led them to it . . .*

—**Shakespeare,**
Henry V, Act IV, Sc. 1

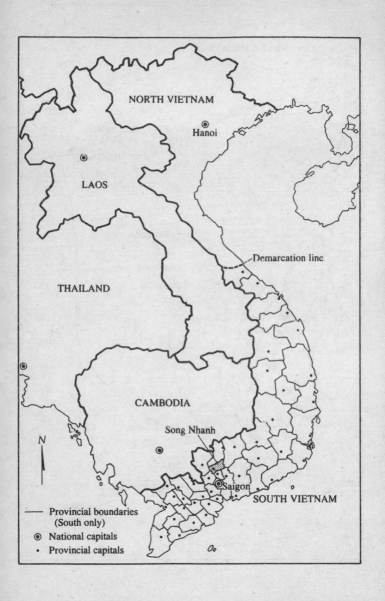

NORTH VIETNAM

Hanoi

LAOS

THAILAND

Demarcation line

CAMBODIA

Song Nhanh

Saigon

SOUTH VIETNAM

N

——— Provincial boundaries
(South only)
◎ National capitals
• Provincial capitals

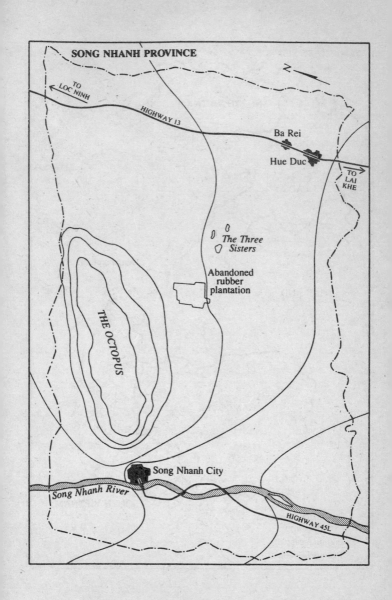

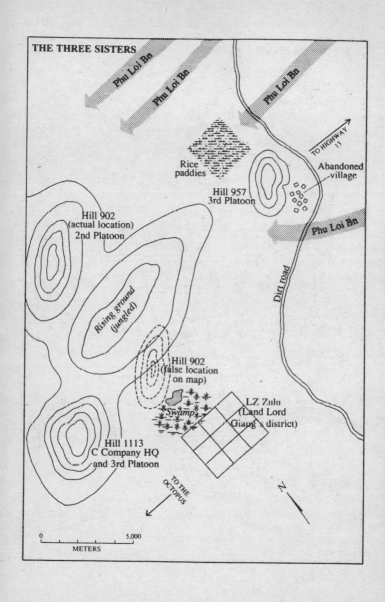

THE THREE SISTERS

Phu Loi Bn
Phu Loi Bn
Phu Loi Bn

TO HIGHWAY 13

Rice paddies

Abandoned village

Hill 957
3rd Platoon

Phu Loi Bn

Hill 902
(actual location)
2nd Platoon

Rising ground
(jungled)

Dirt road

Hill 902
(false location
on map)

Swamp

L.Z. Zulu
(Land Lord
Giang's district)

Hill 1113
C Company HQ
and 3rd Platoon

TO THE
OCTOPUS

N

0   5,000
METERS

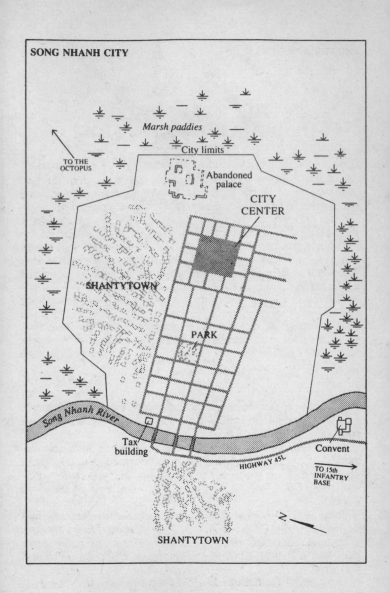

SONG NHANH CITY

Marsh paddies

City limits

TO THE OCTOPUS

Abandoned palace

CITY CENTER

SHANTYTOWN

PARK

Song Nhanh River

Tax building

Convent

HIGHWAY 45L

TO 15th INFANTRY BASE

N

SHANTYTOWN

THE 302D DIVISION,
NORTH VIETNAMESE ARMY

There are 7,000 of them. Burly peasants, mostly from the Red River region of North Vietnam. They're leavened with 500 old soldiers—battle-experienced ex-Viet Minh noncoms and officers.

Many of them are volunteers. Even in 1967, the Army of the Democratic Government of North Vietnam can offer a better life than the drudgery of farming. Some are reluctant volunteers, rootless, uneducated and unconnected young men of cities like Hung Yen or Hanoi. But they are all part of a division with proud traditions:

Formed in 1947, the division fought at Cao Bang, Lang Son, and, seven years later, the 302d was one of the first regular units committed to that hell in a very small place of Dien Bien Phu. Vo Nguyen Giap personally chose them to lead the first assault waves there against the outpost Beatrice, whose fall sounded the first tocsin of French defeat.

After that war, the 302d was built back to full strength and fought in countless jungle skirmishes on the Chinese border against Mao's soldiers. From 1958 to 1960, the North Vietnamese Army underwent intensive self-examination. It was a long, continuing purge that left only the dedicated.

Again the 302d survived. Its personnel were so highly regarded by the Lao Dung's Central Committee that they were filtered into Laos to supervise the opium harvest—a crop that was one of the few major exports of the struggling People's Republic.

They were withdrawn in 1963 and assigned to garrison duty at Yen Bai airfield outside Hanoi. They vegetated there for four years, seemingly ignored while the war drums from the south built into a thunder. But in the spring of 1967, the 302d was reassured.

The Central Committee had not forgotten its elite. The division was isolated in holding camps and built up to full strength. It was rearmed with new weaponry. New officers and new noncoms were assigned. Some of them were a little overweight from time behind a desk. Others had the pallor the perpetual jungle war gave. But all of them had the constantly flickering eyes with the wrinkles at the edges—wrinkles ground in by endless nights staring into blank night and forest. Eyes that were hardened by the war that had gone on since 1944, and might continue for another two generations.

Each man carried, as his personal basic load, about eighty pounds: a pack, one extra olive-green uniform, two pairs of sandals, one set of black pajamas, a raincoat, a shoddy nylon tent, a woven hammock, a mosquito net, a few meters of rope, a wicker helmet, and a very simple first-aid kit. They also carried their individual weapons: Chinese Type 56 copies of the Russian Kalashnikov or AK-47. It was one of the finest assault rifles ever built by any nation. Each man had 200 rounds of ammunition. Specially chosen men also carried radios, the broken-down 82mm or 120mm mortars, and RPD, SGM or Degtyarev machine guns.

The 302d was ready.

In October of 1967 their orders were given: march south.

They were to spearhead the long-awaited General Offensive. The offensive that would overthrow the puppet government of the South and destroy the hated American colonialists.

The attack would begin during the traditionally peaceful celebration of the Vietnamese New Year.

Tet.

1968.

The Year of the Monkey.

In the final hours before they marched, some soldiers of the 302d Division had themselves tattooed: "I was born in the north . . . to die in the south . . . ."

THE TWELFTH INFANTRY DIVISION, UNITED STATES ARMY

FTA was lettered on the back of the infantryman's sun-bleached camouflage helmet cover: FUCK THE ARMY.

The grunt was plodding up a 30-degree slope trying to keep in the ribbed-sole footprints of the man ahead of him. One grunt—lost, pissed off, dirty, smelly and bewildered.

He was one of almost 18,000 Americans who wore the patch of the Twelfth Infantry Division: a black bayonet inside a red, flat-bottomed arch. Since he was a line soldier, there was about a forty percent chance the man was black. He almost certainly had a secondary education or less. He was most probably from the South or Midwest. And he was likely nineteen years old.

This particular grunt was four months into his tour, and he could instantly tell you how many days, hours, and possibly even minutes were left of the thirteen months before he was rotated back to the Land of the Big PX.

The grunt also was eighteen days out of a shower, had worn the same uniform for twenty-two days, had eaten a hot meal twice in that time, and had not fired his rifle in the last month and a half.

He had no idea where he or the rest of the men in his company were. Three weeks ago helicopters had dropped his battalion into a valley somewhere in South Vietnam's piedmont.

Then the 600-man battalion had formed up in company-size elements—around 100 men—and the battalion commander had given this grunt's CO a mission: Proceed so many klicks on such-and-so compass heading to this point (a ballpoint indentation on the captain's map) and form a perimeter for the night. Viet Cong, in estimated two-company strength, are operational somewhere in this area. The ballpoint had easily circled a ten-square-mile area. Search and destroy.

Orders went down the chain, and the grunt heaved himself to

his feet and started to hump. For twenty-two days he had seen nothing but jungle and the sweat-dark back of the man in front of him during the day, and nothing but black silence in front of his scraped-out fighting position at night.

In the Twelfth Division's war diary, the sweep probably had been given some impressive-sounding name like OPERATION LIGHTNING STRIKE, FREEDOM.

The grunt would never hear that name, unless he happened to find a copy of *Stars and Stripes* in the shitter when he returned to base. To him the divisional motto, TO CLOSE WITH AND DESTROY, wasn't even a tired joke.

Most of the 18,000 men in the Twelfth never went beyond their unit's perimeter. They were the cooks, clerks, drivers, runners, specialists, signalmen, mechanics and other support people necessary to put one infantryman in the field.

Few of them had ever seen the division's usually glass-encased battle flag at headquarters, or knew the Twelfth's battle streamers nearly hid the flag itself: Meuse-Argonne . . . German occupation . . . Sicily . . . Anzio . . . Cassino . . . St. Lô . . . the Huertgen Forest . . . Malmédy . . . the Rhine Crossing . . . Inchon . . . the Punchbowl.

Even for the old soldiers those honors were forgotten men and wars. For the Twelfth, there was nothing but Vietnam.

The division's operational area was from just beyond the Saigon Circle (an arc scribed forty-five miles around South Vietnam's capital), stretching north to the Cambodian border—basically covering the province of Song Nhanh.

The Twelfth had three base camps—Division Headquarters and Second Brigade outside the village of Hue Duc, First Brigade at Lang Chu, and Third Brigade at Dau Tien.

By October of 1967, the division had been in-country seventeen months. The men who had come over in the initial deployment had gone home: some in the gray caskets unloaded at Davis Air Force Base in California; some to hospitals in Japan, San Francisco, or Pennsylvania; and the very lucky, the skillful, or simply those who had served far beyond the lines were trying to get themselves back into America and forget Vietnam had ever touched them. Then replacements filtered in, and in turn were educated, became skilled, were wounded, killed, or survived.

The Twelfth Division was blooded and ready. Now all it needed was an enemy. Not one that murdered from the ditch, or from the darkness of night, but an enemy in the open—an enemy the Twelfth, using the sledge of American technology, could "Close With And Destroy."

That enemy was filtering toward them down a thousand miles of trail.

PART ONE:

OCTOBER 3-12, 1967

We're going to win this war if it takes our lives to do it.

**—Lyndon Baines Johnson, quoting graffiti
he claimed to have seen in Vietnam**

We are beginning to win this struggle . . . we are making steady progress.

—Vice President Hubert H. Humphrey

With 1968, a new phase is starting. We have reached an important point when the end begins to come into view.

**—General William C. Westmoreland,
Commander, all U.S. Vietnam troops**

The Viet Cong has been defeated from Da Nang all the way down in the populated areas.

**—General Bruce Palmer,
Deputy Commander, U.S. Army, Vietnam**

Man, I be sayin' to everybody, these dudes in black pajamas, they be winnin' the war. It they bush. It they jungle. They say jump, man, we jump. Sooner come later, they come out they bush and they kick our asses. We be lucky we end up only be in Australia.

**—Anonymous SP/4,
101st Airborne Division**

CHAPTER ONE

SHANNON

MAJOR DENNIS SHANNON sat with his feet hanging out of the Huey. Below him swam the night jungle. He checked the glowing dial of the Rolex on the inside of his wrist and his heart increased its pounding. *Two minutes.*

Two hundred meters away whapped the bulk of the lead UH-ID: the decoy ship. Then his mouth went dry as the Huey nosed down and the pilot twisted the collective. The helicopter moved abreast of the first ship.

Shannon checked the other troops in his Huey. Darkness. Only the sudden grin of teeth from Williams, the LRRP team commander, sitting by the door gunner. One thing the black cats got going for them, Shannon thought, is they don't have to worry about camouflage at night.

The second hand on the Rolex crossed, and Shannon signaled the pilot. The helicopter swooped down toward a rice paddy: the LZ.

The theory was if you wanted to insert eleven troops into Indian Territory without the Bad Guys knowing about it, you took two helicopters and flew like a motherfucker across their stronghold. One chopper would make lots of noise, while the second dropped down and dumped out the Long Range Recon Patrol. Then the second ship would lift back out, and hopefully, nobody would be the wiser. The Lurps would be left to get on about their business.

And how many times, Dennis old boy, Shannon thought, has that theory been proven full of donkey shit?

But the jungle was coming up fast and the clearing was below and the chopper was flaring for its landing . . . ten fucking feet too high, you cocksucker, and Shannon was balanced on the skid, almost overtoppling, and he came off in a classic PLF, but without the roll because this rice paddy ain't as abandoned as it

5

looks on the map, and who wants to swallow shit, but if it *is* dried up I could bust a leg and . . .

He plummeted into five feet of muck. Even over the turbine whine and the slosh of the paddy water from the helicopter blades, he heard other troops falling into the paddy.

And then, thank the good lord, *whopwhopwhop* as the fucking pilot got his finger out and took that shitbird the hell out of it and . . .

Silence. Blackness.

Shannon crouched, ready. Then he realized: Jesus God! Softly moved the bolt of the K gun back until it was cocked. Go in hot, you dumb mick son-of-a-bitch, and you ain't even ready. You're getting too old for this. Almost twenty-eight. Leave this crap for the kids. Or kiss your sweet Irish ass good-bye.

Quit playing old home week.

You're supposed to be back at the Ossifers' Club waiting for word from and I quote your recon elements and I end quote. Drinking beer. What the hell are you doing standing in a rice paddy up to your ass in shit with a bunch of dumbass kids who haven't learned any better?

Aw, shut the fuck up. You're here. Besides, Williams is fifty years old. Doesn't matter. Silly son of a bitch has been recon for three wars now. His brains are fried.

Knock it off! Look at your damned treeline, Shannon. Don't you remember? Watch the trees, asshole. Okay. Get yourself back together. Stop thinking you're a big-time Assistant Division Intelligence Idiot and start playing Cowboys and Gooks. Because that's what they're playing.

Eleven men crouched in the muck, waiting. Shannon started to motion, then caught himself. This isn't your war anymore, remember? He looked at Williams. The man was still waiting. What the fuck is he waiting for?

Then Williams brought up his arm. Held one arc of the tiny LRRP perimeter in place. Motioned for a lead element to head for the treeline.

And Shannon moved. Sloshing, for Chrissakes. Goddamned U.S. technology. How come nobody ever found a way to build good goddamned boots that don't fill up, or else simply rot?

The rice paddy was only half farmed. They came to a dike and Williams's M-60 man crouched. The troopies slithered over the dike like so many crazed tiger-stripe-camouflaged lizards. Put a damned chameleon on a camo shirt and the fucker'd go crazy, Shannon thought, a little hysterically, as he rolled over and came into a firing position. Thank you, God. Dry land.

The patrol assembled. Williams and Shannon quickly conferred over the map boards and lensatic compass, the conversation done completely with long-practiced shrugs, waves, gestures and expressions.

Is that shadow over there where we want to go? Does it look like a hilltop? Damfino, but good guess. How far are we from Cambodia? Good question. Pricks probably dropped us twenty klicks inside. Wouldn't be the first time, would it? Fuck no.

Fucking maps, Shannon thought. "Made from good data." My ass, good data. Basic survey by the Japanese, confirmed by the French . . . and we all know what happened to them . . . so trust this map if you feel like it.

Shannon always figured Army maps, especially the 1:25,000 projections that a LRRP team so desperately needed, should have some kind of a commercial disclaimer: WARNING: FOLLOWING THIS MAP COULD BE HAZARDOUS TO YOUR HEALTH.

Very cute, Dennis, he thought. And followed the shadows toward the treeline and toward the Cambodian border.

CHAPTER TWO

DUAN

THE COMRADE GENERAL'S back was cold. He stood, wet and shaking, outside Sister Marie Teresa's office. Someone kept saying "Comrade General." But he ignored the voice. Duan knew he was really not a general poised on the border of Cambodia, but a terrified schoolboy who had been sent to the Mother Superior, and he was standing in the rain waiting for the rasp of her voice.

The punishment, he realized, would be severe. He had been caught with an indelicate picture of a woman clipped from some German magazine. Sister Teresa was a nun who believed that all girls' breasts should be bound and small boys should eternally sing in the key of C. She was also French. That meant she hated not only the Vietnamese, but Germans as well.

Whatever the punishment would have been for a picture of a nude French-woman, ten extra blows would be added because the picture was of a Boche. Duan stood in the rain, as frightened as he would ever be in his entire life. And the voice kept prodding him: "Comrade General . . . Comrade General . . ."

Vo Le Duan, Commanding General, 302d Division, People's

Army of Vietnam, opened his eyes to see his batman bending over him. As ugly and menacing a face as he had ever seen. But at the moment Sergeant Lau was quite beautiful. Duan was back in the war again and would miss his appointment with the Mother Superior.

"You just saved me from a French nun," he muttered.

The sergeant puzzled, then realized what Duan was talking about. He laughed.

"You fear dreams of nuns. In mine, I am always fleeing angry water buffaloes."

Duan yawned, beginning to come awake.

"There was a man in my village," Lau continued, "who believed bad dreams had a meaning and provided us with a warning."

Duan was interested. "Do you think he was correct?"

"I was never sure. For two weeks once, he dreamed that our village was being drowned in high floods. And so he retreated to the hills, and built himself a hut."

"A prudent man," Duan said.

"Perhaps. But when I took him rice for his evening meal, all I found were the few small bones a tiger had left."

The Comrade General chuckled. "Thank God," he said, "that our current enemies are not immortal like nuns, tigers and water buffalo."

He shifted in his hammock, searching for the first cigarette. And felt the cold water splash against his back. A look on Sergeant Lau's face told him what had happened. Lau was about to explode in laughter. Duan looked about him and realized the ties on his hammock had slipped down the tree trunks while he slept. He had spent most of the night slopping about in a spreading monsoon puddle.

"The man in your village was wrong. I did not dream of floods."

Finally Lau did break into laughter. "Comrade General," his friend said, "it's time to get up. Your ass is wet."

There was no easy way to do it, so Duan rolled out of the sagging hammock into the mud. He creaked to his feet, trying to ignore nearly five decades worth of protest in six hundred and fifty-some-odd muscles.

The sergeant handed Duan a mug of tea, and the general whispered a prayer to whatever gods helped stomachs and took his first sip. The tannic acid hit, curled and rebounded. Quickly Duan took another gulp to settle himself out. He hated tea, especially in the morning. The Comrade General preferred coffee, hot, thick and black. But he was several thousand kilometers away from coffee. He grimaced at his weakness. I might as well wish for Florida orange juice. Or hot French chocolate and croissants.

While the sergeant pumped up the tiny Primus stove for the morning rice, Duan squatted near his hammock, dressed only in his loincloth. He lit the rather soggy cigarette he'd been absently dangling from the corner of his mouth and watched Lau at work.

The sergeant was a short, stocky man, a little older than the general. He had huge hands that worked in small delicate motions as he added spices to the ricewater. Lau crumbled a few tiny, fire-hot Red River peppers into the rice. Automatically, his batman handed Duan one whole pepper. And, just as automatically, Duan popped it into his mouth and chewed. His ears turned to flame as he flushed the pepper down with a huge gulp of tea. Lau handed him another pepper. Duan hesitated.

"One more," the sergeant insisted. "For the crossing. Besides, even that Mongol Mao says that the true test of a revolutionary is his liking for peppers."

The Comrade General ate the second pepper as well. It was only to keep his batman happy, he told himself. A minor peasant superstition. Lau seemed to believe that those peppers cured everything from fever to snakebite to flagging virility. Duan snorted to himself about the virility part. It would be months, if ever, before he slept with a woman again. Thinking about women bothered Duan slightly. It had been a long time since he had felt any desire. Yes, he frequently thought of his long-dead wife and his mistress in Hanoi. But rarely in a sexual sense. Mostly he remembered the nuns when he thought about women. Particularly Sister Teresa, the Mother Superior. The Terrible White-Winged Bat of Hue, the city of his birth.

Lau dumped out a huge bowl of rice for himself and a much smaller portion for the general. Duan scooped up a mouthful with his fingers. It was pungent, and good as only the Red River Vietnamese made rice, but the general had little appetite. He was almost never hungry anymore. The sergeant finished his rice, squatted, farted and lit one of the general's cigarettes, waiting for Duan to give him his leftovers.

The general and the sergeant had been friends for years. They had met near Dien Bien Phu, when the general was a young major and the sergeant was . . . well, a sergeant.

It seemed to Duan that Lau had never changed. Thirteen years ago, he had been just as stocky and had the same round face

9

with the smile that hated officers, distrusted any and all authority, and mocked politics. Comrade was a moderately dirty word on his lips. But Lau was a patriot, as only a farmer can be with generations buried in his own land. Most of all, Lau had remained what he was at Dien Bien Phu—a survivor. Duan thought of him as the universal sergeant. There must have been men like him with Alexander's phalanxes, the Trung sisters' army, the Roman legions, or the Trinh rebels. Farmers, forced from their fields, handed weapons, and ordered to march and die..

Duan thought it odd that Lau still considered himself a farmer, although he hadn't seen the business end of a water buffalo since his late teens, when he was pressed into the People's Cause. Lau was a man of no formal education. Duan had taught him to read and write, both French and Vietnamese. After that major victory, Duan had pressed the classic books on Lau, but Lau's idea of relaxed reading was less Malraux than an after-action report from a stupid officer. The more idiotic the report was and the more flowery the language, the more Lau would howl in laughter.

Like most farmers, Lau was a fatalist. Whatever was going to happen would, and Lau believed he had no control over destiny. On the whole, he would rather live than die—but realized he was unlikely to be consulted in the matter. Duan considered that was what had kept Lau alive for so many years. As it has me, he thought. Duan realized he'd had as little choice in his life as did his batman.

Vo Le Duan's father had been an official in the French-ruled Vietnamese government, and his mother a secondary-level teacher of French history. Vietnamese history, of course, was banned in the colonialist-run schools. Duan remembered childhood as a long, happy dream. He knew it couldn't really have been like that—undoubtedly his mind, over the years of mud and blood, had created those warm, drifting memories as a shelter. But Duan preferred to keep those memories, even though they were false security.

The child Duan had one great talent. Mathematics. At three, he could look at the food on his mother's stove and automatically divide it by the number of people expected for dinner. Since his family entertained often, both sets of numbers were large—giving Duan an interesting set of mental playthings to work with further: If we had sixteen guests, four of them French pigs, and one-third liter of nuoc mam, and the only non-Viet who uses nuoc mam on his fish is that Legion para sergeant, and if that one-third liter is gone, how much more nuoc mam would we have needed, if the colonists knew what tastes good?

At five, Duan kept a running tabulation of the food costs and discovered the cook was padding the monthly bill. Duan was always proud of himself for saying nothing. Of course, the sweets he levied for the silence may have been a significant part of that decision.

Even with his talent, Duan knew by the time he was ten that there would be only three careers for him. He could become a paper-shuffling clerk like his father, teach meaningless imperialist jargon, or work in a shop. But to become a theoretical mathematician like his heroes Einstein, Planck or Heisenberg— impossible. The University of Hanoi, Indo-China's most revered institution, did not even have a science department. Only by emigrating to France or possibly Russia would there be any hope for a career in pure mathematics. Leaving Vietnam was unthinkable for Duan.

When the French surrendered to Japan in 1940, Duan, like almost all Vietnamese, was ecstatic. The Japanese, through their Vichy puppets, upgraded the Vietnamese into major administrative positions, built roads, and even began encouraging Vietnamese writers and painters. But the Japanese were still foreigners. And, by 1944, it was known through the street rumors, they were losing the war.

This meant that the French imperialists would inevitably return. And so, late in 1944, Duan picked his career. A fourth choice. He went north, traveling by foot, and joined the Provisional Republican Government of Vietnam. The nationalists. The tiny group was headed by a tall, thin, polite man with icy eyes and a long, stringy beard. The man was then known as Nguyen Ai Quoc. Later he would change his name to the Vietnamese words for He Who Enlightens: Ho Chi Minh.

Quoc had already formed an alliance with the Americans: Office of Strategic Services/China. Quoc believed that only the U.S. could keep France from returning to Indo-China, after the war's end.

Duan was given an American M-1 carbine, and assigned to a raiding squad. The leader of his squad was instructed to watch Duan very closely, and to report on his performance to the Central Committee. The only measure of ability for a guerrilla is to survive. Duan, after a series of ambushes on Nippon columns, still lived. Then he was ordered to report to the Central Committee. Somehow, Ho and his aides had heard of Duan's talents in mathematics.

They offered him a position as an officer—an artillery officer. The liberation forces' cannon were limited—a few mortars given them by Chiang Kai-shek's robber barons, some elderly WWI French 75s, and two 37mm guns from the American OSS. But even then, artillery was a snobbish, elite position, with historic roots both Oriental and Occidental. A man who could calculate the earth, the sun, the planets and the stars to get a heavenly map that resulted in godlike destruction many kilometers away was to be respected for his abilities. Duan's talent had saved him from death—his raiding squad was wiped out, two weeks after he left them, by being sucked into an ambush set up by the Japanese.

Then the Japanese surrendered. Ho Chi Minh declared Vietnam independent. In October 1945, the French, courtesy of British transports, returned to Vietnam. America was more interested in salving the consciences of the collaborationist French than in any real commitment to the Vietnamese nationalists. The world disavowed any intention of letting Vietnam keep its freedom.

In 1946, Ho went to war again. This time, against the French. Slowly, as the French troops suffered defeat after defeat, the Viet Minh's artillery forces grew. By 1954, Duan was a major, assigned to the 315th Heavy Division, and on his way to the Giap-engineered bear trap of Dien Bien Phu.

But on the march west, Duan was suddenly detached and given a command of his own. He was a battery commander, responsible for three American 75mm pack howitzers, recently captured from the French forces in Laos. Unfortunately, while the troops assigned to his battery were somewhat familiar with artillery, they knew nothing about the jungle, the mountains or the rivers that seemed intent on killing the men and destroying their cannons on the way to Dien Bien Phu.

By the time his battery was two days away from Dien Bien Phu, half of Duan's troops were suffering from malaria, dysentery or jungle sores. The rest were victims of diseases of the spirit.

Two kilometers below Muong Pon, they were ambushed by a roving French GCMA patrol. Duan had been in his share of firefights before, but to him this one would always be the worst. He was within sight of his goal—the mountain of Pha Song and he was already cringing at the cliffs that had to be climbed and the bones that would be broken pulling those damned cannon over them.

Two machine guns stuttered into the jungle noise. Duan's men dropped to the ground, crawling, screaming and dying. Duan

12

was shouting at them to shoot—shoot at the *colons*! And then fall back.

The third Browning machine gun opened up on their only open flank. Duan remembered everything—the black tumble of grenades as the commandos arced them onto the trail . . . thudding rifle fire as his men shot blindly into the brush . . . the double flame spear of a bazooka firing . . . Duan pulling a grenade bandolier from the sprawled corpse of a gunlayer . . . then, on his feet, finger through the ring at the bottom of the wooden handle, and then shouting, running running into that fire spatter.

A hundred years later, he found himself sobbing beside the ruined French machine gun. There were three camouflage-uniformed bodies by the gun. The other Frenchmen had vanished. Half of the men in Duan's battery were dead or useless. Worst of all, one howitzer was lying on its side, the wheel lying meters away. The bazooka round had put paid to the second gun: barrel, shield, sights and carriage lay scattered around the bodies of the crewmen. Only the third gun was intact.

It was the first and only time that Duan had ever contemplated suicide. It wasn't merely a failure—he knew that without those two guns firing into the cauldron of Dien Bien Phu, many of his countrymen would perish.

There was a slight rustling of bamboo. Duan did not care, turn, nor raise his weapon. Another commando might be the simplest answer.

A second later, a short, squat man stepped out of the jungle. He hesitated, then turned the cocking piece on his Mosin-Nagant to safe and knelt beside Duan. There was a gurgle from a canteen, and then a rag mopped mud and blood away from Duan's face.

"Congratulations, comrade," the man said.

"For what," Duan said as he stumbled up.

"For surviving."

Duan did not bother answering that idiocy. The short man wore the rank tabs of a bo-doi sergeant and spoke in the clipped northern Vietnamese accent Duan had always hated, since to even the peasants of the Haute Region anyone from South Vietnam was considered a backward child. It was quite easy for Duan to turn his current wave of self-loathing toward the sergeant.

He tried blustering: "Comrade Sergeant! Where are your men? What are your orders?"

The sergeant seemed to ignore the question and strolled around

13

one of the ruined guns. He also ignored Duan's men, who, still shocked and bewildered, were clustering around him.

"Since you did at least kill a couple of the Tays, and destroyed this machine gun," the sergeant said thoughtfully, "I am sure, Comrade Major, that the commissars will award you a medal. After they shoot you for losing their cannon."

He shook his head, then farted loudly. It may have been a signal, as a moment later fifteen ragged men slipped out of the brush. Duan noticed, as the men began wordlessly tending Duan's wounded, that they may have been wearing rags, but their weapons, which varied from Japanese 7.7mm Arisaka rifles through American carbines to the sergeant's Russian rifle, were all very clean.

The sergeant took a tobacco pouch made from a buffalo's scrotum from under his wicker hat, sprinkled tobacco onto a torn newspaper, and rolled a cigarette. He rasped a wooden match across his rifle barrel, lit the cigarette, and passed it to Duan.

"As to your question, Comrade Major," he said, rolling another cigarette for himself, "I am Lau. Once the worst farmer in all of Bac Can, and now personally chosen by Uncle Ho to lead these fellow pigshit-waders in battle against the colonialist mercenaries."

He blew smoke.

"Do you not admire, Comrade Major, how well I have learned from the commissars' indoctrination sessions?"

Duan was about to explode, when Lau continued.

"As to my orders, Comrade Major, I have no idea. We are lost."

Then Duan noticed how badly his hands were shaking. He left the cigarette in his mouth and pressed his arms against his sides. The sergeant pretended not to notice. "Where are you going, then?" Duan's command voice was returning.

"Who knows." The sergeant shrugged. "We are following the airplanes. Sooner or later, they will lead us to where there are Frenchmen to kill. And I think there will be commissars and officers at that place to tell us which ones to kill first."

And, without a pause: "I can move your guns."

It took almost a minute for Lau's phrase to get through. And it took almost a full day before Duan actually believed him. Only when Duan looked at the line of elephants standing before him in the slow afternoon rain did he start to understand.

Lau said he had purchased them at a local village. Duan did not ask where the sergeant had found money. He was starting to believe that maybe, just maybe, Sergeant Lau could get the guns to Dien Bien Phu.

Duan's men had broken the two surviving howitzers down as far as their limited tools enabled them. Lau had then considered the bazookaed third howitzer and pointed out which pieces to take from the wreckage.

Duan had asked him why.

"With these parts, we shall be able to make at least two other guns function, Comrade Major. Is that not obvious? Perhaps the Comrade Major is still suffering from shock and should lie down under a tree."

Duan decided that the sergeant's self-examination session and subsequent court-martial would wait until they reached Dien Bien Phu. The loading began. Lau cursed at his men as they shifted and heaved. Duan noticed, however, that the sergeant always was lifting the heaviest parts. The problem was that elephants are trained to *push* huge logs, not to carry them. The eight-foot-tall, monsoon-gray monsters watched the little men suspiciously as the pieces of steel were stacked beside them.

Lau ordered the first piece—a barrel—to be lifted onto an elephant's back and lashed in place. The frightened men obediently bent, lifted and strained.

The elephant flicked its trunk absently, as if it were slapping an insect. One of Duan's men went sailing into the brush. The others dropped the steel tube and scattered. Lau hustled them together again.

"Lift," he ordered. The men refused. Angrily, Lau grabbed the barrel himself and strained one end of it off the ground.

"Help me," he shouted.

Still the men did not move.

Duan almost laughed as the elephant waved its trunk at Lau in warning. But the sergeant just became angrier. He dropped the end of the barrel and unleashed a stream of curses.

"Cowards," Lau shouted at the men and the elephants. "Lazy cowards. Give me a pig any day. Or even a water buffalo. You can talk to a pig. But an elephant . . ."

And then Duan witnessed one of the more improbable scenes of his life. The elephant, obviously not used to abuse from casual strangers, bellowed and rose on its hind legs. He towered buildings over the squat Lau. The sergeant took one measured step forward under the rearing elephant and kicked it squarely in the balls.

Duan waited for Lau to die.

He was somewhat amazed as the elephant whimpered, settled

15

back on its hind legs, then, as Lau stepped away, the beast lowered itself gingerly forward. And began moaning. The other elephants—even the females, Duan noticed—quieted down and shuffled into line. Lau, however, was not looking at them. He was glaring at the men. He didn't say a word. Lau didn't need to.

Two hours later, the elephants were loaded and peacefully trundling down the trail, toward the peaks overlooking Dien Bien Phu.

Now General Duan laughed to himself at the memory of the elephant with the furrowed brow, who kept looking worriedly at the squat figure of Lau marching beside him.

While Sergeant Lau cleaned up after the morning meal, General Duan began dressing. He thought there should be some kind of ceremony, as he carefully rolled the olive drab uniform he had worn on the long march down the Ho Chi Minh Trail and pulled on the plain black pajamas of a peasant soldier.

From now on, he and the other men of the 302d North Vietnamese Division would appear to be Soldiers of the Public Regime—what the imperialists called Viet Cong. It was a minor fiction—minor, of course, depending on the point of view—that the diplomats of Hanoi and the National Liberation Front's Central Committee insisted on.

Duan would also wear no badges of rank. How this would supposedly keep an enemy soldier from seeing him as a most desirable target Duan could never understand, since he would always be surrounded by aides, bodyguards and radiomen. Anyone who could not identify Duan as a Most Important Person would be a very poor soldier indeed.

Duan finished dressing, and picked up his AK-47—a weapon he carried quite deliberately, instead of the pistol his rank entitled him to. He had learned long ago that a pistol was less than useless for anything other than parades. Then he performed the final morning ritual, one which it seemed he had done for most of his life. Remove the magazine from the rifle. Check the rounds. Depress the top round slightly to make sure the magazine spring still held its tension.

Move the cocking handle of the Kalashnikov (actually, of course, it was the Chinese-built Type 56 copy of the AK) to the rear. No round in the chamber. Rub the rifle down with an oily rag, and then replace the magazine. Finally ready, Duan slung his rifle and picked up his map case. Lau snapped him a half-salute.

"We followers eagerly await your undoubtedly historical orders, Comrade General," he said.

Duan smiled, and slapped his friend on the shoulder.

"When will you learn to respect officers?"

The sergeant grinned and pointed.

"When the leeches stay in the trees, Comrade General."

Duan looked where Lau was pointing and swore. Lau handed him his cigarette, and Duan pressed its glowing tip to the leech wriggling between his left thumb and forefinger.

"Speaking of leeches," Lau added, "the Comrade Commissar is waiting."

Duan cursed again. The last person he particularly wanted to see was Colonel Thuy.

"He advised me that he had a few suggestions about the morale of our fellow warriors."

"Tell that skinny snake's ass," the general barked, "that I will see him when I am ready."

This time Lau snapped a very proper, very military salute. And this time the general returned it, and the little sergeant wheeled and marched off. It was a message Lau would be delighted to deliver.

CHAPTER THREE

SHANNON

THE WORLD CRAWLED from black to gray to sudden light. Shannon glumly watched the ten bushes around him slowly become people.

The LRRP stakeout was on a hill overlooking the Cham River, which demarcated—more or less—the border between South Vietnam and Cambodia. The patrol was about 400 meters from that border, waiting for something to happen.

For the ten-thousandth time, Shannon wondered what the hell he was doing here. What appalled him almost more than anything was that it was *his* idea. A few days ago, it had all seemed pretty logical. After all, he was acting Division G-2. Instead of sitting on his ass sifting through intelligence reports, he ought to get out there among the grunts once in a while.

Also Shannon thought he had been getting a bit soft. What kind of a badass Ranger was he, anyway? Sitting around shuffling papers and watching his love handles grow.

17

It had all seemed logical at the time. And so he had pulled strings and twisted some arms to join this little Lurp party.

Shannon decided it was probably some fatal genetic flaw in his makeup. Sort of like baldness or leukemia. His father liked to joke that the Shannons as far back as anyone could remember seemed to have had an affinity for testing and retesting the family jewels by sticking their ass into the line of fire.

It was a joke Dennis's ex-wife hadn't appreciated. She'd divorced him after he had volunteered for his second tour in Nam. Actually, Dennis realized, he couldn't really blame Vietnam for the breakup. The divorce had been a long time coming. Lisa had never really been comfortable being a quote Army dependent end quote. Even during their dating years when he was at the Point she'd hated the military.

Dennis couldn't blame her. The Army wasn't much of a life for anyone. He was just used to it.

Shannon had been visiting his parents in California when he'd received the final consent decree. Lisa had been pretty easy on him. The alimony and child support were more than fair. And the terms of the visitation rights very liberal. He could see his sons two weekends a month, and they could stay with him a month every summer. Which in practical terms—since Shannon was a lifer—meant that he could see them almost never. That night, he and his father had gotten very drunk.

The Shannon family was proud of the fact that a Shannon had fought in every war (including some not even on the books) since they arrived from Ireland. Oddly enough, they were not per se patriotic. But the Shannons were highly political. "We like to be involved," Dennis's father had explained.

Physically, there were only three types of Shannons: black hair, with blue eyes and freckles; blond hair with blue eyes and freckles; and deep red hair with blue eyes and freckles. Dennis fell into the first category. And, like his ancestors he stood about six feet, with a 44-plus-inch chest.

His grandfather used to brag that Shannon men could out-pull a mule. They could also out-drink one, too, which his grandfather Emmett demonstrated regularly until the day of his death.

Dennis's grandfather was also considered the black sheep of the family. He was one of the few Shannons since Revolutionary times who had not served in the Army. He'd been a Marine. It was a subject no one liked to discuss—except his grandfather when he was in his cups.

He drank his bourbon neat, in delicate little family heirloom teacups. Dennis kept lookout for his grandmother as the old man

18

dumped out the pot of tea she used to prepare him every afternoon, and refilled it with whiskey.

Dennis suspected that she knew. How couldn't she? By 5 P.M. every day the room reeked of bourbon, his grandfather's face was flushed, and he spoke slowly, enunciating every word carefully. He would also start giving his wife a pinch when he thought Dennis wasn't looking. Dennis liked to think that the old woman traded the bourbon for the pinches.

Most of all, Dennis remembered the stories. Whenever he visited, he watched carefully until the old man had drunk his third cup of "tea." Then Dennis would fetch him his pipe, move up the stool, and wait quietly as his grandfather adjusted his wooden leg, refilled his teacup, and began telling stories.

The whole history of the Shannons was in the old man's head. And since the history of the Shannons was war, young Dennis saw battle after battle through the eyes of each of his ancestors. His grandfather rarely talked about his own experiences. Mostly he stuck to his early days when he had been an Army brat like Dennis growing up in the hot, dry forts of the Southwest. The boy's jaw dropped when he realized that his own great-grandfather had been an Indian fighter just like Jimmy Stewart.

Only once had the old man talked about his own days at war. He'd stopped talking in the middle of some other story. And sat silent for what seemed like hours, staring into the fire. He began talking again, very quietly, and Dennis heard about Belleau Woods, 1918. He walked with his grandfather through the thick yellow fog of mustard gas and heard the booming of the artillery and the clatter of the Maxim guns.

The whole time the old man talked, he rubbed at the place where the wooden leg joined the stump. Finally Dennis felt the bullet rip and then lived through the hours in the shattered forest until the stretcher came. And then the hours more in the butcher's tent. After the surgery was done, his grandfather had nearly died from fever.

The old man paused a moment, fiddling with his pipe. Then he turned and fixed the boy Dennis with his rheumy eyes.

"I think I learned then," his grandfather said, "that God loves war almost more than a Shannon."

He chuckled.

"Otherwise, he would have stopped me then and I wouldn't have bred your father. And where would God be without a Shannon to fight his wars?"

Nearly twenty years later, Dennis realized there was some truth in what the old man had said. He doubted that Lisa, no

19

matter how ardent a pacifist, could keep at least one of his sons from following the road of the Shannons. But after three tours of Vietnam, it was a fact that did not delight him. By now, Dennis would have given his soul to have one generation of Shannons without blood on its hands.

Not that Dennis hadn't had his own chance to opt out of the killing machine. Strangely enough, his own father had been the most opposed to West Point and all that followed. To enter the Point, Dennis had turned his back on a Georgetown University scholarship (won through grades and his father's contacts in the CIA), and a potential diplomatic career. At the time, it seemed like the logical thing to do. Like being here—right now—on a little hill above the Cambodian border had appeared a week ago.

Actually, it wouldn't take even an armchair psychologist to figure out why Dennis had consistently made the choices he had. Because if there was any man that Dennis admired or loved more than his grandfather, it was his father.

Frank Shannon was a big, burly, silent man, who showed his affection to his son by listening whenever the boy wanted to talk. He never spoke of himself, and what little Dennis knew and could guess came from either military histories or when his father's old war friends dropped by.

He knew, for instance, that his father, after himself graduating from the U.S. Military Academy in 1936, had gone into the Airborne Test Platoon in 1940.

These forty-eight men were the guinea pig paratroopers, dropping out of the skies with unsophisticated chutes and cloth pilot's helmets.

Frank survived the Test Platoon as did, unexpectedly, all of the other troopers, and became one of the first officers to volunteer when the 82nd (All American) Division went airborne. He fought in Sicily, the mountains of Italy, Anzio, and he had been one of the 82nd men who jumped into Ste. Mère Église.

Frank had survived that war and then had been recruited by the CIA. During those years, for obvious reasons, Dennis's father had never discussed what he was doing. It was just understood by the family that it was less than safe.

For Dennis, the Cold War years had been heaven. He had once counted the countries he'd lived in and stopped at thirty. He had attended as many schools, and could get by in half a dozen languages. For an American dependent, the Cold War was a time of luxury. Dollars spent like gold in the postwar poverty of Europe and the Far East. By the time Dennis was ten, he could order the proper wine for a seven-course dinner (about $8 per person at a Mediterranean resort).

But what he remembered most about those years was the night in Nicosia when his father had staggered through the door of their home with two knife wounds in the gut. Frank Shannon had refused to let them call a doctor. Instead, Dennis's mother had agonized through a series of mysterious phone calls that eventually brought a taxi and a man Dennis later realized was a CIA medic.

The following day, the whole family—including his father, who was grinding his teeth in pain—had been pulled out of the country. Years later, Dennis understood that his father's cover had been blown.

It wasn't until after Frank had retired that Dennis began to get a vague idea of what a man of contradictions his father was. Frank Shannon had spent his entire career in one military operation after another. And yet he was a bit of a pacifist. He was also strongly liberal, and grumbled for days that Ike hadn't gone far enough when the president warned of the military-industrial establishment. Later, over many drinks and late evenings, Dennis began to learn something about his father's odd world view.

He was antiwar, but had fought in two. He was anti-Communist, but thought that for some countries it was the only logical government. He hated nationalism of any kind, but sounded a little bit like a missionary when he talked about America's destiny in the world.

All in all, Frank Shannon was a puzzling man who looked and talked more like a professor than a warrior. Even in retirement, he stayed close to his past life. When he left the CIA, he had become a Special Warfare consultant for the Rand Corporation, the Los Angeles-based think tank.

One time Dennis had asked his father to explain himself. Frank had thought a minute and then shrugged.

"I can't," he said. "It just always seemed like the thing to do."

"A cop-out if I ever heard one," Dennis had said.

"Is that what they call it now?"

Dennis nodded.

"Good word," his father had said. "Describes it perfectly."

A cop-out. When Dennis Shannon was feeling sorry for himself, that was also how he felt about his own life. He was twenty-seven going on eighty-two and continually wondering why he had ever come to this place. To cop out of a marriage and the instability of being a civilian? Maybe. But mostly he was there because he was damned good. Major Dennis Damned Good Shannon. A man the Army needed.

He was always damned good, even in West Point.

Why West Point? Why not Georgetown or Harvard or even goddam Stanford. Shannon set his mind on West Point as a high school kid. For reasons that he'd forgotten, he'd passed on all the nonmilitary options.

West Point was something to be defeated. There was the Beast Barracks bullshit, the harassment from the upperclassmen, the braces, the premeditated debasement and many, many, many pushups. Shannon the Plebe, who knew better, mocked his tormentors. He had double-jointed elbows and an inherited Shannon family upper body that could pump out thousands of pushups on command.

West Point had mainly been a total waste. Shannon, the young Army brat intellectual, had expected something different. He'd grown up in the service and understood its basic stupidities. But as a young man he had always expected something different at the top. Somewhere there were people who *knew*. Weren't there?

The instructors at the Point *knew*. Knew as only pedants can all the old, dusty wars that would and could never be fought again.

Shannon had a bit of a mouth, and a tendency to speak his mind. During his first two years at the Point, he also had a tendency to get in trouble with the tacs and instructors. When he entered his junior year, Shannon was at the bottom third of his class. And even his roomie was urging him to quit—for the Good of the Service. Then he rediscovered boxing.

When he was ten, clumsy and thud-footed, his father had taken pity on him. Boxing lessons. His father, always the mysterious practical man, had also insisted that Dennis take fencing. Shannon learned how to dance on his toes—to defy gravity—and also learned the satisfying feeling of the punch that goes in with all your weight behind it.

At West Point, he became a middleweight boxer. Sixteen fights: two decisions and fourteen knockouts. When he stepped up to heavyweight even his roommate became his friend. And Shannon waxed the plows of Point men who were twenty to thirty pounds his superior.

Then something happened that Shannon would always be grateful for: he got his ass thoroughly whipped. The Point's boxing team went up against the Third Infantry's team—Washington's honor guard regiment.

"Don't be a showboat," his coach said. "You can kick their butts—but don't go Hollywood on me."

"Hollywood? Come on. I always play it safe."

"Sure you do. And I'm the Invisible Man. Get this: you've been lucky, asshole. You're a dancer. Dancing with college joes. You never had a guy come in flat-footed, cutting you into the corner and then taking you out."

"Joe Palookas," Shannon scoffed. "Nobody fights like that. And if they do, they can be cut up. Run their butts ragged in the ring. Outbox their asses. Last 'em out and then put them down."

The coach thought for a long time. He was a small, thick man in his late fifties. He'd fought in two services, but had never fired a gun in anger. In the Navy, he'd been lightweight Fleet champion. In the Army, he'd been three times Pacific champion. His eyes were knuckled over and his nose was bent in two or three interesting ways.

Finally, he had a grudging admission.

"You're the best brain fighter I ever met," he said. "By the way . . . I met a guy like you once, and he had me for breakfast. Cut me to pieces. By round three, I couldn't see for the blood.

"That sunnovabitching ref tried to call the fight. But I'd palmed some salts. He looked in my eyes, shook his head, and right under his nose I took a honk. Two seconds, and I was a clear-eyed Clarabelle."

Shannon laughed.

"And then you won?"

His coach shook his head.

"Fuck no. The guy still kicked my butt. Beat holy shit outa me. But the fight was a decision. I lost, then headed for the barracks and put ice on my face. Got laid twice 'cause a couple broads felt sorry for me."

"So?" Shannon didn't understand the lesson.

"So . . . the other guy didn't get laid. I broke the fucker up. Six ribs."

The coach passed Shannon his headgear, and signaled across the ring for Shannon's sparring partner.

"What happened to him?"

"He never fought again," the coach said.

"Why not?"

"Because he won. And after he kicked my butt he never had the balls to try it again."

Shannon did not understand—until he got in the ring with Fighting Joe Terrill. Big, black, hungry and a PFC from Louis-

23

ville. A hulk of a man who moved like a tight end and had the sheer power of a halfback.

They came out cautiously in round one. Shannon danced with him. Flicked lazy, point-scoring jabs with his wrist, feeling the man out.

Terrill flicked back. He seemed strangely content to lose the round. The bell rang and Shannon spit out his rubber teeth and sucked in water. He knew he was winning, but wondered why his heart was thudding so. In those days Dennis could run five miles and never change his pulse rate.

In the corner, his coach toweled him off.

"You'd better get him now."

"I already got him, don't I? On points."

The coach nodded. Sadly, Shannon realized later.

Dennis went back out into the ring to win. He danced and cut and pranced and slashed. Scoring point after point after point.

Then he boxed Terrill into a corner. Set himself for the final KO blow. He felt a very gentle hand on his right elbow. He found himself being turned toward the man.

The punch came straight between his eyes, but Shannon never saw it. He only felt a heavy blow, and his head went back. He wondered mildly why it seemed like he'd been hit from behind.

Shannon tried to come back in, but his legs turned to water. He wobbled, dipped, went to his knees, ordered himself back up, and then slid back and back and back. Fighting Joe Terrill, seen double for a moment, was prancing around the ring, his arms high in victory.

Later, Shannon cried in his coach's arms. Then he got dressed and went to see Fighting Joe. The man's face was all plaster, and Dennis was pleased and then shamed when he saw the red blotches, seeping through the bandages.

Terrill stuck out a paw, and Shannon shook it.

"You had me," Terrill said. He took two beers from an admiring Old Guard sergeant beside him, and handed one to Shannon.

"Beat me," Shannon said honestly. "I never had a chance."

Terrill puzzled at him. Then took a very long drink and thoughtfully belched.

"Shit, Lieutenant. I thought you'd gone and broke it off in me!"

Then, slowly:

"I guess you just thought it last, man."

That defeat, that sudden swift shock in front of hundreds of soldiers and fellow cadets, is possibly what helped Shannon survive the rest of the Point.

When Dennis finally tossed his hat in the air on graduation, he was already lying to himself about the misery that had been West Point. After all, he'd made it, hadn't he? And with his somewhat iconoclastic personality intact.

What may have helped was the creation of a dream. The Class of 1962, all 600 of them, were addressed by the President of the United States, John Fitzgerald Kennedy.

As Shannon gradually realized what his commander in chief was saying, he found his adrenaline building.

JFK was using West Point as a platform to create a new military elite—a special force of men who would fight the unconventional-warfare battles that the young president saw in the nation's future.

Kennedy threw his ideas up as a challenge to the new officers. He urged each of them to become a new kind of man, who could become part of a ''whole new kind of strategy, a wholly different kind of force.''

And at that moment, Shannon simultaneously saw his grandfather bleeding in the blood pile next to the old hunting lodge in Belleau Wood and determined to become one of those men that JFK saw in his presidential vision.

> I wanna be an Airborne Ranger
> Livin' off blood and guts and danger.
> I wanna go to Special Forces
> Take my dope an' jungle courses . . .

Shannon snapped back to reality. He nervously glanced about the hill. All the Lurps were quiet, lost in their own thoughts. For a moment, he'd thought he was singing that song aloud.

Guiltily, he scanned down the hill, toward the river. There was still nothing. He shifted a hip toward a more comfortable position. The movement brought eyes flickering toward him, then idly drifting away again.

Shannon realized he really hadn't lost his moves. He'd been awake and alert the whole time, with just a small part of his mind drifting.

The patrol had been positioned on the hill for two days now, never moving except when completely necessary, and they were beginning to smell like overripe goats. Or a latrine. Mentally drifting was just a way to kill time—to keep your sanity in a situation where even the smallest things could become mountainously important.

Right now, all Shannon could think about was breakfast. He shut that side of his mind down. Shannon would wait for the others to eat.

I'm a big-time career officer, right? Third tour in Viet-god-damned-Nam? Aren't I the Young Turk who's gonna save the Army from sinking into its own mire?

Remember, he reminded himself, you are going to be a general one of these years, if the zips don't kill you. And when you get your star, maybe you can show them how to win this silly war, because it'll probably still be going on then. Shannon laughed at himself. He remembered thinking that kind of messianic bullshit when he made first looey.

But now, at this moment, getting a few more people home alive at the end of their tour would be about all the victory he wanted. Because Dennis Shannon was beginning to think that this silly little war was a slip in time. That it'd never end. And he'd spend the rest of his life sitting on this hill, waiting for something to happen. And hoping to God nothing ever would.

Shannon decided that, at twenty-seven, he was too old to do the JC number anymore. He began to wonder why he wasn't back at Hue Duc in his air-conditioned office?

Are you supposed to *like* living in this stinking jungle and eating red laterite for breakfast? You don't mind stinking and sweating and being out of your fucking mind, do you? And maybe a little—change that to a lot—scared that somebody's going to do something out here that hurts? You do remember that pain hurts, don't you?

Unconsciously Shannon rubbed the dent in his chest where the SKS round had gone in, pinwheeled, and slammed up against the back of his ribcage.

Don't think about that. Don't remember, lying there in what we were pretty sure was China with this hole in your chest and some Nung Chinee mercenary trying to remember how the hell you treat a sucking chest wound.

Nice thinking, racist. Chang saved your worthless life, and then sat there with you until the fucking Agency got its fucking control people to wake up and send a dustoff ship out.

And all you can think of is Chinee mercenary.

God bless and keep Chang, wherever he is.

And you're being very silly and sentimental and even worse depressed, because Chang didn't believe in God, Buddha, or Allah, just the old M-1 Thompson gun he slept with.

26

Oh well. Shannon, seeing movement, knew it was now okay to eat breakfast.

He slithered one hand back to the NVA rucksack he always carried in the field, and fished through it. He took out one LRRP ration. Chile and beans.

A great improvement over what Shannon had been issued for chow on his first tour. Elite unit rations then were some Minute Rice in a plastic bag and a can of meat or fish. Canned pilchards. Pilchards, for Chrissakes. The cans weren't even labeled sardines. Shannon never wanted to find out where the Army bought those cans of whatever.

Back then you took this bag of Minute Rice, dumped some water in it, and squooshed it around. The water, sans heat, turned the rice into something like dead oatmeal with little nasty bits in it. Then you dumped your meat or fish or whatever into that mess. Dennis shuddered, remembering the time he got a can of very elderly Japanese crab. That was breakfast. Or lunch. Or dinner.

But the wonders of American technology had come to Long Range Recon. Now there were freeze-dried rations. Wonderfully tasty, and about 3,000 calories per meal. Add water, heat, and they tasted great.

The only problem was that nobody in the field could ever afford to show themselves by building a fire or even setting a chunk of C-4 on fire below a canteen cup. Therefore, you just added water and ate them cold. Even then, they weren't too bad.

Dennis ripped the foil pack open and poured water—his last— from his third canteen. He took the spoon from his breast pocket and then stopped. Sergeant Williams had slithered up beside him. Very good, Sergeant. I didn't even see you move.

Shannon was beginning to understand how Williams had lived through three wars in the "let's go out and get our asses shot off to find out how many bad guys there are" chunk of the Army.

Williams was holding out a can. Why, kiss my money-making ass, Shannon thought in astonishment. He took the C-ration can of Peaches, With Syrup, from Williams, found a P-38 can opener, and started opening the can. Suddenly he realized he was about to cry.

Williams, you stupid asshole, he thought fondly. You could have kept that and scoffed it yourself. And you give it to me. An idiot major who ought to have stayed back at Division.

Crying, Dennis? You been too long in the tules. No shit, brother. No shit. Over a can of peaches.

Yeah, dumb. But maybe now you want to knock off the sniveling and remember why you're doing this whole Nam thing, Denny my boy? Yeah, Shannon answered himself. Yeah, I remember.

Then eat your goddamned breakfast, watch down the hill at that goddamned creek, shut up and realize that you're out doing this because you're doing it with the only goddamned idiots who understand.

Not the only ones, though. Yeah. There are the gooks. They understand. Maybe better than you do.

CHAPTER FOUR
DUAN

DUAN SQUATTED IN the rain, watching his division move up for the river crossing. He saw, with satisfaction, that before any bo-doi moved he looked up, ensuring that his movement was shielded from aerial observation.

A hundred meters or so in front of him, the Cham River snaked through jumbled boulders and fallen trees. It marked the approximate border between Cambodia and Vietnam.

In a moment, the general would give the order, and his men would stream across. He had given his Sixty-seventh Regiment the honor of being the lead unit.

As the scout elements trotted past him toward the river, Duan felt his adrenaline surge, as if he were about to engage the enemy. He smiled at his own fancy, rose to his feet, and caught himself checking the gray overcast skies. His smile grew broader—he had the same reflex as his men. There was really nothing to concern himself with—the monsoon would keep the imperialist bombers grounded.

The crossing should proceed exactly as planned. Duan felt he owed himself a congratulation.

"Congratulations," Lau said.

The general turned and took a freshly rolled cigarette from his sergeant.

"Perhaps premature?"

"Why?" the sergeant asked. "We are alive, aren't we? Now, I know some generals . . ."

"Careful," Duan warned, glancing at his aides who were chattering away under a tree about ten meters distant. "Some-

28

day," he said, "your peasant mouth is going to get you into a great deal of trouble."

"Thank you for your advice, Comrade General. And I understand. They might demote me again. Or, worse yet, send me back to my rice fields."

Lau was difficult to argue with. Besides, he had brought up another area for Duan to feel pleased about. Other generals, indeed. Two months ago, in Hanoi, Duan had received the orders for his 302d Division. Since then, he had marched his 7,000-man division more than 1,500 kilometers, down the sprawling purgatory that the Americans called the Ho Chi Minh Trail. They had survived disease, insects, snakes and air attacks. They had started with Molotova trucks to help them, and ended hauling themselves and their equipment with sheer muscle through impossible mountains and jungles.

Once, on their trek, they had marched for three days through a bombed-out desolation, seeing nothing but mounds of black ash, Dali-esque trees and craters, hearing nothing but the drone of the overhead imperialist airplanes and smelling nothing but the charred remains of the animals and men who had died under that rain of bombs.

Duan felt very proud—his 302d had suffered only seven percent casualties. The average rate for a unit moving south was an admitted ten percent. Duan had reason to doubt those figures that Lau's "other generals" had given.

"A moment, Comrade General?"

Duan recognized the voice, wanted to spin and snarl, and caught and collected himself. The voice belonged to Colonel Vuong Gia Thuy, his political commissar. Of course. He was the only man who would have the temerity to disturb the Comrade General at moment like this.

Thuy was a very powerful man, with important connections in Hanoi. Also a man who desperately wanted to fight against the imperialists—he had volunteered several times to join PAVN divisions moving south.

In a way, Thuy potentially could be more dangerous to the general—personally—than any enemy concentration he might meet. In a revolutionary army, a commissar is at least as and sometimes more important than the officer who leads troops into battle. And so Duan turned, allowing his moment to be intruded upon.

"Comrade General," Thuy began. "I know this may not be the time."

Duan reflexively nodded. It certainly was not.

"But soon we shall be linking up with our comrades in the South, and our soldiers should know how to approach them."

Duan knew what Thuy was leading toward. He was afraid that the men of the 302d would corrupt the valiant freedom fighters of the Viet Cong. They should not be permitted to talk about how miserable their long march had been, how little real support was provided to them, or even how much of the North's life was inextricably woven into the war. Rationing, the lack of luxuries, or even some essential civilian necessities in the North should not be discussed.

Perhaps a little suffering and resolve could be talked about, enough to show dedication to the revolution.

As Thuy ran on, saying exactly what Duan was expecting, Duan scratched his nose thoughtfully. He had to admit the Colonel was right. It took very little defeatism to destroy the morale of a unit, particularly the morale of a unit fighting a losing war deep in the jungle like the Viet Cong. The Viet Cong and the 302d would, after all, be in near-total seclusion for the next few months, waiting for their real mission to begin. It was a problem that had to be faced. But . . .

". . . Not now," Duan snapped, interrupting Thuy's reasoned flow.

The colonel hesitated, then broke off. He was about to turn away when he saw Lau, in the background, smiling perhaps more obviously than he should.

"One more matter. More immediate. When your sergeant . . ."

Oh Lord, Duan thought. Lau *did* call him a snake's ass.

"The sergeant's accent," Duan cut in, "is sometimes confusing. Difficult to understand. I merely asked him to tell you that I was busy."

Thuy frowned, then decided to accept that explanation, and stiffly saluted. Duan turned away, a split second before it was polite to turn, and walked toward his aides, Lau moving in behind him. He made a note to deal with his sergeant later, then put full attention on the waiting Major Vinh.

"Our security squads have secured the near bank," the major said. "We await orders."

"Let us go then, Comrade Major."

Vinh beamed, began to salute, then caught himself. Unlike Colonel Thuy, he realized he was in a combat zone.

Vinh wheeled and barked orders. A few minutes later, lead elements of the 302d Division, People's Army of Vietnam, splashed across the river, into the South.

CHAPTER FIVE

THE BORDER

FOR SHANNON, WHAT had started as a keep-in-touch-with-the-grunts-in-the-field exercise in mild fear had become stark terror.

Unconsciously, he was sliding back from the hillcrest. But his binoculars, hands curled around the lenses to prevent light-flash, were still sweeping the river crossing below the knoll.

Oh, my lord, Shannon thought. NVAs.

Watch the way they move. Very slinky. Rhythm. Right. Now the team with the RPD will go right, provide perimeter security. Now we should see the command group. World of shit.

Shannon counted what was a full North Vietnamese regular company pour across the river below him and realized that in the next few minutes he was about to die.

Part of him was in awe: Jesus, Mary and Joseph. The North Vietnamese Army. The fucking absolute best. How in hell come I've never been able to teach anybody to move that way? Those bastards understand. Look at the way they keep their heads up. They aren't worried. They know it's overcast and there won't be any Arc Lights or gunships, and they're way out of arty range.

Another part of him started calculating: Given the number of people observed in the initial crossing, *personally* observed, estimation of strength would be a minimum of one NVA battalion.

Then Shannon finally came to his senses: You fucking blind idiot! This is a very good way to die.

All his thoughts concentrated as he saw Duan's command group splash across. One squad security.

Command group of . . . shit, there must be twenty-odd officers . . . three radiomen . . .

And now Shannon knew that he was watching an entire North Vietnamese regular division enter South Vietnam. He lowered his binoculars and looked at Williams, who was staring back at him in horror.

A division.

Which means they'll secure a perimeter, which sure as shit will include this hilltop.

Then he was moving, one leg back-crawling and around him the Lurps also were in motion. Lizard tactics were out—the only possibly salvation was to clear the hill and clear the area. And hope like hell they could get a fast extraction.

Please, God, let these fucking Lurps be half as good as the gooks. Then the team was over the crest, shielded, coming up to a crouch and zigzagging back down the hill.

The volume of the PRC-25 was as low as was audible, and Williams's radioman kept constantly tuning the squelch knob. The radio crackled and the men crouched at the edge of the small clearing stiffened.

"Holiday Delta, this is Purple Haze, over."

Williams grabbed the handset.

"Holiday Delta. Receiving you."

"Uh . . . this is Delta. Am outbound. Have Location Maypole under visual. Request location, over."

Great, Shannon thought glumly. By-the-book radio procedure. Which means the fuckin' pickup's either a virgin or scared.

The LRRP team had gotten down the knoll and slid down a creek ravine before security elements of the 302d came in sight. Then it was dead run. Normally, no one but a fool would use a jungle path, for fear of observation, ambush or boobytraps.

But this was different. The team ran down that path, headed away. Shannon pounded along just in front of the last LRRP, trying to keep his orientation for the map location they'd have to give out for the lift-off if the team got clear.

There were only two alternatives: either go to ground and attempt to call in a sitrep (which, beyond artillery reach and with no gunships or B-52s, would not do a helluva lot to stop the NVA); or get out, evade contact, and get extraction.

For once, God was on the side of the Shannons. Somehow they did sneak away, unnoticed, find a possible LZ (a low clearing with an abandoned hut at one side), and get an extraction ship on its way.

Shannon hung over Williams's shoulder, eyeing the map. Maypole was a code-keyed jungle peak about . . . Shannon estimated quickly . . . five minutes' airtime from their location.

"Location," Williams said into the mike, without bothering to ID his transmission, "I shackle . . . Lima Foxtrot Able . . . Tango Delta Yankee." The six constantly changed code letters gave the grid coordinates of the LRRP team.

"This is Purple Haze. I read back your 30 . . . shackle . . . Lima Foxtrot Able . . . Tango Delta Yankee. Estimate your location four minutes, over."

Williams clicked the mike key twice in the standard code: message understood. The less sound, the better their chances.

"This is Purple Haze," the Prick-25 muttered. "Request smoke."

Fuck, Shannon thought. A talkative SOB.

"Negative Haze. This is a negative."

"Are you in contact?" A note of alarm.

"Negative Haze. However we have Victor Charlie about to come out our assholes. Suggest very fast pickup. Will give you visual correction."

"Understood." Very dubiously.

Then Shannon could hear the *whop-whop-whop* of the Huey as it clattered toward them.

"Suggest nap-of-earth, Haze," Williams said dryly. "Victor Charlie estimated as November Victor Alpha units . . . we have you on visual . . ."

. . . And the Huey was in sight, dropping down steadily, and, after Williams's caution, beginning a snake-weave pattern.

"Drop it," Williams screamed into the mike.

The team was up and running into the center of the small clearing as the Huey sank, tail down toward them, and hovered three feet off the ground. Then Shannon was diving into the compartment, one door gunner yanking him into the middle and everyone was aboard and the ship cranked sideways and went, still very low, over the waving treetops, spinning and at full power off and away and clear.

Shannon found himself sucking air like a rescued drowning victim as the air turned cool and then cold as the UH-ID clawed for altitude.

Williams was sprawled, face down, on the deck in front of him. The sergeant lifted his head and carefully felt all of his body. Smiled slightly and then gave his head a woeful shake.

No one can talk in a helicopter in flight, least of all one with its doors off. But Shannon knew what Williams was saying and shook his head in agreement. Why we do what we do . . .

Then, as his adrenaline began shutdown, Shannon began considering his next problem: How in Great God's Name am I gonna convince my brand new division commander that he's about to get hit by 7,000 of the world's best soldiers?

Home.
General Duan waded ashore, then clambered up the riverbank. The exile was home again. He savored the moment. Lau

33

blackened mess of an M-24 light tank. Colonel Sinclair being saluted by some other colonel, with a colorguard drawn up behind; and a photo of a remarkably beautiful woman wearing fox hunting gear, mounted on what—even to Shannon's untutored eyes—was a Thoroughbred.

The general turned and noted Shannon's attention.

"My wife."

"A lovely woman, sir."

"Thank you, Major."

Sinclair adjusted the picture, then turned and walked back to his desk.

"Do you ride?"

"Nossir. Never had time to learn."

"That's a shame. One of life's great pleasures."

Shannon picked a note of sincerity off this. It did not make him feel any more pleased.

There were two files on Sinclair's desk, with a bronze miniature tank between them. One, Shannon recognized, was the report he'd hunt-and-pecked out after the extraction chopper had dropped him at the general's helipad. He had a feeling what the other one was.

Sinclair thumbed through the typed report. He was frowning.

"Your field report. Quite interesting."

"Thank you, sir. We weren't able to ID which NVA units were crossing, sir, but—"

"That wasn't quite what I meant by interesting, Major."

Shannon closed his mouth.

"Obviously," Sinclair said, "you were in the field with this . . . reconnaissance team? So you haven't seen the latest MAC-V intelligence appreciation."

"No, sir."

"That is why I'm having problems with your report, Major. Because MAC-V makes no indication—from *any* source—that any North Vietnamese regular unit is moving south. Let alone what you say is . . . a full division."

"I *did* read that MacVee folder before I went out, sir. That's why I was so surprised."

"Forgive me, Major. Perhaps I should word this more tactfully. But it has been my experience that when troops . . . especially troops operating in small patrol elements . . . observe enemy forces, they can have a tendency to, let's say, overemphasize."

Shannon took a deep breath, calming himself.

"Sir. The Lurpies I was with know what they're doing. We

saw at least two thousand men crossing. Then a command group. One general, aides, radiomen, bodyguards. Standard NVA tactics is for the command element to move immediately behind the forward maneuver element. Sir.''

Stupid prick wants West Point jargon, he'll get it, Shannon thought. He was furious.

"An NVA division. You realize that would mean . . . what would be the strength of such a unit?''

"Assuming three regiments, sir, full strength of twenty-five hundred men per unit. Coming down the Trail, they would lose . . . possibly ten percent of their strength. So we're discussing about sixty-five hundred men. Since they've moved with only about ten percent support troops, we should estimate about six thousand assault soldiers. Sir.''

Sinclair made no comment. He set the report aside. He opened the second manila folder.

"You have an interesting Form 20, Major.''

Shannon wasn't sure what interesting meant to this general. He waited.

"My predecessor, General Wright, thought very highly of you.''

"And I him, sir.''

"Arch is a good man. Even though we have vastly differing ideas.''

I'll bet, Shannon thought.

"I have no plans—at least for the moment—on altering General Wright's command structure. I hope that you and I may reach an understanding—since I would consider you a valuable member of my G-2 staff.''

"Thank you, sir.''

"In fact, General Wright also suggested that if Colonel Frederick's health doesn't improve, that I consider you take over his duties permanently.''

"That was very kind of the general, sir.''

"I must admit,'' Sinclair said, "I find it a bit irregular. For a major to hold that post. However, I have an open mind.''

"Thank you again, sir.''

"Good. And, while we're on the subject of the duties of a G-2, I must tell you, Major, I consider it somewhat foolish for my *acting* G-2 to be in the field with the troops.''

Sinclair smiled. It was a practiced, fatherly look.

"What would the effects be on division policy if you were captured?''

"That wouldn't happen, sir.''

"Exactly what I'd hope to hear from a young officer. But, such eventualities can happen, even to the bravest of us."

Shannon remembered the Lurpie he'd seen in the Ia Drang Valley, crucified with bayonets on fallen trees.

"Yessir."

"You aren't the only one, of course, Major. All my top-level staff will be instructed to consider their personal safety."

Sinclair closed Shannon's file.

"I assume, then, there is no reason that, when you're ready to leave me and take over a combat unit, I won't be able to give you as glowing a recommendation as General Wright."

Sinclair got up and turned back to a footlocker. Evidently the interview was over.

"The report, General?"

"Oh, yes. Very valuable interpretive material. I'll certainly give it primary attention in my planned deployments next week."

There was nothing else Shannon could do but salute.

Sinclair waved a casual salute in return. Shannon pivoted and started for the door. The rain-drum was dying away, he noticed gladly.

"Oh, Major. One more thing?"

Shannon turned back.

"That, uh . . . outfit you're wearing?" He was indicating Shannon's right-from-the-field tigers. ". . . And your personal weapon? In my division we maintain standards that apply to both enlisted and officers. I would appreciate it if in the future you would arrange to perform your duties with authorized gear."

Shannon scooped up the double shot of Jack Daniel's and two cans of Budweiser and pushed his way back through the crowded bar. He found a table toward the back and slumped down.

The only decision he wanted to make was whether to get half-drunk before he shat, showered and shaved, or to get completely polluted right now.

He dumped his Daniel's down while he was thinking about it. Outside the bar, a Cobra gunship thrashed into life, and the snakelike chopper lifted off the strip, canted forward, and clawed for altitude.

As the Cobra passed overhead, the rotorblast sprayed muddy water through the club's wall screens.

"Fuckin' cowboy."

"Get some."

But none of the pilots bothered to look up. They wiped mud off their faces and kept drinking. All pilots are whacko, Shannon thought. He noted, for instance, that the Twelfth Aviation Company's commanding officer was personally tending bar. Where else could you order a drink and be served by a full major?

Shannon watched the major post a FUCK COMMUNISM poster. Then he came to semi-alert as he saw the major pour another double shot and bring it *and* the bottle around the bar to Shannon.

"Personal service, Major?" Shannon asked suspiciously.

"Got to give you the privilege of your new position," the shaven-headed Fu Manchu pilot said. "I mean, Major Shannon, you're now the eyes and ears of the division. Got to treat you right."

"Waddya want *now*, Carruthers?"

"Nothing. Nothing, really. Well . . . maybe you could help us with a little shipment coming up from Saigon."

"Tell me about the little shipment."

"We got a conex full of stuff . . . you know . . . new coveralls. Helmets. Flight jackets. Been stuck at Tan Son Nhut for most of two weeks."

"I'm not in G-4, Carruthers."

"Right. I know that. But we already got the conex skedded on a 123 coming up tomorrow."

"What's the problem?"

"Okay . . . we had to . . . sort of change the manifest to get priority. It's coming up as part of General Sinclair's personal gear."

"Fuck. And you want me to shortstop the conex and make sure you get it."

Carruthers refilled Shannon's glass.

"What's really in it?"

The major looked innocent . . . one finger tapped the bottle of Daniel's . . . and then he went back to the bar. That figures, Shannon thought.

The bar was the Twelfth Aviation Company's officers' club. But since pilots, whether flying slicks or gunships, depended on the goodwill and expertise of their enlisted support, the bar was open to anybody in the unit; also, to anybody Twelfth Aviation was hustling or decided was a good guy. Since it was the only bar, commissioned or enlisted, that *always* had Cold Beer—even when the Viet Cong interdicted the highway—it was very, very popular.

Shannon made a note to himself to get to the airport early the next day.

"This is a private drunk, or you want company?"

Jerry Edmunds slid into a chair beside him. Without waiting for an answer, Edmunds grabbed Shannon's drink and knocked it back. Shannon peered closely at him.

"What happened to the mustache, Jer?"

The last time he had seen Edmunds, there had been a long, flowing mustache—styled after the RAF's night-fighter 'staches of WWII. Now his upper lip was very long and very naked.

"Our new general thinks that Big-time G-3 Flunkies ought to be nit and tiddy."

Shannon had met Edmunds on his last tour, when the captain had been a second lieutenant and running a platoon of the 101st Airborne over hill and swamp. After spending the night pinned down behind a shot-up Chinook and comparing notes on who was the most terrified, Shannon had put the young black officer on his private, very small good-guy list. Now the man was on his second tour, sitting in a Division Operations job waiting for a line company commander's slot to open up.

Shannon took the glass back and poured.

"I just had the pleasure of meeting the General."

"I'm envious."

The anger broke.

"Fuckin' Christ, Jerry! I come back to tell him every zipperhead in the world's coming south—which you didn't hear from me—and the asshole sits there worrying about whether I play polo."

"Figures."

"What's the idiot's problem . . . besides being a fuckin' tanker?"

"General Lee Sinclair," Edmunds recited, "is a fine man. Virginia boy. Old money, my friend. Went to the Point. Class of '38."

"Where he was the goat?"

"Nope. Where he was the eighteenth in his graduating class. Had a helluva rep as an original thinker. Had memorized what ol' Fuller was preaching about blitzkrieg."

This was too much.

"So what the fuck happened?"

"Ever hear of the great Louisiana tank maneuvers of 1940? No? Well, our boy was running a platoon of light tanks. They go sweeping out . . . playing it just like panzer folk. Then they run into a bunch of trucks . . . trucks that had signs painted on them saying they was heavy tanks. A shitpotload of simulated bangs later, he's relieved. Which they tell me happened a lot after those war games. So the guy sits at Fort Knox ponderin'

40

his sins all the way to 1945. Finally, his family puts some weight on some senator and he gets to Europe. They made him some general's personal aide. He got first looie bars week before the war ended."

"Okay," Shannon said. "So he got his whole fuckin' war ruined for him. I still don't get it."

"Stick with me, Dennis. It's worth the trip. Remember, our boy got his nuts cut off doing something original. Time passes. Eventually he makes captain. Then major.

"About then, Korea opens up and he goes off with a bunch of tankers. This time, he ain't gonna blow it. Only problem, Korea's not much different from Nam. Harder'n hell to do a big armored breakthrough when you got twenty-foot-deep rice paddies either side of the road."

Shannon church-keyed a beer for Edmunds.

"Thirsty work, this background briefing shit." Edmunds emptied half the can.

"At any rate, he's there. It's 1950. Every Chinese Communist in the world jumps the border and starts shooting the shit out of the Marines. The Marines didi-mau south.

"At least most of them didi-mau south. Some company gets trapped in a mountain pass. Ol' Sinclair the Fearless hears about this and he blows Boots and Saddles. Gonna save the settlers from the Indians and all that.

"He gets a few klicks up the road. On one side he's got a four-hundred-foot cliff. Straight down. On the other, he's got another four-hundred-foot cliff. Straight up. And in front of him . . ."

Shannon made a guess: "A whole bunch of Chicoms with recoilless rifles, right?"

"Egg-zackle. They tell me about six hero types, including Sinclair, crawled back. Out of two hundred. So they give him a medal, make him a light colonel, and ship his ass over to the ROKs, where all he can get killed is gooks."

He gurgled the rest of the can.

"And there you have it, my friend."

Shannon considered. He believed he was beginning to understand Sinclair: a once young unorthodox officer. He tries trick maneuvers twice—and gets zapped twice. Shannon figured if something like that happened to him, he might be by-the-book and keep-your-head-down too. Not that he still didn't think the general was shit on roller skates.

"How come the asshole never got passed over and kicked out?"

41

"Son. You're part of the West Point Protective Association yourself. You oughta know. They took care of him. Pentagon duty. He finally got his star two years ago."

Shot and another beer. Since Shannon hadn't eaten anything since breakfast, the booze was sinking in fast.

"Gotcha. But, how did he end up as our darling, lovable CG?"

"Ah, my son. You are asking why generals from political families with political wives become generals?"

"Shit," Shannon said softly. "It's gonna be a long war, ain't it?"

"Looks that way."

"What the fuck, over." Shannon cracked another bottle of Daniel's that had mysteriously appeared. "From Sinclair's point of view, *we're* the ones with our heads up our asses."

"You're right. That's why things look so dark."

"Have another drink. Things'll look better."

"Sure. 'Nother drink."

"Yo, Carruthers! Wake us when the war is over."

CHAPTER SEVEN

HUE DUC

HUE DUC, SIXTY miles north of Saigon and home for the Twelfth Infantry Division's Second Brigade and Division Headquarters, was a four-by-eight-mile area of abandoned rubber plantation, a tiny village, disused rice paddies, and scrub jungle.

The rubber trees had been planted after World War II by an enterprising Frenchman. But with the French withdrawal from Vietnam the plantation owner had given up and returned to France, local politics, and Basque absinthe.

The women of Hue Duc who'd been the rubber tappers went back to work in the rice paddies. The curving slashes on the rubber trees healed. The clay bowls, hung by wire tracks from the tree trunks and used to collect the latex sap, filled with rainwater and dead leaves. Huge, bird-eating spiders strung elaborate webs between the trees.

The plantation was quickly returning to jungle. One villager swore he'd heard a tiger cough, deep inside the plantation one night. But he'd been drunk on rice whiskey and was already considered a colossal liar.

The villagers of Hue Duc worked their paddies in silence. The small contingent of ARVN troops—soldiers of the government of South Vietnam—assigned to Hue Duc patrolled loudly enough to make sure everyone knew they were coming. The local Viet Cong sniped just enough to keep the Regional Committee happy. Life in Hue Duc went on as it should and as, God willing, it would go on for many more generations.

But then, in 1966, America committed to the war in Southeast Asia. Part of that commitment was the Twelfth Division. And Hue Duc began changing.

Enormous bulldozers cut lanes around the plantation, to provide hundreds of meters of clear ground. Around the plantation, in an amoeba-shaped perimeter, sweating young American soldiers built and sandbagged their line bunkers. Others strung high coils of barbed wire and laid a devil's garden of mines in the ground. The nearby Highway 13 quickly became rutted with the passage of heavy trucks, self-propelled artillery, personnel carriers, and tanks.

The village of Hue Duc was transformed almost overnight. Several thousand GIs, each of them improbably wealthy, ruined and then rebuilt the economy of the village into a new form.

Many farmers gave up their rice paddies and moved into Hue Duc, setting up shantytowns in the far southern part of the village, where the Americans went. They no longer worked the paddies for various reasons. Some of the fields had been purchased by the Americans to provide clear fields of fire. Others were shelled into uselessness when artillery fire was brought in to chop the occasional Viet Cong probe. But the biggest reason was profit.

A boy could make a hundred times more than his farmer-father polishing shoes for GIs. A girl, if she was pretty, could serve beer and Cokes and, if she could learn a little English, could give the lonely teenage GIs someone to talk to. If she wasn't pretty, she could sell the mysterious trinkets the Americans wanted. A wife could wash the amazing number of clothes the foreigners wore. An ex-farmer could find well-paid work (up to 25 piasters a day—far more cash than he would normally see in a year) digging holes or repairing roads.

Life changed for others as well. The ARVN soldiers, long used to being the lords of the village and accustomed to taking just what they wanted, found themselves ignored by the whores, sneered at by the villagers and, after the GIs realized the absolute corruption and incompetence of the Army of the Republic of Vietnam, headpunched from time to time by a drunk American. They began going armed and in groups.

But the biggest change was for the Viet Cong. With the arrival of what the National Liberation Front saw as a large, soft target, they were forced into action. Within a few months, the du kich xa (village guerrillas) were decimated. The inept, the unskilled or the merely unlucky died in scores of different ways: ambushed, spattered by gunships that dropped out of the sky, countersniped or caught in suddenly very accurate artillery or mortar fire. But the casualties were replaced. Some men were sent in from other areas by the Regional Committee. Some came from neighboring villages looking for adventure. But most came from Hue Duc itself. They differed in motivation, from something as simple as the man who merely hated foreigners to the man who thought they smelled bad and were trying to corrupt his daughters to the few who saw that the Americans were destroying the fabric of Hue Duc itself.

All of them wanted the Americans out.

They might have been surprised to learn that most of the Americans who composed the three line battalions guarding the perimeter would fully agree. There were about 2,400 of them. Each battalion had one-third of the perimeter to secure. The three battalions were Second Battalion, Eleventh Infantry; First Battalion, Twenty-ninth Infantry; and First Battalion, Fifteenth Infantry.

First Battalion, Fifteenth Infantry's sector was the southern part of the perimeter, closest to Hue Duc—about six miles down the road on Highway 13. The grunts of the Fifteenth thought they had the best area. On the southwest they had large, deserted rice paddies to give full fields of fire, then Highway 13, and then on the southeast, fairly sparse jungle that had been mostly torched.

The line companies occupied the outer perimeter.

Behind them, within the rubber plantation itself, was the headquarters of the Fifteenth Battalion and, nearby, in a clear field sat the 4.2-inch mortars, the closest thing to real artillery that the infantry had integral to their unit. The mortars were placed in waist-high sandbagged circles with above-ground sandbagged shelters and ammo dumps on either side.

Under the covering trees, were tents—platoon-size tents that held motor pool people, headquarters, recon, the medics, the supply facilities, and the mess halls.

These just-behind-the-lines men worked in angle-roofed screen-sided sheds, made of the same American-imported 2 × 4s that provided overhead support in the fire bunkers. The officers, including the battalion CO, Colonel Taylor, lived in pyramid tents with duckboard flooring.

Spread along the perimeter were the fighting positions of the line companies. Of the 800-plus men in the 15th Infantry battalion, only about 600 were the cutting edge. These men—divided up among companies A, B, and C, plus Headquarters Company Recon Platoon—were the field animals.

In theory, there should have been about 180 men in each of the three line companies, although they were perpetually understrength. As always, the combat units were the last to get replacements for the wounded, rotated home, detached, and those who were nonspecifically swinging the lead as far away from the shooting war as they could get.

Those three companies manned the two- or four-man fighting positions along the portion of the perimeter assigned to the battalion. These were rectangular holes, about five feet deep by four feet wide, and about ten feet long. The walls were sandbagged, and most of them had an overhead shelter of trucked-in 2 × 4s (from Oregon), Vietnamese tin, and sandbags, as much for weather shelter as shell-burst protection.

Each bunker had a grenade sump—a small, sandbagged hole that was meant for protection if a grenade was tossed some night. Kick the grenade in the sump—praying that it wasn't short-fused like most of the potato-masher VC grenades—and jump on top of somebody else.

These bunkers were for fighting and night watch only.

The men lived by platoon increments—thirty-three men, more or less—in large tents set 100 to 300 feet behind the fighting positions. The tents were elderly, incredibly heavy canvas, lined with mosquito netting and floored with double layer wooden palleting.

Each man had a canvas folding cot with a metal T-bar-framed mosquito net over it. His fighting gear—webbing, weapon and helmet—was kept beside the bunk on the floor.

Most soldiers bought tin footlockers from the local villagers to keep their personal stuff in. These were made of flattened and soldered American beer cans. Personal stuff was not defined as the A and B duffelbags containing useless gear like dress shoes and uniforms. Those stayed under the bunk and rotted.

The bunks were covered with cotton batting mattresses, in colors any New England crocheter would wince at. A small pillow was made out of the same material. At night, soldiers covered themselves with the ubiquitous poncho liner, a camouflaged, six-ounce synthetic blanket that was one of the few Good Things the Army created in Vietnam.

That pretty much took care of the basic individual comforts. The other two basics for grunt contentment were group comfort and light. The latter two were regulated by how sophisticated each rifle squad was at stealing, conniving, bribing, black-marketing and general dishonesty.

Fifteenth Infantry, Charlie Company, Second Platoon, First Squad rated very high on the infantryman's scale of sleazing.

Their tent was buried deep in the brush behind the fighting positions. It was so well hidden that a new second lieutenant once took three days to find where the squad hid out. Being as far as possible from the company CP meant that the universally detested company first sergeant generally found it easier to get men for the crap details from other squads.

First Squad's tent was Army issue for a rifle platoon. In other words, for thirty-three men. First Squad, with eleven grunts, was quite comfortable.

After acquiring the tent, carefully cutting its hidey-hole in the brush, and laboriously pitching the canvas monstrosity, the dirt floor was pounded flat and then sandbagged about six inches high. Shipping pallets stolen from battalion supply provided a softwood floor.

Adding to the comfort was the fact that each man had at least two of the flattened beer can footlockers. Casey, the squad leader, also had a wall closet for his uniforms, as well as a battalion commander's field desk, on which sat the field phone to the CP.

Outside the tent they had dug a tiny bunker, four feet in all dimensions, lined with sandbags and more of the beer can sheeting for shelter. This was always filled with cases of Vietnamese beer—Bier LaRue, Bier 33—one case of Vietnamese Nehi orange drink, and two constantly replaced rice-hull-flecked blocks of ice bought at the nearby bazaar. When the VC cut Highway 13, which they did every now and then out of pure meanness, being out of ice rated very high as the worst kind of war atrocity.

The next to the last luxury was the sign hanging over the tent entrance. It was made from the busted-up wood of a 105mm howitzer's shellcrate. Carved into the wood was the squad's designation and, below it: BE IT EVER SO SHITTY, THERE'S NO PLACE LIKE HOME. The crowning touch was the generator. Combat infantrymen, with some justification, are as afraid of the dark as any three-year-old.

There were basically three ways to hold back the night:

The amateur platoons or squads—those mostly made up of recent replacements or led by horseshit willie officers or non-coms—used candles and Coleman-type lanterns. The white gas lanterns worked, except that they hissed incessantly and, when the positions were mortared—which happened fairly regularly—the mantles shattered. This meant somebody had to partially disassemble the lamp and burn in a new mantle in total darkness and obscenities.

The next most skilled units had managed to run a bootleg electrical line from the battalion headquarter's huge generator down to their tents. They would have one or two bare electrical bulbs at each side of the tent.

Only First Squad had its own generator.

Nobody knew how many kilowatts it put out, or why it was originally sent to Vietnam. How First Squad acquired it was a closely held secret.

Three months before, an Air Force C-123 Provider had missed the airstrip and stacked up in the jungle. First Squad saddled up and sped to the rescue.

The pilots had been killed in the crash.

The crew chief was flattened about twenty meters from the wreck—Mosby could sniff it—crapping his pants.

There were incoming rounds. They were very high rounds that Casey quickly and accurately assessed as coming from their own private sniper. There was little danger in that direction.

They dusted off the crew chief, gave him a shot of rice whiskey, and had Buellton put Band-Aids on the scratches.

Casually they asked what the 123 had been carrying. Officers' Club supplies, as well as the generator, which was headed for a general's mess somewhere up north, came the answer.

Buellton looked at the rest of the squad: they nodded solemnly. Buellton ripped a morphine syrette from his bag and banged the shot into the crew chief's arm.

"Deep, deep shock," he diagnosed. "Couple you dudes wanna take him up to Brigade while we do what's necessary here?"

Buellton marked M on the crew chief's forehead (medic code: The patient has been given morphine), and Martinez and Talia-ferro led him away.

The rest of the squad went to work. The club's supplies—what weren't eaten, drunk or stashed for emergencies—were traded or given away as goodwill.

The generator, however, was lovingly and carefully installed

47

in a deep, sandbagged bunker that DeeJay estimated would take a 16-inch shell without flinching.

First Squad had civilization.

Fritsche dumped two loads of empty sandbags and stepped back, grinning.

"Asswipe," Mosby complained. "You fuckin' stand there and grin and you ain't down here in this goddamned hole, sweating."

"Sorry about that shit, Mosby. Tell you what. Got something for you. Something nobody knows about. Help you get through days like this."

Mosby pitched the entrenching tool into the dirt and looked up.

"Go."

"Gonna give you the bikers' hymn."

"Bikers got fuckin' hymns? I thought all you clowns knew was pillaging and raping?"

"You gotta have something to say when there's no pillage and the only thing to rape is Boys' Town."

"Come on, Fritsche, quit being cute."

"When the world's comin' down around your shoulders—like the first time my knucklehead wasted a crank pin—is what you do is sit there real quiet; assume the proper humble stance; and sing—up to the heavens—at the top of your voice: COCK-SUCKER. MOTHERFUCKER. EAT A BAG OF SHIT. Makes you feel better."

"Hallelujah, brother," Mosby said in his best Burt Lancaster.

"Y'all call that a hymn?" Taliaferro said.

"It don't work for wops," Fritsche said.

"What are you troops doing?"

Mosby winced. He hadn't spotted First Sergeant Ramos come up.

"We are digging a bunker, First Sergeant."

"Are you being smart ass with me, Specialist Mosby?"

"Not a chance, First Sergeant."

"Where is the rest of your squad, Mosby?"

"Working, Top."

"Working where? I see you. I see Brown. I see"—jerking a thumb after Fritsche—"him and I see Taliaferro."

"That's pronounced Tolliver, First Sergeant."

"I know how to speak Cinglish."

"Didn't say you couldn't, Top."

"You did not answer the question. Where's the rest of your squad? Down fucking off at . . . at . . . at the t'ing dere?"

Mosby quickly bent down to pick up the entrenching tool. Otherwise he would have blown it right there by giggling. First Sergeant Ramos was Puerto Rico born. He had been in the Army since nobody knew when. The current theory was since the Philippine war. His English was marginal at best. Any time he couldn't think of the word, he automatically said, "t'ing dere." Mosby had heard from Puerto Ricans in the Second Squad that Ramos couldn't speak Spanish any better.

"I'll tell Sergeant Casey you were looking for him, Top."

"Mosby, you are a fucking poor assistant squad leader. You do not have the right . . . right . . . right . . ."

"Attitude," Mosby supplied. He didn't think he could handle another "t'ing dere." Mosby untied the cord around the bale of sandbags.

"See what I fuckin' mean? Tomorrow, Mosby, you burn the shitters."

Mosby took a very deep breath. Then another. Burning shitters was Ramos's basic punishment: The officers and the headquarters company people had wooden outhouses—screened-in enclosures, seating ten—that looked like midwestern back porches. The back of the outhouse was hinged, and inside were halved fifty-five-gallon drums. Each day the punishment detail dragged those drums out, dumped diesel fuel on the crap and piss, and tossed in a match.

This was burning the shitter.

Ramos had insisted on having a noncommissioned officer or acting NCO in charge of the detail after a particularly ambitious PFC used aviation gas and the ensuing explosion sent the PFC to 93d Evacuation Hospital sans body hair, and, much worse, burnt the colonel's private crapper to the ground.

Ramos waited for any comment. Mosby wisely stayed silent. Ramos snapped his clipboard and stalked away. Mosby stared after him.

"Cocksucker . . . motherfucker . . ."

". . . eat a bag of shit," Willie the Semi-Brown put in.

"I'll be a son of a bitch," Mosby said. "It works. That cocksucker. That asshole. They oughta give Puerto Rico its independence—from *him*."

Taliaferro and Brown concentrated on shoveling. The bunkers were Ramos's latest project. About two weeks before, the battalion headquarters had been mortared by the bad guys. No cas-

ping in the Army, but made him decide to volunteer for a second go-around in Vietnam.

What made him do it? A question, young David, you best not be contemplating too long or too hard. Still, he couldn't help but run it over. It was the only escape from the mind-numbing job of filling sandbags.

It was not easy growing up with a mother who was a society editor and a father who was an absentee bastard.

Sarah Hollings Mosby's grandfather had made a fortune designing and selling hydraulic mining gear to the lemmings who flowed through Portland, Oregon in the last half of the nineteenth century. There had been enough to build a gingerbread-Gothic house on a hill, complete with echoing hardwood floors, sideboards holding multiple sets of dinnerware for guests who never came, and a complete absence of nostalgia.

Mosby grew up in that house with his mother mostly out—she had established her own mini-reign of terror as the Society Editor of the *Oregonian*. It wasn't much of a reign of terror, but what society Portland had at the time did make a point of inviting Sarah to all of its affairs. This meant that Mosby was usually alone in the hanging shadows of his upstairs room.

There were certain questions he knew better than to ask—especially if they involved his own father.

Mosby's first major clash with his mother was just before he turned nine, when the shed at the back of the weed-overgrown garden had burnt down. The tirade from his mother had centered around playing with matches. Even then Mosby knew enough not to admit he'd been dreaming about burning that big echoing house to the ground.

His mother's tirades were unusual—they began in a reasoned tone of voice, built to an almost incoherent stutter rising toward a scream, then broke into tears. One hour later, she would announce that the subject would be forgotten about and David was forgiven. Forgive and forget would last a few more hours, and then the recriminations would begin all over again: this time in a cold, calm anger-hissing tone, complete with words Mosby was sure Sarah didn't use around her pet debutantes.

About nine times in ten Mosby's father would be mentioned as a subject of comparison. David was told again and again that he was just like his father. Just *how* like his old man he was became a subject of intense curiosity to Mosby. Who was the man? Where was he?

Over the years, his mother wept out a basic biography.

Marrying Ross Mosby was the worst mistake in her life, a

mistake she was still paying for. So, David asked, what happened to him? She said she didn't know. He'd joined the Marines during World War II.

Mosby brightened—until she went on to tell him that Ross had made sure he never got overseas. He'd spent the entire war in Hawaii, doing what came naturally to him. David asked what happened next.

"The last time I saw your father," Sarah said harshly, "was in 1944. When the war ended, he never came back. I never heard from him again."

"Is he still alive?"

"I don't imagine so. He's probably drunk himself to death by now."

It was a story David Mosby semiaccepted over the years. He became a surprisingly normal, average-looking young man with the usual number of friends and fairly impressive intelligence.

He also grew up outdoorsy, which was easy and pleasant in the Portland of the late fifties. Unsurprisingly, he also had a taste for the wild side: he figured out how to wrangle drunks to buy him six-packs from the ABC store; was one of the first to discover that a '53 Pontiac, once it gets up on two wheels, will more likely roll twice rather than recover; and that the best way to get laid—contrary to popular theory—was to hang around one of Portland's private girls' schools instead of the docks.

He also figured out early that parents and kids are genetic and mortal enemies. He never told his mother—or any adult for that matter—what he thought, saw, or was planning to do.

It was with this attitude that he first approached the old suitcase he found buried in the debris of the fourth-story attic. The suitcase was made of a cheap fiber and was rope-tied.

It was about half full of an odd assortment of clutter: A battered and filthy set of work khakis. A snap-brim cap. Five very well-thumbed books: London's *Martin Eden* and *The Iron Heel*; Wells's two-volume *Outline of History*; and *Das Kapital*. Under the books was a still shiny longshoreman's hook.

Mosby sat hunched on his knees, staring into the suitcase. The clothes and the hook gave him a pretty good idea of whom the case must have belonged to: his father—the great unknown shitheel and bastard.

He flipped through the books. *Das Kapital* had pencil-scrawled notes in its margin; the handwriting the careful, child-formed script of someone who was self-taught.

Marx. Mosby had never read the turgid German, but had heard enough in his fairly right-wing high school history classes to suppose anyone who read Karl Marx, let alone a dozen times as the ragged book signified, was a Commie. In a few minutes, Mosby learned more about his father than he'd heard in seventeen years.

He slowly unfolded the work clothes and tried to slip into the shirt. The rotten cloth ripped a little. Interesting. His father would have been shorter than Dave, but from the collar size, a hell of a lot more muscular.

He picked up the pants and something fell out. It was a cloth military patch—a shield with a V on it. Mosby studied the patch for a long time. Then he carefully refolded the clothes and put everything away—except for the patch.

The Marine Corps recruiting sergeant's eyes brightened when Mosby walked into the station a few days later. But then they fell when Mosby explained he wasn't there to enlist—he wanted to know something about the patch.

The sergeant studied it.

"World War Two. Fifth Division."

Mosby looked blank—like most teenagers, WWII was to him as remote and uninteresting as anything the Greeks did.

"What were they? Some kind of supply thing, or something?"

The sergeant laughed.

"Whereinhell you get that idea, kid? Naw. The Fifth was formed up real late in the war—'44 I think it was.

"They stuck 'em into Iwo Jima. You heard of that?"

Mosby vaguely remembered a late-night John Wayne movie about Iwo.

"You seen that picture of the flag raising?"

Mosby remembered *that*.

"Fifth Division. Here. Hang on a second."

The sergeant took out a book and flipped through the pages.

"Yeah. Formed up in '44. At Camp Pendleton. Trained in Hawaii. Went into Iwo. There would've been about eighteen thousand of 'em."

He thumbed over more pages.

"By the time they took the island, they'd suffered about seven thousand casualties. The Fifth never fought again."

The sergeant snorted as he closed the book.

"Naw, son. They weren't no supply division."

Mosby pocketed the patch and turned to leave.

"Why you so interested, boy?"

"I think . . . my father was with them."

"You think?"

"Yeah . . . I never knew him."

The sergeant decided not to ask specifics. Instead, he dug out a loose-leaf binder and went rapidly through it, but found nothing helpful.

"You want to find out more, boy, the Fifth's having its reunion in July. Down in San Diego. Here. I'll write down the address of the association. You can get a hold of them if you want."

Mosby folded the slip of paper and put it in his pocket next to the patch. On his eighteenth birthday, the small trust fund set up by his grandfather became legally his. It was money that had been long earmarked for college.

Instead, Mosby systematically drew the account down—to keep the banker from noticing and contacting his mother. Finally he had enough for the plane fare to San Diego. He told his mother he was going fishing for a few days. By now, Sarah was used to three- or four-day absences from her son. It did make life considerably easier for her.

The San Diego hotel was full of loud, brawling, middle-aged men, most of whom seemed to be preparing for the reunion days ahead of time with liquids.

Dave sat in the lobby staring at them—wondering if one of them was his father. He explained his problem to the Fifth Marine Association's recording secretary. The man went through the current files.

"Sorry, Dave. We don't have anything on a Ross Mosby. Not current, anyway."

Mosby didn't know if he was glad or not.

"You *sure* your dad was in the Fifth?"

"I think so."

"Think so? And you came all the way down here on a think so? You got some gumption is all I can say.

"Tell you what. Let's at least take care of the 'think so.' Lemme look up the Division rolls. See if he really was with the Fifth."

It only took a few minutes. The secretary ran a beefy thumb down a long list of names, then his thumb stopped. He looked up at David.

"Lemme ask you something, Dave. You say you never met your dad?"

Mosby shook his head, no.

"Can I ask you something? Personal? Your mom's alive, right?"

"Yessir."

"What did she tell you about your father?"

"She . . . she said he left her. The last time she saw him was in 1944."

"She say much about what kind of a man he was?"

Mosby took a deep breath. He really didn't want to go into it, but for some reason he felt drawn on.

"She . . . I guess she didn't think much of him. Told me he drank. Said he ran around. And . . . she said he was a coward."

The secretary looked back down at the book.

"I don't know about the other shit, Dave. But I can tell you one thing. Sergeant Ross Mosby was no coward. He was awarded the Silver Star. Posthumously for heroism in battle."

The world glazed over. So many conflicting ideas. His mother's apparent lies. The fact that his father was dead for many years. The recording secretary took pity on the boy and took him up to his own room, where he fed David two stiff shots of bourbon. The man got on the phone.

A little later, as David was coming out of the fog, there was a third man in the room—a skinny, short, balding one-armed man whose accent grated New York.

"You Commie Ross's boy?"

"Beg pardon, sir?"

"Sir, shit. I'm a peon just like I was in the Crotch. Call me Angelo. Angelo Cervi. Anyway, Commie Ross is what we called your dad. I guess because he had some real strange ideas about things.

"About, hell . . . lemme see if I can remember. The dictatorship of the working class. The destruction of the boor . . . boor . . . shit, the fuckin' bosses."

The man poured himself a drink and absently refilled Dave's glass.

"Son of a bitch wasn't no pogue. You know your dad was a Raider?"

"I don't even know what a Raider is."

"Right at the start of the war, Marines decided they needed some killers. You know, like them Limey commandos? Guys who'd do shit like find two Japs in a foxhole, cut one of their throats, and leave the body for his buddy to find the next morning. Mean motherfuckers, not criticizing your dad."

Mosby drank, not tasting the bourbon.

"But, pretty soon, somebody said we don't need commandos, what we need is fightin' Marines. And they broke up the Raiders—them that survived, anyway—and used them as cadre for the Fifth. You know, cadre . . . guys with combat experience to show the new gyrenes the ropes?"

Mosby made noises of agreement.

"Right up here at Pendleton is where I met Commie Ross. He was our squad leader. He runs us up every hill in Pendleton twice before he was happy. We hated the prick—'scuse me again.

"Wasn't till we saw how some other sergeants fucked up that we started appreciating Mosby. You heard the crap about how sergeants is fathers to their men? No shit, that was Mosby. Man'd run us for miles, then make us all line up and check our feet for blisters. Make sure we changed our socks. Make sure when we went to Dago we had us our pro kits.

"Course," Cervi added hastily, "I never heard of your old man fucking around any."

"What happened to him?"

"Aw, typical Crotch fuckup. We land on Iwo and every Nip in the world starts shooting at us, 'cause the damned Navy was savin' shells that week. Anyway, we went up that mountain . . . Surifuckinbachi it was . . . and took it. Then they turns us around and we start for the other end of the island.

"By the time we got halfway up the island, there was me, Commie Ross, and one other pogue . . . Hayward, his name was. The rest of us . . . you know."

Cervi poured his drink down in a silent toast.

"Finally we get almost to the tip of the island. We're outside some fuckin' village. Shit. What was the name? I forget. We're supposed to assault it.

"Only, like usual, somebody doesn't get the word. We go forward and get pinned. And then some doggie artillery starts firing.

"Guess nobody told 'em we was there, but they brought in fire right on top of us. And then, right about then, the friggin' Japs had us for breakfast."

Cervi shook his head in disgust.

"We was fuckin' pinned down from two directions.

"Let's see. Three . . . naw. Five guys ate it right then. Including the runner. Somebody's gotta go back to the rear, where maybe there's a field phone, and tell those fuckin' Army people to get off it. Me, I ain't moving, for good and sufficient reasons."

Unconsciously, Cervi rubbed the stump of his arm. "So, up comes Commie Ross, and he goes chargin' back for the rear. Ziggin' and zaggin' like he was runnin' for Brown University. I saw him take two hits. He went down once. Then came back up and went on.

"I didn't see the rest. But they stopped shootin' at us, anyway.

They say Mosby got all the way back to the CP before he fell over. By that time, there wasn't nothin' the medico could do.''

Cervi drained his drink.

"So, that's what happened. Your old man . . . shit, he was a fuckin' Marine. You want to hear more?''

"Yeah. Yeah, I do.''

"Okay, kid. Tell you what. Let's go down to the bar. There's some other ancient fuckers from the Twenty-seventh I saw. They'll have some stories too.''

They got up Dave realized that he was about half-drunk. Cervi stopped him at the door.

"Hey, kid. Kid, shit. You're no older than I was when I joined up. Dave . . . how come your mother . . . never told you any of this stuff?''

"I don't know.''

"Well, didn't she let you read his stuff?''

"What stuff?''

"Commie Ross called 'em his journals. Yeah. Journals. Said he'd been keeping them since he was a kid. When he first went out on the road. Back in the Depression.

"He said they were stories about working stiffs—like us. Commies. Wobblies.

"Hell, he was in the Crotch, he was still collectin' them. Stories about Lew Diamond and ol' John Basilone.

"He said there was no difference between a peasant who's dumb enough to work for the boss class and one dumb enough to join the Corps.''

Cervi peered at Mosby.

"You never saw them, huh?''

"No," Mosby said. "I never did.''

Dave Mosby also never went home again, although he did set out in that direction after the reunion. He played the scene of his planned confrontation with his mother over and over again in his head. There would be tears. Screaming. Half-coherent confessions. And more lies. Mosby knew there would be more lies.

He thought maybe he had heard enough to last him the rest of his life. Mosby drifted for a few weeks, until he finally ran out of money in some now-forgotten town in Northern California. His prospects, he realized, walking down the wind-blown street of the town, were less than pleasing. He had eleven cents in his jeans, he hadn't eaten in a day and a half, and the local cop had been eyeballing him with increasing interest on each pass.

He almost stumbled over the sign in front of City Hall: JOIN THE FEW! JOIN THE MARINES!

Yeah, he thought. Why the fuck not?

Mosby walked into the small city hall. The receptionist directed him upstairs to the recruiting office. Evidently the room was used as a combined-services operation, since it was hung with recruiting banners from all five services.

The only person he saw there was a rather tired-looking man, wearing a dark green uniform with gold stripes on it. He wasn't a Marine. He was Sergeant First Class Peter Thompson. United States Army Recruiting Command.

Mosby explained that he wanted to enlist—but in the Marines. Thompson told him that there wasn't anyone around from the Marine Corps. The military recruits in small towns by sending their representatives on once-or-twice-a-week circuits. Thompson said he didn't expect the guy from the Corps back for days.

Mosby swallowed. He knew he was destined to meet that cop outside the minute he left City Hall. Eleven cents, he was fairly sure, was good for a vag bust.

"Say," Thompson said brightly, "you had lunch yet?"

"Uh, no sir."

"Me neither. Can't stand to eat by myself. Guess it's all those years in messhalls. C'mon. Lemme buy you a burger or something. Maybe I can give you a few tips that'll help you in the Corps."

Over the town's largest porterhouse steak, Thompson continued his slow circling. Fine outfit, the Marines. Problem is, the Marines are kinda small. So they got to put their people where they need them the most.

"Right now, they're short on clerks, I heard. You'd probably end up pounding a typewriter instead of carrying a rifle. I don't know if you'd like that. You seem like the kind of young fellow who wants to see some action."

Even in his deep depression, Mosby knew he was being conned. But he didn't care. There was also the problem of his next meal and that small town cop. Or, if not him, the next cop in the next town.

"Supposing I joined the Army, instead?"

Thompson grinned; the boy was making it easy on him.

"For starters, you'd only have to join for three years instead of four. You also get your choice of any school the Army's got."

David thought this over. Thompson mistook his silence for wavering. So he pressed home for the kill.

"Another thing," he said, "if you wanted to join the Army . . . hell, we could give you that test today. Put you up here in town tonight . . . Tomorrow you'd be on a bus to Oakland.

"You take your physical and so forth down there . . . and four days from now, you're on your way for training. Fort Ord. In Monterey. That's some town. Great restaurants. Great-looking girls."

"Let's do it," Mosby said.

At that point, Thompson wisely shut up. No sense in overselling the boy now. True to his word, Thompson had him on the bus to Oakland the next morning. Four days later, Mosby was raising his right hand. Two days after that, he was on his way to basic training. At Fort Leonard Wood, Missouri, in the depths of summer.

By the time he got over that pissoff, he'd also found that somehow what he and Thompson had discussed about specialized schooling never ended up in writing.

DAVID ROSS MOSBY
RA 19 789 674
MOS 11B10

Translation of the last line: Military Occupational Specialty: Light Weapons Infantryman. Eight weeks of basic, eight weeks of advanced individual training, and, in mid-1966, David Mosby was shipped to Nam as a grunt.

He was surprised to find that he was pretty damned good in the bush. Since the only token of Good in Combat is survival, that was enough. It also surprised him that when his time was up, he volunteered for another tour. He still had no idea why, except that maybe he was as crazy as his father. Also, Mosby had no idea what he wanted to do at this point if he had magically become a civilian.

What the fuck. It was done. Now all he had to do was survive. In the meantime, there was the squad, the bazaar, and Tho . . . His thoughts were broken by a giggle.

"You numbah one man, Mo'by."

He turned to find My, the laundry girl, beside him. Laundry was done by the village women. They charged about 35 piasters, or 35 cents in Military Payment Certificates (MPC), for one shirt, which, since nobody had piasters and the current rate of exchange was 120 to the dollar, meant the villagers saw another profit converting the MPCs on the black market. Shorts were 10 pee, pants, 40 pee and so forth. It was a great bargain, particularly since the gear had probably been worn for a week or so in the field and smelled like a gas attack on Verdun.

The laundry woman, possibly one of the women who'd considered herself lucky to get 20 pee a month tapping rubber trees, might make 1,000 to 2,000 piasters just doing laundry. It was a great deal better than scattering shit in a leech-ridden rice paddy.

Also, it did no one any harm, other than destroying whatever local economy Hue Duc and other similar villages had, and whatever respect people like the village chief (400 piasters a month salary) and other officials had.

This was very hard for anyone to worry about, since no one who'd spent any time in Vietnam labored under an illusion that the South Vietnamese government was *ever* respected by its own people.

"Why you dig hole?" My wanted to know.

Mosby dug a cigarette out of his fatigue pocket and looked at the young woman. He wondered, perhaps for the 1,000th time, why nobody ever fucked one of the village girls. Most of them were prettier than the bazaar whores, or even the hookers that were set up in the new economy of Hue Duc. She was clean, wearing the obligatory black pajamas and white button-front blouse, and friendly. Strange war.

"Dinky-dau First Sergeant say dig hole. So, GI dig hole," Mosby said in that grating GI-Vietnamese-Japanese jargon.

"First Sah-jin numbah ten."

"First Sergeant number fucking one thousand."

"You speakee numbah ten. Tell no dig hole."

"Never hachi. You got laundry?"

"Have laundry. But, you no dig hole."

"Why not?"

"Hole never happen. You go field."

"Aw, fuck me!"

Mosby slumped down on the pile of dirt. Taliaferro looked up from the bunker.

"What's the matter?"

"My says we're goin' out!"

"Shit. Shit. Shit." Taliaferro pegged the entrenching tool into the dirt.

"You talk numbah ten. Field good, you say."

"Bullshit field number one. Field numbah fuckin' ten. Boo-

61

coo Veecee in field. We go field, we get killed. No pay laundry bill.''

"You pay laundry bill now.''

My held the plastic laundry bags behind her.

"You get killed, okay. But you pay now. Get killed, My go boohoo. But have pee.''

"This woman,'' Mosby announced solemnly, "is the most mercenary bitch I have ever encountered in my life.''

He tossed the cigarette aside.

"Come on, troops. Let's saddle up. Fuck this shit. We're going to the fucking bazaar.''

Brown was perplexed. It was only his second month in-country. Taliaferro was already out of the hole.

"But, Ramos said . . .''

"Willie, you are entirely too nice a human being, even if you are from Boston. Here is the way the world works. Take a note, m'lad.

"My, here, says we're going on an operation. She knows. The gooks *always* know. Shit, the fucking colonel probably still ain't been told.

"So, if we're gonna go run through the motherfucking jungle, we're gonna need certain things. Like, I want to go to the bazaar and see if I can get Tho to . . . to . . . fall in love with me.''

"But, we're supposed to—''

"We're supposed to shit and fall back in it. You go get the rest of the squad. We're going to the bazaar.''

"What about the Top?''

"Fuck him. What's he gonna do? Send us to Vietnam?''

CHAPTER EIGHT
THE BAZAAR

WILLIE THE SEMI-BROWN was plunging into the bazaar, way ahead of the rest of the squad, still straggling down Highway 13. His little Minolta—$49.95 at the Brigade PX—clattered away as if it were a motordrive Nikon.

Brown was behaving just like a tourist on vacation. Which, if it weren't for his fatigues, the slung M-16, and the fact that somewhere out there were people wearing black pajamas who wished him ill, was exactly what he was. For Brown, a middle-class black teenager, the bazaar was the most exotic thing he'd ever seen.

It was yet another Vietnamese institution—an institution created and supported by the American Army. The bazaar sprawled across a hillside, about one klick outside the brigade's perimeter. The bazaar consisted of forty or fifty tiny booths, laid out along narrow alleys, all tacked together with scavenged lumber. In looks, the closest comparison might be the annual Our Lady of Martyrs Church carnival—assuming Our Lady of Martyrs was on poverty row.

The bazaar sold everything a born-again village merchant imagined a not particularly bright foreigner could need or might want. Which was a helluva variety, considering that the people of Hue Duc had never heard of Americans until a year or so ago.

Some booths specialized in gifts to be sent back to the Real World—America. There were elephant hide wallets actually cut from the hides of senescent water buffaloes; ao dais, the lovely sensual flowered silk skirts with the white pants that looked good only on Asian women; boxed dolls that were supposed to be the Trung sisters; paintings on metal plates and that sort of thing.

Other booths sold the GI-issue items that somehow the company supply rooms never had, but the black market always did. There were many things like jungle boots in the right sizes, #10 cans of fruit, .45 pistol ammo, and rifle-cleaning solvent.

Still more booths had beer can lockers, go-to-hell hats, or leather goods that only a damned fool or a cherrytroop would buy. Wearing one of those cowboy gun belts or the pinned-back Aussie hat would guarantee Official Death as soon as the grunt wore it in front of his platoon sergeant or higher.

Other booths served food—killer submarine sandwiches with salami from some never-disclosed-nor-asked-about animal, onions, peppers, lettuce, dressing; or noodle soup with nuoc mam, the elderly fish sauce that only the bravest or most Asiatic Americans would touch.

But most of the ten-by-twelve booths, walled off on three sides by cloth curtains, had only two to four wooden tables. They served beer and soft drinks and, the most important thing to American near-teenage soldiers, very lovely and fairly innocent village girls to talk to and flirt with.

The whole bazaar also crawled with kids, pint-size entrepreneurs. Three- and four-year-olds, dressed up like perfect Oriental dolls, selling newspaper cones of peanuts. A zillion seven- or eight-year-old boys, dressed in white shirt and slacks, who would shine your boots whether or not they still had enough leather showing to take a shine. Kids were something the American Army has never been able to resist, especially since the average infantry soldier isn't much out of the lemonade-stand age himself.

So when the troops went to the bazaar, they always ended up with boots that had been shined half a dozen times and carrying enough half-roasted peanuts to feed a Viet Cong company. For those less innocent, the bazaar also had, on its far edge near the jungle's edge, a whorehouse . . .

All in all, the bazaar was a peaceful place where a grunt could forget first sergeants, sandbags, the bush, and whatever problems he had for a few hours, while he drank some beer (rarely getting drunk), told lies, flirted with girls, and even, when the pressures got too bad, got laid.

But peaceful or not, the line animals always went armed when they went outside the wire. Most of the men in First Squad carried their M-16s. Blind Pig, being a machine gunner, carried his .45 auto. Fritsche, the squad's point-man-by-choice, never went anywhere without his sawed-off double-barreled 12-gauge nonissue shotgun.

Walking up to the bazaar, nobody was paying much attention to anything. The argument was far too hot.

It had started as a semirational discussion of their medic—Buellton—and his sexual preferences. Fritsche maintained that, since the medic came from Appalachia and was, worse yet, a short-timer, the only kind of woman he'd be interested in would be about junior-high-school level. And probably related to him. The first, if not the second taste, by the way, was perfectly logical to the Vietnamese.

Since Buellton had decided to stay behind, Mosby was more or less trying to stick up for him, even though a part of him really thought it was funnier than hell to badmouth the tall mountaineer. Because Mosby was sticking up for the medic, Blind Pig, being Blind Pig, took the other side.

"Not that it be necessary," Blind Pig was saying "but this be proof that hillers got no more sense than God give a dead cop. Buellton, goin' for bald legs he don't know shit. Pussy ain't pussy 'thout it have a beard."

At that moment Fritsche turned into a pillar of salt. His shotgun slipped, unnoticed, to dangle from the sling around his waist.

"Well I shall be fucked," he said softly.

"Now there be another area about hillbillies," Blind Pig

agreed. "If they sisters run faster than they, an' the hogs be slaughtered, they be willing to take it out on each other."

Blind Pig then frowned, realizing Fritsche was not paying attention. The rest of the squad also turned, wondering what was going on.

Fritsche was staring, lost in space, at a Harley-Davidson motorcycle, parked near one of the booths. He walked slowly forward, like a priest approaching the Host, and stood staring down at the bike.

It didn't look like much to the other grunts, as they gathered around him. The chrome was long gone. The exhaust pipe was solid rust. The twin gas tanks were brush-painted in ten or more different colors.

"Can you fuckin' believe it," Fritsche said. "A goddamned genuine four-five hog. Must be from World War Two."

"Maybe the French brought it here," Mosby offered.

"Yeah. Yeah. You see what I mean about Harleys?"

"Not especially."

"Mosby, you are a dumb fucker. Man, this little flathead must've been built in '43 or so. Ran all over Africa. Then some Frog must've brought it here, and now a gook's ended up with it. Man, that is American engineering. You see what I mean when I tell you Jap shit like Honda'll never make it in America?"

The discovery of the old Harley 45-cubic-inch bike started a day that would have been better spent filling sandbags. Because, in the next hour: Mosby would not get to fuck Tho; Blind Pig would have some interesting observations about correct English grammar; Speedy Fort would prove there may not be anything wrong with superstition; DeeJay would get half of his long-dreamed-of blowjob; Taliaferro would almost get his head thumped; and the day would go down in squad history as the time that Fritsche went and farted the grenade . . .

Later it would make exact sense that Taliaferro began the wrongness. But that was the nature of Taliaferro.

It wasn't that Specialist Fourth Class Mario Taliaferro was malevolent—he just happened to be a not particularly bright nineteen-year-old who thought quite well of himself and had an absolute ability to step on his social dick every time he opened his mouth. Taliaferro might have been more civilized had his father not owned the only Ford dealership in the smallish North Carolina town Taliaferro was born in.

In the South, car dealers have a lot of clout, particularly when they sell not only cars and trucks, but tractors as well. Taliaferro's father, feeling guilty about the hours spent away from his family, wanted his only son to have everything.

In high school the boy had an allowance approximately equal to the salary of any one of his teachers, plus the first 289-High-Performance Mustang in the town, a hot rod further breathed on with the addition of about half of the parts in the Ford Racing catalog.

The trouble that Mario couldn't outrun, his father could generally buy his way out of. And Taliaferro was lucky, admitted even by the North Carolina patrolman who uncurled Taliaferro and his car from the tree he'd wrapped himself around. Daddy, of course, promptly gave Mario a new Mustang.

Taliaferro might have continued as the town's hell raiser, a man with all the girls and hangers-on that his allowance could buy. Unfortunately biology can't be bribed. The girl that Taliaferro knocked up happened to be the daughter of the local Jay Cee president, and it seemed prudent for Mario to disappear for a couple of years, until the heat died down.

That meant the Armed Forces. But in 1966 any branch of the military that kept you out of Vietnam had a waiting list. Taliaferro had the choice of the Army or the Marines. He chose the Army, picking for his enlistment choice Officer Candidate School. He promptly failed the Officer Candidate Test—Taliaferro and a couple of other enlistees had smuggled some half-pints of bourbon into the Reception Center. The failure wasn't Taliaferro's fault—they should have warned him the all-important test would be the next day. It was never Taliaferro's fault.

Flunking the test solidly qualified Mario to become a grunt. Even then, he might have been able to weasel his way out of getting sent to a line unit in Nam. But his mouth ruled, and Taliaferro successfully pissed off almost everyone he came in contact with, from drill sergeants to personnel assignment clerks.

Taliaferro never learned—even after being in the squad for four months, he was still upset that Casey had chosen Mosby as Assistant Squad Leader. By rights the slot should have been his. The only reason Taliaferro hadn't gotten a shot in the head from one of the squad members was because he wasn't an incompetent soldier. More important, since the squad was a totally interdependent unit in the field, nobody wanted to turn anyone into a complete enemy.

Not that this saved Taliaferro from being grabbed by one of Fritsche's meathooks just as he started to clamber on that old 45 outside the bazaar.

"What the fuck do you think you're doing?" Fritsche growled.

"Gonna see if I can fire this sucker up," Taliaferro said, surprised.

"It ain't your scooter."

"What the . . . it ain't yours, either," Taliaferro said, moderately bewildered.

"Just get the fuck off." Taliaferro thought about arguing, then clammed up as he saw Fritsche's fist ball, his forearm come level with the ground, and that fist turn knuckles flat.

"You're serious," he said.

"Fuckin' A."

He got back off the Harley, confused, angry, and not quite knowing what the hell to do next. Mosby stepped between them before the situation could escalate.

"Jesus, if you guys wanna fight, reup with the jarheads. Come on. I wanna go cuddle Tho."

Taliaferro stepped back. Martinez gave Fritsche, who was still glaring at the Italian, a soothing pat.

"Come on, compadre. Buy you a beer."

The squad split up different alleyways, each member heading for his favorite booth in the bazaar.

The bazaar had songs for street signs. Amazingly current records, played on tiny and very battered portables. And a song for anyone's ear, drifted and mingled together:

> . . . *And the white mouse/Traveling backward* . . .
> . . . *he's mighty handy, with a gun or a knife* . . .
> . . . *call for the captain ashore* . . .
> . . . *sittin' on the dock o' the bay* . . .
> . . . *your chain, chain, chain/Chain of fools* . . .
> . . . *California dreamin'* . . .
> . . . *Go tell Alice* . . .
> . . . *on such a winter's day* . . .

DeeJay was headed for "Come on baby light my fire/Try to set the night on fire." More or less, that was his intention.

He'd been hitting the bazaar whores up for a blowjob since his first visit. With no takers. DeeJay had learned that hookers this far out in the boonies were pretty straight about what they would or would not do.

But lately, he'd been concentrating his attentions on Loan. She wasn't a knockout—none of the bazaar prostitutes were, or they'd be selling Saigon tea down south—but she wasn't that ugly, either. So far, she'd been the most willing to experiment of any

67

of the girls. DeeJay was certain that, for the right price and with a little privacy, she'd go for it.

Money wasn't the problem—privacy was. All fucking was done outside the whorehouse booth, a little ways down the hill and semihidden by a bush or two. In other words, in plain sight for all intents and purposes. DeeJay didn't much care about that, but Loan had made it clear that she was afraid of what the other women would say if they spotted her going down on him.

DeeJay was obsessed with getting a blowjob. Here he was, almost twenty, hipper than anybody else he knew, a big-city kid, and knowing the city was where it is at. But he'd never had his cock sucked.

What DeeJay hadn't yet realized was that whereas he did come from a big city, the part of St. Louis he grew up in had a lot more Baptist churches than knob jobs.

Not that it would have mattered had he known. What other people had or did never concerned DeeJay much. And how could a dude ever be really hip, especially if he planned on being a Top Forty disc jockey, if all he'd done was missionary style. DeeJay was pretty sure that not having had your peepee sucked wasn't admitted to in the flash world of entertainment.

But today he was pretty certain the solution was well in hand. Or anyway in mouth, he thought happily as he hurried through the bazaar. That would turn out to be the stupidest certainty DeeJay'd ever had.

> . . . *and if I didn't love her*
> *I could leave today.*
> *California dreamin',*
> *On such a winter's day . . .*

"Hel-lo, Mos-Bee."

Tho had the softest voice Mosby had ever heard. It matched her height. The girl was so small she barely cleared Mosby's belt buckle. Not that Mosby was exactly a midget. He was well over six feet, with long whipcord muscles. And after being a field grunt for all these months, he was so skinny he looked taller still.

"You come see Tho for soda pop?"

Mosby grinned. "You know why I come here."

Tho turned to the cooler to cover her embarrassment. She fished out a Nehi as Mosby slid into his usual seat at one of the tables. Mosby hated soft drinks, especially the sickly Nehi Orange, but he wanted to be thought of as different, and somehow better than the other troops that came to see Tho. It seemed to be working. Mosby didn't know the profit markup on Nehi was a great deal higher than on Bier 33 . . .

"Do you remember what we talked about last time, Tho?"

"Yes," she said, her eyes lowered.

"Well? Is it yes or no?"

Tho sat down across from him and didn't answer.

"Look," Mosby pressed on. "I'm just talking about a little weekend—two days—in Saigon. You've never been to Saigon, have you?"

Tho shook her head, no.

"I can get a pass. I'll pay for the bus. Meet you at the bus station. We'll have a great time. See the sights. Take in a few shows . . ."

Mosby stopped his sales pitch and nervously sipped orange soda.

"We'll drink a little. Have a French dinner. And then, uh, well, you know."

"You want to sleep with Tho."

"Yeah. Something like that."

She looked at him for a moment, then lowered her eyes again. "Maybe."

"Then it's a promise?"

"Just maybe."

"Great. When we get back from the field, I'll talk to Mr. Chi."

"Man, I do not know where this book get off, spouting this shi . . . stuff."

Blind Pig. Two hundred-plus pounds of Detroit street tough. Hunched over a table, a little book hidden in his massive paws. Perched on his knee was perhaps the tiniest peanut seller in the entire bazaar. She was soberly examining a sentence in that little book—a U.S.-AID English manual—and listening carefully to every word Blind Pig was saying.

"You say it now."

The little girl squinted and very carefully intoned, "Iss there anyoon—"

"Anyone."

"Any-one here who would like to play golf," she said, pronouncing all letters in the last word.

"Golf," Blind Pig corrected. "Is there anybody here who'd like to play golf. Man, dude who wrote this book must be smokin' funny cigarettes. Golf. Shit, babe. You even know what golf be?''

"No, Shefferson. An don't know.''

"You don't want to know, either. Buncha rich honkies waddlin' 'bout smackin' this li'l white ball. Talk about dumb. Next off, they sentence be wrong. Too many words. If you gone do this golf bit, you say 'Wanna play golf.' ''

"Wanna play golf," the little girl repeated.

"You got it. Three words. Just like that." Blind Pig snapped his fingers. "Otherwise, dude be all day figurin' what you be sayin'.

"On the other, maybe that be okay. Dude hear golf, he know this gone be a jiveass date, and he gone tell you get you skinny ass back to momma."

He looked down at the girl.

"You dig what I be layin' down, honey?''

"Yes, Shefferson."

Encouraged, Blind Pig went on.

"Now we be goin' on to the next sentence. 'Do you sell the *New York Times*?' ''

"Do you sell *New York Times*."

"You be gettin' better sayin' these words," Blind Pig complimented. "And these sentences be gettin' better. Me, I might even say 'You got the *New York Times*?' But 'Do you sell . . .' ain't too bad. 'Course, you got a choice, go for the *Free Press* an' fuck—I mean screw that New York shit."

Blind Pig jumped a foot and a half when he heard the first click. Three more clicks behind it. He whirled, to see Brown taking pictures of this remarkable event.

"You. Girl. Get me more nuts.''

He hurriedly pushed An off his knee and hid the book. The child hustled off. Then Blind Pig turned his full glower on Brown, probably ruining all the film in the camera.

"What you be doin' wi' that, nigger?''

"Uh . . . just taking pictures. To send my folks, Blind Pig."

"You be thinkin' that, mo-fucker, plus you be wantin' your skull in one piece, best you be takin' snapshots someplace away from here.''

"Sure, Blind Pig. Sorry.''

Brown lit out as fast as his Boston feet could carry him. Blind Pig grunted, and picked up the book again. He checked ahead for the next sentence. "Where can we see the polo pony you have for sale." Man, man, he thought. And they wonder why these dudes they be Communist.

> *. . . All I really wanna doooo-oooo*
> *Is baby be friends with you-ooo*
> *Baby be friends with . . .*

SNAP. The portable radio went dead.

"Hey, you guys. That's my radio!"

"So what if it's your fuckin' radio. It don't belong playin' in our fuckin' booth. Least of all playin' Armed Fuckin' Forces Radio Stinkin' Vietnam," Fritsche snarled as he picked up Speedy Fort's beer and guzzled half the bottle before the skinny man could say anything.

"Plus," Martinez added softly, "we can do without fuckin' Cher."

Fritsche, Martinez and Taliaferro mildly loomed over Specialist Fourth Class Larry Fort. Fort fidgeted, an obnoxious habit he had, whether he was being loomed on or not. The man had the appearance of being in constant motion even when he was asleep.

"Like Fritsche says," Taliaferro drawled, "you're sittin' in our seats in our booth."

"Fuck you guys. I don't see your names anywhere."

"You know we always sit here," Martinez said.

"Shit, guys. Come on. There's plenty of room."

"Not for no Double Snake Eyes there ain't," Fritsche said.

"What's this Snake Eyes shit?"

"Fort, I knew you were a stupid bastard . . . but I'll explain. Real simple, so even a jerkoff clerk can get the message." Fritsche waited, to see if Fort wanted to take offense. Evidently he didn't.

"You're Second Battalion, right? One and one makes one snake eyes. Eleventh Infantry, right? One and one . . . double snake eyes."

"For Christ's sake," Fort said in disgust.

"That's why we want you to cut a chogie. You know, didimau over to somebody's else's booth. We do not wish the bad luck to rub off," Martinez said.

"Great. Now I'm unlucky."

"Not just you, citizen," Fritsche said. "Your whole fuckin' unit. Man, you cats can't walk out the goddamned gate without getting your ass shot off. Second of the Eleventh's gotta be the hardest-luck grunts in Nam."

"Aw hell," Speedy Fort whined. "You don't really believe that shit, do you?"

"Facts are not hard to believe," Martinez said.

71

"What's your casualty rate?" Taliaferro shoved out.

"What happens to any other unit that goes out the wire with the Eleventh?" Fritsche questioned.

"You fuckers are *that* superstitious," Speedy Fort said in disbelief.

"In this shitheap, it's the only way to keep breathing," Fritsche said, and then pointed a finger. "Out!"

"And es posible it's too late," Martinez mourned. "There is probably a boobytrap already set in the cooler."

Speedy Fort got out, throwing a face-saving if whispered "fuck you clowns" over his shoulder as he went.

The three ignored his whisper, and waved for beer. Class drinkers, tourists and officers drank Bah-me-bah (Vietnamese for 33—Bier 33), which purportedly contained formaldehyde. Grunts preferred the cheaper full liters of Bier LaRue.

Fritsche had one final thought about Fort as he started guzzling. "Ain't just that he's from the Snake-eyes. Gotta tell you, I got no use for any rearechelon motherfuckin' Saigon cowboy like him."

"They cannot help it," Martinez explained. "They take their cojones away when they issue them typewriters."

The three settled down for some semiserious drinking. Fritsche and Martinez talked idly, enjoying the afternoon, away from the omnipresent sandbag detail. Taliaferro was quiet, however. Downing each beer as it came, he was staring down at the oil-cloth-covered table and drawing figures in the moisture rings left by the icy bottles. The southern boy was deep in thought, trying to figure out what he wanted to know without getting a shot in the head. Finally he came out with it:

"Fritsche?"

"Yeah?"

"How come y'll got pissed at me? When I was gonna get on that bike?"

Fritsche wasn't sure he wanted to get into metaphysics.

"Hard to explain to a citizen," he started obliquely.

"Citizen? I don't get it. Since none of us are old enough to vote, what's that got to do with anything?"

Fritsche used the rest of the beer to assemble his thoughts, then waved for another.

"Got to begin at the beginning with you, I see. Okay. A citizen is somebody who ain't a brother. A dude that don't ride and don't carry the patch. Even if he does ride, he's still somebody who ain't a biker. That's the best explanation I got. It's

72

one of those words, you know, that means a lot but there ain't words for."

Taliaferro was desperately trying to follow. "Okay, so I'm a citizen, I guess. But why'd you get pissed."

"Like you said, you ain't a brother. Second, it wasn't your bike. And nobody, especially somebody that don't putt, should fuck with another cat's scooter."

Fritsche was starting to warm up.

"You gotta understand, Tal', ain't much a biker's got besides his ride. A guy puts his whole life into his hog. Puts his whole head into trickin' it up. Works all the overtime he can get to pay the bills, plus whatever he can squeeze out of his old lady. Fuck, man, a bike's a way of life. Mostly your *whole* fuckin' life."

Martinez had been intently listening to all this.

"Ah. Yo comprendo. It's like the bull."

Taliaferro blinked rapidly, really at sea from two directions.

"Hang on a sec. Who was talking about a fucking bull?"

"I was. Me and my hermanos, we bought a bull from Dick Manetti. And we treat el toro like Fritsche was saying."

"Y'all treat a bull like it was a *motorcycle*?" managed the amazed Taliaferro.

Martinez waved him off. He didn't want to get into it.

"Fuck it, man. You just listen to Fritsche. He knows what he is saying."

But Taliaferro, being the blockheaded son of a bitch he was, still wasn't tracking.

"Try me again," he said. "I think I understand, but all that bike stuff's back in America, man. That rusty ol' bike's for sure owned by some buddha-head. So where's the grief if I wanna sit on it and go rumba-rumba?"

Fritsche considered, then found the exactly correct comment to make on Taliaferro's insensitivity. He lifted one ample cheek from his seat and churned out a long, liquid fart, a final plea for international understanding. Almost very final.

As the blast echoes died away, the three heard a thump, from underneath Fritsche's chair.

"Finally went and shit your drawers," Taliaferro said with satisfaction.

They all looked under the chair. Lying on the packed dirt floor was an elderly World War II pineapple-type hand grenade. With the lever still nestled safely against the grenade body.

"What the fuck?"

"Who brought a grenade?"

Martinez, Taliaferro and Fritsche looked at each other blankly, denying ownership. They looked back at the grenade. And this time they noticed some moderately terrible things: Not only was the grenade too old to be currently issued to American troops, but the safety pin was missing; quite recently missing, since there were bright metal scratches through the rust, where the pin had just been pulled through. All that was keeping the safety lever down, Fritsche realized, was rust. And not enough rust, he thought blankly, as the lever creaked away from the body, then flipped clear of the grenade.

A Beatles song blared from the next booth—"Help me if you can/I'm feeling down . . ."—not quite loud enough to keep the three from hearing the grenade begin gently fizzing. At that instant, they came awake. Taliaferro and Martinez flat-dove for the ground. Fritsche scrabbled for the grenade. Picked it up, then looked wildly around for a place to throw it.

"FUCK MEEEE," he screamed and threw it in the general direction of away, hoping to God it wouldn't blow in the air. His mind stuck . . . five to seven seconds five to seven seconds five to seven seconds . . . and Fritsche was in a nosedive, one hand scooping the sawed-off from the tabletop above him.

"A little closer now, miss. That's right. Next to your mom."

Brown was directing a teenage girl, and an elderly lady he assumed to be her mother. It'd make a great picture—the old lady in black pajamas and no teeth, and the girl wearing a pink-and-blue ao dai. They were finally in the proper position, and he clicked the shutter. Brown grinned his thanks.

"Boy, wait 'til Mom and Dad see these. They'll get a bang out of them."

CRUUMMMP. The grenade went off. Yells and screams of confusion. The girl and the old lady ran like hell. All around Brown people were shouting, dropping to the dirt, running for cover, or just plain running.

Brown stood there, dazed, and slowly worked the wind lever of his camera.

Mosby was going for broke. He'd moved over to Tho's side of the table and had both arms around her. He'd kissed her and even managed to get Tho to open her mouth a little.

"We could . . . you know," he said, starting to breathe a little heavily. ". . . Right now. Why wait for Saigon?"

Tho pulled back a little.

"No, Mos-Bee. I said *maybe* Saigon."

"Maybe Saigon is right. Maybe we no go Saigon. Maybe Mosby go field tomorrow and get dead."

Tho looked at him, a bit of her resolve fading, Mosby hoped. It was only a flicker, but Mosby jumped for it.

"You know I like you a lot, Tho. We could go behind the booth. Or we could . . ."

The grenade went off and everything began happening at once, and Mosby found himself staring idly at the sudden holes stitched across the cotton curtain above Tho's head.

"Nigger! Get your ass down!"

Brown finally figured out what was going on. He dropped his camera and floundered behind a cart. Somehow his rifle was unslung and in his hands.

He heard the slow thump . . . thump . . . thump of an M-1 firing, from somewhere out in the brush on the bazaar's edges. Feet pounded behind him, and Blind Pig was headed his way. He had his .45 out and was running, bent low to the ground and covering an amazing amount of ground with each stride. He slid, belly-first, the last few meters and quickly crawled up beside Brown.

"Man, I hadn't yelled, you be dead as you be dumb. Where they be?"

Wordlessly, Brown lifted his head to look. Wood splinters suddenly pocked his face . . . a bullet whee-oowed off the cart, and then Brown heard the flat snap of the carbine firing. Blind Pig shoved Brown's face back in the muck, peered cautiously around the side of the cartwheel, and began methodically returning the fire.

"Oh, baby . . . go, go . . ."

DeeJay's second most important dream was coming true. It'd taken some coaxing, but Loan finally went for it. DeeJay began negotiations by offering her four dollars, which was a lot more than her usual price. Secondly he'd figured out a way to get around the potential exposure.

"We didi-mau across the road, baby. Over there: In the bushes. Nobody see us."

Waving the money, he'd walked out of the bazaar, across Highway 13. Giggling all the way, Loan had followed him. Actually, she was a bit intrigued at this new way of extracting dollars from Americans. Now DeeJay was lying back in the grass, his pants under him for a pillow, and Loan bent over him, working away with increasing enthusiasm.

75

"Oh . . . not so hard, baby . . . a little slower . . . now . . ."

Loan was great at following orders, and DeeJay was in heaven, trying to make this first time last as long as he could.

There was a loud bang from the brush nearby . . . Loan bit him . . . and DeeJay doubled over in agony. He whimpered, grimaced, raised his head dazedly in time to see Loan crawl off into the jungle at approximately Mach 10.

There was a rapid series of bangs . . . shots, DeeJay realized . . . and he peered through the brush. About ten meters from him knelt a young man in black pajamas. He wasn't looking at DeeJay, but was quite occupied firing an M-2 carbine at the bazaar.

DeeJay went from fear into start terror, as he saw two other Viet Cong crawl up beside the first, and rapidly load a bipod-mounted Browning machine gun. On the other side, an automatic weapon chattered, and DeeJay almost shit his nonexistent pants. He was surrounded.

Help me if you click help me if you click help me if you click . . .

The record was stuck and more than anything else Fritsche wanted to get up, stalk into the next booth, and shotgun that record player.

"Whadda we do?"

This from Taliaferro, who was doing his utmost to become a very slender earthworm.

"Mmmph . . . Mmmph."

From Martinez, who had his face in the dirt.

The machine gun across the highway opened up, and the booth exploded around them.

"Motherfucker . . . motherfucker."

Fritsche's contribution.

The machine gun shifted its sights and started converting a small cart nearby into toothpicks. Behind it, Fritsche saw Brown and Blind Pig trying to camouflage themselves in the loose hay as it cascaded down from the cart.

Motion from the ditch beside the bazaar. Fritsche lifted his shotgun . . . fuck, couldn't hit anything at this range . . . and Mosby came straight out of the ditch, sprinted across 13, zigged sideways, and slid behind a low hummock.

Fritsche heard shouts in Vietnamese, and the machine gun turned its fire on Mosby. The hummock became an instant dust cloud. But still Mosby was under cover.

Blind Pig, Brown following him reflexively, took advantage of

76

the distraction and darted out from the cart toward the ditch. Green water spouted, and they were safe.

Somebody shouted "Let's get those fuckers," and Fritsche and Taliaferro and Martinez and some other grunts from somewhere were on their feet shooting and going up the center, M-16s on automatic and Fritsche firing break to reload and shit me I only brought five rounds what the fuck and shouting and . . . Silence. Nothing. No return fire. No movement in the brush. Zed. Zero.

Fritsche heard the screech of sirens and saw two jeeploads of MPs skid around the concertina wire and haul toward them. He realized it was over. Brown, Blind Pig and then Mosby came over to him, Brown bleeding moderately from his faceful of splinters.

"Guess it was amateur night out," Mosby said.

"Fuckin' good thing," Taliaferro said. He tapped the magazine of his M-16. "I'm dry. Anybody bring more'n twenty rounds?"

Everybody checked his weapon. There was a mumbled chorus of "shits." All of them were just about out, too. There was a crackling noise in the brush. Everyone whirled, weapons coming up, hearts somewhere in mid-throat.

"Don't shoot . . . don't shoot . . . it's me!"

They stared, as DeeJay stepped out of the brush, bare-ass naked, waving his pants like a flag of truce. Brown was the first to start laughing.

"It ain't funny, goddammit," DeeJay shouted. "Those fuckers were ten feet away."

Then the MP jeeps were beside them, the armbanded cops rolling out, and a lieutenant, strack-glaring through his glasses, was shouting, trying to find out what had happened. By that time, most of the squad was laughing too hard to answer. But Taliaferro, at that moment, redeemed himself. Keeping a deadpan, he shrugged at the lieutenant.

"Not much. Fritsche here just went and farted a grenade."

CHAPTER NINE

BA REI

ONE REASON THE Fifteenth's sister unit, the Second of the Eleventh, may have been known as a jinx outfit was Ba Rei.

Each of the three infantry units at Hue Duc had responsibility not only for their share of the brigade perimeter, but for a fan-shaped area outward, into Viet Cong—controlled territory.

And Ba Rei was hot.

A patrol going near Ba Rei had about twenty-five percent chance of getting its ass shot off.

Division and Brigade Intelligence had no explanations, but the grunts had their own theory: that Ba Rei was the local R&R center for a couple of main-force Viet Cong battalions.

The area around Ba Rei looked no different from the rest of the area around Hue Duc: tiny village, mostly abandoned; dry rice paddies, their dikes broken and overgrown with weeds; low rolling hills, covered with scrub jungle.

What American intelligence had never learned was that it was possible for a VC unit to move outside the Saigon Circle, all the way north into the "liberated zone" of the Octopus, using for cover the linked passages of jungle that made up Song Nhanh Province.

On this second week of October, such a unit was on the move.

Lead elements of the Phu Loi Battalion, an elite, main-line Viet Cong unit, were moving north, with orders to link up with the 302d North Vietnamese Army Division that had successfully crossed the border and was heading south.

Four klicks southeast of Ba Rei, the jungle opened into a large clearing: about three hundred meters across, and almost a full kilometer long.

Five years ago, the clearing had been a rice paddy. But now the crisscrossing paddy dikes had broken down, barely showing above the low weeds clotting the sunbaked ground.

On the western side of the field there were the ruins of three or four long-abandoned mud-and-straw huts.

One platoon of American infantrymen from the Deuce of the Eleventh was sweeping the area, on a routine patrol.

Sergeant Ed Himes, platoon sergeant of the unit, held one hand up, palm forward, and knelt. Then he moved forward and stopped beside his pointman.

"Anything?"

The rifleman shook his head, no.

The sergeant moved back into the brush and stood.

"Machine gun up. Second squad take point."

This whisper ran back down the thirty-man patrol. There was a loud rustling of brush. Himes took a very deep breath. His radioman was grinning at him. The man covered as the lieutenant came into view.

"Anything out there?"

"Nossir. Never is, sir."

"Why aren't we moving, then?"

"I want to put an M-60 up before we go around the clearing, sir," the sergeant explained patiently. Lieutenant Winters, he reflected, required a great deal of patience.

"Jesus Christ! No wonder we never have any contact. Why the hell don't we just go across it?"

"Because, sir, in Vietnam you take the easy way, you'll get your ass shot off. You always move slow."

"Look, Sergeant. You ever wonder why we take the casualties we do? We move too damned slow."

"Goddammit, Lieutenant. You start patrolling like it's a fucking track meet and you'll run right into the middle of a killing zone."

"Sure," Winters agreed. "That's if they're already set up. But I assume we're bright enough not to walk into an ambush. On the other hand, if we move fast, when there isn't any ambush, we don't give them time to set up some kind of a surprise. Anyway, if there's a Victor Charlie over there—are we gonna worry about one clown with a carbine?"

"I still think we ought to go around," Himes said.

"Thank you for your suggestion, Sergeant. I'll be with the first squad, you tailgunner for me. Now, move 'em out!"

"Yessir."

Across the clearing, Phan Van Tau snapped out of midday sleepiness as the first three Americans trotted out from the tree-line. Tau jabbed his assistant gunner awake and rolled behind the twin handles of the big American .50-caliber machine gun.

The tall grass waved around the ruined huts as the other eighty-four men of the Phu Loi Battalion's Third Company slid into firing position.

Many months before, Phan Van Tau's world had been restricted to his native hamlet of seven huts and his family's rice paddies.

Since the South Vietnamese hamlet was deep in the relatively unjungled rice delta and at least ten kilometers from a major road, the peasants of Vinh Tri VII (as the Americans later called it—trying to clarify the confusion of many hamlets with the same name) had not seen much of the war.

Once an ARVN company had marched through and the company officer had made a South Vietnamese government-approved speech which none of the villagers understood. The company marched back out, taking most of the chickens with them.

A month later, a Communist special activities cell had crept in at night. Tau, lying shivering in his hut, heard the sounds as they beat the headman. Then there was the dull thud of a rifle shot. The headman was never seen again. The next day, an NLF agit-prop team had visited the village and informed the peasants that the headman—a Diem puppet if they had ever seen one—would never collect the land rents again. They also said the tax collectors from the government would never be permitted again in Tau's village.

Even with the occasional voluntary contribution of rice now levied by the transiting Regional VC forces, the hamlet grew prosperous, no longer having to pay rents or taxes. The Viet Cong and their agit-prop teams sometimes helped with the planting and broke the monotony of that endless plod through thigh-deep water, staring up a water buffalo's ass.

In return for the entertainment, where NLF cadre people sang, danced and acted out skits wherein the people of Vietnam invariably triumphed against the Diem (and later the Ky) regime and the U.S. imperialists, the peasants chanted the slogans taught them on each visit: "Struggle against the shelling and the bombing . . . Americans get out . . . Struggle against looting."

Therefore, on one particular night, Tau had been considerably surprised when—at the close of the agit-prop team's visit—one of the cadre announced that Vinh Tri should especially honor one of its own: one who had chosen to join the struggle against the foreign Fascists and the Saigon puppets. He was even more surprised when the commissar said the volunteer was Phan Van Tau.

A moan went through the people. Tau's father stared at Tau in shock. Tau wanted to protest, but remembered the thud of that rifle shot. The party was over.

The members of the cadre helped him collect what they said he needed—a second set of black cotton clothes, his wicker hat, a staff, and a knotted handkerchief stuffed with boiled rice and some slivered dried fish. He was never allowed to be alone with anyone until he left the village for the last time that night.

Tau stood at the edge of the hamlet with his father, mother and sisters. None of them said a word. Finally he turned away and started down the road. The cadre people grouped close around him—they were experienced in dealing with reluctant recruits and family partings.

At the point where the path curved around a hilltop, Tau looked back. There was nothing but a patch of darkness and moonlight on the flooded paddies. On the two-week march into a liberated zone, Tau was desperately homesick. The attention paid him and three other unhappy volunteers by the agit-prop team—constant reassurances, the most select rations—didn't do much to help.

Once inside the Octopus, he was assigned to a du kich chien dau (combat guerrilla) unit, and training began. Endless hours of political lectures followed. Then there were even more hours of rote recitation. Training in cleanliness, first aid, and the use of captured American weapons—even though Tau wasn't permitted to fire any of them.

One day, Tau finally came awake. He was sitting in a patch of sunlight, laboriously tying the endless knotted fiber ropes that would make up a camouflage net, when he realized something: For the first time in his life, Tau was looking forward to the following day. No longer did time run into time, following the cycle of the rice fields from plowing to planting to cultivating to harvest.

Tau sprang to his feet with a howl of happiness. His three neighbors, all bent over their sections of the net, jumped away. Where was the scorpion? Did Tau suddenly think of his girl friend? Or figure out a way they could all go home? Or had he just gone crazy—dien?

It took only a few days for Tau's change to be noticed by his instructors. He was quickly transferred and given different training. This time there was more attention paid to soldiering and far less to politics. An ex—Viet Minh even began teaching Tau how to read. A month later, Tau was assigned to a thoat ly (independent) Main Line unit. The Phu Loi Battalion. Tau felt deeply honored.

The Phu Loi Battalion was among the best of the best—rated even by the Americans as the equivalent of an NVA regular battalion. *All* field grade officers in the battalion were ex—Viet Minh, which meant the battalion had an unbroken record of combat experience stretching back into the 1950s. The battles they fought were always on their terrain and their terms.

Tau spent his first two weeks with the battalion in awe. When he was appointed assistant gunner on one of the captured American .50-caliber machine guns, he paid close attention to what his gunner/squad leader said. He could—and did—recite the gun's statistics: weight, 38.1 kilos; rate of fire, about 500 rounds a minute; muzzle velocity, 893 meters per second; and so forth. He could—and did—disassemble and reassemble the weapon with his eyes closed.

When Tau was permitted to fire five of the .50's huge six-inch-long rounds—before the move began—he was in ecstasy. He never knew that his company commander, Captain Le, saw him one night, crouched over the gun—laboriously polishing each of the rounds. Several days into the march, when his gunner collapsed and died of cerebral malaria, the captain appointed Tau gunner.

Tau, with five other soldiers to carry the gun, tripod and ammunition, was detached to move with the forward security elements of the battalion. He and the other men of the Third company had gone into position behind the clearing near Ba Rei early that morning, expecting—like Himes—no contact. They planned on spending a quiet day recuperating from the battalion's forced pace, while the rest of the unit moved north, covered by Third Company's block.

And now Tau was seeing Americans for the first time in his life. He was looking at them through the sights of that .50-caliber machine gun.

The last elements of the American patrol were coming out of the tree line and headed across the clearing when the .50 opened up.

Lieutenant Winters was standing beside the prone M-60 crew when the first round lashed past his head. His mouth was just opening in astonishment when the second round smashed through his skull—spraying the back of his head into a ten-foot-wide spatter of blood, brain mush, and white bone.

As the lieutenant crumpled backward, Tau corrected his aim. The bullets slammed a steady patter across the two Americans behind the machine gun. They both died instantly.

Then the rifles opened up.

The patrol's medic had time to marvel at the tumble of his guts as an SKS round slashed him open before he died.

The patrol died, looking for someone to shoot back at. And there was no one. The expert riflemen of the Phu Loi Battalion aimed carefully. Even considering the short range of the SKS carbines of the Vietnamese, all the running Americans were down before they made it to the treeline.

Except for one.

Himes. Swearing at his own stupidity . . . goddammit . . . I froze like a fuckin' cheerytrooper . . . He dragged himself behind a tree and stared disgustedly at his leg. A very small hole, Edward. Where's all the damned blood coming from?

He tore an ammo bandolier from around his neck, dumped the clipped rounds out, and tied the cloth around his upper thigh. Then the painwave hit.

Jesusandgodandgodfuckinhurts . . .

The firing stopped. Fucking Christ, they're all dead. Come on, Himes.

He grabbed his rifle by the sling and dragged himself back into the jungle.

In the clearing, one squad of Viet Cong broke from cover and swept toward the Americans.

Procedure:

Approach the body. Fire one round into the back of the head. Turn the body over. Remove all papers, weapons, ammo, grenades and rations.

Next body.

The next body rolled over. Sat up. The American boy held up both hands: pleading. The Viet Cong spoke no English. The soldier fired twice, and the American caved over, blood staining his blond hair.

The Phu Loi Battalion had no time for prisoners.

Himes crawled deeper into the bush. Hide somewhere. Lay up. Maybe when it's dark . . .

One squad of Viet Cong finished checking the bodies near the treeline. Their NCO waved them into the woods. Himes heard the rustle as they came toward him.

The world was starting to tunnel . . . come on, Himes . . . they're going to fucking kill your ass . . . come on, man . . . like that time in Carolina when I was a kid . . . time when the Hatteras wave caught me . . . with my back turned . . . and all of a sudden that wave and all I knew was . . .

The rustling was very close now.

Himes pushed himself to a sitting position. Rifle up. He fired . . . fired . . . fired. The Viet Cong grinned as the first bullet snapped overhead. Slammed the stock of his SKS on a tree and went down.

Himes was moving again, frantically pushing forward. His rifle waved in front of him, like a wand. Yeah. Keep them away. There's another one. Over there. Shoot him, Himes. The thud of another rifle butt against another tree. Himes opened fire and then the M-16 yammered into silence. Man, you're dry. Feed it. Feed the wand. Keep them the fuck away.

The still-smiling Viet Cong soldier stepped out of the brush. Himes stared up at him.

"Well, fuck you, and the horse you rode in on . . ."

The sound of three rifle shots echoed through the brush. The hill became as quiet as the clearing.

PART TWO

OCTOBER 13-NOVEMBER 2, 1967

Swift blazing flag of the regiment
Eagle with crest of red and gold,
These men were born to drill and die
Point for them the virtue of slaughter,
Make plain to them the excellence of killing
And a field where a thousand corpses lie.

Do not weep, babe, for war is kind
Because your father tumbled in the yellow trenches,
Raged at his breast, gulped and died,
Do not weep.
War is kind.

> —Stephen Crane,
> "War Is Kind"

If, in an odd angle of the hutment,
A puppy laps the water from a can
Of flowers, and the drunk sergeant shaving
Whistles *O Puradiso!*—shall I say that man
Is not as men have said: a wolf to man?

The other murderers troop in yawning;
Three of them play Pitch, one sleeps, and one
Lies counting missions, lies there sweating
Till even his heart beats: One; One; One.
O murderers! . . . Still, this is how it's done:

This is a war. . . . But since these play, before they die,
Like puppies with their puppy; since, a man,
I did as these have done, but did not die—
I will content the people as I can
And give up these to them: Behold the man!

I have suffered, in a dream, because of him,
Many things; for this last saviour, man,
I have lied as I lie now. But what is lying?
Men wash their hands, in blood, as best they can:
I find no fault in this just man.

> —Randall Jarrell,
> "Eighth Air Force"

CHAPTER TEN

SINCLAIR

SINCLAIR VOMITED AGAIN, by now bringing up nothing but bile. He was on his hands and knees over his command trailer's small chemical toilet. His stomach settled briefly, then he retched once more. Cautiously, he got to his feet, grimaced, and pulled the handle. He squeezed Ipana on his toothbrush and carefully—counting the sweeps—polished his teeth. He rinsed out his mouth, splashed Old Spice on his face, and turned toward the trailer door. Automatically, he checked himself in the full-length mirror on the door for gigline. He adjusted the creased scarf he wore—the yellow dickey-scarf of an armored division instead of infantry blue.

Sinclair picked up his pistol belt—leather instead of webbing, old-style cavalry belt buckle instead of a clip, and a nickle-plated .357 magnum instead of an issue .45—and buckled it on.

He took several deep breaths, still not sure his gut was under control. A whole goddamned platoon, Lee. Thirty-odd men. No survivors.

Sinclair knew word of the massacre near Ba Rei would spread through his division within half a day. He also knew its effect. A rotten soldier will blanch at ten to twenty percent casualties. A well-trained one can handle fifty percent. But no one can deal with the absolute disappearance of a whole military unit—be it a squad or a division.

Sinclair thought about what it must have been like for the man who took over what was left of the Seventh Cavalry after the Little Big Horn, and felt sorry for him.

It's these damned gooks . . . his mind went on. Fighting them is like . . . like . . . He remembered taking home a bottle of mercury from his prep school lab and found the analogy. The metal flowed through the smallest hole. That's what we're fighting: mercury.

He forced himself to stay in the trailer for another minute. Okay. If these people do not have the guts to face battle, then we'll fight on their terms. I have enough firepower to make sure if the mountain doesn't come to me, I can remove the mountain. Ba Rei.

Sinclair picked up his baseball cap, set it squarely on his head and strode out the door. He was now very much a Major General in command instead of a human being who'd puked his guts out because some people that he was ultimately responsible for had died.

Waiting on the other side of the trailer—on the steps to the villa that composed Division Headquarters—was Ron Mead. His aides had already thoroughly briefed Sinclair on the correspondent.

Mead was Copley News Service, which meant one point on Sinclair's side. Copley, throughout the Vietnam war, defended the military in whatever it did.

Mead was a special correspondent. A contact at MAC-V had coded and telexed what that meant: The publisher, Copley, was an Old Navy man, and had surrounded himself with ex-Navy cronies. When he wanted a Special Report, one of those cronies went—first-class—to the scene of action. Mead was a retired Navy lieutenant commander, a Navy man whose experience was mostly in Washington-level public relations.

After Mead had phoned him through the laborious cross-connect lines that led north from Saigon, Sinclair had made immediate preparations. As he greeted the man, he noted that Mead was wearing overnight-tailored jungle fatigues that were as highly starched as Sinclair's own, plus a blacked-out name tag, and, where the U.S. Army tag went on a soldier's gear COPLEY NEWS SERVICE was sewn on.

Mead tamped out his pipe when he saw Sinclair and walked forward, hand out.

"Good morning, General," Mead said.

"Ron."

"General, I certainly want to thank you. You've done a wonderful job for me. That background briefing put me clearly in the full picture."

Sinclair nodded you're welcome. He and Captain Belasario had handcrafted a backgrounder report for Mead that emphasized the positive. Mead had heard the report while Sinclair was puking his guts out in the trailer.

Mead hesitated, then went on.

"I, uh . . . General . . . I heard about the incident yesterday."

"Pardon?"

"At Ba Rei."

Shit, Sinclair thought.

"I just wish," Mead went on, "that some of those hippies in the States could hear about things like that. They would truly understand Commie brutality, wouldn't they?"

Sinclair angled a glance at the correspondent. Nobody actually talked like that, did they?

"A story like that," Mead continued in complete oblivion, ". . . if it were back in WW II, when Americans knew how to pull together . . . would do something. Inspire people. But, these days?" Mead shook his head. "The last article in the world I'd file would be about the massacre at Ba Rei. It wouldn't be taken right."

Sinclair was very, very relieved.

"However, General, I assume you plan some response?"

"Of course," Sinclair said, feeling a very lucky man. All right, his mind told him, he wants Patton, he'll get Georgie in full flower.

"We're already in preparation. Captain Belasario, of course, couldn't fill you in this ayem. Clearances, and all that."

Mead nodded in sympathetic understanding.

"But . . ." and Sinclair found exactly the proper hesitation, ". . . I think this is important to America. I think they need to know that we are fighting this war the only way we can—honorably, but dedicated to victory."

Now, how did that great lie go down. Sinclair felt his own stomach roil, then he saw Mead nodding and smiling.

"Ba Rei has been a sore spot for this division since it came to Hue Duc. It is a major stronghold and supply depot for all main-line Viet Cong units in Song Nhanh Province. And we shall not tolerate this any longer."

Mead's eyes were alight.

"So you'll . . . ?"

"Within forty-eight hours," Sinclair said, "Ba Rei will be as forgotten as Carthage. These people have shown their contempt for democracy . . . and for this they will pay."

Sinclair was feeling really nauseated now. This was worse than testifying before a Senate committee.

"I intend to obliterate the village," Sinclair said.

CHAPTER ELEVEN

MARCH CAMP

SERGEANT LAU STIRRED the dixie of tea and squinted through campfire smoke at the Comrade General. Duan was nervously pacing through the shadows. They were in the ruins of an ancient temple courtyard, all straggling vines and tumbled, decayed stone, deep in the jungle.

Lau watched as Duan tried to walk off his tension and growing anger. Fifteen measured paces brought the general to an overgrown pool. A statue of some forgotten god had toppled into the pool. Duan ignored it, wheeled, and paced exactly fifteen measured steps in the opposition direction, turned and paced back again.

The sergeant tried to shake off his own building tension. It was an uncomfortable itching at the back of his neck, like waiting for an artillery barrage. He went back to his task, which was to be invisible to his general and to keep the lizards out of the tea.

Lau cursed to himself. In the few moments he had turned his head, hundreds of large, bloated reptile bodies had crowded out of the ruins, and were warming themselves by the fire. Hundreds more baby lizards were perched on the rocks just above the dixie. Before he could react, one of them mindlessly leaped for the heat and plopped its small body into the tea. Lau gently fished it out, set it on its stunned feet, and prodded it away. He waved an angry stick at the others, and they scuttled back into the temple walls.

Lau saw the general's head jerk up as the sound of laughter floated in from a distance. There were other sounds of splashing and horseplay. Duan's 302d Division was hidden in a comfortable march camp and was relaxing for the first time in months.

Duan smiled, caught himself, and paced on. Lau felt sorry for him. Like the general, the sergeant knew this respite was momentary. The original plan was to have the men relax in this secret camp for two weeks after they'd crossed the border. Two weeks of foolishness, repair of gear, and treatment of injuries and jungle sores. Perhaps there might even be a few village girls or nurses to impress.

That had been the original plan. But the sergeant had heard

the new orders. In two hours, the 302d would march on. After the meeting.

The tea was done. Lau carried the dixie of steaming tea into the center of the courtyard. Duan stopped his pacing and glared at Lau.

"What is that for?"

"For your guests, Comrade General," Lau said, glancing around the courtyard for a place to set the dixie. He spotted a large, smooth rock next to the pool and started toward it.

"There shall be no tea," Duan snapped.

Lau looked at him, a little startled. To cover his confusion, he set the dixie down and concentrated on fishing another small, stone-green lizard out. Lau shifted his weight, tugged uncomfortably at the 9mm Browning automatic hidden in the rear of his waistband, and looked up at Duan.

"So, it's going to be that way, is it?"

Duan shrugged.

"Watch me, closely."

He continued his pacing. Lau heard footsteps and saw Commissar Thuy enter with another man. The stranger was flanked by several lower-ranking Viet Cong officers—his aides. The man was Major Nguyen Van Tran, commanding officer of the Phu Loi Battalion, the "guest" Lau had kept the lizards out of the tea for.

Tran was tall and slender, with ropy muscles and deep-set, impossibly gentle eyes. He moved stiffly, like a bo-doi on parade, or . . . the thought flashed through Lau's mind . . . one being marched to a firing squad. Lau shot a very military salute at the approaching officers—a salute that was ignored—and then drifted off, to take up a position behind General Duan.

Tran stopped in front of the Comrade General and saluted. Duan half-waved a salute back. He glanced impatiently at the commissar, who quickly left the courtyard. Duan continued pacing, ignoring everyone. Finally, after a long, uncomfortable silence, he stopped in front of Tran. He blinked at him, as if he hadn't seen the man before, then glanced around at Tran's heavily armed aides.

"We have a poor camp here, Major," he apologized, his voice stiff with tension. "But I am sure we have a few diversions to offer you gentlemen."

Duan looked pointedly at the aides. There was a waver. Lau reached behind him and silently clicked the pistol's safety off. Automatically, he checked which man he would shoot first. Major Tran was unarmed, so he would be last. But Tran spread his hands, and the moment passed. The aides melted away.

Duan squatted by the dixie, picked up the ladle, and dipped tea into a metal cup. He sipped, winced at the taste, and then absently handed the cup to Tran. The major squatted beside him.

Lau slipped closer. He wondered if this meeting would end like . . . some others he and Duan had participated in. Lau checked his target—the space between Tran's eyes, those gentle eyes. Lau prided himself on being not just a good, but an instinctual pistol shot. For an officer, Lau thought, Major Tran did not seem such a bad sort. But the eyes didn't bother Lau at all.

Tran sipped at the tea, made a very ostentatious copy of the general's wince, and handed the cup back.

"I hope you traveled better than that tea, Comrade General," he said. "Perhaps I could assist you from our supplies."

Duan stared at him for a long moment, then smiled a cold smile. He nodded, almost imperceptibly, at Lau. Lau got the message and did an experienced batman's vanishing act. He would take up another position, out of sight, but within range. Lau walked slowly away, trying his best to eavesdrop. The Comrade General's voice scraped across the courtyard.

"Do you know what you have done?" Duan harshed. "Do you know why I am here?"

He did not wait for a response.

"If we do not both think hard and quickly, monsieur, the General Offensive in this province will have failed before it has even begun.

"And all through your actions!"

So that was it, Lau thought, as he disappeared behind a stone wall. It was, indeed, the General Offensive.

The tiger snarled in silent agony, its eyes and teeth flashing below the naked electric bulb. The tiger was in the boy's house, poised, with lashing tail and hollow yellow eyes, for its final leap. The tiger wanted revenge for what had happened. And the boy was waiting.

His father took a stitch through a fluff of hair, all that remained to show where there once had been a gaping belly wound. He softly pulled the waxed thread through the tough hide, gave a gentle pull and the fluff blended into the tiger's skin. Tran's father stepped back from the tiger. He glanced at the boy and smoothed back his son's hair.

"Does it have a ghost, Poppa?"

"We've talked about ghosts, haven't we?" his father answered, and began brushing back the tiger's fur. It was his first large trophy, and the Frenchman who'd gut-shot the tiger had to be pleased with his work.

"There aren't any," Nguyen Van Tran said firmly.

His father also tried to nod away the village superstition. Tran now remembered his father as very old and very wise, though at the time he would have been in his early thirties. His father was slightly pedantic, his voice rising to a sight pitch when he was making a point.

Tran's father had taught him that there were no ghosts. But he also sat the boy on his knee and read Edgar Allan Poe aloud in French. Despite his father, Tran believed in ghosts. He especially believed in this tiger's ghost.

Tran asked his father to tell him about the hunt again. It had happened only a few weeks ago, but still it had become part of village legend. Even in the French hunting estates around Da Lat, it wasn't that often that a man killed a tiger in these times. This tiger had not died well.

The Frenchman who owned the estate had many visitors, all business friends and hunting cronies. They had started the day out very drunk. A Vietnamese pothunter had told them there was a tiger in the area. The Frenchman had ordered out his trackers and beaters (Tran's father being one of the beaters), then had gathered up his elaborate hunting kit—they bring ice for the wine, his father had once told him in awe—and loudly followed the trackers into the heat.

It was a young tiger, not long separated from its mother. The animal had been passing through, vaguely thinking about establishing its own range deep in the forest. It had killed the night before and then holed up. The trackers caught it at the creek. The beaters lined up, with the gunmen behind them, and drove the panicked cat into the Frenchmen's guns. Whoever fired first shot badly, hitting the tiger in the belly. It fled into thick brush.

Tran's father was not proud of what happened next. The young tiger tried to backtrack, but only for a few hundred meters. The Frenchman positioned his friends on a hilltop, then ordered a tracker into the brush to draw the animal out. It charged from the rocks, hating, and blaming the unarmed Vietnamese tracker in front of him for its pain. Six big rifles opened up. Most of them hit their mark. The tiger died five paces away from its hate.

It was an unlucky kill, all gore and gaping wounds. It certainly wasn't a great trophy, so they gave the tiger to Tran's father to work on. Normally a trophy would be gutted, thoroughly iced, and shipped off to Europe for mounting and stuffing. But hunting circles are smaller than their boasts. This was not a proud kill. If the animal had not been a tiger, it would have ended up on the estate's dump.

Tran's father was a teacher, a philosopher, a historian and an amateur taxidermist. In his village, he was a respected rebel. A Vietnamese village is a closed society, not much different in its way from the Bronx or the south side of Paris. To the villagers, this is the ultimate in civilization. What is here, is. What is outside is to be feared and distrusted. Tigers were outside their experience, as was everything else beyond the last paddy dike.

The Frenchman who owned the estate imported his hunters and trackers. The beaters he got from the village, and he bribed and cowed them into their jobs.

Tran never knew why and how his father had learned to read. Before the man considered it was time to tell his son about himself, he was dead. As a self-educated man, he was overly interested in history; why things are. Which led him to the next step, nature, and how things might be.

For as long as Tran could remember, his father had collected animals and practiced the art of taxidermy. He was a nineteenth-century man, who saw all reason in the lifelike statues he created out of gnawed corpses. This tiger was his greatest trust. After this, his father believed, the Frenchman would hire him to mount all his other trophies. To him the bad kill would become his luck.

Tran tried to warn him about the ghosts. But his father just shushed him, threaded the needle by the light of the single bulb in the two-room shack, and worked on. As he worked, he recited Poe in perfect French.

Tran's father was also a Communist. It came with his studies of nature and science. At the agit-prop meetings, his father was always the first to rise and speak. Everyone listened politely, because Tran's father was a learned man. It did not matter that what he was talking about was well outside their experience. The agitator who had organized the meeting would tell them about the oppressors, and how things should be. Tran's father dovetailed perfectly, talking about the beauty of the peasant-village system. All harmony, all with nature. Sans beginning, sans end.

The Frenchman came to get his tiger the day after the harvest festival. It was a lucky time, Tran's father had told him. But the man had been curt and abrupt. He glared at the trophy, nodded once, then ordered his men to put it in the truck. The Frenchman said he would send payment in the next few days.

96

Tran's father was elated. He kept seeing a whole new career opening before him. Tran kept seeing the tiger's teeth and the tiger's ghost.

A week later, the Frenchman had his father arrested. His crimes: membership in an illegal organization and anti-French activities. His sentence: the Frenchman had him shot by the colonial police, before they had even reached the estate. It was then that Tran stopped believing in his father and began believing in ghosts.

Tran put away all of his father's books. He dusted them carefully, then turned his attention to the tools. He cleaned the needles and sharpened the knives. He coated them all with a thick grease and put them carefully away. The last thing he sharpened was the breastbone knife. It was long, curved and waiting.

The Frenchman had a mistress in the village. It was an accepted fact, she was a good and generous woman, and so no one thought anything of it. The village people, good, religious, and quiet neighbors that they were, ignored his visits. They ignored the beatings. They treated her solicitously the next day and didn't mention the bruises.

Three weeks after his father died, Tran was waiting outside her house, with the breastbone knife. He stood when the Frenchman came out, and the man, not recognizing Tran, gave him a friendly cuff to the head.

Tran drove the knife in with all his strength, directly into the man's groin. And, like his father had taught him, he then pulled the knife straight up, to the juncture of the rib cage. He was gone before the Frenchman's guts had spilled out on the ground.

Tran's beliefs changed once more. His father was right. After that, Tran quit believing in ghosts. But he always believed in tigers.

Major Tran glanced down into the murk that was the Comrade General's tea. He fished up two more cups and then tentatively— almost absently—handed Duan one. Tran flashed a look at the brushy area, where he knew the general's bodyguard was crouched, still waiting.

General Duan had just finished what the Party would call a criticism and self-criticism session, and a Western soldier would call an ass-reaming. And Tran had to agree with everything Duan had said.

His men *had* made a terrible error in their victory. They'd wiped out to the man an American patrol. Which meant they had drawn the imperialists' extreme attention to themselves in the Ba Rei area. Duan had explained what all of this meant, at first harshly, then more gently.

Tran admired the Comrade General. He was not a pouty martinet from Hanoi. Tran had unfortunately met more than a score of that kind of officer, who always reminded him of the French. Duan was simply a soldier. Obviously a good one, Tran thought, noting how well Duan's men looked, even after the long torment of the Ho Chi Minh Trail.

All was order in Duan's camp. The air was friendly and relaxed, but with an underlying tension. A tension coming from, Tran understood, their dedication. Duan's men were much like Tran's own Phu Loi soldiers. Called upon, they would face any odds, dying in place if necessary.

Tran nearly smiled, half-listening to Duan. He was now considering both his own men and the fact that the general's bodyguard had been obviously holding a concealed weapon ready when Tran entered the courtyard. Tran had been prepared for instant execution.

He wondered, however, if the Comrade General would have been prepared for the inevitable Phu Loi reaction to the death of their commander. That confrontation, Tran guessed, would only be a bloody victory for the Americans. For that reason, and because of his belief in the terrible revenge of tigers, Tran listened more closely to what the Comrade General was saying.

"What do you suppose they will do?" General Duan was asking. "After this incident, what action do you suppose the American commander will take?"

Tran shrugged, not impolitely. He was too experienced an officer to answer, when a general obviously wanted his own say.

Duan shifted his tone of voice, becoming more kindly, even a bit fatherly. He acted as if, at this moment, he needed the opinion of a younger man who was most knowledgeable in his field. Tran suddenly felt safe. Intellectually, he knew Duan's shift in tone might well be just a sham, but emotionally he reacted like any eager young lieutenant.

"We must put ourselves in the American commander's mind," Duan continued. "What would you do, Major, if you were this General . . . Wright?"

Without thinking, Tran corrected him.

"General Sinclair, sir," he said. "Wright is no longer the commander. The new imperialist general's name is Sinclair. His background, I have been told, is mainly in armor."

For the first time, Duan smiled.

"An excellent choice to fight against a people's war in the jungle. I would appreciate any intelligence you can give me on this Sinclair."

Tran made a note to have his intelligence officer brief General Duan. Besides Sinclair's basic career data, he knew they had a very good copy of the picture of the general's wife. He thought Duan might be enough of a humorist to appreciate some non-essential facts.

"Sinclair," Duan continued, "must retaliate. You have made a fool of him."

Tran nodded. "It was unintentional."

"Regardless. Because of your error, Sinclair must now make a statement to his superiors and to the imperialist press. A military statement."

"Where?"

"Ba Rei," Duan said. "Where else? From his view it is a dangerous area, that his predecessor, for some stupid reason, tolerated. To him it must be a hotbed of terrorist activity. It is also very vulnerable. And, as a Western man might say, an easily acquirable target."

Tran grew suddenly cold. Ba Rei was his men's recreation ground. He had only just approved a dozen or so marriages or engagements before the Phu Loi Battalion moved north.

"What do you think he will do?" Tran asked, already knowing the answer.

"I don't known this general Sinclair as yet. But if I were he . . ."

The Comrade General hesitated a moment. It was a gentle spear he was about to hurl, but he wanted it to sink home.

"Have you ever studied Carthage?" Duan asked.

Tran had. It was a particularly barbaric incident in Western military history.

"I think Ba Rei will look like Carthage when Sinclair is through. Yes, if I were Sinclair I would make Ba Rei a Carthage," Duan said. "We can only hope that he will be more humane."

Duan sipped his now cold tea.

"But after what you did to him . . ." and Duan let the thought trail.

If he were Sinclair, Tran was thinking, and his soul froze for a moment, the revenge would be awful. Tran prayed to whatever gods were left that the American general was a better man than he.

CHAPTER TWELVE

BA REI

SHANNON LISTENED TO the sounds of the night: It was like an Anvil Chorus staged by the First Junkyard Philharmonic—being mostly composed of the noises of the entire Fifteenth Battalion as it circled through the jungle toward Ba Rei.

Being a staff officer without a field command, Shannon could have observed the operation from any vantage point he chose: riding a jeep up Highway 13, for example, or from overhead in a command UH-IB. Instead, he chose to walk in with the Fifteenth.

The Fifteenth's CO was Lieutenant Colonel Lawrence Taylor. Like Shannon, Taylor was West Point and Airborne and Ranger qualified. The Fifteenth's mission was simple: the men were to move out from Hue Duc and provide one side of a pincers movement that would seal Ba Rei. Sinclair had ordered Taylor to march at night. Further proof, Shannon thought, that days of tanker genius began and ended with Patton.

The end result of Sinclair's order was that each of the 600-odd line animals of the Fifteenth had his issue tent rope (about six feet long, with a loop in one end) hung around the combat harness of the person in front of him. The theory was that the unit could move out from the Hue Duc perimeter in silence, without showing any lights, and be able to maintain unit integrity with each man's grasp on the tent rope tied to the man in front.

Shannon could not believe that Taylor thought this tactic would work. But what the hell else could the man do? As both of them knew, the strategy is a valid and standard tactic used by Ranger patrols. However, Rangers mostly move in six- to eleven-man elements and are highly trained in night operations. When the number of men is increased a thousand times, and those men are night-blind at best and night-terrified at worst . . .

The sounds of the night were many, varied and interesting. The crackle of many, many boots crunching through brush. The muttered cursing as someone missed a step and fell into something or other. The occasional thud as a trooper stopped and the men behind thunked helmets. Shannon felt there was a good chance the Fifteenth *would* make contact with some Viet Cong.

100

Mainly, they would be VC who were too paralyzed with laughter to run or shoot back—which would be a classic case of survival of the dumbest.

Shannon smiled to himself, clambered out of the paddy, and gave a heave to the equally buried PFC behind him. He had hooked up with C Company after nightfall just inside the Hue Duc perimeter. As usual, Shannon wore no rank badges and, following orders, had shed his Swedish K gun for an M-16. From jungle fatigues to steel pot, to weapon, to blackface camo, Shannon was indistinguishable from any other grunt. In the event he crossed a sniper's sights, this anonymity could prove valuable. Right, Denny. However, sometimes . . .

The man who came out of the paddy after him was a looming black PFC. He had noticed that Shannon was relatively unburdened and promptly looped two 250-round belts of machine-gun ammo around Shannon's neck.

"You be with us," Blind Pig had grunted.

Shannon had merely nodded.

"Since these honkie fuckers say the Pig don't need no assistant, you be the man's who gone be my AG."

Blind Pig, being Blind Pig, had added assertion to the statement by looming close into Shannon's face. Shannon, being Shannon, had taken the ammo without argument. He was amused. Then the nudge had come down the line and the Fifteenth had ricocheted out of the blackness into Indian territory.

Sinclair's plan was very simple: Two infantry battalions—the Fifteenth and the Eleventh—were to move out from Hue Duc's perimeter. They were to avoid the road and execute a sweeping pincers movement to be in place outside Ba Rei at dawn.

The Eleventh had moved out the previous day, an hour before dusk, and had taken its position by twilight. The Fifteenth played Ranger and went out at midnight.

At 0515 (official dawn), the two units were to move—on line—into Ba Rei. They were to search all the huts and assemble all the villagers. Detached "white mice" (Vietnamese police, so-called because on street duty they wore all-white uniforms) would screen residents and then order them to assemble their possessions.

By this time—0900—the convoy from Hue Duc would have moved up Highway 13 and then the total destruction of Ba Rei would begin—as Sinclair had promised.

Blind Pig stared out through the mists across the field at the plaster huts. The gooks be sensible, he thought. They don't be climbin' out of they rack before noon.

He turned to his appointed AG, not knowing that he had a major at his command. He poked Shannon in the ribs.

"When we be goin' in that fucker," he ordered—spearing a chin at the village—"I ain't prepared to be dealin' with lookin' for no AWOL AG, dude. Best you be hangin' on me like I was yo' momma."

It was now light enough for the man to see Shannon's blacked-out oak leaves. Blind Pig finally knew he was dealing with an officer. He was not pleased.

"Man," Blind Pig said, "I didn't know you be a fuckin' major. Shit. And I only be a PFC for a month, now."

"And you didn't say sir, either," Shannon said, laughing.

"Too late to sweat the small shit," Blind Pig gloomed, fig-uring, what the fuck, he was busted, busted, busted.

"Don't worry, troop. When we go in that vill, I'll be crawling your ass like we were married."

A momentary smile from Blind Pig. This major wasn't half bad. He looked across at Ba Rei. Down the line a whistle shrilled, and the Fifteenth came to its feet. In a long wave they walked slowly out of the jungle, weapons ready and pointed at the village.

"Come on, Mosby," Casey said. "Keep it on line."

Mosby didn't answer, merely increased the pace of his plod across the paddy.

He'd lagged back from the assault wave for a good reason. This was not the first, nor the twentieth time David Mosby had gone in walking—sans cover—into a peaceful village. And at least twenty of those times the village had come alive to the popping of incoming rifle rounds and the chatter of Chicom machine guns. Mosby was being a little slow this ayem because he was trying to pick out something to flatten behind if the village was hot. But, at Casey's urging, he speeded up. Mosby scanned the hamlet. No sign of movement other than a water buffalo restlessly moving about its brush pen and a dozen or so chickens clucking down a dusty path.

To his left, beyond the jungle patch that sheltered the village and also led to the edge of the highway, Mosby could see the long wave of the Eleventh's sweep, closing the jaws. Then a clump of brush flamed black/white and, as tiny soldiers pin-wheeled through the air, he heard the smash of an explosion bend the weeds of the field.

The Fifteenth went suddenly flat and weapons came up. Smooth rhythm as Blind Pig—thirty meters down the line from Mosby—thudded onto his prodigious chest: bipod legs of the M-60 hitting at the same time, operating handle back once to move the gun from half-load to full-load.

Shannon was sprawled beside him, holding up the belt of ammo that fed into the gun. He automatically checked the metal belted rounds for dirt. Blind Pig—ever the expert—left the sights flat and scanned, head up, for any movement from the village.

The explosion's echo died away. No fire from either the brush or the Americans—by now the Fifteenth had learned to hold fire unless there was a target. Then rifle shots spattered from the Eleventh's also down troopies.

"Fuckin' lightweights be shootin' 'thout . . ." Blind Pig grumbled about the Eleventh until he saw a target: a short, slender man wearing black pajamas. The man broke out of a knot of trees about a hundred meters from where the boobytrap had gone off.

Blind Pig scuttled sideways, right hand pulling in on the pistol grip of the gun, left hand firmly clamped on the top of the stock—pushing down. Still, without sights, he squeezed very firmly on the trigger and the M-60 began to sputter. The rounds sprayed dust across the dry paddy and Blind Pig—who avoided tracer rounds like the plague—used the dust spurts to correct fire. Four rounds . . . five . . . and the bullets swept the man's legs out from under him as if by an invisible broom.

Blind Pig clambered to his knees as the VC smashed down. He brought up the twenty-pound machine gun and fired a full six-round burst into the body.

"It best to be sure," he explained to Shannon as he came to his feet and ambled forward to check the body and his marksmanship. Blind Pig was not a cruel man.

The squad leapfrogged efficiently through the village and after a dozen search-and-destroy missions had developed a certain series of moves. Lieutenant Fuller—though not the most experienced of leaders—stayed in the background and let Casey run the operation.

Blind Pig was positioned fifteen or twenty meters from the next hut to be searched—far enough away for his machine gun to cover both the front and the sides of the structure.

Shannon, once the Fifteenth had occupied the village with no further contact, had draped the ammo belts around Blind Pig's neck, mock-saluted, and explained that, with the private's permission, he had to go see how the rest of the war was going.

This left Blind Pig back to his perpetual bitching about not having an assistant gunner, this time to Buellton, the medic. Blind Pig was particularly pissed because he thought Shannon had done an okay job as AG. Taliaferro flanked him by three or four meters, his M-79 grenade launcher providing backup and also an instant way to drop the hut if the searchers started taking fire. Martinez, being the most experienced man in the squad besides Mosby, covered the rear of the hut. Nearby was Willie the Semi-Brown.

"Every now and then," Martinez explained to Willie, "we find ourselves a sorta bright gook, who goes out the back door when we come in the front."

Brown looked puzzledly at the hut's solid rear.

"Don't get it. I don't see any door . . ."

"That hut, amigo, is straw. You put fear in their hearts and they gonna go through that straw like it's not even there. And, if they come through . . ." Martinez gestured with his M-79. "You do what I do—which means better you not shoot before you make sure you ain't shootin' Mosby. Sabe, señor?"

Willie sabed.

Taking the hut went as follows: Two men flanked the open entrance, covering the inside. One man had an M-16, the other was ready with grenades. A third man stood to one side of the doorframe, banging on it with his rifle and shouting. Eventually, either someone came out, or somebody screwed up enough courage to dive through the straw. On each hut, the three men changed positions.

So it was Mosby who slid into the hut and found the three women: they were crouched against one wall, eyes white with terror. Mosby motioned with his rifle barrel to the door. They didn't move. He motioned again. Then in very pidgin Vietnamese: "Di-di. Di-di. Ngoia!" The women rose and sidled toward the exit. Mosby kept the rifle leveled. Even though two of the women were really barely out of puberty and the third woman ancient, unpleasant things could happen when you relaxed.

The women went out the door, and Mosby concentrated on the search. The hut was mostly bare except for a couple of wide straw hats hanging from the wall. There were also three rolled sleeping mats in a corner, a center mat next to the fire pit, and a large pottery rice jar. Mosby saved the center mat for last—carefully lifting the hats away from the wall with his rifle's muzzle and watching for any boobytrap wire. Then he kick unrolled each of the mats. Keeping his head to one side, just in case, he knocked the cover off the rice jar. There was nothing inside but rice.

Outside, Casey and Fritsche guarded the three women. They were dressed pretty much the same: bare, work-horned feet; baggy silk black pajama bottoms; very white and very threadbare button-front blouses. Fritsche motioned the women toward the village square, while Casey went inside the hut to see what Mosby was up to.

Mosby was squatted near the central mat, waiting. They exchanged looks—whose turn was it this time? Mosby finally laid down his rifle, unclipped a grenade, and straightened the bradded-out ends of the pin. Then, with one finger of his left hand inside the right and his right hand holding the grenade ready, he flipped the mat back with his foot. He went nose to the ground as he saw, instead of dirt floor, a gaping hole. By that time Casey was halfway out of the hut, rifle leveled on the uncovered bunker. But he held his fire.

Inside the hole were five bags of rice, two rifles, and one young man cowering against a dirt wall. Casey pointed his rifle exactly between the young man's eyes.

"Gook. Out. Slow."

The kid crept out of the hole, and Mosby and Casey automatically moved to either side of him.

"We got us a zip," Mosby said. "Somebody go wake Lieutenant Fuller up."

By the time the platoon leader had arrived along with the company's own white mouse, Hai, the young Viet Cong had been knocked face down on the ground and carefully pat-searched. Casey made him come up to his knees, put his hands behind his head, and squat back. Hai rattled off a crisp series of syllables. The man looked sullen. Hai kicked him in the chest, sending the man sprawling. Then he repeated the question. A one-word answer.

"He says he is not VC."

"Yeah. Fuck he ain't."

"He says he does not have ID card."

More questions. More semi-lies.

"He says he live in village all his life."

"What's the name of the headman?"

"He does not know."

The white mouse sighed.

"Too bad. He is such a young person. I thought maybe he was telling the truth."

105

Hai unsnapped his holster catch. Before he could draw or even aim the gun, Fuller grabbed his hand.

"That isn't the way we do things," Fuller said.

Hai shrugged. He was untroubled.

"That is not the way Americans do things. So, you do not shoot him. Instead we put him on helicopter send him to Song Nhanh. Let the province chief shoot him.

"It makes no difference to me."

Casey looked first at the young VC, then at the South Vietnamese policeman.

"You ever think, Lieutenant," Casey said, "that mebbe we're backin' the wrong side?"

Fuller chose not to answer.

A tank is a mighty fine thing, Sinclair thought happily to himself from his poised stance in the TC hatch of the M-48A3 tank. Beside him in the gunner's hatch coughed a less-than-happy Ron Mead, who had a handkerchief tied around his nose and mouth to keep out the dust.

Sinclair was riding in the lead tank of the main assault unit as it thundered up Highway 13. It was quite a column—two unarmed jeeps in the lead, two jeeps armed with 106mm, Sinclair's tank, five other tanks and half-a-dozen M-113 Armored Personnel Carriers, and then two tank-dozers, trailed by a D-7 Caterpillar bulldozer.

This was the first echelon. Behind it was the second column— thirty huge, five-ton trucks. Overhead swept the constantly patrolling Hueys and Huey Cobra gunships of an entire air cavalry platoon.

Let them see, Sinclair thought, just what happens when the U.S. Army finally gets its thumb out and decides to move. That's the only thing that impresses these Asiatics. You've got to show them you won't take any guff.

He turned to Mead, who was swaying back and forth in the gunner's hatch, slightly to the tank turret's rear. Mead looked greenish through the dust blanketing his face. He had a red bandanna tied across his nose and a heavy set of driving goggles over his eyes. Jerk looks like a ring-tailed tarsier, Sinclair thought.

"Carthago delenda est," he shouted to the correspondent.

Dusty eyebrows lifted in puzzlement.

"Cathago delenda est," Sinclair tried again.

"What cargo?"

It was Sinclair's turn to look bewildered.

"Didn't you say something about cargoes being delivered yesterday?"

"Never mind."

Sinclair turned back as the tank slowed, swung left off the road and down across a rivulet next to the long-destroyed bridge, then ground its way back onto the highway. Sinclair spotted something and jabbed Mead. The man's eyes followed to where Sinclair was pointing and then widened behind the goggles as he scrabbled his camera up into position. Five shots whirclanked through Mead's motordrive.

"Helluva picture."

It would be, Sinclair thought, as the tank clanked past the whitening bones of the skeleton.

"Viet Cong?"

"Of course," Sinclair lied. "We always pick up our own dead."

Hell, if he only knew. Somebody had told Sinclair that the skeleton had been beside Highway 13 since 1966. Sinclair wondered if Mead's photos would be sharp enough to pick up the Dutch Masters cigar some grunt had stuffed between the skull's broken teeth.

"There it is," Sinclair said, waving his hand in a dramatic gesture. "Ba Rei."

Mead looked disappointed. Evidently he'd expected some kind of VC fortress. Ba Rei looked only like one of a thousand settlements that must've been built by the French for their rubber plantation workers. A handful of plaster huts, twenty or thirty more thatched mud huts, some corrals, and a flattened dirt market area in the center of the village. It was quite a long way from the Maginot Line. Before Mead could comment, Sinclair leaned over to him.

"The search units report significant finds," he said. Mead's expression brightened.

"Whooppie shit," Mosby said, looking sourly at the assemblage of "enemy" weapons and equipment they'd policed up. It wasn't much. The hut-by-hut search had produced two M-2 U.S.-issue carbines in fairly good working order; one SKS carbine with a broken stock; one Tokarev pistol with a rusted-shut slide; one Browning automatic rifle that was so old there wasn't a trace of parkerization left on it.

Shannon grinned across the small pile.

"You say something, Specialist?"

"Negative, Major. Not a word."

"Didn't think so. Now, gimme a hand laying these things out so they look like something. The Division Commander's showing up with some reporter."

They heard gleeful shouting. Both men flinched their rifles up, then relaxed.

"Paydirt! We struck it rich," Fuller was shouting.

Just then the dust cloud out on Highway 13 resolved itself into a column of vehicles. Moments later, Sinclair's tank rumbled up the cart track into the village.

"Your platoon found this, Lieutenant?"

"Yessir."

Sinclair beamed as Mead circled the cache and readied his camera again.

"We'll want you in this shot, General."

Sinclair straightened his gigline, picked up one of the AK-47s Fritsche had uncovered carefully buried under the buffalo corral's dung heap.

It was quite a discovery. The cache itself was built exotically—almost ten meters square and three meters deep. It had been lovingly roofed with cross beams and then the heavy beams covered with plank roofing. Over this had gone three inches of dirt and then buffalo shit. The only reason Fritsche had found it is that he stumbled, groped to recover, said some well-chosen words about getting shit on his boots, and then realized dung heaps don't creak when you step on them. Inside the cache was the treasured trove.

The pièce de résistance was a wheeled, 12.7mm Degtyarev heavy machine gun that looked as if it had fought in every war since the Bolshevik Revolution. There were also several thousand belted rounds. And there was more, including twenty shiny-new Kalashnikov Type 56 rifles with ammo, half a dozen M-16s, two wicker packs of medical supplies, and ten one-hundred-pound sacks of rice, each one clearly stamped U.S.-AID. Rice from the Sacramento delta of California shipped to Vietnam and intended for issue to starving peasants.

Mead was enthralled.

"This'll make people think some about LBJ's program, won't it, General?"

Sinclair, knowing full well which side his promotion bread was buttered on, grunted noncommittally.

"If you guys will get out of the way," Mead went on, "I'd really like to get some pictures."

Fritsche glared at the tubby reporter, then picked up his M-16 and sauntered away to where Mosby was leaning against a tree.

"Wanna bet on who'll end up having personally found that shit," Mosby said.

"Fuck it," Fritsche said. "Medals and that shit don't get me no closer to the real world, do they?"

After being thoroughly photographed, the Viet Cong cache was loaded on a couple of trucks to be returned, with escort, to Hue Duc. There the supplies would become another figure in the mindless statistics America fought the Vietnam war by. The machine gun would probably end up on display in front of some high-ranking officer's billet. The AK-47s would magically disappear. No full auto weapon was allowed to be taken home as a souvenir, but somehow no AK ever ended up being used for anything. The grunts suspected the officers, the officers suspected the CIA, and the CIA suspected the State Department.

The M-16s, the med supplies, and the rice would be returned to the Vietnamese—meaning the ARVNs. And this certainly meant that within a month or two Fritsche might rediscover them, since the ARVNs would most likely resell or even give the supplies back to the Viet Cong.

"What are we doing?" Brown wanted to know.

"We be sittin' on perimeter," Blind Pig said, without taking his eyes off the jungle in front of them. "We be waitin' to get our ass shot off."

"But, nothing much's happened."

"I know. That what be terrifyin'."

"I don't get it."

"Look, fool. Nobody go to Ba Rei without gettin' killed a lot. That be one of God's prime laws. We gone sit here while those engineers trash that place. Sooner or later, we gone get hit and hit fuckin' hard."

Fortunately, for once Blind Pig was a lousy prophet. The men of the Fifteenth sat all day while behind them the destruction of Ba Rei proceeded.

First the peasants were grouped with whatever personal gear they could carry. Then the gear was painstakingly and humiliatingly searched by division MPs.

The village pigs were herded onto ramped five-tons for transport to the new home the villagers would be relocated to. The water buffalo were shot, since the animals tended to go berserk at the scent of an American. Of course, the villagers would be recompensed—American money, converted into piasters, given to the Song Nhanh province chief for "appropriate distribution." The chances of that money's ever showing up in the hands of the relocated villagers were nil.

Then the cruelty of pragmatism went to work. If the United States Army had an ounce of sensitivity, the villagers would have been loaded onto the duece-and-a-halfs and taken south before the next stage. Instead, since the Army wanted to provide "proper security" for the people, they were forced to watch while their homes and village were razed to the ground.

Sinclair was quite correct in his comparison with Carthage. First the D-7 went through the village, its blade cocked about a foot off the ground. When the big Cat smashed into the first hut there was a low moan from the villagers. Subconsciously they swayed forward. Safeties clicked off MP rifles, and the villagers froze again. From that moment to the end, there was not a sound from any of them. Not even the babies.

After the thatched roofs dropped and the walls were smashed down, the dozer dropped its blade to the ground and began leveling the earth itself—scattering the rubble into foot-high mounds.

"Look at them gooks cry," Taliaferro said with satisfaction.

He jumped as two sets of eyeballs daggered at him.

"You be the dumbest motherfuckin' chuck I ever see," Blind Pig said.

"Hey, man. Every time we come up here those fuckers let the VC dump on us, right? Man, this is where the fuckers take their R&R. And you're feeling sorry for them?"

"You know what's gonna happen to those dinks?" Mosby spoke from his crouched position behind the brushline.

"They said they're gonna put 'em in a new village."

"Fuck, you believe that? They're gonna put up some fuckin' tents out middle of some swamp and that's gonna be their new fuckin' home. No farmland, no houses, no shit."

"Fuck 'em," Taliaferro said. "They're gooks."

"I tell you what," Blind Pig said. "Maybe they VC, maybe they just scared shitless, since ain't none of us standing guard over them at night.

"But what the fuck you think you gone be if some roundeye asshole come in, fucks up the home you grew up in, and then say he be on your side? If you not before, you sure gone be one bad motherfuckin' VC after."

110

Mosby almost applauded. It may be the longest speech he had ever heard Blind Pig make. Taliaferro looked for support from Casey.

"You don't win hearts and minds by burnin' down somebody's spread," the sergeant said flatly. He spat.

The squad went back to looking at the jungle and waiting to get hit.

"Come on, mamasan," DeeJay said encouragingly as he boosted the old woman into the back of the truck. He was rewarded with a look of pure hatred.

"Sorry about thàt shit," he said as he backed away.

"This will make a helluva story," Mead said.

"How . . . uh . . . do you plan on writing it?" Sinclair wanted to know.

"The way it was, of course. I think people back home would be proud to see what you've done. These people have lived for years in fear of their lives. And now . . ."

Sinclair relaxed.

At 1600 the troops formed up on the road.

Behind them was a flat, dusty piece of land that looked as if it had been planed. The trees had been blown down for fifty meters on either side of Highway 13, the paths were wiped out by the dozer and the tracks.

Ba Rei had been obliterated.

Casey looked at the dustbowl.

"Makes you real fucking proud," he said. "Okay. Form up. Ten meters. Let's go home."

At 1400 that afternoon, while the Americans were busy destroying Ba Rei, a squad of ten local Cong had nastily buried a boobytrap—formerly a 500-pound U.S. bomb—in the middle of Highway 13. They had covered and packed the hole, trod the ground flat, and repacked it again. Then one VC had carefully run a jeep wheel back and forth over the dirt, so it appeared like a normal section of the heavily traveled highway.

The only clue to the boobytrap was the long green wire that stretched from the detonator across the road and up seventy meters into a clump of brush. One man crouched in the brush, his fingers wrapped around the green wire. Waiting.

The VC allowed the first jeeps to cross over the trap, and the two-and-a-half-ton trucks filled with the Ba Rei villagers.

The next vehicle was an M-13 personnel carrier. Sitting on the tracked steel box were about ten American soldiers. By this time in the war, all Americans had learned that the thin aluminum-armored carrier was a death trap. So the 113s were heavily sandbagged and the troops rode on the top deck by preference. They far preferred the possibility of taking a sniper hit then getting blown up by a mine.

For conventional, small boobytraps, the theory was semivalid. But it did not work for 500 pounds of explosive.

The blast went off just under the driver's legs. The shock first lifted the ten tons of the track almost a foot off the ground. The floor of the track can-openered inward. The driver and the track commander became a slime of red jelly, scattered across the bulged-open track's roof.

The shrapnel from the floor hit the soldiers. Four died instantly. Three more were blown twenty meters through the air to their deaths. Three lived long enough for the screamin'-in dustoff Hueys to get them to 93d Evac. All three would undergo multiple amputation, and two would die of traumatic shock.

The Viet Cong who set off the boobytrap was unseen as he dashed into the deep brush.

The destruction of Ba Rei was complete.

CHAPTER THIRTEEN

DUAN

EVEN AFTER A full day's march, Duan was feeling strangely energized, although his body groaned for relief from the forced pace he had ordered. The 302d and the Phu Loi Battalion had moved out within two hours of Duan's conference with Major Tran. The first haven blown, they were heading toward the Octopus, their ultimate goal.

Oddly, one part of Duan's brain was ready to push him to march on into the night. He hadn't felt like this since they crossed the Cambodian border. It was an imperative, urging him toward some grand confrontation. A very quiet insistence, like the tapping of the rain on the parachute that canopied Duan's hammock.

A figure lifted like smoke out of the shadows, and Duan's heart did a brief, absurd staccato as he recognized one of his aides. Duan came out of the hammock and, in the light of the flickering fat lamp, read the communiqué.

He absorbed the facts. His opponent, Sinclair, had acted as Duan had expected. Ba Rei was destroyed. History moved in multicolored pins across a map. And not all your piety and wit, he thought, can wipe out one word of it.

Duan called for his batman, and dug into his rucksack. He was dusting off the bottle of Rémy Martin that he'd carried all the way from Hanoi when Lau came into the lamplight.

"Are you busy?" he asked politely.

"The Commissar is putting on a show," Lau answered.

Duan nodded. Agit-prop was an important part of his commissar's duties. The show consisted of light entertainment, some jokes, a few puppets and clowns, pretty women when available, and then a relaxed session of kiem thao. Agit-prop worked wonders for morale. It got the kinks and the complaints out. It was an effort at common honesty and self-leveling that Duan wholly agreed with. The problem was that the pressure had been too great lately for him to allow his commissar to perform properly. Also Duan was never very good at a party.

"You'll attend for me?"

"Again?"

"Thank you," Duan said. He held up the bottle. "I think Major Tran and I should have a talk."

Lau admired the cognac. "Talk and French brandy go well together," he finally said. "For officers, I mean." The last a bit wistfully.

"I have one more bottle. For a friend."

"A promise?"

"No. An invitation. But on another night."

"Shall I send for the major?"

"No," Duan said. "Under the circumstances, I think I should go to him."

Lau slipped out of the tent. Duan heard the whisper of a runner. That man would go to the headquarters of the Phu Loi Battalion and tell Tran that the general was coming. Officially, it would be a surprise visit. Unofficially, nervous sentries would pass Duan through their perimeter without putting a bullet between his ribs.

Duan glanced at the bottle of cognac again. He wished he had a whole case to prepare him for what he was about to do.

The puppet waved its black-pajamaed arms and sticked across

113

the tiny stage. It was brandishing an enormous club and whacking at a clump of weeds that represented bushes. The puppet bobbed back, braced itself, and hooted: "Emerge, capitalist fool! Emerge!"

The "bushes" gave a shake and then were still. The puppet turned to the audience.

"How do you remove a cowardly American?"

The audience began chuckling.

"Much like your bowels after a night of long drinking. It comes out easily, but then there is nothing worth fertilizing your rice with."

The laughter spread as Lau entered. He beamed his broad peasant face around, smiled at the joke, and pushed his way toward a seat—carefully chosen, since it was next to a Phu Loi brother. Phan Xuan Cung broke into uncontrollable laughter as Lau settled himself beside him.

Onstage, the puppet was flailing away at the bushes. Moans and shrieks came from the weeds. Moments later, the other puppet was forced out. Obviously an American, with its masque-white face, bauble-covered green uniform, and cowardice. The Viet Cong puppet felled the imperialist, and stretcher-bearer puppets retrieved the American. Before they fled stage right, they dropped him several times, to whines from the puppet and howls from the audience.

Lau nudged Cung and whispered, "Pity it is not that easy."

"How do you find an imperialist corpse?" Cung asked.

Lau gave up.

"You blow up a whorehouse." Cung laughed at his own joke.

"How do you tell a dead American from a dead pig?" Cung went on.

The sergeant waited.

"The dead pig smells better. One more. How do you tell a puppet soldier from shit?"

Lau couldn't wait to hear.

"You can't. They both run."

Now it was Lau's turn.

"What are the three things a starving dog won't eat? Shit, a dead American, and a live puppet soldier."

"Better, comrade," Cung said. "Do you know why the puppet flag is yellow and red? Because everything that is not Red is yellow."

Cung chuckled, but Lau's laugh honked across the crowd. In mid-laugh there was a sudden silence, and the laughter came

114

back to him. The laugh came from People's Commissar Vuong Gia Thuy, as he stepped onto the tiny stage.

"I admire brave men who can laugh at the stupidities and arrogance of our enemy."

There was an instant hush in the clearing.

"We learn by laughing," Thuy went on.

"Kiem thao," Lau grunted under his breath. Self-criticism now.

"But sometimes we laugh too much. We must not forget that while we are sitting here, our brothers of Ba Rei have little to laugh about. Those that the dog Americans let live are now far from their homes and fields. Their only hope now must be that we soldiers are able to liberate them."

Lau cocked a glance at his Phu Loi neighbor. Cung was listening closely.

"There is much work for us before that can happen. We must never forget that we soldiers are at the forefront of learning, through recognizing our own shortcomings in deed and thought."

Lau decided that he would have been better off staying away from the clearing and spending his time cleaning the Comrade General's rifle.

"For instance, in my own case, I recognize that I did not provide sufficient support for my soldiers since we have crossed the border, and perhaps I have not been fully alert in ensuring that our own bo-dois are sufficiently acquainted with their new comrades from the South.

"Perhaps all of us from the North have been overly concerned about our own well-being, and have perhaps forgotten the concern we all share about the upcoming struggle.

"Is that true, Sergeant Lau?"

Lau grunted. He'd been wondering just how the commissar would entrap him. He rose to his feet, head properly bowed, and the thought trickled fast that before you set out to trap the tiger you had best figure out what happens once the trap is sprung.

"Sergeant Nguyen Van Lau. Headquarters Detachment. My pardon, Comrade Commissar, but as you perhaps know, I am but a poor peasant. Also I come from the Bac Can region, and as we all know, Bac Can is the only province where the buffalo must show the farmers which rice plot is their own."

There was a small ripple of amusement. Some of the soldiers of the 302d, who knew Lau, were waiting in anticipation. Lau saw one NVA soldier nudge his dozing Viet Cong neighbor into alertness.

"So perhaps you might be more specific for this poor soldier, Comrade Commissar?"

"I shall," Thuy snapped. "It is my understanding that you spent this afternoon querying some of our tired brothers, after their arrival, as to the availability of rice spirits in this region."

"That is true," Lau sorrowed. "But it was not for myself."

"Then for whom? The Comrade General?"

"Such a thing would never be considered," Lau said indignantly. "It was for . . ." He paused, delicately. ". . . Others."

"Name those who are more interested in their belly fires than in the struggle!"

"Perhaps that would not be wise."

"Comrade Lau!"

"Very well. As a loyal servant of the people, even though the Party has never considered me a worthy candidate for membership, those spirits I was trying to find were to aid my superiors."

"Who?"

"I noticed," Lau said, "on our long march that there were those who had trouble stomaching the simple diet of a soldier. Some of those became most ill, and it became necessary for some of us bo-dois to carry them in litters for long distances. Rice spirits can help them."

Even in the flickering firelight, Commissar Thuy's jaw tightened. He had, indeed, gone down with dysentery and had to be litter-borne for almost six days.

"Bowel sickness can afflict anyone."

"Of course," Lau agreed. "But perhaps it would be less serious if all of us had grown up on the simple diet of a peasant."

Thuy considered.

"That is a valid thought, Comrade Sergeant."

Lau looked for his seat.

"Your thoughts interest me," the commissar went on. "Since you are, as you say, but a peasant, perhaps you would share with us how you, a member of the command group, manage to maintain the proper humility of thought. Or do you?"

"It is easy for me," Lau tried. "Being in the presence of the Comrade General at all times, his clarity and knowledge always remind me of our struggle."

"But is not the Comrade General, with his interest in Western works, perhaps sometimes guilty of what might be called intellectual adventurism?"

You little monkeyshit, Lau thought furiously. You cannot trap me, so you go after my boss?

"How could that be?" Lau answered, in a reasonable tone.

"I have noticed that you spend every possible moment with our Comrade General, even when it might be easier for you to be with the simple bo-dois. With you by his side, how could he possibly fall into that trap?"

Thuy gobbled. Lau was trying to decide how to go for the kill. He was saved as, across the clearing, Sergeant Minh stood, looking equally respectful. Lau made a note to repay Minh the three bottles of beer he owed him.

"Comrade Commissar," Minh said. "Sergeant Lau has brought up an important question. Since I am, like yourself, a member of the political cadre, perhaps we have all spent too much time concerning ourselves with the thoughts and behavior of our superiors. Did you not tell us that the Party flows like a great waterfall over the lives of the people, protecting them like the fish?"

"I did."

"Then I think all of us must be in error. I would call for those of us to consider our own actions first, and to realize that all education and leadership must come from above. Is that not true?"

All that Thuy could come up with was the old saw: Lao T'szu, confounded by the question of an idiot.

Tran's tent—a pegged-down tarp stretched over a line between two trees—was heavy with the night dew. The dew was a sign, Duan told himself as he approached the tent, of heavy rains to come.

Unconsciously he checked the moon overhead, as pure and cold a vision as any man could want. There were no atmospheric rings around it. This meant no rain tomorrow, which meant the American helicopters would be filling the air. More problems.

One of Tran's guards stood in front of him. He recognized the general, stepped back, and saluted. Duan, clutching the bottle of cognac more closely, moved around the sentry. Tran was crouched a couple of meters from his tent, over a tiny pit in the ground. Low, leaf-fed flames flickered, barely visible. He rose as the general walked forward. Tran's face was freshly washed and his eyes were very red.

"Comrade General."

He did not salute. Duan stepped to the other side of the tiny fire and sat cross-legged. He sniffed at the steam rising from the small metal bowl over the fire.

"You eat late, Major . . . The smell is delicious."

"When I was first underground, with the Young Patriot Movement, this was before I became a full soldier with the Kang Chien, I worked as a noodle chef."

"Ah?"

"The restaurant I worked in was favored by de Lattre's officers."

Tran tasted the mixture in the bowl.

"At one time I thought that when the struggle is over I might become a noodle cook again."

Duan did not need to question—neither man truly believed he would live to see Giai Phong.

"You have heard about Ba Rei," Duan said instead.

"I have."

"Noodles may be the answer sometimes. But when the situation is serious we should look toward the West."

Duan took the bottle from his shirt and set it on the ground. Tran smiled slightly and picked the liter up.

"French, hmm? You must have brought this from Hanoi."

"A good soldier knows what is essential on a campaign."

Tran took the bottle and drank, then saluted the air. "To Ba Rei." He drank again, then gave the bottle to Duan.

"A better toast," Duan said. "Ba Rei is dead. To the General Offensive."

If Tran had been holding the bottle he would have dropped it. He turned away to his noodles, recovering.

"When?"

"Soon," Duan said.

"Soon is not a time I recognize."

Duan chose to sip from the bottle and not answer.

"How many divisions have come south?"

"Ten," Duan answered.

"And how many soldiers of the Resistance will be committed?"

"All of the Quan Doi Chu Luc. Half of our Regional Forces."

"The General Offensive," Tran considered, concentrating on tasting his steaming noodles. "From this will come the General Rising, correct?"

"You are correct."

"Did you know our late Comrade General Tanh?"

"I was never so fortunate."

Nguyen Chi Tanh was the highest-ranking general in the National Liberation Front, the only general besides the famed Vo Nguyen Giap to carry the four full stars of a general. He had been critically wounded in a B-52 raid in July '67, carried across the border into Cambodia in time to die, and was afterward buried in Hanoi with full military honors.

"You are aware that General Tanh"—and from here Tran chose his words carefully—"cautioned the Central Committee in Hanoi to not slavishly follow the examples of the past."

"If he had not died a martyr's death," Duan said, "I am sure that Hanoi would have wished him to reconsider that statement."

"You wish a taste of my noodles, Comrade General?"

"Perhaps later. Oh, I seem to recall that your Binh Dinh Province Committee has said this General Offensive will only occur once every thousand years. And that it will end the war and constitute the wishes of both the Party and the people of the South."

"I can only hope," Tran said, "that someday I can clearly see the wishes of the people. I guess that is why I am just a major."

"My sergeant attempts the same kind of pigshit with me, Major. Quelle merde, m'sieu."

"Oui, mon général. En français, suis f'tou!"

"So we are fucked. Why?"

"Because we are sitting here in the damned jungle, Comrade General. We are doing no more than nibbling the Americans as if we were so many rabid ducks.

"Now Comrade Ho and Comrade Giap, from their comfortable palaces in Hanoi, decide, in their infinite wisdom, that now is the time for us to mount the General Offensive, and that all our peasants in the South are going to rise up with their pitchforks and the war will suddenly be over?"

"That is, although your dialectics are incorrect, the theory."

"I will make a prediction, Comrade General. But only if you promise to give me that bottle."

"Here."

"We shall go out," Tran continued, "to confront the imperialists and their helicoptors, and we shall wreak havoc. We shall take their cities . . . how many cities, Comrade General, are we planning to attack?"

"One hundred."

"We shall attack those cities, Comrade General. Not one of us shall retreat and not one of us shall falter. Now, Comrade General, I must also tell you this is very good cognac. I am getting drunk and saying things that perhaps your sergeant shall shoot me for."

"That time has passed, but only if you give me that damned bottle before you finish it."

Tran passed the bottle back, then went on.

119

"We shall, as I said, attack. And then you know what will happen? We shall die very nobly where we stand. Because we are at least four years from the time that our people are aware enough to rise up. I frankly see our Comrade Hero in Hanoi, Comrade General Giap, as trying to do another Dien Bien Phu!"

Duan had, after several conferences with the man, his own reservations about Giap. But he said nothing.

"He," Tran went on, "like most of those who lead us, are realizing they shall die soon. They want to see our country as one before then. Noble thoughts. But do you know who is going to die first, Comrade General?"

Duan just sipped from the bottle. He let Tran answer the question himself.

"You, Comrade General Duan, and myself. I promise you one thing. Because of this misbegotten, mistimed thing called a General Offensive, neither one of us shall live to see Giai Phong. And there is only one thing to do about it."

"Which is?" Duan was fascinated. Tran had passed well beyond any rational borders of insubordination, well into treason.

"To get totally drunk and prepare ourselves for death," Tran said as he took the bottle from Duan and upended it.

CHAPTER FOURTEEN

SHANNON

SHANNON HANDED THE polished and restained AK-47 to Major General Lee Sinclair. He hefted the Chicom rifle.

"Ve-ry fine, Major. Very fine. It'll hang nicely on the wall here."

The wall here of the command trailer was just above the photos of the Korean War Sinclair next to the destroyed tank, and the shots of the yellow-scarfed Sinclair at various obviously peacetime Army awards ceremonies.

"Yessir. Uh . . . I have the poop portfolio ready."

A smile crossed the general's lips. "That's the current term?"

"Yessir." Shannon was still maintaining his basic hostile survival attitude.

"We'll get to that in a moment." Sinclair turned again to look at the rifle. "Did you ever consider something odd, Major?"

"Pardon?"

"Some soldier liberated this weapon. Because it is full auto, he'll never be able to take it home as a souvenir. Correct?"

"That's the MAC-V directive, sir."

"So he gets no souvenir. But, do you know what would happen if I decided to bring it back? Exactly nothing. I end up with a war relic I did nothing to earn, and the man who did earn it has nothing but a memory. We serve in an odd Army, Major."

"We do that, sir."

"Oh. By the way."

"Sir?"

"Our first meeting?"

"Yessir?"

"Perhaps I was a little quick. I was tired. Settling in. Possibly I was a bit testy."

It was, for Sinclair, an apology.

"I was a little wound up too, sir."

"Pour yourself a drink, Major." Sinclair nodded at the containers on the sideboard. Shannon clinked himself a thin slide from the decanter labeled BOURBON.

"More generous, Major. And one for me."

Shannon followed orders. The general took his drink, went behind the leather-topped desk, and sank back into his armchair with a contented grunt.

"Tell me what we have."

"The engagement"—Shannon chose the word carefully—"between the Second of the Eleventh and the VC force appears to have been with a main-line unit."

"That's intelligence? Obvious, Major. No Viet Cong casualties found. All rounds dug out of the bodies Chicom, except for the .50-caliber slugs. No significant reaction when we put our forces into Ba Rei? Do better, Shannon. Sorry. Dennis, I hope?"

"Whatever, sir. You're right. Obvious. From interrogation of the one confirmed VC found at Ba Rei, we have an ID on the unit in question. Mainline Viet Cong. The Phu Loi Battalion. Were you briefed on them, sir?"

"Negative."

"They're called the Phu Loi because, back in the fifties, there was a prison camp full of suspected Communists in that city. The government decided it was cheaper to poison them than try them. They named their battalion as a memorial."

Sinclair shuddered a bit.

"They're just about the best main-line force in the country."

"The best, Dennis?"

"Yessir."

121

"Do you remember, Major, that back during the Big War that General Montgomery issued a directive on discussions of Rommel? Montgomery felt that the Desert Army was turning the man into some kind of demigod. After that he destroyed Rommel at El Alamein."

"Yessir. But I also read that Monty had Rommel's picture pinned up over his cot."

Sinclair drained his drink and made another.

"Your point, Major. We'll return to this in a moment. Go ahead with your poop."

"Interrogation, and other sources, confirm that the Phu Loi is moving north."

Shannon went to the map.

"Toward the Octopus, of course."

"Yessir."

"With orders, I imagine, to avoid combat."

"The VC was only a private, sir."

"Still, a valid assumption. So we have one Viet Cong battalion moving toward thick, heavy jungle. From which we must assume they plan a major offensive."

"No argument, sir."

"Make yourself another one, Dennis . . . Now . . . given this . . . what would you as my acting G-2 suggest?"

Shannon splashed some more bourbon in his glass and added a great deal of ice while considering his response. He decided to bite the bullet.

"All troops on alert immediately, sir. We should insert one battalion outside the Octopus. They would have orders to sweep north, in platoon- and company-size patrols. We should insert a second battalion as a blocking force to the east in case we are in error. We should hold the third battalion as the response force."

Sinclair sipped at his drink, then smiled.

"One exception. We shall also deploy one company of armor up Highway 13, on roving patrol."

Armor, again, Shannon thought. But still: "Yessir."

"Now"—Sinclair moved his hands theatrically across the map—"we have one unit . . . the Fifteenth, I would think . . . headed north . . . straight down the throat of the Viet Cong. We have the Eleventh to the side in case of error . . . and we have the Twenty-ninth back here at Hue Duc. I like it."

He gave Shannon a wolfish smile of satisfaction.

"Now, we return to my initial point. We appear to have the entire Phu Loi Battalion in a trap. Is this true?"

"Yessir."

"Then, how do you expect me to listen to your stories about them being the best? If you were they, Major, is there any way you could picture yourself ending up with your ass in this kind of crack?"

Shannon was startled. The crudeness was unexpected.

"My point is," Sinclair continued, "that I have no respect for this heroic Phu Loi Battalion. And I propose to bring them to battle and destroy them."

Shannon lifted his glass in a toast. Sinclair responded, smiling.

"You were somewhat vehement," Sinclair went on, "about the quality of this unit. Personal experience?"

"Yessir. About three months ago."

"Tell me about it."

Shannon got up, went to the map, oriented himself and, as he spoke, his hands sketched unit movement.

"We inserted a LRRP team about . . . here . . . And they found the Phu Loi base camp. Everybody was home."

"I read the operation report, Major."

"Yessir. But, here's what really happened. We put the Twenty-ninth on their west. The Eleventh on their east. Up the middle we send the Fifteenth. Up here we had a B-52 strike zone."

Shannon's hands roughly sketched an oblong box around the map points.

"The operation report said contact was tentative."

"Yessir. That was CYA. Because we went in . . . swept the area . . . We went right into their base camp . . . and do you know what we found, General? We found shit. Not a goddamned thing! Something near three-hundred men slipped through this net, and not one of them was even seen."

"Spider holes? Caves?"

"Nossir. The Fifteenth's a very good unit. They looked and didn't find a blessed thing."

"Good story, Dennis. Let me make you a final drink. Because it would appear we're about to do the same to the much vaunted Phu Loi Battalion as we did to Ba Rei."

Shannon took the drink and drained it. He hoped Sinclair was right. But the back of his grunt brain suggested: You wish, General. Wish in one hand and shit in the other, and see which one fills up first.

CHAPTER FIFTEEN

THE SQUAD

"WHY ARE YOU not in Tho's booth?" Mr. Chi asked delicately.

"Because I wanted to talk to you," Mosby said, wondering why the hell he found it necessary to talk like a character out of a Charlie Chan movie. He was, after all, on his second tour.

"Ah?"

Mr. Chi was slender, good-looking, with a carefully manicured Gable mustache. About twenty-four. He dressed invariably in black French shoes, white slacks, and as obnoxiously loud a Hawaiian-style shirt as he could procure from the American PX in Saigon.

He was also widely known to the grunts as the local Viet Cong agent. He was, however, never wasted "accidentally," nor finked on by any of the GIs to officers, White Mice, or ARVN intelligence. There was a very good reason: Mr. Chi concentrated what energies and intelligence he had more on feathering his own mattress than on furthering the cause of Communism. The grunts figured if Chi was blown, the VC Regional Committee might replace him with a qualified agent. So, Mr. Chi was permitted to survive and prosper.

Chi's mission was to befriend the GI in order to seek intelligence. In Vietnam, the line grunt had almost no friends, so he took what he could get, where he could get it. Chi could advise on what noodle shops were the best, which whores were "sick," and how to buy silk ao dais for girl friends back home. Most importantly, he could advise them on how to be successful black marketeers.

Chi fished a Salem cigarette from his pack and decorously offered it to Mosby. Mosby shook his head. The man spoke very good—if sometimes oddly structured—English, which is why Mosby found himself talking in the same stilted manner.

"You have a problem, David?"

"Sorta. It's about Tho."

"Ah. She is pregnant?"

"Fuck no. *That's* the problem."

"I beg pardon?"

"If you don't fuck somebody, they don't get pregnant."

"Now, I understand. You wish to fuck her."

"Uh . . . no shit." For some reason, Mosby found himself a little uncomfortable.

"There is no problem, then. I will speak to her father and she will remain all night in her hooch. All you need do is find a way to stay all night in Hue Duc."

"No fucking way. If I go into her hooch, the VC might be waiting."

"That would not happen. You have my word."

"Yeah. Well. Also, Mr. Chi, I do not want to . . . to fuck her with mamasan in the next room."

"That is a problem," Chi solemnly agreed, lighting another Salem from his half-smoked cigarette.

"I want to take Tho to Saigon. Show her a good time."

"And?"

"Yeah . . . And . . . I do not want to offend anybody."

"I do not comprehend."

"Tho is a good girl. Perhaps a virgin?"

Chi just stared at him.

"She comes from a good family, right?"

"She does," Chi agreed. "Her father runs the same store for ten . . . fifteen years."

"So, if I ask Tho to Saigon I do not want to offend her or her father."

Chi puzzled at him.

"What do you want me to do?"

"First, is it OK if I take Tho to Saigon? I do not want to marry her. Will this make her father angry?"

"No. Vietnamese understand. Remember . . . her father is not a Catholic."

Mosby heaved a vast sigh of relief and chugged down half a bottle of Bier LaRue.

"That is all you want? For me to ask her father?"

"No. One more thing. You know we are going to the field?"

"Everyone knows."

"Okay. When we get back, I'll try to get a pass. I want you to buy a bus ticket for Tho. Then I want you to put her on the bus to Saigon. I will meet her at the station."

"I see no difficulty, David."

"You'll take care of the tickets now?"

"Not now."

"Why not?"

"I will buy them after you return from the field."

"Why not now, goddammit?"

"Because . . . and the Army did not tell you, but your officers know . . . the Fifteenth goes to the field and there is the Phu Loi Battalion waiting.''

Mosby's shocked response was echoed over the next twelve hours through the Fifteenth's entire base camp:

"Aw, fuuuuuuck!''

Screams there were—but the Fifteenth got ready to bump the boonies with efficiency. At least the experienced grunts did.

There were three men in First Squad's tent: Willie the Semi-Brown, Fritsche and Blind Pig.

Brown was staring disconsolately at the enormous pile of gear on his cot. Across the tent, Fritsche and Blind Pig were sitting in companionable silence. Fritsche had his sawed-off shotgun broken in half and was carefully toothbrushing around the ejectors. Blind Pig had his M-60 machine gun torn down—far beyond authorized field-stripping—and had the gas plug out and was running a pipe cleaner into the gas cylinder's port. If crud blocked that tiny interior hole, the M-60 becomes a rather ineffective club, instead of a helluva machine gun.

Blind Pig was a very skilled and talented gunner. Finally, he got it cleaned to his satisfaction. As he began reassembling the weapon, he noticed Brown's huge pile of gear and groaned. Fritsche glanced at him.

"Problem?''

"Yeah,'' Blind Pig said. "That dude.''

Fritsche also looked and also groaned.

"Shit.''

"Fucker's like that dude in Treasure Island, dig? Got him a Black Spot.''

" 'Fraid so,'' Fritsche said.

"Whyn't you show him?''

"Me? Shit! I ain't no brother. What's the matter with you?''

"Man, machine gunners be too mortal as it be. I ain't gettin' near no dude who got a death angel on his shoulder. 'Sides. I hear you bikers be fuckin' *immortal*.''

"We are,'' Fritsche agreed, dumping oil down the shotgun barrel and soaking the action. As he thought over Blind Pig's request, he inserted two #4 buckshot rounds into the chambers and snapped the shotgun closed. Contrary to orders, Fritsche's shotgun was always loaded, whether inside the perimeter, in the bazaar, or out in the field. He made up his mind and set the alleysweeper on his cot and got up to help Willie the Semi-Brown pack his gear for combat.

"You got all the looks of a man that's lost in space," Fritsche said.

Brown gloomed once again at the pile of gear.

"I don't understand how I can carry all this. Hell, it's got to weigh . . . what, eighty pounds?"

"More like ninety."

"I can't carry . . ."

"No shit, Dick Tracy. Where'd you park your squad car?"

"So what am I supposed to do?"

"First thing you're gonna do—with a twisting, pulling motion—is pull your head from your ass, rock back, and throw. Come on, Willie. You better start listening or somebody's gonna toast your cookies out there in the boonies."

Obediently, Brown sat down to listen. Fritsche fingered through the foothigh pile of gear on the cot.

"We'll start on the essentials."

Fritsche pulled the Gillette razor from the pile and set it to one side. This was item number one that Willie would be carrying. Brown gaped at him.

"Colonel Taylor, chickenshit motherfucker that he is, wants the troops to be clean-cut at all times. So you take the razor. But you don't take the lather can, you don't take the spare towel, and you don't take that Aqua-Velva."

"Why the hell not?"

"Gooks swear they can smell aftershave, just like we can honk out that nuoc mam they eat. Prob'ly they're fuckin' lyin', but who wants to take the chance? You go out, it's best to stink like they do.

"Second essential. Your rifle . . ."

By this time, the only rifle carried in Vietnam (with the exception of some Marines, Special Forces, and snipers) was the Colt AR-15—misnomenclatured the M-16, correctly nomenclatured the M-16A1. It was nylon and steel and was superlight, supereffective and totally recoilless. It fired a necked-down high-velocity .22-caliber round that, when it hit, would normally tumble and create awesomely lethal wounds. The weapon fired either semiautomatically—one shot each time the trigger was pulled—or fully automatic. This was dubbed rock and roll by the grunts. Pull the trigger back and the weapon kept firing until the twenty-round magazine was empty. While very lethal in an instant brush encounter, full auto quickly depleted the number of rounds the troops carried.

There were two main criticisms of the M-16. The first was that in its early days, it jammed in combat, which produced the uncomfortable condition known as death on the part of the jamee. This was due to the military's use of the wrong kind of powder and the propaganda that the M-16 never had to be cleaned. In fact, the M-16 needed to be cleaned and oiled as thoroughly as the most exotic weapon in the Army's arsenal. Maintained in such a manner, it never malfunctioned. The second objection was that the weapon was incapable of making the previously mentioned nasty holes in the enemy beyond a couple of hundred meters. This was somewhat true, but insignificant, since the average jungle combat occurred at about a twenty-meter range.

Willie the Semi-Brown semirealized, as Fritsche went through the ritual, that each piece of field gear that a grunt carried was deliberately chosen, deliberately modified, and deliberately carried and used in a certain manner. The rapid learners made it through the tour. The others . . . the others did not.

The survivors learned that the M-16 should be kept drenched in oil and torn down every night for recleaning, which included total disassembly of the bolt housing group, something that was supposedly unnecessary oftener than once a month.

In the rifle's butt was a snap compartment, which contained the weapon's cleaning gear—screw-apart rod, a small amount of 20-weight oil, and some cloth patches. The wiser grunt carried no patches, but much more oil—preferably 10-weight sewing machine oil (Singer brand by preference). The patches would be made from torn-off bits of bandolier cloth made up in the field.

Then the nylon stock and forehand were wound with two-inch-wide green duct tape. One turn went around the forehand at the top, then the tape was wound down, in one full wind, to the rear of the forehand. Two turns sealed that. On the butt, one turn went around the rifle sling clip, then, again up and around the stock—winding twice around the stock's end. This provided both visual camouflage (a break in the sight outline of the black nylon stock) and sound prevention. While the nylon elements were far more weather-worthy than wood, if they smacked into a tree they made a loud clonk. Infantrymen do not consider loud clonks desirable—especially during a night patrol.

Special Units—such as the Lurps—taped over the carrying sling entirely. On patrol, their rifles were *always* in their hands. But for the line grunts, who spent more time standing and waiting than shooting, the sling was a necessary way to get rid of the rifle when both hands were needed—like when standing in a mess line.

Trivia. But trivia that might give an infantryman—even as new as Willie the Semi-Brown—a slight edge.

And so it went from nose to toes:

The helmet, which consisted of the fiber helmet liner with canvas straps that fit around the wearer's skull plus the WWII steel pot. Over that went a greenish camouflage cover, held in place by a light brown rubber band. Dumb grunts kept their cigarettes, matches, and C-ration toilet paper and so forth in the rubber band. Dumb grunts also wrote graffiti on the front of the cammie cover.

Smart grunts learned quickly that anything that showed on the helmet might be defined by an unseen sniper as officer's insignia. So nothing except the brown C-rat paper matches would be carried there and any graffiti—FTA, peace emblems, NUKE THE SLOPES, or whatever—went on the helmet's rear. The grunts also learned the supposedly lubiquitous steel pot wasn't all that universal. It could, indeed, be used as a washbasin, and everybody did. If used as a pillow, the head fell off a lot. If a grunt used it as a seat—to keep his ass out of the red ants—his butt tended to develop wear rings around the edges in short order. Also when the pot encountered a tree or fell off, it made loud noises. Few successful night patrols went out with the grunts wearing their pots.

The pot was also useless in its main purpose—keeping the wearer's skull reasonably intact. Against shrapnel, it worked fairly well, or even against an angled rifle slug. But when a Viet Cong took decent aim and dumped one 7.62 x 39 bullet straight into the helmet, the owner was guaranteed a new home in a body bag.

Nose-to-nose care . . .

"Willie, Willie," Fritsche moaned. "Only two canteens?"

"That's all they gave me."

"*They* sent you to Nam! You gonna listen to them or me?"

"You."

"Fine. Go scout the supply tent. Get yourself two more. You'll need 'em."

The canteens by this time were no longer the steel/canvas WWII abominations. They did still have the canvas covers, plus the inserted canteen cups that were guaranteed to taste like tin, burn your mouth if the coffee was hot, and then chill the coffee tepid in ten seconds. But, now, the canteens were made of plastic. Tasteless. Odorless. Odorless, unless a grunt made the mistake of trying to make the heavily chlorinated water palatable by adding Kool-Aid. Then the canteen would taste like Kool-Aid for the next six months. This was particularly obnoxious to a man who dumps a bottle of I. W. Harper inside.

The necessities . . .

Very few grunts wore underclothes. The jockey shorts that most Americans wore would ride up and produce instant crotch-rot inside a two-klick walk. Boxer shorts, on the other hand, did provide some measure of comfort. No one wore T-shirts, since they were hot, stinky, and dyed green—stupid looking. Socks, on the other hand, were highly prized—no grunt went without at least one and generally two spare pairs of socks. The best socks available came from the Aussie units in-country. They were made of pure, virgin bullet-proof wool. Standard Army boot socks wore out inside a week.

Fritsche sorted through Brown's potential contents for his ass-pack—the low pack that hung down from the web belt the Army called a pistol belt, whether a pistol was used or not.

"Spare fatigues . . . shit, man, you don't need those. Underwear . . . fuck that shit. A Bible. Yeah. Whatever. Hope it's got a bulletproof cover. Foot powder? That shit don't work. Hustle your ass up to the medics. Get some crab powder. Works great for everything. Insect repellent. Get three more bottles. Good for leeches.

"Socks. Okay. Man, get rid of those jockey shorts. Make your cock fall off. Writing paper? Okay, but it's gotta be water-proofed. Get some plastic bags."

One thing good about Vietnam: postage was free for GIs. For the first time in the twentieth century the grunt in the field didn't have to worry about his stamps sweating themselves together. Of course, envelopes were very interesting. The trick tip there was to slit the flap open carefully with a knife, then use sap from a rubber tree for glue. There were lots of rubber trees.

The jungle fatigues were also good—fairly lightweight cotton/ synthetic that adequately absorbed sweat off one's body. A grunt wore a set of fatigues on one operation, generally ripped the dark-stained and sweat-soaked clothes off at the end of the mission and threw them away. Nobody had balls enough to ask the Vietnamese laundrywomen to wash those fatigues.

The jungle boots also were of good design. They were leather-bottomed and canvas-sided, with Vibram soles that could plow through the thickest mucky hillsides. They had been supposedly designed for Special Forces use early on in the war and had steel insoles to keep the man who stepped into a punji pit (bamboo spikes covered with shit) from getting his feet impaled.

For night comfort, the grunt carried a poncho, which was a horrible rubberized sheet with a hood. It was waterproof, which meant that it sweated incredibly. It was also the only protection a grunt had against the rain. Nobody ever wore it, since it also swished loudly when walking. The grunts used it in very creative conjunctions with their friends when they needed to build a tent.

What was useful was the poncho liner—a synthetic, super lightweight blanket, camo green. It not only was warm, but maintained its warmth when soaked through. It also dried out in any kind of a breeze in a few minutes and was rated as a stone winner by the infantry.

Pot, gun, fatigues, boots, personal gear . . .

Ammo.

There was no such thing as too much ammunition. American soldiers carried incredible amounts of ammunition. Their web belts would be lined with ammo pouches, and they would use any carriable container to lug more.

In World War Two the "basic load"—the amount of ammunition every soldier is expected to carry into combat—was 200 rounds. In Vietnam, it was not uncommon for a man to carry twice to three times that number, even if it meant excluding everything except the extra water canteens.

"Brown. You better learn you can't carry enough rounds. First time you run dry in a firefight and start hollerin' for momma when you need a case of .223, you'll know I ain't blowing smoke up your young ass."

The basic method the grunt had to carry his gear was the ring-holed canvas web belt—again a survivor from the past. On the web went a set of canvas suspenders to help support the load. On the belt itself went the asspack, a small, six-by-ten-by-twelve-inch canvas pack, then the canteens, then the magazines. The small first-aid pouch, which contained one very lousy bandage, generally was emptied and used to carry cigarettes.

Bayonets were also supposed to be carried. But, since the bayonet for the M-16 was only about six inches long, made of the worst high-carbon steel (meaning it couldn't be sharpened), and nobody in his right mind could see charging any armed individual with this stubby little object, bayonets were mainly used for throwing into rubber trees. Instead, combat knives were carried—either a very expensive custom knife special-ordered from the States, or else a scrounged Air Force/Marine K-Bar fighting knife.

After all this, as Willie the Semi-Brown pointed out, were the rations.

"Fritsche. How the fuck am I supposed to carry twelve meals, for Pete's sake?"

Brown was getting to be intuitive, now. On his bunk were a

dozen little boxes of C-rations. Two boxes alone would fill his asspack to overflowing. Fritsche showed him how.

C-rations were organized into three meal groups: B-1, B-2, and B-3. One was intended for breakfast, one for lunch and one for dinner. They were creatively organized to give the grunt a variety—unlike the single-choice field rations of earlier wars. However, no one ever figured out how these little boxes could be conveniently lugged on the back of one lousy infantryman.

If was very necessary to filter through the C-rats so only the best and tastiest were carried. There were three cans in every C-rat box, as well as one brown foil container of accessories. The three cans broke down as follows:

The main course:

Ham and eggs, chopped. Loathsome. Almost inedible.

Turkey loaf. Fritsche had gone through a momentary fascination with turkey loaf, until he realized it tasted like canned cat food.

Boned chicken. Boring but palatable.

Chicken and noodles. Okay.

Beefsteak with juices. Dead pot roast—somehow lumpy—in grease.

Ham with water added. Palatable. (Palatable being defined as something an amateur field chef could fuck with.)

Beef slices with potato gravy. Potato in the singular. Since beef slices were indistinguishable from beefsteak with juices, this was not a serious favorite.

Meatball with beans and tomato sauce. Edible.

Beans with franks in tomato sauce. Okay.

Spiced beef with sauce. Try the above beef slices, some catsup, MSG, and ooze generally thought of as essence of ptomaine.

Pork slices with juices. Best be very hungry.

Then, the high point:

Ham and lima beans. Generations of young men came out of Vietnam with a lifelong loathing of ham and lima beans. The canned ham and lima beans were so ghastly that not only would no one eat them but they would deliberately leave the cans by the trail for the Viet Cong to pick up—sans booby trap. The Viet Cong never touched those cans. Ham and lima beans was then replaced by a new addition—spaghetti and meatballs. Both very deceased.

The second can—available only in the B-1 (breakfast) packs—was fruit:

Fruit cocktail. Nice.

Pears. Not quite.

Apricots. A serious loser.

Peaches. Extremely popular, since the can was filled with juice and was perfect for the total parched throat that was produced from humping the hills.

The third can contained:

Crackers and cheddar cheese spread. Mosby had once told Fritsche about the ship's biscuits that Nelson's Navy lived on—suitable for cannonball substitutes—and the biker instantly understood the honorable heritage of C-rat crackers. The cheese was called cheddar. The grunts thought of it as ultra-modern plastic.

Fudge brick. Eat and die. It was a small, cookielike piece of candy that even the Vietnamese beggar children would throw back. Which hurt. No one in his right mind was ever known to take a second bite.

Peanut butter and crackers. Good peanut butter. For crackers, check above.

Date nut pudding. This was the ham and lima beans of desert.

Fruitcake. See above.

Pound cake. Correctly described by weight.

Cocoa powder. See below.

Jam spread and crackers. These could be spread with grape, apricot or pineapple. The jam would be scraped off and spread on the pound cake. This crackers would be spread on nearby bushes.

The accessory pack contained picnic-style packs of salt, pepper and sugar; an instant cream packet; one plastic spoon; two pieces of chewing gum; one napkin; one taped roll of toilet paper; and four wrapped cigarettes.

At the beginning of the war the cigarettes were elderly. Mosby swore—and was completely disbelieved—that he'd opened a C-rat pack and found a pair of Lucky Strike Greens—abandoned with much fanfare in 1941. By this time, the cigarettes were mostly Marlboros, Winstons, many Salems, Pall Malls, Luckies or Camels in a great while, and every now and then some poor unlucky sod got the pack that contained Viceroys.

The final item in the pack was instant coffee. This was sit-up-and-take-notice coffee. Amphetamines—found only in Special Forces packs—were considered far less effective than C-rat coffee.

The gourmet amateurs took two packs of coffee, three packs of cream, and one pack of cocoa and made field cappuccino. Heated in a canteen cup over a C-4 explosive fire, it had something. Especially tasty after two weeks out of a bath, three weeks in boredom/terror, and four days short of sleep.

The problem became how to carry all these goodies to the field.

"You get . . . three, no, four pairs of socks," Fritsche told Brown.

"You already put the socks out."

"These are not for your feet, my friend," Fritsche said. He unrolled the socks that Willie had dug from his footlocker. "You sort out the cans, right? Take all the plastic parts apart. You want to keep one spoon, a couple of salt and peppers, three asswipe packs, the cigarettes and cream. Junk the rest of the shit."

"But I don't smoke."

Fritsche pocketed the smokes for himself.

"See, we're making you lighter by the minute," he said.

Then Fritsche sorted the cans.

"Keep the fruit. Dump this fuckin' B-3 pack. Open the can and take out the cocoa pack, first. Now. Main cans. You got ham and eggs. Throw those fuckers away. Chicken and noodles. Fine. Another chicken and noodles. You got lucky on the draw."

Troops chose their C-rats by a draw. The case was opened—the old-style M-16 barrel flash suppressor worked wonders as a wirebreaker—and the case was turned over. Grunts then wandered by and picked out rations by random.

In theory, this kept the first troops in line from picking out the most highly desired ration packs (B-1 with the fruit). Actually, since the C-rat cases were always packed the same, the more sophisticated memorized which pack went where. Upside down or backwards, they knew.

Fritsche finally got the cans down to a manageable pile. Then he stuffed the cans into the socks. The socks, when filled, were tied shut and then fastened with shoelaces to the back of the combat pack suspenders. They wouldn't clink if tied tightly enough.

Willie looked at the end result and frowned. "Fritsche . . . we're supposed to be carrying twelve meals."

"Yup."

"I don't think I've got more than four or five there."

"Yup."

"I don't want to starve to death out there."

"Lemme clue you, son. There is no way we'll go four days without resupply. We ain't Sneaky Petes, for Chrissakes. Besides, if we get hit, think of all the extra stuff you can pick off the bodies."

While Brown blanched, Fritsche went through the rest of the gear—the stuff that was "support equipment" for the mission. Support equipment entailed bits and pieces of gear the grunt

134

carried to help somebody else. Things such as spare machine-gun ammo belts, LAWs, explosives, mortar rounds, etc.

Willie had been given two 250-round belts of machine-gun ammo, two blocks of C-4 explosive, a ten-meter coil of orange nonelectric fuse, plus grenades and two LAWs.

"You got to take the C-4. We'll cook with that. Carry it behind you on top of your asspack."

"Why there?"

"Because it's white, dumbshit. Never carry anything that makes you into a target. Now, the grenades."

Fritsche ripped open the round cardboard canisters of grenades. "Fuller said carry four. Take two."

"But . . ."

"You ain't gonna need but two, or else we're all fuckin' dead. The others'll rust on you. The fuckin' M-26s rust if you just whisper water at 'em. These two . . . hang on your ammo pouches. Clip 'em. Don't hook them by the goddam handles. If the pin falls out you're fuckin' dead.

"Nobody gets a fuckin' Congressional for falling on his own grenade. Take some more of that duct tape and tape the handles down. Unscrew the fuses, and rub a little Vaseline on the threads. Now, you're strack. These fuckers . . . leave 'em."

"These fuckers" were the two cardboard containers of LAWs, the M-72 rocker launcher (Light Antitank Weapon)—one of those good ideas that don't work. They replaced the old familiar bazooka. The LAW came two generations of tank weapons later. The LAW was a cardboard, one-man throwaway bazooka. It weighed about five pounds and was only a couple of feet long in its carrying position. When a grunt wanted to take on a tank or a pillbox—instead of digging a hole with his teeth—it was only necessary to open the sealed pack, pull the safety pin—at which point the launching tube could be extended to its full length. Now. Aim and fire. A perfect theory.

LAWs, however, did not work in Vietnam. About one-third of the 66mm rocker launchers failed to fire. Fewer still could accurately hit a target within less than 200 yards. Junk.

"Leave 'em," Fritsche said again.

"But Lieutenant Fuller said—"

"Fuck him. You notice he don't carry no M-72s either. Now . . . the important shit. Blind Pig's ammo."

"Tell him, brother," came the rumble from Blind Pig's corner.

Fritsche gave it to him, brother:

"The only thing we got going for us if we get hit is Blind

135

Pig's M-60. It's gonna eat ammo like there's no fuckin' tomorrow. So, everybody carries spare belts.''

Fritsche snapped open an ammo can and reverently lifted out the brass-bright linked bullets.

"One problem the Army ain't figured out yet is how to carry these motherfuckers. You ain't gonna lug that ammo can, right? So, how do you think you're gonna hump this?''

Brown hesitantly took the belt and started to lift it over his head.

"Sure," Fritsche sneered. "Just like a bandido. You ever think that belt is goonna make you shine for a sniper?''

Brown looked scared.

"Plus, you fall on my fuckin' ammo," Blind Pig broke in, "you gone tweak them rounds in they belt. I kill you, you do that.''

"Fine. How do I carry them, then?''

"You go find Buellton and get him to score a medic pouch. That's the only way we figured out. If you come up with a better idea, you be sure and tell us, because we're blanker than dogshit.''

Fritsche examined his teaching aids.

"That's all she wrote, Willie. You're ready. Strack. Stupid Troopers Runnin' Around in Circles.''

The acronym STRAC originally stood for Strategic Army Corps—the designation for the Army's standby combat troops that would be the first to save Democracy from itself. By '68, strack was used mockingly, with various definitions such as Shit, The Russians Are Coming.

"You got it?''

"I think so. Thanks.''

"No problem. Now, haul your ass out there and grab me a beer. If we're going to the field tomorrow, I'm gettin' fucked up tonight.''

Brown headed for the ice bunker. Fritsche watched him go, then muttered and went back to his cot.

Blind Pig: "Like the man said, thanks.''

"For what? The fucker's gonna go out there and die a lot. You know that, don't you?''

"Yeah. But you helped a brother.''

"Fuck you," Fritsche said, embarrassed. "All I done is what people did for me.''

"You dudes be that close?'' Blind Pig was speaking of Fritsche's biker brothers.

"Yeah.''

Brown came back through the tent flaps with Bier LaRues.

Fritsche snapped the caps off them with the side of his K-Bar knife and handed them around. The three men—nineteen-year-olds—drank in silence. Then Brown decided he had a question:

"Hank? Can I ask you something? Were you really a Hell's Angel?"

Blind Pig flashed Brown a warning look, this was a touchy point with Fritsche. The big biker brooded for a moment and then grinned broadly.

"Nope. But I did party with them. Righteous, righteous dudes . . ."

Henry Charles Fritsche was, by anybody's judgment, a righteous dude himself—at least in the judgment of everybody except his parents, the courts, the Bureau of Narcotics and Dangerous Drugs, and, ultimately, his fellow outlaws.

Everyone has some kind of seminal shock when growing up— a personal incident, a book, or even a movie.

For Fritsche, it was when his folks let him go to the Saturday-afternoon kids' matinee. Before that, Fritsche had figured—if a ten-year-old can figure—that there was no life beyond the small Ohio farming town of his birth.

The film was the old Marlon Brando classic *The Wild Ones*.

As all the other kids sailed popcorn boxes, booed, cheered, shouted and generally paid no attention, Fritsche sat in supreme focus. He found himself fascinated with the film's unredeemable villain—Lee Marvin. That might help explain why, a few years later, Fritsche hocked his potentially state fair calf to buy a flogged-out 1948 Triumph motorcycle. The townspeople and his folks found a simpler explanation. "That boy was born bad."

Bad is as bad does, and Fritsche did a great deal to justify predestination over the next few years, as he threw up on the prom queen, suckerpunched a PE coach, got tossed out of school, and then was in the "vicinity" during a number of store break-ins.

He ended up riding prospect for an outlaw motorcycle club. A "prospect" is a prospective member. During the prospect time, a potential new member is expected to do all the demeaning requirements of a fraternity pledge, plus more. The prospect must also be approximately brave in any situation that your basic Audie Murphy might be able to handle, and be generally available at any hour—like when a drunk full member wants a pizza at 2 A.M. There are no excuses in such a request, even though the town might be closed solid and surrounded by the National Guard.

137

Hank eventually got his patch. This was the club emblem, to be sewn on the back of a Levi jacket with its sleeves removed.

And then Fritsche fucked up.

He discovered speed and then that the methedrine rush was better if you shot it. It was fun—he could run for hours and days on amphetamine, getting stronger and smarter by the minute.

He also could not support himself. By 1966, drugs were penetrating the U.S., even into the Midwest. And speed was such a seemingly innocuous substance in that time and also very profitable—especially at the local college.

Fritsche became a dealer/user. He was making a great deal of money. Fritsche also was becoming an obnoxious, stumbling fool.

The first realization for himself was at a club meeting, where his brothers, who had warned him many times before, pulled his patch. There is no greater shame for anyone who has gone through the massive testing it takes to win that patch than to be thrown out of a club.

Fritsche could have gone home, regrouped and—after a period of straightening out his act—rejoined the club. This always was a possibility. Instead, he went home and shot more speed. Then set up a big scam.

The scam involved people from California and people from Miami. Fritsche stood to get very rich from this deal.

Instead, when the people met, guns, not deals, came out. Hank Fritsche stood there in a small apartment—ears ringing—staring down at four bodies. He knew that each body had minimum one friend.

It took him several days of hiding out in a welfare hotel before most of the speed washed out of his system. Then he took only two major hits—orally—and walked into the recruiting station and said he wanted to enlist. He was lucky. By 1967, recruiters weren't looking too hard at volunteers—particularly if they wanted to go to Nam. Vietnam was the safest possible place for Hank Fritsche. He could stay there until the echoes of that sour drug deal blew away.

But, since bikers always dare the gods, Fritsche became the perpetual point man. It was something he always volunteered for—no, insisted on. After a while, it just became accepted. No one thought it was strange, except perhaps Mosby, who didn't question out loud, because Mosby knew it was suicide to always walk point.

It was also in the nature of bikers to be favored by the gods, since Hank Fritsche had now walked some 150 patrols as point man. Without a blemish or scratch.

And now it was time to try it again.

138

CHAPTER SIXTEEN

LZ ZULU

DAWN FOG LIFTED over the rubber trees. The world was very gray as the fingers of fog climbed, circled, and then were caught in the swirling rotor blades of the choppers.

Twenty Hueys lined each side of Hue Duc's PSP airfield. Casey's squad crouched at the side of the strip as their chopper cranked slowly—reluctant in the morning air, blades groaning in the mist. Finally, the chopper's turbine caught, and the rotor blades whined up into invisibility, their tips catching and tossing stray wisps of gray, and the sun pinpointed through their wake. The UH-ID's crew beckoned and the squad double-timed forward and boarded the chopper.

Mosby, sitting next to the door gunner, saw the world tilt forward through the scratched windshield. The fingers of fog became a blur as the forty helicopters—each carrying a squad of grunts—ground ahead, swung slightly, and then lifted up at a 45-degree angle, straight into the mist and oblivion.

Mosby's chopper climbed to 2,000 feet, and he could feel the sweat dry and chill on his body as the Heuy broke out of the early morning clouds.

Imagine an old electric fan.

Imagine that fan—with one bent blade—so that its sound becomes not just a drone, but a drone with one crashing whap every beat.

Now, imagine that fan forty-eight feet larger.

Imagine forty of those fans.

That is the sound of an air assault.

For more than a decade, the area had been called Landlord Giang's district. However, after Giang made the error of visiting his district to inquire why the rice rents had not been paid for twenty-two months, the NLF answered his query with two .30 M-1 carbine slugs in the throat. After that, the one-kilometer by three-kilometer segmented rice paddy had become open territory.

The villagers gleefully began farming this open space, and then an old farmer—working with his plow and buffalo—was machine-gunned by an American helicopter. Then the area had been abandoned by all but fools. So, for four months, Giang's district had been ignored.

Now the paddies were renamed Landing Zone Zulu, and the war descended on them.

The first choppers were Huey Cobras and armed B-model gunships. Overhead orbited an Air Force spotter plane and, still higher, two flights of Phantom Fox-Fours.

The gunships were the first out of the cloud cover, coming in over the treeline, their guns chattering, yammering into the silence. Then there was the period-bang of their grenade launchers. There was no return fire.

Forty helicopters, and behind them forty more, and behind them forty, plus forty, as the Twelfth Division went to battle.

The juggernaut of war.

The juggernaut became men as they spilled out of the Hueys into the rice paddy muck. The Huey lifted away and the LZ was silent, except for the shouts of noncoms and officers as they hustled their troops out of the clearing toward the brush. Two men hesitated: Willie the Semi-Brown and the platoon leader, Lieutenant Fuller. They were bewildered. Disoriented. Casey hurried to Fuller. He grabbed him by the elbow.

"Come on," he urged.

Fuller stared back at him blankly. His eyes were wide and frightened. He was gaping at the empty horizon that had only moments before been filled with choppers and guns and men.

"Let's go, sir. We can regroup at the tree line."

He manhandled his platoon leader toward the brush.

Charlie Company's mission was a three-platoon sweep assigned to Karl Harris, C Company's commanding officer, by the Fifteenth Infantry's battalion commander, Lieutenant Colonel Taylor.

It looked easy on the map. From LZ Zulu C Company was to split in three prongs. Each prong consisted of one platoon. The objective was also in threes. In this case, three small hills. To the peasants in the area, they were known as the Three Sisters. To the U.S. Army they were Hills 957, 902 and 1113.

The numeral names where chosen from the purported height— in meters—of the hills. You could see the figures on the military map, which was oriented from a 1952 French Army survey. The French based their details on the original Japanese Army cartographic survey of 1944. Translated, the figures meant that the map the Army was planning to use in its assault was approximately as accurate as the one Columbus used when he tried to sail to the Indies.

According to this map—and therefore incorporated into Colonel Taylor's command briefing—the Three Sisters sat to the north/northeast of the projected landing zone. The farthest west—Hill 1113—was about 3,000 meters from the LZ. The second and lowest of the hills—Hill 902—was some 6,000 meters from the LZ; while the third and most distant hill—957—was about 10,000 meters away. That was what the map said, adding that the farthest hill was very close to a currently used dirt road. At the base of 957—again, according to the map—were the remains of a village.

According to Taylor's orders, each platoon was to move—as expeditiously as possible—to one of the hills. They were to search as thoroughly as possible on either side of their direct routes to the hills. If engaged by the enemy, they were to fight back. Once the hills were occupied, Charlie Company was expected to "aggressively patrol" to the front and flanks. This would hopefully fulfill General Sinclair's expectations of bringing the Phu Loi Battalion to battle. If no contact was made within forty-eight hours, C Company could expect to be helilifted out and relocated to a second landing zone some ten klicks north.

Sinclair called the plan—a bit dramatically—OPERATION SWIFTSURE.

The orders went down after being structured by Shannon and his G-2 staff as well as the officers and men of the other G-sections. From there, Colonel Taylor, given his Area of Operations for Swiftsure, gave each of his company commanders their various operations orders.

After the briefing, Charlie Company's CO, Captain Harris, gave the word to his platoons. Harris, feeling that after five months in a combat unit and less than thirty days away from being reassigned to the rear, he was justified in ghosting it a little. He gave his own command group and the First Platoon the task of taking and holding the nearest of the Three Sisters—Hill 1113. Third Platoon—his current favorite—got the second-best job: flanking down the old road and occupying Hill 957. Second Platoon, Mosby's group, got the shitty end of the stick—Hill 902.

It did not appear—even on the map—that this would be a fun day. But what the map, as bad as it made Second Platoon's route to be, didn't show was that the original survey was slightly in error: Hill 902 was more like 11,000 meters from landing, rather than 6,000. The map also did not say that between the low hillock and the LZ lay fields of kunai grass, secondary jungle, and other unpleasantries.

Second Platoon thought they were in the shit when they were briefed.

They didn't know the half of it.

CHAPTER SEVENTEEN
THE SQUAD

FRITSCHE LED THE squad along the almost invisible trail of an overgrown paddy dike. The men moved swiftly, with only Brown and Fuller occasionally stumbling at places where the ancient dike had crumbled. They were already beginning to drip sweat, and their mouths dried to the old tin can taste of body salt.

Martinez kept his eyes constantly moving, glancing forward once in a while to make sure Brown was okay. Already his heart was settling down from its LZ-thunder, and his legs were beginning to untense into a smooth and steady stride. He saw the river of sweat beginning between Brown's shoulder blades and then streaking down the shirt toward his pack. Within minutes the stain had spread outward, until Brown's entire shirt was dripping.

Fuck, Martinez thought. The last thing he wanted to do was play nursemaid. At this rate, the kid would keel over from the heat before he'd even started. But then he started feeling sorry for Brown. Everybody has to have a first time humping the bush. Martinez took one of his canteens out and passed it to Brown. As Brown slurped, Martinez noticed that his light chocolate skin was already beginning to dry and flush. Fuck, Martinez thought again.

They bumped to a halt at the edge of the field.

"Five minutes," Casey said, and everybody sprawled. Including Fuller. If Brown looked bad, Martinez thought, Fuller looked like he was going to die. Casey walked over to him.

"Uh, Lieutenant," he said. "I think we better talk."

Fuller stared at him a second. Then reality groaned back, and he clambered to his feet. Casey pulled him aside and began talking. Martinez couldn't hear what he was saying, but he could guess. Fuller was feeling in his side pockets for a forgotten map.

Casey pulled his own out and began leading the platoon leader through the motions.

Fuckin' huerro, Martinez thought. Couldn't find his huevos with two hands and a fifty-dollar whore. But Martinez wasn't worried. They had Casey. That was enough.

A moment later Casey had them on their feet and was lining them up, drawling orders in his low-key style. They moved forward again. If anyone had the time and inclination, there would have been some awe, seeing the pristine wilderness stretching out into a low, steady rise in front of them. Rolling, heavily overgrown hills that climbed to soaring two tiered jungle. It would look great in a *National Geographic* picture. But if you had to hump these hills, it looked like pure hell.

Fritsche again took point, like always. Taliaferro moved forward to back him up. Fritsche gave him a look of total disgust and waved him back. Martinez smiled in satisfaction, patted his M-79, and slipped into the slot behind Fritsche. It was a helluva lot safer this way. The only real itch he had now was Taliaferro was behind him.

Now clear of the LZ, Casey put them into marching order: after Fritsche, Martinez, Taliaferro and Blind Pig he put Willie, the greenhorn. Willie's job was also to hump ammo for Blind Pig's M-60. Then Casey, Mosby, Buellton the medic, and after him the supposed command group, Lieutenant Fuller and his radioman, DeeJay. Behind came the platoon's other squads.

Casey had a slice of a moment of indecision about where to position himself. Normally, Casey would have positioned himself as far away from Fuller as he could. Lieutenants died more than a bit in this war, and then you needed somebody to take over, meaning Casey.

Martinez guessed that things were so bad in this instance, however, that Casey wanted to be just far enough out of booby-trap disaster and near enough to keep track of the doomed lieutenant.

And doomed he was, Martinez thought. If there had ever been any man with big black birds hovering near him, it was Fuller. Martinez shot a small prayer of thanks to the Little Flower that he wasn't anywhere near the sombitch. From here on out, he would be subconsciously braced for the big loud bang way in back of the squad that would signal Fuller's demise. Too bad about DeeJay.

As Martinez moved on, he absently tapped the letter in his shirt pocket. It was from his big brother. The family was fine, thank you. And his brother assured him that Martinez's novia was completely faithful. Martinez and Rosa had been engaged for two years, and the only time they had even Jesus, Mary and Joseph kissed was when Martinez had gotten his orders from Nam. Rosa had three hulks for brothers. And after *her* brothers he had his own two.

Nobody but no-pegpants-body would even get near his lady until he got home. Not that Martinez was worried. If there was anyone in the world he was certain of, it was Rosa. Like him, she was modern, with a broadminded view of human possibilities. With her, Martinez was sure he could achieve anything. The only hesitation he had was that Rosa was so modern that she still didn't have that love for the huge, squabbling warmness their two clans would provide after Martinez and Rosa were married.

But they had never, for instance, argued over the size of the family they wanted for themselves. Two children. Sex didn't matter. Only the number. One for each of them. Not too many to interfere with their plans for the future. Future, meaning the ranch.

The ranch was a pact he had made with his brothers. Martinez had almost his entire check held out and mailed to a bank in Santa Maria. That would buy the ranch, which they would call Rancho Guadelupe.

Guadelupe was also Martinez's hometown. Picture the smallest of small California towns, about ninety miles north of Santa Barbara, bordered by sprawling ranches and farms on one side, and cool pacific breezes on the other. It was also one of those strange little hidey-hole towns. A slice out of the Old West, where gambling was not only legal, but almost a civic duty. It had been founded by the Spanish and built by tiny waves of immigrants—the Swiss, the Chinese, and then the Italians.

The town's entrance is marked by one of the world's strangest graveyards, with odd stones and edifices from each race and generation. Ornate bulky mausoleums with many plaques for the Swiss. Strange, twisted sculptures for the Chinese. More traditional stones for the Italians and Mexicans. There is another item worthy of note—just how many of the tombstones stand over the graves of Mexican-Americans who died in American wars.

In fact, one of the first things Martinez could remember was a full military service at the graveside of some cousin. He couldn't remember for what war. But he did remember his dead cousin's picture, imbedded in the stone. A fat-faced baby Marine. That was one of the reasons that Martinez, unlike his big brother, had avoided the Marine Corps. His brother also had the shit shot out of him in 1965. Martinez, although very modern, was superstitious.

He comforted his M-79 and concentrated on the jungle around him. Unlike Fuller, Martinez was very sure he would make it through this fucking war.

Everyone, including the laconic Casey, had tried to explain it to him, but Willie the Semi-Brown still didn't have the faintest what was going on.

It was a three-platoon sweep. Willie wasn't too sure what a platoon was, much less a sweep. But he was learning fast. A platoon was him and the guy in front of him. And also somebody panting just behind. A sweep was slogging through 100-plus heat and learning to hate every raw-rubbing stitch of clothing on his body. At this moment he particularly hated his underwear.

It kept molding itself to the inner portions of his thighs and hitching itself up into the crack in his ass. For the first time in his sheltered life, Willie was wondering what the purpose of underwear was, anyway. What the hell use was it, except to change every day to keep your mom happy? Fritsche was right. The next time they stopped Brown was determined to shed the pair he was wearing immediately and swear off underwear forever.

He started dreaming of shedding all his clothes and diving into a cool, clear spring. He would dam it up and create a ten-foot pond. He would swim in five feet of it and drink the rest. Then he started dreaming about the soap and deodorants of all kinds, humming TV jingles to himself and listing the various brands. Willie was already starting to stink. He as yet had no idea how bad the squad would smell by the end of the mission.

Willie was sure he'd reached the ultimate when he imagined dumping a truckload of baking soda into his ten-foot pond. Now *that* was clean.

Something jabbed into his back.

"Move, motherfucker," Blind Pig low-growled.

And Willie the Semi-Brown realized he'd come to a complete stop. He moved obediently forward, choking on the thick mucus and jungle pollen in his throat.

After he shed the underwear, he swore to himself, he would score some ice cream. Yeah. Ice cream. Like when he was a kid and had his tonsils out. Right. Underwear first. And then ice cream.

One talent Mosby had was humping the bush. After all this time as a grunt, he should have. Part of the talent was mental preparation. For instance, Mosby was normally an inveterate

145

daydreamer. Once moving, however, the first thing he did was shut down his imagination. He didn't reflect on past or future possibilities. There was only the present, lifting one foot and putting it in front of the other while trying to stay alive.

Mosby was not one of those people who had to fool himself with the *another five klicks and I'll fall down*, then *another five* and so forth. He just walked until it was time to stop. Mosby could do this for days on end. This left his mind completely free for mundane thoughts like survival.

Mosby *saw* everything around him, making note of things that were odd, slightly out of place, or even moving unexpectedly. When the oddities reached a peak Mosby either went flat or started shooting. It was an ability David Mosby was quite proud of. There were very few grunts who were as good at that as he was. Except possibly Casey.

Casey was something else. He seemed to *know* things were going to happen a moment before they did. Mosby kept a particular eye on the sergeant.

Casey was moving easily in front of him. As each meter passed under his bootheels, he seemed to move more easily still. The man was a superbly toned walking machine.

Suddenly Mosby heard the slight snick as Casey's safety came off. A heartbeat later, his own rifle was in firing position. He saw Casey swing to the right. Adrenaline spurted, and two heartbeats later there was a loud whirr, as a cloud of tiny yellow-marked birds took flight.

All around him people were hitting the ground, and Mosby was first, his thump clicking his M-16 to full auto. Mosby heard cracks, as some 'cruits popped a few nervous caps. Shit, Mosby thought. Now they know where we are. And he got ready for the whole world to come down on him.

Muffled orders went down the platoon line, and then a long silence. Mosby watched those birds, hovering just a breath above the trees, like mosquitoes hanging molecules away from repellent. And then, by some invisible command, the birds settled peacefully back down on their roosts. Casey was back up and moving again.

That incident broke Mosby's concentration. He noticed the tiny throb of a blister on his right heel. As he slogged on, the little nagging began growing, until his whole heel felt raw. It was hard to shift his mind. Mosby even caught himself limping, which was unncessary—you *always* got blisters in the field—and foolishness. If he didn't watch himself, his leg would start cramping.

Mosby tried to push himself back into the rhythm of the hump again. He started running subjects through his mind, searching for something that wouldn't take his attention totally away from his job. Then he found it.

Mosby started wondering who would get it this time. Let's see now. Start at the front. Fritsche on point, and in theory, most vulnerable. No fucking way. People like Fritsche didn't die in any damned jungle. They ate the weenie on freeways, during bar fights, or maybe in the gas chamber after a nice comfortable last meal.

Okay. How about Martinez? Naw. Too good.

Taliaferro? Fuck no. Too big of an asshole. Mosby, unlike most people, did not believe that assholes are self-eliminating. Also, Mosby grudgingly conceded, Taliaferro knew how to soldier.

Now, how about Willie the Semi-Brown? Yep. Definite body-bag type.

Blind Pig? They don't build anybody mean enough to sell him the farm.

Casey? Shit no. Don't even think about Casey. If he goes, we're all in the shitter . . .

Which brought Mosby to Mosby. Maybe. He'd been stretching his luck lately. Going for another tour. Dumb, dumb, dumb. Come on, David. Best you keep moving.

Buellton? Hell, yes. He's short, isn't he? So short that prick Ramos shouldn't have even let him go out this time. Poor Buellton. Mosby glanced back. The medic was slogging along with the best of them. His face was peaceful. Mosby bet himself a beer that Buellton was toe-tag city.

Fuller? Dead, dead, dead.

DeeJay? Now there was a guy to feel sorry for. Fuller was sure to fuck up. And if he got it, his radioman was a goner.

Mosby was feeling a lot better about the world when Casey called for a lunch break. He put one squad out around the platoon to watch while the others chowed down.

Mosby didn't even taste his C-rats. They were just fuel he had to shove in his face and then later on empty out the other end, squatting behind some bush with his pants around his ankles and his rifle ready, scared to hell that this was when he'd get it. Mosby wasn't too hot on dying. But getting it when he was taking a shit was even lower on his list of the ways to go. On the whole, he much preferred a nice comfortable heart attack at, oh, age 102 or so.

Mosby crushed his empty cans, so they couldn't be used by

the bad guys to make up booby traps, lit a stale C-ration cigarette, and walked over to Buellton, feeling a bit guilty about his
mortality game.

"Got a problem, Doc."

Buellton gave him a sarcastic look.

"Fuck you, Mosby. I ain't medevacking your ass. Anybody
goes out, it's gonna be me. Hell, I'm so short I can walk under
a snake with a top hat."

Mosby squatted down beside the medic. He lit another cigarette and passed it over.

"Hey. Lighten up. I got a blister is all."

Buellton snorted.

"On the brain?"

"Fuck you. It's on my heel."

"Poor baby. You want me to kiss it and make it all better?"

"You got some blister shit, don't you?"

"Sure. Which means you're gonna have to take off your boot.
Which means it'll never go back on. Which means mean, evil,
and definitely not very nice bugs are gonna start chewing on
said blister. Then I gotta medevack you.

"Fuck you, like I said. Shoot yourself or something. Then
I'll dust you off. Hell, I'll go out with you. Make sure you got
the right scrip. Them self-inflicted wounds get tricky. You go
and put a round through your foot, and we could be hoisting a
few to my imminent departure in a couple hours."

"Sorry Doc. Loud noises scare crap out of me."

"Pity."

Mosby got back up.

"Jesus. You are short. Cranky sonofabitch."

Buellton laughed.

"Hey. My rights. Next week about this time I'm gonna be
crawlin' up the skirts of some barmaid in Nashville."

Buellton finished his smoke and began field-stripping the cigarette, as he reflected on his near future.

"Shit," he said, shaking his head in awe at the partying that
he was planning.

Mosby smiled to himself. Buellton was *ready*. He was so short
he could walk under a door. Mosby made himself another bet.
Two beers now that Buellton wouldn't make it. He almost wished
he was willing to shoot himself. Then he could help Buellton
out.

Then the column was up and moving again.

Fritsche moved cautiously along the thread of the trail. He

was starting to tire now, and although he hated anyone walking point except himself, he knew he was getting a bit dull around the edges. Pretty soon, he'd have to call somebody else up. He mopped sweat from his forehead as his eyes searched the rising countryside around him. He moved cautiously around a bend in the trail and then stopped, raising a hand to signal Martinez.

Just in front of him, an ancient tree lay across the trail. It was lightning-blasted and had obviously been lying there for years—a huge clump of dead and living vegetation covered it.

Fritsche moved slowly forward, his sawed-off ready. This was a place that smelled of nasty things. He reached the tree, and carefully scanned the thick vines, looking for booby traps. Nothing.

Fritsche began clambering over the tree trunk, feeling a bit naked, but not so anxious to get to the other side that he didn't study everything around him.

The punji pit was just on the other side of the tree trunk, right where he knew it would be. Fritsche breathed a sigh of relief. It was a very old pit, with the covering twigs and leaves sagging down onto the now-gray pointed bamboo stakes at the bottom.

Fritsche stepped around the pit, waited until Martinez caught up with him, pointed down. Martinez saw and hand-signaled the word back. Fritsche moved on.

Lieutenant Fuller stood knee deep in the muck, a miasma of swamp gas and biting insects rising around him. He kept cursing the map, folding and then refolding it. He was studying the circled area where he was theoretically at and scanning the terrain around him. Behind him, DeeJay was on the radio, talking to Citation Six—the Fifteenth's battalion commander, Lieutenant Colonel Taylor. He was stalling for time, as Fuller tried to figure where the hell he was. Finally Fuller grabbed the handpiece.

"Uh . . . this is Whirlaway Duece Six. We got a small problem, sir."

"Quite correct, Whirlaway. The problem is you. Get moving. Your platoon is way behind line."

Fuller started to gobble a weak excuse as Casey came up. Casey motioned a finger across his throat. Helplessly, Fuller handed the map to Casey.

"Shit, Lieutenant," Casey said after a minute. "You're doin' fine. You ain't lost, the map is."

Fuller looked at him is disbelief. Casey ticked off some major points that Fuller had missed. Suddenly Fuller's mind cleared. There was no swamp on the map, but here he was standing in one. There were a lot of other things that the map was missing as well. Like many thick-treed hills, brush-choked canyons, and ravines, for openers.

"Hell," Casey said. "Uncle Ho himself couldn't find his way with this topo. No wonder the French got their asses shot off."

"Yeah," Fuller gloomed. "But Big Six is all over my ass. We're supposed to be on our objective now."

Casey shook his head.

"No way. We got at least another five thousand meters to go, which means at least another day's humping."

"What do I tell Colonel Taylor?"

Casey snorted.

"Lie to him. He's up there in his chopper. He don't know what's going on."

The radio crackled again, and DeeJay was shoving the handpiece at Fuller.

"This is Citation Six Actual, Deuce. Give me your map coordinates."

Fuller did, properly coded. There was a pause. Obviously Taylor, overhead in his Command and Control ship, found the map as puzzling as Fuller did.

"Whirlaway Deuce Six, this is Citation Six. Throw smoke. I can't see you."

Fuller took a smoke grenade off his harness, but Casey shook his head and disappeared. Fuller, puzzled, lit a cigarette while Casey went about his mysterious business. Before he'd finished the Winston, Casey was back and hustling everyone back in motion.

The smoke took a few minutes to clear above the trees, and Taylor finally spotted it.

What Taylor didn't know was that, thanks to Casey, the smoke had been thrown at the rear of the platoon, not its center. Many meters behind Fuller's actual location. The next time Taylor asked for smoke, which came this time from Fritsche at the head of the platoon, he saw real progress.

Taylor congratulated himself. The new platoon leader just needed a little ass-busting to realize his men were a lot better grunts than he was, and capable of far greater effort.

And, below, was the young second looie feeling guilty about the deception? Hell no. Fuller was smiling to himself even as he felt a leech slither down between his shoulder blades. You're learning, son, he thought. You maybe are even gonna get out of this thing alive.

Up ahead, Martinez was now on point. Unlike most of the

grunts, walking point was something he didn't mind. He started to clear some vines in front of him, routinely checking them for booby traps. And just as routinely, he spotted the thin strand of wire strung at helmet height. The wire ran across the trail and ended no doubt tied to a U.S.-made artillery shell.

Martinez ducked under the wire, pointed to it so Fritsche would see it, and walked on. Fritsche also ducked, pointing as he went to warn the next soldier in line—Taliaferro. On it went, down the line, each grunt ducking and each grunt pointing. All in a day's work.

Mosby, too, cleared the wire and pointed. Then Buellton. Lieutenant Fuller saw Buellton point, looked around for maybe the pretty bird, and walked straight on, into the wire. A split second later, he was lying on his back, looking up, bewildered at DeeJay's angry face.

"Jesus fuckin' Christ, sir. You almost killed us!"

"Huh?"

"The wire, man. The trip wire. Didn't you see Buellton point?"

Fuller saw the booby trap, realized what it was, and almost shit his pants.

"I'm sorry," he muttered. "I'm sorry."

DeeJay didn't answer. He helped Fuller to his feet, pushed him under the wire and on his way.

Fuller felt very much a fool. It wasn't that he was scared, although of course he was. He wasn't *that* much of a damned fool. But it wasn't thoughts of mortality trampling through his brain. It was the fear of failure. That was why he'd frozen back at the LZ, and why he'd been fucking up by the numbers all along.

Fuller was just a dumb jock from Florida State. A little baseball. A little water skiing. A little ROTC. He was a dumb jock with a smart accountant father who'd done something successfully dangerous in WWII. Fuller had been proud when he'd gotten his commission on graduation. His dad had exploded the balloon for him—just before Fuller left for Nam. His old man had gotten a bit tight at the send-off party, and had taken him aside.

"Of all the dumb-fuck things to do," his father had slurred. "You a goddamned lieutenant. Listen, do me a favor.

"Just don't kill anybody, okay?"

Fuller had been too stunned to do more than gulp an answer and get the hell away. His cold, aloof father had finally told him his real opinion. If Fuller lived long enough, he might grow up

151

enough to get his head straight, go back to Florida and kick his father's ass for the wonderful send-off party and parting remarks.

But right now, Fuller was just trying to do his best and not kill anybody. Unfortunately, his best was sadly lacking. And it looked like he might prove his father right.

Casey pulled them up about 5 P.M. Everyone was grimed, grim and exhausted. They were thousands of meters away from their first day's objective, but there was no other choice. Five thousand meters, in that terrain, was no brisk evening stroll. It'd taken the platoon a full day of ball-breaking humping to get this far. And they had another day at least as hard tomorrow.

It was a nasty little knoll that Casey had brought them to. It was a place of hard ground, bad cover, and prickly shadows.

It was also the best place there. Fuller picked up the horn to call Taylor. And he was so tired he really didn't give a damn what kind of ass-chewing he was in for.

Casey looked at him with a small glint of approval.

CHAPTER EIGHTEEN
BLIND PIG

THE KNOLL WAS indeed a rotten-crotch place for a platoon base. Not only was it low—only twenty meters or so above the surrounding terrain—but the knoll was flanked on two sides by bamboo overgrowth and brush. Plus it became obvious that somewhere out there was swamp since, as it grew closer to dusk, mosquitoes began practicing for some night-long stuka runs.

Once they'd gotten the word that this crappy hilltop would be their new home, Second Platoon went into motion. Sort of. Since they were experienced grunts, their motion could be compared to that of a geriatric lizard.

The first move was to crap out. Troopies' tongues lolled like reptiles as they gurgled down the last of the chlorinated water from whichever canteen they'd been husbanding. But being experienced and having the gut feeling that somehow Lieutenant Fuller would fuck up and not get them any water, nobody went into his second, third or fourth emergency canteen.

The squad leaders met with Fuller, who'd of course set the platoon's command post on the center top of the knoll, and each squad was assigned a pie-shaped wedge for its area of perimeter responsibility.

After the briefing, the squad leaders moved their people into position around the hilltop. Again, like so many reptiles in the setting sun, the men moved slowly and reluctantly into their positions in the scrub below.

Blind Pig scowled at Casey, eyeing the position Casey had selected for the machine gun. "Man. This field of fire ain't shit."

"That's what it is," Casey said flatly. "Look. I got you overlookin' the only high ground we've got."

"High ground, my man? This ain't high ground. This place be a swamp with ambitions."

Casey didn't bother to answer. He just dumped the 250-round belt he'd been lugging beside the M-60, and walked on. Blind Pig was right. This was not a very good setup for the machine gun. A machine gun is the closest thing that a grunt has for a deus ex when the shit hits the fan. A machine gunner should have a position that provides covering fire for the other men in his squad. He should also have a fair amount of open terrain that his gun can deny the enemy.

From the small finger of land that Casey set Blind Pig and Willie the Semi-Brown on, there was perhaps twenty meters before the bamboo brush started. Laterally, Blind Pig could see Mosby's position to his left and, to his right, the position taken by Taliaferro and Martinez. The other members of the squad were hidden.

"This shit sucks," Blind Pig observed to Willie, as he dumped his webbing beside his gun.

"We better dig in," Willie said.

"We better shit and fall back in it," Blind Pig said. "First we eat."

An amateur might think, seeing the scattered line of soldiers out in the open, that they were virgins or damned fools. This was not the case—all of the grunts in Second Squad had already found something to duck behind if they got hit, and all of them had their weapons ready. Like lizards recovering from the desert sun, they now ate, stretched, gagged down salt tablets, and slowly came alive as the shadows crawled across the hill.

Blind Pig finished his can of peaches, belched, and got to his feet.

"Now we dig in."

Willie, obedient to his training, puzzled slightly. Fritsche hadn't let him bring his entrenching tool. Then he brightened.

In case of emergency, one sergeant back in Advanced Infantry Training had said, you can use your helmet as a shovel. Willie took off his pot, yanked the helmet liner out, and started to remove the camouflage cloth cover.

"What you doin', fool?"

"You said . . ."

"I said shit. You go down and scout for some logs in front. For one night, we ain't diggin' no holes, cherryboy."

Brown put his helmet together, then started down the hill.

"Man forward," Blind Pig semi-shouted. Brown ambled downslope and never noticed that the minute he walked forward Blind Pig was flat behind his machine gun, right hand over the cocking lever. If there was somebody lurking on Brown, Blind Pig was ready to ruin that individual's entire day.

Brown panted three somewhat rotten logs back up the slope, and Blind Pig quickly lopped branches and wide-Ued the logs around the M-60.

"This be all we need. If we get hit, we be too busy shootin' an' shittin' to worry about not havin' some hole."

"But we're supposed to dig in."

"Man, Brown, why you got your head so far up? Fuckin' Army say all kind shit. That don't mean you be listening, do it?"

Brown started to argue, then looked at the other positions. The other members of the squad were doing exactly the same as Blind Pig. The only people in Vietnam who actually dug foxholes were the bad guys, the Marines, the fools, and the Rear Echelon Motherfuckers. After a hard day of humping the bush, nobody had the energy to dig a hole in the ground, regardless of what Army regulations, military practice, or common sense dictated.

The lizards continued coming alive. From each position, always with the "Man Forward" words, grunts went out to plant their Claymores.

The Claymore mine is a nasty piece of potential carnage. It's made out of greenish plastic, and contains a third of a pound of explosive and about a zillion tiny steel ball bearings. It's shaped like a wide V, about six inches tall by two inches thick by two inches wide. There are two spikes below the mine, plus a steel third spike behind the body.

The Claymore is directional. It's pushed into the ground, and then the third spike is used to "aim" the Claymore in the desired direction at the desired angle. The top of the mine has a fuse well. A fuse is screwed into that well, and then wire is reeled back to the plastic detonating level (or the mine can be wired into a det box, or set as a booby trap in a number of interestingly perverse ways).

When a Claymore is detonated, it fires like an enormous, V-winged shotgun. Anyone within twenty meters is filled full of those steel bearings. This is a very lethal little gimmick, which gives line animals a little bit of security when they're trying to sleep, out beyond the wire.

Claymores were never planted before dusk because, in the early days of the Vietnam war, soldiers would put them out as soon as the took their night positions. Observing Viet Cong would slink in later and then turn those Claymores around. Then they would retreat to a safe distance and fire a round, hurl a rock, or do whatever would make the soldier behind the trigger of the Claymore push the lever.

Since the mine was turned around, that soldier would then blow his own head off. Undoubtedly the Viet Cong got serious chuckles from that.

The tables were turned, however, when soldiers got hip to what was going on. So their revenge was to plant dummy Claymores. Those Claymores, unfused, would have very taut wires leading from them to the night positions. Then, after dark, a second Claymore would be planted, aimed so its killing zone was pointed at the first, dummy mine. The grunt then retreated to his position and kept one hand on that taut wire to the dummy. When the wire moved, the soldiers would trigger the second, real Claymore. Several Viet Cong practical jokers got splattered learning that the U.S. Army also has an evil sense of humor on occasion.

Blind Pig preferred to set up his own perimeter. He put Willie behind the machine gun and went forward, just after nightfall. He planted two Claymores on either side of the finger, pointed down the hill's edges.

Then Blind Pig continued down the finger, moving cautiously in the now almost total blackness. From his fatigue side pockets, he took four C-ration cans, which he'd saved after the troops finished eating. Each of them had a handful of pebbles in it, and Blind Pig had punched holes in the tops of those cans with his K-Bar knife.

The cans were hung on bamboo shoots. If anyone came through the bamboo, the cans would shake, the pebbles would rattle, and Blind Pig would level the surrounding terrain. Blind Pig set out two flares with their trip wires just where the finger disappeared into the bamboo-blanketed flatland. He considered his work, scratching his crotch thoughtfully.

One more precaution. Blind Pig took a hand grenade from his shirt pocket, hefted a small boulder up, and position the grenade under the rock. He tested it. There seemed to be enough weight. Blind Pig pulled the pin on the grenade. Anyone scrambling up that finger would undoubtedly hit the boulder and activate the grenade.

Blind Pig tiptoed—as much as anyone six-three and 240-plus can tiptoe—away from his handiwork back to where Willie waited behind the M-60.

"What were you doing down there for so long?"

"Seein' that I be alive to greet the dawn," Blind Pig answered. "Now move over."

Blind Pig slid behind the gun and continued his preparations. Around the perimeter, all the other lizards were fully awake, finishing their own preparations for the night. Some were more, some were less elaborate than Blind Pig's. But no one on the knoll who'd been out on more than one sweep trusted to God and luck to keep him alive that night.

Blind Pig ripped two small branches from the log in front of him and dug them, vertically, into the ground on either side of his gun. These were aiming stakes. He could now tell, even with his eyes closed, how far he could swing the gun before he might be shooting into Mosby's or Martinez's position.

In near-total darkness, Blind Pig checked his gun. The 250-round belt that he'd carried all day was removed, to be replaced with another belt, a clean, oiled belt that he'd husbanded in his asspack. He went over the M-60 by feel. There were very few damned things in this world Blind Pig loved. Children. Lost causes. Deacon Rayburn, the Detroit mobster who'd promoted Blind Pig from street thug to backup. And the M-60 machine gun.

The M-60 replaced, in the early sixties, the World War I vintage Browning machine gun, a heavy, solid-iron clunk of a gun that, to any of the soldiers who carried it into innumerable wars, was a weapon that had corners in places that most weapons don't even have corners.

The M-60 was somewhat different. It weighs about twenty pounds and looks a bit like a very fat rifle, with swing-out bipod legs up front. The M-60 can be mounted on a tripod, but no one in Vietnam ever took that tripod or its T&E mechanism on an operation. The M-60 is actually based on the German WWII

MG-42. Due to the extensive use of nylon for the stock and forehand grip, it was dubbed the Mattel Toy by GIs.

It is a wonderful gun. It can be fired only by right-handed shooters, since the weapon throws its hot shell casings back to the immediate right, into the face of the left-handed gunner. It is .308 caliber (7.62 x 51 in NATO cataloging).

The M-60 eats 250-round belts at the cycling rate of fire of around 600 rounds—bullets—per minute. Of course if the machine gunner actually tried to fire at that rate by holding the trigger back, the barrel would get white hot, droop, melt, and then blow up.

Any machine gun—except one that is water-cooled or multi-barreled—can only be fired in short bursts, to prevent damage to the gun. So the actual number of bullets that an M-60 could deliver, per minute, was from 75 to 100. Which was still enough to make the gun the heaviest cat on the battlefield.

Blind Pig had first seen the M-60 in AIT, and had fallen in love. He wistfully thought about what he could have done, back on the block, with the gun. Even now, he was trying to figure a way to steal an M-60, strip it down, and ship it home to the Deacon.

Most infantrymen-in-training keep their opinions to themselves about the alternative weapons they're trained on. Mostly they realize that, if they do very well on a certain weapon, they're going to have to carry that heavy sucker into combat. Not only is the M-60 a pain to carry, but the survival rate of a machine gunner in combat, back to WWI, is only slightly longer than that of a second lieutenant.

Blind Pig did not give a shit about all that. He qualified expert on the gun. His Senior Drill Instructor, who'd been trying to set Blind Pig up for Fort Leavenworth Federal Prison, grudgingly admitted that, in all his years at Fort Gordon, no one had ever qualified higher on an MG. So Blind Pig went to Vietnam as he wanted—as a machine gunner.

Blind Pig knew the M-60's supposed defects—if a barrel had to be replaced in mid-action, there was no way the gun's sights would be accurate. And the sights themselves weren't much at night. If the gas plug was not safety-wired in position, it could vibrate out and the gun would stop working. None of this mattered to Blind Pig.

The gun was light (at least to him), could be sling-carried and fired from the hip, the barrel change could be done with the flip of a switch, and, most important, the guy with the M-60 was the Man. He ran the battlefield.

Now, behind the logs, Blind Pig ran through his ritual with the gun he loved. With the ammo belt out, he pulled the operating handle back twice, letting it ease forward. The gun was clear. He then pulled the buttstock, buffer yoke and buffer, then slid the rod and bolt assembly back until they dropped into his hand.

He took a large can of 10-weight oil from the spare parts gear he carried in a gas mask container, and drowned the receiver and bolt in oil. The gun was hastily reassembled, and the new belt fed into the gun. Blind Pig ratcheted the operating handle twice. The M-60 was now fully loaded and ready.

The safety was perpetually off on Blind Pig's gun—as he reasoned. "I come to this stinkin' country to kill folks. There be no need to be hesitatin'."

The nightly ritual completed, Blind Pig moved to the side of the gun and positioned two grenades and his .45 pistol on top of a log. He was content.

All that would make him happier, he decided, was a bath, some Chivas, a blowjob, and eight lines of good snow. In his content, he farted loudly. Brown, lying beside him, sniffed distastefully. Blind Pig, having no other sign of trouble, took offense.

"Hey, nigger."

"What do you want."

"Get your black ass over here. I don't be shoutin' to the world."

Brown slid over a bit.

"Got a question, Brown. What kind of nigger you be?"

"I am not a . . . nigger," Brown said. "And why do you talk that way, anyway?"

"Why the fuck not?" Blind Pig wondered.

"You're doing everything these people want us to do."

"Shit. Me do what *anybody* want? Best you explain."

"Jefferson, all these white people, they expect us to be . . . well, be spear chuckers. They want us to be what the fucking Klan says we are. Apes."

"I don't dig. But keep talkin'."

"What I'm asking is why the hell do you have to behave like you're a goddamned gorilla?"

"Oh, man." Blind Pig sighed. He took a Camel from his pocket and stuck it in his mouth, unlit. No one smoked after nightfall. But still, there was a bit of comfort.

"Okay. I got your bitch. Now you through?"

"I guess so."

"Fine. Now it be my podium. So listen up. First I tell you I owe nobody shit. Nobody white, nobody black. Whatever I be, there it is."

"I don't think you—"

"Shut up, nigger. I listen to you, now you give me back. I gone clue you. These chucks—man, it don' matter you sound white on white on white like they want. They still gone think you a nigger. That's right, mister man. To them you be a nigger, no matter how much you say you don't want fuck they women or live in they neighborhood. I tell you truth, Willie."

"Jesus Christ, Jefferson!"

"That white man god got shit to do with us, either. Best you be learnin'. The only way anyone leave you alone be by shovin' a gun up they fuckin' nose an you say move on, dude.

"Otherwise, they be fuckin' with you from now till they lynch your fool black ass for not bein' white enough. Second thing you best be thinkin', friend man. Since you be in the squad, all you do is cry blues an' whine. Shit, dude. Ten years gone, you be lookin' back an' thinkin' this be the best time you ever live."

"I sincerely doubt it."

"Why not?" Blind Pig wondered. "Man, here you be fed. You carry the biggest gun on the block. All you be asked is be ready to be the baddest nigger on the block. What be better'n that?"

Brown thought about answering, then shook his head. He forgot that in the blackness Blind Pig couldn't see him.

"You got no answers, nigger," came the sandpaper whisper. "Tell you what. Ten years now, I gone be set. I gone have people. Have my part of town. That give me any bitch goin', she be black, white or green, it don't matter.

"I gone come back from this war. An' when I do, I gone be big dope man. Now you ain't answerin', is you, Brown? You shocked and all that shit. But I gone ask you. Ten years gone, where you gone be?"

"I guess, I'll probably go to college. And then . . . I don't know. Maybe medical school."

"You shittin', nigger. I gonna make a prediction. Crystal Ball Blind Pig, so you best listen close.

"The way you be goin', snivelin' an' such, you ain't gone see no ten years. You be dam' lucky you alive an' come back, you don't get your head out and start worryin' less what they devil motherfuckers be thinkin' an' more about what your own black ass be doin'! An' that be solid advice you best be takin' to heart!"

The conversation finished to Blind Pig's satisfaction, he spat into darkness and rolled back behind his machine gun.

CHAPTER NINETEEN

THE THREE SISTERS

OPERATION SWIFTSURE WAS about twenty-four hours old.

As per Sinclair's orders, the Twelfth Division was deployed. The Eleventh was put on in a blocking position ten kilometers east of the sprawling complex of forests that was called the Octopus.

The Fifteenth—Mosby's battalion—had been successfully scatter-gun-dropped slightly south of the Octopus and was slowly sweeping north looking for the Phu Loi Battalion.

What Sinclair, Shannon, and the rest of the intelligence apparatus did not realize was that the Phu Loi—moving at speed—had already crossed Highway 13 and had linked up with General Duan's 302d North Vietnamese Division. From there—after Duan's realization that the Americans would be hunting down the Phu Loi—the two units had moved due west toward the Octopus.

The 302d was being screened to the south by the Phu Loi Battalion. Duan had correctly understood that if contact was made with either the Americans or South Vietnamese, there would be far less alarm—and therefore less chance of exposing the imminent General Offensive—if the engagement was with a Viet Cong unit.

The units were moving under forced-march conditions. All cells had been told that if any soldier fell out during the march, he was to be stripped of his combat gear, identification and then abandoned. None of the hard men of the Phu Loi—let alone the men who had come down the Ho Chi Minh Trail with the 302d— were upset by the threat. None of them fell out.

Twenty-four hours in. Both forces were moving like two blindfolded boxers—neither knowing for sure who was in the ring with them.

So far, Sinclair was drawing a large blank. The tank unit he'd sent up the highway had been very easy for the NLF soldiers to avoid. Since the NVA and the VC were moving almost due west, they were not seen by the Lurp patrols inserted on the fringes of the triangle.

Duan had few initial problems. He anticipated moving the 302d and the Phu Loi into the sanctuary of the Octopus within seventy-two hours. Since his hand-drawn maps were even less accurate than the American maps, General Duan never saw the three hillocks that the peasants had dubbed the Three Sisters.

CHAPTER TWENTY
MOSBY

"KEEP ON KEEPIN' on, sports fans. Standing by in the wings we've got Hendrix, the Airplane, Quicksilver, Otis and the Doors. Doo-dah, doo-dah . . . all the hits that give lifers shits!"

DeeJay was motor-mouthing into the handpiece of his PRC-25.

"But now listen up, campers. It's time for our Boss Radio Eye-in-the-Sky early aaa emmm traffic report. Don't touch that dial, wage slave, or you'll be sittin' in the middle of the Turnpike Blues!"

DeeJay unkeyed the mike and checked around for a reaction. The squad was saddled up and ready to move. Blind Pig glared at him. Fritsche turned away with a grunt. Martinez grinned broadly.

DeeJay giggled to himself, then turned serious as he became the Traffic Reporter and opened his mike again.

"Looks pretty bad at the MacArthur offramp, Jack. They just opened up a new whorehouse there, and we got us some convoys backed up on top of each other . . . okay, now we're hangin' up here in our Spad over the Westmoreland Turnpike.

"Good news for you east-bound commuters. That little traffic jam's clearing itself out. I can see the tow trucks hauling off that dead water buffalo. Sorry, got a correction here, Jack.

"That wasn't a water buffalo. The tie-up looks to have been caused by a second lieutenant trying to read a map. That's him they pulling away now . . . Now over to the Patton Thruway . . . all the tanks are moving smoothly again . . ."

DeeJay unkeyed the mike, trying to keep from laughing while he searched for more inspiration. At that moment the speaker crackled.

"This is Citation Six Actual. Who made that last transmission?"

Oh shit. It was the old man. Colonel Taylor.

Not that DeeJay was fazed; he was after all, the budding genius of the airways. He went back on the air.

"Ah, so, Imperialist Pig. You like Running Dog Broadcast: I

161

expert on American ways. I go UCRA! Fuck big tit coeds. Ris-ten KFWB all time. Bill Ballance my hero! Good-bye, GI! Fuck you up ass!''

He hastily broke transmission and turned the volume down, so he couldn't hear the sputterings from Citation. Martinez and Fritsche were now laughing, and even Blind Pig had a slight smile on his face.

"That be bad shit," he admitted.

Now *that* was Top Forty praise. DeeJay wandered off to see what Lieutenant Fuller was doing.

"This is a lot of shit, Casey, and you know it," Mosby complained. "Our squad's gotta take point two days in a row?"

Casey shrugged.

"That's the way it is."

Mosby snorted.

"I wish Fuller'd get his head out of his ass before he kills us all.''

"Not Fuller's idea."

"Oh yeah?"

"Yeah. Mine," Casey said.

Mosby gaped at him.

"I just got a feeling," Casey explained.

"Jesus, Casey!"

"Something else, Dave. I want you on point."

"Fuck you, Sergeant! I got your feeling right here." Mosby cupped a hand around his balls.

"Just do it, Mosby."

Mosby sighed and got to his feet.

"Okay. But what if you're wrong?"

"Sue me."

Mosby laughed.

"How could I? Where's I ever find a jury of my peers? In case you ain't noticed, they're killing them all."

Mosby closed his pistol belt and moved forward to take point.

Mosby pushed his way through the endless elephant grass that towered over his head. He couldn't tell what was in front of him or behind him, as the grass sprang back as soon as he pushed through it. Mosby could be walking into a big goddam rock— or a big goddam ambush, for that matter. The only way he could tell whether they were going up or down was by the tension in his legs.

The elephant grass had saw edges that lacerated exposed flesh.

First there was the sharp, thin pain of the cut, and then it burned like hell as sweat streamed into the wound. Taliaferro's body pushed up to him.

"Five minutes," he panted.

Mosby sagged, leaning on his rifle. Casey rustled through the grass toward him.

"What the hell do we do with this Hill 902 if we get there?" Mosby wheezed.

"We take it, hold it, and patrol aggressively forward," Casey recited in a mock Regular Army drone.

"Alright. Next question. How do we know when we get there?"

"Got a big sign on its side, sayin' Hill 902."

"In English or Vietnamese?"

"You talk too much, Mosby."

"I love you too, Acting Platoon Sergeant Casey."

Just then, to make Mosby's morning complete, it started to rain.

For a change, the map now appeared to be correct. It said they ought to be climbing right now, which Mosby was doing his damnedest to comply with. The ground rose sharply before him, loose rock and rotten shale, slabbed with mud.

Swearing to himself, Mosby wiped rain from his eyes, placed a tentative foot forward, found purchase, and moved his other foot. Great. One step down. About a thousand more, and he'd be there. At this point, the only thing keeping Mosby and the other members of the platoon going was that Hill 902 was just on the other side of this rise. At least, that's what the map said.

Mosby took another step, and the ground crumbled into a shower of rocks. Somebody cursed below him, but Mosby paid no never mind, as he fought for balance. There. Safe. Now, another step. Mosby was starting to get his climbing moves down. That was when gravity ambushed him, and a heartbeat later he found himself sliding back down the hill, his nose scraping a furrow in mud and rock.

He felt a sharp pain in his side as he careened off a boulder, and then he caromed into something soft and yielding. It was Taliaferro, who'd watched in some awe as Mosby's body skittered down the face of the rise into him. After the thump, Taliaferro then went ass-over-teakettle down the hill.

Mosby clung to an outcropping, keeping himself from sliding any further. He thought about just lying there for the rest of the day. To hell with the fact that he was lying there in the open. Maybe some VC would spot him and put him out of his misery.

He felt a prickling along his spine. Jesus, Mosby, he thought, are you going nuts? Goosed by fear, he started scrambling upward again.

"This ain't Hill 902," Casey said, checking the map against the sheer cliff yawning below them.

"The hell it isn't," Mosby argued. "Says so right on the map."

"The map's wrong again."

"Okay. Then where's our disappearing hill?"

Casey pointed to a towering, tree-covered mount in the distance. To get to it, they would have to negotiate down this cliff, then through a brush-choked canyon, and then somehow go up that hill through what Mosby suspected would be the thickest scrub jungle he'd ever walked through.

"That's another couple thousand meters, Casey. This can't be right."

Casey studied the map carefully.

"Yep. That's our hill."

"Howinhell we supposed to get there? Take us ten years to cut through those trees."

"Bound to be some mouse deer trails," Casey said.

Mosby was aghast.

"You mean we're gonna *crawl* up that sucker?"

"What the hell," Casey said. "It'll give our feet a rest."

On that cheery note, he turned away, to hunt down Fuller and break the news.

Casey had been right. There were hundreds of tiny mouse deer trails, mazing through the brambles.

Mosby's knees and hands were pulp, and his head pounded from eyestrain. It had been hours, he thought, since he'd been able to see for more than a foot or so in front of him. And about the third of the time, he'd taken the wrong trail.

This was a fact only discovered after many minutes of crawling as you suddenly realized you were going downhill again. Then you had to wait until you hit a crisscrossing trail, checked your compass, and hoped this trail would turn out to be the right one.

The trails were only a meter or so high, roofed with thorns that grabbed from every direction. The undergrowth climbed all the way up into the branches of the low-slung trees, reducing

164

visibility to twilight. And while it'd stopped raining an hour or so ago, thick gray drops still cascaded down as Mosby moved. Each drop felt cold and slimy, like a leech. Mosby did not want to think about how many of them *were* leeches.

At first, Mosby hadn't really thought about how spooky the trails were. He'd been too busy finding his way and mourning his aching body. The feeling came as a gradual creeping depression. Mosby would have given anything for one ray of sunlight, or a breath of fresh air. He felt the trails closing in on him, and it seemed like he'd spent his entire life in this limbo.

Sometime later, he realized that his heart was pounding, doing double-duty as fear-pumped adrenaline fed the engine. What was he afraid of?

The answer crawled out. What if there were other people on these trails, listening to the crackling of the brush and the low muttering of swearing GIs? He would never see them. Never smell them. And he probably wouldn't hear the shot that killed him.

Adding to his jumpiness was the persistent sound he'd noted about halfway up the hill. It began as a low moan, growing louder the higher they crawled. Mosby couldn't figure out what the hell it was, other than it didn't sound human-caused.

This should have relieved to the fear, but instead he kept wondering about it, imagining silly little-kid-at-night thoughts. He wasn't sure what he was afraid of most, stumbling on a gleeful Viet Cong or finding the source of the sound.

Mosby was not a particularly superstitious man. But he'd learned long ago that when a grunt encountered the mysterious, it never turned out to be anything nice. What the fuck. At least it'd stopped raining.

He slithered around a twist in the trail and broke out of the brush so fast that it left him gaping and blinking into the sunlight, like some bewildered mole. Mosby came up to a quick half-crouch, weapon ready. He turned this way and that, trying to get his eyes to focus.

Just in front of him was a tumble of moss-strewn boulders, about three meters high. Little rivulets of water streamed here and there, down the side of the rocks. As he saw them, Mosby realized that the moaning sound had turned into a full-blasting thunder, coming from just beyond those boulders.

Mosby found handholds and very slowly lifted himself up. His scalp felt very tight under the helmet, against his skull. He was so tense he knew he could duck faster than any rifle could hurl a bullet at him. Fuck the speed of sound—Mosby was quite prepared to hit Mach 2 getting back into the safety of those nice, comfy mouse deer trails.

He was so busy looking for bad guys that it took four small forevers for what he was seeing to register. Mosby smiled at God's very strange sense of humor.

The source of the sound that had terrified Mosby on the long crawl was one of the most beautiful things he'd ever seen. Hill 902 could have illustrated a travel poster.

The thunderous, mysterious beast was a waterfall, spilling down mossy rocks into a small pool. That waterfall cast a constant rainbow that arced over a tiny meadow of soft grass, sprinkled with a carpet of pinhead-sized wild flowers. Flitting over the meadow was a cloud of pure yellow butterflies.

A cool breeze drifted toward Mosby, filling his nostrils with the perfume of the flowers and a slight, delicious musty smell from the moss.

Around the waterfall were many small caves, and one grotto that appeared to be hand-hewn into the rock. Peering out from the grotto, staring directly into Mosby's eyes, was a small, ancient Buddha, with kind stone eyes and a gentle smile.

"What the fuck you doing?" came a low voice from behind and below.

"Shut up," Mosby hissed. "I think we just found paradise."

He scrambled the rest of the way over the rocks, came to his feet, and zombie-walked across the meadow to the edge of the pool. Then without a breath of hesitation, he dropped his rifle and helmet and marched into the water. It rose up his body, cool and delicious, until he found himself paddling around like a puppy.

Hill 902 had been secured.

As soon as Fuller had the platoon deployed to Casey's satisfaction, he let the men go crazy, in staggered bunches. Some were just lolling in the grass, chewing on flower buds like so many Ferdinands in sweaty OD green. Others were cleaning out caves for hooches, lining the floors with the soft, sweet-smelling grass. But most of them were splashing around bare-assed in the pool.

Fuller felt like he was in one of those old war movies, midpicture, when the sounds of battle fade and the soldiers cavort in an innocent stream. This was where they always had the beautiful nurse walk out of the jungle and the "what does it all mean" sequence.

He caught himself looking over at a clump of trees wishing a tawny beauty into existence. Fuller was suddenly pleased with himself. Maybe he was learning enough to relax a little. Careful, man. You're getting way too relaxed. But still he couldn't wipe that silly grin from his face.

It was Willie the Semi-Brown who invented the waterslide. He'd tired of playing in the pool, dodging people, ducking people, splashing people and getting splashed. He climbed up the side of the waterfall, to the top of the hill where the spring burst from the ground.

He was sunning himself on a rock, staring up at the sky and wondering how long those black clouds in the distance would take before they were on them. To either side of the falls the rocks dropped down to the pool in a fairly gentle swoop. Brown noticed that the moss covering them was inches thick and slick from the constant spray.

Then it came to him that the fall was just like the giant plastic waterslide they had at the amusement park just outside Boston. His dad and mom had taken the family there every summer. The slide was Willy's favorite attraction, better than the roller coaster or the haunted house. Gingerly, Brown got to his feet and dangled his way to the far side of the falls. He positioned his bare ass on the moss.

"Look out below," he shouted.

He pushed off. Ten grunts in the pool below gaped as he plunged down the rocks, twisting and turning and then splashing into the water like a cannonball.

Minutes later, half the platoon was lined up atop the rocks, waiting for a go.

Just before dusk, Mosby and Casey strolled along the edge of the now-empty pool. The water had settled, and Mosby could see the fat silver shapes of carp patrolling the bottom. He pointed one of them out to Casey.

"Imagine that guy on your plate."

Casey casually admired the fish.

"Too bad we don't have any tackle."

Mosby had the tickle of an idea.

"See that little cave over there?"

Casey saw the indicated tiny opening to one side of the falls and nodded.

"Might be some VC in that cave, Sergeant Casey. Maybe I ought to clear it."

Casey frowned, then got the idea.

"Sure is a possibility," he drawled seriously. "Probably

167

twenty, maybe thirty guys holed up, just waitin' to leap on our asses tonight. Go ahead. Clear it.''

Mosby unhooked a grenade from his pistol belt and pulled the pin.

"Fire in the hold," he shouted.

He then carefully lobbed the grenade.

"Ooops," he said, as the grenade missed the hole by a mile and plopped into the pool.

Mosby and Casey went flat, just as the grenade sent a water-spout high in the air. They climbed to their feet and examined the mistake. Half a dozen stunned fish floated on top of the pool.

"Cleared that hole, alright," Casey allowed. "Now get your ass in there and get those badass gooks before they come to."

Laughing, Mosby waded into the pool to collect dinner.

The closer night came, the more peaceful the meadow was. A wind brought the scent of rain from an approaching storm. Fires were lit here and there across the meadow and in the caves. A few birds made last-minute passes over the camp, gobbling insects drawn by the fires.

Taliaferro watched with greedy eyes as Martinez spread a gut-ted and butterflied carp over the coals of their fire. Martinez was whistling softly to himself as he worked, sprinkling some spices borrowed from Mosby over the fish.

To one side, Willie, DeeJay and Fritsche were talking about old times in the land of the Big PX, each waiting patiently for the other to finish his story, laughing at the right point, and then waiting a gentlemanly moment to make sure the man was done before beginning his own tale.

Taliaferro was feeling pretty pleased with himself. He'd made a discovery that morning and had been waiting all day for just the right time to announce it. Now he could not hold it back any longer.

"Hey, Martinez," he blurted. "Guess what?"

Martinez and the others turned toward him.

"Que pas', chingo?"

"You know what tomorrow night is?"

Martinez considered, then shook his head.

"Thursday? Monday? I don't know. Who cares."

"Let me tell you," Taliaferro said pedantically. "Tomorrow night's All Saint's Night."

Martinez looked at him blankly.

"Halloween, dummy," Taliaferro went on. "You know. Ghosts and goblins and things that go bump in the night?"

A sudden and total chill enveloped the group. They stared at Taliaferro with glittering eyes.

"You know, you're an asshole, man," DeeJay said.

"Hey," Taliaferro said, not understanding. "Really, I figured it out this morning. Tomorrow's Halloween. It's gotta be."

"Just shut the fuck up," Fritsche snarled.

"What's wrong with you guys? I thought . . ."

Fritsche was on his feet and Taliaferro almost bit his tongue in two shutting up.

Martinez shook his head and turned back to the fish. And that moment, the clouds opened. Martinez yelled, grabbing his fish as the water torrented into the fire. Within seconds, dinner was ruined. Dripping and miserable, the grunts headed for shelter in their cave.

"Fucking Taliaferro," Martinez said. "Fucking huerro cock-sucking asshole."

"Jesus, y'all," Taliaferro said. "I didn't have anything to do with this rain."

"The fuck you didn't."

Taliaferro sat in the tiny cave, trying to figure out what he'd done wrong.

Mosby listened to the rain thrumming outside his cave. He liked the sound, a steady peaceful beat that would have let him drift off to sleep. But tonight it made him feel uneasy and isolated. He felt that way despite the cheery, crackling fire (the mouth of the cave shielded with a poncho), and the two pounds or so of fish tucked safely behind his ribs.

Perhaps it was the presence of Casey, who sat silently across the small fire from him, endlessly stropping his knife on his boot and staring into the embers. In the firelight, Casey's eyes glowed yellow, and his deep, weathered tan looked like carefully oiled hardwood. Mosby thought Casey was way up there on the list of the strangest men he'd ever met.

No one in the squad knew how old Casey was. He could have been twenty-five or forty-five. Casey never talked about himself, and you got the idea that he didn't welcome questions. Nobody knew how long or how many times he'd been in the Army. Sometimes he let little things drop that led the listener to believe that he might have been in WWII or Korea. No one knew if he had a family, or where he was from. His drawl placed him somewhere between the Texas Panhandle and Montana.

Mosby dug his stick into the fire again, stirring and stirring the embers.

"Jesus, Casey," he finally exploded. "You don't talk much, do you?"

Casey studied the question awhile, considering.

"Nope," he finally said. "Guess I don't."

"Well, say something, for Chrissakes. I'm going nuts from nobody to talk to."

Again, Casey rolled this around in his mind awhile. Then he nodded, as if discovering for the first time that speaking had some use beyond passing information or telling somebody what you needed done. Mosby had always suspected that Casey was much more comfortable with the hand signals they used on patrol than the English language.

"Okay," Casey said. "What you aim to talk about?"

"Shit, I don't know. Whatever people talk about when they're sitting in a fuckin' cave in the middle of a monsoon in Vietnam. That's what I want to talk about!"

"Fine with me. Go ahead. Shoot."

Mosby was at a total loss. He hunted around for a topic, then decided to take a wild chance.

"I heard some guys say you used to be a cowboy. You know, a rodeo-type cowboy."

"You did?"

"Yeah. I did."

"Oh."

"Well?"

"Well what?"

"Were you?"

"I know one end of a horse from the other, if that's what you're askin'."

Shit. Mosby tried another approach.

"You got family?"

"Sure, I got family."

"Well?"

"Well what?"

"I mean, if you got family, where are they from? You got brothers and sisters, a mother and father, uncles, aunts, a rich cousin? Do they write to you? Do you write to them? Does anybody care if you get your ass shot off? That's the kind of shit I mean!"

Casey thought about this, then nodded.

"We write," he said. "Not a lot. But we write."

He thought a moment more.

"I guess a couple of folks might be upset if I kicked. Not surprised, you understand. But mournful, like. Yeah, I suppose so."

Mosby gaped. This was the most that anyone had ever gotten out of Casey. He was being downright loquacious.

"You feel better now?" Casey asked.

"Better about what?"

"We talked some, right?"

"Uh, yeah. I guess."

Casey yawned.

"Well, if that's enough talk, I think I'll get me some shut-eye."

"Fuck me, Casey. You act like talking is some kind of prescription. Like a pill that's gotta be handed out."

"You mean we ain't talked enough yet?"

"Isn't a matter of enough. People talk because they like to. They need to."

"That's the difference between you and me, Mosby. You like to talk."

"And you don't?"

"Not much."

"Well, shit, why did you talk to me in the first place, then?"

Casey looked at Mosby for a long moment.

"What's eatin' you, son?"

Mosby also considered, then shook his head.

"Fuck, I don't know. Scared, I guess. Don't you ever get scared?"

"Huh. Yeah. Yeah, I get scared. When I think about it."

"Haven't you been thinking about it tonight? I mean, I don't want to surprise you and all, but this is not a Boy Scout Jamboree. We're in the deep bush, and there are people out here who want to kill our young asses. Don't you think about that?"

"Not much."

"Why the fuck not?"

"Because it scares shit out of me."

Mosby fell into silence, chewing this over. Then it came to him.

"It's like the feeling you got today? When you put me on point?"

"Yeah. Like that."

"I shall be a son of a bitch," Mosby said. "You're human after all."

Casey started to say something, then stopped. Then started again.

"I put a lot of store in what I feel. Saved my ass a few times."

"And?"

"And that feeling I had?"

"Yeah?"

"I still got it," Casey said softly.

"Even here?"

"Especially here."

Casey pulled his poncho liner up around his shoulders and settled back against the wall of the cave.

"Now. Enough talk. Go to sleep. I got to check the guards in two hours."

He closed his eyes and was instantly asleep. Mosby stared across the dying fire at him a long time, listening to the drumming of the rain outside.

Normally, Mosby liked that sound. But not tonight.

CHAPTER TWENTY-ONE
CUNG

PHAN XUAN CUNG was a prankster. He looked his role, being moonfaced, thick-bodied (as thick as the low-caloric diet of the Phu Loi Battalion permitted), skinny-legged and constantly smiling.

"Of course I smile a lot," he once said. "How else can a man who claims to come from generations of fishermen live with the fact that the last four generations of my family never hauled a net?"

He was not quite exact, but the nets his family hauled did not catch fish.

His great-great-grandfather had, indeed, been a fisherman, captaining a leaky sampan, setting fore and aft throw nets from Nha Trang, fishing for the shrimp that the French found extraordinarily tasty and were willing to pay high prices for. But like any decent fisherman, he had no aversion to making a profit on the side. He generally brought back to Nha Trang not only shrimp, but a few flintlock muskets or pistols hidden in the bilges, for sale to a certain Chinese merchant in the city.

Unfortunately one night the sampan was boarded by a French revenue cutter, captained by an eager young ensign and a crew of Binh Xuyen pirates, who were getting very well paid not to listen to excuses or bribery. Cung's great-great-grandfather went over the side after the searchers found the muskets, carried down by his own netweights and one .44 caliber Colts pistol ball in the guts.

Cung's great-grandfather heard of the murder, burnt the family's waterfront fish shop, and went north to join De Tham in the upper regions of the Red River. He took the precaution of sending his pregnant wife and their only daughter south, to join relatives in Saigon. When De Tham was betrayed to the French in 1913, Cung's great-grandfather died with him.

Cung's grandfather was a street urchin, hustling cyclocabs for drunk Frenchmen staggering out of the Cercle Sportif. When he turned fifteen, he went into the bush and joined the Trotskyite Ta Thu Thau. Since the Trots are nowhere near as puritanical as main-line Communists, it was possible for him to marry and father a son before he was shot down by a Vietnamese policeman, for cheering on the day that the French colonialists were forced to surrender to the Japanese, in 1941.

Cung's father, in his mid-teens, also went into the field. By now the Cung family had nothing but legends of their former home in Nha Trang. For three generations none of them had seen the town.

Cung's father was an excellent soldier and was chosen from the volunteer regional Viet Minh to join the elite 803d Viet Minh Regiment.

Cung's father had been on a very short leave when the French fortress at Dien Bien Phu fell. Cung would have been three years old, and vaguely remembered his father as a slender, very nervous man who spent every minute of that leave with his son. Then he went north, to rejoin his unit.

Most people assume that after Dien Bien Phu surrendered all fighting stopped in Indo-China. They aren't aware of the long, slow Golgotha a French unit called Groupement Mobile 100 went through over a month later, in a retreat through the central highlands south of An Khe. There were 3,500 of them, highly experienced tankers, artillery- and infantry-men, most with experience in the recently ended Korean War, three battalions of the finest Cambodian and French soldiers.

They began the retreat down Highway 14 in June 1954. As they moved south, they were hit again and again by the 803d. On June 29, GM 100 reached Pleiku, having traveled some fifty miles. There were fewer than 1,700 soldiers left by then. GM 100 had ceased to exist as a military unit.

But the 803d had also been decimated. In the confidence of victory, they'd moved out of the jungle and left themselves open for the napalm strikes from French B-26 bombers, planes that ironically for Cung's father were flying out of Nha Trang. One of the Viet Minh who died, and whose fried-mutton fragrance spread across the coastal plain, was Cung's father.

With this heritage, for Phan Xuan Cung the world was nothing more than war—first against the French, then against the puppets, then against the Americans.

And Cung, like his father, was very good. Good enough to be a first scout for that finest of all Viet Cong units, the Phu Loi Battalion. His abilities as a joker were also prized by his superiors.

But at this moment, Cung was feeling less than humorous. Flanked by two fellow scouts, he was crouched in one of the ruined huts just to the south of Hill 957. Even though dusk was falling, he could see the American soldiers still moving about, around their perimeter atop the hill.

Were he leading a company-size or smaller formation, it would be simple for Cung and his fellow Main Unit bo-dois to slip past, unnoticed.

But the entire Phu Loi unit was on the march, in four roughly parallel columns. Cung spearheaded the most southerly. The problem was that the second column, he knew, was supposed to pass just *north* of Hill 957, across a wide expanse of abandoned rice paddy. As soon as Cung had spotted the American unit on the hill, he'd passed word back to Captain Le, his column's commander. A runner had been immediately dispatched to warn the second column to the north. Cung wished they had the elaborate radio gear of the Americans and their puppet soldiers.

Captain Le had given orders, orders that Cung considered obvious. His column would hold in place, with its point in the ruined village until full darkness. When the storm looming overhead broke, the column would move past the hill, then break north. Le was assuming that the other Two Sisters were also garrisoned by imperialists.

Le had moved two RPD machine-gun teams and one 82mm mortar element up, in case their column was seen. The machine gunners were positioned on the edge of the bamboo clumps outside the ruined village, and the mortar behind the sagging wall of one hut.

Cung had little respect for the Americans' ability at night—he'd outmaneuvered too many patrols and led enough sapper teams through base camp perimeters not to know that the giants were children when the sun went down, crouching behind their weapons, terrified of the dark.

The problem would be not Cung's elements, but that second column as it moved across the 500 meters of open paddy to the north. Cung might have prayed, but the only gods he had were Doc Lap (independence), his battalion, and Ho Chi Minh, none

174

of whom he felt were in the business of listening to whines from the jungle. Cung just wished the storm would hurry, and that when it arrived it would be the grandfather of monsoons.

Waiting, he estimated the number of Americans on the hilltop. It wasn't hard, since Cung knew the imperialists invariably put two men in each fighting position, more for their crew-served weapons. And since all Americans felt it was safe to smoke until full dark and sometimes even then, the estimates were easy.

Cung thought there were about twenty-eight men on Hill 957.

He involuntarily crouched as a helicopter broke through the low cloud cover, flapping past to the south. He smiled at his own overcaution, knowing that the pilots would be intent on their waiting whores and steaks, not looking for one peasant lying prone next to a paddy dike.

Cung was always amazed at the imperialists' loud pronouncements that they fought a jungle war as well as any Viet Cong. This was true for a few of their soldiers, men who moved and lived in the bush for weeks on end. But mostly the Americans went to war as if it were a parade, long columns of men stumbling along, their gear clinking as if they were so many belled water buffalo, their presence signaled for miles by the overhead metal birds, their flares, and smoke grenades.

Major Tran had once told the battalion that the Americans still thought they were fighting their fellow Fascists in Europe, a place that Cung could vaguely point to on a map, but had no other knowledge of or interest in.

Full night had fallen, according to Cung's watch—a Hamilton talon from a dead American—by 20:20. Rain sheeted down at 21:17.

Cung slid back through the mud to his fellow scouts. A touch on each shoulder, and a motion forward. Cung could hear the slight clinks as the gunners folded their bipods, ready to move. Then Cung hesitated as the rain intensified, cascading around him so that he could not see the dim faces of his two fellows, less than two meters away.

PFC Edwards, 2d Squad, Third Platoon, Charlie Company, 15th Infantry, clicked the starlight scope off and shoved it back into the pack.

The light-amplification scope, in spite of its nearly four-pound weight, was a prized tool for the grunts. It gave its user, at least in theory, 300 meters of eerie green nightsight under starlit conditions, 400 meters of see-in-the-dark capability under a full moon.

Actually in practice the range was limited to 250 meters maximum, given the worn condition of the scope. But in the overcast and the rain, Edwards's starlight scope was just four pounds of dead weight. Edwards grimaced invisibly through the rain toward his platoon leader, Second Lieutenant Walker, who was in the position with him.

"Darker'n hell's hinges. Whole fuckin' Charlie Army could be out there, for all I can see."

Walker keyed the mike of the Prick-25 next to him.

"Whirlaway Six, this is Trey Six, over."

"This is Whirlaway Six. Go ahead."

"Trey Six. Visibility my position zip. Do we have a Smokey?"

There was a pause as, miles away on Hill 1113, Captain Harris consulted his SOI.

"That's an affirm, Trey. Switch to Freak Four. Call sign is Smokey One Niner."

"Trey Six. Switching frequencies. Out."

Walker, by feel, changed the preset frequency selector of the radio.

"Smokey One Niner, Smokey One Niner, this is Whirlaway Three Six, over."

A bored drawl whispered through the speaker.

"You got him."

"This is Whirlaway Trey Six. Position Tangerine. We need some light, over . . . sorry . . . continuing transmission . . . authorization Foxtrot Yankee."

"On the way, Three Six. But it ain't gonna give you much, since I'm droppin' blind in this shit."

In the distance, the men of Third Platoon could hear the throbbing drone of the incoming plane.

Cung had held up the advance because the increased rainfall might be the monsoon increasing its intensity. Or it could portend a sudden break. Cung's caution was correct. The Phu Loi's second column, to the north of Hill 957, had not been nearly as wary. They were a quarter of the way across the bare paddies when the rain suddenly stopped as if someone had cut a switch. Their first piece of bad luck.

The second piece was that, just as the rain stopped, Smokey the Bear was overhead. Smokey ships were unarmed, WWII-vintage C-47's, unarmed—except for superintensity aerial flares.

176

Smokey's first flare dropped through the overhead clouds, and an instant overhead searchlight lined out the men of the Phu Loi Battalion in the open.

Cung saw the flare, and almost simultaneously heard the chatter of the American machine guns as they opened fire. Then came the thump of grenade launchers, the crackle of rifles firing from the hilltop and, sporadically from this distance, spattering return fire from the Phu Loi column.

Captain Le was beside him, his angry face reflected in the flare's light, bouncing off the overhead clouds.

"Cung," he hissed. "What watch are the imperialists keeping to their rear?"

"Now, none, I would think," Cung said carefully. "They're too busy slaughtering our comrades."

"Very well. Position one of your scouts here as guide. Two platoons, you and I leading, will attack up this hill, before the Americans can bring in their cannon and aircraft."

That was the only option. Cung pushed the safety/selector switch on his rifle to center position and, half-crouched, moved up Hill 957 toward Third Platoon.

CHAPTER TWENTY-TWO

THE SQUAD

DeeJay, Lieutenant Fuller and Casey crouched around the PRC-25, listening to the broken transmissions from Third Platoon. The distant flare in front of Hill 957 cast flickering shadows across their faces. Over the mile-and-a-half distance, they could hear the crackle of fire.

"Estimate . . . engaging . . . companies . . . hell, we got . . . shitpot of . . . out of here . . ."

"Walker, this is Six. Do you need arty? Over."

"That's affirm . . . request . . . movers . . ."

"I'll relay. Arty's on your frequency, Deuce. Bombard Seven-Three."

"This is Bombard. Go ahead."

"Coordinates . . . 567 . . . troops in line from . . . to, uh . . . 345569 . . . gimme some Willie Peter . . . will adjust . . ."

"Sounds like they're havin' themselves a real turkey shoot over there," Casey said.

"This is Whirlaway Six, Walker. Negative on Fast Movers. They're socked in. Will see if I can get out a Cobra flight. Over."

"Whirlaway Six, this is . . ."

The radio went dead.

Over the distance between their hill and 957, they could hear the firing suddenly intensify.

"Shit! They're taking fire from the rear!" Casey's eyes could pick out the tracer rounds spearing at the hill from both sides.

The radio came alive again.

"Whirlaway. This is Bombard Seven-Three. On the way. Wait."

Nothing but static followed . . . then:

". . . Gooks coming in . . . us . . . taking . . . heavy casualties . . . Chrissakes! Somebody . . . something!"

"Trey, Trey. This is Whirlaway Six. What happened to Lieutenant Walker?"

"Dead . . . CP . . . This is Avery . . . They're right on top . . ."

For years, DeeJay imagined the unheard rifle shot that broke off the transmission. Then the artillery rounds exploded in front of the hill—graceful white flowers through yellow-black smoke.

". . . This is Bombard. Can you correct?"

Nothing.

"Three . . . goddammit . . . this is Captain Harris. Is there anybody receiving? Come on! Answer me!"

Static.

Firing from Hill 957 died, then there were two single thuds clearly identifiable as AK-47 rounds.

Fuller gaped at the radio.

"Jesus fucking Christ," he said. "Just like that?"

"I'll get the troops up," Casey said. "We'll move at first light." He slid off through the mud toward the platoon's perimeter.

The rains swept in again.

Second Platoon went back down Hill 902 in the gray dawn and the rain, red clay greasy under their bootheels. The grunts were tight-faced and silent. There were 5,000 meters of jungle to cover to relieve whatever was left of Third Platoon.

First Squad felt it was by god their right to lead. They were, after all, the best. March order was unusual. Casey himself walked point, with Fritsche behind him for backup. Behind him was Blind Pig, a belt half-loaded into his M-60, the rest of the 250 rounds slung over one shoulder. Fuller and DeeJay were a full squad behind the first. Lieutenant Mel Fuller was bone-scared. He'd spent most of the night alternately on the PRC-25 with either Captain Harris or Colonel Taylor, becoming more afraid and more confused by the minute.

Somehow the colonels and generals in Vietnam, contemplative with their staffs, grease pencils, and wall charts in air-conditioned Tactical Operations Centers could never understand the problem a second lieutenant—out in the dark and the mud with the Bad Guys—had getting the Big Picture.

To Colonel Taylor and General Sinclair the answer was obvious—given the contact with Third Platoon, the Phu Loi Battalion must have evaded Second of the Eleventh and the tanks, and have crossed Highway 13. Of course the Phu Lois were moving at full speed toward the Octopus.

The solution, according to the rules of high-technology airmobile warfare, was simple: a unit out of combat, such as Second of the Eleventh, should be airlifted between the Phu Loi Battalion and the Octopus, as a blocking force. Then the scattered elements of the Fifteenth should be gathered and reinserted as a maneuver element, which would catch the Viet Cong in a classic pincers movement. Meanwhile airpower should slow the Phu Loi down.

But the jungle and the monsoon were not ruled by high technology or by West Point tactics. The rain kept the slicks—the troop helicopters—and the gunships grounded at Ba Rei. The few fast movers, Air Force or Navy fighterbombers, that were able to get off their fields were flying blind, high above that solid cloud cover that extended from Highway 13 across the Three Sisters to the Octopus.

Grand Strategy became nothing more than relieving Third Platoon. Sinclair's Maneuver Elements were Captain Harris with one platoon and company headquarters, and Lieutenant Fuller's Second Platoon. Artillery was firing H&I—Harrassment and Interdiction—missions. But with no observers and no observed targets, the shells were just shredding empty jungle.

All this left Fuller and his men feeling very naked. Again the radio came alive.

"Whirlaway Deuce Six, this is Citation Six Actual, over."

DeeJay passed the mike cord to Fuller.

"This is Deuce Six, over."

"Fuller, this is Colonel Taylor. Look, son. I want you to move careful. I know how you feel about Third Platoon, Mel. But I don't want you to end up the same way they are. Take care, boy."

179

Fuller wondered how Taylor had found out his first name, considered a response, then just keyed the mike open.

"Roger, Colonel. Thanks. Whirlaway Deuce Six. Out."

He gave the handpiece back to DeeJay.

"Once more onto the fuckin' breach," he muttered from his English Two class. DeeJay was uncomprehending. They moved out again.

Trying to move fast in the bush, Mosby knew, was suicide, stupidity or both. Vines pulled at you. Unseen branches caught your webbing and your rifle and dragged you back. And the faster you moved the more you knew that Charlie was sitting only meters away, waiting.

Mosby wanted a cigarette, a chance to catch the breath rasping through his lungs, or maybe just somebody to call this whole thing off. Assuming . . . just for drill . . . he thought sourly . . . the gooks don't ambush us between here and there, what is going to happen when we get to that hill?

Mosby found himself hoping that they would find something other than what he knew was there.

The column stopped, and the whisper came back.

"Mosby forward."

Mosby slid past Taliaferro, toward point. Blind Pig crouched at a wide place in the trail, his M-60 aimed forward, vaguely between Casey and Fritsche. In front of them was a solid wall of bamboo. But the two men were looking down at the muck in front.

Mosby moved up, saw the blood, still pooled, in spite of the rain beating it into the ground.

Casey dipped his fingers. "Gun shot," he muttered, running the thickness across his palm. He straightened.

"Fuck it," he said. "They know we're comin'. We're gonna surprise 'em. Mosby, flank us."

Mosby nodded and pushed himself sideways, into the thick brush. Casey had his bowie, and Fritsche the squad machete out, and they started.

Ten minutes later, and the platoon had moved off the trail and ten feet forward through the bamboo clump. Mosby and Taliaferro relieved Casey and Fritsche cutting trail.

Slash down, 45 degrees to your left. Recover. Slash again, 45 degrees to the right. One step forward. Heave for air and wipe the rain draining down your helmet onto your face. Slash, slash, a second step forward.

Second Platoon cut their way forward through the bamboo

until they hit a clearing. Blind Pig was through the cutters, M-60 covering the far side of that clearing. Casey went back on point. He led the platoon, almost at a dogtrot, around the edges of the clearing, to its edge. He checked his compass, then pushed his way into the bamboo again.

Mosby, sucking new blisters on his hand, was just behind him. Crawling, pushing through brush . . . chopping through bamboo . . . dragging up, pulling up a slope, using breakaway brush for handholds. Realizing that somewhere one of your ration socks was gone and lost. Draining a canteen, and realizing it's your third and you do not remember drinking the other two . . .

It took eight hours for Second Platoon to cover the few thousand meters to Hill 957.

CHAPTER TWENTY-THREE

DUAN

GENERAL DUAN AND Commissar Thuy crouched over the map, spread over rocks piled atop the mucky ground. Duan's command tent was his large rubberized sheet, tied between trees. Outside the tent Major Tran waited in the rain.

On the map was a collection of broken-off twigs, each representing a unit of either the imperialist forces or the People's Army. Duan was too security-conscious ever to mark a map that might easily end up in enemy hands.

It was simpler, he mused, when we played this General Offensive as a map game, in that warm, comfortable high-ceilinged room in Hanoi. Entire units could be committed to battle, destroyed, and the pasteboard marker would be dropped back into its box, awaiting the next round.

"Comrade Giap has said that he would climb over the bodies of one hundred thousand countrymen to reach final victory," Thuy observed.

"He just may," Duan muttered.

Thuy perhaps should have remarked on the insubordination. But the march south had changed him, as it had every other bodoi in the 302d.

"Comrade General," he said formally. "I am a novice at tactics. But I don't see any other option. I concur with your decision."

He paused.

"Shall I be present, Comrade General?"

Duan shook his head.

"I wish," Thuy said, "I were marching with them."

Duan looked at his young commissar. He should ream him out good now, for even mentioning something that smacked of adventurism. He couldn't bring himself to do it. The Comrade General let silence do the job for him. Thuy flushed, rose from his haunches, and ducked under the edge of the groundsheet. He told Major Tran to enter.

In the distance, Duan could hear the thunder of the American bombers and, closer to him, the occasional crump of the blind-firing artillery. Not factors to concern himself with at the moment. Tran was waiting for his orders.

"Major Tran," Duan began slowly, without preamble, "circumstances force a change in your unit's mission."

The lean commander of the Phu Loi Battalion scanned the map and the twigs on it. He touched one stick.

"I would assume this represents myself and my comrades?"

"It does," Duan said.

"You have us in contact with the imperialists, yes? And if this stick . . . here . . . represents your division, it is far closer to the Octopus than our forces are presently."

Duan decided that this was being overly subtle.

"Your orders, Major Tran, are to remain in contact with the Americans."

"For what period? Until Giai Phong?"

That was too much. Duan's voice hardened.

"You are to engage the imperialists for a period of seventy-two hours, in the areas where your Phu Loi comrades are presently fighting. I leave the method of engagement to you. But I will remind you that orders from the Central Committee are that, under no circumstances, is my division's presence to be discovered.

"So, we're to be thrown away?"

No, Duan thought. He was handling this incorrectly.

"During the days of the French," Duan said with seeming irrelevance, "I once found myself commanding a platoon of bodois. Our objective was a small post, occupied by some of France's mercenaries. The Foreign Legion."

"But, we are discussing my men, Comrade General . . ."

"Perhaps there is a point to be made in this," Duan said.

"These Foreign Legionnaires were very proud. Very efficient. They were commanded, our agents told us, by a young officer

182

who treated these men as if they were his sons. His unit was most effective in patrolling this area, denying us our mission.

"And so, one day, we ambushed a small squad, one which we obliterated to the last man. We then removed the heads from these five mercenaries and, under cover of darkness, put those heads on stakes outside the French base. That marked the end of that unit's efficiency in combat."

Tran felt like shouting. Why in God's name was his Comrade General blathering like a temple mandarin? He cooled himself down.

"I would have thought quite the opposite," he said quietly.

"You might have," Duan went on. "For certain, the mercenaries were frenzied, wanting to kill every Viet they could see, bo-doi or civilian.

"But we did that not to affect the mercenaries, but rather their officer. The young lieutenant, who thought of these soldiers as his sons, could not stand the personal hurt of seeing any more of them killed and their heads staked in front of him. And so, from then on, he patrolled only during the hours of daylight, and in areas visible from the fort."

Now Tran understood.

"You think I have that attitude toward my battalion?"

"Not consciously."

Tran was angry . . . and then he considered.

"It is true that all of us have been fighting so long we think of ourselves as family."

"We are all family," Duan said softly. "A family with a purpose. Fulfilling that purpose is the only way our family can survive."

Tran looked again at the map. "If the rain continues," he said, "the Americans will not be able to insert their soldiers ahead of us—and my mission will be useless."

"I cannot operate on that as a certainty."

"No," Tran sighed. "You can't."

The two men stepped out into the rain.

"I suppose," Major Tran said wistfully, "that my main objection to your orders is it makes it unlikely my comrades shall survive to see Giai Phong."

Duan remained silent.

"Oh well. That was what I said over our cognac. And none of us should have lived this long anyway."

Tran stepped back and saluted, as if he were on parade.

"I shall give my unit the orders."

183

Duan returned the salute and Major Tran pivoted and disappeared in the gray rain.

CHAPTER TWENTY-FOUR

THE SQUAD

MOSBY LAY FLAT behind Casey, staring up the brush-covered slopes of Hill 957. The abandoned village was to their right. There was no sign of life.

Casey waved an arm. Fritsche and Taliaferro came up and doubled forward. They dropped into firing position. Mosby, Martinez and Casey ran up the line. Mosby tried to console himself: If they're up there, this friggin' rain will cut their visibility.

No sounds. No birds. No insects. No human voices. Not even the croak of frogs from the rapidly swelling paddies they lay in.

Casey came up. Without a word, Mosby and Martinez flanked him as they went into the village. Again they held firing position. Nothing. Nada. Zed. Casey turned back to the treeline. He waved. Blind Pig led the rest of the men toward them. Casey bent and pointed. In the muck—half-buried under the imprint of a sandal heel—was a shell casing. It was an AK round.

"Their LD was here," Casey said. He hand-signaled the platoon. The men moved out, up the hill. Fuller, buried in the middle of the group, felt a slight burn of resentment. Then, he marveled. Jesus, son. You don't know how to do this. Think about what your old man said. Don't get anybody killed.

The hill rose through the same scrub brush Second Platoon had been fighting all day, a gentle rise toward the crest. Through the brush—flashing almost like slow animation—Mosby could see the green and rain-blackened motion of the grunts snail-walking their way up Hill 957.

Fritsche found the first body. Instinctively, he crouched. His shotgun swept in front of him—a pointing finger. Fritsche vaguely knew the man: Spec Four . . . Turner? No. Turnbull. The man's eyes still held a look of wonder at the fist-size hole below his sternum.

Casey was beside Fritsche. There was no weapon and the body had been stripped of all webbing and ammo. Personal papers—letters, a couple of pictures—lay scattered and rain-ruined.

"Phu Loi," Casey noted. "They didn't fuck with the body."

Fritsche nodded and they climbed toward the crest.

Moonscape with bodies, Mosby thought. He looked around the hilltop. A rifle bullet can cut an inch-wide tree down. A grenade can rip out several square meters of brush. A machine gun can be almost as effective as a machete in clearing brush.

There were two bodies sprawled at Mosby's feet. The gun was gone, but the bits of linked metal and the piled casings told him this was one of Third Platoon's machine-gun positions. Two . . . three . . . Mosby continued the body count.

Fuller was glad it was raining. Maybe the tears wouldn't be that noticeable. Five days ago, Sam Walker had sat in the Officer's Club, drawing lines with a wet beer can on the tabletop and explaining how the bar he was gonna buy in Lincoln was gonna knock them dead. Five months until ETS. Walker would take his discharge in Oakland, lay over in Frisco to get the hot tips on music and dancers, and the joint he'd open would be light-years ahead of anything Nebraska had ever seen.

Now Fuller was glad he couldn't see Walker's face. The grenade had blown Walker almost in half.

"Least he went quick."

Casey was beside Fuller.

"No big thing, Lieutenant," Casey said. Fuller realized after a moment that Casey had seen his tears. He didn't feel ashamed of them anymore.

"Is anyone . . ."

"Nope," Casey said. "We've found twenty-six bodies so far. No weapons. No ammo on any of them."

"Third Platoon had twenty-nine effective."

"Three missing. Still looking."

Fuller glanced around for DeeJay. It was time to call in an update. Then he heard the shouting.

Second Squad had found him—face up—halfway down Hill 957's forward slope. The grenade that blew PFC Rafer Smith off the hilltop had also saved his life. Any bo-doi who'd seen Smith—unconscious, his face looking like chopped steak—would have assumed death.

Smith was alive and talking.

Since the man had lain with his head under a heavily leafed branch, out of the rainfall, his bleeding wounds had caked into a red-mud mask. Buellton had Smith's head on his knee and was gingerly giving him sips of heavily salted water.

"You're the doc?"

"Sure, Rafe. You know me . . . Buellton."

"They were all around me, Doc. I just laid there. Was that okay, Doc?"

"You did fine, babe."

"I can't see anything, Doc. I just can't see anything at all."

"You just got crap in your eyes, Rafe. Now, I'm gonna clean you up. You ain't bleeding none, so you're just gonna have to terrify the nurses the way you are."

"You sure my eyes are okay, Doc?"

"Hell yes, Come on, man. White trash like me are too damn dumb to lie."

Casey looked at Buellton—eyebrows lifted. Is he? Buellton nodded, then turned back to Smith. He resecured the taped-in syringe from the plasma bottle that hung on the overhead branch.

"I do okay? They were everywhere. Nobody else was shooting, Doc. Is anybody else . . ."

"Hell if I know," Buellton said. "I'm sitting down in this friggin' bush with you and the leeches. Anyway, don't worry about anybody else. We got a dustoff on the way. I gotta tell you, Rafe. You're a cheap prick. You're gonna be back in the world before me. I thought I was the ultimate short-timer."

Casey had already gone back up the hill and grabbed the mike from DeeJay to call in the dustoff.

There was no reason for the second man to be alive at all. One AK round had almost torn off his arm at the shoulder, and the second had squarely impacted through his right lung, then had shattered the shoulderblade. But, somehow, Sergeant Gonzales had managed to drag himself undercover, gotten his aide pack open and the tinfoil cover pressed over his sucking chest wound. He used the tape on an M-16 bandolier to tourniquet what was left of his arm. Now, he and Smith lay on ponchos. Troopers were holding other ponchos over them to keep the rain off.

DeeJay gave Casey a skeptical look.

"You really think we're gonna get a dustoff in this weather?"

Casey didn't answer. He had done what he could.

"Citation Six. This is Nightingale. Weather our end zero-zero. Sorry."

Colonel Taylor swore to himself and opened his mike again.

"Nightingale. This is Citation Six Actual. Be advised we have two Whiskey India Alphas. Advised one critical. Come on! We just can't leave them on that hill!"

Pause.

"This is Nightingale. Have your people cut a Lima Zula?"

Taylor lied: "Affirmative."

"Citation Six . . . I've got a pilot here who says he'll try to get in. But, if he can't . . ."

"This is Citation Six. Tell your pilot if he gets these two out he can drink on me for the rest of his tour."

"Citation Six. Nightingale One Eight says that's a big Roger on that. His Echo Tango Alpha your area approx one-three minutes. He says he drinks Hennessey. This is Nightingale, clear."

Whirlaway Deuce Six. Whirlaway Deuce Six. This is Nightingale One Eight, Over."

Mosby wrapped six strands of primer cord around the last tree blocking the hilltop. He crimped the blasting cap on it, lit the fuse, shouted "Fire In The Hole," and walked unhurriedly away. Then he dove for the ground. The explosive cracked and the tree jumped into the air and fell. Martinez and Blind Pig dragged the log out of the way and kicked it down the hill. As his ears stopped ringing, Mosby could hear the dull whoppings of a Huey somewhere above them in the clouds. The rain had slackened to a drizzle.

"This is Deuce," Fuller said, trying to keep his voice as calm as the studied boredom of the medevac pilot. "I think you're just above us."

"You guys got nasty surprises for me—like big mother mountains or zips?"

"That's a negative, Nightingale. We're on the tallest hill."

"Don't be lying to me just 'cause you want my bod, Whirlaway. Alright. I'm comin' down."

The whapping became louder and more distinct.

"Hey, Whirlaway, old buddy. You know it's rainin' like a cow pissin' on a rock in your part of the world?"

Fuller kept off the radio, figuring the pilot would have his hands and mind very busy.

"There he is!"

Martinez was the first to spot the chopper as it broke out of the cloud—about 150 feet high and maybe 300 meters from the hill. Instantly, three grunts popped smoke grenades. The violet smoke rose about a foot, sizzled, and then drifted away.

"I see you, Whirlaway."

The helicopter drifted in over the hilltop, flared, and settled—spattering mud and sheets of water over the whole platoon. Buellton hastily pulled ponchos over the two casualties. The Huey touched and the medevac's crew chief unclipped his helmet and jumped out along with the ship's medic. They unshipped the stretchers and started loading casualties.

Fuller ran up beside the pilot's window. There was a pinched face staring back at him. Above the face was a helmet with MCGRAW stenciled on it.

"Thanks!"

"What?"

"I said, thanks!"

"No problem."

"What?"

The blade wash and turbine whine wiped out any other attempts at conversation. McGraw lifted both hands in a hopeless motion. Smith and Gonzales were abroad. McGraw cocked his head, listening to the crew chief, who was plugged into the cockpit circuit. Then he looked back at Fuller and waved bye-bye.

Fuller, bent over, splashed away from the Huey as it lifted and tilted forward.

It was seventy-five feet or so clear of the hill when Phan Van Tau opened fire on it with his .50-caliber machine gun. Of the fifteen-round burst, ten bullets stitched through the dustoff ship's red crosses and crew compartment.

Mosby remembered it oddly. First he saw the Huey rock sideways, then he smelled the stink of spilled JP-5 fuel. Then was a flash of seeing the Huey sideslip toward the ground, hearing the hammer blows of the VC machine gun, seeing the chopper smash into the ground and then pinwheel down to the foot of the slope. The next thing Mosby remembered was Blind Pig charging up— M-60 held like a rifle—and a scream of Motherfucker and a burst shred out from the gun and then Mosby found himself going down the hill with four other men, wondering why the fuck he was running toward something that was going to explode any minute.

Casey was slashing with his bowie at the remnants of the helicopter's shattered windshield. McGraw's helmet was split down the center and gray/white/red seeped through the crack. Most of the copilot's chest was gone. The Huey had crashed and skidded on its side some twenty meters downslope. Somehow—maybe he'd tried to jump and gotten dragged down by his helmet mike cord—the crew chief had ended up between one skid and the ground. His body was jellied along the twenty meters.

Mosby clawed his way over the aluminum body. He peered down into the troop compartment. Then he gaped as he saw something move among the gore. He heard a voice:

"Doc? Doc? What happened? Is anybody there?"

Private First Class Rafer Smith was still alive. It was his second miracle of the day.

"I say again. Dustoff went in. Five Kilo India Alphas. One Whiskey India Alpha. No other casualties. Over."

"Whirlaway. This is Citation. Can you estimate the size of the unit?"

"Negative. Dustoff hit with fifty cal. Heavy rain now. We observed troops—estimate one company-size—on rice paddy across from hill. Over."

"Are you in contact now?"

"Light sniper fire only."

"Whirlaway Deuce, will provide arty. Other units will support as permitting. Stay on this net. This is Citation Six Actual. Over."

Fuller lifted his chain out of the muck and looked at Casey. The two were prone behind the only large log on the crest of Hill 957. The rest of the platoon was spread out in fighting position—flat and motionless.

The lieutenant checked his watch. Minutes until night. One Viet Cong company—at least—with heavy machine guns. Against his platoon. Fuller supposed that he should have something heroic or even funny to say. But his lips stuck together and his tongue was firmly glued to the roof of his mouth.

CHAPTER TWENTY-FIVE

SHANNON

MAJOR GENERAL LEE SINCLAIR stared at the black grease-penciled circle on the plastic-covered wall map that represented Hill 957 and C/15's besieged Second Platoon. The huge map covered most of one wall in Sinclair's command center—the villa's ballroom. He tapped his fingers on the plastic, then hand-spanned his way across the map to the beginnings of the Octopus.

"This Phu Loi CO," Sinclair asked of Shannon, "what was his name again?"

"Tran, sir. Nguyen Van Tran."

"Thank you. Either this Major Tran is four kinds of a damned fool . . . or he thinks that I am."

Shannon considered the observed behavior of the Phu Loi Battalion, and agreed that what they had evidently done during the last forty-eight hours made little conventional sense. But his theory was one that Sinclair wouldn't want to hear. Fortunately, Sinclair was continuing.

"Let me mutter at you, Dennis," he said. "Feel free to interrupt if I get myself out on a limb.

"We saw the Phu Loi Battalion moving from here, near Ba Rei"—his fingers tracing the map again—"up to here . . . across Highway 13, then making contact with the Fifteenth Infantry at Hill 957. Correct?"

Shannon nodded.

"They destroy one platoon of the Fifteenth there, then disappear. This did not hold Hill 957, nor lay ambushes for the rescue units. Why, Major?"

Sinclair went on, before Shannon could answer the rhetorical question. Dennis had learned that his CG had the habit of talking through his own reasoning. That was as much of a staff conference as General Sinclair felt he needed.

"Perhaps because he is moving flat-out for the Octopus. Sanctuary. So far, I'm in agreement with Major Tran's thinking. Question, Major. How far could Tran have moved his unit yesterday?"

"Thirty . . . maybe even forty kilometers, sir."

"That would put him within one day's march of this Noir Massif. But instead he turned back and hit us again, back on Hill 957."

Sinclair puzzled, then looked away from the huge map as Captain Shapiro, the Air Force meteorological specialist, approached.

"Captain," Sinclair said. "I could really use a CAVU day tomorrow."

"With my fingers crossed, sir, maybe I can give you one. Do you want to look at my charts?"

"Negative, Captain. The last time I tried to read a weather map it took twenty minutes before I figured it was upside down," Sinclair said.

"Excuse me," he went on. "Major Shannon, would you chase down Captain Edmunds?"

Shannon nodded and went out of the command center. Sinclair returned to the weatherman.

"If you played poker, Captain, what would be my chances on blue skies tomorrow?"

"Actually, sir, a little better than even. We picked up a report from a Steel Tiger flight up around Neak Luong saying it was wide open as his . . . uh, that there wasn't a cloud in the sky. Tomorrow, there'll be southerly winds . . . might be a patch of high cumulus south of Tay Ninh. But I'd expect the weather to break as early as 0300, maybe 0500 at the latest."

190

"Captain, it surely is nice to have a piece of good news for a change," Sinclair said. "By the way, Captain Shapiro. That Steel Tiger pilot over Cambodia? Curiosity. He actually said the sky was as wide open as what?"

"Uh . . . as his hoochmaid's pussy, sir."

Sinclair half-smiled, dismissed the weatherman, and went back to studying the map. He glanced up as Shannon and Captain Jerry Edmunds approached.

"Gentlemen. Captain Edmunds, tell Colonel Brown to get G-3 up and bushy-tailed. It's 2345 right now. In half an hour, we'll need an Ops order."

"Yessir."

"Hang on a minute, Captain. You should hear this. Major Shannon, I think I just figured out what's going on.

"Your Major Tran is trying to play me for a sucker. He turned back and hit 957 hoping that I'd dump the rest of the troops in there. And while I did that he's going to be turning back for the Octopus at flank speed, with nobody in his way. But that is not what will happen. We are going to ruin his whole war. We're going to take every single bird this division has, and every other Huey G-3 can scrounge up, for a lift by 0400. Dawn, by the way, is at . . . ?"

"0456, sir."

"Thank you, Major. We'll get Second of the Eleventh off their tails at three, ready for liftout at . . . 0515. They'll be inserted here."

Sinclair slapped the map about five kilometers outside the Octopus.

"This battle on Hill 957 is being waged by a rearguard. All we need is to put in the rest of Charlie of the Fifteenth at dawn for backup. That's all that'll be needed, since the Phu Loi is now moving away from the area. Second of the Eleventh, landing and moving in company-size blocks, will sweep east. And then we shall have them."

Shannon had also considered the puzzling movements of the Viet Cong force. He agreed with Sinclair's battle plan—but for different reasons.

"Before the Eleventh makes contact, we'll have the Fifteenth in, across here." Sinclair's hand ran across the map.

"We shall then have Phu Loi Frederick in a world of hurt."

Sinclair paused in satisfaction.

"All right, Major. Since you think these super-Viet Cong are capable of all kinds of subterfuge, what other options do you perceive?"

"He won't go south," Shannon mused, unconsciously echoing

191

Sinclair's habit of thinking aloud. "He knows we're below him. He might disengage, and head for Tay Ninh. Not real likely. And he sure can't go south."

"*Can't,* Major?"

"Nossir."

"An explanation?"

And Shannon knew he was in the crapper. But somehow his mouth, which had always led entirely too free and open a life, was fully in gear.

"I agree with you, sir, that Tran is trying to suck us into committing on Hill 957. But I don't think it's just to cover his own movements. Sir, I think the Phu Loi Battalion is screening for that NVA unit I saw crossing the border."

Shannon reddened.

"Captain Edmunds? If you'll excuse us?"

Sinclair took Shannon by the elbow and led him toward a corner.

"Major Shannon. I have heard all that I wish to about this North Vietnamese unit that you and ten other people supposedly saw."

Supposedly? Shannon got angry.

"My situation, right now, Major, is that I seem to have an entire Viet Cong battalion by the short and curlies. I am not interested in chasing, not thinking about some NVA will-o'-the-wisps at present. Is that clear?"

"Yes. Sir."

"Secondly, I'll remind you of something. Once before I emphasized my belief in team playing. I thought you understood what I was saying at that time.

"Considering that you occupy a slot that half of those lieutenant colonels chairwarming at the Pentagon would give half their retirement for, aren't you being a little, shall we say, thick about your situation?"

"Nossir, General Sinclair. I assumed the General would appreciate *any* intelligence input, sir."

"Come on, Shannon. Knock off this thee-thou shit. I am trying to fight a war with a division I don't even remember the units of, and you aren't making my job any easier."

"Yessir. Sorry, sir."

"After this operation, we may need to discuss this more thoroughly, Dennis. But right now I'd like you to consider whether you really feel that you're working to your full capabilities here at Division."

Sinclair was finished. He returned to the map and Edmunds. Shannon trailed him. Straighten up, Dennis, and fly right, he thought. That was a pink slip he just waved at you.

Shannon gave himself the luxury of one teeth-grinding, then went back to planning Armageddon for the Phu Loi Battalion.

CHAPTER TWENTY-SIX

HILL 957

THE PHU LOI BATTALION's Third Company attacked seconds after the medevac helicopter crashed. They were halfway across the open paddy when the first artillery rounds came in.

Phan Van Tau followed orders. He and his men rushed across the paddy with the big .50 still mounted on its tripod. When they hit the base of Hill 957 they were ready to continue fire.

Tau's job was to provide the assault fire for the first wave. Once the first two platoons crested the hill, the machine gunners were to come up and complete the destruction.

"Tien-lien! Tien-lien!" The shouts began and the soldiers stood and rushed the hill.

"Motherfuckers don't need to be advertisin'," Blind Pig said. "Didn't figure they gone sit down there playin' whist."

Willie kept his teeth sensibly clamped together. This would keep them from chattering.

"Don't leave me forget," Blind Pig said, "to beat Taliaferro into dogshit. Sumbitch give us notice about Halloween. Now the shit be comin' down."

Willie managed a weak "Huh?" Blind Pig was holding Taliaferro responsible for their current problems.

"Motherfucker didn't figure tonight be Halloween, none of this shit be comin' down. Now, when I be workin' the gun, you be watchin' me an' the ammo. Don't go worryin' about no gooks comin' up on us—you hear, nigger?"

"I hear."

"Long as you keep feedin' belts and the gun don't jam, ain't no zips gone appear."

Then Willie heard—over the spattering of rifle fire—the sudden CLANG . . . CLANG . . . and he screamed: "Incoming!"

The first mortar rounds impacted just behind the platoon's fighting line, then walked the perimeter. Casey, Fuller and DeeJay—at the platoon CP—dove for cover.

The ground and air shivered. Come on, Fuller thought. Don't

193

make a complete jerk of yourself. He pulled a hand-held flare from his pack, and then a round landed on the other side of the log they were hiding behind. In the photoflare of the blast, Casey saw Fuller go down.

"Medic! Medic! Six is down!" DeeJay was screaming as Casey went over the log and—in the darkness—ran his hands over Fuller. A red flashlight went on and Buellton was beside them.

"Shit! Lieutenant! Lieutenant! Fuller, can you hear me?"

Buellton's combat knife ripped Fuller's rolled-up shirt sleeve away and black welled in the dim red light. Fuller was muttering: "Don't kill anybody! Don't kill anybody!"

"Come on, Lieutenant," Buellton said. "This ain't no time to be a peace creep." Fuller came back to awareness.

"They hit me."

"No shit," Buellton said, as his hands—working independently—cleaned and then bandaged the wound. "You got yourself a War Story *and* a Purple Durple." Buellton kept working. "They missed the bone, and you ain't bleedin' bad enough for them to have hit an artery. You hurtin'?" Buellton readied a morphine syrette.

Fuller was in pain, but he suddenly realized it was no worse than when he had dumped his roommate's Honda back in college. He waved away the shot and pushed himself up.

"Casey . . . how long was I out?"

"Couple seconds. They're still comin' in."

"All right." Fuller tried to stand, then reconsidered. "You pull Second and Third Squads' M-60s and put 'em up on the line."

"You want to leave our ass hangin'?"

"Casey, if they're coming in everywhere, we're fucking dead anyway."

Casey caught the logic and doubled off into the darkness. This lieutenant might work after all.

"DeeJay. I need the horn."

DeeJay handed over the mike.

"Bombard . . . uh . . . Seven Three . . . This is Whirlaway Deuce Six. Over."

"This is Bombard. What happened, Whirlaway? You went off the air."

"Bombard. I got every Victor Charlie in the fucking world coming up my hill. We're gonna kick their ass back off it. And, I'm gonna need a Tango Oscar Tango when I do."

"Roger your Tango Oscar Tango. What coordinates?"

"From previous coordinates, drop one hundred. Same azimuth. Over."

"Drop one hundred. Same azimuth. Roger."

* * *

Martinez was pressed against one tree, his eyes closed. The VC mortar CLANGed from downslope, and his eyes opened. He peered down the hill. His M-79 was aimed over a shattered tree limb at where that—possibly imagined—red circle was.

Uno mas, cabrone, Martinez thought. And you're one muerte slopehead.

Maybeflash . . . CLANG . . . and Martinez's M-79 chugged. Trying to hold the barrel on target, he snapped the grenade launcher open . . . slid in a flare round . . . Snap . . . Chug . . . and there was the shattering blast as his grenade set off the mortar's stacked ammo supply.

Through the drizzle, the explosion outlined the attacking Viet Cong.

Blind Pig—lips drawn back in a grin/snarl—crooked his right finger. Six rounds chattered. Blind Pig shifted . . . six more rounds . . . shift right . . . six more . . . walk right in, you jive mother-fuckers . . .

The rounds spat across the advancing Phu Loi soldiers, aimed at waist level. Blind Pig always figured you took more troopies out when you wounded them than when they were nice and quietly dead. It was an accurate theory.

Mosby would never remember what he was muttering to himself as the VC came up the hill. What he was saying over and over again was: "Luck be a lady . . . Luck be a lady . . ."

Just below him, two AKs sheeted fire and rounds whip-cracked past him to one side. Mosby heard the scream from the rear. His four grenades—pins already bent straight—were in front of him. He yanked one pin, let the handle come off, and "luck be a lady" two-second delay and the grenade went out into the night.

The M-16 was pointed and Mosby slammed four rounds through the grenade flash and then he rolled over once.

"Luck be a lady . . . Luck by a lady . . ." There was more blackness to one side and two rounds went into it and the shape went down. Downslope, Mosby saw the fuse-sputtering as a Char-lie pulled the ring out of a stick grenade and lobbed it toward him. It bounced once and Mosby rolled again. The grenade exploded. Mosby became night-blind. Still praying "Luck be a lady . . ." as his M-16 yammered at this fucking gook who had the brass balls to want to *kill* him and the rifle chattered dry. The bolt locked open. Mosby's thumb hit the release and he scrabbled a new twenty-round

195

magazine into place, tapped the bolt release, and the bolt slammed the new cartridge into the chamber.

Sound to the front—heard even through Mosby's blast-ringing ears. He bellycrawled back and another grenade arced down the hill and went off. Two screams. Mosby definitely saw the Viet Cong come out of the night in front of him. The man walked into his bullet spray and went down. Mosby found time to shout: "They're in the perimeter!"

"They're gonna kill us. They're gonna kill us, Doc. Don't let 'em kill me." This was from Rafer Smith.

"They ain't even close," Buellton said, trying to sound as if he wasn't thinking the same thing. He pushed the wire down the Syrette's needle, breaking the seal. Then he pulled the wire out and squeezed to remove air bubbles. He shoved the morphine into Smith's arm.

Probably OD the fucker, he thought. What the hell. Easier getting killed stoned than straight. Then Buellton was headed back for the perimeter and new shouts for MEDIC.

The bayonet looked ten foot long as it slashed at Fritsche's chest. The Viet Cong was at full lunge. Fritsche brought his rifle across, parrying the bayonet, stepped back, tripped, and went flat.

The VC recovered and brought his rifle shoulder high, ready to split Fritsche as he squirmed on the ground.

One-handed, Fritsche clawed his sawed-off up and pulled both barrels. The recoil almost broke his wrist—but the double-blast of #4 shot blew most of the VC's head and chest off.

"Fuck with the bull you get the horns!"

Fritsche broke the shotgun and two-fingered new rounds from his ammo pouch into his gun.

"Enough of this shit!" Blind Pig squeezed both detonators for the Claymores. Blind Pig had positioned his Claymores so they fired across-slope just moments before the dustoff chopper was hit. The blast from the directional mines caught the Viet Cong's first assault wave squarely, turning almost thirty meters of hillside into a hail of shrapnel.

Among the casualties was the Third Company's commander— Captain Le. The assault wave hesitated almost at the summit of Hill 957.

Blind Pig had his half-empty ammo belt out of the gun and a special belt loaded as he came to his feet.

"Anybody who ain't a gook get flat!" He pulled the 60's trigger.

His special belt was 250 rounds of tracer, fired just above waist level. A tracer round is very inaccurate—but the incoming red streak will produce an automatic duck from even the experienced.

The solid sheet of tracer rounds broke the assault line—already hesitating from the Claymore shock on one flank. The Viet Cong stumbled back down the hill.

Buellton turned the M-60 gunner over. He was as dead as his assistant. Buellton felt his own heart wince and then he was scurrying on. Guess I'm the only sawbones in Harlan County makin' housecalls tonight. He scrambled on to check the next casualty.

Mosby suddenly realized he was muttering something and there was nobody coming at him and only spattering fire coming overhead from the base of the hill. He set his rifle down.

He discovered he had time to breathe and time to notice that the rain had stopped and the clouds had blown over and the moon glimmered over the shattered hilltop.

Then a face—a solid mask of blood—came around a tree stump at him. Fingers clawed and there was a gurgling scream. Mosby was never sure who screamed.

He had his M-16 by the handguard and was swinging it—swinging at that mask of horror.

The nylon butt hit the Viet Cong solidly and shattered. Mosby had the rifle reversed and one round fired as the bolt came back against the bent recoil spring and then jammed.

The face was gone. There was only the sound of a corpse rolling down the hill.

"This John Wayne shit be gettin' wearisome," Blind Pig said as he flattened beside Willie's motionless figure.

"This barrel be done burnt, nigger. Get off your hunkers and get me a spare."

No response.

Blind Pig growled deep in his throat:

"Aw you dumb motherfucker, you didn't go and . . . fuck . . . you did." His exploring fingers found the hole in Private First Class William Brown's chest.

"Shit . . . Shit . . . oh, man! Now I gotta train me another assistant. Man, this war is gettin' unreal."

"Whirlaway . . . This is Deuce . . . On my command . . . fire!"

"Fire. On the way. Wait."

Count . . . count . . . and then the rustle into scream as the shells roared in overhead. Fuller never heard the radio crackle "Splash. Wait" as the Time on Target barrage—all shells calculated to arrive at exactly the same moment—blew the world at the base of the hill apart.

Casey was beside Fuller.

"Goddammit! Give us some warning next time, Lieutenant!"

Fuller was on the horn.

"Repeat range. And could you walk it down the same line you're on?"

"No problem, Whirlaway. Same range. Will fire one-zero degrees either side of our azimuth."

Fuller unkeyed the mike—realized what Casey had been saying— and shouted: "Incoming! Friendly!"

Somebody down on the line had recovered enough to yell back: "No shit!"

"What we got, Mosby?"

"Willie's dead. Fritsche got himself cut."

"How bad?"

"Messy. But he's too pissed to feel anything."

"How's the ammo?"

"Shitty. I'm down to five magazines. Everyone else has about the same. Blind Pig's got two belts. Plus he scored another one off West."

"Fuckin' great," Casey said. "Okay. Next they'll be trying to infiltrate us. Tell your end of the line to keep it on semi-auto. First bastard that goes rock and roll's gonna burn the shitter for a week."

Mosby had to laugh. If all the ammo got wasted firing full auto, the only shitters anybody would be burning would be in hell.

Casey went one way, Mosby the other. Both were on their way back to their positions when Tau's .50 caliber opened up. It was grazing fire—five inches above the ground. Somehow the VC gun crew had come silently up the hill and positioned the gun on a finger of the hill just beyond the platoon perimeter.

Rounds raked back and forth. The whole unit was pinned down. Mosby found himself staring into Casey's eyes and wondering if his own were as flared and scared-looking.

"Fine," Casey said, spitting words. 'You got the squad. When the gun shuts off, the gooks are gonna come in on us."

Mosby was about to ask what the fuck, and Casey had his webbing off, a grenade in one hand, and the long bowie knife flickered once as the sergeant eeled into the night.

Casey's orders were shouted/whispered down the line. Mosby had the pins on both his grenades half-out. A soldier screamed as a .50 round tore through his foot. Four more rounds shredded the rest of him.

Mosby heard the whack of AK rounds. He knew the Viet Cong were bare meters below the hillcrest. A grenade boomed. The .50 caliber's fire rose. The big gun was firing almost straight up. Then it seemed to jam. Silence.

"Grenades," Mosby shouted.

He had the pin out, arm back, and he threw . . . and in the seconds before the explosions he could hear men yelling from where the .50 had been.

He went forward again. He sprayed bullets down the slope. The artillery rounds howled in.

Thunder and ears ringing and then the clatter and dimly heard shouts as the Phu Loi company broke and ran.

CHAPTER TWENTY-SEVEN

SINCLAIR

SINCLAIR, ORBITING IN his C&C chopper high over Hill 957, was feeling very much like a modern major general. With the exception of minor wrinkles, everything had gone as planned. Even the monsoon had broken as predicted.

The only somber note was the Chinook grounded on Hill 957's crest. Sinclair could see a thousand feet below the small figures lifting the last of the green, limp body bags into the huge, twin-rotored helicopter. To make up for that he could also see the patrols Harris had out, combing the ground for enemy dead. Even from 2,000 feet, Sinclair could see some scattered bodies in the open.

Initial reports from Company C had confirmed over forty enemy dead. It was accepted practice to factor a body count by four, to calculate total casualties. In other words, for every dead VC body seen, four others were either wounded or killed and their bodies removed. Although Sinclair knew the correct factoring should be by two, he was more than happy to use the larger estimate.

The Chinook lifted away, and Sinclair's chopper settled in to land on the now-barren hilltop. He was quite content—everything was in motion. He'd already leapfrogged the Second of the Eleventh in front of where he knew the Phu Loi Battalion was. Soon the Fifteenth would also be air-assaulted into position, to complete the pincers movement.

* * *

Captain Harris was not pleased with his new orders. He felt—correctly—that Charlie Company had done more than enough. One platoon wiped out, another decimated. All that Harris had left was First Platoon and his own headquarters element, which had been lifted onto the hilltop shortly after dawn. They should police the hill and be sent back to Ba Rei to reorganize.

Instead, Sinclair had ordered the company into combat again within a few hours. Harris didn't like it.

"I understand your concern, Captain," Sinclair was saying. "But I need every available man from the Fifteenth. We're about to strike a blow that the enemy will not soon forget."

"My troops, no offense, General, aren't real good at the big picture, sir. They're all expecting to get pulled out. They need a rest. Sir, they deserve it!"

"Under normal circumstances," Sinclair said, "I'd agree with you. But these aren't normal circumstances."

Harris yessired in defeat.

"One thing," Sinclair went on, "that I've done, however, is to bring in some hot chow with the resupply."

He indicated a second Chinook that had crowded itself onto the hilltop, next to Sinclair's C&C Huey. Men were already hauling out marmite cans of steaming food. Sinclair smiled, then:

"And I'll tell you, Captain, after what I've seen of C Company so far, I'm sure they're the kind of men who just need meat and potatoes behind their ribs, before they're ready to fight again."

Harris blanked at him. There was no sense in this. But he had lost.

"We'll be ready, sir," was the best he could say—although his response should have been a refusal of orders and a request for relief. Not that it would have changed things—Sinclair would merely have brought in a new CO. There were no options.

"Fine," Sinclair said. "Now, I'd like to meet some of your men."

Fuller, slumped against a stump waiting for dustoff, felt as if he were looking at Sinclair through the wrong end of a pair of binoculars. The voice also sounded far away. But he listened and tried to react properly.

He felt no glow, hearing Sinclair's words of praise. He flatly did not feel anything, physically, or emotionally. Fuller was only just aware of the discomfort from his arm, and he also had no sense of feeling in his other limbs. There was only one moment of semi-reality, and that was when he heard Sinclair say that the platoon would be moving on. Without him, of course.

"I'm sorry, sir. I can't do that."

"Can't do what, Lieutenant?"

Fuller's mind was stumbling over even simple words, but he desperately pressed the thought.

"Sir . . . they can't go without me. I'm their platoon leader, sir."

Fuller realized that Sinclair was staring at him, and he fought to pull his mind together.

"My arm can wait, sir. Sir, I've seen it in this far. I can take it through to the end."

Sinclair smiled kindly down and then looked over at Captain Harris. The captain nodded. Fuller should be medevacked, but his wounds weren't *that* bad. Sinclair felt a welling inside him. With men like Fuller, his luck could never go wrong. He felt an ungeneral moisture in his eyes.

"Okay, son. I'm going to grant your wish. I'm prouder than hell to do that. And when you come back from this action, there'll be a Silver Star waiting."

Fuller was suddenly and massively terrified. What the fuck was he doing? If his big mouth hadn't run away with him, he could have been in a nice safe dry clean hospital. Then he was horrified at himself. After Casey, Willie and the others, he was quite ashamed. Ashamed, he sort of recognized, for even being alive.

"Nossir. Thank you, sir. But I don't want any medals."

Sinclair, again misunderstanding, was again deeply moved. He gently patted Fuller on the shoulder.

"I understand how you feel, boy. But you leave those kinds of things for other people to decide." He moved away.

Jesus, Fuller thought. A Silver goddamned Star. What would his old man say? At that moment Fuller determined that his father would never find out.

Buellton had never thought much about generals, one way or another. Now, with only ten days left in hell, he was *really* unimpressed with this two-star asswipe chatting amiably in front of him. Buellton just wished the man would go away, so he could finish resupplying his aid kit.

The only thing on Buellton's mind was staying alive long enough to rotate out. He'd been a madman last night, running around like Audie Frigging Murphy every time somebody yelled "Medic." Patching asses up while the slopes were trying to shoot a giant hole in his. You are a stupid son, Buellton my boy. You're too short for hero moves.

Buellton had almost shit when he found out that Top Sergeant Ramos, contrary to policy and orders, was gonna send him out in the bush again. He'd resolved then that he was going to find the fattest cat in the platoon and walk behind him. Or else find a fat hole to hide in.

Either way, he was going to let those last ten days of war go right on by. Buellton almost told Sinclair—after the general'd complimented his stupid-ass hero moves the night before—the only thing *that* proved was that Buellton was ready for a 208 Psychiatric Discharge. Instead he said thank you sir a lot and wished he would go away.

"This your first tour, boy?"

Boy. I got your boy swingin', General.

"Excuse me, sir?"

"Is this your first tour?"

"Yessir."

"Are you planning to make a career out of the Army? We could use more men like you."

"Nossir. Sorry, sir. But I'm figurin' on gettin' back to my folks."

Sinclair smiled in understanding.

"What kind of career are you planning on?"

"I'm thinking of medical school, sir. I'd like to be a doctor."

"So, you're trading the jungle for a golf course, eh?" A Sinclair joke.

Buellton gave him a diplomatic, meaningless smile.

"Don't aim to be that kind of doctor, sir."

Sinclair laughed.

"No. I guess you wouldn't. By the way, when *is* your DEROS?"

"I got ten days left, sir."

Sinclair's face froze. He spun, angry eyes sweeping Harris, then they settled on a very nervous Ramos.

"What is this man doing in the field, First Sergeant?"

"Uh . . . sir . . . uh . . . sir, da t'ing dere is, sir . . ."

"Aren't you aware, First Sergeant, that no man is supposed to be sent to the field with twenty days or less remaining on his tour?"

"Well, sir, I . . . uh . . ."

Sinclair shut him off with a glance, then turned back to Buellton. "Son. Get your things together. You're flying out with me. I'm making sure you see your folks again."

Buellton gaped at Sinclair. All of a sudden, generals were impressing him . . .

Mosby only heard bits of the exchange between Sinclair and Buellton, but what he'd heard was enough to put him into shock. Now he watched as the general approached him, flanked by Captain

202

Harris, First Sergeant Ramos, and a still shocky Fuller. A joyful Buellton trailed them.

Mosby had figured Buellton for a dead man. With only ten days left, there was no way he could survive the odds. Just like Willie had been doomed. Guys who were shiny-new or mossbacked-short always ate the green weenie. There were exceptions, of course. Like Casey.

Although, Mosby thought, they still didn't know what had happened to him. They'd found the blasted-out .50 caliber, and the grenade-shattered bodies of the Viet Cong. A couple of the dead gooks also had their throats slashed, Casey's handiwork with his big bowie knife. But there was no sign of the man. They'd searched the area thoroughly, but with no luck. Blind Pig and Fritsche were at this moment downslope, combing the brush for their squad leader. Hopefully, he was wounded and had managed to find a nice safe hole to curl into, until it was all over. Mosby did not really believe that. Things just never worked out like that.

Mosby figured they'd find the body momentarily. Which put, to his mind, just another check in the KIA column, even though he had liked the man. For a flash Mosby wished that Casey'd been an asshole. Mosby realized that his chest hurt and there was something solid stuck in his throat. But experience took over, and he put Casey back behind the door and locked it tight. The man was dead, god-dammit.

By the time Sinclair had stopped in front of him, Mosby had himself together again. He even enjoyed Ramos's look of stark terror and Buellton's shit-eating grin. He damned near laughed. Keeping from doing that, he missed Sinclair's lines.

"Sergeant Mosby?"

"Uh . . . nossir, sir. The sergeant's a Spec Four, sir."

Sinclair chuckled, Harris politely joined in, and even Fuller managed a smile. Ramos's face, however, stayed grim.

"You just got yourself promoted, Specialist. At the recommendation of Lieutenant Fuller.

"Thank you, sir," Mosby croaked.

"He's also put you in for a Bronze Star. I approved it, of course. The lieutenant thinks quite highly of you, Sergeant. You'll do a good job leading your squad."

Mosby now knew that the Army had gone crackers. Or maybe it was just a new and interesting way to kill him. As squad leader, they were figuring that Mosby would take all kinds of chances trying to keep everybody else alive. Mosby hated Sinclair et al., because he knew they were right.

"One thing more, Sergeant Mosby," Sinclair said. "I'm sweetening the kitty. When you get back, you've got yourself a three-day pass.''

That was it. Mosby knew he was dead. He would not be coming back from this operation. Not with a three-day pass waiting for him.

"Thank you, sir," he managed to shudder out.

Then Sinclair and the others were walking away. Buellton lagged back. Mosby was thinking about all the things he could do with a three-day pass, and started ignoring the death thought. Shit, they don't shoot brand-new sergeants who just got themselves a tin medal, do they?

"If I can make it, you can too," Buellton said, reading Mosby's mind.

"That's obvious, huh?"

"I read you like a comic book."

Blind Pig's voice grated behind them.

"Chuck, you be one lucky mo-fucker," he said.

They turned to see Blind Pig and Fritsche clamber from behind a pile of charred, mortar-blasted trees.

"Where the fuck you been?"

"Soon as we spotted that two-star asshole," Fritsche said, "we determined to keep low till he left."

Blind Pig had more important thoughts.

"They be plannin' on the zips be gettin' another try at us, ain't they?"

"How you figure?" Mosby inquired, still not absorbing what was going on.

"Soon as I see those C-rats bein' offloaded, I see they have plans for our unlucky asses. They don' resupply us field niggers. So they gonna be puttin' us back out there."

"Sorry about that shit," Fritsche added. "Maybe you clowns are staying out, but not me. Here, see. I been wounded." He pointed at the bandage across his chest. "I need some serious med-evacking."

Buellton and Blind Pig nodded in agreement.

"Maybe Fuller'll pick up my bar tab at Di An."

"Wrong, babe," Mosby said. "He won't be there. He's insisting that he's fine. The general went and kissed his arm and made it all better. He's stayin' out."

"That dumb motherfucking son of a bitch," Fritsche said emphatically.

"No shit."

Fritsche was suddenly gloomy. "Fuck."

"What's wrong? So the lieutenant's got the brains of a lieutenant. Got shit to do with you."

Fritsche sighed, overcome with Biker Morality.

"I ain't goin' out neither," he said. "If that pansy-ass is stayin', so am I."

"Don't be a dumbass," Mosby said.

"I'm stayin'," Fritsche's face was a portrait of stubbornness.

Mosby suddenly felt better. With Fritsche along, he might live to get his three-day pass after all.

"If that's the way you want to play it," he said, pretending reluctance.

There was a shout, and they looked, to see Ramos waving for Buellton. Sinclair was loading onto his helicopter. Very formally, Buellton shook each of their hands, saying good-bye, wishing them luck, promising everyone that he would stay in touch. They all stood there awkwardly, watching him walk toward the Huey. Buellton turned back.

"Hey, Mosby!"

"Yeah?" Mosby shouted over the building whine of the Huey's turbine.

"Take care of those feet!"

Buellton sprinted for the chopper. In a few moments Sinclair's ship lifted and turned back toward Ba Rei. Mosby slumped down on the ground and lit a battered C-ration cigarette. The world was a little too impressive right now. And speaking of that . . . he looked up at Blind Pig and Fritsche.

"You didn't find Casey, huh?"

Blind Pig reached behind him and pulled something from the top of his asspack. He handed Casey's Thorpe bowie knife to Mosby, who automatically took it in one hand.

"That's all there was," Fritsche said.

Mosby stared at the knife that Casey had so lovingly polished-sharpened, hour after hour.

"I figure that be yours," Blind Pig said. "He liked your honkie ass."

"Yeah," Fritsche said. "He was tighter with you than anybody else."

"Okay," Mosby monotoned.

Blind Pig and Fritsche went back toward their positions.

Yeah, Mosby thought. We were real asshole buddies. As he shoved the knife into his buttpack, Mosby had the insane thought that perhaps Casey had been a ghost . . .

CHAPTER TWENTY-EIGHT

THE PLANTATION

THE TIGER'S GHOST had finally found Major Tran. Tran could almost see the cat now, just as his father had posed it in its snarl of agony and revenge.

Tran remembered his tiger when the Phu Loi Battalion entered the huge rubber plantation. The area was much like where he'd grown up, except this plantation was long-abandoned. Still there were the same trees, planted in perfect kilometer-long aisles. The aisles were now overgrown with thick brush, and dimly lit by the sun. This plantation was a place of ghosts, and so Tran remembered the tiger.

Less mystically, the plantation also offered very little real cover for his men, and so Tran had pushed the battalion to move through as quickly as possible. It was the last place he wished to meet the Americans. But wishes, as they say, are just wishes.

The Second of the Eleventh caught the Phu Loi Battalion just as the lead elements emerged from the trees. Tran knew better than to try to face-to-face the imperialists, and so had begun leapfrogging his men backward, company by company, through the plantation. The Americans went in pursuit. There was some consolation in the fact that Tran was inflicting heavy casualties on the imperialists. If his men had little cover to fight from, neither did the Americans. But Tran was also taking heavy casualties, casualties in a unit that had few men to spare.

The Phu Loi Battalion's only hope was to escape the plantation and break contact. So, as they retreated, Tran hurled suicide platoons against the enemy, praying for time, praying for an advantage, praying most of all that he would survive long enough to be alive for Giai Phong. But the part of Tran that believed in ghosts also knew that tigers do not listen to prayers.

Phan Van Tau watched the enemy soldiers sweep toward him. They were moving fast, which forced them to stick to the narrow trails that wound through the brush between the rubber trees. They were springing booby traps almost as fast as they were moving, then pausing only long enough to concentrate their awful firepower against Tau's comrades. Then they attacked again.

It would not be long before they reached Tau's group. Tau hefted the weight of the B-40 rocket launcher. He would be ready when the imperialists came. But the tube gave no comfort. If he only had his beloved machine gun, then he would show them. Tau and his group were perfectly placed for an ambush. If they had the .50-caliber gun, the Viet Cong would let the Americans move past them, and then reap a harvest. The image of the enemy soldiers screaming and dying as he raked them was so real that Tau could smell the blood.

Tau would die, of course, but he always assumed death in every engagement. Somehow he'd survived, but the fact was a surprise. Tau had thought he was dead for certain two nights ago, when the wildman American had slipped through their lines and attacked his gun emplacement.

There'd been a flash of sudden light, the simultaneous shock of the grenade that had kicked him away from the gun. When Tau had been able to see again, he'd watched the tall lean American move from comrade to comrade, slitting each throat. The man turned and saw Tau. But instead of attacking him with that terrible knife, the man had dropped to the ground and disappeared. Tau experienced the mild surprise of still breathing.

He checked again that the spare rockets for his RPG were piled at hand. Then the attack came. He saw the Americans fire and rush forward. He saw a grenade arc toward him and then explode. He saw this, but he didn't hear it—the grenade that Casey had thrown two nights before, destroying Tau's gun, had also shattered the man's eardrums. But he didn't need hearing. The Americans were in range now. Tau lifted his weapon, sighted, then fired.

He laughed into silence as he saw the squad disappear in a cloud of smoke and a shower of debris. A man beside him quickly slapped another rocket onto the B-40's snout. Tau aimed and fired again, and once more. He felt the crackling rush of the air around him as Phu Loi brothers fired at the enemy.

Tau felt a hammer blow strike him in the abdomen. He was floating backward. The ground cushioned his fall. After that first blow, there was no pain, just a sudden coldness spreading outward. He saw a face over him. It was an American, pointing his weapon down at Tau. Tau looked at the man curiously. He'd never really seen an imperialist this closely before.

How ugly they are, he thought, as his enemy squeezed back on the trigger.

Phan Xuan Cung lay very still, a few meters away from Captain Phong's body. He wasn't sure, but Cung believed that he was the only man left alive in the platoon.

Cung lay face down on the ground, his mouth open, trying not to twitch as various insects investigated his gums. The trick in playing dead, Cung was sure, was to be a dead fish. He'd kept that image large in his mind as the imperialists had stalked past his motionless form, their heavy boots thudding on the packed soil.

Once someone had kicked him, but Cung had kept that picture of the fish close, and let his body flop lifelessly. The other image he had in mind was his little joke. It was a joke that he hoped would let him live. Cung almost smiled at the thought, then pushed his building laughter down. He would look at the prank analytically. That was the trick. Examine it carefully, so that he could tell it correctly later.

When Cung realized his group was surrounded and that his brothers were dead or dying around him, he'd quickly come up with the idea of becoming a corpse. He also knew the idea would work only for a small time. Sooner or later, someone would examine him closely.

However, before they checked Cung, they would examine the bodies of the officers. That would be Phong. And that was also what gave Cung his plan. He'd pulled the pin from an American grenade, lifted Phong's body, and then propped the grenade under the man. To further entice investigation, Cung had slid the captain's prize Makarov pistol from its holster and put it slightly under the corpse. Hopefully a souvenir hunter would not be able to resist the pistol, and would lift Phong to get it. The grenade would then activate, go off, and kill the stupid souvenir hunter and anyone else near him.

Cung might then be able to slip away in the confusion to appreciate his joke. There was only one large flaw in the trick. For it to work, Cung required an inexperienced soldier. A true professional would never touch a body without first checking for boobytraps.

Cung heard footsteps close by. They paused at his body. Cung thought fish, fish, be a fish, Then he heard voices exclaim, and the footsteps moved past him, toward the captain. Cung wished he could understand what the men were saying. He knew there was little chance, if there were two Americans, that *both* of them would be unprofessional soldiers.

Fish, fish, fish, please, fish, please.

A moment later Cung was on his feet and sprinting for cover, the sound of the explosion ringing in his ears. He had lived to tell his joke.

Major Tran raced along the trail.

Besides his three surviving aides, he had about twenty men with

208

him. They were in flight, toward the edge of the plantation. Just beyond the tree line was the sprawling plantation house and its many outbuildings.

Tran would make his stand there. It was the perfect place to fight from, covering the retreat of his battalion. There was not much time. He could hear the sound of fighting behind him. He sprinted around a bend and saw sunlight dappling through the last stand of trees. The plantation house was just beyond. Tran shouted encouragement. Just a few minutes more . . . just a few meters more. Then they could turn and fight.

His father was right, Tran thought wildly. There was no such thing as a ghost. He had just proven it, hadn't he? He had beaten the tiger, hadn't he?

Major Nguyen Van Tran, Commanding Officer, Phu Loi Battalion, never heard the shot that killed him.

The Phu Loi Battalion died in place, and died hard.

The blast of gunfire that killed Tran and most of his command group would have paralyzed any conventional infantry unit, either North Vietnamese or American.

But the Phu Loi, like most main-force Viet Cong, were far more familiar fighting in small units rather than as a cohesive battalion. Moving almost instinctively, the remnants of the battalion perimetered around the ruined plantation house, set up hasty fighting positions, and began shooting back.

Company B, Fifteenth Infantry, went flat, pinned down where the plantation ended and low paddies began. And, as reflexively as the Viet Cong, the other American companies spread wide, and closed in on the surrounded Viet Cong battalion.

"Citation Six Actual, this is Splatter Six," Carruthers drawled into his mike, in the mock-southern that all pilots seemed to adopt.

"Got us a buncha slopeheads down here. You want to have your fellers toss some smoke? Over."

Carruthers's gunship flight was orbiting 500 meters above the plantation housing. Colonel Taylor, the Fifteenth's CO, who was hovering nearby in his Command and Control helicopter acknowledged.

The word was passed down, and yellow smoke drifted up, then, through the fringes of the plantation. Carruthers switched his radio to the grunts' ground frequency.

"Observed yellow, confirmed yellow. You folks hang on. I got a whole bunch of zips we're gonna reincarnate."

Carruthers went back to his flight's frequency as he kicked the C-model gunship over on its right side, full right pedal and cyclic, and chopped the collective. The Huey began its slow spiral downward.

"Splatter Flight," he said, "y'all want to come on down and get in on this? Run in southeast to northwest, over."

Above Carruthers, the rest of the gunships came down after him.

"Uh . . . Splatter Six . . . this is Splatter One-Four. Do you have any observed fire, over?"

Nervous chickenshit, Carruthers thought, mentally noting to get one-four transferred As Far As Possible.

"That's a big negative, One-Four. All we got is buddha-heads panicking in place."

Carruthers restored power, brought the UH-1C straight and level, watched the plantation's buildings rush up toward him, and thumbed the rockets. Twenty-four 2.75-inch rockets rippled out, and Carruthers lifted the cyclic and allowed the plantation house to come into and then out of his sights.

"Got some," he chortled into his open mike as below the plantation paroxysmed in smoke and fire.

Under other circumstances, Major Dennis Shannon might've been amused. He'd been in General Sinclair's command ship as the battle began, the Huey flying endless circles over the vast rubber plantation. Then, abruptly, Sinclair had ordered the ship to land, back on Second of the Eleventh's LZ. Now Sinclair paced, ten meters in front of the grounded Huey, studying a small-scale map in its clear plastic board.

Shannon knew the reason for Sinclair's anger—there was no way his general could reconcile that green sameness he'd seen from the air with the precision of the map. General Sinclair was in danger of losing his mental picture. Sinclair'd be in better shape if he threw that map in the bushes and played it by ear.

Directly in front of them came the fire from 2/11, as they swept forward, grimly maintaining their contact with the Phu Loi Battalion. The burst of explosions over there came from the Fifteenth, now in contact with the VC, and also from the gunship strike.

To the south, dimly, Shannon could hear the clatter of helicopters, slicks bringing up a response force—First Battalion, Twenty-ninth Infantry.

Sinclair had totally committed the Second Brigade. Dennis Shannon desperately wished that, for ten minutes, he could be the Twelfth Division's commanding general. Right now, he'd be pulling Deuce of the Eleventh back out of battle, and dropping in the Twenty-ninth on the Octopus's perimeter. Let the Fifteenth take care of the Phu Loi Battalion, and use the rest of the brigade to go after those North Vietnamese he'd spotted crossing the border.

Shannon reconsidered. Supposing he was CG, and did exactly that. And suppose again that the always elusive Phu Loi Battalion managed to break contact and disappear once again while the rest of Shannon's division was looking for something that might not even be there? That could be an excellent way for the mythical General Shannon to end up suddenly reassigned to Goony Bird Commander, Wake Island.

As Sinclair came back toward the Huey, his face now firmly in Command Set Profile, Shannon disconsolately realized that, were he in command of the Twelfth Division, he would be doing exactly what Sinclair was, and no more.

"Come on," Fuller shouted. "Let's go!"

First Squad came reluctantly to its feet. Mosby heard Blind Pig chatter a burst off to the left, then he saw movement toward his front, and sprayed rounds. There was a low wall ahead of him, and the crack of AK fire.

Mosby's hand was off the rifle, snapping the release from his ammo pouch, and the grenade was in his hand. Left finger came away from his rifle's handguard, and the grenade's pin was out, and the grenade underhanded toward that wall, hitting and bouncing back and Mosby going down as the blast rang shrapnel over his head.

Another grenade off, lobbed over this time, and the explosion and the fire stopped, and Mosby was up to his knees, then back down as RPD fire cut brush around him, rolling away toward a depression, and firing, firing, firing. He changed magazines, wondering what the fuck he was shooting at, and then the roar from the flank as Blind Pig ran a solid fifty rounds through his M-60. The RPD was silent.

Mosby was up and moving forward, looking, trying to see someone else. To one side movement, half-swinging to aim, recognizing Martinez, and swinging back to his front to see two black-clad Viet Cong break cover, darting toward a building, and his rifle was up, thumb bringing the selector back and the blast/springback of the rifle four times, and the two men going down and then moving forward again and seeing bullets spray dirt and diving down, down behind a stupid bush that couldn't stop a rock and out of sight out of aim and safe for the moment.

Mosby very slowly lifted his face from the dirt and looked ahead. There was a clearing on the other side of the brush and, beyond it, the smoking ruins of the plantation housing. Enough. His face went back in the muck.

Fire spat from the ruins, more and more heavily. Return fire pattered away, as GIs stopped shooting and went for cover. Mosby looked for something to shoot at beyond fireflashes, vines, stone, but found nothing.

Come on, man. If you were Casey you'd be checking the line. Fuck you, asshole, I ain't Casey and I didn't ask for this fucking job and I am going to stay right here until this fucking war is over.

"Two Six! On me!"

Mosby identified the shout as coming from Captain Harris. Mosby crawled back, and was able to see, through the brush, Fuller, DeeJay behind him, zigzag toward the company commander's position.

Martinez was the only one to see the B-40 gunner push out of his cover and aim at that target of a lifetime—three radio aerials and below them a command group.

He snap-pointed and fired his M-79 one-handed, recoil snapping his wrist back. He fired just as the RPG belched its double spear of flame. Martinez thought he could see the rocket's fins snap open. The two explosions came almost simultaneously. Martinez's grenade sent the Viet Cong gunner spasming back out of sight. The four-pound Soviet rocket from the B-40 hit a tree, five feet away from Captain Harris's command group. Harris and his two radiomen were killed instantly.

Lieutenant Fuller was very lucky. The shrapnel that should have sliced his skull open merely can-openered his helmet. More metal scythed through his legs, Fuller went down, and Mosby could hear the agonized scream from Ramos—"Maricone motherfuckers!" but Mosby's eyes were on Martinez.

Martinez had his grenade launcher open, the grenade casing out, in the air and spinning toward the ground, his left hand fumbling a new round from the ammo vest when the burst of RPD fire stitched him across the chest. Mosby was on his feet, then down again as the machine gunner sent a burst across Mosby's bush. But he still kept moving forward, on his elbows and knees.

Mosby saw Martinez's body move slightly, then the bullet line walked back across him and there was no motion. Mosby had a smoke grenade off his harness, pin out and lobbed forward over the man's body. Again, he was moving.

Then, through the smoke, walked DeeJay, eyes glaring, helmet gone, rifle gone, radio and webbing gone, but still holding his microphone, cord dangling, stumbling toward the Viet Cong lines.

Taliaferro flat-dove out of the brush, sending DeeJay down as more machine-gun rounds swept through the wisping smoke.

Mosby was out of the brush, on his feet, and beside Taliaferro as the man dragged battle-shocked DeeJay back toward cover. Taliaferro was swearing in a monotone, "You fuckin' nigger you want to get yourself killed do it on your own time you fucking nigger not on mine come on move you asshole," and they were over and behind a blown-down tree.

Mosby and Taliaferro stared at each other, and Mosby wasn't sure if either of them recognized the other.

Mosby was up on his haunches as the last of the smoke ebbed away, and saw, to one flank, First Platoon charged the plantation. Mosby was also in the open, going forward, run, dive sideways behind cover, mind seeing and body finding the tiny dips and folds of the ground. A grenade—Mosby noted it was his last—went over a wall, and then Mosby was around the mud-brick line.

Rifle up, ring-and-pin seeing, aiming eye seeing a squad of Viet Cong coming out of the blasted building, selector still on full auto and rounds clanging out, into them. Grenade smoke greased, and then there were more VC charging into the American fire and going down, and Mosby was firing, reloading, firing, and then there was nothing left to shoot at. All he could see were sweat-darkened, ODs as the grunts came into the plantation's center, crack-spatter of fire into wounded but still-moving Viet Cong.

The body count, Mosby heard later, was 292 confirmed Viet Cong dead, 14 wounded and captured. Against 76 American KIAs, 240 WIAs, 2 MIAs.

The Phu Loi Battalion died very hard.

But they died.

CHAPTER TWENTY-NINE

DUAN

GENERAL DUAN, FLANKED by Commissar Thuy and Sergeant Lau, stepped away from the column and looked southeast, as if somehow he could see what he could dimly hear, the dying battle sounds of the Phu Loi Battalion.

To either side, the columns of his division moved swiftly into the draws and narrow ravines that marked the beginnings of Le Noir Massif—what the Americans had dubbed the Octopus.

During this forced march, Duan's 302 Division had taken about thirty casualties. Most of them were heat-stroke victims, stripped of weapons and papers, and abandoned in villages along their march. Others fell victim to boobytraps, some NLF, some imperialist-planted. Two men died from snakebite. A handful of others from accidents along the jungle paths.

And the Phu Loi Battalion had 583 effectives before he sent them out to delay the Americans . . .

Who, Comrade General, Duan thought, is climbing over the stack of bodies? You or Comrade Giap?

Duan looked at Sergeant Lau, whose face was as masklike as his own. The Comrade General found nothing to say. He turned back and rejoined the column.

PART THREE:

NOVEMBER 3, 1967-JANUARY 30, 1968

1. All actions are subject to command.
2. Do not steal from the people.
3. Be neither selfish nor unjust.

1. Replace the door when you leave the house.
2. Roll up the bedding on which you have slept.
3. Be courteous.
4. Be honest in your transactions.
5. Return what you borrow.
6. Replace what you break.
7. Do not bathe in the presence of women.
8. Do not without authority search the pocketbooks of those you arrest.

**—Mao Tse-tung,
Three Rules & Eight Remarks**

1. Remember we are guests here: we make no demands and seek no special treatment.
2. Join with the people! Understand their life, use phrases from their language and honor their customs and laws.
3. Treat women with politeness and respect.
4. Make personal friends among the soldiers and common people.
5. Always give the Vietnamese the right of way.
6. Be alert to security and ready to react with your military skill.
7. Don't attract attention by loud, rude or unusual behavior.
8. Avoid separating yourself from the people by a display of wealth and privilege.
9. Above all else you are members of the U.S. Military Forces on a difficult mission, responsible for all your official and personal actions. Reflect honor upon yourself and the United States of America.

**—U.S. Military Assistance Command,
Vietnam, Nine Rules**

CHAPTER THIRTY

NGHI

NGUYEN TRUONG NGHI'S fingers automatically slotted the Campagnola's gears onto their shaft. This was a rote task that he performed automatically. It was a job he particularly enjoyed because it gave him time to take stock.

In any other army his command would cover kilometers of space and consume endless liters of fuel. Instead the seventy-five vehicles he was responsible for were stacked, handlebars interlocked, in the rear of his shop.

Nghi was not only a National Liberation Front provincial section chief, but a logistics expert for the Viet Cong's units throughout Song Nhanh Province.

This meant bicycles. Hundreds of bicycles, some kept in the shop but hundreds more of them in constant use. Some of them Nghi thought of as "white"—they were the conventional two-wheelers used by couriers and agents; while others were "black." These illegal cycles had sprockets, pedals and chains removed, the frames beefed up, and bamboo or metal extensions on the bars. They were not to be ridden, but used for supply transport—loaded with well over a quarter-ton of rice or arms. The vehicles were wheeled over jungle paths to their destination. Nghi's responsibility—not his main duty within the NLF—was procuring, modifying and maintaining these bicycles. Unlike many assignments given out by the NLF, Nghi's job was exactly what he would have been doing in peacetime.

But unlike all too many assignments given out to those who joined the fight for liberation, Nghi's job was exactly what he wanted to do.

Nguyen Truong Nghi had grown up with two dreams: to attend university and someday to compete in cycling's premier race—the Grand Prix de France.

His father had considered both dreams unrealistic. The family were little more than shopkeepers, even though their bicycle shop was the largest in Song Nhanh City and the only one capable of working on the exotic French bicycles favored by the city's elite.

University was quite out of the question—Song Nhanh's Mandarins ensured that no one beneath them would be permitted to attend a real lycée. And who, his father questioned, would provide the money for Nghi to go to France? Nghi persisted—and discovered his father was correct. The dreams were possibly only for Nghi's children, and only then if the entire social structure changed.

For a few years, as American involvement in South Vietnam grew, Nghi and his father hoped that social shift was possible. But all they saw, as Nghi's father observed, was the "changing of which pig was permitted at the trough." Their only option was the National Liberation Front.

Nghi's family were Cao Dai, the somewhat unusual sect revering spirits as diverse as Buddha and Charlie Chaplin and known, at least through the 1950s, for adamant anticommunism. Nguyen Truong Nghi was an ideal recruit, never tainted by open contact with avowed Marxists. Instead, he continued working in the bicycle shop and slowly created and ran an intelligence network throughout the city.

The Vietnamese have a natural fondness for secret societies and subterfuge, but Nghi proved exceptional. In all the years, in spite of various secret police and intelligence sweeps by the puppet government and the American imperialists, Nghi was never even close to exposure.

Six months previously, the province committee's vice-chairman had instructed him on certain tasks: most of them involved the exact structure and capability of the ARVN forces assigned to the capital; what potential existed for reinforcement; and, most important, to what degree imperialist forces might respond in an emergency.

Nghi obeyed, realizing that such orders could only mean that the Central Committee was preparing for a major offensive. Nghi was very glad he was a native of Song Nhanh rather than Saigon or Hue, because such a major offensive would inevitably involve battles in the cities, battles that could well destroy them. But Song Nhanh should be relatively untouched. Nghi loved his city.

Song Nhanh had slept peacefully for centuries. It was founded in the twelfth century as a trading center for the Meos inhabiting the massifs to the north. It was used as a fortress to guard against invasion from Cambodia as well as a port on the river of Song

Nhanh (from which both the town and the province took their name). It was also a vacation center for members of the imperial family. A ruined palace still crumbling near the swamps on the eastern edge of the city paid homage to this asterisk in Vietnamese history.

But the roads were bad, the river had silted up until it was now navigable only by small boat, the opium trade was no longer as open and profitable as it had been, and so change provided only passing nods to the city. To other Vietnamese, someone who was a native of Song Nhanh was considered somewhat less than ambitious. Such a man, the saying went, would rather wait for a breeze to rise than brush a mosquito from his nose.

Song Nhanh City covered about twenty square kilometers, and, including nearby hamlets, had a population of around 60,000, plus an estimated 20,000 refugees who fled from the increased fighting in the southern part of the province. Song Nhanh, like almost all Vietnamese cities, owed some sort of debt to the French occupiers, who'd maintained a small presence from the 1890s until the end of the First Vietnamese War in 1954.

There were still a few hundred foreign devils in the city—missionaries, rubber plantation owners and specialists, and the nuns resident in a small convent a few kilometers outside the city. The owed debt was architectural—the French had razed the center of the city and relaid it in the characteristic wide boulevards, centrally grouped stone administration buildings, and for the rich—villas. The rest of the buildings were typically Vietnamese—apartment buildings that looked as if they were designed for Southern California, wood single- or two-story ramshackle buildings and, of course, the peasant housing that was improvised from any building source: from split steel drums to bamboo walls to thatched roofing to flattened and soldered cans.

The city center was about a kilometer to a side, built around an open, once-grassed square. Now the square was mostly a marketplace, with a recently built barracks at one side housing the province official's communication center.

Around the square were the main South Vietnamese government offices. The province chief had taken over the old French admin building for both his headquarters and residence. Across an open area were the barracks for the ARVN soldiers whose sole function seemed to be to keep the province chief from being assassinated. Thick-piled barbed wire and sandbagged walls surrounded the center and the barracks. Also around the square were police headquarters (housed in what was formerly a primary school building), post office, treasury building, and the revolutionary development headquarters.

Both the city and the province were actually ruled by the National Liberation Front. The Saigon government, reasoning that nothing ever happened in Song Nhanh, staffed it with incompetents, grafters, and exiled officials. To be "Song Nhanhed" was to the members of Thieu's government the same as for a French official, in an earlier time, to be "Limoged."

For the NLF, this was ideal. It gave them an area to train both soldiers and administrative people, a safe operating base for their soldiers, and even a place to experiment with ideas that might be used country-wide after the inevitable liberation of the country.

There had been only two major irritations for the Viet Cong in South Nhanh. The first, in 1966, had been the appointment of Nguyen Van Thoan as province chief. On arrival, he had made large waves, requiring the battalion of ARVN infantry to smarten up, requesting and getting the assignment of one company of Vietnamese Rangers to the city, and adding sophisticated communication gear to his headquarters.

The NLF's central committee feared that a firebrand was now heading the puppet government. But rather quickly they were reassured—Nghi's operatives, several within the administrative headquarters itself, had discovered that Thoan was interested only in showmanship. He would never dare risk his red-scarfed Rangers or his drill-and-parade qualified infantrymen in combat.

The second shock was far more serious when, later in that same year, an American division was deployed in the province. Fortunately most of its combat operations were restricted to the southern area, and NLF strategists were fairly sure that the imperialists were more interested in guarding the approaches to Saigon than in the area around the city itself. And, as yet, there had been no significant attempt to pacify the Viet Cong's stronghold: the Octopus.

This was very good, Nghi thought to himself as he finished assembling the derailleur mechanism onto the bicycle. There were only three things he liked about the Americans—the canned orange juice he was able to blackmarket which he used on his daily ten-kilometer rides on the Peugeot racing cycle; the superb lubricants that were so easy to obtain; and the fact that there were no more than a handful of imperialists in the city.

Song Nhanh was like many other South Vietnamese cities (Da Lat and Hue being the largest) that were off-limits to most Americans. The few in residence were the American captain and his sergeants, advisers to the ARVNs, and half a dozen men who claimed to be part of some American civilian effort to help the people. Nghi and his cell assumed them to be agents of the Central Intelligence Agency. This was not far from the truth. Three of them actually were spooks.

Nghi broke off his thoughts as a slender girl, wearing an ao dai and a mournful expression, wheeled her bike into his shop, the chain dragging in the dust. Nghi tsked.

"Co Tram," he chided. "A chain without oil is like a kiss without a mustache." Nghi was inordinately proud of his—he sometimes felt it made him look like one of the velodrome racers of the past.

The two reflexively scanned around them, then dropped the charade. Tram was the province chief's secretary and mistress. She was also in charge of the subcell reporting from the province headquarters.

"Thoan has been in communication with Saigon six times within the last twenty-four hours. The last communication was directly to the Presidential Palace."

"Coded, of course." If the transmissions had been en clair Tram would have delivered them immediately.

"Second, he has been trying to study maps of areas south of our city." She giggled. "I had to tell him that the map was upside down. He was looking for an area that was not populated, an area with a hill that could be fortified."

Nghi considered. "Thoan is too cowardly to ever consider moving his own body outside the city, so he is not building a summer vacation home."

He loosened the axle of Tram's bicycle and reinstalled the chain on the sprockets.

"Thank you, sister. I shall pass along the report. This could be important. Any further information on this should be sent to me directly. Do not use drops."

Tram pushed her cycle back toward the door, then paused.

"Comrade," she asked, her face turned away from Nghi, "have you heard any more information about the Phu Loi unit?"

"None, as yet."

Tram mounted her bicycle and rode off into the near-noon traffic, back toward the city's center. Nghi watched her disappear and returned to his work. Tram's brother was serving with the Phu Loi unit. All that Nghi's superior had told him was that the Phu Loi unit had bravely resisted a massive attack by the imperialists and that the unit would need reconstruction and would not be participating in the General Offensive.

Nghi translated that as decimation at the least, complete obliteration as the most likely fate of the unit. Another debt incurred. Nghi had not been told when all those debts would fall due, but he felt they would be within the next three months.

He theorized sometime during Tet, at the start of the Year of the Monkey. And if Nghi was correct, his cell would emerge into the open and become part of the Liberation Army itself.

Nghi knew what their task would be—he had helped create it. There was a list, numbering more than 1,000 people. Turncoats, supporters of the puppet regime, opponents of the NLF who could not keep silence, suspected weak links within the movement, and others.

At the proper time, Nghi and his fellows would be well prepared to deal with them.

CHAPTER THIRTY-ONE

HUE DUC

THE GENERAL WAS gorgeous, Tarpy thought. He was a military work of art. He wore perfectly creased combat fatigues, now set off by a robin's egg blue infantry scarf, carefully tucked into his blouse. His boots gleamed as if they were lacquered.

Cast in bronze, Sinclair could be put in a park and draw pigeons for miles around. Yes, Tarpy thought, gorgeous was definitely the word. He waited with some glee for the helicopter to make another pass for the television crew and spoil the whole effect. Like grunts, combat reporters—especially Associated Press combat reporters—like to see their generals mussed.

Cliff Tarpy gave Edmunds an elbow to make sure he wouldn't miss it. It wasn't necessary. The captain was already in near hysterics. He wasn't upset at all that his work helping Belasario set up the press conference was on the brink of being destroyed by the Evening News. Edmunds was too busy laughing.

The press conference thing had begun innocently enough. The general had just got through kicking some serious VC ass, and quite naturally wanted some ink. His superiors also wanted the ink, as did their superiors all the way to Washington. Since good ink was a bit of a rarity in Sinclair's career—as Tarpy was well aware—the general's ideas on press conferences were rather antiquated. In other words, he did not anticipate television.

Sinclair had enlisted all his G-sections in the project. They had drawn up dozens of charts, graphs, maps, and body-count score cards. Then they'd redrawn them again and again until they were just right. Someone had even tracked down a pointer for the general to flourish and had it choppered in from Saigon. There would also be the usual victory press conference words of praise for "the men," and medal pinnings.

Belasario *had* mentioned television several times, but Sinclair just kept nodding, yes, yes, invite them too, and he had missed the fact that when Belasario said television had special needs, he meant *special needs*.

Tarpy figured he was in luck the minute Belasario ushered him and the other print reporters into the yawning ballroom of the old villa. The command center had been spicked and spanned and was hung with elaborate maps. At the far end was a hastily erected stage, and several covered easels which Tarpy was sure held the general's chart ammunition. Tarpy gave a swift look around the room to make sure he was right. Yep, besides him and that military suckbutt Ron Mead, every single swinging Richard in the room was print. Not a TV news dolt in sight.

As usual, they were fashionably late. Which meant they had lingered over the fourth or maybe fifth Bloody Mary in Saigon before catching the chopper to Hue Duc. Tarpy knew, soon as he saw the layout, that the TV guys would sneer. Talking Heads shit. No visuals for the folks at home. I mean, Jesus, a boob tube guy had once told Tarpy, if you're covering a war, people expect to see a fucking *war*!

Tarpy suggested that, if that were the case, maybe he ought to get his ass out of the bar and go to the field with the grunts. That's where the war is, asshole. For some strange reason, the TV guy had taken offense at Tarpy's professional advice and he'd had to deck the S.O.B. Wasn't welcome in that bar any longer, either. But, what the hell, he had been looking for a bar when he found that one, so what's another 86?

But, back to the point, Tarpy told himself, soon as the TV crew saw the layout, they would insist on some changes. An interesting background outside—stacked ammo and captured weapons, that sort of thing. And, if Sinclair wanted his General mug on cans of film on the next flight to New York, he'd have to go along with it. What this all added up to was a perfect opportunity to strike before the confusion started.

Tarpy edged his way up to Sinclair, who was having a hasty where the fuck are TV people conference with Edmunds, Shannon and Belasario. Edmunds spotted him and gave him a quick good-luck grin. Tarpy had always been tight with the captain.

"Excuse me, General Sinclair," Tarpy said, and as soon as the man turned his head, he jumped right in.

"There's a couple things I don't understand. Maybe you could clue me in before the shindig begins."

Sinclair pretended to recognize him immediately, which is a good trait, Tarpy thought, for an ambitious officer.

"No problem," Sinclair said. "That's what we're here for."

Sinclair didn't see the warning look from Belasario. Tarpy did, so he decided to get in and get out fast before the PIO officer cut him off.

"Okay. You had yourself a whole VC battalion between a rock and a hard place and you proceeded to wax their plow, right?"

Sinclair grinned.

"I wouldn't exactly put it that way, but that's about the size of it. What's your question?"

"What the hell were they even doing there?"

"I don't understand."

"This was the Phu Loi Battalion. Pros all the way. It's pretty hard to believe they'd make that kind of mistake."

Tarpy noticed Shannon giving him a thoughtful look. So, he wasn't alone. Other people were thinking the same thing. What he wanted to know now was whether this included Sinclair.

"Battles hinge on mistakes," Sinclair said.

"True. But weren't they acting out of character? I mean, to be caught in the open like that?"

"I forced their hand," Sinclair said.

"Maybe so," Tarpy pressed on. "But don't you think—"

Belasario saw which way this was going and broke in.

"Good question, Cliff. But maybe you ought to save the rest until the press conference. Can't leave the other guys out, can we?" Belasario gave a weak giggle to show that he wasn't pissed.

"I agree wholeheartedly," said a booming voice behind them.

Tarpy turned to see Ron Mead.

"Don't be greedy, Tarpy. I'm sure all will be revealed in good time by General Sinclair."

"I intend to be absolutely open to all lines of questioning," Sinclair agreed.

"*When* the press conference begins," Belasario said.

"Besides," Mead said, "we should wait for television compadres, don't you think, Cliff? Wouldn't be fair, otherwise."

Tarpy just grunted, thanked Sinclair for his time, and headed back with Mead to join the rest of the pack. But he couldn't resist a last shot.

"When the fuck did you start working for CBS, Mead?"

He had stalked off for the long wait for the stars. And when they finally arrived, things had happened pretty much the way Tarpy had called it.

TV grumbled. The general listened to these representatives of 20 million viewers and adjourned the press conference to a more "colorful setting" . . . not that we'd want to interfere with the news, you understand, General Sinclair, but this is a visual medium, you realize, and ratcheta, ratcheta and once again real events took a backseat to the red-eyed beast.

Sinclair was so cowed by the specter of offending that he even let the CBS team shoot their "color" before the press conference got underway. Which meant, Tarpy thought sourly, that they had decided what had happened before it was even announced. After the shots of the general posing nobly beside the captured VC paraphernalia, with a busy airfield in the background, CBS asked Sinclair to skip to the medal-pinning portion of the agenda. That way, they'd have some impressive footage and would need only a few seconds of press conference film. Then they could call a wrap and be headed back for Saigon while the rest of the press corps did the dull job of gathering the news.

Tarpy's eyes swept the line of about-to-be honored men and noticed that it included a good number of hastily cleaned-up grunts from the lower ranks.

"Is that part of the show?" he whisper-questioned Edmunds.

"Nope. Believe it or not, Sinclair *does* have a soft spot for the enlisted men."

"Bullshit," Tarpy said. "Generals don't bleed for troopies until they write their memoirs."

Edmunds buried a laugh.

"I'm not saying he's a populist general, for crying out loud. He likes to think of himself as a father figure. General El Patron Sinclair, if you catch my drift."

Tarpy recognized some of the men in the ranks, including whatsisface, Mosby Something, or Something Mosby. Tarpy had joined a couple of patrols that included Mosby. Guy told a helluva story. Tarpy had even interviewed him once, but Mosby's answers had been so cynical and to the point that Tarpy hadn't even bothered to type them up.

Even the night desk would have thought he had made Mosby up. Still, he owed Mosby some. On one of the patrols, Tarpy had found himself in the middle of a firefight. He had been taking a shit at the time, and in the undignified scramble for cover he had a choice between losing his cameras or his .45.

Old habits die hard—if you don't bring the camera back, kid, you better still have the strap—and Tarpy found himself in the unfortunate position of only being able to take wonderful black-and-white photos of people trying to kill him. Mosby had tossed him an M-16 belonging to a recent casualty. Tarpy didn't know if he had actually hit anybody with the thing, but it proved to be an aid and comfort to his instantly advancing old age. Nice guy, that Mosby.

It was his turn to get the elbow from Edmunds, and Tarpy woke up to see the press conference finally beginning. Now, Sinclair was semi-in-his-element. Despite the unanticipated handicap of not having his charts and other visual aids, Sinclair handled the background briefing like a jovial commander sharing his thoughts on the preceding action with his junior brother officers. Tarpy got the details down in the unreadable shorthand he had developed over many years and as many conflicts.

Sinclair quickly sketched in the problems he had faced, his initial reactions, and then the setting of the trap. Then he filled in the body count, nearly 300 VC dead, fourteen wounded *and* captured, which meant he was probably being honest, and then the high American casualties. The last was given without hesitation or shame. More than seventy U.S. casualties was a helluva lot.

"This is no bullshit?" Tarpy whispered to Edmunds.

"Uh, uh. He's being straight."

The first question came from Ron Mead.

"General, after this—and I think I can frankly say this—admirable and timely victory, what does the future hold for this area? To be specific, could you address yourself to how this action fits into the scheme of things, vis-à-vis the pacification program?"

Tarpy almost groaned aloud. What a suckass question. What a fucking setup. Go ahead, asshole, give Sinclair a platform, why don't you?

"I'm glad you asked that question," Sinclair said. "I believe the major defeat the enemy just suffered will set back their efforts for months, if not permanently.

"And we intend to follow up immediately with an intensified mopping-up action that should eliminate every bandit VC in the province.

"For the first time in recent history, the local farmer will be able to go to the fields, knowing that he and his village are safe. He will also be able to take his goods to market, with the assurance that his roads are safe.

"And, if we can continue our strong presence and cooperate

fully with our Vietnamese colleagues, the present I just outlined
will become a permanent future in the lives of these people.''

Sinclair paused for effect, and Tarpy came in blazing again,
but this time with little hope.

"General Sinclair, I'd like to return for a moment to my earlier question . . ."

"I caught Tarpy trying to slip one in on us guys," Mead said,
laughing. There were some polite titters from the other reporters. Tarpy didn't give a shit. What he *did* care about, however,
was whether Mead and Belasario had been able to clue in Sinclair before the press conference.

"Oh, yes," Sinclair said, "your question on why we happened to find the enemy where we found him . . ."

Tarpy got a sinking feeling in his stomach.

"The answer is simple and complicated at the same time. We
succeeded because our entire thrust in this region—dating back
to able commanders well before me—was to drive the enemy out
in the open. To make him confront us. Fight on our ground,
head-to-head. This is a confrontation the enemy cannot permanently avoid. If he wishes to press his own cause, he must eventually slug it out with us.''

Sinclair now looked directly at Tarpy and smiled a fatherly
smile. Oh, fuck, Tarpy thought, I bet he even knows my name,
now.

"In other words, Cliff," Sinclair said, "we caught 'em because we caught 'em.''

The general had made a joke. It took a minute, but then the
press corps roared with laughter.

Shit, Tarpy thought, it wasn't that good. But he had to smile.
He had been deftly outmaneuvered. Not bad for a rookie, he
thought. Then he put away his notebook, because, as far as he
was concerned, this press conference was over. For Tarpy,
the fat lady had finally sung her song.

Shannon had delivered the appropriate orders to have press
conference props put away and was getting ready to hitch a ride
to the Officers' Club. Many large cool beers loomed largish in
his mind.

He guessed the press conference had gone pretty well, and he
had enjoyed the sparring match between Tarpy and Sinclair's
staff, which seemed to include that Copley reporter. He also
wished he knew the answer to Tarpy's question. Shannon understood *what* had happened, but the *why* was up for speculation.
As acting G-2, it was Shannon's job to speculate. Although he

was pretty sure Sinclair wouldn't be pleased with his attempting any line of reasoning.

"Major, a moment, if you please."

Since it was Sinclair speaking, Shannon knew he'd better have many, many moments.

"Yessir."

"I'd appreciate it if you would meet me back at the villa, Major," the general said. "I think's it's time we had a long talk."

"Right away, sir," Shannon said.

Shannon had reasonable cause to believe that by "long talk," Sinclair didn't have hosannas in mind.

Later, Shannon eyed the double shot of Jack Daniel's and the can of Carling's Black Label, half of which was poured into one of the Twelfth Aviation Company's few unbroken glasses. He had the feeling he'd been set up. Across the table sat Edmunds and Carruthers. The Twelfth's CO, Shannon thought, had the poised anticipation of a divorce lawyer. Shannon took the precaution of downing the shot and chasing it before he said anything.

"All right, you bastards. Why do I feel like a lamb at the shearing?"

Edmunds looked innocent. Carruthers didn't bother.

"We just thought . . . since you had a conference with our dearly beloved division commander . . . that you might need a drink."

Shannon got it, drained the beer, and motioned for a refill.

"Got a call on the odds?"

Edmunds, staring carefully out at the chopper pad, said: "Three to one you're relieved. One to two you're transferred to Mac-Vee. Six to four you're going to the 101st."

"What about me getting confirmed as G-2?"

"No takers on that," Carruthers said. "But I'd go, oh, fourteen to one . . . against."

Edmunds got tired of playing games.

"Come on, Dennis. What did that evil cocksucker do to you?"

"I seem to have gotten myself promoted," Shannon said. The other two officers waited for clarification. It wasn't easy. Shannon was grudgingly developing a certain respect for Sinclair's ability to manage people—especially people he wasn't fond of.

"You are now looking at the new executive officer, Fifteenth Infantry. Said appointment to be effective immediately after two weeks' R&R. Said R&R personally ordered by Major General Lee Sinclair.''

"Shit," Carruthers said. "They done killed the messenger."

Carruthers could be right. On the other hand, possibly Sinclair had a point. Shannon certainly was not and *would* not fit into the Capital Letters Command Concept of Sinclair's Team. But, thinking about it, Shannon had little to bitch about.

He was acting G-2, a light colonel's slot. But a senior lieutenant colonel's position. Which meant there must be hundreds of chairwarmers in CONUS eager to get their ticket punched with a divisional staff post and that good right-shoulder combat patch. His chances of keeping the post, even under the previous CG, were almost nonexistent. Also, since the Pentagon promotes officers in its own unique mysterious ways, occupying that slot was no particular quick way to get bumped a notch.

To the outsider—and, Shannon had to admit privately, even to himself—moving Dennis down to a line unit was, indeed, a promotion.

The Fifteenth was, Shannon knew, a good unit. Its commander, Lieutenant Colonel Taylor, was a leader who specialized in going in harm's way. One sniper, one mortar blast, and Shannon could end up commanding an infantry battalion in combat, a situation that would look very good on his Form 20.

Still, Shannon realized he'd been sent into exile. As did Edmunds and Carruthers. They drank, and then Edmunds started laughing.

"Looks like the pool doesn't pay off anybody, does it?"

Carruthers was unamused.

"Sorry to bring up the small shit—but what about that last CONEX you promised?"

"Already up at the strip," Shannon said. Carruthers finished his drink and near-double-timed out of the bar—fortunately forgetting the bottle.

Carruthers's assistant barman, a crew chief, started to field it.

"This stays," Shannon said, getting a firm grip on the Jack Daniel's. "It goes on your fearless leader's tab."

Edmunds was again amused, then turned serious. He hoisted his glass.

"Isn't this what you wanted, Major?"

Shannon shrugged and drank. Edmunds was right. The next stage in Shannon's career—and what he wanted more than anything else—was to command a large combat unit. It could also turn into a wonderful way to get killed, and Shannon again pondered the irony of a profession where success required putting

231

yourself into danger. This was, he decided for the nth time, an area not to be dwelled upon. He changed the subject.

"Oh, by the way, Captain. I have some orders for you, too."

Edmunds waited, warily.

"Pack, soldier."

The smile grew across Edmunds's face.

"Seems as if Charlie of the Fifteenth's looking for a company commander. Thought you might be interested."

"Major Shannon," Edmunds said. "If I kiss you now, people are gonna start talking."

Edmunds was up, shouting for a round on him, and Shannon wondered if he'd just arranged for his friend's death. Fuckin' Army, he thought to himself, pouring another shot.

Fuckin' Army.

CHAPTER THIRTY-TWO

MOSBY

MOSBY CLIMBED OFF the Tan Son Nhut–Saigon shuttle bus and tried not to look like a hick in the big city.

Mosby suspected that his pegged gray slacks, Beatle-winkle-picker boots, and op-art jersey were more than a little out of style back in the World. But in Saigon he was ultra-hip, since most of the grunts who made it to the capital city were restricted either to khaki uniforms or civilian clothes run up by some outback Vietnamese tailor, working from the pages of *Playboy* magazine to the customer's specifications.

Mosby, however, was one of the few who, when initially assigned to Vietnam, had ignored the orders that civvies were forbidden. He was proud of the fact that he wasn't wearing what everyone else was wearing.

What he didn't realize was that, to the Vietnamese, there were only three categories of Americans: soldiers in uniform; soldiers in strange civilian garb; and civilians in a third and suspicious category (embassy types, reporters, CIA, and so forth). In any category, to the citizens of Saigon they were all easy marks.

Mosby dodged a cyclo and moved farther up the sidewalk to momentary safety. He considered his situation. The shuttle had dropped him outside the heavily sandbagged and guarded Brink's BOQ, on Ra Trung Street.

From here, Ra Trung led into the GI shopping and bar district.

He was half a block away from Saigon's center—the sprawling, open-air Continental Palace with the high-rise and plush Caravelle hotel across from it, and, between them, a stupid monument to some ARVN soldier or other.

He figured the monument—which vaguely resembled Fort Benning's *Follow Me* statue—was dedicated to the first and only South Vietnamese troop who'd made the mistake of charging the VC instead of hauling ass for the rear.

Mosby also wondered if any high-up American had discovered that the billboard above the monument—for Park Lane cigarettes—was actually advertising filter-tip pot.

He leaned up against the Brink's sandbagged wall and ignored the nearby MP's glower—after checking to make sure his DA31 (the three-day pass)—was securely tucked in his front pocket. David Mosby had problems.

This was not his first time in Saigon—it was his sixth. The CO of his previous unit, unlike a lot of other American commanders, had little objection to letting his men go to Saigon. So Mosby knew his way around. A little.

That was the problem, because the little bit of Saigon he was familiar with was party town. He knew three good whorehouses and five or six bars where the girls didn't hit a grunt up for Saigon Tea (tea, sold as whiskey, in shot glasses for one dollar) every five minutes.

He also knew one good souvenir store where you could buy a doll or an ao dai to send home at reasonable prices and one very loud restaurant that served steaks—made from what Mosby was fairly sure was elderly water buffalo. These were excellent places for a GI with money and only a short time to get drunk, fed and laid. Totally useless, now.

Mosby checked his watch. If Mr. Chi hadn't gotten confused, Tho's bus should arrive soon. Mosby was beginning to regret his romantic impulses. He had no idea where the bus would arrive; he had no idea whether Tho would be aboard it if it did; and, worse yet, he had less than no idea how to entertain the girl.

He was pretty sure that just taking her to the nearest hotel and banging her lights out was not going to be acceptable. Plus— and Mosby would not yet admit this to himself—the reason he had wanted to take Tho to Saigon had little to do with just getting laid.

A good noncom, Mosby reminded himself, takes one problem at a time. He straightened off the wall, ignored the neon signs just down from him promising undreamt-of delights inside, and walked across the street looking for a cyclo.

Brakes screeched and Mosby reflexively put one hand over his watchband as a motorscooter broadslid up beside him. The rider was a smiling young man—about twenty—wearing blue slacks and shirt.

"Hi, GI," the cao boi said. "You want to get fucked up?"

A cao boi was just that: a cowboy. A young Vietnamese civilian staying one step ahead of the cops and the draft by using false ID, family connections, or bribery. They were the lightweight street criminals of Saigon, specializing in minor ripoffs—from speeding past an American foolish enough to wear his wristwatch on a breakable band and ripping it off; to the old Murphy gambit of setting a GI up with the most beautiful girl in the world ("you give me money—she has apartment down this alley") and then disappearing; to being an Instant Connection.

"No," Mosby said firmly. "No skag."

"Okay. Maybe, Number One marijuana? Excellent quality."

Mosby was about to tell him to fuck off, when a possible solution presented itself. The cowboy's English was better than most. Mosby decided to take a chance.

"You know bus station?"

A vigorous nod. "Yes. Bus station. I know."

"How much you take me there?"

"Aaaah . . . 200 pee."

"Bullshit. You think me cherryboy?"

"Okay . . . 100 pee. You get on."

Having the feeling that he was making a horrible mistake, Mosby clambered on the back of the cowboy's niftyshifty-Honda50 and the Vietnamese gunned away. At full throttle, the young man sped between two cyclos, cut in front of an MP jeep, then almost rear-ended a Citroën. He shifted, then looked back over his shoulder at Mosby.

"My name is Pham. You are?" He stuck his left hand back to shake."

"David—look out!"

"Ahh. David." And Pham veered around the five-ton truck turning across the intersection in front of them.

"You will like bus station," he promised. "Very pretty ladies. All good friends of Pham."

"Aw, shit!" Mosby swore. "No. Not boom-boom. No ladies. Bus. You know?" Mosby took one death grip off the bottom of the Honda's seat and pantomimed a steering wheel.

"Ah. Bus." Pham changed his mind and direction—180-ing across the street, narrowly missing three bicyclists, and down into an alley, almost hitting a scrawny dog.

"Bus very good for GIs," Pham said. "Have good odds. Lucky GI make much money. Pham go there all the time."

"Goddammit, stop!"

Obediently, Pham stopped. Mosby started again.

"Look. Bus. You know truck?"

"I know truck. You don't think I speak English?"

"Okay. Bus like truck. But . . . carry people . . . People. Man. Woman. Babysan. Many, many. Bus big truck with cover. You know. Bus go to Hue Duc . . ."

"Ahhh. No go Hue Duc. Hue Duc numbah ten. Beaucoup Veeccc Hue Duc."

"Goddammit. I no go Hue Duc. Meet girl. She come from Hue Duc."

"Ah, now I understand. My apologies."

Pham waved Mosby back onto the seat and roared away. From that point on, things became confused. Mosby had a rough idea of Saigon's major points—but why was the Saigon River suddenly on his right? And if that were so, was the embassy also on the right? Why were they driving down Le Loi, past the Brink's? Most important, how was Mosby going to survive this insanity?

His other puzzlements were cut off as Pham turned off a tree-lined boulevard Mosby had never seen before, onto a rutted semipaved street, and from there into a very narrow dirt alley flanked by wooden shacks and a nasal blast of nuoc mam sauce. Pham stopped.

"In here," he directed.

Mosby got off the scooter and backed away from Pham until he bumped into a wooden fence that he was reasonably sure did not have a gate.

"What here?"

Pham possibly did not understand. "David, you know you have to be careful in Saigon. Many bad people here. Some take you wrong places. Maybe even . . . to Veecee."

At that point, Mosby took the Buck knife from his pocket and snapped out the blade. Pham's eyes shot open.

"Why you do that?"

"This not bus station." Mosby, knife held loosely in his right hand, took a step forward.

"You no understand," Pham protested. "This where new girls

235

come. Some maybe from Hue Duc. This where girls come learn about Americans.''

"Bus station," Mosby said, taking another step forward and getting ready to cut Pham if he moved.

"Okay, David. Okay. I did not understand." And Pham kick-started the Honda. Mosby was on behind him; this time he held the knife against Pham's back. Pham found the Saigon bus depot a few minutes later.

After fifteen minutes of careful observation, Mosby thought he had the bus situation down. The depot was a huge, muddy square, with incomprehensible stone buildings with even less comprehensible banners and signs posted upon them.

Into this square would roar buses of every configuration: from repainted new ex-American vehicles, to trucks converted with brightly painted sheet metal sidings, to vehicles that looked as if they had once been Japanese armored cars. None of the buses was marked as to its destination or point of origin. As each bus slowed, an insane number of people would pour out, followed by their pigs, ducks and chickens.

A new driver would leap in, and instantly a second horde of people, also with their livestock, would board and the bus would be gone. About as much elapsed time as one of Richard Petty's better pit stops at the Darlington 500.

Mosby looked vainly for somebody in something resembling a uniform, but there were only a few ARVN soldiers. They seemed to be the most ruthless in boarding—able to ace even a pig from his position.

The final rule of the terminal seemed to be that everyone was shouting at the top of his lungs and communicating with no one else.

Mosby pushed through the crowd, looking for somebody who looked as though he knew what he was doing. Finally he spotted a tall, dignified man who was taking money from people and chattering away at them. A ticket seller, Mosby hoped. Although he glumly thought that with his luck it was somebody selling tickets to the Irish Sweepstakes. The man politely turned away from a babbling old lady when Mosby got his attention. Mosby figured on starting at ground zero.

"Bus," he began.

"Hah. Bus," the man agreed.

"Bus Hue Duc?"

"Hah. Bus. Hue Duc." The man considered, then translated: "Bay chuc dong?"

236

"No. I do not want to buy a ticket to Hue Duc. When bus come Saigon?"

"You no go Hue Duc," the man cautioned. "Cong"—and he mimicked shooting, pointing his imaginary rifle at Mosby—"on duong."

Mosby sighed, thinking about saying the hell with it. He gave it a final try.

"Hue Duc." He motioned, pointing to an imaginary spot on an imaginary map. "Saigon." Another point. "Bus . . ." He traced the route with his finger from one point to the next. "When?" Tapping on his watch.

"Aaah." The man understood. "Hue Duc bus. Aaah."

Mosby felt he was in an Abbott and Costello routine—and he'd always hated Abbott and Costello.

"Bus come . . ." and the man took Mosby's wrist and pointed to one number.

"One hour?" Mosby said.

"Yes," the man agreed. "One . . . hour." Then he frowned. "No. Maybe . . ." and he held up three fingers.

Mosby groaned.

"Maybe . . . one day?" The man smiled hopefully. Mosby swore under his breath, thanked the man as best he could, and went back to his post across the square. He watched every incoming bus, trying to pick out Tho from the endless stream of ao dai clad women and praying that this was not the most insane idea he had ever had.

And the long shadows of the afternoon crawled across the square.

Mosby thought the shoat the mamasan was lugging in her arms was very beautiful. As was the crate of chickens unloaded behind her. Mosby even grinned happily at the drunk ARVN sergeant who shoved past him. The second most beautiful thing in the world was that rotten, stinking bus—a rusting chunk of iron that looked like it placed fifty-third in a demolition derby. The last bus coming from Hue Duc.

But the most beautiful thing going was Tho. She stood, smiling shyly, wearing what must have been her best ao dai. She carried a small, briefcase-size rattan purse. Of course, Mosby didn't know what to do. He knew enough about Vietnamese customs not just to grab her and kiss her and hug her. Leaping and whooping would make him appear like a damned fool.

"I am very glad you came," he managed in total inadequacy.

Tho just smiled once more. When in doubt, punt, so Mosby

covered his confusion by waving frantically for a cab. A thing that looked like the bus's little brother chugged up, and Mosby got himself and Tho inside and told the driver "Continental Palace." He settled back in his seat—ignoring the looks of speculation the driver was giving him in the shattered rearview mirror—and considered the next step.

The problem was that Saigon—and South Vietnam—existed on two levels. There was a place for the Vietnamese and a place for the Americans and the Vietnamese who catered to them. The two never came together. David Mosby, on his sixth trip to Saigon, had stepped outside the limits. For an American, the city offered little opportunity for romance.

He was just beginning to understand the depth of his problem fully when the taxi dumped them at the city center. He tried to attack the thing one step at a time. First, they would need a hotel that wasn't a bordello. This meant finding, for a change, someone who spoke English better than Mosby spoke Vietnamese. He started down the line of taxi drivers outside the Continental Palace, quizzing each man as Tho patiently waited.

The hotel looked good. It was a three-story concrete-block building, painted brown, with iron railings on the balconies. There were no GIs evident, the room was clean, and the bed made with fresh sheets. Mosby probably should have wondered why the woman clerk so eagerly took dollars—Military Payment Certificates—instead of asking for piasters. Or perhaps he should have stuck his head into the hotel bar. But he didn't—he was absurdly feeling an almost teenage embarrassment about what Tho was thinking as she sat in the cab outside.

So he paid the woman, put a mental checkmark on one more problem solved, and went to the next. Dinner. He figured he should take Tho to a real Vietnamese restaurant. None of the American-oriented brawling joints that might upset the girl.

"Some wine, Tho?"
"No, Mosby. I do not drink."
"Uh, this is French champagne, Tho."
"Maybe . . . one glass."
Mosby poured. Tho sipped and grimaced. She was just as beautiful in Saigon as she was in the bazaar. Tho set the glass down and took a deep swallow from the water goblet. Then she returned to her meal, her head down, never looking around, concentrating on her food. He was actually grateful for her

seeming single-mindedness. Because he was as uncomfortable as he'd ever been in his life.

The restaurant he'd been steered to *was* Vietnamese. Vietnamese expensive. Mosby was the only American customer.

The patrons either wore military uniforms or dark suits. Their women wore silk—either Parisian or custom ao dais. And while the men, Mosby thought, were all in their forties, the women were either the same age or else ostentatiously in their late teens. And—Mosby must have been wrong about this—they all seemed to be glowering at him whenever he happened to look up. He picked up his chopsticks and went back to the paper-wrapped dumplings—bo nuong no chai. The chopsticks seemed to twist in his fingers and the dumpling hit the ebony tabletop, bounced once, and plopped into his lap. Mosby put the dumpling back on his plate and swabbed at the stain.

Mosby looked over at Tho and grinned, trying to shrug off the incident. Startled, he realized she was almost in tears.

"Mosby," she said, ". . . I do not like this place."

Wonderful, Mosby thought. And I figured my junior prom was a bust.

"Why not?"

"Because . . . these people think . . . I am your whore."

Mosby thought about his options: to run for the door; to toss a grenade he hadn't brought with him; or to break into tears too. Instead he called for the check. Now, back to the hotel, he thought. I wonder what great surprises God has in store for me there.

The first was the lizard, sleeping comfortably under the sheet. Mosby was already to toss it out the wide-screen window, but Tho insisted on soothing it and then placing it next to a wall. No big deal, he realized, lizards kept flies away and were a necessary part of any Vietnamese building.

The second surprise was the loud shouting coming from down the hall. Mosby was glad that Tho's English was limited—although how limited he wasn't sure—because the shouts were in American. Drunk GI American.

The third surprise was the tap at the door. Mosby, who by now was trying to find a way to undress without stripping in front of Tho, answered it. The woman at the door looked twenty-five going on fifty-five. She grinned seductively through teeth that alternated gold and rotten. Then she noticed Tho.

"Ah. You have short-time girl." She smiled again and went next door. Tho looked lost and scared. Mosby *was* lost and scared. Then he found out that the light switch didn't work, and the only way to turn the light off was to clamber up and unscrew the bulb.

Darkness, except the neon flashing from the next-door bar, the car headlights flickering across the wall. Silence except for the yodels from the soldiers down the hall.

"Fuckin' wonderful," Mosby said for maybe the thousandth time that day. He undressed down to his shorts and rolled into bed. "Just fuckin' great."

Springs creaked, and Tho slid into the narrow bed beside him. She was naked. They lay side by side for a few moments. And then Mosby realized the girl was crying. Feeling more helpless than he could ever remember, Mosby took her in his arms and held her.

Eventually she stopped crying. Eventually she fell asleep. And eventually dawn came.

Tho reached out and patted Mosby's hand. He looked up from his espresso and croissant, and tried to smile at her. It wasn't a very good smile—he was feeling sorry for himself. She smiled back. Mosby wondered what in the name of the Lord she was thinking. Although he could guess.

Hell, if he were Tho he'd figure him for every kind of a dickhead. First he brings an inexperienced country girl across dangerous terrain to Saigon, where she gets looked at as if she were a boom-boom girl. Then he takes her to a hotel that sounds like the Ugly American with a hard-on. Shit. Shit. Shit. Christ, David, you're a fine one. Howinhell if you ever get back to the World are you gonna be fit company? You don't even know how to treat a lady unless she's got two-dollars-can-do tattooed on her forehead.

He tried a better smile at Tho.

"Maybe . . . when we finish breakfast, I put you on bus for Hue Duc?"

Tho's small teacup jiggled and a splash of tea went unnoticed on the table. Tho looked down at it.

"If that is what you want," she said.

Aw, goddammit, that isn't what I want, Mosby mourned, staring out over the Continental Palace's railing at the early-morning Saigon traffic. What I want is to walk across the street to the Caravelle—if I could afford it—get us a suite, and get caviar and champagne and a fuckin' violin player and Jesus Christ I can't do anything right.

"Ladies and gentlemen, this is your typical AP hack, conducting your typical man in the street interview with an exceptionally ugly leg whose name I think is Mosby Something, or Something Mosby.''

Mosby turned to see Cliff Tarpy. He didn't recognize the reporter for a minute. Instead of his usual sweat-stained and faded fatigues and camera, Tarpy wore suit pants and a silk shirt, and carried a coat over one shoulder. A tie dangled from the coat pocket. Mosby started to greet him, but Tarpy didn't let him get a word out.

"The question we're asking today," he went on, "is how anybody so ruint could end up with a fox like her?"

Mosby found himself smiling for real.

"Co Tho, this is Tarpy," he introduced. "He is a journalist. You know. Photographer?" He mimed taking pictures. "He is dinky-dao."

"Nice talk, GI," Tarpy said, pulling up a chair. Then he turned to Tho and began speaking in fluent Vietnamese. Tho grinned for the first time that day and, looking down at her teacup, answered Tarpy—at first in monosyllables, then more expansively.

Mosby sat wondering what the hell was going on. Tarpy tsked, and, without looking away, beckoned. Instantly a waiter sat a glass half full of Scotch and an unopened bottle of Perrier on the table. Tarpy built himself a drink and then addressed Mosby.

"Do you know," he said, "I almost got my head thumped."

Mosby wondered.

"Here I was all ready to ask where you scored this fine unit here, and how much. Shows you gotta have all the facts, ma'am." Tarpy poured down half the drink.

"Is Mosby, by the bye, your first or last name?"

"Uh . . . last. David's my first."

"Just like to know my reference points. Looks like you're using Sinclair's three-day pass in fine style."

"Yeah." Flat.

"Uh-oh. What's the problem?"

Mosby found himself narrating the debacle of the last dozen hours. Tarpy was gentleman enough not to laugh, although it took another drink-and-a-half to do it.

"And you think you've got problems, pal," Tarpy managed in a parody of the Old Philosopher. "All you have is the love of your life and nowhere to go.

"Me, I've got to go to Hong Kong and explain howcum I keep filing stories on what batshit the Five O'Clock Follies is to some

241

dickhead from New York who's an ex-jarhead who's voted the straight Fascist ticket for the last two hundred elections."

Tho suddenly asked Tarpy a question. He answered. Tho stood.

"I come right back," she said, and threaded her way through the restaurant.

"A woman's gotta whiz when a woman's gotta whiz," Tarpy said, watching her go. Then he took a key ring from his pocket, popped a key off, and put it on the table.

"Like I said before, I owe you. This is the key to Room 506, Hotel Caravelle. My hooch. Take it and sin lots more, my son."

"I can't . . ."

"Why the fuck not? AP's gotta pick up the tab whether I'm there or out in the bush, or in fuckin' Hong Kong—which I'm headed for momentarily if I can get drunk enough."

Mosby fingered the key and tried to come up with a response. Tarpy saved him. "Check the sheets, babe. Make sure the maid got the worst of the cumstains out. Oh, yeah. One other thing."

Tarpy took two business cards from his pocket, scribbled on them both. "This one is if that prick Indian at the door of the Caravelle gives you a hard time.

"This one is to a real good restaurant. You can walk to it— it's just over on Pasteur Street. You know where that is?"

Mosby nodded.

"They owe me, so you shouldn't have any problems."

Tarpy saw Tho coming back toward the table and stood.

"Two things, Mosby. First, relax. Second, remember the Vietnamese think that getting laid is one of man's—and woman's—basic rights."

And he was gone.

Mosby was sure that in the next ten seconds he would wake up and find himself squatting in the mud next to, say, Blind Pig. And so he savored what must be his dream.

A dream of clean sheets in a large Western room, a dream where traffic buzzed and honked four stories below him across Tu Do Street. A dream where Tho's naked brown body flickered tantalizingly across the open bathroom door.

Like all good dreams, it was a little blurred around the edges:

Mosby was in a shop on Trung Street, a shop he'd discovered on a previous tour, buying Tho an ao dai that was nearly as beautiful as she was. Mosby remembered being slightly embarrassed when Tho cut the price three hundred percent below his best bargaining effort.

He was in another shop, buying Tho some jewelry to go with the ao dai, and the haughty salesman telling him that this jade necklace was indeed a bargain at only $4,000, and almost trying to buy it.

He was in Room 506 at the Caravelle, with a bellhop and the manager making sure the room was exactly the way it should be.

Later, he was smiling with Tho at the French restaurant on Pasteur Street, eating Danish caviar and something not too far away from a steak, while Tho champed heavily on something the waiter had said was a "very special dish."

Tho had even drunk two glasses of the "French wine. Very old. Very good" with David.

The bathroom light went off.

A silhouette left the room, crossed in front of the drawn curtains, and slid in beside Mosby.

Scented smoothness touching him, and his hands and lips moving, meeting eagerness, and his body finding moistness and Mosby as he started down the whirlpool roar found a moment to wish that this dream would never end.

For the rest of that night, it never did.

CHAPTER THIRTY-THREE

SONG NHANH

SINCLAIR WAS IN a firing squad mood. As his jeep and escort vehicles drove across one of the graceful bridges that spanned the Song Nhanh River, he was not charmed by the ancient beauty of the city.

There was nothing exotic in the smells he smelled, or mysterious about the crowds of Vietnamese who jammed his path and were honked out of the way by the lead vehicle in his caravan. What filled his mind were the frankly bullshit orders that he had gotten from his superiors. Said orders had all come down from Westmoreland's office, instructing him to provide a battalion-size presence to protect the capital of the province from possible enemy incursions.

The general's arguments against the orders were twofold: 1. There had been no appreciable enemy activity in or around Song Nhanh. Nor was there any intelligence to suggest otherwise. The only significant activity within III Corps's area was the attack on Loc Ninh—and that city was far out of Sinclair's AOR. 2. The danger was in the south, where he had won his recent victory over the Phu Loi. By splitting one full battalion away from Second Brigade's base at Hue Duc, he would be left with only two to follow up on his blow. His other two brigades were too far distant to provide the rapid response that Sinclair needed.

Both these arguments fell on polite but equally deaf MAC-V ears. He was to meet with the province chief, one Nguyen Van Thoan, and to provide full cooperation and support to their ARVN ally, despite the fact that the man already had a full battalion of South Vietnamese infantry and at least a company of Vietnamese Rangers at his command. Like most American officers, Sinclair was cynical about the fighting abilities of those men, but to him, even the number of ARVN troops in the area was more than enough to guard against a nonexistent threat.

He also was not looking forward to his meeting with Thoan. He had a pretty good idea, again cynical, about what kind of man he would be. Sinclair probably would have been surprised to know that his idea of Thoan and his ilk was shared by the very men he was fighting. His mood was further soured by the American captain who met him outside the province headquarters building. Captain Charles Drew was one of those irregular Army cowboys that Sinclair detested. The man wore tailored tiger stripe fatigues and sported a jaunty green beret on his head. Sinclair did his best to be civil during the introduction. Drew was, after all, Thoan's American adviser and might have a great many enlightening things to say. There was also the fact that although he was a lowly captain, Drew might be able to exercise enormous power through Thoan.

"I'm glad you're early, sir," Drew said. "I was hoping we could discuss the situation before the meeting."

"That's *exactly* why I'm early, Captain!" Sinclair said. That it came almost as a snap embarrassed him. To cover, he looked casually around at the ARVN barracks, sandbags, barbed wire, and heavily armed troops protecting the admin building.

"Looks like someone is expecting a siege."

Drew caught the attempt at humor. "Yessir. Thoan is a bit on the edgy side. We tried to tell him this wasn't the way to deploy his guys, but . . ."

There was no need to complete the thought.

"You know," Sinclair said, "Thoan's turned his headquarters into a dream target. Give me a couple of eight-inch SPs and . . . it would be like shooting skeet."

"You're right, of course, sir," Drew said. "Fortunately, that's not likely to happen around here. Hell, nothing happens around Song Nhanh.''

''That's precisely why I'd hoped we could have a talk, Captain,'' Sinclair said.

Drew ushered him into the bowels of the admin building.

''We have plenty of time, sir,'' he said. ''Thoan's having his weekly powwow with some of the merchants, right about now. Sort of like a royal audience. They air their problems and he makes like Solomon and settles things.''

Drew shrugged. ''He clears more piasters on one of these days, sir, then a general makes a year. No offense intended, sir.''

Sinclair was neither offended, nor shocked. Bribery, he half-guessed, was what this was all about.

''To be frank with you, Captain,'' he said, ''I have more than a few reservations about this Thoan. Almost as many as his approved request for one of my battalions.''

''I advised strongly against it, sir,'' Drew said.

He was so emphatic, Sinclair was inclined to believe him. ''Why was the request made in the first place?''

''Bucks, sir. Pure and simple. Sure, Thoan pulls down a bundle as province chief. But you gotta keep in mind, he's in this province because he's a fuckup.

''His family's real tight with Thieu's people, sir, and so, instead of being gigged, they put him where he won't be in the way, but can still live like a gentleman.''

Sinclair had heard that Special Forces people tended to call a spade a fucking shovel no matter how many stars they were talking to, but this was his first experience with their outspokenness. Drew stopped just outside a large, ornately decorated anteroom. Thoan's office obviously lay just beyond.

''Trouble with Thoan is he's a greedy so-and-so. He's been seeing all the money other people have been raking in off the American presence, and he wants some of it too.''

''So that's what's behind all this,'' Sinclair said.

''Yessir. Between your battalion, and all the support guys, this city will clean up. All those hungry GIs with no place to go to spend their money. That's what Thoan's after.

''Course, the way it works, sir, is that he'll have to pay a lot more juice up the line, but . . .'' Drew made with the shrug that said it all.

Sinclair found himself sitting across from Thoan, sipping from a thimble of tea. The cup was made of exquisite, paper-thin

245

china, and the soft chair was of hand-tooled leather. The province chief's office was not an office at all. There was no desk, no files, no in-and-out baskets. There were no pens or papers, or reports waiting to be read. There wasn't even a phone in the room. If Thoan had an important call, his secretary—a beautiful young Vietnamese girl, who had introduced herself as Miss Tram—politely interrupted, and if Thoan desired the call, she brought the phone into the room and plugged it into a convenient receptacle.

The "office" itself looked more like the living room of a fabulously wealthy bachelor who indulged his every whim. There was nothing garish about the opulence around him. In fact, Sinclair noted some French period pieces that his wife would have slain for. And, although not educated in the arts, Sinclair was sure he recognized some of the paintings on the walls as being originals.

Thoan's main interest seemed to be kept in a large glass cabinet in one corner of the room. It was filled with toys. Not ordinary toys, but antique toys that seemed in some cases to date back several hundred years. All but a few, Sinclair guessed, were European. One of them, in fact, seemed to be a toy guillotine—built to scale—and complete with a tiny victim with a presumably removable head. Thoan was playing with one of his toys as he talked. It was a small top that, as it twirled, spread flowering leaves that revealed a ballerina on point. It was almost hypnotizing. The top twirled, the girl appeared, and then as the top slowed, she was enfolded into the leaves again.

The province chief himself was also not as Sinclair expected. Although he wasn't too sure what he had expected. Thoan was tall for a Vietnamese and slender. He was impeccably tailored in clothes Sinclair was sure he had made up in Paris. His hair was stylishly cut, and his cologne faint, but masculine. Thoan did share the Vietnamese penchant for jewelry, and although he wore—to Sinclair—way too much, each piece seemed to have been carefully chosen for simple beauty. The general was not looking at oily flash, but at a carefully constructed facade of a well-bred cosmopolitan man. Even the man's accented English seemed to have been developed for charm. Sinclair thought he had never met a man he hated more.

". . . I'm sure, General, as a man of sophisticated reasoning abilities, you realize your presence in Song Nhanh will provide much more than just protection—badly needed as it is?"

"Really," Sinclair said.

"Yes. You see, the very fact you are able to provide a battalion of men to so remote a city will prove that the tide has turned in this unfortunate conflict.''

"Prove to whom?"

"Why, our dissidents."

"I wasn't aware," Sinclair said, "that Song Nhanh was exactly a hotbed of Communist activity."

Thoan dismissed this with a wave of his hand.

"Of course not. To be sure, there are a few VC in Song Nhanh, but we know who they are, and keep careful track of their activities. By dissidents, I mean men who are on the edge. Who are waiting to see which way the tide of events is churning before they commit themselves."

"I'm glad to hear you say that," Sinclair said. "Some of my younger officers—I have my own dissidents, you realize—suggested that profit was your only motive."

Thoan laughed. It was just as smooth as his speech, and Sinclair felt his skin crawl.

"If I were guilty of all the sins the young wish me to have done, I would have burned in hell years ago. Although I think it would be worth your while to discuss with them the opportunities that Song Nhanh can provide."

"Such as," Sinclair asked dryly.

"Without too much trouble, I can arrange to have this city placed back on limits. Unlike Saigon or Vung Tau, we have no resident terrorists, nor are our bars or entertainment disease-ridden."

"Aren't we putting things ahead of themselves," Sinclair said, trying to keep the anger out of his voice. "First there's things such as where my battalion will be based, the amount of logistic support, and so forth."

"True," Thoan said lightly. "One of my biggest faults is I tend to see too far into the future. By good fortune, my staff prevents any possible oversights."

"Yes."

Sinclair stood, hoping to end the conversation before he did something he might regret—like putting a .357 magnum round through Thoan. "I'll have my staff officers start discussing our problems immediately and coordinate with your people."

Thoan looked disappointed as he, too, rose.

"You are not staying for lunch?"

"No. I have a conference in Saigon this afternoon regarding the transfer," Sinclair lied.

"A shame. But this has been a pleasant chat."

"Yes," Sinclair said. "It has been an experience, hasn't it?"

247

* * *

General Duan bent low over his bowl of noodles, staring at the Song Nhanh province headquarters building across from the market shop. Like Sinclair, he noted the new barracks, the fortifications, and the lolling ARVN troops.

"I thought they only made targets like that," he said to Nghi, "in whatever paradise artillery officers go to. If only I had my old 105s from Dien Bien Phu. Poof! Song Nhanh would be ours for the asking!"

"Some might argue," Nghi said, "an artillery round is not quite the fate they have in mind for the man inside."

"You're probably right," Duan said. "I think I even remember feeling that angry myself, once. Sergeant Lau says I'm getting squeamish in my old age. I told him he was wrong. Blood just bores me. Possibly both of us are right. Who knows?"

"Would you care to stroll the marketplace?"

The two of them left the small thatched building that housed the noodle shop. Nghi was thrilled the general had insisted that he personally tour Song Nhanh. To him, it meant that he had a military commander not only very brave but aching to launch the promised General Uprising. The fact that Duan also appeared highly intelligent and sophisticated was just added spice. He was in the company of a philosopher, Nghi felt, like himself.

The two men were dressed identically in open white shirts, slacks, and sandals. It was the basic uniform of a small Song Nhanh businessman. They had toured most of the city on foot or bicycle in the past two days. Duan had noted carefully the possible problems his troops would face during the uprising, and the two men had spent long evenings discussing ways around them or methods that Nghi's people might use to ease the soldiers' way. Nghi was particularly proud that Duan listened intently to his ideas, argued strategy, gave ground when he saw he was in the wrong, and politely pressed home points when he saw a flaw in Nghi's thinking. He wished his father were alive to witness all this. Nghi had confessed all this to Duan. He had told him of his dream of being an engineer. Duan listened sympathetically.

"It can still be, my friend," the general had said. "And it *will* be very soon."

"Do you really think I could return to school?"

"Why not? Unless you prefer politics. I detest politics. I have to be political. But I don't like it."

248

"That's how I feel," Nghi had said. "I think I'm very good at politics. But I'd rather be good at machines."

The two strolled on through the marketplace, seeming nothing more than two tradesmen relaxing after an excellent lunch.

CHAPTER THIRTY-FOUR

SHANNON

SHANNON SAT ON his B-4 bag, his head and back crammed against the tin wall. The slight overhang from the airfield storage building provided about six inches of shade, and Shannon was trying to take advantage of every second of it while he waited for his ride. The heat steamed through the PSP on the runway, creating a waving oily haze that turned things slightly out of focus beyond thirty meters.

Across the Hue Duc airfield, he could make out a large number of miserable grunts. Even from here, Shannon could tell that they were fresh meat. Some of the men were being loaded into trucks, while others were just standing there melting under the tropical sun, waiting for the next convoy of trucks. Shannon knew they would wait for hours before the last man boarded the last truck. He saw several men turn away and vomit on the PSP, from nervousness, or the heat, or maybe both. One part of his brain made him glad to see them. God knows they were desperately needed. The other part felt sorry for them, because he knew that a great many would never make it home again in one piece. Welcome back to the war, Dennis, he thought. Oddly enough, he was almost glad to be back. His two weeks' R&R had been one of the stranger experiences of his life, and he wasn't too sure he had actually enjoyed it.

His ex-wife, Lisa, had set a little mind-trap for him. Strange how some people take years to let go. Although Lisa had been the one to file for divorce, sometimes she acted like he had been the one who had split. When she felt that way, she liked to stick it to him. Usually, Shannon caught on and ignored her. This time, he had missed all the signals and walked right into it. Although he wasn't sure how he could have avoided it, because Lisa had caught him on the most basic of levels: his kids.

Well before Sinclair had ordered Shannon to take two weeks' leave, Lisa had written to him with what seemed to be a pretty nice offer. She had suggested that when he went on his next

R&R that he take it in Hawaii. Lisa said she'd fly the kids out to meet him. She'd worked out all the details, even calling his father and conning him into escorting the boys, figuring, she said, that her presence might be a little painful, considering what had happened, and besides, she didn't want to quote cramp his style end quote. How could Shannon refuse? He'd be a beast if he had. Also, it had been months since he'd seen his sons. He was looking forward to the visit. Yeah, one helluvan idea.

The moment he walked off the plane to be met by his father and the boys, Shannon realized what Lisa had done. He'd changed on the plane into civvies, hoping to avoid what he had heard was an increasing hostile reaction to soldiers from the folks at home. His father had given him a traditional Shannon-family bear hug that almost cracked ribs, and then Dennis had turned to sweep his boys into his arms. But he had been stopped by the cold stare from his oldest son. Dennis Jr. fixed him with a superior look that Shannon instantly recognized. Hell, it was Lisa looking out at him from that six-year-old head.

"Where is your uniform, Father?"

"Uh . . . I changed on the plane."

"So people wouldn't know what you're doing?"

It rocked Shannon back on his heels. Jesus Christ! This was his kid! His namesake, for crying out loud! Where did he get that kind of idea? Six-year-olds don't talk like that, do they? "Father," not "Dad," or "Pop" or something! What in blazes had Lisa done to his boys? He didn't know what to say or how to say it. He just wanted to crawl back on that plane. Christ, even if the doors were shut, he felt so small he could probably slither right under them. He looked at Emmett, expecting the same.

The small three-year-old figure was glaring at Dennis Jr. Then the boy turned to look at his father, and his face almost shattered into a loud whoop of laughter.

"Daddy, Daddy," he shouted, and leaped into his arms. Emmett wrapped his legs around him and began hugging him and kissing him, saying "Daddy" over and over again. Shannon felt his father embrace both of them. A moment later, they broke apart. Emmett slid to the ground. Shannon saw him give his older brother a dirty, so there, look.

"Daddy, I want to be a soldier too. Will you teach me?"

"Uh . . . sure, son," Shannon had said.

"Okay. Rule number one of soldiering, Emmett," his father's deep voice had boomed. "When on leave, the first thing you do is crawl into a hot shower and then a cold drink. Come on. Let's get this soldier in motion.''

Shannon was hustled out of the terminal, into a cab, then to the cool, cool safety of the Hilton Hotel. Frank Shannon had taken charge. Dennis Jr. seemed to relax for a while after that, taking a little boy's delight in the tropical scenery of Hawaii and the lushness of the hotel. The only other incident during the first few hours was when they'd entered the taxi. Shannon had gotten into the back first and slid over to let the boys in. His dad was going to sit in front with the driver. Dennis Jr. got in next to his father, but little Emmett had grabbed his shirt.

"I want to sit next to Daddy," he insisted.

Dennis Jr. had rolled his eyes in exasperation. "What do I care."

Even now, two weeks and thousands of miles later, Shannon felt the words claw at his heart. Thanks a lot, Lisa, he thought. Thanks a fuck of a lot. Shannon lit a cigarette and dragged in the smoke. With the airfield temperature soaring, it was almost too hot for his lungs. Still, he exhaled and pulled in deeply again, puzzling over the two human beings his sons had become. One thing he had to admit, Lisa hadn't done all that bad of a job overall. Both kids were superbright, spoke way beyond their years—at least Shannon liked to think that—and were well behaved. But she sure as hell had tried to turn the boys against him. Shannon wasn't sure how consciously she'd done it, but he had seen the result. Thank God kids seemed to be individualists almost from their first breath out of the womb. He smiled to himself. That Emmett was something else. Thought his old man walked on water.

Dennis Jr., however, was another matter. What hurt wasn't so much that the boy disliked him, Shannon realized, but that the disliking was such a struggle. At certain moments, Shannon could see him waver, wanting to love his dad, wanting to look up to him. But the boy always fought it back. Then the bitter sarcasm would leak through.

It reminded Dennis of the last days of his marriage to Lisa, when she was wavering between love and hate. One day she'd be biting his head off, and then that night she would make love with him furiously, weeping after she climaxed and then whispering his name until she fell asleep. Shannon remembered that it hadn't been his idea to name the first boy after himself. In fact, he'd always thought that kind of thing was sort of egotistical. He'd wanted to name the boy Emmett, after his grandfather. But Lisa had always been a pretty traditional sort of person and had insisted. The name war, if there is one, is something mothers almost always win. So Shannon had said okay, but the next one, if it's a boy, is Emmett, right? And Dennis Jr. and then Emmett it became.

Now Dennis Jr. was nothing like Dennis Sr. at all. He was an exact duplicate of his mother, from looks to temperament. Emmett, on the other hand, was just like his father. No, not exactly, Dennis thought, in small flashes the child really reminded him of his namesake. There was a certain stubborn tilt to his chin, the way his eyes fired up when his big brother pissed him off. It was the old man standing there in a little boy's body.

On that first day, Shannon's father had put the boys down for a nap and then had come out to have a drink with Shannon, fresh from the shower. Frank Shannon had mixed a couple of tall gin and tonics—heavy on the Rose's lime juice—and then had sat down at the small table set up by the window in the hotel suite. Shannon had looked around the room for the first time. It was tastefully plush and must have cost two small fortunes.

"Jesus, Dad, you really went overboard!"

"Don't worry about it," his father had said, "your mom and I can afford it."

He drained his drink in one long pull, and then motioned to Shannon to do the same. Dennis drank it down, his teeth aching from the delicious cold. His father rose, took the glasses, and went to the wet bar to make two more.

"How is Mom?"

"Great. As usual. And everybody else is great as well, so let's drop the polite talk and get down to the problem at hand."

Frank Shannon had always been absolutely direct.

"You noticed the kids have got some problems. And those problems involve you."

"Probably my fault. I didn't really handle . . ."

"Just listen, for a minute, will you," his father commanded. Shannon listened.

"Whose fault, why fault doesn't matter. What I'm trying to tell you is that you may or may not want to deal with it while you're on leave.

"If I were you, I'd leave it alone. Just be yourself. Have a good time and enjoy the kids. They're just normal kids, no matter what you may be thinking right now. Next. You only have two weeks. I intend to see they're good weeks. Have a ball with the kids during the day. If you want me along on anything, fine. If not, I can amuse myself."

Frank smiled at his son.

"Night is another matter. I'm the baby-sitter. You get yourself out of the room and find yourself a girl, or two girls. I don't care. Get drunk. Get laid. I'll cover for you in the morning."

Shannon laughed. "Sounds great. But I hope you don't expect me to plunge in right now."

"No," his father said. "It's best you un-jet lag. Falling asleep whilst nibbling on m'lady's knees isn't considered gentlemanly."

For the remainder of his leave, Shannon had followed his dad's orders. During the day, he and the boys played. The kids burned, peeled, burned again, and then turned deep brown. By the end of two weeks he had taught them both how to swim, how to build sand castles with elaborate tunnels and dungeons, and he introduced them to the mysteries of paddling a kayak in a reasonably straight line. Emmett plunged into everything full force. He would watch his father and listen carefully to his directions, and then repeat his motions move by move.

Dennis Jr. usually kept his distance. He seemed to be measuring Shannon, trying to find some fault. Shannon noticed that sometimes it was difficult for the boy. His son would start laughing over some antic. Then he would realize what he was doing, and pull back. After that he'd be sullen for the rest of the day, going through the motions of play.

Shannon also did pretty well during the nightlife portion of his leave. He met a tawny, long-legged stew on his second night. She was much better looking than he thought he deserved, listened with few interruptions, laughed at the right moments, and kept up a fairly interesting conversation. The lady wasn't the greatest companion he'd ever had in the sack, but was about average—which is just about where Shannon placed himself. It wasn't love, but it was nice and it was comfortable, and Shannon thought they'd even become friends of a sort when she left a few days before R&R ended.

There was only one incident with his oldest son, although it really wasn't that big of a deal as incidents go, Shannon thought, but it hurt, just the same. The boys were getting ready for bed, and Shannon was saying good night before he went to meet the stew. He had made the mistake of asking the boys if they were having a good time. Emmett was effusive, but he got something very odd from Dennis Jr.

"I guess it's okay," the boy had said. "But, isn't this what divorced fathers always do? Try to show how much fun they are?" He looked up at Shannon defiantly. "We have fun with

253

Mom, too. Lots of fun. But she doesn't have as much time. She has to work. Take us to school. Go to the grocery store. She worries about us all the time. You just play soldier.''

Shannon had almost slapped him, he was so pissed. Instead he just gritted through his teeth:

"I'm not in competition with your mother. We're two different people. Divorced people. And the only thing we have in common is you two.''

"I'll bet you think she talks about you all the time,'' the boy had said. "Always saying bad things. Well, she doesn't . . .''

Emmett's scream of anger broke it: "Shut up, you! You're a liar! She's always saying things! Always! Always!''

Emmett turned to Shannon and burst into tears.

"She does, Dad. She thinks she's so nice. But she isn't. She's . . .''

Shannon pulled him into his arms, shushing him. This was the last thing he needed.

"She is nice, son,'' he said. "Dennis is right. She's just busy and all. Probably she gets tired and angry. That's okay. I get angry too. You should hear me when I'm mad.''

He forced a laugh, and tickled Emmett until he was giggling through the tears. He looked up at the other boy, who was staring at all this. Shannon thought he looked sorry.

That was something, anyway.

Neither Shannon nor his father had brought up the war during their few chances to talk. In fact, Frank seemed to be carefully avoiding the subject, confining himself to humorous Rand gossip, stories about the family, and a few tall tales about himself, which all ended with his getting the short end of the stick through his own stupidity.

It wasn't until the last night of his leave that the subject had come up, and it was Shannon who had mentioned it. All of a sudden, he found himself pouring out the whole sorry mess about the phantom NVA unit to his father. He went through it from the moment he spotted them, to Sinclair's disbelieving him, to his promotion up and out of the way of his commander. Frank listened closely, asked a few probing questions, and then settled back to think. Shannon had learned years ago always to stay as silent as his father during moments like these.

Frank Shannon always went about this sort of thing the same way. He sucked in every speck of information, then leaned back in his chair, closed his eyes, and ran it through again—nodding to himself once in a while as points were made or unmade.

Finally, he opened his eyes again, got up, and poured them both hefty slugs of brandy.

"You have to understand," he said finally, "that this general of yours has no choice but to think you're full of ham hocks."

"I don't get it."

"Washington doesn't want this NVA Division there, that's why. Don't you read the papers? We're winning this thing. If a unit that size had holed up in the Octopus—nice name for a mountain, by the way—then it turns things upside down. Washington would have to admit there are problems that may not go away."

Frank Shannon sucked at his brandy, then he shook his head in disgust.

"Christ," he said. "They're having enough problems with this Dak To business. I understand the NVA are kicking some serious behind there, right? But they're painting it as a last gasp thing. An all or nothing fight. What you're suggesting is that the NVA can infiltrate large numbers of men and equipment with impunity. If that's so, then the 'light at the end of the tunnel' is a big goddamned train."

"Fuck," Shannon said. It wasn't a word he used often in front of his father, but it was all he could think to say.

"So this Sinclair fellow has got to believe the way he believes. Because if it were the other way around, he'd have to convince his bosses, and those bosses would have to convince their bosses, all the way up to LBJ. And, son, Mr. Johnson cannot be convinced of anything that is not already a firmly held belief of his own. He tends to dump on people who don't fall in line."

Frank Shannon finished off the brandy and brought the bottle over to the table so that he would not have to get up again for a refill.

"I suspect Sinclair," he said, "would find himself relieved before it got beyond the first step."

"Just like he did me," Shannon said.

"No, I don't think they would be quite that kind," his father said. He stared at the bottle awhile. "Rand is full of all this we've-got-it-won foolishness," he said after a moment. "But there are people who are trying to turn in honest reports, even though no one is thanking them for it.

"What I have been able to glean, however, is that we lost this thing from the get-go. We can't win. Hell, to do that, we have to invade North Vietnam. And anybody with even half a wit knows that will bring in China."

Shannon's stomach lurched. He had discussed things like this with his officer friends before, but from his father's mouth it seemed real, not boozy theory. Shit. The Chinese. The only thing that could stop them would be . . .

"Which means our only hope would be nukes," his father said, unconsciously finishing his thought for him. "And no administration of either party is going to push the button. Not in our lifetimes."

Shannon was having trouble taking all this in, and he sure as hell couldn't assimilate it into his own situation. But that, he realized, was because there was nothing he had to do with it. Major Dennis Shannon just carried the spear. Other people told him when, where, and how deep to stick it in.

"It'll be over in two, at the most three years," his father said. "As thick-skulled as we are, it will take that long for us to get the message."

"What the hell," Shannon said. "At least I've got a job for a while."

"There is that," his father said. "But, to be selfish, I thank the good Lord that you are nowhere near the Octopus. Let someone else encounter your elusive NVA."

The roar of a jeep missing on about half of its cylinders brought Shannon out of his haze. He looked up to see Edmunds squeal up beside him, carrying along with him the foul smell of a flogged engine and scorched brakes. He swept out of the jeep and gave a low, formal bow to Shannon.

"Your carriage, sirrah," he said.

"Where the fuck you get Old Smoke and Choke?"

"It's all I could scare up. They're getting ready to move everything else."

"Move? What the fuck for?"

"Beats the hell out of me," Edmunds said. "I am but a lowly company commander, thanks to a certain buddy of mine. But that doesn't entitle me to the confidence of my asshole superiors."

"At least you gotta know where we're going," Shannon said, a bit exasperated.

"Got you covered there. We're moving to Song Nhanh, boss. Only moments away from bright lights, music, and sloe-eyed and willing maids of the mysterious Orient."

"Song Nhanh?"

Shannon slumped back down on his B-4 bag. So much for his father's good-will wishing.

If Dennis Shannon were the type of man who spat, on a good

day, with a reasonably brisk wind, from Song Nhanh he could just about hit the Octopus.

CHAPTER THIRTY-FIVE

DUAN

GENERAL DUAN COULD not have found a better place to go to ground than the Octopus, which was called, on his maps, Le Noir Massif. It was a natural fortress, set upon high plateaus covered with thick, three-tiered jungle. This made the Americans' favorite tactic of aerial assault nearly impossible without paying a high cost in men and equipment.

Adding to the difficulties for any enemy was the fact that it was crisscrossed with rugged canyons and thundering mountain streams that could sweep all but the largest boulders before them. It was not the sort of place that welcomed the modern, mechanized army, as the Americans, and before them the French, had learned the hard way.

The Octopus was the traditional hiding place for the Vietnamese guerrilla fighter. Here he could retreat, rest, lick his wounds, and ready himself to fight again. The fact that the enemy had a good idea that he was there made little difference, because he would always be fighting on the guerrilla's ground, a ground that had been well prepared for decades.

To begin with, the area was honeycombed with tunnels—although nowhere near as elaborate as the Chu Chi region—that a waiting soldier could pop out of to do terrible damage to his enemy and then disappear into with little chance of discovery. The tunnels were boobytrapped with devices as simple as trip-wired bombs and as elaborate as deep wells, flooded with water, that hid secret entrances and switchbacks and walls that collapsed on cue.

Over the years, the Viet Cong had also established huge ammunition and food dumps that they kept constantly supplied, so an invader would confront not only a secretive enemy who could strike from any direction at will, but an enemy whose supplies were nearly inexhaustible, and close at hand. In the past, the Americans had sent in their elite LRRP units, but each patrol had ended in disaster, or near disaster. Now, no American went there. In fact, the only men at all who walked the jungles of the Octopus were the Viet Cong and now Duan's soldiers.

Sporadically, the Americans would lash out. Planes, returning to base, might drop any remaining bombs there, or strafe the jungle. Or, equally as futile, an artillery unit might fire a few rounds at map coordinates. But this was all done in the blind, and only a very unlucky man suffered any real harm.

The Comrade General knew he was many things, but unlucky certainly wasn't one of them.

The camp Duan and his division were in had been well prepared. Local units had known for months that a large force was expected from the North and they had acted accordingly. Long-abandoned tunnels had been reopened, and new ones dug.

A large base hospital had been constructed, partially underground, with recovery rooms set out in the fresh air and shielded from the elements by woven bamboo roofs and roll-up screens. Mess facilities and recreation areas had also been built, and his welcomers had partially completed aboveground shelters for his men, all connected with small tunnellike paths cut into the jungle.

When Duan arrived he had immediately set his men to completing and expanding the work. Lau had personally overseen the construction of command headquarters, as well as the small, attached hut that Duan made his home. Lau had also attempted to stock it with a few small luxuries, such as captured American rations, but Duan had a bad habit of mostly giving these things away. The sergeant kept complaining that the general was more softheaded than softhearted, and, besides, if there was any giving away to do, didn't the Comrade General see a worthy man right before his eyes?

So much for the advantages of friendship in the high ranks.

Duan shifted in his hammock and then stifled a groan as the motion sent spears of pain through him. Even in the cool of the hour before dawn, the hut felt stifling. He was also horribly thirsty, but he dreaded getting up to find a flask of water. Like most of his men, Duan was suffering from malaria and he hadn't slept well in several days, although he had tried to hide it from Lau. He knew the sergeant would nag him unceasingly to have himself hospitalized.

Hospitalized! As if he could afford the time. The past month had been a blur of planning, exhorting, and driving the men under his command. He had only a little more than two months to ready his troops for the General Offensive. There could be no failure now. Duan knew that failure was a very real possibility and it would not necessarily come on the battlefield.

He might meet it here in the Octopus, because the fortress

was also a deadly prison. Disease was slowly whittling away his forces, despite his efforts to fill out the ranks with local recruits and the remnants of the Phu Loi Battalion.

Malnutrition was also a problem. Certainly there was plenty of stored rice, but there was almost no protein, which meant that all of his men suffered from severe anemia—a condition afflicting most Vietnamese, even in times of relative peace and plenty.

Then there were the huge practical problems. The Octopus was relatively safe, but it was also just as strange and frightening to his NVA regulars as it was to the Americans. His men were either peasants or children of the cities. The jungle with its diseases and horrifying plants and animals was slowly eating away at their morale.

Rumors based on ignorance swept the camp sometimes only minutes after the first man babbled one hysteria or another. The rumors ranged from a snake that would smell out a man kilometers away and then hunt him down relentlessly like a tiger, to a tree that would entice a man with its delicious fruit and then seize him with its branches and slowly devour him. It was all Duan and his officers could do to keep a half-step ahead of the rumors and then explode them.

His men's fear of their surroundings included the tunnels. Ideally, most of the camp should be underground, but Duan knew that his men would fall apart if they were forced to live in those narrow confines. Even his own batman, Lau, refused to go underground, except when absolutely necessary, and then he would pop to the surface like a spring-loaded puppet and flee to his hut to recover.

It was all very well, Lau liked to say, for these Southerners—he used the word like an obscenity, perhaps forgetting that his general was from the South—to live like rats. After all, it is a well-known fact that they are closely related to the rodent. Look at their sharp little teeth and beady little eyes that never look a man straight in the face.

Lau's distaste for the locals was shared by the other NVA, which led to Duan's next difficulty. Somehow, he had to blend his men, the Viet Cong regulars, and the local village sympathizers into a cohesive fighting force. The only way to achieve this was to train them constantly.

Duan went at this task with subtlety. For instance, he would team one of his best squads with a squad of locals, then present them with some war problem. Following the lead of his men, the locals would defeat the mock enemy—usually to their surprise—and then glow with pride. It was a way of making the men feel a real part of an elite fighting outfit.

All this, of course, assumed some spirit and dedication on the part of the locals Duan was recruiting from the villages. As Commissar Thuy pointed out—accurately—many of the men might only be pretending allegiance. They might be bandits at heart, taking advantage of a situation. Ferret them out, was Duan's answer. And then kill them on the spot, his commissar sensibly suggested.

No, Duan said. Once we know who they are, then we have to make them ours. The commissar nodded in understanding. It was one of Mao's dictums that to waste a potential soldier of the revolution—even a bandit—was a crime. Duan was not a devotee of Mao Tse-tung—although an officer would have to be a fool to ignore his writings on warfare—but Mao's logic on handling troublemakers was impeccable. Besides wasting needed manpower, troublemakers have a way of deserting and joining your enemy.

Duan heard a rustling near the door of his hut. It would be Lau with his breakfast. Ignoring his aching body, Duan swung up to sitting position as the sergeant entered. His head swam, but he fought everything into focus and greeted his sergeant with a great cheery grin.

"Good morning, Sergeant," he said, just a bit too loudly. "You slept well, I hope."

"You're sick," Lau said, instantly suspicious.

"No. I feel fine. What makes you think I'm sick?"

"You're acting glad to see me," Lau said.

"I am. I'm also looking forward to your excellent tea."

"You hate tea in the morning," Lau said.

"Since when?"

"Since always."

"When did I ever say . . ."

It was too late. Lau was at his side and testing his forehead with a meaty arm. Duan found himself being pulled to his feet.

"What are you doing," he spluttered.

"Taking you to the hospital."

Duan tried to protest, but Lau raised an authoritative hand.

"You don't have to stay there," he said. "I know better. You'll just drive me crazy sneaking around."

Duan had the insane picture in his head of a general slipping through the dark to avoid this own batman. Something about this impossible role reversal struck him as funny. He started to laugh. Then he looked at Lau's face. The man was really upset. Duan felt bad about this; he didn't want to worry his old friend needlessly.

"All right," he said. "I'll go. But it isn't anything. Just a touch of some sort of virus."

Lau snorted. "A virus. That's your story on everything. You don't eat right, that's your problem. If you'd only listen . . ."

Lau broke off and sighed a long-suffering sigh.

"Now let's go see that pig's behind we call a doctor."

He hustled the Comrade General out of the hut.

The main base hospital was administered by a doctor whose roly-poly appearance and nearly bald head were the exact opposite of his personality. Dr. Nguyen Van Quot was that great rarity of the Communist jungle hospitals, a highly skilled, French-educated doctor, who made up for his total lack of bedside manners by being a medical genius.

In the short amount of time that Duan and his officers had known the man, Dr. Quot had managed to irritate every person he came in contact with. He not only hated his fellow human beings without fear or favor, but he seemed to go out of his way to inspire hate in return. He was proud and loud about the fact that he was a capitalist, who found all Communist thinking foolish, and the only reason he had not been placed before a firing squad was that the man was saving hundreds of lives.

Quot's genesis as a guerrilla doctor was remarkable in a world where the strange is commonplace. He came from a prominent Saigon family who believed that civilization began and ended with the French. After he had graduated from medical school and done his surgical residency in France, Quot stepped into a wealthy practice that catered to the rich.

His fees were as huge as his ego and proven skills, and Quot flaunted them both. During the day, he drove his medical colleagues wild with broad statements of medical fact that flew against common belief. That he was almost always right, or could quickly ignore a minor error and explain it away, didn't make him any more popular. During the night, Quot attended the theater, or opera, and ate at fine restaurants. He also considered himself an expert on all three of these subjects, and would argue long and loudly on the merits of a wine or the exact note hit by a soprano.

The doctor probably would have gone on like this for a long and fruitful life, if he hadn't made a nearly fatal error. Quot also considered himself an expert on politics, and thus, with his connections among the wealthy Catholics of Saigon, he would be assured a seat in the parliament. It never even came to an election.

It was one thing for the authorities to ignore the doctor's crisp dinner-table analysis of the corruption of the ruling regime so long as he was content with merely being a doctor. It was another to hear them on the radio or see them in political broadsheets.

Quot was only a half a step ahead of the tiger cage when the soldiers came for him. He barely managed to grab his bag of surgical tools and flee the city. The hunt for him had gone on for several months, with Quot calling on the favor of family friends, who were fortunately more loyal to his father's memory than interested in betraying his decidedly unpleasant son.

Quot wasted the first few weeks plotting his victorious return. But then a few basic realities began to occur to him. He couldn't go back to Saigon as long as the current regime was in power. As an Asian, he could never enjoy the prestige he believed he deserved if he fled to Europe and attempted to set up practice.

Only one solution presented itself: the American-backed government of South Vietnam must fall. The only possible way that could happen was through the Communist North. Although he made no secret of his view that they would soon be replaced by his beloved French, Quot was welcomed by the Viet Cong. They could not afford to spurn the help of any doctor, much less a doctor of his talents.

And so, during the next few years, a legend was born. He became the "Bac Si"—The Doctor. Tales were told of fantastic operations performed with a common household drill or with surgical knives constructed from helicopter blades.

Men who in the short past would have almost certainly died from their terrible chest wounds and shrapnel injuries, now had a very good chance of survival if only they could live long enough to be operated on by him and his team. It was also said that the Bac Si had invented fantastic medicines, relying on the jungle for his pharmacy.

The fact was, when you stripped away the propaganda, almost all of this was true. Just as, despite his outspoken behavior, the fact also was that if Dr. Quot survived the war he was assured a high place in almost any government that followed. Pig's asses, as Lau liked to say, were not necessarily guaranteed to end as bacon.

The problems jungle doctors like Quot faced were enormous. There were diseases ranging from beriberi to the bubonic plague, which was rife throughout Vietnam even before the current conflict. Most Viet Cong also suffered from body parasites and cerebral malaria, which did not respond to traditional treatments.

Supplies were always almost impossible to get in the early days, and even though the system of theft improved, things like penicillin and other antibiotics don't keep well in a jungle environment.

Disease was the first problem Quot had to combat. Even the most remarkable surgeon can't ultimately save a wounded man if he is also suffering from malnutrition and/or malaria. He was constantly exhorting political officers to educate the men on basic nutrition and sanitation.

Quot prowled the camp during his few off hours, personally searching out violators of his health laws, and he recommended stiff punishment for any examples he found, earning him the eternal hatred of the common soldier as well as the officer. Still, when wounded, men prayed to whatever gods they favored that they would be carried to the site of the Bac Si's operating theater, instead of some lesser man's.

In the Octopus, Quot had sensibly placed his operating rooms underground, figuring the dangers of the tunnel-bred bacteria were far less than trying to operate in the open, under the enemy guns and bombs. He had the walls lined with parachute nylon, and he and the rest of his team operated with flashlights attached to their heads. The recovery rooms he had placed outside, to escape the chances of disease and so the patients could benefit from the sun and fresh air.

To stave off malnutrition, he forced his patients to eat as much protein as they could hold, which usually meant rats and occasionally captured or stolen American rations. He also experimented with the edibility of different kinds of insects, which he had his kitchens mash into the rice to disguise them. The result of all of this was that, like the American soldier, if a Viet Cong was wounded he was almost assured of survival—if he could reach the Bac Si's hospital.

The difference, naturally, was that the GI could be helicoptered out almost instantly, while the VC had to carry their wounded through the jungles on makeshift stretchers, sometimes for days.

When Duan had first encountered the Bac Si, he was already trying to counteract this. Using his usual imperious means and snarled orders, Quot was gradually establishing an elaborate system of movable clinics, where a soldier could be stablized before the long journey to surgery. To meet the doctor, Duan learned, was to find yourself instantly in a contest of wills. The Comrade

General lost the first one, and was sure he would lose the next if he was ever so foolish as to engage the Bac Si again.

One of the first things Duan had done, after he and his men had escaped into the Octopus, was to tour the hospital, to check on the condition of his men. He and his commissar, Colonel Thuy, accompanied by Sergeant Lau, had been walking through the bamboo-screened recovery areas, giving words of encouragement to individual men, and taking mental notes on the changes for the survivors of the badly mauled Phu Loi. They had barely begun their tour when they heard a man screaming high-toned obscenities at the top of his lungs.

"You syphilitic penis . . . you weeping pustule . . . you green-slimed bottle of feces! I want this to stop! Instantly, do you understand!"

The three men rushed to one of the recovery areas to see what was going on. Duan saw a tubby little man whose face was swollen and purpled with rage. He was screaming at another man whom Duan vaguely recognized as one of his own medics. The tubby man, Duan guessed from what he had heard of his reputation, was Dr. Quot. The Bac Si was digging through the medic's kit, hurling things in all directions.

"What else do you have in there, you insufferable quack? Are you trying to kill my patients, or what?"

"But, Doctor," the medic was protesting, "those things are Issue. We have orders to carry them."

"I don't care what your orders are. I'm overriding them, do you hear!"

The sound of a countermanded order triggered the commissar into action. Before Duan could stop him, Thuy strode forward, his chest swelling for a bellow.

"Here, now. Leave this man alone!"

The Bac Si whirled at the sound of his voice, and for a wild moment, Duan almost thought the doctor was going to go for the ancient pistol he carried holstered at his side. Instead, the doctor drew himself up to his full, insignificant height.

"Are you addressing me? Remove yourself. What business is *my* hospital of yours?"

Thuy exploded.

"You are in the presence of your superior officers. How dare you talk to us like that?"

The Bac Si looked him coldly up and down.

"I'll speak to you as I like," he said. "Now, quit sputtering like a newly removed foreskin and leave. You can return when you're shot, a fate I'm sure you deserve."

Thuy was floored. This was unbelievable. Duan noted with some interest that his commissar was sputtering incoherently, a situation he himself had never produced in a political officer. Still, Thuy was his man, and he'd better stop things before they went too far. However, if this was the legendary Bac Si, perhaps a little diplomacy was in order.

"Excuse me, Comrade Commissar," he said quietly. "Perhaps we should see what is going on."

Thuy buried his anger and nodded curtly.

"As you wish, Comrade General," he said, with the emphasis on the general. Since neither he nor Duan wore any semblance of a badge of rank, he wanted this pig doctor to know whom he was dealing with.

Instead, Quot turned to give Duan a hostile glare. Duan thought for a minute that the man would say something unfortunate, thereby forcing his hand. Duan didn't believe in having doctors shot unless absolutely necessary. Quot, however, held his tongue—or at least toned down as much as was possible for the man.

"General, is it? Good. Finally, someone with the authority to end this nonsense."

Quot scrabbled for something inside the medic's kit and held it up for inspection. Duan recognized it as the lump of medicine all medics were required to carry to treat snakebite. After being bitten, you broke it in half, swallowed one portion, and applied the other to the wound. Duan knew it was a fake, and its only use was for morale purposes. He also understood the reason for Quot's anger.

"I thought you trained medics in the North," Quot said, his voice shaking. "Not witch doctors. This stuff is as useless against snakebite as a sugar pill."

"Quiet," Thuy hissed. "The men will hear you."

"Oh, so you admit it then."

"I'm not admitting anything."

"Good! Then tell me what this is for?"

"Snakebite!"

"Any particular breed of that species, or is it intended for snakedom in general?"

Thuy was folding under this attack.

"I'm not a doctor," he said. "I'm a . . ."

"Finally! The crux of the dispute. You are not a doctor. And I am."

Quot turned back to Duan.

"You see, General, this small matter of witchcraft—which I

find surprising, since you Communists are noted atheists—is merely symptomatic of the overall problem.''

"Which is?'' Duan was curious despite himself.

"There are two forces at work here. The medicine—poor as it is—that you bring with you, and the medicine I provide. Only one can prevail.''

Thuy was horrified. "Are you suggesting that we put our medics under your command?''

Quot shrugged. "It's only logical. Do you want superior medicine or witchcraft?''

"I see your point,'' Duan said.

"And?''

Duan could tell that the little man was waiting for him to concede the point. If not, he was ready to withhold his services.

"I'll talk to my staff, see what can be worked out,'' he said.

"And until you do,'' Quot pressed.

"Until then, you're in charge,'' Duan snapped. He waited for just the correct amount of time, and then said: "But only of the hospital. Not my men.''

He turned on his heel to stalk away. Lau caught up to him within a few steps.

"This doctor,'' the sergeant whispered. "Is he good?''

"A genius, apparently,'' Duan gritted.

"Good, then I'll talk to him later about your malaria.''

"I don't want to see that man unless I absolutely have to,'' the Comrade General said. "He is a . . .''

". . . pig's behind,'' Lau finished for him. "But a genius nonetheless.''

Duan felt as if he were back in the nuns' clutches as he sat uncomfortably on the plank examining table, stripped to the waist, while the man he had vowed to see as little as possible thumped on his chest, peered into his eyes and mouth, tsk, tsk, tsking at his middle-aged condition. Duan could see Lau hovering anxiously in the background, like a squat, beefy peasant mother. The Bac Si shook his head one more time and stepped back from the table.

"It's malaria, of course,'' the doctor said.

"I know that,'' Duan snarled. "I've had it for years.''

"Temper, temper, Comrade General,'' Quot admonished. "Just because a quick temper is an early symptom of your condition, does not mean you have to give way to it.''

"Under the circumstances, it's very difficult,'' Duan said sarcastically. "Has anyone ever told you about your bedside manners?"

Quot looked at him, honestly puzzled.

"No. Why should they?"

Duan groaned inwardly. The only thing worse than an asshole is one that doesn't even realize he is one.

"Just get it over with, Doctor," he said. "Give me whatever pills you have in mind, and let me get out of here."

"It's not that simple," the Bac Si said. "You obviously need a great deal of education in your health care. Don't you listen to your own political officers? I have supplied them with information on diet, work stress, personal sanitation. I've seen to it that they lecture your men on these simple rules at every opportunity."

"I've attended a few," Duan said. Then, grudgingly: "You're doing an excellent job, Doctor."

Quot ignored this. Of course he was doing an excellent job. Why discuss the painfully obvious?

"Let's begin with your diet," he said. "From now on I want you to consume at least four thousand calories per day. At least half of those calories should be protein."

"I can't eat that much," Duan said. "And as for the protein, I'm not really that fond of meat."

"Nevertheless, you shall eat it," the Bac Si said. "Now, for liquids. Whatever amount of water you're now drinking, I want you to double it. And juices. Plenty of the citric juices."

Duan gaped. The doctor obviously thought he ought to slosh around the camp like a swimmer of the English Channel. And as for juice . . .

"Next, sleep. You're not getting enough, and what you do get is apparently not very deep. I'll prescribe something."

"My God," Duan said. "I can't fight a war doped on sleeping pills!"

"Of course not," Quot said. "I don't believe in sleeping potions, anyway. I'll recommend a good, relaxing herbal tea that your batman can brew up for you every night. It's also good for regularity."

Duan spotted Lau's broad grin in response to all this. His chief torturer was taking careful notes.

"What else . . ." the doctor went on. "No alcohol, of course. Bad for sleep. Bad for the constitution."

No alcohol? The man was a fiend. Duan couldn't even begin to imagine what hell he had risen from. The Comrade General, however, decided not to utter a word of protest. He wouldn't give the man the satisfaction. Instead, he struggled off the table and began pulling on his top.

"Where are you going?" Quot asked.

"Aren't you through?"

"With you, yes. But there are some other things I want to discuss."

Duan had been dreading exactly that during the entire examination.

"Take it up with my commissar," Duan said. "I'm sick, remember?"

"Come now, Comrade General. You're not that sick. Just a touch of malaria and appalling neglect of your body."

"All right. What seems to be the problem?"

"If you want your medics trained properly," Quot said, "I must have more authority over them."

"We've discussed that before," Duan said. "I understand your logic, but this is the military . . . we don't do things that way."

"Then I'm afraid I can't be responsible," the Bac Si said. "Frankly, I have a great deal of doubt about the ability of your medics to care for the awesome casualties I estimate you face in the coming General Uprising."

"Oh, you're an expert on casualty estimates now?"

"Don't be sarcastic. Any fool could work it out with even a minimum of knowledge."

"Very well," Duan said. "I won't argue. Now. What's wrong with my medics? They have been provided the best training possible."

"In the North," the Bac Si said, "where the medical facilities and talent are notorious. Besides, they suffer from overweening egos. You can kill a patient if you think you know too much. I blame it on the Communist system. No profit motive. In a capitalist system a doctor listens to his patients because they are *paying* him."

Duan wasn't too sure how many times he had just been insulted.

"What is your point?"

"They don't listen to their patients. Nor do they learn from experience. They commit error upon error, without ever correcting themselves. Instead they congratulate each other on the few paltry lives they save, instead of being horrified at all they are losing."

In Duan's experience, the pig's behind was right. It was a fault that self-criticism sessions never seemed to solve. He would be damned, however, if he would admit it.

"You know I'm right, Comrade General," Quot said. "You're too intelligent of a man not to see."

Oh, so Duan was intelligent, now, was he?

"I'm afraid we'll just have to live with the system we have, Doctor," Duan said.

"What a pity," the Bac Si said.

"Now, is there anything else, Doctor?"

"A great deal," Quot said. "To begin with, I have a plan to greatly expand our aid stations . . ."

Duan settled back on the table and let the man go on. He didn't like the idea, but he was sure as the man was a gold-plated penis that whatever plans he had might save many lives in the 302d Division.

CHAPTER THIRTY-SIX

THE OCTOPUS

VIEN SANG FELT the shovel bit sink into the ground, gave it a slight cutting twist, and in the same motion lifted up, feeling the earth come away easily. He dumped the load on the growing mound of dirt on the straw mat, then turned back to attack the ground again.

Sang understood vaguely that he and his digging mates were widening a tunnel for one of the guns his division had transported from the North. He didn't really much care what the reason was, he just dug. It was a task he enjoyed. After the long march, anyplace permanent—even the Octopus— felt like home. The hot sun on your neck, the play of muscles working smoothly, the comfort of a full belly at the end of the day, and a little time for ease in the cooling evenings. At any other time or place, Sang would be a perfectly happy man.

The trouble was, he was as lonely as only a seventeen-year-old could be lonely. Also his comrades seemed to be shying away from him lately. He didn't understand the reason, but if an older man had taken pity on him he could have easily explained: Sang talked about being lonely unceasingly. No matter what the conversation, Sang would find a way of bringing his wife into it, or the child he had never seen, or what a most remarkable woman his mother was, and how beautiful the growing fields surrounding his village. No man, the way Vien Sang told it, came from such a paradise as he.

Sang was born in a small agricultural port near Thanh Hoa, a city noted for its massive bridge, railroad spur, and the fact that it was a vitally important and centrally located trade and transportation center. This also made it one of the favorite targets of American bombers. The bridge was always being destroyed and then raised again seemingly overnight. The rail line leading out of the town and down the coast to the city of Vinh was also a bombing favorite. Since Sang's small village lay just near the track and about midway between Thanh Hoa and Vinh, bombs had a way of straying over the fields and thatched homes.

"Paradise" is not a word most people would have used if they were describing Sang's hometown. But to young Sang, bombs had become as familiar as his plow. They were something to be feared, of course, and the damage they did was tragic. But life still had a way of going on pretty much as normal. When the planes came, most villagers leaped into the small concrete-lined shelters honeycombing the area and waited for the planes to pass. Some crewed the antiaircraft guns and fired back at the Americans, while others joined the fire and rescue brigades. When the raid was over, life went back to the way it had been for several years. Regional Party leaders had a slogan that had been passed down from Hanoi: "Combat and Construction."

A local village wag, however, had dubbed it "Shit and Shovel Out." The second slogan had made the rounds of the entire village within minutes, and Sang remembered everyone having a good laugh about it, even the local chief, who swore he would pass it along at the next regional Party meeting. Knowing the chief, Sang was pretty sure he had.

In only a few years, Sang had seen village life alter significantly around him. More and more men were drawn into the war—as soldiers, or as part of the massive construction gangs that roamed the countryside rebuilding what the bombers had destroyed. His own father had been pressed into military when Sang had been about thirteen, and when Sang had finally followed in his footsteps nearly three years later, no one had heard from him for some months.

In the last letter Sang had received from his wife (dictated to the chief, because she, like most peasants, was illiterate), his father still hadn't been heard from and his mother had just about given up hope.

Another thing, besides the bombs, that had changed was the drain on the menfolk had produced a society consisting almost entirely of the very young, the very old, and women. Women ran almost everything of importance. Women did all the farm work, repaired the village, and made up most of the local militia. The result was a matriarchy, since most of the women, Sang's mother among them, delighted in these new responsibilities and declared quite loudly that things were not going back to the old ways if and when their men returned.

He had received two letters from his wife, Tham, since he had left home. He kept them wrapped in a small piece of waterproofed canvas, and was always pulling them out and reading them at every opportunity. They were crammed with the ordinary detail of a farmer's life. Such-and-such number of eggs gathered, how much or little rain, and the expected harvest. He had to read between the lines for any affectionate feelings, because she was dictating the letter to the chief and it wouldn't be proper to reveal herself.

One proud note was the news that not only had she joined an antiaircraft team, but that her team shared with another the successful shooting down of an American plane. In one of the letters was the news that he was to be a father. Sang had been proud at first, but then had been terrified that something would go wrong during childbirth. By the time the letter reached him, he realized without comfort, the child would have been born and, in fact, might be near to walking.

He had asked every man he knew who had a child what his chances were of the baby's surviving. Then he had nightmares about his wife. What if Tham died? He had many sleepless weeks over that. An older man, a corporal, had finally taken him aside.

"What if she did die?" the corporal had asked. "What if your nightmare comes true?"

"Then I will be the most miserable man in my village."

"So miserable that you'd do something . . . like kill yourself?"

Sang had been shocked.

"Of course not. Tham is the most beautiful woman in my village . . . the kindest . . . the hardest working . . . But . . ."

"Will you quit quacking like a duck. We all have heard of the many virtues of this legendary Tham. Answer my question."

"I have responsibilities in my village," Sang had said. "People depend on me. My mother, for instance, she—"

The corporal shut him up about his mother, and continued. "Now, let's consider the alternative. What if she is alive?"

"Then I would be the happiest man in my village," Sang said quietly.

The corporal had nodded, sliding another small twig under the bubbling pot of rice.

"Then you must assume she and your child are alive and well. If you don't . . ." The corporal shook his head as if in great sadness. "If you continue this way, young Sang, you are going to die. And if you die, you'll never find out what happened."

Sang considered this the rest of the day. He thought of himself as a good soldier, but lately . . . since the nightmares . . . That night he dreamed about his village again. Tham was fat and smiling and he was the proud father of a beautiful boy. The next day he fell into step beside the corporal.

"I want to thank you, comrade," he said.

"The nightmares stopped?"

"Oh, certainly. You were absolutely correct. But, now, I have one small question . . ."

"Go on."

"Do you have any children?"

"Several."

"Good. Then you must know. My son should be nearly walking right now . . ."

The corporal merely nodded, waiting.

"What if he walks too early? I have heard their little knees bow and . . ."

The corporal had nearly killed him. Unfortunately for the others, Sang hadn't learned his lesson. He merely stopped speaking to the corporal.

Lau surveyed the bare aluminum cans stacked in endless rows before him. There were thousands of them, some labeled, but the identities of most had been rusted or washed off by the climate of the Octopus. The array of canned goods before him was only a small portion of the liberated American supplies the Viet Cong had stashed. Lau was looking for citric-based juices, as per Pig's Ass's directions.

Over the what seemed to him like centuries of stealing from the West, he had learned that nice things like orange juice, grapefruit juice, and even papaya juice came in cans that had a certain configuration. Lau thought of his knowledge as little different from learning the configuration of enemy planes. The can could produce something that would bomb the guts, or it could merely observe, with occasional harmless gunshots. Prune juice, for instance, is always in a smaller elongated can, usually just enough for one and a quarter servings. Lau had no idea why all liberated prune juice seemed to come like this, it was just so. This can was to be avoided.

The second thing you had to look out for was tomatoes. Different nationalities seemed to package tomatoes in dangerous ways. Tomato paste, for instance, tended to be small, but you could pick up a tall slender can that was bound to be orange juice, and it ended up being merely lots of tomato paste—a completely useless condiment in Red River cooking. Out of the can, tomato paste tasted like old ground-up snails. It also gave you the shits.

Lau learned the hard way that evil-tasting products also tended to be packaged in cans that were just outside the size they should be for normal consumption. Things to be avoided were never produced in cans for less than two or three.

The sergeant eyed one particularly interesting can: grapefruit juice, or at the very least sliced grapefruit in juice—pulp in too-sweet sugar water vs. bitter liquid. The can was a bit squat, as if it contained manufactured slices, but it was also tall enough to contain pure juice. He was as unsure about the age of its contents, but he did understand that the Americans had been adding large quantities of vitamins to their latest efforts. The choice was a chance he would have to take.

No. It was a chance *Duan* would have to take. Lau swore to himself that whatever it contained, the Comrade General would eat it all.

"My pardons, Sergeant," came the voice behind him. Lau knew the voice belonged to the commissar. Therefore, pretending no looter's guilt, he carefully put the can in question into his pack and turned as casually as he could.

"Comrade Commissar," he said with pretended surprise. He waved a disdainful hand at the carefully lined-up cans and packages. "What disorder. I was just making notes for the next self-criticism discussion."

The Commissar ignored the oddly shaped heap bulging from the sack dangling at Lau's side.

"How is the Comrade General?" he asked. "I hope that you are making him obey Dr. Quot's instructions."

And now he nodded approvingly at Lau's sack. The man knew what it was about—looting stores, perhaps, but for a good cause. Naturally, they both understood that Duan needed merely to order that the proper dietary supplements be provided him. But that was something they both knew he would never do.

They shared a small silence of respect for their superior, and Lau was aware that the commissar was not pretending. Despite the man's bluster, Lau realized that Thuy saw Duan as a hero: privately indecisive; outwardly calm; an inward potential coward; publicly without fear; a child in disdaining his own needs; a father, or even a favorite uncle or older brother, when talking to his officers. More important for Lau: why was the commissar, vastly Lau's superior, suddenly standing in front of him, almost hat in hand?

"He still has the fever," Lau said, "but I think it will break soon."

"You are very close to him, aren't you, Sergeant?"

"We met at Dien Bien Phu," he said.

He didn't mean to say this flat, or boasting, or anything. It was just so. The long silence that came afterwards made him realize a few things. Dien Bien Phu. Was this some kind of magic to these young people? This pig's behind of a commissar? Was this the boy peasant, shedding his sandals and carrying the Buddha across stormy waters?

It was pigshit. He was alive—Duan was alive—because they got the guns above the French. Lau studied the Commissar through his large cow eyes. He measured the man: could this fellow have stood with him at Dien Bien Phu?

Pigshit, he said to himself. Great long green streams of sick pigshit. Lau was not an introspective man, but he knew that what lay behind him was phony history and what lay before them would be Dien Bien Phu.

"You want me to send your kind greetings?"

Thuy nodded, nodded, nodded, and finally his voice pressed out.

"Sergeant Lau, in the spirit of self-criticism, would you say that I have done my duties well?" Thuy didn't wait for an answer. "Would you say that I have indoctrinated the men so that they are at the height of their abilities? Is there anything more I could do?"

Lau pretended to consider this for many moments, waiting just a bit longer than was comfortable for the commissar.

"You are one of the best men I have seen at your job, comrade," Lau said. "If ever a single man could improve the morale of our fellows . . ." He let his voice trail off in admiration. Lau noticed with interest the boyish look of glee on Thuy's face.

"Sergeant, I have been giving a great deal of thought to the difficulties that face us. Perhaps my job is done. Perhaps I could be put to use in better ways?"

"You have some thoughts on this matter, of course, Comrade Commissar?" Lau said this very dryly. He could get away with it now.

"Well, you travel about this camp as much as I . . . perhaps there is some unit . . . some underutilized unit . . . a unit that will be sorely needed in the General Offensive . . . that I could . . ."

". . . command?" Lau finished it for him. So, he was to ask his general to put Thuy into a combat command.

"Yes," Thuy said. There was no shorter way he could admit it.

Lau was long practiced at hiding his cynical grin from superior officers. Sure the man wanted to command a combat unit. You make Politburo points with that kind of a background. Did Lau care? Not in a dog's ass. Did Lau want this Commissar leading other men into battle? He looked his skinny snake body over. He was ready, that was for sure. Lau envisioned the Commissar screaming for his men to fix bayonets and charge! It had happened at Dien Bien Phu, the taking of Beatrice or Isabella: suicidal frontal assaults.

Sure, they had kicked those French behinds from here to the International Dateline. But at what cost? Fuck you, Commissar. Fuck you up your skinny behind.

"What a remarkable idea," Lau said. "I will be sure to mention it to the Comrade General."

Lau watched with great delight as a colonel tried to bow himself humbly out of the presence of a lowly sergeant. One bright note. He knew that Duan would enjoy the hell out of the joke.

The assault force waited nervously at the bottom of the hill for the signal for the attack to begin. The enemy was well dug in. They had taken position atop a 15- to 20-degree slope. The slope itself was a jumble of concertina wire that they would have to go under, around or through, exposing themselves to a potentially withering fire. The defenders were in sandbagged foxholes.

It was a classically American hilltop position and they had prepared the ground with care. There could be no surprise in the attack, because the enemy knew they were there, just as well as they knew from which direction the attack must come. Lau smiled broadly at the young VC lieutenant beside him.

"Excellent job, Comrade Lieutenant. Your men have studied the American mind well."

Lieutenant Lam beamed. This was high praise from the veteran sergeant. He and his men had trained for weeks with Lau and the other NVA troops. It had been enough time for him to realize with pride that the men from the North were among the best-trained troops he could ever hope to meet. He could not imagine any enemy capable of standing before them.

Lau gave the training ground one more professional glance. He pointed a stubby finger at one almost imperceptible lip of ground about halfway up.

"If you can get a few men just to that point," he said, "it should give you enough cover to bring up the rest."

Lam's eyes widened slightly, then he nodded, yes, that could work. He turned to find a few likely candidates.

"Phum Phuong," he barked, and in a moment a bulky figure scrambled over to his side.

"Yes, Comrade Lieutenant," the voice whined.

Lau looked at the man with a small start of surprise. The whine in his voice at first did not match the size. Phuong was almost as big as Lau himself, with massive arms that disappeared into a nearly nonexistent neck. A thick knife scar roped down one cheek and partway across his neck.

The lieutenant explained to the man what he wanted him to do. He was to take four men, and when the signal for the attack began, Phuong and the others were to take advantage of the confusion and take the lip of ground Lau had pointed out. Phuong followed all this carefully, nodding in continuing agreement, but Lau noticed that the man was really measuring just how difficult the climb was going to be, and from the glint in his eye, Lau was sure he was also thinking about how to get out of it.

"With pleasure, Comrade Lieutenant," came that whiny voice again. "And I am honored that you have chosen me for so important a task."

Here it comes, Lau thought.

"But . . ."

Somehow Lau knew there would be a "but . . ." followed by a meaningful pause.

"But, what, Phuong? Quickly. We haven't much time."

"Well, I was only thinking, Comrade Lieutenant, since I have spent so many hours training on the machine gun wouldn't it be best . . ."

Now Lau had his game. What Phuong was proposing was that he stay behind and man the RPD machine gun providing covering fire for the assault force. Since no one would actually fire during the game—there wasn't enough ammunition to spare for live-fire practice—Phuong could loll back behind the gun and take his ease while everyone else sweated and grunted up the slope.

276

In actual combat, for Phuong to volunteer to be with the machine gun would be either a very brave or very foolish thing to do. People you are trying to kill tend to get angry, and what better target for their anger than a gun that is continually hammering away at them, making them shit their pants? But Lau doubted that Phuong was either very brave or very foolish. From his accent, he seemed to be from one of the large cities of the South. Lau also guessed the man made his living as a civilian in ways other than totally legal. The knife scar hinted that the man also wasn't above using a little applied force to earn a piaster.

Lau shot the young lieutenant a glance, wondering just how long and how well Phuong had been using his civilian skills.

"Yes, yes, I see your point," Lam was saying. "Although you realize the risk you're taking. Your position could be eliminated in the first exchange."

Phuong gave a small shrug.

"It is only my duty, Comrade Lieutenant," he said.

Lau laughed silently to himself. He was pretty sure Phuong wouldn't be so noble when it came to a real fight. He decided to teach the man a lesson.

"With spirit like that," Lau said to the lieutenant, "maybe we can put a little pepper in this stew."

"Such as?"

"If in the first minutes of the attack we could get a machine gun up that hill . . ."

The lieutenant quickly got his point, as did Phuong, with increasing dismay. Now, instead of merely toiling up the hill with the others—an effort he had been doing his damnedest to avoid—he would have to lug the RPD. Phuong listened, his face darkening gloomily, as the lieutenant quickly adopted Lau's tactics and added in a few twists of his own.

A few minutes later, the attack was launched, and the men stormed the hill, Phuong stumbling and swearing under the weight of the gun. Lau enjoyed all this immensely, although he had encountered too many men like Phuong to believe that any lesson had really been learned. He imagined that for the remainder of the war, Phuong would manage to duck almost anything thrown at him. The man was an expert on survival.

Lau strolled away from the training area, reflecting on this and life's other little mysteries. He was far too fatalistic to get angry at men like Phuong. Also, he had been a sergeant for so many years in so many battles, that Lau noticed that he almost always got the Phuongs of the world to do what he wanted. And, if they didn't . . . too bad for the Phuongs. Lau had buried his share and had also written the after-action report describing how the poor man, while engaged in a frontal assault, met up with a bullet in the back of his skull.

The point was, when this silly fight with the Americans was over, Lau fully intended to be alive. He had imagined the scene of his victorious return to his home village thousands of times.

Although he had been a professional soldier his entire adult life, Lau still considered himself a farmer. He dreamed of the little plot of land and the rich smell of a buffalo hard at work. If pressed, however, Lau would have to admit that the dreams of his homecoming had changed. Naturally, he would be welcomed home as a hero. Just as naturally, the people would urge him to take on the duties of village chief. He would humbly refuse, oh maybe three times, just for form's sake. No. Make that two. Farmers tend to take you at your word too easily.

The other part of the dream required that Duan stay alive. This wasn't the full reason why Lau worked so hard to guard the Comrade General's back, but it certainly helped. In this part of the dream, Duan also got a hero's welcome, except in the rarefied atmosphere of Hanoi.

Most of the current crop of leaders was starting to get creaky-jointed. It was only logical that Duan, a relatively young man, and a bona fide fighting general, would move quickly up the ladder. Naturally, he would remember his batman's long years of faithful service. Lau wondered if a position on the regional politburo would be too much for an old sergeant to ask? Or, maybe even . . .

The hero of Dien Bien Phu suddenly found himself lifted from the ground and hurled through the air by a huge shock wave. He didn't have time to register what was happening to him. Lau's body slammed into the hard ground, and then he was curling up into a ball, sensing rather than hearing large objects ripping and tumbling past him.

A hundred tiny insects were stinging as small rocks pelted him. Lau lifted himself up on his elbows and looked wildly about for cover. Around him, the pristine jungle was charring stubble surrounding a gaping, smoking hole. Entire trees had been ripped from their roots, and thrown hundreds of meters. Lau heard a few screams of pain from the wounded. The back of his mind told him that a bomb had fallen—as usual dropped from a plane flying so high that no one had heard it approach. The front of his mind said where one bomb had fallen, another should follow.

Lau's eyes focused on a small hole a few meters away—the entrance to a tunnel. Lau crammed his large bulk into it and kicked his way down just as the world exploded again. He felt the ground rumble under and around him. His ears and mouth and nose were clogged with dirt, but still he dragged himself down, down, down. And then he just stuck there. He realized that he was at a bend in the tunnel, and that there was no way he could negotiate it. He was stuck. Outside the thunder of bombs continued. Here, at least, he was probably safe.

Lau remembered a terrible thing. He was absolutely terrified of close spaces. So terrified, that only under direct orders from Duan had he entered even the larger tunnels during his time in the Octopus. Slowly, he began muscling his way backwards, out of the hole. He hoped like hell that the bombing would be over by the time he got out. If not, fuck it. Lau would rather face the bombs.

For Vo Thi Mo, the bombing raid was manna from heaven. Just like the gods brought rain when they pleased, they also brought bored American pilots who decided to drop their 500-pound gifts onto what appeared to them as empty jungle. Mo knew there was no grand purpose behind the exercise. The planes had merely been flying home from a raid on the North, and the pilots had a few bombs left over. The Octopus was a free-fire zone. So they dropped the bombs, expecting to accomplish nothing more than scaring a few birds.

She also knew her prayers had been answered when she spotted the first unexploded bomb. She motioned her team over to it and quickly began her examination. There were a few things they had to find out, before they began digging into it for pure gold. First off, was the bomb on a timer? In other words, was it possible that it hadn't exploded because of some fault in a timing mechanism, and was ticking away at this precise moment? Over the years, Mo had seen too many people guess wrong at this point. You never got a second guess.

There, that was out of the way. Next, identify exactly what kind of fuse the bomb employed, as well as see if the bomb was boobytrapped.

Finally, she declared it relatively safe for them to go to work. Two of her team began sawing the bomb in half, while another poured a steady stream of water over it to keep it from getting too hot. In a very few minutes, they would be inside, and Mo would begin harvesting the explosives. With a shudder, she remembered the days when they had to steam the explosive out and then dry the highly unstable mush.

Vo Thi Mo was highly skilled at her profession. At twenty-eight, she was also a middle-aged member of a very elite group. It seemed like centuries ago, but thirteen years before she had been the happy new wife of a young villager.

Really, it had been a case of mistaken identification. At least that's what she told the ARVN troops that had come for her husband. They said he was Viet Cong. She had cried, and pleaded that her husband was not even political. He never even entered the discussions in the village square at night. All this was true. But, when the soldiers had left an hour later, Vo Thi Mo was a young widow. The ARVN made two mistakes that night. The second one was that they had left her alive. Mo was now a thoroughly political woman who comforted herself at night with the thought of the thousands of clever devices she had built over the years to avenge her husband.

Mo smiled to herself as they worked on the 500-pound bomb. She whispered sweet endearments to it, cooed to it, like a mother comforting a child someone had left behind.

CHAPTER THIRTY-SEVEN

THE SQUAD

SERGEANT DAVID MOSBY was tired of a world made up of fuck-ups, fear, boredom and sorrow.

For the last two weeks he had been stuck on this hilltop, ten kilometers outside the city that he could see in the distance—a city that the map told him was named Song Nhanh. Fuck Song Nhanh, fuck the Army, fuck First Sergeant Ramos, fuck . . . aw hell, he mourned. Fuck whatever might've happened with Tho.

Mosby had returned from Saigon full of puzzlement, wondering what was going to happen between him and Tho. After he'd put her on the bus for Hue Duc and gotten himself to Tan Son Nhut, he'd had hours to worry as he sat under the tin roof, waiting for a lift north.

He wasn't at all sure what he felt toward Tho and was very unsure he wanted to take the next step. In fact, he was very unsure of what the next step would be. He'd cringed, thinking about what happened to the few GIs who decided they wanted to get married. On the other hand, he realized that he couldn't just walk away from what had happened to him in Saigon.

The United States Army had made up his mind for him. Mosby was back less than an hour before he was called to the company CP, informed that the unit was relocating, and that he was going to be part of the Advance Party. He and Taliaferro. Be ready to move in two hours, Ramos had said.

Mosby, walking back toward the squad's tent, came as close to crying as he had in years. Tho would return to Hue Duc, back to her booth, and wonder what had happened.

Somehow Blind Pig must have known or figured, because he met Mosby outside the tent.

"We got your shit together," he growled. "An' you owe me seventy-five bones."

Mosby was in no mood for games.

"I don't owe you shit, man."

"You keep talkin' like that, you're gonna get your head smacked, asshole," Blind Pig went on. "I sent My down to the bazaar. Tol' her give the money to Tho when she comes back."

Mosby then really felt like crying. Fortunately half an hour with Taliaferro solved that. By the time the Huey put them down on the hilltop below Song Nhanh, he was back in a nice safe killing mood.

The Fifteenth's new base camp was on Hill 134, a wide knoll sloping down to the Song Nhanh River. The highway—a one-and-a-half-lane blacktop called Highway 45L—crossed the river on a low Western-style concrete bridge. The highway ran along the hill's east side, and the bridge was located almost due north of the hill. The river ran to the west of the hill. Between the river and the hill was a quarter-kilometer of paddies, now forcibly abandoned by Province Chief Thoan's orders.

About 100 grunts made up the Advance Party. Their orders were to secure the hilltop and, as ordered, to begin laying out the to-be-constructed perimeter.

It was a dismal place. Of course Thoan hadn't picked a hill that could conceivably yield any benefits to him, and so the hill, an amoeba-shaped bulk a half kilometer north-to-south by a quarter kilometer east-to-west, was solidly overgrown with secondary jungle. The rice paddies below would provide immediate mosquitoes as soon as the grunts moved in.

And the Advance Party made it worse: a handful of noncoms who were either incompetent or on somebody's shit list; grunts who were guaranteed to be on the shit list; and too many goddamned officers. Not to mention the fact that these 100 men were just enough to provide a succulent target if there were any Viet Cong around but not enough to adequately secure the perimeter.

The first night had been a terror, with the 100 men scattered around the enormous perimeter hoping that nothing would happen. Fortunately nothing did.

The next morning, the officers had arrived. Mosby had three seconds to meet Charlie Company's new CO, Captain Edmunds, and then was getting the word. C Company was getting the worst of all possible worlds, he learned. The company would occupy one-third of the hill's arc—unfortunately the northernmost sector.

This meant, Mosby realized, that not only would they get the mosquitoes, but they'd be responsible for providing checkpoints out on Highway 45L. And Mosby knew full well who'd have the job of keeping that fucking bridge from getting blown up by any ambitious young gook.

About the best Mosby could do for himself and his people was to jigger the platoon AOR within the company's sector. His squad would have a thick clump of brush to set up in and located only a dozen meters in front of the line there was an artesian well.

Then there was Taliaferro. Taliaferro talked. Incessantly. All Mosby wanted to do was sit sullenly in the hasty position he'd dug, stare out at the stinkin' river, and fell sorry for himself.

Okay, motherfuckers, he'd resolved. You gonna treat me like this all I'm gonna do is let these fuckin' days pass. I don't want to know if it's Monday or Sunday or whatever day it is. All I know is I'm gonna do it one day at a time and I'm not gonna make any waves.

Taliaferro, of course had managed to fuck that up yesterday by solemnly handing Mosby a can of C-rat boned turkey loaf and wishing him Happy Thanksgiving.

Now Mosby stood at the edge of the hill and watched the long column of trucks, dust boiling around them, move up the highway and turn left toward the hilltop. He spotted the two deuce-and-a-halfs with the members of his squad and all their gear, and waved the trucks toward a prestaked position.

Mosby wondered a minute—there were some guys in the trucks he didn't know from shit, and then realized. Fuckin' wonderful. Cherrytroopers. These clowns were gonna be his responsibility. No more sergeants. No more Casey. Mosby felt less like a leader than a man barely out of his teens who wanted to go somewhere—like maybe Canada—where the world wouldn't keep fucking with him so much.

But at least for the next four hours he didn't have to deal with that much, since Edmunds, First Sergeant Ramos, and the new platoon leader, a black guy named Wilson, all gave their new noncom help.

Mosby didn't want help, but somehow he got everyone arranged in something resembling fighting positions. Tomorrow, he promised, all this shit'll sort itself out, and I'll figure out who's gonna go where.

Mosby wanted nothing more than to sleep—to sleep, if possible, through the remainder of his tour. Instead, he hunted down Fritsche, whom he'd put at the left flank of the squad, to find out what the fuck was going on. Fritsche was sharing a space behind a paddy dike with one of the new men, somebody named Diaz. Mosby'd told Diaz to go up to the squad CP and mind the phone, then tried to find out what he was facing.

Fritsche lit up a hand-rolled cigarette the size of a Roi-Tan cigar and sucked it into life. Mosby sniffed at its acridity, bristled, and started to say something.

"Babe," Fritsche interrupted, "don't play kid sergeant. You know they ain't gonna hit us tonight. So if I want to get fucked up, what do you care? You think discipline is fallin' to shit since you been gone or what?"

Mosby had the grace to smile, and to take a hit off the joint. The effect of the weed didn't make Mosby feel any better, but it seemed to make everything fit into some kind of pattern.

"Dunno about this new second john," Fritsche said. "Don't seem too bad for a nigger. Seems like his head's somewhere else."

"What about the new platoon sergeant?"

"Blake? Watch the fucker. He used to be SDI in some basic outfit. Told me I better shave more often."

Mosby took the joint and inhaled again. Maybe the world was just miserable and not totally fucked.

"You ain't seen the new medic yet. He'll come in tomorrow. Big sucker. Oh yeah. I think he's a faggot."

"Totally fucked," Mosby muttered.

"Huh?"

"Never mind."

"That guy—Diaz—he also don't seem too bad. Least he knows which end of a 79 goes pop."

"What about that runty little fucker?" Mosby supposed as a buck sergeant he shouldn't be calling his troops things like that.

"Grubb? Cat's a real piece of work. Two minutes after he

meets Blind Pig he's telling him what he is gonna do and not gonna do bein' assistant gunner."

"Shit. Hope Blind Pig kills him quietly."

"That other guy—Arledge, he's the cat with the glasses—he's a clusterfuck. Went and got into a poker game with Da T'ing Dere and the supply sergeant first night. Took 'em for a hundred fifty each."

Mosby laughed.

"Yeah," Fritsche went on. "Had his own Bicycle deck. Other cats—dunno what they're like. One of 'em's named Godfrey. Black dude. Other one's Masters."

Mosby had sucked the joint down to a roach. It went out.

"Don't suppose," he began.

"We ain't smokin' no more shit tonight," Fritsche said firmly. "Big-time squad leaders gotta be strack tomorrow."

Mosby started to argue, then stumbled to his feet. He giggled, remembered his M-16, slung it, and walked off. "Hey, Mosby. You're headed the wrong way." Mosby giggled again, corrected his point of aim, and crashed through the brush toward his poncho liner and the end of one more lousy day. Tomorrow, he dimly realized, was gonna be a motherfucker.

General Sinclair, or somebody on his staff, had picked the name that Hill 134 would be known by on all documents—Camp Jeb Stuart. The name was personally picked by Sinclair not only in honor of his cavalry branch of service, but in consideration of the area he and his wife lived in. The grunts might have preferred the camp be named for the anonymous sentry who'd blown Stuart away at Yellow Horse Tavern, but they weren't consulted.

Mosby, walking with a slight dope buzz, would have been content to stand around in the sun for an hour and suck on an icy Bier LaRue until his head was straight. He and Taliaferro had already made provisions with the local kids from Song Nhanh to get beer and ice.

Instead, Mosby was what would have been called in a stateside outfit Standing Tall, listening to Sergeant First Class Roger Blake tell him what he'd done wrong. Blake's finger wagged down the hill, toward the lower point of land where Blind Pig and his new assistant gunner, Grubb, were carving out a position for the squad's M-60.

Mosby was damned glad that Fritsche had told him where

284

Blake was coming from, because he felt a lot like the way he did in basic, listening to the crooning ass-chewing.

"Sar'n't Mosby," Blake was saying. "Whyinhell'd you put the squad gun over there. The book says that you're supposed to emplace your MG so it can cover your entire line."

Mosby goggled at the man. He'd actually said emplace and MG. Christ, he thought. This wasn't AIT. Next he'd be asking about indirect fire.

"I put the gun there," Mosby explained, "because it's the only way we can get covering fire down on the road and on both sides of the slope, Sergeant."

"The M-60 machine gun can deliver accurate fire up to a thousand meters, Mosby. Is there something wrong with your gunner?"

"For Chrissake, Sergeant. That's all manual shit. Fact is you can't hit a bull in the butt with a 60 beyond three hundred meters. Our barrels are damn near shot out, the tripods have been used to pound tent stakes, and nobody's seen a fuckin' T&E mechanism in a year."

Blake took a moment to simmer properly, and Mosby continued his evaluation. He was beautiful. Somehow his jungle fatigues had something resembling a crease in them. His boots were highly polished. Mosby had the idea that with another couple of days' work Blake would have them spit-shined. Even his fuckin' belt buckle looked like it was Brasso-ed.

Mosby stared left, trying to figure out how the new platoon leader was taking all this. Second Lieutenant Wilson was listening, but with all the disinvolvement of a man watching a movie. Mosby felt a little better about things.

"Sergeant Blake," he started before Blake had time to simmer up to operating temperature, "you ain't never been in Nam, have you?"

"What works, works. Anywhere in the world."

"Bet me. Lemme give you a tip. We ain't in the fuckin' world, we're in Vietnam. And nothing works here the way it should. So maybe you oughta listen to people who've been here a while before you start jumping airborne ranger."

Mosby had just hung himself out.

"Lieutenant," Blake growled—Mosby could almost hear the words across a parade ground at Fort Leonard Wood or wherever—"I can't deal with this man. You better take him by the stacking swivel and straighten him out."

Wilson looked mildly at Blake. "Maybe Sergeant Mosby has

a point. Maybe you better check the ground before you move in.'' He half-smiled and walked away.

Blake's jowls bulged and he moved inches closer to Mosby. ''Okay. Now I know the rules. That nigger's a pussy, Mosby. So we'll deal with this man to man. You want to step back in the bushes and take our shirts off, and have a little conference?''

''Fuck you,'' Mosby said tiredly. ''Look, asshole. Before you start talking like that, get the lay of the land. You better learn nobody fights over here. Fuck around and somebody's gonna shove a grenade up your ass and frag you. This ain't basic training and you ain't John fuckin' Wayne, trickbag. You got 366 days just like the rest of us, and that's all there is.''

Blake narrowed his eyes but stepped back. He glowered at Mosby, then turned and stomped off after Lieutenant Wilson—walking a bit like Gabby Hayes—leaving Mosby to wonder what the fuck had gotten into him. It sure as shit wasn't the stripes. What the fuck, maybe it was missing Tho and not knowing what to do about the whole fuckin' mess. Maybe it was the hangover. Fuck, maybe it was the generator they'd had to abandon at Hue Duc, or even the loss of their dream club that Casey had come up with. Who the hell knew?

Mosby did not want to consider the possibility that he was now the Man, and that there suddenly were people depending on his ass. That was far too heavy for a glaring winter morning in Vietnam, where the temperature was already getting near 100 degrees and not the slightest breeze came from the river.

''Sar'n't Mosby! Sar'n't Mosby. Come here. I want you,'' came the high-pitched yell. Mosby winced, realized he would never get that beer, and headed toward the sound of First Sergeant Ramos's voice.

''So when do I get to fire the gun?'' Grubb asked, a note of belligerence in his voice. Blind Pig took two more deliberate shovelfuls out of the deepening bunker before he answered.

''On'y time you get to shoot, fucker,'' he said, ''is when Blind Pig be dead or too fucked up to half-load.''

''Goddammit, how'm I ever gonna get to do it?''

Blind Pig had just about enough. He buried the shovel in the bottom of the pit, took six deep breaths, lit a cigarette, and mopped sweat from his forehead before answering.

''Listen, you midget fuckin' honkie. You be here for one job. That be carryin' belts plus, we ever take it out, that motherfuckin' tripod. Other jobs you got is diggin' holes, keepin' belts clean, an' jumpin' when Blind Pig say frog. That be the beginning, that be the end. You want anyelse more, you gone get this shovel alongside your head. Now shut the fuck up and keep digging.''

PFC Patrick Grubb looked at Blind Pig, who somehow, even though he was in the half-dug bunker and Grubb was on the surface, managed to loom over him. Grubb brushed a dirty hand across his red hair and smeared muck across his freckled forehead.

"Somethin' else," Blind Pig finished. "Best you put your shirt back on 'fore you get sunstroke. Fuckin' Army court-martial your skinny ass you get sunburnt."

Blind Pig wasn't into confrontation, he decided. After all, for the first time in months, he actually had what he'd been sniveling about—an assistant gunner. Even if it was some mick-looking chuck from Jersey or somewhere. Blind Pig tried a joke. Of sorts.

"Grubb, best you be takin' everything slow. Nam, this gun, the sun. Just lay back, and soon's you know, you get a tan like me."

He waited for some recognition. Blind Pig was not a man who made frequent jokes. Grubb, however, stared at Blind Pig, flushed as if he thought Blind Pig was making fun of him, picked up the entrenching tool, and started spading the loose dirt into a sandbag. Blind Pig shrugged, spat against the side of the bunker, and went back to digging.

He could play any game any honkie came up with and shit fire on the side.

Noon chow brought more C-rats. According to the company cooks, they hadn't had time enough to set up the mess hall. Mosby noticed, though, that the officers were served some kind of hot food on the company's metal cafeteria dishes.

Mosby wasn't surprised. At least one thing—he'd finally gotten a bit of peace and his beer.

Correction. Half his beer, as Taliaferro suddenly shouted at him, "Hey. Mosby. You better rescue the fuckin' medic."

Mosby downed the rest of the LaRue, shouldered his rifle, and went to see what was happening now.

That shithead Casey had to go and get himself wasted and give me all this crap to deal with. For another seventy-five bucks a month, who needs it? And by the way how'd this guy Hank said was a queer manage to get himself in trouble already?

Mosby cleared the bushes at the top of the hill, looked down, and spotted his medic. That wasn't hard—he was indeed as big as Fritsche had said. A fuckin' basketball player. And he was in trouble.

For some reason the guy—Mosby thought his name was Geiger, or something like that—had wandered outside the single roll of concertina wire that marked the Fifteenth's outer perimeter at the base of the hill, a roll that would soon be supplemented with dozens more rolls of wire, mines, Claymores, foo-glass containers and tripflares.

He was surrounded by at least fifty kids—Mosby found a moment to wonder where all these goddamned kids came from way out here in the boonies—and resembled a statue.

Mosby plodded down the hill toward him, still wondering about his own problems. Christ, all he had to do was tell Ramos he didn't want to be a sergeant, and Da T'ing Dere'd be happy to bust him back to a Speedy Four. And then, David? Then they turn the squad over to somebody else.

Like who? Taliaferro? He's got time in grade. No way. Not even Ramos is that dumb. Fritsche's too damned bright to take the job, and Blind Pig'd kill anybody who tried to take him off that gun. So they'd bring in somebody else, some cherrytrooper Blake would go through like a dose of salts. Fuck me, Mosby realized. All these jerks need me. Not that they're ever gonna tell me or realize it. Shit, all of a sudden I'm just the fuckin' sergeant to them. Mosby was starting to get the impression there was no justice in the world as he hit the base of the hill and advanced on his medic. Geiger was standing, dripping kids. One little boy had his helmet on his own head, another had Geiger's aid bag slung over one shoulder, and half a dozen more were searching through his pockets.

Mosby eyeballed the man. Definitely a moose. Looked like somebody who ought to be playing football, not basketball. Christ, the guy's got shoulders you could land a Huey on. Mosby suddenly realized whom the guy looked like. Jeff fuckin' Chandler. All he needed was a headband and a grunt that white-eye speaks with forking tongue and he'd be perfect. Great. That's just what I need, a fruit who happens to look like a movie star. Then Mosby realized that (A) he had no idea if Fritsche was right and (B) what the fuck did he care so long as the guy knew how to be a proper chancre mechanic.

After all, growing up in Portland and spending a lot of time on the docks, Mosby was not inexperienced with homosexuals. A couple or three had made passes at him, and Mosby had found, contrary to what the whispers were in high school, that once he said no they left him alone.

Enough of that shit. There was also a C factor—Geiger didn't seem even vaguely aware that Mosby was standing five feet away from him.

"Who the fuck do you think you are, Saint Francis?" Mosby managed. Beat . . . beat . . . beat and Geiger turned his head—the beatific smile still wreathing his face—to recognize Mosby.

"Afternoon, Sergeant," he said cordially. He had a voice like that guy on the radio—oh yeah. Orson Welles. *The Third Man.* "Thought I'd come down here and see what these kids needed."

He beamed around, and Mosby felt slightly like either kneeling for the blessing or smacking Geiger with his rifle butt. He tried the military median.

"Geiger, I'm your squad leader. You can call me Dave." Geiger extended a hand, and they shook. Mosby suddenly realized, with some astonishment, that he hadn't shaken hands with anybody since . . . hell, since he joined the Army as best he could remember.

"My name's Steve," came the bass voice.

"Right . . . uh . . . the perimeter's off limits, Steve. And you better tell the kids to didi-mau outa here, because we're gonna be putting up some shit that could ruin their whole fuckin' lives if they keep hanging around."

No registration.

"Anyway," Mosby said. "You better get up to the CP, and figure out where you're gonna hooch. Get your shit."

Geiger bobbed his head obediently and collected his gear from the kids, trading candy bars—PX candy bars, not the shit in C-rations, Mosby noticed—and then patting the children on their way. "Where's your weapon?"

Geiger turned a look on Mosby full of paternal sorrow. "Didn't Lieutenant Wilson tell you? I'm a conscientious objector."

"Wilson didn't tell me shit," Mosby said, as he started back up the hill. "Where you from, Doc?"

"Iowa. But I was living in San Francisco when my draft board caught up with me."

"Frisco? Nice town."

"It is. Marvelous people. I had this absolutely wonderful apartment near the end of Market. My roommate and I had the decorations perfect when Mr. Johnson decided I was entirely too happy."

Mosby grunted. Man, they shake the Army by the heels and everybody who ain't nailed down tight slides all the way to Vietnam.

Which made him wonder why he himself was in-country and kept him silent for the rest of the walk.

Phan Xuan Cung decided that the vacation was over. It was time to go.

In a normal, Western army his survival of the destruction of his unit, and making his way solo through kilometers of hostile territory, would have been received with medals. And after the award ceremony Cung would have been given a copious amount of leave and then reassigned as training cadre to a new unit.

But the National Liberation Front, in common with all Soviet-style units, used a man to the last. Cung's leave had comprised three days in one of the Octopus's camps. He conceded that the rear cadre had gone to a great deal of trouble to find out his favorite foods and drink, and provided them. Cung had even been allowed to drink himself into insensibility on two of those nights on the rarely seen whiskey. And then a commissar had informed Cung that duty called.

Fortunately for Cung, he was aware that Marxist sentiment is allowed only after the battle is won. Also fortunately, three generations of combat made him unaware that things could be handled differently. And finally the assignment piqued both his humor and his pride.

He was assigned three bo-dois—North Vietnamese privates from the 302d—under his command. Soldiers from their reconnaissance unit. Cung could preen slightly—it was a rare honor.

Cung, being a realist, knew there was little to gain in mourning the past. The Phu Loi Battalion was as if it had never existed. Perhaps later the Central Committee would re-form the unit and tell a new group of willing soldiers the history. Or perhaps not. The struggle went on.

Cung's orders were simple—to investigate the new American presence on what was named, on the American map he had been given, Hill 134.

The NVA major who had given him his orders and the map had needlessly instructed Cung on its value—Cung knew. Of all the patrols he had led, this was the first time he had been given anything more than a rough sketch, or worse yet a to-be-memorized drawing in the sand before he went out. Even better were the rations provided—tinned food and freshly cooked rice. Cung knew this assignment was most important.

For the past few weeks Cung and his soldiers had crouched

in a hide just across the Song Nhanh River from the hill and watched the imperialist presence build.

The hide had been most carefully constructed—it was centered in a bamboo clump centered on a small rise barely 150 meters from the bridge where Highway 45L crossed the river. The regional forces had tunneled into the clump and built a two-level shelter, whose upper level had observation windows, cleverly reinforced with bamboo for a roof and to line the observation slits.

But the stroke of genius, Cung thought, was whoever had the brains to then cut down half the bamboo atop the clump and finally to shroud the entire clump with rusty barbed wire—exactly as if that clump had been used by maybe ARVN forces in the past and then been abandoned.

The first American patrol to work the area had slashed its way through the bamboo to stand atop the observation post, Cung and his men huddled five feet below trying not to laugh, as the Americans crashed back out like so many drunken buffalo. Thereafter, the clump was ignored by subsequent patrols—the imperialists must have reasoned that there was no way anyone could or would want to occupy such a spot.

Cung used his time well. He showed the North Vietnamese soldiers exactly how the imperialists established themselves. How they considered that their machines could replace the vigilance of man. And how deadly those machines could be, given a moment's inattention by a stalking force.

He also found time to mourn slightly the death of the only real home he had known. And more rationally that there was no way to prepare the meals freshly each day. He fondly thought of the possibilities if only there were some impressionable young quy chanh had been assigned to them, a quy chanh with smooth skin, wide eyes, and pert breasts, who would be interested in hearing the heroic story of the death struggle of her elder brothers in the Phu Loi Battalion and one who perhaps might, once darkness fell, might have her own feelings about a certain nondoctrinal willingness to sacrifice for the Revolution . . .

But the dreams had never happened. Now it was time to leave. At nightfall Cung and his men withdrew from the hole, taking all their discarded trash and the plastic American bags they had defecated into with them. Even if the hide were discovered, there would be no way of telling that it had been used in the last year.

Now there was only one task, and Cung, skilled scout that he was, knew it would be easy. To traverse, undiscovered, the kilometers between Hill 134 and the Octopus. He wondered, as he crept along the paddy banks, what that senior NVA general would make of his report.

CHAPTER THIRTY-EIGHT

HILL 134

Vo Le Duan responded quickly. The decision was obvious, since there were few options available to him. They were: to ignore the imperialist presence below Song Nhanh (an impossibility); to attempt to wipe them out (equally impossible); or to create what Duan called "fortress-think," just as he had done, on a far smaller scale, years before to that Foreign Legion unit.

The last seemed his only possibility.

Sapper Ngo Dinh Cuu gifted his twelve men at full darkness. The gifts were a ball of sugared rice and a two-inch square of smoked fish, plus the instructions they were to be eaten immediately. He had disobeyed policy and let the men gather around him, even though he knew one mortar round would destroy the entire squad. But Cuu knew that, once a soldier learns his SOP, it is made to be broken.

He had told them how proud he was, and how he would be honored to have them part of his own unit. He felt it was only a moderate lie and justified under the circumstances. As a matter of fact, Cuu felt rather proud of himself. He had been seconded from Battalion N-10 only three months ago to help the Song Nhanh committee ensure their own sappers were as skilled and capable as the N-10 unit.

Cuu's comrades had roared at the impossibility of his task. Song Nhanh? Such a man would prepare a fuse that would give him time for a nap before it went off. Cuu had smiled, frostily, then reminded his comrades that perhaps Cuu himself came from Song Nhanh. Their jokes ended uncomfortably. Perhaps a political officer had overheard what Cuu said, because when he was given a squad, after trekking into the Octopus, no political officer had been assigned to ensure that he was properly indoctrinating the new sappers.

Cuu felt that he had borne up under the strain well. To be reassigned from the best anti-imperialist unit in South Vietnam and given a short amount of time to build a new elite was preposterous. Because N-10 was as good as it thought itself. Stationed both inside and outside Saigon, with their operations and intelligence officers in the city itself, N-10 specialized in impossible and high-value missions. They were proud that their men and women had destroyed targets such as nightclubs that catered to the imperialists and, as well, imperialist officers' barracks.

Sappers were possibly the most skilled soldiers produced on either side in Vietnam. The popular concept was of drug-crazed kamikazes carrying satchel charges, kamikazes who sought nothing more than death itself. They were high-casualty units, but no more so than American formations such as SOG or Marine Recon.

The stories seemed based on that block the American military had always had—that the enemy cannot be as motivated and dedicated as they are. Perhaps to believe otherwise would require an American to consider that justice is not always on his side.

Cuu was very proud of being a sapper, and equally proud that his team of fifteen men had suffered less than four casualties within the past six months. Pride was an emotion very new to Cuu. Fear, shame and hatred were far more familiar to him, emotions battered into him by the fathers and their lay brothers.

Ngo Dinh Cuu was an orphan, taken in from the streets by the kindly priests of Duc Lap. He wondered, as he grew older, why he had been taken in—the priests seemed unbothered by and uninterested in other children he saw starving on the streets of the village when he was permitted outside the orphanage.

Cuu's first explanation was that he must have come from a wealthy or powerful family. Perhaps his father was a famous soldier who would return some day and rescue him. Cuu might have told one of his friends of this constantly varying dream, had not three or four of them told him that they also came from monied families.

Cuu figured that there couldn't be that many rightful heirs to Bao Dai's throne, not in one orphanage. Of course, none of the priests told him of his origins. They were more interested in the cleanliness of his ears, the extent of his devotions, and how hard he worked when they used him as contract labor with the local farmers.

Cuu listened to their words about gentility and peace on earth carefully. He thought he understood what was wrong, why the fathers were so quick with their bamboo canes, why they were so fat and he and the other children were so skinny, why the statue of Mother Mary had gold on it and on Jesus' birthday he and the other children spent the day praying and fasting.

The orphanage had been set up by the French. Then, when they left, their underlings had taken over. Cuu was positive that, one day, the French fathers would return, take those canes away from their flunkies, and use them on the priests.

Second shattered dream.

The third, developed when Cuu was fourteen, was that the Americans would change things. The priests were very fond of showing the children pictures in tattered American magazines, pictures that showed happy and fat children. Cuu wanted more than anything to one day have so much food on the table that he could push it away.

In 1965, he saw his first Americans. They arrived in a jeep. One, he was surprised to see, was dark brown. He drove the vehicle. The second man was tall, dignified and gray-headed. He wore, on his shirt lapels, a cross. Now, Cuu knew, things would change.

This dignified man was more than capable of whipping all the fat-asses in sight. Perhaps the brown man would hold them. Instead, the tall American ate with the priests, drinking, Cuu disapproved, entirely too much of the priests' wine. Then he gave them piasters, got back in his jeep, and drove away.

Cuu clung to the hope that those piasters would improve the food. Thus died his last myth.

At that point, Cuu discovered the first real way out. Literally. Behind the orphanage, where the dike path went toward the or-phanage's fields, there was a gap in the barbed wire. From there, it was only 200 yards to the outskirts of the village. And since going to the village was condemned by the fathers, it must be good, Cuu reasoned.

No one bothered the skinny teen-ager who wandered the dark streets after curfew. Cuu was looking. If nothing was happening on the streets except an occasional drunken soldier or whore, the secrets must lie in the huts themselves. Before he got clubbed for being a peeping Tom, Cuu was lucky enough to encounter the Viet Cong. The word had been very clear from the fathers. Something was going to happen that night, something evil in the village. It was most important that all of the children were pres-ent, and the fathers would spend the night making sure they were in their floor-spread blankets.

Cuu giggled at that—the priest in charge of their room could not stay awake beyond ten o'clock. His snores had barely begun when Cuu was headed for the fence.

The Evil was a tuyen van giao—agit-prop—team. Cuu was entranced. The team leader explained very clearly what was wrong with life. And it made sense. Of course it made sense for those who were fat to keep people like him skinny, so they would work harder.

Cuu thought that if he had been nothing but fat his whole life he wouldn't care less about anyone else. And of course the French were gone, and of course the Americans had not changed anything. For the first time he saw the truth, that all over the world the fat would never want change.

It was, the team chief clarified, very well set up, from the landlords who never let the peasants have a chance to breathe free, to the government who took the young men for the army, to the church who taught people they should be honored to be exploited.

The agit-prop team leader was very tired, as was his speech. He stared out over the torches onto the blank faces of the peasants. He and his team members had already met with the hamlet's cell members, building their morale and trying to convince them that they were as important to the Party's grinding juggernaut as Ho Chi Minh. After that, there came The Speech, to be followed by their playlet. Following that, the team leader would select four volunteers to join the struggle.

He had heard the elderly joke about the men sent to a province committee with a note: Please find six wildly enthusiastic fighters against imperialism and for freedom. Please return the ropes.

He was somewhat shocked when the skinny boy stood in the middle of the crowd and shouted out his desire to join the fight. To be a fighter against the imperialists and their puppets. He looked at one of the guards, who was also goggling. Then he promised himself a beer as reward

Cuu's volunteering was the spark. Five other young men from the village also volunteered. The agit-prop team then took advantage of the village cell's seldom-accepted hospitality and got thoroughly drunk before they moved on.

Cuu was a sponge. Marxism, to him, explained the world as thoroughly as Catholicism, but without needing invisible gods or virgin births. Of course, he never considered whether the inevitability of class struggle and the dictatorship of the proletariat weren't gods just as invisible. For him it was enough to belong.

Ngo Dinh Cuu was never sullied with the training methods used on the normal Viet Cong "volunteers." Instead, he was immediately asked if he cared to volunteer for a sapper battalion. The cadreman who asked him seemed truly interested. This was not like being pressured to be an altar boy by a brother who fancied his buttocks.

There were ten others in his training class. The first stage of training lasted a month. He and his fellows—of both sexes—learned how to use a knife. A grenade. A length of sharpened bamboo. Some of them stood guard while others learned to creep past them without discovery. And endlessly they learned more of the truth, the truth of how history was moving inexorably toward the victory of communism.

They ate well. During that first month there was only one thing missing. Sleep. Cuu would be yanked awake after one hour's sleep and then told to walk a guard post. Or to crawl through a barbed-wire fence without disturbing its intrusion devices. Then he would be given half an hour's sleep, pulled to his feet again, and queried on the correct interpretation of why the Trung sisters were not able to free their country.

Cuu won praise and the chance for a full night's sleep by remembering Christ's principle about a rich man entering the Kingdom of Heaven, and pointing out that the Trung sisters were aristocrats and, while the people hated the Chinese, they recognized they would be merely trading a foreign whip for a native one.

Eight of them survived that month—the other two were regretfully sent to a main-line force and told never to forget they were still fortunate in having been considered as prospective sappers.

The next few weeks were spent learning the tools. The sapper units were armed with AKs, B-40 rocket launchers and light mortars. But their main weapons were explosives. By the time that block of instruction ended, Cuu and his fellows could identify and disarm any explosive used in Vietnam from artillery duds to land mines; modify those devices for their own purposes; and set them off using anything from the most sophisticated imperialist fusing to devices as simple as tin cans or bamboo spikes.

Their classroom was a jungle clearing, their training aids were live explosives. Only one man died, when he attempted to force a rusted primer from a mine and set it off. The Viet Cong picked their recruits for the sapper units very carefully.

Emotionally, Cuu might have welcomed any home that would have been offered. But he knew he had made the correct choice after the death of his classmate, when one of the instructors stood that night and said that the death was his fault, and that he, the instructor, was no longer qualified to be a sapper. Catch a priest, Cuu thought, ever saying that a man's fall into sin was the fault of that priest.

The graduation exercise was the infiltration into an American supply base and the theft of fifty kilos of unwatched explosive. The imperialist guards were never aware their perimeter had been broken into.

Cuu felt himself able to handle any task the Central Committee could give him. He was somewhat shaken, after being assigned to the N-10 battalion, to discover that he still had much to learn. How to reconnoiter before a mission. How to build a model of that target, either in miniature or full-size. Each man knew exactly his post and his goal.

Cuu had survived a full year with the battalion, before being detached and sent to Song Nhanh. Now he, and the other experienced sappers assigned to Song Nhanh, had almost 100 men trained, about half the strength of a full-manned sapper unit.

He felt honored that his unit had been the first to be told that they were not merely part of an NLF buildup in the province, but that the long-promised General Offensive was soon to occur. But the first task, the task that Cuu had prepared himself for, was the attack on the new American positions.

While he recognized the probability of death, he vaguely hoped that he would see the day of the offensive. Perhaps, he thought, if his new unit did well enough, he would be permitted to rejoin his parent unit in time for the fall of Saigon.

But before that, he sternly redirected his mind, there was this hill and these invaders to deal with. At dusk, he had moved across the paddies 2,000 meters north of Guardian Hill—Camp Stuart—Hill 134, keeping his men below the dike. None of them had sworn as they hunched through the thigh-deep mud, hunched below the weight of the explosives and weapons.

Bamboo rafts had been previously prepared by village fighters and hidden in the rushes at the water's edge. His sapper squad had pushed their way across the river four at a time, their satchel packs tied to the rafts.

The road had been crossed crawling. Cuu could have sent his men across in one line, taking the chances on inattention. But crawling, no matter whether the imperialists had night-vision devices or not, made it very unlikely they would be seen.

Once across Highway 45L, only a hundred meters separated them from a tree line that they used as cover to move toward the American's western perimeter. At the final resting position, Cuu had given out the presents. There were four hours until dawn.

His men would move into position, just in front of the perimeter, before the sun rose, and disappear. Other sappers were doing the same. During the next day, three companies of mainline Viet Cong would take position in the tree line Cuu's men had left. At dark, they would move in.

Cuu was grateful that the lazy Americans had not prepared the perimeter as they should. There was enough dead ground in front of the hill to hide a thousand men.

He crept down the rim of the dried paddy, moving closer toward the perimeter. Red/yellow flared ahead of him, and Cuu smiled. Four guns, just as he had seen. Their destruction would be an excellent graduation for the new sappers.

Once Mosby had realized that he was, until hit or busted, the Man, the next problem became how to break in his new virgins.

Since the Fifteenth's new position appeared to be as safe as a rear echelon, the answer was night patrols. Every American unit in Vietnam, regardless of the area they were based in, ran patrols or observation posts at night. They went outside the perimeter at nightfall, lurked somewhere until dawn, and then returned. Generally, nothing happened. But these patrols were a way to learn your moves.

Mosby had thought—okay, if you're gonna be one, be a big red one. And so he started volunteering his squad for night OPs, beyond the wire. Each night, either Fritsche, Blind Pig or himself would take out a group of the new guys, stay out all night, let them get terrified, and then come back in the morning.

What would keep David Mosby alive this night is that, once he'd decided to run these patrols, he hadn't made them into a walk-through.

The plan was to move out beyond the perimeter sometime after nightfall, travel a certain number of meters either on a compass direction or toward an observable point. The patrol would hold in place until daylight, then return to their positions. Taliaferro, of course, had complained because Mosby wouldn't let him run any of the OPs. Mosby, short on sleep even though he pulled rank and took first and last watches, told him to fuck off. The last thing he needed was a Taliaferro-indoctrinated virgin.

He'd run through his program with the new troopies three times for each man. Tonight, he was taking out Diaz and Arledge. In the dying light, they sat glumly atop Mosby's bunker. They'd followed orders and had left their steel pots behind, smeared cammie cream on their faces, and removed everything from their web gear except two canteens, three magazine pouches, and six grenades. Their rifle slings were also left behind. Mosby had also told them what to bring along in the way of goodies—candy, PX peanuts, C-rat date nut bars and chewing gum. No cigarettes, no matches.

Mosby was crouched behind a line bunker, staring out at the rice paddies, tree line, river and highway in front of them, trying to figure out a new way to go. Suppose, he figured, we cross the river—Mosby had already learned where the waist-deep fords were—and head for that little copse of brush. Move maybe fifty meters north of those bushes, and set up along the paddy dike. That didn't sound bad—in fact, it got a flicker from Mosby. Of course there weren't any VC out there, but just maybe they could nail a sniper who would be dumb enough to head for that copse.

Mosby grinned—he was getting good at kidding himself to keep boredom away. He made a final compass sight, put his boonie hat back on, and started for his bunker to pick up Diaz and Arledge. He found three people instead of two. The other man was his new platoon commander, Wilson. Mosby saw that Wilson was wearing a soft cap, had an M-16 instead of his .45, and wore webbing. Trouble.

"Uhh, Sergeant?"

"Yessir?"

"Umh, Captain Edmunds said you were taking out OPs."

"Yessir. I've got a whole shitpot load of new guys, sir. Is there anything wrong with that?"

"No, no. I, uh, just wondered if I could go out with you."

Mosby tried to be diplomatic. "Sir, no offense and all, but I think if they went out under you they'd get confused. Sir."

"Mosby," Wilson said, "I'm trying to tell you I'm a goddamned cherrytroop like they are. I'm Private Wilson."

Yessir. Sure, sir. Wanna bet, sir.

"Sorry I got it wrong, sir."

"The name is Wilson."

Ho. Ho.

"Hang on a second. Lemme tell Arledge and Diaz what's the hot skinny."

Wilson waited and pretended not to hear Mosby's instructions to the other two. "Six is gonna go out with us. Gotta tell you, that means no fucking up. This is strack time. Don't blow it."

Mosby walked back to Wilson. "Joe and Arledge're glad to have you. By the way. You got second watch."

Wilson's reaction was concealed by the now-total darkness. And Mosby did not give a shit. After a tour-and-a-half, he'd seen second johns come and go. Quickly. Wilson, whatever he did or was, would not be around long enough to matter. Either he'd get wasted or he'd get transferred up. Either way, it didn't matter.

"Gather around, people." Mosby wondered what Casey would think of his briefing. Then he wondered if Casey was alive, a POW or what. There was a brief flicker of pain over Tho. Something else unknown, that Mosby was starting to think would never be finalized.

"We're gonna go out the wire out there. Just in front of Fritsche's hole. There's a lift-out chunk of the concertina. Wilson, you take rear. I'll be on point. After we're through, you put the wire back. Only hook up one piece of baling wire.

"I want you guys down outside the wire. We'll wait there until I say go. Then we go straight for the water. You see that big fuckin' clump of bushes out there? Yeah?"

Mumbles.

"Arledge, goddammit, did you see it? Fuckin' great. You follow Diaz. Okay. The water's only about waist-deep. We go straight across. Diaz, you and me go either side on top the bank. From there, we're gonna hook over toward the road, until we're past that bunch of bushes. Then we're gonna run back toward the trees. We'll set up along a dike.

"The position's gonna be about halfway down that dike. I don't want anybody to stick his fuckin' head over the dike. Try to get your asses out of the water.

"You got it?"

Mosby assumed nods in the darkness.

"Okay. Here's the bit. I take first watch. That's till midnight. Lieu—sorry. Wilson, you take it from midnight to two. Joe, you and Arledge got it from two to four. Then wake me up. You got it?"

Arledge protested. He was pissed that Mosby didn't trust him enough for him to have his own watch. Mosby couldn't believe it. There was an answer—several nights earlier, Mosby had caught Arledge stone-ass asleep when he was supposed to be standing guard. All he'd done was hit him as hard as possible with a steel pot.

What the fuck did Arledge think the comeback would be? There was a fuckin' officer standing there, and if Mosby said what he wanted to, Arledge would get at least an Article 15 and maybe head for Long Binh Jail.

"Shut the fuck up," Mosby found as his diplomatic response. "Diaz, you take the radio. We're gonna be Whirlaway Deuce Oscar Poppa. Citation Deuce is the monitor. Check-in is once an hour. We're gonna use click code. You two clowns remember that? 'Kay. It's darker'n a welldigger's ass. Let's move.''

Wilson followed the other three away from Mosby's hole. He was trying to remember click code. Oh yes. You keyed the transmit button on the PRC-25's mike once to respond to a call. Twice meant you were okay. Three clicks meant . . . you needed help? Wasn't there something else?

Ahead of him, Mosby almost started laughing at himself. That cheap shit really sounded like he knew what he was doing. But howcum none of it sounded like it came from Audie Murphy?

The four dim figures stopped at the wire. There was a subdued grate-KLACK-snick. Wilson jumped, then loaded his own weapon and put the safety on. They moved through the wire. Wilson stopped, clear of the three-tiered concertina roll, and put the wire coil back in position. He tore his finger on a barb before he got the baling wire hook relocated properly.

The figures were almost lost in darkness in front of him. Hurrying to catch up, he nearly slammed into Arledge, stopped where the bank went down to the river.

Okay, man. Do it right. Rifle up, over your head, keep your feet apart, and dammit, I forgot to take out Marjorie's letter, and you're up to your ass in brown water, Lieutenant, a little too late to worry about it. Drip up out of the river, squelch and slide through the mud, following Arledge, then crouching, and Diaz and Mosby moved out from the bank top. Why that Diaz? Why not me? I am an officer. That Mosby is playing games.

Even more awful. All that stuff that Mosby rattled off. Mr. Wilson, you don't even know what half of it means. How come Mosby knows exactly where to go? I should have asked him if he ran an azimuth. And what it was. Not that it would have done any good—it's too damned dark to read a compass anyway.

This time Wilson *did* slam into Arledge, who whined inarticulately. There was a glower of blackness to their right, and Wilson guessed it was the clump of brush.

They moved on, splashing on through the paddy. Wilson figured out that if he bent over, he could see the outline of the others in front of him. This time, when Mosby brought the patrol to a halt, he was ready. He followed Arledge as they crawled halfway up the paddy dike that sat two feet above the paddy's waterline.

Suddenly Mosby was beside him. He held his illuminated watch dial in front of Wilson's face. He moved a mucky finger over the dial, then put both hands together, Dürer's praying hands, except to the side. Sleep now. Wilson nodded. Mosby swished through the water back to Diaz.

Very quietly:

"Citation Deuce, Citation Deuce, this is Whirlaway Deuce Oscar Poppa. In position. Out."

And the long night began.

Diaz seemed to become a corpse. Arledge started a low, burbling snore. Wilson knew he should be asleep, but there was simply too much happening. He was actually beyond American lines, in a combat zone, for the first time. He didn't identify the feeling, but he was somewhat disappointed. So far, all it was was like what he'd seen and done back in Infantry Branch Training. More skillful, with less bullshit and more mud, but still just like a training exercise.

Wilson's mind was caught up in the smell of the shit-fertilized paddies, the worry about leeches finding their way toward his cock, the cold from his water-soaked fatigues, the very slightly pebbly plastic of the M-16's stock in his right hand, the round bulk of a grenade digging into his stomach on his left side, and the amazement that lying here on this tiny piece of mud he could honestly feel the whirl of the stars above him.

But more than that was the wonderment of being in a rice paddy in Vietnam at all.

This was not the way the world had been planned.

Jeff Wilson's parents were people who, in the best sense, planned their lives. Of course there was inequity. An inequity that was unlikely to change in their lifetime. Of course there had been Lincoln, the Emancipation Proclamation, W.E.B. Dubois and the Niagara Movement, and then the NAACP. That was one thing, and both the Wilsons gave as they could. These goals would happen eventually, probably not in their lifetime. And so they provided for themselves. They both recognized that the first part of America that would provide advancement for blacks would be government service. For Wilson's father, that meant he became a heating engineer for the City of Chicago. His wife taught grammar school.

They were certainly middle-class and movers in the black community. For the next generation, their son, another jump would be made. Jeff Wilson would be a lawyer.

College costs a great deal of money, especially since Wilson wanted his son to attend the best school affordable. Since Jeff had no major athletic skills, a way to help pay was ROTC. The plan the three of them had was that Jeff would take Reserve Officer's Training for his four years of college. That would pay

302

off in his senior year, when he would begin drawing a salary as a future officer of the United States Army. From there, the plan went, Jeff would apply for law school.

On graduation from law school, he would do paybacks to the Army and serve a couple of years as a junior man with the Staff Judge Advocate's Corps. He would gain trial experience and hopefully make some good connections for after the service.

The problem was that Jeff Wilson was not particularly bright and, worse, not quick. He was the student who ground the books for two hours per one hour of classroom instruction, receiving a B— for his labors.

He graduated from the University of Chicago in the lower middle of his class. And then failed his law school entrance exam. Perhaps, in other days, he could have restudied under a tutor, reapplied, and made it. But not in 1967.

Jeffrey Wilson became a second lieutenant, United States Army. The pressing need for officers in 1967 was in the infantry. Wilson felt that he was probably competent to run thirty-three or so men in peacetime, probably competent to manage a small office, probably competent to do whatever job someone gave him. And goddammit, goddammit, goddammit, here he was stuck in this stinking jungle worried—not scared, worried—and the only role model that came to him was Sidney Poitier being disgruntled and refusing to drive a truck for Jeff Chandler.

And by the way, what the hell did *Red Ball Express* have to do with him being up to his balls in a rice paddy listening to some kid sergeant who probably had a great future as a welfare hippie telling him what to do.

Wilson was moving from worry through disgruntlement to anger when the first rocket exploded—behind him, within the perimeter that was the only part of this new and strange world he thought of as being safe.

Ngo Dinh Cuu had never heard, but would have appreciated, the American infantry demi-slogan of "Take the high ground."

He prized the imperialists' abilities to scout their area and then to build fighting positions to command every inch of that area. Dead ground—ground that could not be seen from the base area—would have a machine-gun post set up above it. The post would be heavily sandbagged and even elevated so that under any circumstances the soldiers within would be able to open fire on that particular section of the perimeter.

This also meant that those posts were easily recognizable from a distance. Also merely the existence of those posts meant the Americans would be complacent.

They never bothered, Cuu knew, to move outside their perimeter and look at their line from the point of view of a prospective attacker. Nor would they send their soldiers against that perimeter as if they were attackers.

Cuu had never heard of the Siegfried or Maginot lines, or the seaward-aiming guns of Singapore, but if he had he would have understood the continuity of stupidity.

The sapper had spent the day's broil curled around a brush heap, ten meters in front of the imperialist wire and thirty meters from that machine-gun bunker. He kept his mind in a controlled drift: No, he could not sleep, but neither should he be alert and awake. Cuu had defecated just before dawn, and the stink bothered him all that day, almost as much as the stink of the rotting cans of food the Americans had hurled over their perimeter. Had he been an American officer, Cuu would have forbidden that practice.

He watched a lizard scavenge one can, and then the lizard crawled over his own body. The lizard's tongue licked once at the sweat on Cuu's skin, then crawled on, without alarm. The sapper could as easily have lain on an anthill for those hours, mind floating, body nonexistent.

As night came, the problem was bringing himself from that drift, back to reality. Cuu knew the Americans would expect to be attacked—if they expected anything—just at dark, at 0300 in the morning, or at dawn. Mechanical minds. Cuu was surprised, each time he killed an imperialist, that their bodies did not contain gears and wheels like their aircraft.

Ten o'clock. The Americans would be changing their guard. The old guards would be preparing for sleep, and the new soldiers would either be half awake or possibly drunk. There would be people moving back and forth from the sleeping positions to the bunkers. Ten minutes before, Cuu had heard the slight rustle as one of his teammates bolted together the last two pipes on the bangalore torpedo and slid it forward, under the concertina wire.

The attack would be signaled by one of Cuu's comrades. He and another soldier had circled around the American camp and were now waiting for the hour. When the second hand crossed, Cuu's friend was to fire one American five-starred flare. This would be visible to the Viet Cong forces half-encircling the American perimeter.

The hand of Cuu's watch swept forward. He came to his knees.

Against policy and probably orders, Cuu was overly armed for his task. Slung around his neck was his satchel charge—almost twenty kilos of explosive. The explosive could be detonated either by an instantly set-off pull fuse, or by a time pencil. Cuu, not suicidal, had wired the pull fuse so that it would require his full force to yank it free. Comrades of his had become instant heroes of the revolution by leaving that pull fuse dangling, only to catch it in their crawl toward the attack or on the enemy's perimeter barbed wire.

Cuu's second weapon was a folding-stock AK-47. His third weapon was an RPG-7. This, the successor to the B-40 (RPG-2), was newly arrived for the Viet Cong. If he followed policy and orders, Cuu would have used it as his sole weapon for the assault. But he was never comfortable with the idea of carrying a single-shot weapon—a weapon that would take at least five seconds to reload. Cuu would prefer not to die while attempting to fit a tiny notch to a percussion cap.

The cardboard propellant cylinder was already attached to the grenade itself, and the grenade fitted into the RPG's long tube. At darkness, he had removed the nosecap and pulled the safety wire. Cuu now gazed through the sight at the bunker across the wire in front of him. Dim mutters. Then a light flared, outlining the bunker's rectangular firing port. Cuu corrected his aim. And then the bunker was outlined, as the flare exploded to the south. Cuu two-fingered the trigger. The rocket exploded out, back blast and flame double-spearing, and Cuu was then twice night-blind as the bangalore tore through the concertina wire.

Cuu came up and clambered through the gap in the wire. He saw flames leap and explode from the American bunker. Very good indeed, as his slung AK came into firing position, and he went up the hill into the Fifteenth's position, feeling the others behind him, knowing that other liberation fighters were coming across the paddy he had crossed the night before.

Now for the guns. There was a white glare of an undervest and face in front of him, hands pleading toward him. Cuu triggered two rounds into the middle of the white and it went away.

Ten . . . fifty paces forward, beyond the American front-line positions. Cuu veered right, toward the line. He let go his rifle and pulled two grenades from his side pouch. Pulled the cord on the first, counted two, and pitched it toward the piled sand-bags—the source of the tracer fire. Counted twice more, then sent a second grenade in the same direction. Without waiting to see if his grenades were effective, Cuu went forward.

The American guns were firing flares overhead. Cuu was

grateful for the illumination, even though he did not need it. There was the dark mouth of a bunker, and another grenade went into it. Cuu pressed on, the satchel charge dragging on the ground, the walls of sandbags ahead of him. Another pinpoint of flame, and Cuu went sideways, into the shelter of:

Sandbags. Bullets pierced the bags in front of him. Shelter.

Cuu crept around the edge of the sandbagged wall. He was very close to the gun he had chosen. Cuu took the satchel charge from his neck. He began to unwire the instant pull fuse, then realized what his arm was touching. Wood. He investigated, night-blind. More boxes. He hefted one. Full.

Evaluation. Cuu was behind a low, three-side-sandbagged wall, behind which were those boxes. Ammunition for the guns. Cuu's fingers found the time pencil, and he crushed it. On his knees, he came out from behind the 105mm cannons' ammo dump, then was up, and crouched and running. There were others around him, racing in every direction. A green tracer—a friend, and then a yawning hole.

Cuu threw himself into it just as the satchel charge went up. Flame mushroomed, and a typhoon came down the hill and Cuu realized he was not the only one in this hole. Someone muttering, crying, in an unknown language. Cuu ignored him for the moment and blinked, trying to see again as the flame-front became a fire.

Cuu could see two of the guns, one on its side, the other with its barrel pointed directly upward. Cuu expended one magazine toward the guns, reloaded, and vaulted out of the hole. His hearing was returning. This man's whining was an annoyance, for some reason, and his finger crooked on the trigger and the crying was gone.

He retreated back toward the wire. At the bunker he'd destroyed, Cuu again took up a firing position. Counting, ready to cover the retreat of those comrades who were able to withdraw.

Two hundred . . . two hundred and ten . . . and Cuu went back through the wire. There were two black-clad bodies next to the passage. There would be two more new men to train in his squad before the General Offensive.

It was a very long night for David Mosby.

The slopes had either ignored or missed his OP. That left only two other people trying to kill him—plus his own unit.

The first one had been Arledge, who when he realized the perimeter was getting hit had wanted to run for cover. Straight

306

back toward the wire. Diaz had landed on his chest and cold-cocked him. Then Wilson had wanted to play officer. Mosby had told him to shut the fuck up.

The patrol lay there, listening to shots, screams and explosions. Whatever was going on back up the hill Mosby didn't want any part of. Eventually the shooting and the screaming let up.

Mosby was quite pleased that the zips hadn't bothered to scoop him up as either an appetizer or as dessert.

Then the U.S. Army decided to try to kill him. Citation Deuce started calling around, trying to find out how many of the battalion's OPs had been nailed. Wilson wanted to answer. Mosby shut the Prick-25 off. They weren't going in before full light. Anybody left alive inside the perimeter would ice anything that moved. Wilson seemed to understand, and was quite ready to lie in a big, dead pile until the situation sorted out.

After that, Mosby got Spooky. The gunship growled over-head, flares turning night into photo-glare.

"Don't even fuckin' move," Mosby said. The four men lay together, heads only a few feet apart. "They got flares, they got starlight scopes, and anything out here's gonna be a gook to them."

Arledge started bawling—but since he did it quietly Mosby left him alone.

Spooky fired a few million rounds into the tree line, just for General Principles. By then the Viet Cong were long gone. All that was left between them and going back up the hill was the mortar H&I fire dumped outside the perimeter, and the fact that, for the rest of the night, everybody on the hill shot at every shadow that breathed hard.

The night took only half of Mosby's life to end. He collected his people and went back toward the road. They were going to walk down the middle of that fuckin' highway, singing "Yankee Doodle" at the top of their goddamned lungs and just maybe nobody'd shoot them.

They made it. It didn't look as if Mosby's line had been hit. Most of the damage looked to be on the other side of the hill, and there was a gawdawful amount of smoke coming from the center of the perimeter.

Mosby didn't give a fat fuck about what else had happened. Wilson headed for the company CP without saying anything, and Mosby told Diaz to get Arledge out of his sight.

Fritsche had a Bier LaRue uncapped as Mosby stumbled toward the position. He and Blind Pig looked at their squad leader and considered.

"Christ, Pig. This cat looks like he's gone and seen the elephant."

"Naw," Blind Pig disagreed. "He just be pissed nobody let him sit up here an' get another medal." Mosby had enough energy to drain the beer and give them the finger before he died on his cot for a full seventeen hours.

CHAPTER THIRTY-NINE

THE SQUAD

ON THE TWELFTH day before Christmas, the Fifteenth Infantry counted its dead and started rebuilding. Twenty-seven men, mostly from A Company's sector, where the Viet Cong had broken through the wire, were dead. Fifteen artillerymen had been killed, and two of their guns were destroyed. Over ninety Americans had been wounded. They found eleven dead Viet Cong. The bodies were searched, stripped, and piled.

Captain Jerry Edmunds stood by the pile of VC bodies, waiting for the bulldozer to show up and dig the burial trench. The stink didn't even register—he was intent on the long, pistol-gripped tube he'd found outside the wire.

It was the first RPG-7 launcher he'd seen this far south. The only other one he'd handled (outside of a familiarization briefing) was way north, in the A Shau valley—and it had been the former possession of a North Vietnamese regular.

Edmunds decided that Dennis Shannon might be very interested in seeing this—and in considering how well equipped their attackers must be if they could abandon a nearly new launcher.

On the eleventh day before Christmas, Shannon put the word out.

He and Colonel Taylor had sat up late in the officers' mess tent, looking at an assemblage of exhibits. There was everything from the RPG tube to unexploded and now disarmed sapper satchel packs to oil-gleaming AK-47s. To one side were the documents taken from the bodies.

It was quite a haul. Taylor, however, was far from pleased. There was something wrong. He laid out his doubts to Shannon.

Fact: The unit(s) that attacked the Fifteenth were experienced. They were spearheaded by sappers. Shannon had a pretty good idea that some members of the N-10 Battalion had at least trained these sappers, and maybe even taken part in the attack itself.

First question—there were supposedly no main-line Viet Cong forces in Song Nhanh Province. Where did these experienced troopers come from?

Second question—if the sappers were from N-10, what were they doing so far north?

Second fact: The excellent shape of the weapons and canvas gear indicated that whichever unit was responsible for the attack had been recently resupplied.

Third question—resupplied by whom?

Third fact: The bodies had provided the usual collection of letters and diaries. But all of them were written by or to South Vietnamese. Four of the bodies had no identification or personal documents at all.

Fourth question—why had the VC hit the Fifteenth at all?

"Makes no sense to me," Taylor said. "Even an idiot could see they didn't have a prayer. Why not leave us alone? Do a little road interdiction, hit some patrols. That kind of thing. Fuck us up where they can hurt us."

Shannon considered, then poured himself another shot of his battalion commander's whiskey. It didn't help, he still didn't know the answer.

"Maybe they're trying to make us play turtle," Taylor said.

Before Shannon could answer, Taylor made one of those wild leaps of logic that Dennis still hadn't gotten used to.

"You still think there's NVA over in the Octopus?"

Shannon did not know whether to bristle or change the subject. After two months' worth of doubt, he was starting to wonder if he really had seen that NVA division come across the river.

"Reason I'm asking," Taylor went on, "is I can't figure out why nobody's seen your boys. And there sure aren't enough NVA around that Hanoi'd let them come south just to sit in the bushes."

This kind of linkage is the reason why Shannon was gradually becoming thoroughly impressed with his battalion commander. It made him wonder why he had put up with the batshit at Division for so long, even before Sinclair's arrival. This is where he belonged, a line unit.

The Fifteenth Infantry, even though it wore no trick badges or uniforms, was a fairly special unit. Its battalion CO, Taylor, made it such. Primarily because Taylor was a fairly special man.

He was one of those career officers who had seen the Army from the bottom up.

As an enlisted man, he had been a Ranger in Korea and had seen the beginnings of helicopter warfare. He'd later read about air mobility experiments by the French in Algeria, the British in Malaya, and even the tentative Army work in the field. The minute a helicopter went into service that was capable of delivering a squad of soldiers by air, Taylor knew the always absurd parachute was obsolete.

He was bright enough to realize, however, that the best he could hope for was to finish his career as a hardass parawhoopie first sergeant. Not bad, but he'd still spend his twenty or so listening to fools with commissions. He determined to become one of them.

In the fifties he left the Army and put himself through college, majoring supposedly in history, but actually in ROTC. Four years later, he returned to the 101st Airborne as a second lieutenant. He stuck with the paratroops until he made captain, then got out. Taylor had reasoned that rank came very slowly in the elite units. More important, elite troopies are viewed with extreme suspicion by the always-conservative military establishment.

Taylor moved steadily upward, his Form 20 unbroken by anything other than Excellents. Now, as a CO of an infantry battalion, he was almost guaranteed his eagles and then promotion to brigadier general. Assuming, of course, that he didn't make any minor errors such as getting his unit wiped out, forgetting the divisional commander's birthday, or possibly even getting himself killed.

Shannon ran all this through his head while he waited for Taylor to make up his mind on what to do next. The answer delighted him.

"Tell you what, Major. Whyn't you grab my slick and go blow in people's ears. See if anybody else has heard anything. Damn sure G-2 won't give us the real skinny."

That was probably as close as Taylor would get to criticizing his commanding general's tactical sense.

"You get any good poop, maybe we better think about somebody going in the Octopus and nosing around.

"I'm starting to feel like I just took my pants off, and the lady can't remember if it's today or tomorrow her husband comes back in town."

* * *

It was the tenth day before Christmas, and the night sky was a wondrous thing.

On this particular night, the observation point was a two-man foxhole, just far enough outside of Song Nhanh so the stars and the planets weren't obscured by city lights. The foxhole in question was occupied by Privates Arledge and Grubb. Several hours had gone by and the nervousness of being on a perimeter watch had subsided just enough so that even Arledge found himself wiping his glasses and gazing up at unfamiliar stars, instead of looking for evil slopes in the bushes. Arledge pointed a finger at a low-hanging bright star.

"Hey! Look at that. The North Star!"

Grubb sighed a weary sigh. Arledge had been a probable expert on everything since they first climbed into the foxhole together. He wasn't too sure what the man was pointing at, but whatever Arledge said, he had decided in self-defense that it wasn't.

"It ain't the North Star, you asshole. Any fuck knows you can't see the North Star in Vietnam."

"Why not, it's there, isn't it?"

"Too far south," Grubb said, "Besides, it's too low on the horizon. Probably a planet. You know, like Venus . . . the Morning Star."

"Fuck you and your Morning Star. It's midnight, man. How do you see a 'morning star' when it's midnight?"

"Because we're so far south," Grubb said. He said it with a huge question in his mind and absolute conviction in his voice.

"Yeah, well I got your south hangin' right here." In the darkness Arledge cupped something below his waist.

Grubb decided this was going to be a very long night. He ran a hand through his thick red hair, a self-soothing gesture he did unconsciously.

"So what's your story, Arledge," he said, doing his best to sound friendly. It came out as an accusation, but this was a quirk Grubb would never pick up on.

"You got a real problem, Grubb," Arledge said. "Always pushing, like your shit don't stink. What'd I do to put you on my case?"

"Just trying to be friendly," Grubb said. "Nothing behind it."

Arledge considered this for a minute, then nodded in the blackness. Maybe the little jerk was just as dumb as the rest of them.

"What'ya think of these assholes we're stuck with?"

311

"Assholes," Grubb confirmed. "Except maybe that big black sonofabitch. Blind Pig. He's okay. Especially after I let him know who *I* was."

Arledge was also stricken by the stars enough to let this slide. Besides, he had an idea the crazy motherfucker beside him would start swinging with anything he had at hand if Arledge said the wrong thing.

"Yeah, you always got to let the fuckheads *know* you're around."

Arledge shifted his seat, looking for a new uncomfortable place.

"That's why back home I drove a Vette. Standout car, sure. But what the fuck, fast is fast. But a Vette looks fast, if you know what I mean?"

"Who the fuck can afford a Corvette?"

The crucial question was asked and Arledge was off and running.

"Me, who, that's who. My old man's a banker. Practically owns Langley Park. That's in Maryland, just outside of D.C. And you know what that means . . . ?"

"I know where the hell it is. Okay. If you're so hot shit, how come your ass is sitting here beside me?"

"Just temporary. I fucked up. Kid shit, you know. Had me a killer-diller car. Great fiancée with a pussy like a country club golf course. Then I flunked outa college. Maryland State, right? Baseball scholarship, the whole shot. Got too busy with the slash, so they flunked my ass. Then drafted it."

"What happened to your old man? Thought he was connected."

"Fucked up again. Scared to tell my old man. By the time I got around to it, I was in Basic."

"Great story," Grubb said. "So how does it end?"

"Fuck you! You'll see. My pop's working on it right now. Two weeks max and he'll pull me out. He's got Congressional connections, babe, and you know what that means."

"Yeah. They'll make you a general."

"What? You don't believe me? I can show you some letters."

Grubb started laughing. He couldn't help it. Arledge was such a bullshitter he probably had pictures and notarized documents that somehow would back up this preposterous crock. The capper, he was sure, would be a sworn-to shot of a pussy as smooth as a country club golf course.

The funny thing was, Arledge was insulted. The foxhole, the bright stars—to him the whole thing added up to a sharing of honest thoughts and experiences. The mere fact that all of his comments were fictitious affected him not at all. Therefore, Arledge sulked. It was the kind of a sulk that was hard to ignore. He shuffled around in pockets for cigarettes he couldn't light. Tugged at his crotch to move his balls. Grubb took pity on him.

"What you want," he finally said, "is a nice safe place to hide for thirteen months. Like in the rear, right?"

"I'm no chickenshit."

"Gotcha. But you're really counting on this congressman bullshit, aren't you?"

Arledge squeezed out a pimple of trust.

"Yeah. My dad really is writing letters."

An admission.

"No way, unless you want to claim queer, are you gonna get out of the Army, correct? So you wanna play REMF."

Grubb raised a hand to shush any objections.

"No shame. No complain. But I'm here to tell you, pal, there's nothing safe about the rear. That's where you *really* get fucked with.

"Right now. In this foxhole. What are my actual chances of getting my ass shot off? Not much. But I'm here to tell you that Private First Class Grubb was two hanks from a dog hair from getting shot when he was in the rear."

"Oh, yeah. Heard you were a colonel's driver. Soft fucking duty, man."

"Not so soft."

"What'd you do? Take a wrong turn in Saigon?"

"No, not exactly," Grubb said. "What I did is punch out the colonel."

Arledge chewed on this for a very long while.

"They normally hang you for that kind of shit," he said. As a consummate liar, Arledge believed every word Grubb was telling him.

"Or send you to the crunchies," Grubb said. "Fuck it, I'll take my chances with Blind Pig."

Arledge thought that Grubb was two cunt hairs from a Section Eight. He wisely decided not to mention his opinion at the moment. Instead he just grunted a non-answer and settled back to gaze at the stars. Somehow, he knew there had to be a way out.

On the ninth day before Christmas, the squad briefly came in possession of a living Christmas tree, complete with chiming

bells and painted balls. Mosby was the one who found the tree—
at the new bazaar.

Mosby never stopped being amazed at how fast the Vietnamese small businessman could get his hands into a grunt's pocket.
In just the short time the Fifteenth had been at Song Nhanh, a
small bazaar had already started to spring up just down the road
from the camp.

Although far from complete, the bazaar merchants already had
set up their hooches and booths, offering everything from the
usual gaudy souvenirs to booze and broads. As he hurried into
the bazaar he noticed that someone had even scored a record
player, which was blasting rock 'n' roll from two huge speakers.

Mosby spotted Fritsche and a couple of other guys drinking
beer and shooting the shit at one of the open-air bars. Jesus, he
could use a cold one now himself, and it was with great self-
control that he passed them by with a wave of recognition and
headed deeper into the bazaar. Duty was calling, and Mosby
wasn't too pleased about it. Taliaferro had alerted him to the
brewing problem in his usual mocking manner. He had strolled
into Mosby's hooch and had found him with his feet up, reading
a tattered paperback.

"Hope you ain't at a real excitin' part about now, Sarge,"
Taliaferro had said.

Mosby peered up at him. As a matter of fact, he had been
thinking about taking a little snooze.

"Why for?"

"Because any minute now, you're gonna be interrupted. The
shit is about to hit a very big fan."

Irritated, Mosby put the book down and sat up.

"Knock off the mystery garbage, Taliaferro. What shit and
what fan?"

Taliaferro snickered. "One of the new guys is over at the
bazaar, getting his ass all measured for the sling. Way he's carrying on, bound to draw MPs like roaches on toothpaste."

"Which new guy?"

"Oh, you know, the Rhode Island kiddie. Masters."

This set Mosby back some. Although he didn't know the man
very well yet, Dan Masters was the last person he thought would
cause trouble. The man seemed like a damned good trooper, for
a cherry. A real quiet kind of a fellow who didn't seem that
bright, but always had a smile on his face and did what he was
told with little grumbling.

"What the hell is he doing?"

"He's all drunked up. Yelling, singing, screwing every whore

314

he can get his hands on and begging for more. The dumb fuck's so rowdy, the old lady's gettin' ready to toss him out and call for reinforcements."

That *did* sound serious. Mosby hastily pulled on his gear and shot out of the tent. The last thing he needed was to draw the law down on a member of his squad. The MPs would figure the whole group for troublemakers and be constantly down on them. Besides, there were certain slightly as well as highly illegal comforts they had all busted their ass to get.

Mosby didn't have to look far to find Masters. Just outside one hooch was gathered a small group of concerned Vietnamese. They were in a huddle discussing some problem furiously. From inside, Mosby heard Master's booming voice:

"Let's get this party in gear! Danny Masters is here!"

Masters began singing: "Jingle Bells, Jingle Bells, Jingle Bells Rock. Jingle Bells Roll . . ."

Mosby groaned to himself and entered the hooch. The first thing he noticed was not the piled bottles of beer and hard liquor surrounding Masters. Nor was it the smell of a burning illegal substance. He also paid no mind to the two whores playing firstups on Masters's jutting cock. It was PFC Daniel Masters himself that caught Mosby's newly critical squad leader's eye. The man was standing straight upright in the debris of what appeared to be an awesome party. The fact that he was buck naked under these circumstances was old news to Mosby. But what grayed his temples was *how* Masters was buck naked.

Someone, whether it was Masters himself or an accomplice, had painted the man in Christmas colors. His body was striped green. His face a several-colored star. Masters was standing there Christ-like, his arms outstretched, with aluminum strips hanging from his hair, his ears, and his fingers. Tiny silver bells hung in loops from his shoulders and wrists and ankles and waist. The capper was his groin. One ball was painted red, the other blue, and his cock a shocking kelly green.

Masters bleared into reality and spotted Mosby. A big grin wreathed his face from left hairline to right.

"Lookit me, Sarge, I'm a Christmas tree."

"Oh God, Masters. What the hell are you doing?"

"Partying, Sarge. Hey. You got to help me. I'm going outside. *Really* celebrate Christmas."

He peered at Mosby, conspiracy in his eyes.

"Except the girls won't let me. Hell, they won't even let me paint them."

Despite himself, Mosby was curious.

"Why'd you wanna paint them, Dan?"

"For a surprise, of course. I'm planning on surprising the squad. With three Christmas trees."

Masters gave the girls an owlish look.

"I ain't figured out the balls yet, but I was gettin' to it. You got any ideas?"

"Dan. Partytime is over. We gotta go home."

Masters, ever the willing soul, brightened even more—if this was possible under the rainbow job he had done on himself.

"Sure, Sarn't Mosby. Right away."

He started walking toward the door.

"Christ!" Mosby jumped and pulled him back.

"You can't go out like that! We gotta get you washed off. And dressed."

Masters gave him a long, mournful look.

"But, what about the Christmas tree, Sarge? I went to a lot of work."

"Sure you did, Dan," Mosby soothed. "And I'm sure the guys will all appreciate it. What I'm worried about now is MPs. They don't tend to get into the Yuletide spirit."

Masters stiffened to his full height. He curled one arm into a bulging muscle, bells tinkling as veins jutted.

"Fuck 'em, Sarge. Let 'em come. Hell, I been thumped by Providence fuzz lot tougher'n they are."

Mosby suddenly realized that what he had on his hands was a jolly Jekyll and Hyde. The quietest and maybe the best new member of his squad was the Jolly Green Giant. All he needed was a short beer and SHAZAM! The party kid!

Somehow, Mosby got the man dressed. Somehow he calmed the angry mamasan and her cohorts. And somehow he got Masters through the bazaar without incident to where Fritsche was counting beer bottle caps and holding forth on the very latest in Harley top-end conversions.

Fritsche took one look at the star burst on Masters's face and jumped to his feet.

"Holy shit," he said.

"You should see the rest of him," Mosby said.

"I don't wanna. Probably got his balls painted red."

"One blue, the other red," Mosby corrected.

"I'm a Christmas tree," Masters shouted. "A living Christmas tree! Let's party!"

"Get him home," Mosby pleaded with Fritsche. "I've had enough of this squad leader shit. I need a drink."

Fritsche took pity on Mosby, and, ever the point man, grabbed

Masters by the elbow, lifted enough to get the man on his toes, and frog-marched him out of the bazaar and down the road.

Mosby ordered a beer and drained half of it down on the first go. Instead of sitting down, he began pacing back and forth—filled with nervous energy—nursing the rest of the bottle. What the fuck next, GI? Being a squad leader was not a wonderful way to spend a nice peaceful war. Aw, shit. Masters wasn't *that* bad. Just blowing off steam. Fucking Christmas tree. Shit, they were probably all certifiable. Who was he, Buck Sergeant David Mosby, to cast the first ding on a man's 201 File?

He finished the beer, picked up another, and wended his way through the streets of the bazaar. Gradually coming down, gradually becoming slightly grateful that nothing serious had happened. A man's profile moved through the crowd. Mosby stopped. Didn't he know him. For some unknown reason, his heart fluttered a little. Then he got it. The man wore white slacks, black French shoes, and a very loud Hawaiian shirt.

"Hey! Mr. Chi!"

Mosby's voice cut through the crowd. He was sure that Chi heard him, because the man turned his head slightly in his direction, then firmly back, and marched on. Mosby sprinted after him.

"Chi! Yo! Mr. Chi!"

This time Chi stopped, and Mosby panted up to him. The man brushed at his drooping mustache, covering his surprise at seeing Mosby. Mosby got the idea he was not very happy about the situation. Then Chi smiled his small, charming smile and gave Mosby a pretended start of pleasurable recognition.

"Ah, Mosby! What a surprise."

Now, absolutely relaxed, Chi fished into his pockets for a pack of Salems. He offered one to Mosby, a sort of substitute greeting for shaking hands, Mosby guessed. This time, Mosby took one.

"What are you doing here, Mr. Chi?" Mosby asked, trying to keep his voice casual.

Chi lit both their cigarettes and took in a long draw. He breathed out the smoke slowly before he spoke.

"You know how much I like the Fifteenth, Mosby," he said. "When you and my other friends left Hue Duc . . . things were . . . not the same."

"So you followed us," Mosby said.

"Of course. Business must be a pleasure, otherwise it cannot be business."

"Good to see a familiar face," Mosby lied. "Lots of ins-and-outs you can help your old buddies of the Fifteenth with."

317

Mr. Chi brightened.

"Oh, yes. Most certainly. Already, I have found some bargains. And the women . . . there are a few . . . although not like Tho, Mosby."

Mosby's eyes narrowed. He had to be very, very careful now. "How is Tho?"

Chi lit a cigarette off his Salem.

"She sends her best, Mosby," Chi said. "She said to tell you what a wonderful time she had in Saigon."

Mr. Chi offered Mosby another Salem. This time he refused.

"She wants to know when she can visit you."

Mr. Chi bowed his head slightly as he said this, using the excuse of flicking an invisible speck of ash off his pure white trousers to avoid Mosby's eyes. Careful, asshole, Mosby warned himself. That was a fucking threat, not a promise. Mosby barked a harsh laugh.

"You know me, Mr. Chi. Got a new girl already. Just as pretty as Tho."

"Does she have a father I should speak with for you? Like with Tho?"

"No," Mosby said. "This honey doesn't have any family at all."

Mosby made his polite good-byes and got the fuck out of the bazaar. He had a damned good idea what Chi was doing in Song Nhanh. The problem was, what should he do about it? Whom should he talk to? Or, should he just play it safe, as Chi had so explicitly advised?

Merry almost fucking Christmas, Mosby.

On the eighth day before Christmas, Shannon got a gift from Emmett. It came in an envelope addressed by Lisa's perfect hand, and so for a few minutes he was afraid to open it. The last thing Shannon needed right now was a downer from his ex. But, after a few moments, perverse curiosity took over, and he slit it open. There was a single onionskin sheet inside—figure Lisa to be practical under any circumstances—and Shannon unfolded the thin sheet. On it was a crayon drawing: a big yellow sun and a heavily scraped-on blue sky. Like Hawaii, Shannon thought. Just under the sun, almost touching it, was a Christmas tree, decorated in many colors with heavy crayon blobs. On top of the tree was a small stick figure, with little points for eyes and a crooked smear for a smile. The figure was waving at him.

318

Oh so carefully inscribed, under the figure was his present: MERRY XMAS DAD. LOVE emmett.

Suddenly the closeness of the tent became too much for him. His own odor gave him a slightly sick feeling. He had to get the hell out of there. Before he did, he carefully refolded the onion-skin drawing and placed it back in its envelope. He got to his feet, brushing at now-damp eyes. Just then, someone outside cleared his throat.

Shannon took a long minute to compose himself. Somebody someplace really did love his ass, no matter how misguided their feelings. On this eighth day before Christmas, Shannon was not feeling very loving about himself.

"Yeah!"

Mosby entered the tent. The expression on his face immediately calmed Shannon down. The man looked . . . scared? What was there to be scared about? Shannon never thought about himself as a person another guy might fear. Oh, shit. Shannon knew right then that Mosby had a personal problem. A Dear John letter, a dead mom or dad. Some shit like that. There was no way Shannon could handle anything so mundane and delicate at the moment.

Shannon sat back down. "What'd ya need, Sergeant?" He motioned for Mosby to grab a pew.

Mosby got right to the point. He told him about Chi, maybe a VC, who somehow had got the correct papers to be transferred from Hue Duc to Song Nhanh. Mosby let Shannon fill in the blanks. After the recent incidents, what the fuck was this son-ofabitch doing here?

"I got one more question," Shannon said. "And I don't think you know what it is."

Mosby slumped in his seat.

"Yeah, I know, sir, I'm way the fuck out of the chain of command."

"No, shit," Shannon said. "I understand you skipping Wilson and all that. But, how come you didn't go to Edmunds? He's your CO."

"Sir," Mosby said, "all I can say is . . . I *know* you."

Both of them realized this wasn't true. Shannon barely knew Mosby at all. There had only been that one real contact, back when they . . . Yeah. Shannon remembered Ba Rei.

"Edmunds is damned good," Shannon said. He said it quietly, but with enough force so that Mosby understood he was personally vouching for the black captain.

"Yessir."

319

Shannon leaned closer to Mosby.

"What do you think we ought to do about this Chi? Phoenix his ass?"

Mosby thought about it. He imagined Chi in his sparkling white trousers, rainbow shirt, and carefully trimmed mustache. A jerk, yeah. But he had a hard time thinking of him as an enemy across his sights. Still . . .

"There's a girl I know involved," Mosby said. "But, honest to fuck, that's not really why I came to talk to you. It . . . the situation . . . just . . . just I don't know, sir."

"I'll take care of Mr. Chi," Shannon promised. And that was the end of goddamned that.

On the seventh day before Christmas, General Sinclair had his old friend Nguyen Van Thoan over for dinner. Knowing the province chief would be on the hustle, Sinclair had prepared for him. To begin with, he had politely declined Thoan's own invitation to a celebration of the Christmas cease-fire. This meant Thoan had to fly to him in Hue Duc. Secondly, he had set the stage for the dinner so that Thoan would be as much out of his element as possible.

Sinclair had taken as much care over the preparations as his wife would have at a country club affair. Except he had reversed the order and look of things. Instead of snow-white tables and glittering ware, he had ordered all the tables in the officers' mess stripped bare. Thoan would eat on bare boards. He would also eat, like Sinclair and his officers, off a steel tray. The food, instead of the usual delicacies that could be available at a general's table for important affairs, was straight from the mess halls. High in calories, but low in taste buds.

Sinclair also decreed that there would not only be no fine wines, there would be no spirits at all. Just water and mess hall coffee. To greet Thoan, he had all of his officers dress in field uniform, complete with sidearms. His thought was to present Thoan with as Spartan a view as possible. Thoan would be speaking to a U.S. soldier, surrounded by other American soldiers; and each and every one of them would be by-god combat ready. Sinclair was through with being any man's perceived toady.

As Thoan traced his fingers across a map, pointing out suspected Viet Cong villages surrounding Song Nhanh, Sinclair was far from sure that his plan was working.

"We could probe here, and here," Thoan said, stabbing his finger at the map.

"Exactly what do you mean by *we*, Mr. Thoan? Are you suggesting a joint exercise?"

Thoan frowned, as if considering a thought he had never exercised.

"No. As admirable as that idea is, General, it would leave the city unprotected," he said. "I'm sure I couldn't spare the men."

"But you think I can spare mine?"

Thoan smiled his smoothest smile.

"It would be in both our interests if you could. A few small sweeps now, and we would almost certainly catch the VC off guard."

Sinclair knew there was no damned way he could accede. First off, it was unnecessary. Hadn't he just recently whipped the Phu Loi Battalion? The only enemy left, Sinclair knew for a fact, was a few locals. He viewed the sapper attack on the Fifteenth's base camp near Song Nhanh as the last-gasp effort from the last shards of the Phu Loi unit. Also, if he agreed, putting his soldiers basically at the command of this bandit, Sinclair knew he would be deservedly relieved. Especially since he would be in violation of the recently agreed-upon Christmas cease-fire.

Sinclair was especially pleased that Thoan had gone about the whole thing stupidly. No matter how connected Thoan was, Sinclair could turn him down with impunity.

"Mr. Thoan," the general said, "there is no possible way I can help you. And I would strongly advise against your taking matters in your own hands at this time."

Fat chance this chickenshit would ever launch his own sweeps. Still, no sense in daring the gods of dim-wittedness.

"Then you are rejecting my request out of hand?" Thoan was plainly pissed.

"No. Not out of hand. I assure you that we'll kick the idea around." He waved his hand around to include all of his officers. It was a somber, a very military picture. "Then we'll see if we can staff it."

Even Thoan knew what that meant. It was the military way of saying it was permanently shelved. The province chief glared at Sinclair, as if attempting to stare him down. Too bad for Thoan. One thing Sinclair had been thoroughly trained in was a general's glare back.

Fuck you, Sinclair thought, shocking himself a little at the intensity of his own feelings. Thoan's glare wavered and his expression became bland once more.

"Shall we join the others for dinner?" Sinclair said, gloating as he led the province chief to the appalling cafeteria-type odors that awaited them at the tables.

On the sixth day before Christmas, Fritsche was stricken by the terminal glooms. He hadn't had a piece of mail for months, a situation that normally didn't bother him. Who the hell would write to him anyway? But, Jesus, it was almost Christmas! What depressed him even more was the thought that there also was no one *he* could send a card or gift to.

Feeling unloved, the big biker looked up Mosby for company. Fritsche had noticed that Mosby also never received anything at mail call. He found the man in his tent, sulking over a beer. Happily morose, Fritsche took a seat across from Mosby, fishing out a joint for the two of them to share. He exchanged a few appropriate "fuck Christmas" comments, and was pleased to see Mosby sink deeper into self-pity.

"You ever have a *real* Christmas?"

Mosby thought back over the empty attempts his mother had made over the years. He couldn't remember getting a single present he had ever wanted or hinted strongly about. To Mosby, Christmas was a big dark house that groaned and settled in the rain.

"No."

"I did. Few years ago the club did it up big. And I mean fucking big!"

"A biker Christmas?" Mosby was interested despite himself.

"Best kind, man. Then you're really with family. You're with all your brothers, you know?"

Mosby didn't, but he prodded Fritsche on.

It was when Fritsche's club was still young and growing in membership. Everyone was full of piss and ideas to keep it growing. And at one particularly dope-hazed, boozy meeting, just before Christmas, somebody brought up the bad press the gang had been receiving.

"Fucking newspapers, always got us fucking wrong," Fritsche said. "All we ever wanted to do was party. All they ever wanted to do was bust us. Bullshit stuff. Always accusing us of thumping heads and smuggling dope."

"Untrue, of course," Mosby said.

"No. It was true, alright. It was *how* they said it that made us mad."

Anyway, the membership decided they had to change their

image, preferably in one bold stroke. Somebody brought up the plight of a group of frizzly old farts who lived in a slum building downtown. The guy had heard about them on the Evening Snooze.

"There must'a been twenty–thirty of these old motherfuckers," Fritsche said, "freezing their asses off in this building. Asshole landlord had cut off the gas and electric 'cause they'd pissed him off by not paying the rent. Seems he'd raised it already three–four times in the past year, and they all got together to tell him to fuck off."

Fritsche anted up the makings for another joint and started rolling.

"We decided to throw them a party. Bikers got big hearts, you know? Like we just pretend to be bad asses."

"And you really aren't?"

Fritsche considered. "Naw. We're bad asses. But not the kind of bad ass you're thinking."

"I wasn't thinking shit," Mosby said in dead earnest.

"Good. So, what we did was have a charity drive. You know, collect money and gifts and freebies from all the merchants in town."

"Fuck me," Mosby said. He was honestly amazed. "How'd you do?"

"Fuckin' great, man. Nobody, but nobody turned us down. We must'a collected twenty or thirty grand's worth of shit."

Mosby considered this sudden outpouring of love from cold-hearted city dwellers.

"Pretty awesome," Mosby said.

"It was easy, man. Surprised nobody had tried it before." Fritsche was being humble now. "What we did, see, was use the personal touch. We split up the job into squad size, you know? Five–six guys on their bikes would visit each merchant on the list. Hit him up for a buck or three."

Mosby could imagine a small storekeeper being confronted by a thunder of engines and a clatter of boots. Yeah, he guessed they'd dig and dig deep.

"How many heads did you have to thump?"

"Not more'n one or two. Then the word got around what a worthy cause we had, and, shit, people got really Christmasy, like."

"I imagine the newspapers and television people came all over themselves after that," Mosby said.

"Hell, yes. Especially after the party."

"You had a party for them, too?" Somehow, Mosby couldn't

see all these suffering old folks dancing the polka with a bunch of hairy bikers.

"Shit, yeah, we had a party. Blocked off the whole street. All the booze and dope and food you could eat. Had a big ceremony, handing over the presents and money to the old fucks."

"Jesus! I can see all the reporters there now," Mosby said.

"Well, not right away. They showed up later after we burned the landlord's house down."

"You did fucking what?"

"Burned it down, man. See, while we were having the party, he sent over some rent-a-pigs. Tried to run us off as a nuisance. Kind of pissed us off, but it *really* pissed off the old fucks."

Fritsche took a toke, reflecting back on the incident.

"Just 'cause a guy's old," Fritsche said, turning philosophical, "don't mean he ain't got balls. Actually, it wasn't a guy at all. It was an old lady. She started screaming and waving her bottle—we got 'em all little pony jugs for their stockings—and saying we ought to all go over there and burn the fuckface out."

"Oh, shit!"

"Real cheery fire, too," Fritsche said, dreamily. "Real Christmas-like, burning there in the snow."

"What happened to the landlord?"

"That was the great part. Publicity was so bad, the city finally busted his ass six months or so later. Fuck, we had a *big* party then. Everybody drinking, and yelling and cheering, watching him get his fat ass cuffed and thrown in a squad car. They had the whole damned thing on the TV news."

"And nothing happened to you guys?"

"Not much. We got busted and the cops beat us up a little, but nothing big, you know? I mean, how hard's a cop gonna smack you for something like that? Their hearts weren't really in it."

"Some Christmas," Mosby said.

"Yeah. Best Christmas I ever hope to have."

It was on the fifth day before Christmas that Grubb was attacked by a pie, and Blind Pig became the most popular man in the squad.

"Fuckin' A!" This was said in total awe, as Diaz watched Grubb gingerly examine a package from home.

The reason for the awe was not the size of the package—it was fairly small, about as big as a couple of hardcover books—but the shape and smell of it. The brown-paper-wrapped box was smashed in at the sides and seemed to be swelling from some great inner pressure. And the smell. Diaz instantly thought of a rice paddy, then shook his head no. It was much worse than that.

"Who's it from?"

"My mom," Grubb said. "It's my Christmas present."

The other members of the squad had caught the smell, and gathered around Grubb in perverse curiosity. What could someone's mother send that would smell like that?

"What do you think it is?" Godfrey wanted to know.

"She promised me a mince pie. My mom makes the greatest fucking pies you ever had. Especially mince."

Fritsche sniffed the air suspiciously. He had a few good comments in mind, but decided to pass. Even Fritsche wouldn't say anything about another man's mother. Especially if the mother belonged to Wild-Man Grubb.

"Maybe you oughta take it outside to open it," Fritsche suggested.

"Naw. That smell's just the wrapping paper. Probably got dumped in some shit or other," Grubb said.

"When she mail it?" someone else wanted to know.

Grubb examined a myriad of stamp marks all over the paper.

"Can't make it out. Looks like it went to Saigon, and then all over hell's half-acre."

Grubb started tearing at the paper.

"I think I hear Sergeant Mosby calling me," Masters said, heading for the tent door.

"Hey! Hold on. I tell ya it's just somethin' on the paper, man. Wait'll you guys get a taste of my mom's pie."

Grubb ripped the package open the rest of the way. First there was a slow hiss, then a whoosh, and then the sound of men screaming as the pie exploded. Everyone had ancient mince in his hair, and Grubb himself was one big gooey smear. The stuff dripped from his eyebrows, and his mouth was a large, surprised O.

"Fucking wonderful," Fritsche said. "Booby-trapped by your own mom."

He picked a fleck from his arm and tasted it. Everyone stared at him, waiting for him to keel over.

"You're wrong, Grubb," he finally said. "It ain't mince. It's cherry."

"Ho, fuckin' ho," boomed a voice outside the tent, and everyone turned to see Blind Pig and Mosby stagger in.

They were staggering under the weight of two huge packages.

Godfrey looked at the cartons, and then at the remains of Grubb's exploded pie.

"Incoming," he screamed, and dove for the floor.

"It ain't fucking funny," Grubb said, and everyone looked at the misery on his face. Even his Irish freckles were drooping.

"Fuckin' Army," Diaz said.

"What the hell is going on?" Mosby asked, sniffing at the air and smelling the evil smell.

"They fucked up Grubb's Christmas," Fritsche said.

"Well, I be here to tell you," Blind Pig said, "long as Blind Pig be here, be nobody's mo-dickin' Christmas fucked up."

He dumped one large carton on the floor. Mosby set the other one beside it.

"This from my main man, Deacon Rayburn," Blind Pig said. "An' if I know the Deacon, there be plenty for all."

Much hooting of laughter later, the tent was cleaned up, and the squad was happily playing grab-ass and pushing close into Blind Pig as he peered into the contents of the two cartons. Inside was an assortment of gaily wrapped packages, ranging in size from teeny to fairly large. Blind Pig hefted one of the packages, musing.

"What the fuck this be?" he asked. He handed it over to Grubb. "You be my backup," Blind Pig said, "do some backup moves."

Grubb hesitated, then he started stripping off the paper. A few second later they were all staring at a small, inexpensive portable stereo set. This was a very strange present indeed. To send a stereo to Vietnam, the land of super-cheap high-quality stereos, was very much coals to Newcastle time.

"Wonder what the Deacon has in mind?" Blind Pig mused. Then, his face brightened. "Give her a shake."

Grubb did. Something rattled slightly.

"Maybe it's busted," Godfrey said.

"I don't think so," Grubb said, picking up on Blind Pig's grin of satisfaction. "Anybody got a screwdriver?"

A couple of Phillips heads later and the *real* present was revealed.

"Not one bottle of fucking Rémy Martin," Fritsche said with much reverence, "but two of the motherfuckers."

Sure enough, the Deacon had hidden two bottles of cognac inside the stereo.

"Do my man know how to wrap a present, or do he not?" Blind Pig said.

"You think they're all like that?" Godfrey wanted to know.

"Be your skin black or is that just shit on it?" was Blind Pig's answer. And then: "Open the rest. Come on. Give a nigger some help here."

There was much yelling and ripping and tearing after that. In a short period of time, the tent was littered with Christmas wrapping, and sitting in the center of the floor was the most bizarre pile of presents anyone could ever remember having seen in his young life.

There were jars of cocktail olives and onions. Except the juice had been replaced by gin. A large, very stale loaf of French bread had a bottle of champagne hidden inside. Cheese cartons, boxes of candy, everything but everything had some sort of spirits hidden inside. The final box contained about five dozen rum balls.

"Would you fucking look at that," Grubb said in a hushed voice, as he picked up one very moist ball. "More shitting Bacardi in that than they got in all of Cuba."

"What be you waitin' for, a personal invite?" Blind Pig asked, and he stirrup-cupped a bottle of cognac and raised it high in a toast. "Deacon, wherever you be," he boomed, "Merry Christmas, you motherfucker!"

"Merry Christmas, you motherfucker," the other men chorused. They proceeded to diminish the pile and their wits with copious quantities of Christmas cheer.

On the fourth day before Christmas the squad rested. They spent the day in a throbbing hangover blur.

On the third day before Christmas everybody except Grubb and Godfrey got to see a movie. This pissed the two of them off to no end, because they were playing *Combat* at the battalion HQ theater, starring Vic Morrow and Rick Jason. Nobody liked Jason much, but the producers who compiled the TV series into movie form threw most of the good shit to Morrow, the tough-talking sergeant.

"That fucker is real, I'm tellin' ya," Grubb was grousing.

Godfrey did not contradict him. Vic Morrow was also one of his heroes.

"What the hell, Grubb," he said. "Somebody's gotta be on perimeter. Mosby'll make it up to us."

Grubb sighed. What the hell indeed. Still, sitting in a foxhole just inside the perimeter wire was not his idea of getting in the

Christmas spirit. It didn't make him feel much better that there were many other men in identical foxholes spread out in the darkness along the perimeter.

"What really fries my ass," he said in a last-gasp grouse, "is this whole thing is full of shit. Nothin' gonna happen. All we're gonna do is sit here all night smelling your own farts."

At that moment there was a scream.

"MOTHERFUCKERS! COME ON YOU MOTHERFUCKERS!"

It jolted them out of their shorts. Instantly, Godfrey scrabbled a flare into the night. In other holes, other men equally as startled and scared hurled out flares of their own. The night became eerily lit by spots of fizzling, smoky light. And, right in front of them, they saw . . .

"Fuck. Don't shoot! It's goddamn Blake."

Grubb said it just in time, because Godfrey was getting ready to go to rock 'n' roll. Instead, he gaped at the ghostly figure of a man who seemed to have gone mad. Blake was dressed in full combat gear, pacing and screaming into the darkness past the wire.

"COME ON YOU ZIPPERHEAD MOTHERS. I'LL FUCKIN' WASTE YOUR SLIMY ASSES!"

He was waving something in one hand. Godfrey at first couldn't make it out. Then he could see it.

"It's a grenade. A fuckin' grenade!"

He could also see that Blake had the pin out and a not very tight grip on the lever. Around him other men were shouting at Blake, who ignored them, and kept shouting into the night. The man was obviously drunk.

"He's gonna kill either him or us . . ."

Grubb's voice died in midstream when they all heard the unmistakable sound of the lever pinging away and then the firing pin falling. Blake had somewhere between five to seven seconds to live.

"Jesus!" Grubb yelled, and then he saw an incredible sight. Godfrey leaped from the hole and sprinted for Blake. The sergeant just stood there, blearing with horror at the grenade in his hand. Somehow Godfrey covered the meters separating him from the man, then jumped in a full low dive. Blake's breath exploded out as the two men fell, the grenade dropping from his hand. Godfrey rolled with him on the ground and then:

"It went kafuckingpow," Grubb later told the awed members of the squad.

"And then what happened?"

"I'm not sure. I ducked just like everybody else. Then I stick my head up and see Godfrey gettin' to his feet. Me and half a dozen other guys go runnin' up, expecting to find guts all over the place, but there wasn't one drop of blood. They must have fallen in just the right place, because not one bit of shrapnel got to 'em."

"Why'd you do it?" Masters asked Godfrey, who was sitting gloomily in the corner, trying not to listen to all this. "Whyn't just let the sorry ass kill himself?"

"I don't know," Godfrey hissed. "Just leave it alone, okay?"

And everyone left it alone. Some people were not too sure how to treat Godfrey after that. Mosby, for one, decided to keep a close watch on the man.

On the second day before Christmas, Diaz opened the mountain that was his Christmas presents. Every Diaz on both sides of the border had remembered him, and the gifts were stacked two to three feet on top of his bunk.

Diaz did what came naturally. He started handing presents out to every man in the squad. They weren't the kind of gifts you could drink, like the Man sent Blind Pig, but they were interesting just the same. There were two main parts of the huge Diaz family. An aunt headed the part gathered on the Ensenada side of the border. She owned a five-and-dime type of store. So there was a whole lot of little presents from her people—mostly wind-up toys, wallets, aftershave, belts, you name it.

An uncle was the el patron on the San Diego side. He owned an insurance agency and was considered a man of great wealth. So all of the presents from his part of the family were eminently practical: books, men's magazines, Mexican food and spices that he knew Diaz would miss. His uncle was an ex-Marine, so there was one last present that Diaz kept for himself. The package had a great deal of heft to it and beneath the Christmas wrapping paper there was a layer of aluminum foil. Slowly, Diaz opened it.

"Oh, my God," someone breathed in awe. "Would you look at that."

Diaz was. His mouth was open. His uncle had sent him a Colt Python .357 Magnum. It came complete with shells.

"I guess my uncle really was serious about that job offer," Diaz said.

"How's that?"

Diaz waved the gun around in glee.

"Man, he's makin' sure *this* Diaz gets home."

* * *

On the night before Christmas, Mess Sergeant Kerley, his crew of three, and many many volunteers went into overdrive. They had already been up and steaming in 140-degree-plus heat for nearly thirteen hours at this point, but they knew they had at least another twenty-four hours in front of them.

On Christmas Day, the Army becomes a different place. The entire organization is focused on the grunt and his well-being. Morale is paramount. All the old virtues of home and hearth are underlined in reports that careers can sometimes swing on. In other words, a man has to have a meal *just like home*. Duty would be light—the perimeter and other key positions would be manned with the least number of people possible. And the food would be plentiful and good.

Staff Sergeant Kerley, a lifer, was determined that he would get nothing but the best of reports for the Christmas dinner that he served to Charlie Company. For Kerley and the rest of the mess cooks responsible for serving the battalion, the convoys had been running and the planes had been flying for several days. You cannot serve a traditional American Christmas meal out of the normal mess supplies.

To begin with there would be turkeys. Frozen turkeys to be sure, but there must be more turkey available than any man could possibly hold. And then ham, canned, but cooked with the special crust that Kerley prided himself on: brown sugar, basted heavily in pineapple juice. The turkeys also would be constantly basted—every twenty minutes on the minute . . . he had worked out the basting with his underlings like it was a dress military parade. Sergeant Kerley never never served a dry turkey or ham on Christmas Day.

But this was only the beginning of his plans. Turkey and ham alone do not create a groaning board. There would be cranberry sauce, which came in no. 6 cans, that he had chilled as soon as they arrived so the cranberry could be cut in ample slices. There would be peas and canned corn, all delivered in the huge no. 10 cans, but which Kerley touched up with a bit of cinnamon and ginger to cover the taste of can.

"You can't taste either one," the mess sergeant liked to tell his assistants, "they just take away from aluminum-bitter. Kinda like MSG."

There would be potatoes, dehydrated, but with a heavy hand on the white pepper to cut the dryness and a great deal of re-constituted milk and margarine so they'd be "just like home."

330

For the all-important gravy, Kerley slipped in great quantities of salt and pepper and bouillon cubes—"always use beef, not chicken, in turkey gravy. Chicken taste like shit." Then he got really heavy on the MSG. He would also have string beans. Except what Kerley did, was that he fried up canned bacon, sautéed canned tomatoes in the bacon, and then added the whole thing to the huge pots of string beans.

Following that came his real pride. Like most Army cooks, Kerley believed he was the best baker known to man. There would be breads and rolls, for sure. But the pies. Lord, the pies. Nobody, but nobody could make a pie out of canned ingredients like Kerley could. There would be both pumpkin and apple. And Kerley had a way of finishing off a crust with a little margarine and cinnamon—"a bit of sherry makes it brown just right," he told his people. He never told them, however, where he got or kept the sherry. Sergeant Kerley was an ambitious man. Ah, yes, and then the ice cream. Flown in just last night. Kerley had a way of keeping the pies just hot enough so that if you wanted it "fuckin' a la mode, it'll melt right in like cum."

On Christmas Day, Mosby and the rest of the squad went through the mess line with enormous grins. The smell of the food and the quantity would make your gut drop to your knees, just getting ready.

"I'm gonna have thirds," Mosby announced dreamily.

"Not in that skinny butt, you ain't," said Blind Pig. "You best be a heavyweight like me. I be doin' fifths, mofo, when you still be dawdlin' with yo' peas."

"Fuck a bunch of peas," Fritsche said, "look at what we got at the end of the line . . . no . . . no coffee . . . keep your canteen cups empty, boys."

This was very wise advice. Because Edmunds had set up station at the end of the mess line. Stacked up beside him were many crates of wine. No one knew it, but they were paid for out of his own pocket. It wasn't great wine, but it was good enough to keep Edmunds grunting away pulling corks. As each man exited the mess line, Edmunds was filling up his canteen cup to overflowing with wine.

"Merry Christmas," Edmunds kept saying. "Merry Christmas. We got red or white. Vintage Saigon PX. What's your pleasure, monsieur?"

"I'll take the red, Captain," Mosby said. "And Merry Christmas to you."

"Make mine white," Fritsche said.

Blind Pig paused for a long moment before Edmunds, mock considering. "Red or white, Cap'n?"

Edmunds laughed and then carefully poured a measure of both in Blind Pig's cup.

"Now, that's nice'n pink, like Uncle Ho," Edmunds said.

"This man do not discriminate," Blind Pig said, and he followed the others over to a table they had picked out ahead of time.

Mosby took the first ceremonial bite. Savored it. Kerley had done good.

"Thanks, God," he said after a second. Then: "Hey, anybody bring any cigars?"

In the Octopus, Christmas Day was a day like any other. It was business as usual.

CHAPTER FORTY

SHANNON

SERGEANT FIRST CLASS WILLIAMS had finally run out of war. Shannon stood over his cot, staring down at the Lurp sergeant. Tubes ran in his arm, out his ass, up his nose, and Shannon didn't want to know where else.

Ninety-third Field Evacuation Hospital was a helluva place to look for information. Williams opened his eyes, closed them, then reopened them toward reality.

"I fucked up," he croaked.

The last thing the sergeant wanted to hear was reassurance.

"No shit," Shannon agreed.

"I got casual, Major." Williams breathed through his lungs and his tubes. "I shoulda known better. Those bastards in the Octopus were lookin' for us.

"We come off the slick and they let the birds lift off before they nailed us. First thing I knew was going down. Funny thing, Major. You forget what it feels like to get hit, don't you?

"Next thing I knew is some white bitch, sorry, Major, was pushing on my chest telling me if I don't breathe I'm gonna die. Major, anybody else make it out?"

Williams' eyes curled back and he was back out, saving the reply.

There had been three survivors of the Long Range Recon Team that Williams had taken into the Octopus before Christmas—the RTO, Williams, and one M-79 man. All of them were hit to a greater or lesser extent. The only reason Williams' patrol had any survivors at all was that orbiting nearby was a gunflight of Huey Cobras, looking for trouble.

They'd heard Williams' cry for help, come in, and gunned the treeline around the team, enabling the lift-out ships to extract the survivors. Six of Williams' people were still out there. Hopefully dead.

Shannon told the ward nurse that the black sergeant was a very special friend. And he'd appreciate it if he got nothing but the best. The second lieutenant, barely bothering to curl her lip, told Shannon that all her patients got the best, and by the way Williams would go out for Camp Zama, Japan, sometime tonight.

That was the best Shannon could do for Williams. He headed for the airstrip and Colonel Taylor's Huey.

Six hours later, Shannon was feeling very redundant. He'd assembled his facts, his rumors, and his friends' reports. Taylor had told him to scout the ground, and, short of going into the Octopus himself, he'd done exactly that. He'd talked to the SF Commander at the Forces base in Loc Ninh, ground info out of intelligence people in Ban Me Thuot and Saigon, and read intelligence reports from every swingin' grunt that ever had anything to do with anything around the Octopus.

His assumption, verified by the zero information from anyone going into the Octopus, was that The Bad Guys were still in place. He'd barely begun what he—fatal error, sure sign of thinking like a staff donk—thought of as The Appreciation, when Colonel Taylor grinned at him.

"Shit, Dennis. Didn't I say you might have to go in and have a look-see? Why're you giving me all this shit?"

Shannon felt deflated. He had the long con ready, and it wasn't necessary.

He sat in his tent considering, then brightened. He still had a con to do. It was just a little different. This time he didn't need maps and reports. All he needed was a bottle of cognac and a lot more intelligence than any Army situation normally required.

After a tour and a half, Dave Mosby had learned there were only a few things in life that were unalterable. Among them

333

were: the Army sucks; the only good zips are the ones on the other side; the only person you can depend on is somebody you've been ambushed with; plus minor points.

One minor point, confirmed after the staggering drunk before Christmas, was that Blind Pig never got visibly loaded. He was therefore less than pleased when Blind Pig slumped up and announced that he was fucked up. It was just at dusk, and Mosby was looking forward to his first beer of the day, already icy in the sandbagged cooler. Then chow, putting his guards out, and maybe seeing if Fritsche had any of that killer weed left. Mosby, even after all this time, didn't handle surprises that well.

"Motherfucker sandbagged me," Blind Pig complained. Mosby didn't have the foggiest. Then Blind Pig took a third-full bottle of Courvoisier from his side pants pocket and planted it atop Mosby's bunker. Mosby had sense enough to grab the bottle and take a slug before inquiring.

"Who?"

"Fuckin' Shannon."

Mosby was on alert. Why would the battalion XO go see a machine gunner, especially without going through anywhere close to the chain of command. Mosby was beginning to think that maybe this was gonna be one of those days. Except that somehow it'd be worse.

"Dude comes down the trail. I be contemplatin' the world. Sent that fuckin' Grubb off to the PX. An' that motherfucker shows up. Say he wants to talk.

"Man, momma done taught me better. But this dude, he have the bottle, so I be listenin'."

Mosby was appalled. Something very bad was coming down. Blind Pig was telling the story. No grunts, no monosyllables, no easy way out.

"First thing he say is he never got th' chance to thank me, back Ba Rei. What the fuck he got to thank me for, he never say. Then he dig out the bottle.

"Tell you, Mosby, I ain't seen Corvasier since I left th' Motor City. I ever tell you you honkies drink shit?"

Mosby took the invitation to grab the bottle from Blind Pig. Hell, he'd only had Courvoisier about twice in his life before.

"Then Shannon he start askin' about me. Wonders what I'm doin' as a leg. He says he was Sneaky Pete, and wisht he'd had a dude as bad as me on the gun before. This shit I discards. Figurin' he wants somethin'.

"Next, he tells me about what happen a few months ago. Dude went up with Lurps up near Cambode. They be sittin' on

334

the border, an' they sees a whole cluster of NVA come diddy-boppin' across. Shannon says they be headin' for the Octopus. He says this why we go through the shit with the Phu Loi. Say they be maskin' the movement. That be his words, right?''

Mosby had not the foggiest where this was going, except toward trouble.

"So he tells me about lyin' on this hill, watchin' these dudes come through, an' he ain't saying' or doin' shit. Man, it be rainin' an' misty an' stuff. It sound like when you granny be tellin' ghost stories.''

"So you asked him what happened next?''

"Yeah. An' the dude he veers on me. Goes back to how I be the best pig gunner he ever see.''

Mosby thought that Shannon was certainly right on that at least.

"He say, that as far as he can see, these NVAs be lurkin' still up north. What he wants is go find them.''

"Oh fuck.'' Mosby grabbed the bottle and drank. Then considered his words. The last thing he wanted was to get smacked by Blind Pig sober for saying something wrong. He thought it'd be worse if Blind Pig was bagged. He set the bottle down on the sandbags, then saw a white paw grab it. It was Fritsche, who'd come up, unnoticed in Mosby's masochistic listening.

"So you and him are gonna saddle up and invade the fuckin' Octopus,'' Mosby said optimistically.

"Don't be that simple.''

It never was.

"Dude go on, about how he thinks I got moves, and how he thinks you an' the rest of the squad got moves. How maybe we want to go out one time an' not be draggin' the dog of all these legs with us.''

"Motherfucker knows how to put it,'' Fritsche said with admiration, swallowing, then surveying the empty bottle with regret. Blind Pig saw the empty and snarled. Mosby knew that a full bottle turns away wrath even better than a soft answer, dove in his bunker, and took out the Jack Daniel's he'd been saving for a major catastrophe. Come to think about it, maybe *this* was the catastrophe.

"Man, I'm getting fucked up,'' Blind Pig said after taking three straight swallows and no recovery breath.

"Come on, Blind Pig. Keep talking.''

"Shannon, he say he want to go in and nail these NVA motherfuckers cold. Find out where they be, an' then we take 'em out like we did the Phu Lois. On'y take five of us.''

335

"You cocksucker," Mosby said with deep feeling. Right then he didn't give a fat fuck if Blind Pig did moose over the sandbags at him. This asshole appeared as if he'd found a new way to get everybody killed.

"Sure be trick if we could go out," Fritsche interjected, "and be only carrying our own load for a change, instead of having all these cherrytroopers getting us killed like they do."

That made perfect sense. Stupid goddamned biker, stupid goddamned point man. Of course he'd be interested in playing Shannon's game. Mosby groaned to himself. He himself felt that echo. Damn, he was good, and going out without backup'd be one way to prove it.

Stupid, stupid, stupid. That's how you end up in a bodybag. Stupider, stupider, Mosby realized that two of his friends were gonna go for it. Hell, he'd have to go along just to keep their foot out of the shit.

"Blind Pig," he tried. "If you want to play games like that, whyn't you go Special Forces?"

"They be nothin' but country rednecks under those beanies," Blind Pig said.

"Whoopie shit. Who else did you and your fuckin' major end up drafting?"

"Me. Fritsche. DeeJay, since Shannon say he be needin' the best radio around."

"How the fuck are you gonna con him into going for it?"

"Don't be worrying about DeeJay. That skinny nigger gimme any shit, I gone shove his antenna up his butt. Oh yeah. We gone take Diaz."

"We," Mosby questioned, all his squad leader and sergeant moves blocked. "You got a mouse in your pocket, Blind Pig?"

"On'y reason I figure you oughta go is to keep us out of trouble," Blind Pig said.

"All right, motherfucker. You put me and Hank and your own ass in a trick bag. Why?"

There was a long hesitation.

"Aw, Mosby," Blind Pig confessed. "That honkie dude got a line of shit that won't quit."

"Captain Edmunds, sir, I have a problem."

"No kidding, Lieutenant Wilson. The bastard didn't tell me he was stealing some of my company, either."

"Sir, this isn't the way the Army's supposed to work."

"You got that right, Batman. Also that shithead major didn't

336

ask me if I wanted to come along. Is there anything else, Lieutenant?''

"Nossir."

"Mosby, how come Diaz gets to go, and I don't?"
Hesitation.
"Hell if I know, Taliaferro. But Major Shannon specified he wanted Diaz. Maybe he wanted somebody left back, in case we, uh, you know."
"Oh. Okay. I got it."

"You never gimme all the skinny, Major."
"Nope," Shannon agreed cheerfully.
"If you tell me I couldn't take my gun, you think I would'a been your fool?"
"Probably not. You want to back out?"
"Tell you one thing. Somebody get Blind Pig in, they ain't nobody but Blind Pig gone put him out."
"Then quit bitching and try it again."
There was no way that Blind Pig could lug the weight of his M-60, plus all the ammo it would require, on Shannon's patrol. But there still was the need for firepower.

Shannon had scored, for a box of pantyhose, two bottles of Chanel #5 (gotten from the Saigon PX), and fifteen dollars in MPC, an old Browning Automatic Rifle from the ARVNs in Song Nhanh.

The BAR was first invented for use in World War I as a way of giving an infantry squad semiportable firepower. And since nobody in the American Army came up with a better weapon, it had continued in use until the mid-sixties. Not that the BAR was any good. It weighed, fully loaded, almost eighteen pounds.

It fired the now-obsolete .30-06 rounds from a twenty-round box magazine. Fired from its barrel-mounted bipod, the gun crawled forward in spite of the gunner's best efforts to hold it back. Fired from the shoulder, it climbed irresistibly. Fired from the hip, it was even worse. But it did give a grunt a somewhat transportable weapon that could deliver heavy-caliber automatic fire.

Even stripped down, without bipod, carrying handle, rear shoulder rest, and so forth, it weighed about fifteen pounds ready to roll. The only people who could fire it accurately needed the body weight and musculature of an enraged moose and a conviction that they could shoot anything. Shannon correctly figured that Blind Pig qualified on all three counts. The praise didn't

337

please Blind Pig. He squinted through the knock-down sight at the E-silhouette propped 100 meters beyond the perimeter, then pulled the trigger. The gun chattered, and the barrel tried to climb up and to the right. Blind Pig ground it back down and watched his four rounds tear into the target at mid-chest level.

"I be zeroed, Major," he snarled. "Best you hope I don't be findin' other uses for this crowbar when we be out in the bush."

CHAPTER FORTY-ONE

THE OCTOPUS

"GOTTA LET YOU citizens in on the hot skinny," Fritsche said after some cogitation. "We don't even look like we're in the American Army anymore."

"And what be the matter with that," Blind Pig asked from the corner of the tent where he was sitting, morosely polishing the BAR.

Once the five men were committed, Shannon had moved them off the line, into a squad-size tent near Charlie Company's CP. To First Sergeant Ramos' fury, he'd also ordered them exempt from any detail. Then he'd spent a week fine-tuning his patrol. They slept all day and patrolled all night. Shannon would pick a map point, generally a klick or two outside the perimeter. The route would be laid out on a map and, at full darkness, the six of them would head out. Shannon would assign someone else as patrol leader. None of the five knew it, but Shannon was putting them through a very half-ass, very speedy version of Ranger School.

No talking and no smoking outside the wire. Commo checks were done by click code only, run on a separate net. This meant that whichever route Shannon selected was closed off for any H&I fire.

The only break that Shannon had allowed them was a loud protracted drunk on New Year's Eve, and then followed it with a mile run down Highway 45L the next morning. Mosby and the others were adjusting to a whole different way of fighting a war, not the least surprising of which was that Shannon had moved into the tent with them.

Even their gear changed. Fritsche was modeling, late in the afternoon of the seventh day of training, the New Look. Their jungle fatigues had been blotched with spray-on flat black paint.

The steel pots were abandoned for floppy boonie hats. Dyed-green towels went around their necks. Black and green cammie cream was issued.

Even the web gear had been altered. Shannon had taken away their asspacks and issued brown canvas NVA rucksacks. Each man carried three canteens on the back of his belt. In front was an aid pouch, plus another, Special Forces issue aid pouch, containing never normally issued items such as morphine Syrettes, salt tablets, and codeine and Dexedrine tablets. The last two Blind Pig and Fritsche had already decided would somehow get lost in the field.

Instead of ammo pouches up front, each man carried two empty canteen covers that held far more magazines than the conventional heavy and noisy-to-open issue pouches. Normal pouches—three per man—were hung on the belt's sides. Their bayonets were replaced with K-Bar fighting knives for everyone except Mosby, who had Casey's Randall.

In the rucks went five days' worth of pouched LRRP rations, crab powder, mosquito repellent, and a spare battery for Dee-Jay's radio, cased in plastic. Instead of ponchos or poncho liners, Shannon had gotten dark blue Air Force windbreakers, pointing out that everybody would be too scared once they were in the Octopus to feel cold.

All of them already had their M-16s camouflaged with tape, so Shannon had no changes, other than to pull their rifle slings off and tape the swivels down.

Diaz's M-79 was replaced with a cut-down version Shannon had scrounged from one of his A-team friends. The stock was cut just at the curve, the front sight removed, and the barrel chopped just in front of the handguard. Diaz was carrying only four grenade rounds—the other twelve in his neck-hung apron were multiple-projectile rounds, turning the 79 into a 40mm super-shotgun. Fritsche had declined with firmness the idea that his personal sawed-off be replaced with a 79 like Diaz's.

Diaz carried his .357 Christmas present and DeeJay lugged a .45. The others felt that in combat by the time you were close enough to hit anything with a handgun you were dead anyway.

Shannon would carry his much-beloved K gun, the Swedish Carl Gustav firing thirty-six 9mm slugs per magazine. He also carried a handgun, even though he agreed with the grunts as to its uselessness. The piece was a suppressed (silenced) .22-caliber Colt Woodsman automatic that had originally been built for OSS use in WWII. The pistol would be used only if there was a fuckup—Shannon had no intention of letting any bad guy know he was within a thousand kilometers if he could help it. The patrol was to go in, find the NVA, and haul ass. After all, six men got into a shooting match with zillions of enemies only in John Wayne movies.

Each man also carried a spare magazine of .30-06 rounds for the BAR, one Claymore mine, two frag grenades, and one smoke grenade taped to his webbing harness.

It was still too much shit, but at least their load was down around a reasonable forty pounds (not including DeeJay's radio or their personal weapons).

But Fritsche was right. None of them looked like members of the American forces.

"Well, whataya think," Fritsche continued.

Diaz grinned. "Those fatigues look like you went one-on-one with Earl Scheib, my man."

Blind Pig looked at Shannon, who was across the tent from him. "Got a question, Major."

"Go."

"All this trickshit? It cost the honkie taxpayer any more'n the regular stuff?"

Shannon considered. "Nope. Not much."

"The way you been teachin' us to move? That be any harder to teach a grunt 'stead of the runnin' around they give us in AIT?"

"Maybe a little bit."

Blind Pig considered again.

"Gotta wonder why we got all this shit with battalion sweeps and search an' shit and playin' chargin' cowboy all the time instead of what you be preachin'. That shit be fucked.

"I remember . . . back in basic . . . some cat told us there was three ways of doin' shit."

Shannon nodded. "The right way, the wrong way, and the Army way."

"Yeah. Well, they coulda made it only two ways."

Blind Pig dropped the trigger mechanism back into the BAR and stuck the retaining pin in place.

"Tell you something, Major. We gone lose this war. An' we gone lose it bad."

Dennis Shannon had seen something that, seemingly, no one else had recognized yet. The fact that the Twelfth Division's Lurp teams were getting their ass shot off could be ascribed to a number of theories, from inept personnel to very ept VC awaiting them on the ground.

340

Shannon wondered if maybe there wasn't another reason. For years the old system had worked fine, send two slicks over your patrol zone, drop one down and kick the grunts out, then keep on going, no one the wiser. Shannon was wondering if maybe the baddies, whom he never made the mistake of thinking of as dumb, hadn't figured out the method on their own. He knew that the most critical times for a patrol were on insertion, on contact, and during extraction.

Shannon determined on something new. Basically there were three ways into the Octopus:

The first was to sneak in on foot. That'd work great, if Shannon was willing to live with the probability he'd be eligible for Social Security by the time they hiked back out. The second would be by river. Maybe if he was a SEAL his team could slither up one or another of the rivers that flowed out of the Octopus. Shannon remembered the one time he'd gone white-water rafting with some other drunk Ranger friends and shuddered at the idea.

So the best way in was by air. But there had to be a trick way to do it. Shannon puzzled at that one while he studied the high-resolution medium-level aerial photos he'd cozened out of Air Force Recon. Because he also had to figure out where to go.

The Octopus, even if it had not been semi-vertical, thick jungle massif, would have taken about ten years to investigate properly. Shannon, using the photos and contour overlays, narrowed the search. I am looking for a North Vietnamese Division. The commander of that division is evidently holding his troops in place for some unknown task. Therefore, he won't break the unit up too much. This means I need an area where it is possible to quarter, say, 6,000 men. That was the first level of search, and many small valleys and plateaus were eliminated.

Second requirement is water. Shannon, hoping to Christ there wasn't a whole bunch of unmapped springs in the Octopus, cut the field further.

Third was resupply. Dennis Shannon knew that the idea that anyone—Viet Cong, Special Forces or human beings—could live off the jungle was total bat guano. The jungle may be neutral, but it will fuck you in an instant if you aren't a native. Even the native Montagnards live short, painful survival existences. Any unit required to stay in the Octopus would slowly, inevitably deteriorate unless resupplied from the outside. So the box canyons, blind draws, and such on the map also were ignored.

Finally, since Shannon was assuming the NVA unit had come in from the southwest, carrying all its gear, there must be passable terrain. Again, this reduced the area. Shannon thought he had it.

Of course, being Dennis Shannon, he felt that most likely he and his semi-willing sneakies would fall in this carefully selected area and go through it for five days and the only military presence they'd find would be a long-rotted French Foreign Legionnaire's kepi from 1952. If that.

Ah well. Shannon's area did look promising. And still better, close examination with the stereo viewer suggested a trick way in. One of the dots in the photo turned out to be, under examination, a crashed Huey. It sat on its side, about 400 meters up a looming massif.

If Shannon had still been division G-2, or in charge of the division's LRRP teams, the next stage would have been simply a matter of issuing orders. Instead, since this patrol was at the very least irregular and at the worst something that would cause General Sinclair to ruin Shannon, everything had to be done from left field.

Left field was a crawling drunk with Major Carruthers. Yeah, one of the Twelfth AvCo's Hueys disappeared about two months ago, coming back from Tay Ninh. Carruthers was grateful that the missing chopper had been found. He wondered if anybody had made it out, looked closely through the viewer, and grimaced.

"Looks like they went straight in. Zero-zero. Pretty badly crumpled up on the nose. Uh, Denny . . . is there any way we can go in . . . get the bodies out at least?"

The operation then became a lot more elaborate. All Carruthers had to do was provide six D-model slicks, one flight of Cobras, and oh, yeah, a Shithook.

"Why the fuck do we want to lift that bird out? Fucker's tinfoil."

Shannon explained. He couldn't determine whether Carruthers went for his plan because Shannon promised to recover any bodies if they were there; because it was an excuse for him to put gunships into a free-fire zone like the Octopus; or just because Shannon's plan was so sneaky.

At least Shannon thought it was.

At false dawn, two platoons from A Company stood shivering next to the tiny LZ in the center of Camp Stuart. Among them were Shannon and his five men, taking a ration of shit about how their mother dressed them all funny. None of the A Company grunts got too serious—they were all scared shitless of going into the Octopus, had no idea why they were being sent in in the first place, and were just hoping they could get out and keep at least some of their ass from getting blown away.

Huey blades thudded against the dank morning air, and the slicks came in two at a time, loaded eleven men, and lifted away. They formed up over Song Nhanh, then turned east. Shannon, sitting in the lead ship's right seat, spotted the dark bulk of the CH-47 coming up toward them from the south. The Chinook fell into formation at the rear, as the Cobra flight took covering positions on either side of the troop-carrying slicks.

Below them was the Octopus. Shannon lifted the visor on his helmet, and stared down at it. He'd seen a fair chunk of scary turf in his life: Bad Tolz, the A Shau valley, Michelin plantation, the Superstition Mountains, the California redwoods deep in fog. But nothing like this. Shit, he thought. All you need is some fucker banging a gong and this'd be the opening of some cheap-ass horror movie. Velcome to Transylvania, Meester Shannon. Vould you like to visit my crypt?

The intercom crackled.

"You actually gonna take a stroll down there," Carruthers wondered.

"You got a better idea?"

"Shit yes. Let's see if we can't get a nuke Arc Light. Those hills look scarier'n West by God Virginny."

"You're doing wonders for my morale."

"Sorry about that shit. Hang on. I got your hill on visual."

The hilltop rose out of the fog blanketing the canyons below, trees, even in the growing dawn light, standing dark and very still, trees that could hold every nightmare a boy could imagine and every nasty reality Vietnam could provide.

The Cobras made two passes over the broken Huey halfway up the hill. No return fire. Carruthers ordered the slicks in.

The Hueys hovered on the steep slope, trying to keep one skid on the ground. The grunts doubled away from the ships and took up a defensive perimeter around the crashed Huey.

Shannon keyed his mike.

"See you around, Carruthers," and he had his flight helmet off, bush hat held on, the right door open and was out, Mosby and the others tumbling after him.

Crouched, they went straight down the hill, through the platoon's perimeter, fifty meters down. Shannon saw an impenetrable thicket and waved his five men into it.

The last ass—Diaz's—crawled out of sight. Shannon looked at the ground. No marks.

Shannon heard the Chinook thud in above him. Shouts—that should be A Company hooking up the slings to the wreck. Wonder if they found any bodies.

Shannon followed his team into the thicket. Rotor blades got louder, shriek of metal, more shouts, several helicopters coming in, prolonged blast as the slicks lifted away with the Chinook. Shannon chanced a peer upward and saw the cargo chopper climb away, the wrecked Huey swinging underneath it. The troopships were behind and below the 47. Finally the smash as the Cobra flight made one final pass—Shannon could have sworn whoever was flying one ship stuck a skid into Shannon's thicket—and then silence.

For almost ten minutes.

And then crashing, slithering, and Vietnamese voices. Like ducks fucking, Shannon thought, deep in the heart of the thicket. More voices. Disappointment—there were no imperialists to ambush. Why did they land here. Explanation, finding the remains of the wreck. Laughter. Then the feet came back, headed downhill, moving more quietly this time. There were no voices. If they bust us now, we're just fuckin' dead.

They did not.

Eventually the Viet Cong voices and sounds disappeared. Shannon gave it another full hour and ten minutes. He took the radio mike from DeeJay.

"Citation Six, Citation Six. This is Whirlaway Zulu, over."

"Six Actual. Go." Colonel Taylor was on the other end of the radio link.

"Zulu," Shannon whispered. "Moving. Click. Out."

He shut down the radio, hoping that whoever was in the Octopus wasn't using a sweep RDF, since the link with the Fifteenth's CP was on a totally unassigned frequency.

Shannon took point—to Fritsche's annoyance—out the thicket and down the hill. All the bullshit, from staff to ex-wives to R&R to strategy, dropped away. It's hide and go seek. Wouldn't it be fine, Dennis, if war was played like that? No fuckin' guns. If you found them before they found you the penalty would be . . . let them pick up the bar tab.

That, too, fell away, and Shannon's body took over. The delicate step, very slowly, up and toe-down down, cushioning the downhill shock, hand lifting the wait-a-bit thorn before they clung, letting the rhythm, the slow 2/4 clogstep time sing through the universe. Behind him silence, none of the swearing, clanking and thuds he'd come to know as the American soldier in the field.

Damn, we're good, he thought happily. When we want to be. The monkey goggled indignantly at him, half-eaten fruit dropping away. Two-legged things should not move so quietly, and the monkey was too frightened to chatter a warning until the last man was past.

There was a trail of sorts, and Shannon used that as a guide to lead them down into the canyon. Nothing could go wrong this day—there was even a slight clearing that gave Shannon a chance to shoot exact triangulation bearings. Careful, Dennis, he reminded himself. This is going entirely too easy. There's probably a booby trap in somebody's future.

Shannon stopped about 100 meters above the canyon floor and motioned Mosby up toward him. Again, Fritsche looked pissed. Shannon frowned at him—he'd told the man that he wanted to save him for when the shit really came down. Hang tough, Mr. Fritsche. You'll get just as much of a chance to commit suicide as any of us. He indicated on the map where they were, and that he wanted the patrol to move along the canyon walls, until—and he pointed to a rift a kilometer or so ahead.

Mosby was feeling very strange as he moved ahead. Christ, maybe Blind Pig was right—maybe this was the way to fight a war, not hurry up, hurry up, with the gunships overhead and the 500 or so grunts banging into each other and sounding like a demolition derby.

Every bush Mosby saw as the patrol crept forward was an enemy and a friend. Each clearing was to be avoided. Step. Pause. Step again. Wait and listen. Every few minutes stop and wait for a long time. Stop when you see where you could be ambushed and listen. You have more to lose than they do. If there is someone behind that clump of rocks they will fart or light a cigarette or cough before you do. Mosby was starting to understand what it was to be a Viet Cong.

The patrol moved possibly a kilometer and a half before dark closed in. All according to plan. Shannon had pointed out a large boulder about 500 yards before they hit their night's final position. This boulder, if they were hit during the night, would be the rendezvous point—the RP. The bivvy site, Shannon decided, would be about twenty meters away from a stream that curled down from the hills.

They moved about 200 meters past that point, swung back on their trail, and took up ambush positions. Nothing. They were not being followed. At full dark, they moved back in their tracks to the bivouac position.

The check time was 2100. Shannon missed it by only a few

seconds. The radio whispered. "Whirlaway Zulu, this is Citation." Shannon clicked the mike twice, then shut down.

The perimeter was very tiny. The six men lay, starfish-fashion, their legs almost touching. They added water to the packs and ate, eyes never moving from the darkness beyond them.

Mosby was quite astonished. All this time the night had been his enemy. How many times had he started out and watched a bush fix bayonets or prime a grenade and come toward him? But that was because, he thought, they always knew where you were. We're here, he thought, and there isn't a single swinging zip around us who's got the foggiest.

You hope, troopie. You fuckin' hope.

Shannon had the watch before dawn. Again, he checked in with battalion on click code, then had nothing else to do but wait for the world to lighten. Just like back on the border. Shannon sort of wished that he had brought a camera. Maybe Sinclair would be convinced. Yeah, but what kind of pictures would he need. The only shot that'd move him would probably be an NVA officer pinning a Hero of the Soviet Union on some grunt, with three Russian commissars chuckling in the background.

Dawn was the mist of gray, and Shannon's people were awake. Dennis yawned and thought that none of these legs realized how lucky they were. Nobody snored, nobody had to take a smelly shit in place, and so far nobody had gotten the hiccups. All his people were still entranced with newness, and that they were in a guerrilla war as they should be. Ah well. Time to be moving.

Their route followed the canyon that had become a valley and became a canyon once more. The rock walls rose steep above them, and the streams were waterfalls on either side. Shannon kept them above the valley floor, moving on the ages-old remains of rock slides.

Now they moved slowly, perhaps 100 meters in an hour. Step and listen. Step and listen. Take two breaths on each step. In the silence.

Shannon was getting worried. The low jungle they were moving through was desolate and waiting. No animals meant people—and so far there was no one to be seen.

They broke for lunch where a stream cascaded down the hill, pooled, and then ran down to the river in the valley below. Fritsche surprised an otter, hunting in that pool. Blind Pig stared at Shannon. Took his BAR by the butt. Mimed tying on a line, adding a fly, and then casting out into that pool as if he were fishing. Now whereinhell did that street dude ever hear about

346

fly-fishing? A thought to avoid thinking about the mush he was shoving in his face.

One hour, and then they were moving again.

DeeJay went on point and was, Shannon was startled to see, the first to spot the faint trails that led downhill, toward the valley floor. The patrol flanked the trailside. Shannon considered, then took compass readings in the bright sunlight. If the map's right . . . we're here. He listened, holding the radio mike in its waterproof bag on his shoulder. No sound but the sleepy buzz of an afternoon jungle.

"Citation Six, Citation Six, this is Whirlaway Zulu, over."

The response was instant—Taylor must have the battalion's best radiomen on watch.

"This is Citation, over."

"Citation, this is Zulu. Present position from Mike Alpha up six, left two. Have indications. Route from given toward Mike Delta. Out."

"Zulu, this is Citation. I read back, present position Mike Alpha up six, left two, direction toward Mike Delta, over."

"Zulu, roger, out."

The tracks became a trail became a path became a foot-hardened dirt track, leading toward a village, nestled near the river. The village appeared abandoned and shot up. The thatched roofs were burnt black and torn away. Shannon scanned the village, looking for something. Red peppers on a rack waiting harvest. A central firepit with white ashes.

There was nothing.

Shannon doffed his ruck and webbing. He pointed at Fritsche, who did the same. They paced forward, along the trail, eyes on the trodden dirt in front of them, eyes on the huts, eyes trying to be dragon-fly vision.

The village *was* abandoned. But the village was not a village. Each of the shot-up huts was carefully reinforced as a supply bunker. The dirt floors were dug down five meters. The roofs above were framed with five-inch mahogany logs.

Shannon filtered the dust outside one hut with his fingers and found rice grains. He tasted one. Still bitter, still resistance.

A large supply dump, camouflaged as a shot-up village. A supply dump that had been cleaned out quite recently. Question—why? Shannon waved the patrol forward. Taking a chance, he grouped the five near one hut and told them what they were seeing.

Blind Pig was the first to evaluate it. The BAR resting on one leg, he held up two hands, palms apart. Then sketched a question mark. How far are we away from them? Shannon spread his hands. Who the fuck knows? Then he pointed. The track they must follow led up the valley, deeper into the Octopus. Now he put Fritsche on point. Okay, my man. You been wanting. Now let's see you earn your pay.

Fritsche, perhaps more than even Shannon, felt the rhythm of the jungle. Once you learned it, and it maybe was gonna kill you learning, it was easy. It felt right, just like the way it felt when you finally figured out what tranny sprocket, balance ratio, and rear sprocket to run at whatever speed you were gonna cruise at.

Silence but for the hum, and Fritsche lifted, stepped and moved, a picture he could see like Davy Mann or that French fucker, everything in place, and nothing out of motion. He hoped he didn't run into a gook or a mine—it just wouldn't fit. If he did, he wished he'd have Casey's knife that Mosby had or Shannon's silenced piece. The noonday hum was too perfect.

The trail wove left, and a sunlit clearing opened. Fritsche checked to see if there was an intersection, if there was anybody there. The whole world was asleep. He crouched, ready to cross the clearing beside the trail.

The king cobra reared.

Fritsche was ice in the sun as the snake came three feet above the ground and slowly flared its hood. The snake's mouth yawned and its sensing tongue flickered.

The king cobra and the biker were perhaps four feet apart, the cobra ready to lunge, Fritsche's shotgun aimed and klickklick cocked, and then they were, perhaps, in mutual admiration.

To Fritsche the cobra was the perfect thing in this sleepy clearing. It was the beauty of his cat licking itself in the morning, a long line of bikes snaking down a mountain road, Clapton's fingers on "White Room," the perfection of life within death.

Fritsche thought that maybe the best thing that would ever happen to him was if the snake came in.

Yeah, his mind exulted. This is the picture. If nobody fuckin' kills me here, this is what I'm gonna remember about the Nam. And yeah, there's everything here, realizing that nobody behind him was moving or doing anything. If that fuckin' Taliaferro were here he'd blow the snake away and we'd all be in the shitter.

Fritsche did not want to pull the trigger.

The cobra—Fritsche had the insane thought that it was probably taking its nap and got woke up—deflated its hood and decoiled. Then an equally insane thought, as the snake lowered to the ground, hissed once, and coiled away into the underbrush, that he wanted to pat its head.

Jolt.

Shannon was beside him. Eyes asking.

Fritsche shook himself back to the real world. No problem, Major. Just waiting. Shannon nodded approval—you didn't shoot, you didn't panic. He didn't have, Fritsche realized, the slightest idea of what had happened. Fritsche determined, as he crept forward again, that if he made it back to the world he would have a cobra painted on either side of his fatbob tanks.

The trail became a road and there were other people in the world. The six Americans went flat, hearing the thump of feet come down it. Mosby lifted his head to see two khaki-clad Viets, carrying a stretcher with a bandaged man on it, trot past. Four other helmeted soldiers ran behind them, AKs at port arms.

DeeJay saw them, as he fetus-curled around his radio. This is DeeJay here, reporting some major traffic on Giap Way, and cats and cracks out there, this isn't something I am gonna confess, but we're all partners on the air aren't we and I just did an FCC in my pants because this ain't part of all the hits that give you shits and the world I am trying to keep myself alive for so I can be part of it and that fucking nigger Blind Pig if he wasn't the size of the *Hindenburg* I'd frag him. Aw hell, he thought. Bill Drake never went through this. Man, I want to be a platter spinner, not a fucking helicopter traffic reporter. Helicopters and, he was afraid, DeeJays, fall down a lot . . .

Shannon held them in the position on the trail crossing that night. RV point would be back at the ruined "village." Piss-poor, Major. You are getting yourself in very, very deeply.

Diaz always thought that he would see a Viet Cong up close. But the follow-up would be that he would kill him—with a knife, with a rifle or, since his Christmas present, with the .357 Magnum. He never thought that he would lie on his belly in the middle of the jungle and watch Commies pass on by. Pass on by, wait on the corner . . . Joseph, you are cracking up. Es verdad, y porqué, María mi madre y la madre de los todos, did you let me get into this insane fucking position in the first place. I would have made a great insurance salesman. Josef, Josef, why did you let this fucking gringo con you into going on this patrol in the first place? And in Christ's holy name, if we have to do this at all, why is this goddamned major keeping us here all night? He is not macho enough to want to go in in the daylight, is he?

Shannon wasn't macho—he just knew that no one, on any side, can move quietly at night. And also he was getting angry. Why am I going through this again, finding these gooks when I already did it once? I went and told it very clear that there was a whole shitpot load of NVA in the world, I went and shouted in their ear. And now I am going to get killed. Just at dawn, when he awoke, he was dreaming that Sinclair's wife was just confessing to her husband that she was leaving him because she liked getting gangfucked by a bunch of black privates at Fort Knox.

Blind Pig took point as they moved out, moving beside the trail, keeping twenty meters away in the brush.

The day passed very slowly for David Mosby. Quite literally. It took them ten hours to move 300 meters, and, with every step, Mosby was considering himself a total fool for ever thinking he belonged in the jungle.

The high point of the day, Mosby thought to himself wryly, was that he got to examine a North Vietnamese Army heavy machine-gun post. Ah yes. That is the Degtyarev heavy machine gun. What an unusual sight it has. Looks like it's intended for antiaircraft. Sure, especially when you look at the mount. Do you want to think about those five very alert zipperheads standing around it? Or maybe those belted rounds that look to be about three feet long going into the gun? No, Mosby. You just want to keep crawling through this brush following this insane fucking major who somehow got you into this. Hell, Mosby, eventually it's going to get dark and safe.

Then all you'll have to worry about is being in the middle of an NVA camp and also what that fruitcake with the oak leaves can come up with to make it worse.

Eventually it did get dark and the smell of the charcoal fires and the murmur of voices died away from the valley below, and Dennis Shannon, probably not sane, considered what to do next.

Were this a rational war, he would withdraw his patrol. He had found a large enemy force. His patrol should pull out, and other patrols should be sent in to identify this unit, get some idea of its strength and hopefully its intentions. Or else massive artillery or airstrikes would be brought in to destroy this unit.

For that kind of action, Shannon and even his battalion commander lacked clout. Sinclair would want more before he'd be willing to get the B-52s from Guam sent in. And even if he did, who was to say that the Arc Light would hit the proper valley at the proper time?

Dennis Shannon wanted more proof—and became less than sane because he was not sure what more was. The head of the NVA commander? A letter from Ho Chi Minh saying all imperialists smell funny?

So, as the camp below them fell into silence, Shannon went looking. Without words, he moved the patrol out of its bush cover and flanked them down the path that led toward the middle of the camp.

Hand signals, done inches in front of each man's face. You, Blind Pig. To the left of this trail. You, Diaz, on the other side. You will know what to do. You, Fritsche, below Blind Pig and to the side. You, DeeJay, beside Blind Pig and on standby and do not answer the periodic checks from Citation. You, Mosby. Shed the webbing. Motion. The knife.

Mosby, in awful fascination, drew the bowie, dropped his pistol belt and rucksack, and followed Dennis Shannon down the trail.

Shannon had the .22 tucked inside his shirt and the K-Bar knife in one hand. He went down the trail, moving like a curious gibbon toward the flat land. Shannon saw to one side of the trail the banked darkness of a machine-gun post. Mosby behind him, Shannon, on hands and knees, went around a bush, hands lifting, knees lifting, expecting a snail with racing stripes to smoke past him momentarily. You can't be that crazy, Shannon, if you can still make jokes.

Mosby stopped before he slammed into Shannon's butt. Shannon reared, not unlike that cobra seen the day before, and swept like a scanner over the brush in front of them. Shannon turned. Tapped Mosby's hand once. Waved a finger in front. Then he scuttled forward, across an open space.

Mosby, with no options, followed. He was astonished to realize he wasn't even vaguely scared. This whole situation was so far beyond reality, beyond anything any grunt should expect, there was no fear reservoir to work on. Lord God, he thought wildly. Maybe this fucking Shannon thinks I should have this knife between my teeth.

Shannon fell—almost literally—into what he was looking for. It was a low, semi-dug-in bunker, dug down below its thatched roof about five feet. Shannon slid down the wooden steps, motioning—Mosby thought—to watch his rear.

Inside was the roar of snores, coming from the far end of the bunker. Shannon's fingers, surgical in precision, ran across the dirt floor. Found a straw mat. Crept across the foot of that mat, finding no warmth of a sleeping body. He moved his hands upward. Roughness. Canvas. His fingers, moving independently, found the catch of the pack and sought inside. Papers. They went inside his shirt.

A second unoccupied mat. Another pack, this one with more papers. Some soft—letters. Stiffness—photographs. A large, folded paper. Then cloth.

Shannon came back to rationality. This is enough, Dennis. If it isn't, Major, what the hell would keep you happy. Time to go home. He crawled back up the bunker steps, pausing only long enough to take that cloth, billed object—a Mao cap—from his fatigues and put it on Mosby's head.

Time to go home, son.

Vien Sang walked his post in a military manner, pouting all the while. He had not failed in his duty. He had been active with his squad. And so why should that corporal put him out, tonight, on the edges of the camp, with orders to walk back and forth for half the night.

This would be the last time, he decided, he ever would consult a superior about his own life.

Walk back from this tree to that tree, and then repeat it again. What a stupid thing to do, as if the imperialists would somehow materialize like so many animal ghosts in the heart of this camp. Sang felt there was no way anyone could penetrate this far, especially at night. He knew that out there were tigers and the fearsome creatures of the jungle. All that he could do was walk back and forth, mourning his child that he felt he would never see, feeling sorry for himself and being bored.

For this reason he was startled when Phum Phuong loomed up at him. He almost brought his AK down and challenged the man. That would have been even foolish, since he thought Phuong considered him nothing more than a whiner.

"Comrade," Phuong whispered. "When we ate tonight, I thought you looked sick."

"No. I feel fine."

"Ah. I was wrong. Maybe you just haven't written to your wife lately."

This was true, Sang begrudged. How would his words sound, by the time they made the long miles north? Also, how would they sound to the commissars who would read those letters?

"I learned something, comrade," Phuong went on. "When I am upset about something, I write a long letter to someone. I do not have the advantage of a wife like you, so I write letters to someone I knew long ago, a beautiful girl who is now dead. That helps me to think clearly."

Sang wondered—he had never thought to find this in Phuong. He stammered as if he understood.

"You go back and write that letter," Phuong said. "I shall stand your guard for you. Isn't this what comrades are for?"

Sang, relieved of four more hours of blackness outside and inside, agreed, and left for their squad bunker.

Phuong took the unheard applause from the night. This Sang was criminally stupid. First he had spent long tiring weeks talking about this water buffalo of a wife of his, a wife that Phuong knew was probably fucking anyone who showed up with a red star on his cap and a hard cock in his hand. He would probably be most surprised if he ever returned home to discover that his wife had three children since he had been gone. Phuong also figured that Sang would become a believer in virgin birth at that point.

Sang, a weak man, gave Phuong his strength. And his salvation. Phuong, for the first time since he had made the mistake of attending the rally and cheering loudly enough to be noticed and recruited into the People's Army, felt that he was about to control his own destiny.

Phuong had recognized that his division would be the first to fight in what Phuong believed—in spite of there having been no briefings as yet—would be a General Offensive. Phuong, as a boy, had heard of the bravery of the Viet Minh units at Lang Son and Dien Bien Phu and had been the only one who had asked the comrade teacher how many of those comrade heroes had survived. Phuong was feeling that he was in the position of being a potential comrade hero, and had no interest in being mentioned, posthumously, in dispatches. For this reason, it was most important that he manage to get out of this infantry squad he was forced into.

He had a plan. First, with Vien Sang on the good corporal's and on Lieutenant Lam's reeducation-through-work list, that created a weak point. If Phuong encouraged that thinking, Lam would insist that Comrade Sang be present to realize his Marxist duty in combat. Especially if Comrade Sang was a bit of a slacker on a simple duty like walking his guard post.

Phuong knew that the comrade corporal or hopefully Lieutenant Lam would check this guard post soon. Would they not be surprised to discover loyal Phuong walking that post, and being very knowledgeable about what the terrain was like? When the unit moved out for the General Offensive, Phuong knew, it would be necessary to leave some members of the 302d Division behind as rear guards. Who else would be more motivated and capable than Comrade Phuong?

It was a perfect, flawless plan.

For this reason, Phuong was most surprised when he stepped on something that his sandaled feet told him was a man's leg. A living man's leg.

He was about to exclaim his surprise and indignation about the comrade corporal sneaking up on him when they were in a combat zone when Shannon's knife went in below his sternum, driving his breath away, and then the black night turned red and turned black and Shannon caught the body and eased it down to the ground below.

Shannon took the knife out, wiped it reflexively on Phuong's fatigues, came around and beckoned Mosby, and in a crouching run, the two went back up the hill toward the rest of the patrol. It was just then that Comrade Lieutenant Lam *did* check his guard posts.

Blind Pig didn't need hearing the frantic scuttle as Shannon and Mosby came back up the trail to know the deal was blown. This was the way the world worked.

The illuminating flare that Lieutenant Lam threw after stumbling over Phuong's body, finding wetness at the corpse's gut, and realizing somehow, someway the imperialists were among them was only further indication that when you walk on the wild side, the shit gonna come down.

One jungle is like another, and Blind Pig was reminded of the first time Deacon Rayburn had made him gun cover when they took off a small-time dope man. Instead of a tree-hung jungle there'd been a narrow street and brownstone apartments. But the scrabbling was the same as the two men came toward him. What was different was that there wasn't a gutshot boy screaming on the steps of the brownstone. Blind Pig got mildly pissed when Shannon paused by him and told him not to open fire.

Shit, man. He knew about not giving away his position. Things, of course, had been different back on the block. He'd leveled a full magazine from his carbine at the brownstone's open door as the three of them smoked for their ride. But boogyin' be boogyin', he knew, hearing Shannon and Mosby shrug into their gear and the patrol went back up the trail, hunched black backs in the dying light of the flare.

Fuckin' Shannon done out-tricked himself. Man, I have my gun, I could put max hurt down that trail. Be hours afore them gooks come up after us. This smokepole Shannon be stickin' me with be impossible, he continued as he spun and, last man, rearguarded up the trail.

The first rule was to break contact.

Behind them, Shannon heard the stir and saw occasional lights as the NVA camp came to life.

Which means move, goddammit, which was why Shannon was on point. He was systematically breaking every rule that existed on patrol movement. He kept them on the trail, moving at a near lope. Fritsche grumbled at his rear. Maybe Shannon would lead them into a booby trap—but that was less deadly than the NVA elements he knew would be coming after them.

He'd made an estimated 500 meters from the NVA perimeter when he halted the patrol. Come on, now. Adrenaline, slow down. I need a second or so to think. Where are we? Trail led up, along the fringe of the jungle. What, Shannon tried to remember, was above them? Oh-ho. A nice, solid rock formation, he recalled from the map. A great place for a last stand. Not too far from it another hillcrest opened out—an ideal place for a panicked extraction. Below them—the river. No one in his right mind would head for the valley floor.

Shannon waved them down.

The trees broke into scrub brush and the ground became cracked granite rock, and then there was nothing in front of Shannon's investigating toe but air and the river roar.

He turned and slid, face toward the cliff, over the edge. Found a footing. Explored it.

Solid.

A ledge. Silhouetted against the whitish-gray rock, he beckoned and the other five followed him. Along here, he silently instructed . . . wide ledges have brush on them I hope and he felt the feathers of leaves against his searching, waist-high hand. More exploration. He thought there was a wide clump of brush on the ledge. Wide enough, he hoped, to hide them until dawn. Shannon took his men to ground on that narrow ledge.

Diaz had a vague idea of what Shannon was doing, since a couple of times he'd played coyote to get friends and relatives across the border. If Immigration got on your trail, it was time to think.

You must assume that the man chasing you—Diaz knew that the NVA, just like the Immigration nazis, worked as a team, but it was best to consider the bad guy as a single person. Then perhaps you could out think him.

Diaz envisioned whatever gook was directing the search as a

355

man standing in a well-lit tent, holding a very good map. He would think, Diaz continued, that it was possible to cover a certain amount of ground within a certain time. The only way he knew to elude such logical pursuit was to be illogical. Either you must run like the wind, moving faster than the sweeping net, or you must hide within that net. Hopefully the empty net would discourage whoever was after you, and they would give up the pursuit.

Diaz huddled on the ledge, trying, like the others, to make himself look as much like an innocent bush as possible. He was very grateful that his uncle had sent him that pistol. Diaz had the correct idea that if they were found, their future would be either short and unpleasant or very long and very unpleasant. Joe Diaz preferred to go out in the former way.

Near dawn, Mosby heard the rustle of men above him and shuddered. The rustle passed on.

False dawn, and Shannon briefed them, using fingers on the map, fingers on his watch. DeeJay wanted to scream for help— the radio was the only link to life and civilization. Shannon, a veteran of several badly blown patrols, knew better. Think like a rabbit, he wanted to say. There is nothing out there but the hawks and the foxes. Don't scream for Big Daddy Rabbit to come in and save your ass, because it's only going to make it worse.

Shannon was right in picking the ledge. It was ignored during the day. It was also an oven.

Fritsche sucked at his second canteen hoping that maybe there were a few drops left in it. It was dry. He lay, back to the beating sun, his shotgun aimed straight up the cliff above them. If any gook spotted them, it'd be the last thing he would ever see. Sucking at a stone, he took his mind off the sound of the river below him, and, perversely, his mind then began figuring what would happen if a VC spotted them on that ledge and just rolled a grenade? Don't do that, told himself. Think about something else. Think about the bike you're gonna build when you get back to the World. You know, if you took this new shovel engine Harley's got, stuck it into a straight-leg frame, that might be trick. Yeah. Use ULH tanks, take that XA springer you've got, and run a 21-inch wheel and drag bars. Wonder what it'd look like if you painted the rear legs of the springer to match the frame, instead of chroming them?

Half asleep, half in staring terror, the day crawled past.

Shannon's easy way out was destroyed in midafternoon, when he heard the sound of troops moving on the path above him.

Okay, he thought. They think we're still inside the net. Next thing they're going to do is fine-tooth whatever perimeter they've established. After they give the troops a break. Let them relax.

They'll figure that we'll move just at dark, and be waiting for any kind of noise.

Bet me, ziphead.

Shannon nudged the other five out of their stupor. Now. We move. Down.

He was the first to go over the cliff, hanging by his fingers and a belt buckle. Handhold . . . footing. Now. Ten feet down. Stand by. Somehow the other five also came over the edge to the notch Shannon was on.

Again.

The patrol crept downward, toward the river.

They hit flat, muddy ground, and knotted up behind a low tree. Now there wasn't anything but the rush of the river in front of them. It would be cold, deep and wet. If I had a Mike Force, he thought, we'd go across on a poncho raft. If I had an A-Team, we'd probably do some kind of Ranger toggle bridge.

Yeah, Dennis, and if you were an angel you'd just spread your little wings, too. Come to think about it, Major, aren't you being a little fuckin' arrogant? You've just taken a bunch of legs out and dumped 'em in the shitter, and look at how well they're doing. Maybe you better take your head out and stick it in the creek, huh?

Shannon did just that—and found the way to get across the river. Slightly under the river's surface were rocks, piled to a foot or so below the water's surface. Which you should have spotted, Dennis, since it looks a little like a dam. The rock bridge was typically Viet Cong in cleverness—a way across a seemingly impassable stream, but a way that would never be visible to aircraft, casual patrols, or aerial photographs.

Shannon held his men until that moment when the falling sun moved across the river. That sudden dimness would blind—he cross-finger-hoped—any observers. Okay, you people, this is the way you cross a stream, moving facing into the current, moving sideways, finding a secure foothold, and holding on to that toggle rope the next man has got and you best hope he doesn't lose balance if the river catches you.

He cheated a little by arranging to get his head underwater in the crossing, letting the rushing current cut through the crap and salt and dried sweat on his body, knowing that he'd have to put about a ton of WD-40 on anything metal before it rusted. Who

357

cares, he exulted, they're probably gonna kill us before anything rusts anyway.

They reached the opposite bank and, with full canteens, moved into a thicket. Okay, Shannon thought. We made it. We went across the river while they were chowing down. Fine. What do we do next to perplex the fine Oriental mind?

He hoped that the NVA search was confined to the far bank of the river. Assumption. Now what? Either A we move further into the Octopus and try to clusterfuck their thinking, or B we try to get out. Mmmh. If you go deeper, you might really hit something. Shannon felt he'd rather not stumble into this NVA unit's command post and try the explanation that he just got lost. And at gut level he wanted out of these mountains, with their low threatening clouds and overhanging jungle.

Mosby's thoughts were in the same vein. Anybody who says he is at home in the jungle is a stone fucking liar, he decided. Homo Mosbius. Native habitat—hell, where would it be? That blonde back home—what the hell was her name? Denise. With her own GTO and apartment. Or maybe the Caravelle with Tho. Not here on this river edge watching the leeches hump toward you and thinking that maybe you can smell your own crotch stink. What a fucking armpit this is. Jesus, Mosby thought, if this is the home turf these zips want, why don't we just let them have it?

I want silk sheets and watching somebody else's ass in the crack on the tube. And no, it ain't no satisfaction thinking that if you make it you can get a helluva good war story out of this one. I want to go to Berkeley and smoke dope and organize a commune is what I want. Mosby was too scared even to be pissed at Shannon or Blind Pig, who'd gotten him into this idiot situation in the first place.

Shannon had the mike open.

"Citation Six, Citation Six, this is Farmer Bravo, over." He'd switched to a prearranged code that he hoped to Christ whoever was sitting on the radio at Camp Stuart remembered.

Shannon and Taylor had set up their SOI skillfully—or at least Shannon hoped so. Since his patrol was using an open frequency, Shannon had thought it might be cute, if they made contact and were blown, to switch call signs. If their frequency was monitored, Shannon wanted to sound like a nice, safe Civic Action team, somewhere way outside the Octopus.

"This is Six Actual, Farmer. What's the livestock situation, over?"

358

Taylor was on the other end. Farmer was the arranged call sign if Shannon's patrol found the NVA unit.

"This is Farmer," Shannon tried to drawl, trying to sound as if he had all the time in the world. "Looks like these guys got one buffalo and a clump of pigs. All of 'em are real healthy."

Simple code: one chicken equaled one Viet Cong platoon; one pig equaled one Viet Cong company. A buffalo was a regiment. "Also they tell me they got a real good elephant they're using." A NVA Division.

"Farmer, Farmer, this is Citation Six. I read back, one buffalo, several pigs, one elephant, over." Shannon had the insane desire to chant "I got pig iron, I got pig iron, I got pig iron/ And the Rock Island Road is a mighty good road . . ." and just clicked his mike twice.

His gut was screaming at him—the zips heard us, and they're getting bearings right now. Let's move, goddammit.

They were only half a kilometer away from the thicket when the first mortar rounds exploded behind them. Okay, fuckers, you're good, Shannon conceded. My little trick didn't work. Let's see if you can outrun us.

Somewhere above them was a path, Shannon knew. But he kept the patrol in the brush, moving as fast and as silently as he knew how. It didn't work staying inside their sweep, now we're gonna outrun them. Exhaustion crawled through their bones, as one bush holding them back became another, and slippery shale became sand became shale again, and lungs on fire trying to breathe quietly, trying to run if you could without making any noise, and then, near dawn, hearing the pad of running footsteps on the trail above them, passing them.

Shannon got pissed.

Give it another try, he said, body a solid ache.

He led them up to the trail. Motioned to DeeJay. Take the Claymore out. Stuck it into position, detonator in place. Pull-release fuse screwed in. Wire across the path. Now the nylon cord, tied around a cigarette, and shoved over a flare's lever. Shannon pulled the pin on the flare. The cord held the lever in place.

Mosby almost shot Shannon when he saw the man crouch and, with shielded hands, light that cigarette. No. I don't know what's happening, his mind caught his tightening trigger finger.

The cigarette lit, Shannon beckoned them on, now moving alongside the path, toward where those running footsteps had gone. Shannon was counting to himself. A long, long time ago he had figured out exactly how long a cigarette took to burn down—it was as reliable a fuse as it was possible to come up with.

The second hand of his Rolex crossed the one-minute mark, and he took the patrol back into the brush. Ten seconds later, the cigarette must have burned down to where it let the nylon cord slip, and the flare's handle flew away. Behind them in the night was the sudden glare of white and then ahead of them chatter, footfalls, and the clack of weapons being readied. Wait . . . wait . . . wait . . . now. The last man has passed and I hope there's no stragglers and Shannon led his patrol out onto the path itself, into a wheezing, racked doubletime as behind them somebody hit the trip wire and the Claymore exploded amid screams and blast of gunfire.

The path curled and turned, following the valley's curve as the patrol staggered, lungs afire, toward the east and flat land.

DeeJay found, to his considerable amazement, that he was able to keep stumbling on after his body had said enough. Who cares. Let them take you. Hey, his mind went, moving itself away from this horrible now of fear and fatigue, you could get a good riff off this one. "People, people, my mind an' my PD told me I couldn't play my main man Smokey three in a row, but my body just took over that tone arm . . ."

Shannon moved them back down toward the river just before dawn. He took out a ration pack and tapped it. Headshakes. There was only thirst. Mosby felt his stomach be a walnut, and then he was down on the ground, sucking in water, not giving a shit if Joshua thought this was bad tactics.

Fuck him anyway. All he had to worry about was a bunch of Philistines. These zips, he blindpigged, be *bad*.

Shannon was earnestly plotting in two ways. He'd taken compass sights off the two mountain peaks that he could see. Hoped like a sonovabitch that the map was somewhere close to being accurate. Now, let's try our next move.

His mind refused to work. All it wanted to do was curl up and sleep. And the patrol was looking at him. Waiting.

"They stone you when you're dancin' cheek to cheek," Fritsche whispered, his hands going into the pouch, coming out with the bag containing dexedrine, and shoving two of the tablets into his mouth.

Shannon had the desire to finish the line. Shut up. He nodded. Speed does more than West Point can/To justify the zips' ways to man? You *are* shot, Major.

Blind Pig had his own Claymore out, rigged and planted across the space between two trees they'd moved between.

"You conned 'em we be smart," he half-explained, wiring the booby trap. "Maybe this turn we be stupid?"

Shannon got it, and motioned the patrol into the edges of the river. Hopefully he had the NVA convinced they were after some experienced soldiers, soldiers who knew damned well that nobody tried the old hack move of traveling in a stream, least of all down it.

An hour later, hearing the splashes behind him, he thought that perhaps the NVA weren't as good at double-think as they should be.

Try it again. They went out of the water, back up, over rocks, toward the trail. Try again for the heights. Shannon left a clear track up from the track toward the hillcrest high above, then doubled the patrol down, and went back along the sides of the trail toward the NVA base.

He moved only a hundred meters or so before taking them out to the side. Now he regretted having taken the dexies—half the patrol should be asleep while waiting to see if the NVA were still after them.

Too late now.

DeeJay, eyes glaring in a brown face, beckoned him over. Murmured in his ear—"Citation's been trying for us every ten minutes."

Shannon decided to chance it.

"Citation Six, this is Whirlaway Zulu. In contact. Zero Kilo, zero Whiskey India Alpha. Need extraction on standby. Present location from Romeo down three up one point five. Monitoring, out."

Then the calm whisper from safety.

"This is Citation. Do not roger this transmission. Your location from Romeo down three up one point five. Have slicks and pink flight one zero minutes from your position on standby. Citation, out."

Shannon was relieved. Now he just had to lose these persistent North Vietnamese Regulars, find a nice flat place, and Big Daddy would show up to save him. All he needed now was John Wayne to make a hero last stand, Natty Bumppo to lead him, and a battalion of SeaBees to build an airstrip.

Small shit, really. Fatigue plus fear plus dexedrine produces an amazing amount of not giving a shit. Generally followed by sudden death, Shannon cautioned himself. When it gets dark, we'll try again.

Just before it got dark, the NVA moved. This time it was quite openly. Shannon, cursing his curiosity, stared through the brush down at the trail, seeing what he estimated to be two full platoons of North Vietnamese soldiers move down the trial.

A sergeant—or maybe an officer, Shannon couldn't tell in the dying light—halted the column. Waved two men to one side. Motioned the column on. Just before it went around the bend in the trail and out of sight, two more men were dispatched as guards. Okay, Dennis. What now? You know they've got some kind of direction finder. They know about where you are. What they're going to do is keep you pinned down tonight, and then sweep the area with everything they've got tomorrow morning. Your chances will be zip-burp.

Shannon had another idea, and hoped like hell that this NVA unit was as good as he thought it was. Verification would come at 2000 hours.

It did, as four men came up the trail, paused by the two guards below him, then moved on. Shannon timed those four men. It took them about twenty minutes before they came back down the trail. Every two hours you check your guards, right? God bless the military mind. He mimed what was to happen next. Blind Pig glowed. He was ready. Let's get some.

One hour and fifteen minutes later, Shannon moved the patrol down onto the trail. Lined his troops up, and marched them forward. Jesus, Jesus, he thought. If we get away with this I'll go back to the church. I'll never wonder if God is really up there again.

Make promises, Dennis. God doesn't care if you sound like a panicky ten-year-old kid about to get his ass reamed. God's used to that. God's great, God's good, and goddamn, we just went past what I think were a couple of guards, pistol ready, black finger pointing into blackness. Ahead of him shadows beside the road, and the glint of a machine-gun barrel.

A quiet phrase from the three men around that machine gun, a phrase ending, Shannon hoped, in a question. He hissed back, nonsense garbled s-inaudibles, ending with a command-sounding rasp. Silence from the position. The RPG muzzle did not shift. Then they were past—the trail climbing and then flattening.

Somehow Shannon knew they were beyond the fine net the NVA commander had cast for them. Now all that was left was to avoid contact with whatever Viet Cong elements garrisoned the edges of the Octopus, find a suitable LZ, take the position, call for extraction, and hope the Hueys got there before the gooks did.

No problem at all, the patrol knew in a gestalt composed equally of bravado, fatigue toxins, and amphetamine.

Relief was just a lift-off away . . .

Shannon listened to the sounds of Blind Pig heaving his guts outside the tent and considered empty gestures. His own mind being empty and speed-whirling, it was as good as anything while he waited for his system to finish shutting down.

Blind Pig finished vomiting, stumbled back into the tent, looked at Shannon, grunted, and collapsed on his cot.

Empty gestures . . . in World War II, before aircrewmen or intelligence sorts went on a mission, they were served two eggs, a very special treat in an England where eggs were almost totally unobtainable. Those eggs were frequently not eaten or puked up before the plane took off—but it was the importance of the gesture.

Any cost-efficient commander would have canceled the program and fed the soon-to-be-slaughtered lambs pablum, most likely. Colonel Taylor also understood the importance of a seemingly empty gesture.

The Huey that had grabbed them from the heart of the Octopus had been met on landing by Taylor and a truck. Mosby and the others had been taken immediately to the Fifteenth's officers' mess. Taylor's cook had steaks on the grill and fries ready.

Shannon joined them later, after he'd given Taylor a rough debriefing, and made arrangements for the documents he'd found in the base camp to be translated on the qt by a friend of his at Division.

Most of the steaks had gone uneaten—the men were more interested in alcohol. Taylor had provided that, too—two cases of Budweiser were on ice in the patrol's tent, and several bottles of I. W. Harper.

Fritsche had made it through half a bottle before he passed out. DeeJay and Mosby had about a shot apiece. Somehow Dee-Jay managed to strip off and fumbled out for a shower. Diaz hadn't touched a drop before he caved in.

Only the bulletproof Blind Pig had gone through two steaks and four beers chased with bourbon, chattering away to Shannon like a cement mixer on overdrive before the reaction hit him, too.

And so here I am, the last of the noble survivors. Now I gotta figure out, Shannon thought, how I'm gonna handle this hot poop.

Somehow he had the idea that Major General Lee Sinclair was not going to appreciate having his nose rubbed in his wrongness. On the other hand, those documents might only be love poems. Bullshit, bullshit, Dennis. You saw the map. Sinclair'll probably ignore it. So what? Do you care? Not much, his mind suddenly bleared, and Major Dennis Shannon sagged sideways, half-undressed, into oblivion.

CHAPTER FORTY-TWO

SHANNON

MAJOR GENERAL LEE SINCLAIR toyed with the tiny bronze tank for a moment, then lifted his attention to Major Shannon. Shannon had been summoned to Sinclair's trailer. Entering, he'd winced. The only things on Sinclair's desk, besides the model track, were photocopies of the map and papers Shannon had lifted from the NVA camp, plus appended typed translations.

"George Patton would have known what to do with you, I suppose," Sinclair finally said.

"Yessir." Absolutely neutral.

"He would either have had you relieved and on the next transport for England, or else given you CCB.

"You know, Major, about the only thing you learn, the older you get, is what you aren't. I have had to concede, over the years, that I am not a Patton."

This conversation was not going in any of the directions Shannon had anticipated. He kept silent.

"Take a moment, and look at the situation from my side of the desk, Major. Some months ago, you came dripping out of the monsoon, looking like a scarecrow, to inform me that you had just seen an entire North Vietnamese division. Your information was unverified by any other source. Am I correct?"

"Nothing Grade 1," Shannon sort of agreed.

"But you kept beating the drum. That, as you're probably aware, was one of the reasons I transferred you. So then you manage to convince Taylor to let you run another patrol. Major, as my ex–G-2, don't you think it was unwise for you personally to be on that mission?"

"Nossir."

Sinclair smiled frostily.

"Whether it would have been possible for anyone to extract

information from you, had you been captured, is another subject. I continue. You carry out this patrol, fortunately without any casualties—my congratulations, by the way—and produce this information."

Sinclair's hand swept over the documents.

"Intelligence that seems to indicate that, at the very least, I was remiss in not following up your original report, correct?"

There was no way in the world Shannon was going to agree or disagree with that.

"What we have here are letters addressed to two men, one a private, one an officer. Both of them coming from North Vietnamese sources, both not less than six months old. This map shows positions indicating the presence of at least a regimental force, a regiment part of a division.

"Finally, we have this officer's diary in which the man mentions how proud he is to be under the command of one General Duan, and how excellent the 302d Division, Vietnamese People's Army, is and so on and so forth."

Sinclair's hand became a fist, started to come down, then stopped. An index finger tapped the diary.

"Major Shannon, I had the chance to destroy them when they were out in the open. And I fucked it up."

Shannon was startled—he didn't think Sinclair had ever used the word fuck in his life before. Sinclair swept the documents into a pile, collecting himself and coming back from anger.

"Major, like I said, I don't know what Patton would have done. But for whatever it's worth, I apologize. I should have listened months ago. I don't propose to spend any more time thinking about what I should have done then.

"For your information, this is what I want to do next. We have the 302d nailed down in the Octopus. This Vietnamese New Year . . ."

"Tet, sir."

". . . is five days away. We will honor the truce. But within one week, we are going in after the 302d. We missed them the first time. Now, I think they have trapped themselves. This is going to be a very large operation, Major. Tomorrow morning, I have a meeting at MAC-V to begin discussions on the operation.

"Roughly, assuming command-level approval, I would like to send the entire Twelfth Division in on the south and west of the Octopus. Another division—possibly the First Air Cav—should cut off any possibility of retreat to the north. The third division will be the anvil on the east.

"As I said, a very large operation."

Shannon was still lost in realizing that Sinclair wasn't quite the stick-general he thought him to be, and that Dennis Shannon wasn't about to be made the division's new PX officer.

"This is to be kept quite confidential, Major. I have already informed Colonel Taylor of my plans, when he brought these documents to me. I do not wish either of you to discuss it privately, nor in any way to begin prepping the Fifteenth for the offensive.

"There will be time enough for all that after Tet. That's all."

Sinclair was quite wrong.

There was no time left at all.

CHAPTER FORTY-THREE

SONG NHANH

30 January 1968.

Tet.

The Lunar New Year.

The beginning of the Year of the Monkey.

Even though the Lunar New Year is a Chinese tradition, and no one can hate the Chinese more than the Vietnamese, Tet had become a tradition.

An odd tradition, one that celebrated not only the new, but the old.

This was a time for new friends and new clothes, but also a time to honor the friends of the past and the long tradition that enabled a man to look at the years of struggle past, the years of struggle to come, and to accept them.

A time to celebrate life is/life was/life gone.

A time of peace.

Or at least a time of peace in Vietnam since the first Tet truce, declared unilaterally by the Communists in 1963. They had also proclaimed truces for Christmas and New Year's. In 1965, both Saigon and the U.S. forces followed suit. So, for the incoming Year of the Monkey, the Tet truce was a given. After all, both sides had honored the Christmas and New Year's truces.

Tet would be a celebration of peace and plenty.

For one week Death, in his own kingdom, would not reign.

Item: In 1789, Quang Trung struck at Hanoi during Tet with

hundreds of elephants and thousands of soldiers. The attack stabilized relations with China.

Item: In 1960, during Tet, NLF soldiers attacked the province capital of Tay Ninh, successfully, an attack some feel was the beginning of the Second Indochinese War.

This Tet, Death could find his own throne.

Merchants had been busy for the weeks before Tet ensuring that every family had gifts and new clothing for the holiday to come.

The bicycle shop owner, Nghi, and his comrades had also been busy, making sure the location and the identity of all the imperialist collaborators, the local despots, and other poisonous snakes were recorded.

Street salesmen had ensured that every family in Song Nhanh had a ready supply of fireworks, enough to drive away evil spirits for the upcoming year.

The National Liberation Front had also ensured there were enough fireworks to drive away evil spirits—but these spirits weren't the laughed-at myths, but very real men wearing jungle fatigues. They were only to be driven away for a few days, long enough for the long-suppressed rage of the people to build, and for the people to gain courage and then rise up.

The Americans pulled their soldiers from the Vietnamese cities and villages so the people could celebrate properly. The Viet Cong and NVA moved in, to celebrate in a somewhat different fashion.

Twilight closed in on Song Nhanh shortly before 7 P.M. Now Tet would begin, with bands and firecrackers and the young celebrating life. In the streets of Song Nhanh there were the bands and the explosions—but the young were somehow absent.

This, again too late, might have provided a clue.

It did—but for only one man.

Captain Charles Drew had been invited to a friend's house, to celebrate Tet. He had been humming happily, getting into his best tigerstripes, and looking out the window at the people in the street below when he noticed something. The people in the street were either old or very, very young. Where were the cowboys and ladies?

Drew thought that he was being ridiculous—they were probably waiting for the action to really get going.

But instead of heading for his friend's party, he went downstairs and brought back a case of C-rations, six grenades, and a wooden box of .45 rounds. He put the teak desk he was very proud of and planned to ship back to the States across the door, put a full thirty-round magazine in his archaic Thompson gun, and sat waiting.

He consoled himself with tiny sips from the bottle of Cutty Sark he'd planned to take to his friend's. To entertain himself, he put on, at very low volume, a record on the PX stereo set in the room.

"Paranoia strikes deep," Stephen Stills intoned. "Into your heart it will creep . . ."

Drew's paranoia would keep him alive through the next few days, when a large part of the city of Song Nhanh would die.

General Vo Le Duan knew that imperialism died with la belle époque.

He had seen the paintings with French officers, saber in hand, breastplate gleaming, one tiny shard of blood heroically down the sleeve, waving for the attack. He had seen the paintings of the British officers in khaki, again with their sabers, the Gatling down, readying themselves as the wogs came in. He had even seen the paintings of the American Remington, where sweat-stained soldiers stood against the North American natives.

All this was very wrong.

But, God Damn It (he consciously chose English to swear in), being a general should have *some* perks. This was the climactic moment of his life. He knew the philosophers of war would laugh, but somehow, he wanted to stand in front of a host of cheering soldiers. They would wear polished bamboo armor— his mind veered—and have bright banners above them. The time would be just at the setting of the sun.

Duan would wave the tattered banner of the Trung sisters, and, with a Napoleonic—the moral is to the physical as three to one—roar, his soldiers would charge.

Instead, General Duan stood on a paddy dike, one kilometer north of Song Nhanh, scraping water buffalo shit from his boots. Standing behind him were his runners, his radiomen, Commissar Thuy, Sergeant Lau, and the squad of bodyguards.

His division, the division that he had lovingly cradled down the Ho Chi Minh Trail, cleverly brought across country and cuddled in safety in Le Noir Massif, was about to attack. With no more drama than watching the second hand of his watch cross the top of the dial.

"Let us go," he ordered briefly, and started toward Song Nhanh.

The General Offensive began.

PART FOUR:

TET

O Lord! Thou knowest how busy I must be this day:
If I forget Thee, do not Thou forget me.

—Sir Jacob Astley,
October 23, 1642

What the hell is going on?
I thought we were winning the war!

—Walter Cronkite,
February 1968

CHAPTER FORTY-FOUR
CHI

FIRST VIET CONG to die was Bui Vo Chi.

Mr. Chi delicately squeezed himself off the bus near Song Nhanh's city center, taking care not to soil his white trousers against the chicken cages. He stepped to one side as an old woman coaxed her pig down the four steps off the bus and then led it on a rope leash into the marketplace crowd.

He glanced around at the gossiping peasants, their arms filled with baskets of livestock and produce. He smiled to himself. For the first time in many weeks, Mr. Chi was a happy man.

These poor ignorant fools, he thought, had not an inkling that great events were about to intrude on their lives. Such silly little lives. The babble around him concerned itself solely with prices and harvests and plans to spend dreamed-of profits. There was also a holiday anxiety underlying all this, and Chi casually wondered how many profits would be squandered on the first night of Tet during an ordinary year.

Although Chi was not privy to the confidences of his superiors, he knew that the Year of the Monkey would be far from ordinary.

Chi started pressing through the crowd, glancing at unfamiliar alleyways and streets. Song Nhanh was still new to him, and he had to take special care in following the directions that had been slipped to him a few nights earlier. Although he was far from impressed with the ancient city, he was not so inexperienced that he would get lost and miss his appointment.

Chi was to meet his cell leader at such-and-such tea shop to receive final instructions for the role he was to play in the weeks to follow. The message had lifted his spirits from gloom. Mr. Chi had always been deeply disappointed with his orders moving him from Hue Duc to the new bazaar. He had always considered his Hue Duc assignment as a sort of apprenticeship for greater things to come. And hadn't he done a wonderful job keeping track of American troops, as well as the minor stuff of fingering potential difficult villagers?

His intelligence, he was sure, had always been reliable. Chi figured that when the word came down, he would be moved to a more important post, in Hue or Saigon, even.

But then he had been ordered to follow the Fifteenth. For weeks he had searched his soul to understand why he rated such a demotion, from spying on a division to a mere battalion. Still, he told himself now, he had not flagged in his new duties. He had handled the merchants at the new bazaar with aplomb, and had easily wrangled his way into the trust of the barbarian GIs that cavorted at the bazaar.

What disgusting people the Americans were, Chi thought. He couldn't understand how they could ever be respected in any place in the world, much less Vietnam. They were worse than pigs. Pigs at least had some intelligence, ask any man that. Americans, on the other hand, were so simply fooled. Chi knew that not once had he ever been suspected of being a Viet Cong agent. And he had always worn his bright shirts, white pants, and gleaming shoes with as much ease as he wore his smile.

Mr. Chi spotted the alley that marked his first turn. He never noticed the two men who followed him into it. Nor did he notice that the alley was oddly empty of any traffic.

The two Vietnamese who followed him kept up their casual chatter until they were just behind Chi. Then they quickened their steps, one drawing just ahead of him, and casually turning to ask Mr. Chi directions to the square.

Chi smiled at the man and began to apologize for his ignorance. He was new in the city himself. At that moment, the other man pulled a heavy cloth tube from his clothing. It was filled with sand.

He hit Mr. Chi sharply just at the base of the neck. Chi slumped without a gasp into the arms of the first man.

"Quickly now," the second man said. "The car is at the corner."

The first man tried to straighten Chi up. The Phoenix team's standard operating procedure at this point would be to help the seemingly drunken Chi into a car and then spirit him off to some nice quiet place where they could do unpleasant things to him until he decided to talk.

He would talk. The interrogators of the PRU were very skilled at that. Unfortunately, the man with the sap was either not fully trained in his craft or was feeling a bit nervous when he hit Chi.

The first man wrinkled his nose in disgust as Chi voided his bowels. He let the body fall to the ground.

"You hit him too hard," he complained to his companion.

"What do you mean?" The second man bent over Chi's body. ". . . Oh. He's dead!"

They left his body where it fell and hurried out of the alley. They didn't talk. Both men were busily figuring out how to tell their stories in the best light.

It was unlikely that the stories would agree.

CHAPTER FORTY-FIVE

SONG NHANH

AT MIDNIGHT, AS if it were a medieval masque, the real faces appeared in Song Nhanh's square. Shopfronts came open, and young men poured out. Tiny bazaar stands had their tin walls kicked away, and smuggled-in explosives and arms were brought out.

Troops loitering in the streets as drunk ARVN soldiers tore away their rank tabs and unit patches and, shouting, mounted the red star.

There were real ARVNs around the square, who died before they were given a chance to change sides.

The blank ants, now fire ants, closed on their targets.

Police headquarters was captured silently—less because of orders than that none of the Viet Cong or NVA wanted the puppet white mice to die easily. The few gunshots were buried under the wave of fireworks being set off in the street.

Action squads moved in behind the soldiers and began looting the police files.

Task Two was the province radio station.

This, too, feel soundlessly. Those broadcasters the Liberation Front wanted as quislings were not in the station as the soldiers took the building. The radio technicians were soothed under the gun—the General Offensive would need all of the competent people it could find and convince they were unfortunately on the wrong side.

The station continued broadcasting music. It was not yet time for the NLF to take over the airwaves.

Task Three was to surround the barracks containing Thoan's bodyguard—the company of Rangers—and the ARVN garrison. Again, those soldiers were waiting for the signal.

The waited signal was the beginning of Nguyen Van Thoan's personal New Year.

It was not long after midnight that it came.

CHAPTER FORTY-SIX

THOAN

NGUYEN VAN THOAN poured the cognac from the silver flask into the tiny sterling cup that was its cap. It held just enough for a gentle swallow. He raised it to his lips in a silent toast and then drank it down. The cognac settled nicely in his already warmed stomach.

The Province Chief was waiting patiently for his mistress at the entrance of the province headquarters. Thoan was in a party mood. It had been a long time since he had felt like this; in fact, it had been since his exile from Saigon. It was so difficult to make conversation, he mused, among the locals. Tonight would be different. Tonight he had been promised stimulating company in the warmup party that would be the first of many in the New Year celebration.

Thoan's young cousin, recently returned from a Grand Tour of Europe, including Paris, had accepted his invitation to spend the holidays in Song Nhanh. The cousin was in favor with the family, and so the acceptance of Thoan's invitation was on the surface surprising. Thoan had to believe there was something more behind it. Why else would a man of quality choose to spend Tet in Song Nhanh? Perhaps Thoan was about to be recalled. The thought put him in a fine mood. He sipped a great deal of cognac to celebrate it. To top it off, his cousin had brought along his own chef—he swore the man was French-trained. Yes. Tonight would be a fine night.

He turned as he heard the sharp tap of footsteps coming down the hallways. It was Tram. She was dressed entirely in white: highheeled white pumps with four-inch heels. Dangling white jewelry at her ears and caressing her throat. Thoan remembered buying the pearl set. It had been very expensive. Best of all, however, was the silk dress that sleeved over her body, hugging it in just the proper places. It was slit almost to her tiny waist. Tram paused just in front of him. She had a childlike look on her face as if begging him for approval.

"I am sorry if I've kept you," she said in a small voice.

Thoan could smell her musk drifting through the hall. He smiled his most gentle smile.

"It was well worth the wait." He made his voice husky. He pulled her to him for a kiss. Her lips were soft and moist. He pulled back.

"Ah, yes, my Tram," he said. "Now I know tonight will be very special indeed."

She gave him a sexy grin. "Oh? You have plans I haven't heard of yet? Am I involved?"

Thoan chuckled. What a woman she was. What a wonderful lover. He had done exceedingly well in choosing her. There was no waste of his attention on this woman. She appreciated his many kindnesses. His gifts. The post he had given her as his personal secretary. Thoan was sure that he would not be ashamed of Tram as his mistress even if they were in Saigon. Well, probably not Saigon. There were women there who . . .

"Perhaps I do have a few surprises in mind," he told her.

He led her to the door. Outside his jeep was waiting. Thoan always drove himself. Of course, being no fool, he never went out alone. There would be two other jeeps following him filled with heavily armed soldiers. He escorted her outside and then took her toward his jeep. Tram hesitated, then turned toward him.

"The entire time we are at the party," she said teasingly, "I want you to know what I am thinking."

"And what is that, Tram?"

"You know," she said, girlish again. "You always know what I'm thinking."

"Perhaps we'll leave early," Thoan whispered to her. "Perhaps we'll never even find our way home."

Tram giggled. "On the roadside?"

One of the things Thoan liked about Tram was that she had a great deal of imagination. She especially liked spontaneity in their sex life, and liked him to plant ideas that might or might not be played out.

"Your underthings," Thoan suggested. "You could take them off now. Then . . . you would never know . . ."

Another delicious giggle. "Oh, you *do* have ideas for tonight, don't you." This, very taunting.

"A few."

"Well," she said, "if there are those kinds of thoughts for the night, you'll have to be patient just a few moments more, my darling."

She slipped away and hurried back into the palace. Thoan didn't ask the reason for the momentary delay. A gentleman does not inquire about such things. Instead, he slid into his jeep. It was his habit to warm it up thoroughly before he drove it like an Italian on the Swiss border. Tram ran down the hallway and slammed through a side door. She kicked off the stupid high heels, pulled her dress up to her waist, and sprinted for the gate. A man in an ARVN uniform waiting. Just another young guard. Except, sprawled beside him, were the bodies of the real guards.

"Hurry," he hissed at her, as he opened the gate.

Tram had barely cleared the compound when Thoan turned the ignition switch and the 200-pound bomb exploded in his jeep. The blast also killed every man in the two vehicles behind him.

The Year of the Monkey was born.

CHAPTER FORTY-SEVEN

SONG NHANH

SAPPER NGO DINH CUU set off the next explosion, while the square of Song Nhanh was still echoing to the blast that had killed Thoan and destroyed most of the main administration building.

He triggered the charge running to the ARVN barracks with an American detonation box. Very good, he proudly observed. The woman Mo and I determined our charge correctly, as the three pounds of American plastique lifted the sandbags, wire, and barricaded door away from the barracks building. Just enough.

Cuu still thought the puppet soldiers should have been killed as they stumbled, half drunkenly, out the door, their hands flailing the air. But his commissar had corrected him—no man not a criminal should die without having the chance to correct his mistakes.

Cuu realized that he still had things to learn about the revolution. Perhaps the long-nosed Catholics still influenced him too much. There were only two men who emerged from the barracks with guns, and Cuu recognized that one of them was far too drunk to realize what he was doing.

Then he brightened. Perhaps he was wrong.

But now the next task was the barracks of those red-scarfed BBDQ. The debt, for those who were so misguided as to have "Sat Cong" tattooed on their bodies, would be paid in full.

It was.

"Dai-uy?" came the question after the hammered knock.

"Ong can chi?" Drew asked, in his best drunken-American slur, bringing the bolt handle back on the Thompson gun.

"Ong co ranh khong?" came the question.

378

Unfortunately for the NVA sergeant and the four men who stood, weapons ready, against the wall outside Drew's room, Captain Charles Drew was enough of a linguist to recognize the difference between the harsh northern accent and the more familiar southern softness.

"Co no gi?" he slurred again. Without waiting for the reply he held the Thompson gun sideways, left hand wrapped around the gun's sling, and pulled the trigger back.

The 230-grain slugs ripped through the wall of the building into the hall. Drew let the weapon chatter empty, riding up, pulling down, just at waist level. There were satisfying screams and moans. Drew came up from his kneel, pulled a grenade from the box, yanked the sharded door open until it hit the desk, and rolled the grenade out.

The grenade went off, and the walls bulged a little inward. The moans outside stopped. Drew, in ear-ringing silence, shoved a handful of grenades in one pocket, a new magazine into the M-1A1, four magazines into another pocket, cranked the volume up on his stereo set, and rolled out the back window.

A story below, he hit, did a PLF, and crouched away into the tracer-and-explosion-lit night, hearing, behind and above him, Steve Stills try again:

"Somethin's happenin' here/What it is ain't exactly clear . . ."

CHAPTER FORTY-EIGHT

SHANNON

SHANNON'S FATHER HAD smuggled him a bottle of Ancient Ancient Age. He had put it in a package of books clearly marked "The RAND Corp." with an accompanying note: "Use with care on a happy night." Shannon looked at the note again and then at the bottle and measured his feelings. Outside, he could hear the distant pop-pop-pop of firecrackers sounding in the Vietnamese New Year.

On his first combat tour, the sound had made him edgy. He hadn't yet learned to separate the difference between caliber and coziness. This time, the sharp reports made him think of celebration and company, even though it wasn't his holiday. It was time to crack the bottle and it needed to be shared. Who, he wondered, would enjoy sipping at the smoky flavor of Ancient Ancient Age with him?

Edmunds, he knew, was on duty on the perimeter. Taylor? Yeah.

Maybe it was time to see what was really in Taylor's mind. Perhaps Taylor was feeling the same way Shannon was: waiting for events to turn his life around. Shannon hooked the bottle of bourbon between two fingers and strode out of his tent. The night in Vietnam was something Shannon still hadn't become used to. You could easily see the glow of the nearby city of Song Nhanh and it was a gentle gleam, illuminating the sky like a candle, instead of the neon glare of American cities.

There were so many stars in the sky that they lit the way between the path of tents. He could clearly see the light from Taylor's tent. The man was still up. Shannon made his way toward the tent, sensing the presence of many men—all friendly—around him. He was comforted by the thought of the black line that marked the perimeter wire not so many meters away. There were some good people there, he thought warmly, guarding the night.

Just before he reached Taylor's tent he saw the night light up over Song Nhanh with an incredible display of fireworks. A few seconds later, the sound of the explosions thundered in. A little early, aren't they? he thought. At the same time a terrible coldness cut through him. There was another flash and then he was rocked again by the sound. Shannon gaped at the display of pyrotechnics.

The Province Chief was sure outdoing himself this time, wasn't he? Taylor charged out of the tent.

"What the fuck?"

They both automatically looked at the glow in the sky over Song Nhanh and then just as automatically turned their heads to look down toward the wire.

On the perimeter, someone threw out a flare. Then another and another followed. They bloomed up, illuminating the way too close horizon.

In a misty, smoking vision, Shannon and Taylor saw what appeared to be hundreds of men poised just beyond the wire.

"Jesus," was all Shannon managed.

At that moment, Blind Pig opened up with his machine gun. What seemed like a thousand or more rifles answered.

Shannon remembered that he was unarmed. The hell with that—what the hell is going on?

It's Tet—and we're getting hit.

Shannon saw the foo-gas canisters blow around the perimeter and then bloom out toward the attacking Vietnamese.

Taylor and Shannon sprinted for the flash of guns.

CHAPTER FORTY-NINE

MINH

SERGEANT MINH AND the rest of the 300-odd men of the Sixty-ninth Regiment were set up on a hillside below Song Nhanh, six klicks below the American base camp. Even at night, the view was spectacular.

Minh and the others watched in some fascination as enormous balls of light exploded over what they thought had to be the city, and then closer to them, the exclamation points of fire that had to be the battle being carried to the imperialist infantry.

Minh was a terribly disappointed man. That pig's behind Lau, he was sure, was getting in on all the glory, and, more important, the loot of an entire city. Lau would be a very wealthy man when this was over. Minh was not feeling very philosophical about the whole thing. Certainly he was a top NCO of the Sixty-ninth—the pride of all of General Duan's regiments. And they had been given an important task.

Everyone assumed there would be an instant response from the ARVNs. Minh could almost see the column of South Vietnamese armor being gathered at this moment somewhere south of them to be hurled up the road to relieve Song Nhanh.

The ambush that the Sixty-ninth had set up was perfect. They were positioned on a hill just above the highway to the city. The ARVN's column would have to cross a bridge across the river, and then negotiate another a few hundred meters later.

The Sixty-ninth would catch them in between the two bridges. They had an absolutely clear field of fire from the hill, since the only thing between the regiment and the highway was long-abandoned rice paddies. Their main worry, Minh realized, was not the ARVN. They would kill them like flies on buffalo patties.

But they had to be careful. Minh, and the officers and other NCOs of the regiment, had specific instructions on this part of the operation. They were to destroy the attacking force and bring as many tanks and personnel carriers as they could back to Song Nhanh.

Meanwhile, Minh complained silently to himself, that rectum of a batman to the general would be loading up on the spoils of the city. There was one consolation, however; with that kind of richness, Lau would be impelled to pay him the eight beers he owed him. Minh retracted that: actually the general's batman owed him six—that cheap pizzle Lau *had* managed to come up with the money for two.

Minh looked down the road again, thinking about how good those beers would taste.

CHAPTER FIFTY

SINCLAIR

"WHEN ALL ABOUT you are losing their heads"—General Sinclair caught himself, standing in the sudden chaos of the command center. Two deep breaths. What do we have? Somebody's hitting the Fifteenth hard. All commo lost with Song Nhanh. Probes on our own wire. Sinclair glanced at his new G-2, waiting for some kind of analysis.

Lieutenant Colonel DeFrance looked lost.

Right then, Major General Lee Sinclair had the one absolutely clear picture he would ever be granted. It was as if he stood in COSVN headquarters, looking at their grand map. Ah. First you hit here . . . then there . . . now you will back it up. At that point Lee Sinclair touched humility.

Lee, my friend, you had better quit dreaming about four-star rank and JCS and all that shit. All you are is a slogger. Except this once. Yes, his mind said fiercely, but this once. This once I have all the time in the world.

"Did you ever," he said conversationally to Colonel DeFrance, "hear Churchill's story about the man who went to the vet with the sick bull?"

DeFrance's mouth hung open.

"The vet diagnosed the disease and gave the man this enormous pill and a tube. The man was supposed to shove the tube down the bull's throat, put the pill in the tube, and then blow hard.

"The man leaves. About a week later, the vet is walking down the high street, and he sees this man again. And he's tottering. Looking like he just came off his deathbed. And the vet asks him what in God's name happened. The man says, 'You remember what you told me—about how to give that pill to my bull?' Of course, the vet says. 'That's what happened to me. I did it just like you said, Doctor . . . but the damn bull blew first.' "

Sinclair waited for some kind of reaction.

DeFrance looked at Sinclair as if the general had suddenly begun speaking High German.

"Oh," he managed. "Yeah. Good story, sir. I understand."

No you don't, you simple . . . Sinclair wished at that moment there was a way to undo his changes. That irregular mick Shannon would have gotten what I was talking about.

Enough.

Orders now.

"Colonel DeFrance. We're canceling the Tet truce. I want every manjack up and out.

"I want Second of the Eleventh on standby at the strip by dawn.

"I want an operations order. We're taking our armor up that highway . . . what is it?"

DeFrance had to check the map.

"45L, sir."

"I want the armored cav ready to roll tonight. First we relieve the Fifteenth. Then we're going to roll into Song Nhanh.

"Shannon's NVA are going to find out that the farmer's got more than one blow to him."

More bewilderment. "Move, Colonel. Move," Sinclair growled. Just this once, while he had that picture, he was going to respond, and the hell with what happened all those years ago in the war games in Louisiana.

CHAPTER FIFTY-ONE

CUU

PROBABLY THE ONLY two men who might have understood the death of the ARVN Rangers in Song Nhanh City would have been General Duan and Sergeant Lau. At Dien Bien Phu they had seen many men choose to die instead of surrendering or retreating. But they were still three miles outside the city when the last of the Rangers sat up and spat a mouthful of blood into the medic kneeling over him.

Cuu's sappers had led the assault on the Ranger barracks. Satchel charges at the front and rear had begun the fight—and two of Cuu's best trainees had died before the charges were set off.

From inside the barracks, the BBQD had opened fire. First a sheet of bullets, then well-aimed shots as the ninety-odd men of the company saved their ammo. There were calls to surrender from the most honey-tongued of the commissars.

Ignored. Worse than ignored, used as targets. Perhaps the Rangers knew the offers of amnesty and forgiveness were lies. Perhaps they were believing their own mystique. Perhaps the world of Song Nhanh—the world of the future where the imperialists would be gone—was a world they could not believe in.

Perhaps this was all bullshit, and the Rangers had so conditioned themselves that all they knew how to do was die.

But they did it quite well. Two squads debouched out from the semiruined barracks and took up fighting positions. They accounted for almost a full company of Viet Cong regulars who attempted a frontal assault. Behind them, Ranger snipers took out the Viet Cong commanders.

The decision was made by the Viet Cong commander to pull back and reduce the barracks with rocket fire.

More Rangers died as their building was blown down around them. But the rubble made it easier to fight from.

The first NVA company from the Sixty-seventh Regiment to enter the city square was ordered to destroy the Rangers. They lost half their force assaulting the ruins. The company pulled back, into the shelter of the administration building, to regroup. At that point, one platoon of Rangers attacked. They made it across the boulevard, into the ruined yard of the admin building before they died.

Their counterattack destroyed half of that NVA company. And then there was silence from the rubble. Until the next wave of Viet Cong went on line and attacked. Again there was the solid blast of fire—this time from AKs and SKSs taken from the bodies of the Viet Cong around the ruins, since ammunition for the Rangers' own weapons was by now expended. But the Rangers were driven back into the wreckage. RPG gunners fired rockets until it seemed there was nothing left to shoot at.

Once again, silence.

And then, from the smoke and haze, four men emerged, their red scarves around their necks as black as the blood from their bodies.

Four men.

Attacking.

They made perhaps twenty meters while the NVA regulars stared in awe. And then the sheet of fire tore them apart.

It was over. The ruins were swept. Ten more NVA soldiers died. Wounded Rangers had tucked grenades under their bodies, pins out, as they died. Others, near death, chose to take someone with them.

But it was over.

The final resistance inside the city of Song Nhanh was obliterated. The city was now openly a liberated zone. Stage 1 of the General Offensive in Song Nhanh Province was a complete success.

Ngo Dinh Cuu watched the smoke drift upward and tried to understand what made these enemies of the people do what they did. He decided it must have been drugs or the conditioning of the imperialists. He would never understand. Besides, there was now important work to be done.

CHAPTER FIFTY-TWO

DUAN

GENERAL DUAN ENTERED Song Nhanh with a prayer on his lips: "Little Flower, in this hour, show your power."

It was a child's prayer to St. Theresa, his family's patron saint. His mother considered her the good-luck saint, the person to appeal to whenever fortune or misfortune hovered just out of sight. Although he was many years an ex-Catholic and a dedicated Communist, the little prayer came instantly to mind when Duan was under stress.

Chanting the prayer, the Comrade General led his forces through the last of the swamps and into the ancient province seat.

It was just after dawn. This was the moment he had dreamed of months before on a similar morning when he had waded across Cham River from Cambodia.

Despite the occasional sounds of gunfire, he knew the city was his. The question on his mind now was how he could hold it. The taking and keeping of Song Nhanh was the keystone of his plans. On the surface, everything seemed to be going well. The city had been won, and he had successfully pinned the Fifteenth—the only immediate hope for relief—some ten kilometers below Song Nhanh.

Duan pictured himself as being in a chess game—a sport he had always been extraordinarily good at. Chess is a skill, he reminded himself, that requires one to keep a firm portrait of the enemy in mind. Otherwise the puzzle will always remain unsolved.

In this case, the opponent was Sinclair. Duan was pleased with the fact that he had not underestimated the man, despite reports that Sinclair was an old-style Western general more at home leading a tank column through Germany than in the difficult terrain of an underdeveloped land. Look at Sinclair's handling of the Phu Loi Battalion. True, the man had fallen for Duan's desperate tactics and had fought at great cost to himself to take what he thought was a rook, when all Duan offered was in fact a pawn. Still, Duan was impressed with how Sinclair had approached the problem. Always, in the back of his mind, Duan had hoped that more men of the Phu Loi would survive. But the luck had been with the American.

Luck? Duan hissed a warning to himself. A general has to make his own luck. This is the reason why he was wary of Sinclair. Duan had to accomplish some fairly difficult objectives, and the failure of any single one could endanger the rest.

First the city. Then the Fifteenth. This appeared to be going in his favor. When he had ordered the attack on the Fifteenth, Duan had cautioned his officers. Intelligence indicated that they were attacking about 600 soldiers. So Duan had attacked Camp Stuart with 1,400 men.

He wanted to overwhelm that base in the initial attack. But it was not planned as a suicide mission. If the defenders held firm, his men were ordered to pull back and keep the Fifteenth pinned within the base camp, giving Duan time to unfold the rest of his plan.

Song Nhanh played an important role in the overall strategy of the General Offensive. Ultimately, it was to be a safe way station for supplies to move down from the North so that the final fight could be carried to the enemy.

To accomplish this, Duan needed many more men than were available to him. He would have to recruit many thousand fighters from the people of the province. This was an absolute dictim of the General Uprising, so basic that it was the final definition of the phrase.

The People, that great mass of patriots, would rise up to join in the fight against the American oppressors. Duan needed minimum 6,000 patriots. His commissars were already preparing to go to work across the city and outlying areas, recruiting men and women for the cause.

Now, while he was accomplishing this, what would the enemy do?

Duan assumed, with a great deal of reason behind him, that the ARVN would instantly send a large armored force to relieve the city. That is why he had placed a full regiment of his very best troops in ambush on the road. It was an ambush that could not fail, considering not only the surprise element, but the poor quality of any ARVN force.

Duan was also sure that by the time Sinclair could react to the ARVN disaster, Duan would be ready to defend Song Nhanh. Sinclair would be hurling regiment after regiment first where the NVA would have ambushed the puppets, and then to relieve the Fifteenth

Infantry, ignoring the occupation of Song Nhanh until it would be impossible to conquer. Considering that the very nature of the General Offensive was that the Americans would be fighting across the breadth of South Vietnam, there was little hope that Sinclair would be able to resupply himself with fresh men or equipment.

On any chessboard, Sinclair was doomed. It was a thought that Duan took great comfort in as he entered the city.

He was mistaken on only one count: the portrait he had of his opponent was in error.

Sinclair did not play chess.

He played checkers.

CHAPTER FIFTY-THREE

GODFREY

IN FASCINATION, THE NVA soldier's eyes followed the muzzle of Godfrey's rifle as it swung down and pointed at the middle of his chest. Godfrey tasted all the moments of this death—the gutshot enemy, the brightness of the morning, the smell of gunpowder and cooked pork.

"You be touching that trigger it gone be the last major move you make, motherfucker."

The growl did not fit in with the dawning day. Nor did, as Godfrey whirled, the sight of a glaring-eyed Blind Pig, his M-60 across one knee, the barrel an enormous tunnel inviting Godfrey to walk down.

"Hey, man. This guy ain't gonna make it."

"Ain't for you to play God. We got enough clowns already got that complex. Don't be justifyin', motherfucker. Back off or go for it."

Al Godfrey's finger moved away from the trigger, his thumb moved the switch to safety, and he stepped carefully away from the wounded NVA soldier. He turned and hurried back toward his bunker.

Blind Pig was in command of the battlefield. Or of the butcher's floor. He stared out, across the wire, over the carpeted bodies of the North Vietnamese soldiers. Best, he thought, you be tryin' to make sense of this nonsense. All these gooks come in on us once. Once only. But they come like it not be a probe, like they really want our young asses for a late-night snack. We kick them back and then they go away. This ain't the way them PAVNs do things. Something weird be goin' on.

Blind Pig decided the only thing he liked less than not understanding the bad guys' moves was the fact that the squad seemed to have a killer in its midst—Godfrey. Blind Pig, in spite of having killed his man both in Detroit and in Nam, was shocked. Maybe he best talk to Mosby about this shit, he thought. For a honkie, he ain't got no moves, but he's tryin' to get some.

Blind Pig lifted the latch of the M-60, took the belted ammo rounds out of the breech, and set the gun back on its tripod, on his bunker.

"Grubb," he said. "You be the gunner now. Any of those corpses get up, you deal like I taught you."

Grubb, ignorant of what was happening between Blind Pig and Godfrey, had brains enough to nod okay and move behind the gun. Blind Pig unsnapped the holster catch on his .45 and headed out, looking for somebody to help him figure out what was really going on.

CHAPTER FIFTY-FOUR

THUY

By 0900, SONG Nhanh's square was packed. Commissar Thuy was letting what in the West would be called the warm-up man—the second-in-charge of Song Nhanh Province's Central Committee—prepare the crowd for his speech. He felt truly sorry for the people of this city. They had lived so long under the puppets that it took soldiers to collect the people from their houses and convince them they had nothing to fear. This was the day of liberation.

His South Vietnamese comrade finished with shouts:

"Song Nhanh is free!"

"Long live the heroes of the Revolution!"

"Long live Ho Chi Minh!"

The crowd cheered loudly and correctly, Thuy noted. He let the comrade clear the platform, then counted thirty. Very deliberately, he climbed the steps. Thuy felt that he presented a correct figure—khaki uniform, scarf, and AK slung across his chest. He waited for silence and scanned the crowd. Thuy had been trained to never speak to a crowd. Single out one person in that crowd, and address him—or her—as if that person was alone.

His eyes found the person. He was a stocky, somewhat taller-than-average man, standing near the front of the throng. His open face, Thuy thought, reflected his honesty and the honesty of the peasants. This man—and hopefully 10,000 like him—were what Thuy wanted.

"Comrades," he began. "I stand before you as the spearhead of the forces of freedom. This day, we of the North, with our comrades, your friends and fellow workers, have lifted the yoke of the puppets from Song Nhanh.

"This is the first step toward freedom, toward the vision of no imperialists in our country. This is the beginning of the end of terrorism!"

The cheers came freely, and there were chants, Thuy could distinguish, of some of the correct slogans—"Americans get out" . . . "Struggle against shelling and bombing" . . . "Struggle against the puppet government."

"Struggle, my comrades—we have all struggled. And now our biggest struggle will begin. Across the face of our beloved country, our comrades are rising, in an unstoppable wave, in righteous anger.

"With the aid of the men of the North, and the heroes of your own land who have fought against imperialism for most of their lives, the end is in sight."

More cheers. Thuy noted with pleasure that the husky young farmer he was speaking to was cheering more loudly than anyone around him.

"But the struggle is not yet over. This is the day of battle, the day that we will need every one of you, each in his own way. We need men and women who are not afraid to face the imperialist soldiers with guns. We need men and women who will help the comrades in the trenches.

"Comrade Ho and Comrade Giap have correctly named us a People's Army, and this is a People's War. Now it is time for you to prove the truth of this, by joining us now in this great moment. There is a place for the grandmother and for the child. There is a place for the schoolgirl and the husky farmer.

"Who will be the first to step forward?"

And Thuy extended a hand directly at that young peasant.

The young peasant beamed at Thuy and shouted, most loudly, "Yes! Yes! Let the first hero step forward!" And moved not a pace.

Thuy covered his reaction and eyed the crowd. There were cheers indeed. But the crowd—as an entity—moved not one step forward.

Something had gone very wrong. Perhaps his words were wrong. Perhaps the Central Committee's agit-prop teams had not properly prepared the word. But the General Uprising—Khoi Nghia—was coming most reluctantly to Song Nhanh.

CHAPTER FIFTY-FIVE

HIGHWAY 45L

MAJOR GENERAL LEE SINCLAIR blundered into heroism. His after-action report would never reflect the series of errors that, on the first day of the Tet Offensive, would begin the destruction of the 302d North Vietnamese Division.

The lucky blunders started at the wire just outside Hue Duc. Sinclair saw the wall of refugees already clamoring around the division's perimeter, and realized that the highway north would be cluttered with fleeing civilians. Sinclair, thinking in terms of public relations, saw that his division should not be thought of as if they were German panzers, bulling through France, 1940. A bit of his mind, he was honest enough to admit, wanted to have the freedom of schrecklichkeit. Civilians seemed to spend their entire lives getting in the way of war. But they were a fact.

Sinclair made a rapid decision. Instead of his own tank leading the column, he put in front two jeeploads of white mice—ARVN police officers. Behind them was a three-quarter-ton truck with American MPs. All of them, of course, were in combat fatigues. Then he rolled the armored cav squadron, headed north, to relieve the Fifteenth. He was as puzzled as Blind Pig that "his" battalion had been hit only once that night. Sinclair assumed that, somewhere on the route north, there would be a waiting ambush.

Sinclair welcomed the idea. *The Communists really haven't seen what we can do when we get the chance. But they are going to.*

At 20 mph, the tanks growled north, toward Song Nhanh. There were fifteen tanks in that column, with two companies of infantry, carried in M-113 personnel carriers. And they were ready. The role of armor in Vietnam was a joke. Mostly they drove up and down roads—tanks don't work too well in most rice paddies—getting blown up. Or else they were used as semimobile artillery to support the grunts. Since tankers are no brighter than infantry types, those men assigned to the Twelfth Infantry Division's armored unit thought their tour was a bitter waste, rather than being grateful for not getting wiped out nearly as regularly as the crunchies did.

Their M-48A3 tanks were technically obsolete—but they were also the best tanks the Americans built in the 1960s. The forty-seven tons of steel were pushed forward by an 850-horsepower diesel engine. The four-man crew—tank commander, driver, gunner and loader—had for killing power sixty to seventy-five rounds for the tank's main 90mm cannon. Firing coaxially with the gun—which meant aimed and fired in the general direction of the cannon—was a 7.62mm machine gun. A .50-caliber machine gun was also mounted atop the tank's turret. Plus most tank crews had mounted a second 7.62mm M-60 on the turret.

The M-113 personnel carriers had a .50 MG, plus one or two M-60s added to the gun, as well as the guns of the infantry squad riding in the back.

A list of firepower can be very impressive—and very meaningless, since no gun works if nobody's willing to shoot it.

Unfortunately for Sergeant Minh and the Sixty-ninth Regiment, their ambush worked perfectly.

The NVA were very ready for the convoy—the boiling dust clouds had given everyone more than enough time to move into position.

Sergeant Minh's commander stared through binoculars at the sweeping curve that led to the first bridge. A jeep appeared. Its occupants were clearly South Vietnamese. Behind it came a second jeep.

Possibly the last chance the regiment's commander might have had was if he could have deciphered the white numbers and letter on the jeep's bumper, or if he knew that very few ARVN units had the M-151 jeeps. He did not.

He was too busy counting down to realize there were imperialists in the three-quarter-ton truck and in the hatches of the tanks and personnel carriers behind the leading vehicles. That probably was an impossibility—after the miles of roiling dust everyone looked brown-skinned. The column stopped before crossing the first bridge. No one got out to check the underside of it. Minh smiled—typically inept puppets. The tracks rumbled forward.

Minh wished then that he were in charge of the regiment. He would allow the unit to bunch up on the curve before the second bridge—ah, just as his officer was doing—and then allow the jeeps to pause at the second bridge.

There was a longish pause. Minh held his breath. Perhaps they were about to get out and check the second bridge for explosives. Not that it'd matter at this point, but that might keep the ambush from being the artistically perfect creation it was becoming. A hundred and fifty meters away from Minh's position, the jeep gunned forward, over the bridge. The second jeep . . . the truck . . . and then the first tank. Now, Minh pleaded. Let it be now, as he came to his knees, fingers closing on the RPG's trigger, reminding himself to lead the personnel carrier by one full length.

Both bridges blew up at the same time, and Minh's fingers flexed on the firing lever. Minh's rocket sputtered and dove slightly, ricocheted off the ground ahead of the personnel carrier, and then exploded above the track. There was no time to worry about this miss, as Minh had a second RPG ready and his regiment boiled out of the tree line toward the trapped tanks.

Sinclair ducked forward, into the turret, as the bridge blew just behind him. Then he was shouting orders, half-deafening his driver. The M-48 spun and roared down into the smoke, fording the shallow Song Nhanh River.

Dryly, the after-action report would say that the tank gunners and their commanders found "targets of opportunity" as the North Vietnamese charged forward, across the dried-up paddies. More correctly, if still coldly, it could have been described as a massacre. Most honestly to the tankmen, it was ecstasy. Somehow, someway, they had something to shoot at. Something that was shooting back and something that had the sheer balls to attack them.

Sergeant Minh was killed four times before he had run twenty-five meters—a track commander leveled a burst from his .50, as, almost simultaneously, a tank gunner pulled his firing lever on his coax machine gun and two tank gunners touched the firing buttons at that oncoming small man carrying the tank-killing rocket launcher.

The first rounds fired by the tanks were high-explosive shells that were intended to burst and destroy any nonarmored target. The next shells fired were canister rounds. Canister has an ancient and somewhat dishonorable history, originally consisting of one charge of powder rammed into a cannon, all the scrap iron available loaded on top of it, and the shot fired against unarmored infantry. Canister existed as rounds for the M-48s' 90mm cannon. The result was a very large shotgun, with a barrel 3.5 inches in diameter.

The effect of the rounds from the ten tanks cut off by the blowing of the bridges and now rumbling forward into the oncoming NVA was obliteration. Men caught by those rounds ceased to exist, except as a hose spatter of red and gray. Those on the fringes of the blast had time to see an arm or a leg disappear before they died.

Within fifteen minutes, the entire Sixty-ninth Regiment, 302d Division, People's Army of Vietnam, ceased to exist.

The wounded would almost all die. Those unwounded—physically—were almost catatonic. It was a famous victory—not unlike the fame a man might feel by pouring gas into an anthill and tossing a match.

The rest of the column could clean up. Sinclair ordered the lead column back on the road north.

Years later, he would tell of the battle with satisfaction—it was, after all, not different from what the Chinese Communists had done to his unit in Korea in 1951.

But for some reason he lost his former taste for duck season.

CHAPTER FIFTY-SIX

NGHI

THE POET WAS waiting for Nguyen Truong Nghi. The door to his villa was open and there was a pot of tea and a bowl of fresh fruit on the table. He ignored Nghi's leveled Tokarev pistol and Nghi's two AK-armed assistants.

"You, then?" he asked—a nonquestion.

The poet would be the fifteenth man that Nghi was to kill this first day of Tet. Some had screamed, some had tried to flee, some had pleaded for mercy or understanding, others had died fighting. Nghi was on his third group of assistants, and there were still hours before dusk.

The poet poured two cups of tea and indicated one to Nghi. Nghi accepted—it was the least he could do. Possibly this man might truly understand why it was necessary for him, as for so many other collaborators and puppets in Song Nhanh, to die. Actually, it was somewhat of a pity, Nghi thought. Here was this man, one of the South's most respected writers. Certainly a man who could never be accused of supporting the shameful governments that Saigon and South Vietnam had suffered under.

And his writings had been repaid by Saigon with imprisonment and then banishment to Song Nhanh. Nghi wondered why this man also rejected the cause of liberation, and wrote about it as caustically as he did the regime of the South. Of all people, Nghi thought, a man who writes poetry should realize there is no place for one who straddles the fence.

"How many others are on your list?" the poet asked.

Nghi did not answer—that was no one's except the Province Committee's business.

"I have been sitting here," the poet said, "for two days now, attempting to realize a proper epigraph. Without result. I think I've been reading too many bad Russian and American poets."

Nghi just understood the first of what the man had said. "Two days? Who told you about the Offensive?"

"A man at the market, when he said there was no more American whiskey available."

Enough of this. A poet could have confused the Buddha. Nghi lifted the pistol.

"One request, Comrade Nghi. Perhaps you would read this." The poet indicated a slip of paper with brushed writing on it. Then, without being ordered, he turned away from the pistol. The bullet entered the back of his head and took out most of the poet's foreskull. The poet stiffened, then sagged sideways. There was no need to check the body. Nghi picked up the paper and read:

A HAIKU

Bao Dai, Ngo Diem
John Kennedy, Uncle Ho
What a stupid list to join.

Nghi shook his head. The poet was obviously quite mad. He crumpled the paper and walked to the door. It was getting late, and his task was only half completed.

CHAPTER FIFTY-SEVEN

HILL 134

IN THE MOVIES, the good guys know they've been rescued from the Indians by the cavalry when they hear the bugle blow and then see the horses charge over the hill. In the movies, weary, bloodied men rally to fire a few shots into the enemy horde and then raise dusty hats in a cheer.

It was a scene that Sinclair might have dreamed of since he was a child. There is rarely such a scene in warfare. So when Sinclair "rescued" Hill 134, people were beginning to have second and even third thoughts about it.

First off, what was there to rescue? There had been one major attack, and then the enemy had withdrawn, leaving only a few snipers to buzz the air. VC snipers were notoriously poor shots and were counted only as a minor irritation in the life of a grunt. Still, to be fair, there were slightly mixed emotions on this point. Everyone was expecting another mass attack again that night. Sinclair's action had made that an impossibility.

But then again things were getting damned crowded. A camp built for a battalion was hastily being filled with the forward units of a division. Helicopters were ferrying men at a blinding rate, and people were jammed onto the small hill until it was approaching the critical factor of assholes to kneebones.

There was some fun to all this, however. The men of the Fifteenth got a ringside view of many many gunships prepping Sinclair's entrance. An enormous amount of Uncle Sam's good money was spent shooting thousands of rounds at a few snipers.

Even Taylor enjoyed the show. There were bushes and trees surrounding the camp he hadn't had time to deal with, and the gunships were doing a great job of removing them. Taylor had been the first to hear the news of Sinclair's breakthrough and subsequent destruction of an entire NVA regiment. Sinclair's cavalry charge had met and defeated the best and the brightest.

Still, as Taylor told Shannon and Edmunds, he had mixed emotions about their imminent rescue. What would Sinclair do next? The logical answer made Shannon feel like a snake had just crawled into his stomach to die.

Out on the wire, Blind Pig and Fritsche came to the same conclusion. Their thinking, however, did not come until much later when they first spotted the column of tanks push into sight. Sinclair's tank was in the lead, and he was standing tall in the turret for everyone to see.

"Cocksucker, motherfucker, eat a bag of shit," Fritsche intoned.

"What be the matter with you, Fritsche? You seein' somethin' I not be seein'? We bein' rescued!"

"Uh, uh. We're being invaded. By the goddamned top brass."

Blind Pig considered this, then saw the wisdom in Fritsche's words. The Fifteenth was soon to become a command company, with all that entails.

"Asshole gone make us shine our boots."

The two men did their best to hide as Sinclair's tank creaked toward them. They had a previously successful history of hiding from this general and now was not the time to change their luck. Fritsche had the presence of mind to grin back and do a half-ass rat-in-a-foxhole salute.

"What do I do?" Blind Pig moaned. He was sure Sinclair was looking right at him. He couldn't know that Sinclair was so elated that he couldn't see anything but vague shapes.

"Flip him off," Fritsche said.

395

And so Blind Pig did. As a flip-off, it was kind of impotent and curled. Still, no one noticed it, and the general waved back.

"Asshole, I'm gonna get you. What you be playin' with me like that?"

Fritsche knew better than to double over with laughter. After all, he was between a general and Blind Pig. So all he said was: "If you don't want my advice, fucker, don't ask."

Blind Pig was too shocked at what he had just done to kill Fritsche. Also, it was the kind of incident that makes one ponder the future. He lapsed into silence, thinking. The silence became so lengthy that even Fritsche got nervous. Was death being considered? You piss off this sonofabitch, and you don't know how it's gonna come out.

"I was just fuckin' around, man," Fritsche threw out as a peace offering. "Don't get fuckin' moody on me."

"What's that?" Blind Pig pressed for an apology.

"Screw you." Fritsche never groveled twice.

"I be thinkin'," Blind Pig said.

Fritsche avoided the obvious comeback. He was still feeling diplomatic.

"Yeah?"

"What's that motherfucker gone do to our young asses?"

"You said it already. Make us spit polish our boots. Wash behind our ears. Cut off our beer. Declare the whores off limits. That kind of shit."

Fritsche gloomily contemplated a lengthly period of sobriety and chastity. He wasn't too sure which he would miss most. Probably the beer. The whores around these parts were mostly dogs.

"No, no, no, my man. Besides all that."

"What could be worse than that?"

"Motherfucker, don't you get it? We be only ten klicks from Song Nhanh!"

Fritsche got it.

"Shit! He's gonna attack the city!"

Blind Pig shook his head in a negative.

"Uh, uh, brother. *We* gone be attackin' the city."

"Oh, fuck!"

Both men had been in the Army long enough to understand what that meant. They would have to take Song Nhanh back street by alley by street. In city fighting, the blood runs in minor lakes. Fritsche, the man who always walked point, couldn't see how he could do his job. There would be no comforting trail signs, no smells drifting on the breeze, no sounds subtly out of place.

"Christ, what're we gonna do?"

Blind Pig shrugged.

"The man ain't gone be askin' our opinion."

Fritsche decided to confront the evident inevitable, and changed the subject.

"What do you know about city fighting?"

Blind Pig thought about this, running over his various skills. Then he chuckled.

"Song Nhanh be nothin'. Shit, man, last summer *we* took Detroit!"

Tarpy sat jammed up against Mead, hating him so much that he was sure that even over the kerosene fumes of the Huey he could smell the man purposely farting.

The chopper banked, pressing him closer to the Copley correspondent's rotund body, and he felt Mead shrink away from him. It comforted Tarpy to think the hate was mutual. Hell, for him, would be that Mead would think he was your friend or colleague. Tarpy hoped this was a fate he'd never deserve.

Yeah. But what if he'd just fucked up by heading north instead of staying in Saigon? What if Tarpy'd fucked up so bad that AP would pinkslip him?

Cliff Tarpy had a sudden nightmare of going, hat in hand, to Ron Mead, begging him to put in a good word to his boss and asking for a job, just to keep covering this fucking story until it ended. It didn't matter that Mead might be on the same wrong errand he was. Copley forgave ignorance by firing it, then hiring it back as a consultant.

Besides, Mead was safe since Old Man Copley was dedicated Navy. Copley would forgive any kind of journalistic error made by a man who'd made the supreme sacrifice to his God, Country, and Chain of Newspapers to cover these second-class citizens who were in the Army instead of the Senior Service.

Jesus, Mead thought, the man's been drinking. He could tell it from the flushed look on Tarpy's face and he could smell it on his breath every time he turned his face Mead's way.

Mead was pissed because he was sure that Tarpy had horned in on his show. Soon as they had gotten the news in Saigon that his pal Sinclair had smashed through an overwhelming enemy force to rescue the Fifteenth, Mead knew he had a story. Fuck, not a story. He could milk this thing for a week or more, and then do several columns and maybe even an editorial or three—guaranteed publication in the twenty-two dailies and host of weeklies owned by his good friend and patron Captain Copley.

The two men heard the busy muttering of the pilot as he cleared himself through other military traffic and got set for a landing at the Fifteenth's base camp. Mead clutched his B-4 bag.

Tarpy slid out his notebook and his flask. He took a long drag off the flask and then scribbled a few notes. From the helicopter's erratic approach and the constant chatter through his headphones, he guessed that maybe his instincts were right. Maybe there really was a story here.

The two newsmen had decided to head north after a briefing given some hours ago at MAC-V headquarters.

MAC-V was known as Pentagon East. This is where all "news" for the grunts and stars of the media emanated from. There were some fifty or more men, under a general, who were responsible for feeding daily briefings on American actions to the press. The briefings came morning and afternoon. Except under exceptional circumstances, no one attended the morning briefing.

And in the Year of Our Lord 1968, there had been so many lies told that almost nobody attended the afternoon session—set for four thirty so that everyone who cared, or was a duck enough, could make it by five. Even Ron Mead agreed with what his colleagues of the Fourth Estate had dubbed the afternoon briefing: the Five O'Clock Follies.

The main press room was Spartan—a small stage and some fold-out chairs. There were not even any major electrical outlets for the TV people. They had to snake their cables down a long hallway and stumble them into the room. There were also rarely any visual aids: no maps or charts pinned to a board; no framing angle to put behind the minor Army functionary who would deliver the dry daily briefing.

Even Mead was irritated by the briefings. He had a point to make and the Army rarely supplied him with any help to make it. When they dressed the stage like a Mexican birthday, colored boxes denoting bombs dropped, maps and pins showing *real* American progress, the U.S. had just lost a battle.

Ron Mead was not a fan of the Five O'Clock Follies. He had attended today, however, desperately looking for a story. Mead wasn't sure he would find it. The briefings mostly consisted of dry, almost police log statements—with no pressure that the report would someday have to turn into court record.

Mead was pissed because another Copley man—with a full-time photographer—had been assigned to the battle at Khe Sanh. Mead knew that neither man was even getting near the action.

Like any sensible journalist he was filing safely from Da Nang. Mead would do the same in his place. There was no sense taking chances when the American public could be more properly informed from the cool perspective of behind-the-lines thought. Still, the dateline was Khe Sanh. That is what counted.

There was no way Mead would allow some young hack to get the better of him. He'd heard rumors of Sinclair's success near Song Nhanh, and he was hoping, with a little ferreting and his special relationship with the general, to impress Jim Copley. Mead had become increasingly aware that he was getting short in his assignment, especially with the punks like that Khe Sanh fellow crowding in. A nice story right at the edge would easily position him for a slot as, say, bureau chief in Sacramento.

California politics. Now, that was something Mead knew. You could get some prestigious sidelines out of that. An article or two in the *California Journal*. A little consultant work for the *Field Poll*. Acceptable things. Mead was a Newsman. He couldn't be bought.

When the young captain took the stage and began mumbling over the latest stats and other lies, Tarpy was sure that he had steered himself wrong.

He'd heard the same rumors of a report that Mead had, but his motivations were entirely different. He listened patiently as the captain, drinking frequently from a pitcher of water, hoarsed over the day's alleged activities. About a dozen or so reporters were in attendance, and they asked desultory questions, filling notebooks with something—anything—to dump. There was no television.

Tarpy spotted Mead and knew the man was basically after the same story he was, except with a much different twist: Sinclair. Mead would see the trashing of the NVA regiment—Tarpy could only guess at this point that it wasn't VC, it was NVA—as a great victory by a brilliant tank officer. It would be a story right out of the tradition of the great tank end-runs in World War II. He could see Mead's lead. It would play especially well in a Hearst newspaper of 1944.

The captain droned on, then hit the part about Song Nhanh. He confirmed in theory what Tarpy had heard: an overwhelming force hitting a lonely outpost a dog's breath from the provincial seat. An entire regiment wiped out by an armored column. The rescue of the Fifteenth.

Tarpy had already filed that story in three paragraphs. Sources can say a helluva lot, if you have imagination. He wasn't interested in Sinclair's dramatic breakthrough. What Tarpy was fumbling for was Tet. He had been through too many truces.

In his newsman's bones, Tarpy was sure that the Vietnamese New Year would presage a moment in history. To hell with "presage," he thought. You use words like that in the Opinion Section when you're trying to write off a vacation on your taxes. "Fucked" was much better, although unacceptable.

The captain's rote lies confirmed Tarpy's idea. Something was happening up north. Several major cities were already under attack. Had Hanoi finally and firmly committed itself? He had been hearing and reading the speculation of a (quote) General Uprising (end quote) for some weeks. If so, could Uncle Ho carry it off? Another "If so."

The key might be in Song Nhanh.

When the captain concluded his pitch, most of the newsmen busied out, heading for the nearest bar. Tarpy noted that Mead was slow to get started. Shit, he thought. The fuckhead wants to write about Sinclair. Slight sympathy—it was well known that even Copley thought of Mead as a lightweight. Mead was the kind of newsman who when pissed said "browned off," instead of "fuck you."

And so the two men found themselves jammed into a helicopter bound for the Fifteenth's camp ten klicks from Song Nhanh. From the pilot's constant chatter, Tarpy and Mead realized that the traffic was much more than intense. Troops and equipment in fantastic quantities were being moved, quickly. It would be difficult to land.

Their helicopter circled, and then found a landing spot on the tiny hilltop at Camp Stuart.

Both Mead and Tarpy tumbled out, now sure they had their stories.

CHAPTER FIFTY-EIGHT

DUAN

THE COMRADE GENERAL chose the treasury building for his headquarters. It was a logical choice. As the central bank for the province seat, the French had built it low and strong. Its walls were exceptionally thick and reinforced with steel. Each floor in its three-story structure was of high-quality cement.

When Duan chose it he had two major thoughts in mind. The building was centrally located, and just enough off the city square to be an obvious target. At this point, all Duan had to worry about was an air or artillery strike. So he put his team in motion to turn the structure into a fortress.

He paced back and forth in a large ground-floor office, watching the men at work. He could see them clearly, since the cloudy glass of the office door had been removed.

All around the building, men were removing glass from doors and windows and from the ceiling vents on the top floor. Glass equals shrapnel when explosive force is applied. It was a textbook fact that Duan remembered very very well.

There were a few other ideal things about the treasury building. It had a deep and strong cellar. At the moment his men were cutting through the ground floor and turning the cellar into a sandbagged bunker. He heard loud thumping overhead as other teams placed sandbags over the second-story ceiling.

If the building was hit in an air attack, the collapsed rubble from the third story would provide an additional shield. Duan also noted with satisfaction that several teams of men were ripping away the ceiling plaster. Falling plaster has a way of spoiling consistency in thought. It can also crush bones.

General Duan had been surprised but not completely shaken by the news of Sinclair's destruction of his ambush regiment.

He immediately accepted the blame for the error. He had been expecting a response from a South Vietnamese unit. He should have understood the nature of his opponent. Sinclair was cavalry. Historically, cavalry successes come in do-or-die strokes. Besides, there probably had been little possibility of an ARVN response. When Duan's own force had hit Song Nhanh, most of the soldiers had been on leave, celebrating the New Year. He had been opposed by about one-third of the available force.

Why should he have supposed that other ARVN units would be different?

Now. Now. How to turn the failure into victory . . . Consider it a pawn sacrifice? Think of the situation as the middle game? Could he wear his opponent down?

Try it this way: Sinclair would follow up by bringing most of his forces to bear on the city. Song Nhanh had to be an irresistible temptation, sitting as it did only ten kilometers from Sinclair's rapidly growing stronghold. Intelligence said that Sinclair could bring about 9,000 men maximum to bear on the city. Duan had about 6,000 trained men to oppose him, and about 3,000 or more new recruits. The recruits that should have volunteered from the populace of Song Nhanh hadn't materialized, but Duan did not blame his commissar. It was just a failure to understand the nature of peasants who had been dealing with constant warfare and changing positions for several generations. Still, it made 9,000 against 9,000.

Basic rule of attacking a city—something Sinclair surely must know: You must have to have three-to-one odds. For a successful attack, Sinclair would require 27,000 men.

Add some more factors to the equation. His troops were not

thoroughly integrated into the division. There were volunteers, there were the few remaining soldiers of the Phu Loi Battalion, and there were the activated Viet Cong soldiers. The training was not, by Duan's reckoning, complete. On the other hand, each man had been walked through that sand map of Song Nhanh. They knew the terrain, and, at least he hoped, they knew their tasks.

Variables . . .

Consider the situation throughout the country.

The General Uprising would be nationwide. Sinclair would assuredly attack. But how long could his superiors allow him to press the point? Saigon itself would be under attack. When Westmoreland understood this he would withdraw Sinclair and shift his attention to a target much more important than a lowly province capital far to the north.

Therefore, Duan only had to hold the city for a few days. Could he do it? He considered his strength and the terrain. He had five regiments remaining. How to place them?

Think of Song Nhanh as an island. Swamps in three directions, a river to the west. Sinclair could only come at him across the ancient main bridges into the city.

And it came to him. It was one of those beautiful ideas that are handed to you like jewels.

Song Nhanh was an island. Duan would pattern his defense after the great Japanese tactician who defended Iwo Jima at terrible cost to the Americans. What was his name? Strange how you ask those questions at times like this. Oh, yes. General Tadamichi Kuribayashi.

Duan felt very good about remembering this.

So. Iwo Jima Song Nhanh would be an island.

Five regiments. How to deploy them?

It was simple. Two would be blocking forces in the east and north. One unit he would keep as a mobile reserve. The other two he would place directly across the river from where Sinclair would attack.

This meant that he would delay blowing the river bridges. Yes, he would have them prepped and ready to go. But he would wait until Sinclair advanced, say, a company-size probe. Then Duan would have the bridges blown, slamming the door on the company. He would slaughter them all.

It would take all of Sinclair's attention to deal with this matter. Especially since it would require several days for him even to bring his entire force to bear.

The Comrade General was absolutely correct in his tactics. There were no errors in his thinking. Duan's tragedy was a simple mis-understanding of the situation.

CHAPTER FIFTY-NINE

SINCLAIR

GENERAL SINCLAIR RAPPED on Taylor's tent pole just after 4 A.M. The colonel was huddled with Shannon and Edmunds, going over last-minute preparations and stealing a few minutes for a hot cup of coffee.

The move on Song Nhanh would begin at first light, and outside the night was filled with the sounds of men getting ready, shouted orders, and the constant roar of incoming and outgoing helicopters.

"Gentlemen," Sinclair said as he entered, "I have news from Saigon. I thought you'd like to be the first to know."

Shannon looked at the general curiously. His voice was solemn, but there was something else . . . was that an amused sparkle in his eyes?

"They've just attacked the U.S. Embassy." Sinclair waited a second to let this sink in, pouring himself a cup of java.

"Jesus," Taylor intoned.

"Yes," Sinclair went on. "Apparently the situation is pretty terrible. Diplomats' lives threatened, and all. Including the Ambassador himself." Sinclair finally allowed himself a grin.

Edmunds couldn't bear it.

"Well, get some," he murmured.

Everyone in the tent burst into laughter, including Sinclair.

Sinclair perched on the edge of a trunk, waiting until the laughter died down and then growing serious.

"Of course, to speak selfishly, this does leave us with a few problems. Communications with Saigon are, shall we say, spotty at best."

Shannon imagined "hysterical" would be a better word, but then Sinclair couldn't say that. He also saw Sinclair's main difficulty.

"No chance for air support," he said.

"Exactly," Sinclair said. "No one is going to care about our little war way up here when it looks like the whole country is about to go up.

"And, to make matters a little more ticklish, I haven't been able to reach anyone who is willing to give me permission to use our own artillery as intensively as I would like."

The men thought about this in silence for a moment. Song Nhanh was an ancient province seat. There was no way Sinclair could let loose his big guns to bombard strategic areas of such an historic city. That was a decision that would have to be made at the highest levels.

Sinclair shrugged, as if it were only a minor disappointment.

"Of course, I really wasn't that sure I'd get it anyway," he said. "I hope I've planned accordingly. Also, with Saigon out for all intents and purposes, we have a free hand up here. That could play in our favor."

The general put his coffee down and rose to his feet. He began pacing up and down, reviewing his strategy out loud to help him think.

Taylor, Edmunds, and Shannon were completely familiar with the overall plan. Sinclair believed in keeping his officers briefed to the last detail, but it was still helpful to hear it again to clarify their individual roles.

"The whole operation hinges on three things," Sinclair said. "Speed, speed, and faster still. We have to bring our entire force to bear on Song Nhanh."

"But that will leave us with no reserves, sir," Taylor said, instantly falling into the devil's advocate role that Sinclair needed right now.

"True," Sinclair said. "But if we don't take the city in the first few days, there won't be time for reserves anyway. Besides, the enemy has the advantage of an equivalent force defending positions of his choice within a city."

"We have to hit them now," Shannon said, "before he can *really* dig in."

"Exactly, Major," Sinclair said. "I'm also betting that our opponent has no idea how fast a modern army can move its troops and supplies.

"If I were him I'd be playing for time. And that, gentlemen, I have no intention of allowing him to do."

Sinclair changed from strategy to tactics. He would strike up the highway with his tank column, bringing with him elements of the First of the Fifteenth to secure the slum area of the city on the west, just across from the bridges.

They would quickly establish LZs for the helicopters and then ferry in the rest of the Fifteenth and the Second of the Eleventh. These elements would attack across the river.

Sinclair assumed here that Duan would blow the bridges, and he already had engineer units on the way from Hue Duc.

To the east and north, he would chopper in his third battalion—

the First of the Twenty-ninth. This unit he would position on the edge of the marshes in case Duan decided to break contact and flee.

"I firmly believe that this man—Duan, isn't it?—has built himself a lovely trap," Sinclair said.

Shannon could see the map in his mind as clear as if it were hanging on a command center wall. Yes, from Sinclair's point of view, the NVA general was in a trap of his own making. But from Duan's viewpoint, it would be a virtual fortress that Sinclair would have to mount a potentially costly siege against.

"It could be pretty dicey, sir." Shannon said. "Once we get across the river we're gonna have to take Song Nhanh street by street."

"You're absolutely right, Major," Sinclair said. "But, you see, I've trained for this kind of fight my whole life. I doubt whether this Duan has ever defended a city in his long and apparently honorable career."

Sinclair walked to the tent opening, getting ready to leave. Shannon thought his face looked very much like a fox about to carry off the farmer's fat goose.

"He's on *my* turf, now," Sinclair said.

As Sinclair hurried away, Shannon almost felt sorry for Comrade General Duan. Then he thought about tomorrow, and Song Nhanh and attacking the city, and all thoughts of sympathy vanished.

He had a feeling that the farmer might take a good piece of the fox's hide.

CHAPTER SIXTY

THE SQUAD

AT FIRST MOSBY thought the four bodies in the courtyard were children—tiny contorted figures with flesh peeling away as if the people had been feathered in life.

Then he realized, and looked away.

Captain Jerry Edmunds had taken only three other men with him into the smoldering ruins of the convent—Mosby, Blind Pig and Fritsche. He'd had two clues on what to expect as the Fifteenth moved up the highway toward the city of Song Nhanh—none of the refugees clotting the road turned toward the scatter of buildings atop the hill, and black smoke still whispered from the ruined roofs.

There was no movement inside the convent walls.

Edmunds should have called them back.

But the four of them, weapons dangling, forgotten, walked through the courtyard into the chapel.

Coals still glowed from the sharded benches.

Blind Pig knelt beside a body and gently turned it over.

Under the burnt surplice, bandages could be seen. Blind Pig moved them aside.

"Gooks come in first," he whispered.

Fritsche's eyes closed.

"Motherfuckers."

He went to one wall and heaved bile. Came back.

"Then they had time to put on bandages before . . . shit. C'mon, Pig. I've seen enough."

Blind Pig let the body flop over and stood.

"Best we be thinkin' about paybacks, my man."

Fritsche touched the stock of his sawed-off, as if discovering it for the first time.

"You know something, partner," he said. "The hell with the zips. I'd like a piece of whoever called in the airstrike."

Blind Pig put an arm around his shoulder.

"You got it. But it gone be easier to ice zips than lookin' for jet jocks."

"Come on," Edmunds said, his voice dead against the blackened stone. "There's nothing here for us."

And Mosby never knew what part of his mind wanted to say "Thank you, Mr. President" as he and the others went out of the napalmed convent, trying not to let their minds see what their eyes registered.

CHAPTER SIXTY-ONE

SONG NHANH

To THE AVERAGE soldier, being a scout was an invitation to suicide. Phan Xuan Cung looked at his new comrades and knew better. At least a scout had a choice whether to commit suicide or not. These comrades didn't have the option of not. He wondered if they realized they were hand-picked as bait. No, would be a good guess. The men were selected from the newly volunteered fighters of Song Nhanh and local Viet Cong units. To them, their task was a possible moment in glory.

To Cung it was an invitation to die.

He and the other ten men were crouched next to a few huts

clustered on the west side of Song Nhanh River. To their front were the slums of the west bank and, at the end of the rutted dirt road, the intersection with Highway 45L, the road the imperialists would come up.

That was Cung's hope, at any rate.

If he were in charge of the Americans, he would have abandoned the road where it swept away from the river half a kilometer below them and moved directly along the riverbank. But the Americans, with their lumbering machinery and lazy soldiers, loved the straight and level. He knew he was right, since, for the last ten minutes, American helicopters had figure-eighted up toward the squad's position from the southeast.

Fifty meters behind Cung, the broad stone deck of Bridge #2 stretched across the river into the city. To the south, the blown ruins of #1 lay collapsed in the muddy current. One hundred and fifty meters above #2 was the still-intact Bridge #3, and Cung realized there was a squad identical to his waiting, with the same orders.

He saw the flicker of black-green at the end of the street. Cung took a moment to evaluate. They move in with infantry first. Another flicker. Two imperialists bolted across the street end, one carrying a machine gun.

Cung approved—they seemed to be sending one of their best forward. Perhaps it was the unit that Cung had scouted earlier on the hill below Song Nhanh. Next there should be men moving alternately forward, on either side of the road. Yes, yes. Now the machine gun will come up. Now there will be a pause, as some sort of vehicle—probably one of their armored reconnaissance vehicles—should appear. There it is.

At this point, Cung violated orders. He should have been moving back across the bridge, but he waited until the American APC hit the mine. The bang was satisfying loud, and the metal walls of the tracked box bulged correctly. Smoke boiled out of the vehicle. Cung had always wanted to see a track killed. Now he was moving, ignoring the spray of bullets coming up the street. The orders said he was to report to the division command center when the first imperialists approached the bridges.

He didn't want to see his men obey the orders.

"Come on, Grubb. You ain't dead yet."

The voice came from a tunnel. Grubb was sprawled in a ditch about fifteen meters away from the burning M-113.

Crouched over him were Geiger and Masters. The blast had pinwheeled Grubb into the drainage ditch beside the road. Grubb ran thoughtful fingers over his body, then sat up, and spat blood. Masters handed him a canteen. Grubb swallowed gratefully, then goggled and wheezed.

"Why, you motherfucker," he marveled. "Would you like to marry me?"

Masters just smiled and put the canteen away. It held a full fifth of Old Crow. Grubb got to his knees just as the Viet Cong at the end of the street opened fire. Everybody went flat. Grubb was face first into what smelled a lot like the air around Perth Amboy.

"Come on, goddammit, let's get some fire," Blake shrieked.

The squad obediently blazed a few rounds down the street. Then: targets, as six . . . eight . . . nine black-clad figures came up and retreated across the broad bridge.

"Let's move, troops," Edmunds was shouting, and the squad was on its feet as a tank ground around the corner, shoved—metal screaming—the burning PC out of the way. Charlie Company hauled toward the river.

The Viet Cong squad died as they went across the bridge. The expectation was that the imperialists would pelt after these decoys into the heart of the city.

But Charlie of the Fifteenth had been sucked in too many times like that. They hit the banks of the river, spread out, and went on line. Mosby found an overturned haycart to hide behind. Ahead of him stretched that thirty-foot-wide bridge, arcing gracefully over the river and beckoning them into the city.

Mosby knew if he put foot one on that bridge, he would die. A few feet away, Edmunds had the company CP, and was on the PRC-25.

"That's an affirm, Citation."

After a pause, the radio crackled.

"Whirlaway, this is Citation Six Actual. Big Six says move out."

Edmunds buried his reaction. The radio spoke again: "We have fast movers on the way, Whirlaway. But we need those bridges."

Edmunds was up, shouting at the puzzled tank commander in the M-48A3, "Come on. We're gonna play Remagen," and was moving out, across the wide open bridge, his company gaping and then up and moving.

Mosby felt everything most acutely—the muck under his feet becoming fine, level pavement, almost slipping into a pothole. Seeing the stone balustrades on either side of the bridge—I'll bet this bridge looks like one of those in Paris. Be nice to see sometime. Wonder if those lights work—bet this'd be really pretty at night. Hearing the scuffle of feet and the clatter of the tanks's treads about ten meters behind him.

The bridge was many miles . . . a lifetime . . . long as Mosby and the rest of the squad sprinted across the wide-open bridge. On the other side, the city rose. To one side of the bridge was a large, light-brown stone building with arched windows.

They're in there, Mosby thought.

At one window he could see a brown face, black uniform, and hands poised on the handles of a detonator. Mosby knew there must be ten tons of TNT wired just below his scraping feet—TNT that would go off as he reached mid-span.

He was half right.

There were about eight-and-a-half tons of explosive wired on the middle span and the two central piers of Bridge #2. But the person waiting was not in the old tax building across the bridge.

Vo Thi Mo was crouched just under the bridge's abutment—on the *west* bank of the river. She had heard the scuffle of feet above her, and then the rumble of a tank. Not enough. Mo waited. Calmness.

Somehow Mosby, and the rest of Charlie Company, made it across the Song Nhanh River. They instantly spread out into a rough perimeter. Edmunds was on the horn.

"Citation Six . . . this . . . this is Whirlaway. We're across. And we'd like all the goddam backup you've got."

"On the way."

A platoon of trucks rolled around the corner and down the street toward the bridge. Mo could hear the sound of the engines. This was the moment.

Al Godfrey was pissed—why had Mosby ordered him down? Hell, he saw those gooks pulling back. Man, they should have gone after them. Godfrey heard the sound of the tank platoon coming toward the bridge. Curious, he turned toward it. He saw someone hanging on one of the bridge's stringers. Godfrey shouted as his rifle came up and fired.

The round hit Mo in her thigh, pinwheeling and ripping most of the flesh away. Mo was thrown back—the detonator falling out of her hand—and she was falling away . . . falling . . . as overhead she heard the engine roar fill the world.

Across the river Godfrey was shouting and pointing. Lieutenant Wilson, the nearest to him, was the first to see the small moving object under the bridge, and was also shouting, as two . . . three . . . four tanks crossed the center section.

There was only one thing in Mo's world, the detonator hanging at the end of the wire, only inches below her body, which kept wanting to roll off this cold steel into the brown, inviting water below. Her fingers stretched, and a part of her saw bullets strike copper off the steel, and fumbling she had it. Her hand closed on the switch.

The next tank was in the middle of the span when the charges went off. Tons of steel lifted, hung, then dropped with the tons of the bridge into the muddy Song Nhanh River, the blast echoing and then reechoing as the charges on Bridge #3 also went off.

This left five M-48A3 tanks and the ninety-three men of C Company, First Battalion, Fifteenth Infantry trapped on the wet bank of the Song Nhanh River. Then, with perfect timing, the 300-plus men of the Sixty-seventh Regiment, 302d Division, People's Army of Vietnam, closed the trap.

One company of the Sixty-seventh came straight down the bridge street that led from the bridge to the city square. One more came in from the north, attacking between the three-story brown tax building in which Mosby had "seen" a waiting bomber, and the waterfront.

The main thrust came from the south, from the long warehouse and sheds along the riverfront itself, as two full companies attacked in a khaki wave.

Charlie Company's Third Platoon, previously wiped out in the battle on Hill 957, was mostly composed of new blood. They saw waves of NVA regulars come in on them. Their training, their belief as Americans, and their own courage killed them. This should not happen. Most of them did not even fire back. Those who did open up, shot as if they were on a stateside firing range.

They died.

The tank supporting that side of the flank was killed as quickly. A skilled RPG gunner, crouched on the warehouse roof, pulled his rocket off, a rocket that hit exactly on target between the M-48's hull and turret. The explosion of the round and ammunition frisbeed that ten-ton turret forty feet in the air, and then sent it skidding back down, grinding across paving stone and wounded Americans to splosh into the riverbank mud.

First Platoon, traditionally lucky, held their good fortune, as they instinctively jumped backward. They went over the destroyed bridge's parapet, down onto the mud of the Song Nhanh flats. Seven feet below the roadway, they held, crouching against the masonry riverbanks.

Mosby's squad, and platoon, scurried for the shelter of that three-story brick building. It was a very wrong move to make, since they were facing, on their flank, a full company of oncoming NVA regulars. They lived for only one reason. The track supporting them happened to have, against orders, its 90mm cannon loaded with canister, and the turret was pointed north, along the waterfront.

The tank's gunner saw oncoming gooks and fired. The canister round sharded and sent the oncoming NVA reeling back.

Mosby knew none of this. All he knew was that he hit the ground, and slammed into solid brick: the tax building. He turned, looking to his side, and his memory, even years later, presented still photographs; photographs taken from his childhood leafing through old issues of *Life* magazine:

Above him the metal tube coming out of the second-story window of the tax building and a black blur blasting from a tube's muzzle.

The flash of the tank's cannon firing a second time.

Men dead, men dying, men screaming, men running across the cobblestones.

Then an etched picture, all unique:

The RPG gunner firing from the window above Mosby dying in the rocket backblast, his well-aimed rocket going through the top of the M-48's rear deck.

Modern tank-killing rounds work a number of ways. Most commonly, and most effectively, they hurl a carefully constructed amount of explosive against a tank's armor. The explosive punches a very tiny hole through the tank's armor, and then converts the tank's own metal into molten steel, sending it in a spattering stream into the tank's crew compartment.

Mosby heard a muffled explosion as the RPG rocket detonated on the tank's rear deck. He saw the driver's hatch come open, and the driver clawing his way upward.

And then the next picture, as the inside of the tank caught fire and blew up:

The track's commander was turning the .50 machine gun up and toward the gunner that had just fired on him when the tank went. Mosby saw a cone of flame shooting through the tank's hatch—a red X-ray silhouette of a human being—his bones black against a Halloween silhouette of red and the fire turning life into black and being whisked away as a grinning, crumbling skull fell forward, flesh turning into ash as Mosby watched.

This is when Charlie Company should have died to the last man, one platoon decimated, a second platoon driven down onto the mud flats, and a third platoon pinned down in the open.

However it was then that Major Oreste Carruthers, CO of the 12th Aviation Company, potentially earned himself a General Court-Martial, the Distinguished Service Cross, and a lifelong debt from every line animal on the spot. Carruthers, with three elderly, B-model hogs—gunships—came in low and slow, across the waterfront, totally in violation of orders and without the proper clearances.

A UH-1B gunship had four crewmen—the pilot, copilot, and two door gunners. It was armed with two M-60 machine guns hung on the doors, six 2.75-inch rockets on either side, dual quad-60 machine guns in pods, and an automatically firing 40mm rocket launcher hung below it nose. In theory, if all of those guns were fired at once, the hog would stall and fall out of the air. It was a theory seldom tested, since almost never was a target found which was that choice.

Carruthers, cyclic full forward, collective rolled all the way, wondered what would happen.

The Huey slammed down.

If it were a fixed wing, it would have stalled out of the air. Being an illogical helicopter, it merely tried to rear, then tucked its nose down. Carruthers, at the moment, didn't give a shit what happened, watching what he could only describe as a hose from hell sweep across the oncoming NVA soldiers below him.

Fortunately for Carruthers, the miniguns spat empty before the helicopters lost more than twenty meters' altitude. Since they were at no more than 100 feet above the ground, that meant their skids were almost slashing across the waterfront cobbles. But helicopter pilots, especially gunship pilots, are not normal. It was a perfect run.

Carruthers would end up getting the DSC from Sinclair instead of a court-martial. And anytime he walked in a military bar and vaguely mentioned Song Nhanh, he would not be able to pay for a drink.

He also was awarded, for the rest of his military career, his call sign as a nickname.

Splatter Six.

It was well earned.

To duplicate what happened, find a sunny section of pavement, with three columns of ants crossing. Sprinkle the column with firecrackers and then gasoline. Fire across those ants with a blackpowder shotgun charge.

Now, those ants are North Vietnamese infantrymen.

Men.

Mosby found himself panting inside the tax building, a body over his shoulder. In the office chamber was his squad, Lieutenant Wilson, Blake, and most of the rest of Second Platoon.

Mosby eased himself down, half his body and most of his mind feeling like he was under novocaine. Geiger helped him. Mosby saw the body was Captain Edmunds. Very dead.

It may have been a fragment from a B-40 (RPG) round, or it may have been from the airstrike. Regardless, most of Jerry Edmunds's lower skull was missing, and his gaping jaw sagged down onto his chest.

Mosby felt the syrup-wet on his fatigues.

Goddammit, he thought, goddammit, why are you guys all looking at me? Goddammit, I don't glare any worse than you do. I don't look any more scared than anybody. It's just this fucking blood.

"Okay," Taylor said. "It was worth the risk. Now what do we do to get them out?"

Shannon's answer was interrupted as Sinclair's helicopter dropped down. They were on the closest LZ to the river, an LZ cut from rapidly burnt huts near the highway's cutoff into Song Nhanh. Other LZs had been burnt out, and Hueys, bringing in the Eleventh and Twenty-ninth, landed and lifted off again on a continuous shuttle from Hue Duc.

Sinclair came out of his chopper as it grounded and paced toward them. "I've got the Twelfth Engineers halfway up the road," he started, without preamble. "Colonel Taylor, how many men do you have on the other side?"

"Not sure, sir," Taylor confessed. "We're still trying to get through. We lost all four of the tanks, and about, I'd guess, half of Charlie Company. I've got, as far as I can tell, most of one platoon on the edge of the waterfront.

"And we're holding that"—he pointed down the road, toward the tax building on the other side of the river—"building there. I don't know how many are in it."

"Right now," Sinclair said. "I'm trying to get clearance from the ARVNs for arty and air. They're stalling us. Colonel, is there anything we can do to support your troops over there?"

Taylor and Shannon looked at each other. Sure. A nuke strike. A miracle. John Wayne's Seventh Cavalry. Sinclair read their expressions.

"The engineers will be here by 1800. They can put a bridge across by dawn. Let's hope our people can hold."

Platoon Sergeant Roger Blake stared down from his window at the two corpses. As the shadows grew, he fantasized about how they died. Yes, he had first thought. That man collapsed with that chunk of steel coming from his chest. The other man died, shot, trying to pull it out.

413

Then his perceptions changed: Maybe those two men hated each other. Maybe the second man shoved it into the first man's chest. Maybe that man was screwing the other man's wife. Maybe they were both running. Maybe that chunk of steel killed the second man, then buried itself into the other man's chest.

Blake was, fingernails unnoticed, tearing across the brickwork in front of him, pulling himself apart. As he had always torn himself.

Roger Blake was not a man for great events. Born differently, he would have made an excellent Rotarian, an owner of a dry-goods store in the Midwest, a Babbitt at his best and most useful. But not in West Texas. And not as a sharecropper's kid.

In West Texas, you hear about the heroes of the Alamo a lot. As a sharecropper's third son, post–World War II, you heard about Audie Murphy a lot.

So Blake joined the Army, in 1949, not knowing what the hell was going on, or what the hell he should do; but anything was better than getting the stray clout in the head on Saturday night when the old man was drunkenly trying to beat the crap out of Blake's mother.

Without talents, without education, without drive, Blake found himself in Korea, as the war started, in the first retreat, manning a machine-gun position on the Naktong.

Blake did not know what he was doing behind the gun and, worse yet, didn't know how to get out. As far as he knew, all his friends were dead around him. Facing him were running men in brown.

Behind him were those people, people who, except for their almond eyes, reminded him of where he came from. There were no options, except to hold the trigger up on that 1919A4. He broke the North Korean assault and piled bodies in front of him before he collapsed of wounds.

In Japan, in hospital, the Silver Star was pinned to his pillow by Douglas MacArthur. That award closed down the options for Blake. Now, it was better to stay in the Army rather than return to that dust hole in West Texas.

Since the Army is very forgiving to a hero, he managed to skate through another eighteen years' worth of duty. Never satisfactory, never more than adequate in his performance, Blake managed to clamber up the ladder to Sergeant First Class.

If it had not been for Vietnam, he would have finished his twenty years in some unimportant post and retired to a mobile home outside Fort Benning and massive lies at the local American Legion. But someone saw that Silver Star and decided that SFC Blake would make an ideal training NCO at Fort Ord's Advanced Infantry Training. On the Machine-gun Committee.

Blake lasted seven weeks. Then, drunk on his ass, he was found on Fort Ord's back forty, carrying an M-60 and swearing that he was looking for a good deer for dinner.

Of course, being a Silver Star hero, he wasn't even given an Article 15. Instead, he was shipped hastily to Vietnam, with a sealed envelope in his 201 file. Blake, the instructions from the colonel in charge of the Machine-gun Committee suggested, needed a combat assignment.

He got it: Fifteenth Infantry.

Because of his rank, Blake was made a platoon sergeant. A command position he had never held nor thought of holding.

SFC Roger Blake listened to his fingernails shred and tried to keep from jumping out that window and running, running in any direction that would not make him have to do something.

Because what he wanted to do was what he had done after being beaten—to stagger out to the shed, put his arms around the long-eared mongrel, and cry, cry without making a sound that might wake up his father.

"Man," Blind Pig growled as he trashed the last pieces of glass out of the window, "you see how them Hollywood fuckers went and lied to us?"

Grubb yanked chunks of grating away from their second-story window and perplexed at Blind Pig. He was learning to let the man take his time to make the point.

"You went an' saw those cavalry movies when you was a kid, right?"

Grubb guessed so.

"And you still don't hold the problem? Man, you micks be dumber than I thought. You not be considerin' the situation, my man."

Grubb didn't answer. He was realizing that somehow, someway, Blind Pig had promoted him from chuck and cherry to my man.

"We be sittin' in a building that looks like the Old West. Man, I expect to be seein' Henry Fonda come up those steps any time."

Grubb saw the tax building with new eyes. Yeah. Three stories of sandstone, gratings over the windows. Fucker did look like some kind of Hollywood set. Shit, he realized, it was the bank.

"No, babe," he said. "This is where that fucker with the mustache—what the hell was his name—Donlevy. You know, the banker. This is where he tells the bad guys they're gonna go out and shut down the widow's ranch."

Blind Pig considered. The mick was right. He roared in laughter.

"Man, man," he rollicked. "We be sittin' here, with but twenty of us, on the bad side of town, waitin' for all those zips to come in an' ice us, an' all we can come up with is John Wayne shit. Dude, I tell you, we be weird. Just plain weird."

Across the body-strewn blackened square below, the Sixty-seventh came in again. Blind Pig had the M-60 up on its bipod.

Tacktacktack . . . there went that cat lookin' like he was an officer. *Tacktack* . . . the guy behind him, must've been a platoon sergeant . . . fine, fine . . . bend a little . . . *tacktacktacktacktack* . . . right across that line of those fuckers who want to kill me. Man, I guess I be a corpse. But this be just like home.

William Jefferson—Blind Pig—had never been under any illusions about the chances of seeing old age. And he didn't want it. Who the fuck, he pointed out, wants to be some old nigger sitting around the club waitin' for some dude to buy him one. Livin' on the white man's handouts—naw. Best you go out hot and young.

Blind Pig was irretrievably bad. On the streets, it was real clear, real young, that the kid built like a brownstone did not care about pain—his or yours. Walk small around this dude, or you will regret it.

Blind Pig's first option was boxing. He was thrown out of Golden Gloves not only for lacing—twice—an opponent, but for kidney punching the man after he had been ordered to a neutral corner. Suspension might have been temporary if Blind Pig hadn't sought out and thumped the man who'd refereed the fight.

Awright, Blind Pig resented. This ain't payin' no rent. But I got the name. Lots of blind pigs—illegal after-hours bars—need some weight, don't they?

They did—which gave Jefferson his nickname.

Unfortunately and ultimately fortunately, William Jefferson never learned when to walk small.

There were four dudes in the joint, getting rowdy, and Blind Pig decided that was enough of that shit. Three of them made the mistake of dragging iron. One died, one was crippled, and one would limp for the rest of his life.

The fourth man was Deacon Rayburn—one of the first hardcore crooks in Detroit to learn that the money and prestige wasn't pimping anymore, but in being the Jones Man.

Rayburn could have had Blind Pig wasted for his temerity in trashing the Man's bodyguards and ruining the Man's night. But Rayburn, always a wild card, thought it was funny.

He hired Blind Pig two days later to be his main man. And taught him that a gun was not only quicker to solve problems but didn't leave you with bruised knuckles or witnesses.

Rayburn, having moves, also believed in cooperation. He laundered his money carefully, and then declared it on his tax returns.

He was one of the first dope men to drive a Mercedes instead of a pimpmobile.

"Pig," he counseled. "You got to realize. These honkie fucks don't be carin' what happens down here. They just don't want to be confronted with the reality.

"It be just like down south. We stay down in our part of the world, doin' what we want, an' then they leave us alone. But we gots to remember, every one of these charlies want to kill us. Kennedys, Johnsons, Stokes—man, they all be joinin' the movement that say us niggers best never be big in their eyes.

"So the rule I learn, an' I be tryin' to teach you, is live yo' life like you be a big black submarine. Submarines only end up fucked when they come up for air. You hear?"

Jefferson did—which was why he showed up for induction when he got his draft notice. Besides, as Rayburn pointed out—these cats be willin' to pay you to learn the best tools of killin' known. This be like somebody hirin' you to go to . . . shit, what's that honkie school? Harvard. My man, for the streets, Vietnam be like that.

Blind Pig wasn't sure he understood—but he followed the Man's orders. And so far Deacon hadn't been wrong. Rayburn kept him on the payroll, made sure when Blind Pig had his passes and leaves before he went over that he was treated like king shit, sent regular checks to Blind Pig's mom, and generally made it right.

Blind Pig realized he was probably going to die right now, in this isolated building on the far side of nowhere, in a city that no one had ever heard of. But if he didn't, he was getting some serious ideas about what would happen back in the world.

The Deacon was all right—but he was a little bit behind the times. Blind Pig thought that, after a year or so of getting his moves back, there might be a new, very big Jones Man in Detroit . . .

Dennis Shannon, on the opposite bank of the river, watched Sinclair juggling three radio communications simultaneously. It reminded him of the phone sequence in that movie. What was it? *How to Succeed in Business Without Really Trying.* Yeah. Now who the hell was the actor? It was a good thing to puzzle over. Shannon and Taylor were trying not to consider the death of Edmunds, because all of the options ended as tragedy.

Yeah, Shannon would understand later, we sent Jerry to his death. But what else was there for him? He wanted to be a soldier, and soldiers get killed. But what an awful waste. Why a waste? Soldiers die, don't they? Sure they do, but not for a stupid fucking reason like trying to retake Song Nhanh, a city that won't even appear in the footnotes in the history books.

417

It may have been at that moment that Dennis Shannon first thought of himself as a man committed to riding a juggernaut rolling downhill to the destruction of itself and whatever purpose that juggernaut—the Armed Forces of the United States of America—should have. But all this would be later.

Sinclair, on one radio, was trying to patch from MAC-V headquarters through to the ARVN high command, trying to get permission to fire artillery into Song Nhanh.

On another, he was trying to get, at a time when Tet was stretching the military's capabilities very thin, air support committed to his division. On a third, he was blustering at units of his own division—most of DivArty's self-propelled units and the long column of five-ton trucks headed north from Hue Duc.

Shannon wondered whether, if the guns arrived and Sinclair still didn't have clearance, the general would have the balls to call for fire missions. He rather hoped that he would not have to find out.

"Sir," Shannon tried to Taylor. "It'll be dark in about an hour or so."

"Yeah?"

"There's enough loose lumber for rafts," Shannon began.

"Negative, Major. This is not Point du Hoc, I'm not running a cluster of Rangers, and neither one of us is named Darby. Drop it, Major."

What might have been an interesting ass-chewing was broken by one of Taylor's radiomen.

"Got Whirlaway again, sir."

A shattered voice through the static.

"Whirlaway, this is Six Actual. Lieutenant . . . Wilson, right?"

"Yessir."

"Hang on, Whirlaway. We're trying to get across to you. What I need is your effectives, over."

Wilson's voice steadied.

"This is Whirlaway. I have eighteen effective, three Whiskey India Alphas, unknown Kilo India Alphas, over."

"What's your situation, Whirlaway?"

"Uh . . . position is secure. We just beat them back again. Our ammo is . . . I have my acting platoon sergeant making an ammo check at the moment. Sir, are you gonna be able to get us out?"

"This is Six Actual. Hang in there, Lieutenant. I ain't never let anyone swing yet. And you ain't gonna be the new tradition."

Shannon wondered if—were he in Taylor's boots—he would have the ability to drop into that take-all-the-time-you-want drawl Taylor was using. He pictured what must be going on in that sandstone building across the river.

There'd be mud, blood, and panic, about one inch below the surface. A commanding officer—Lieutenant Wilson—who was in his first real battle, and one that looked entirely too much like Bastogne. A platoon sergeant—Blake was his name, Shannon remembered—who looked to be every bit a pussy. The squad leaders . . . and Shannon saw a spark of hope. Mosby was over there. If he wasn't dead, maybe that would be what would hold things together.

Dennis Shannon wanted, very desperately, to be in that building. Because without help, he was very afraid that every man in it was about to die.

Mosby had seen Blake crouched in that upstairs window, and had felt no anger or hatred. He thought the man was responding quite sensibly to an impossible situation.

Mosby was wondering why his own responses were quite illogical. Here he was, moving from man to man. Smiling. Voice quite calm. Mosby, you jerk, you are gonna die right now, and everybody here is going to die with you. Nobody is ever going to know how you died. What a dumbass thought. Nobody ever dies well—it's always fuckin' messy. Just some get it faster than others. So why am I acting like I'm in some stupid movie about jerkass Limeys with stiff upper lips in In-jah?

There were a dozen-plus unknowns in the tax building from other squads in the platoon. Mosby couldn't know if they were good, bad or terminal sloughers.

He took inventory of his own people.

Blake in a second-floor corner; Arledge near a first-floor window. Blind Pig and Grubb well positioned upstairs, covering the open area in front of the building; Wilson and DeeJay in front of the door on the first floor.

Geiger and Diaz had windows on the riverfront, and Taliaferro and Masters covered, from the first floor, the northern area.

Fritsche was alone on the third floor, gleefully sniping down any zip who came into view, a one-man Zeusbolt. Godfrey was here and there and anywhere on the second floor.

The ammo was plentiful, surprisingly enough. Mosby thought it was because they'd been hit so hard and fast that nobody had quick enough reactions to blaze out a basic load.

The only problem Mosby saw was that they were stuck on the far side of a river, with every gook in the world plus all their friends coming in. And there was no way he could see that the rest of the battalion could get across the Song Nhanh River in time to save their young asses.

At least Wilson wasn't blowing it. His voice was calm, level, and he seemed to be carefully considering everything he said.

Mosby knew the answer. Wilson the cherrytrooper could not know just how deep in the shitter they all were.

Mosby was dead-nuts wrong.

Wilson was very aware of what was most likely going to happen. But he was very damned determined that this time he was not going to fail. Two disappointments were enough. Wilson was beginning to understand that he was very much his parents' child, and his failing to get into law school was as big a defeat to him.

Plus there was Marjorie.

Wilson, as his mind began going through that, was obscurely grateful that at that moment the NVA mounted their third assault.

The ultimate failure of Communism, like any other entrenched bureaucracy, is that it rewards and promotes agreement.

Vo Le Duan was correct in considering the Sixty-seventh Regiment his corps d'elite. Its dedicated soldiers would die to the last man in accomplishing whatever mission was assigned to him.

But this dedication also required direction. Splatter Six had arranged that the Sixty-seventh command structure was mostly dead—his first pass had destroyed the regiment's entire command group. Now the Sixty-seventh's highest-ranking officer was the supply captain. The assignment from Duan was to destroy the American presence on the riverbank. That would be done.

There could have been other, easier ways to accomplish the mission. Artillery could have been brought up and the tax building leveled. Or, at full dark, the Sixty-seventh could have filtered in on the building and taken it in a sudden, screaming assault.

Supply officers are normally not schooled in tactical thought—at least tactics more immediate than keeping their men fed and clothed. The Sixty-seventh's de-facto commander, then, had no other ideas than to keep assaulting the tax building—across open ground.

This is an acceptable way to win a war and a battle. Grant destroyed the Army of Northern Virginia by repeated frontal attacks. But not in Song Nhanh. The Union in 1863 had a limitless number of grunts to throw away. The People's Army of Vietnam needed every warm body it could get. And so the Sixty-seventh began destroying itself, attacking a three-story building held by half a platoon of Americans.

CHAPTER SIXTY-TWO

THE SQUAD

AT DUSK, THE Viets made their fourth attack, this time with RPGs and grenades. Four B-40s crashed around the entrance to the tax building, and then five sappers, who'd crept close under the cover of the still-burning tank, cascaded grenades toward the building. The blasts sent Wilson and DeeJay stumbling back away from the door and then an NVA squad was inside the building.

Mosby saw the glint of the AK's bayonet, as Casey's bowie was swinging forward. The steel buried itself in the wooden handguard, and the knife was ripped from his hand. The NVA spun in a half-circle, Mosby watching the muzzle come back toward him, his own rifle coming up far too slowly, and then Fritsche, bellowing like a bull in heat, buried the blade of his entrenching tool in the back of the man's neck, wrenched the shovel free, and shotgunned another soldier into gore.

Mosby was on one knee, firing now at the rectangle of lessening light across the building, hearing the blast of two more rifles beside him and then Blind Pig was halfway down the stairs, 60 barrel balanced on the staircase's shattered balustrade, sending most of a belt into the oncoming NVA. The NVA assault hesitated and then, from the second-story window, Grubb dumped the white phosphorus grenade on top of them.

Mosby saw the can hit and rolled for shelter, as the grenade detonated in white smoke and pluming fire. White phosphorus—Willy Peter—goes off like instant napalm. The lucky ones are killed by the blast. Since phosphorus burns, in tiny flakes, for at least sixty seconds and atomically combines with carbon atoms—the human body—getting wounded by WP is a singularly awful way to die. Phosphorus can only be stopped in its searing passage by removal or water immersion. The handful of NVA on the fringes of the grenade's blast dervished blindly toward the river's edge—and died as they stumbled.

Mosby changed magazines, then automatically found the AK lying on the floor and yanked his bowie knife free. He noticed absently that the blade was not even chipped.

A voice croaked behind him. It was Deejay. Mosby crouched beside the bloody mess that was the RTO. Blood trickled from the wound that was his face, and air whistled from his chest. Mosby moved automatically, fingers going to his belt and taking out one of his aid pouches. The foil packing of the kit was pressed flat and forced against the shrapnel hole in DeeJay's chest. Then, in spite of DeeJay's semiconscious grunts, Mosby had him up and the bandage against the foil, its ties around DeeJay's shoulders, and pulled very tight.

DeeJay was unconscious by then. Geiger'd come downstairs unnoticed and rammed a Syrette of morphine into the man's arm. The two of them managed to lug the RTO upstairs, to where Geiger had his aid station set up.

"You probably," Geiger said after they'd put DeeJay down and he'd covered him with his own poncho liner, "should have waited."

"For what?"

"Any man who wants to be a disk jockey," Geiger said, "should have been able to whistle 'Bugler Boy of Company C' through his lungs."

Mosby found time to give Geiger the finger before he went back into the machinery of death, checking his troops.

Fritsche, on the third floor, had a pile of AK-47s beside him and was experimenting as the last light died.

"Y'know, babe, the sights on these gook guns ain't worth sour owl shit."

Fritsche, as far as Mosby could tell, was absolutely unbothered by being trapped. The man looked like a casualty—the bloodspatter from the NVA soldier had pasted his jungle fatigues together, and the entrenching tool's blade beside him was black.

Mosby crouched away. He was fucking up. Downstairs was his lieutenant, who must by now be in the middle of the screaming meemies.

Lieutenant Jeff Wilson had considered the option. After he'd realized that no way was he going to be an Army lawyer, but was going to be a junior infantry leader, he figured he'd thought of all the various awfulnesses—freezing under fire; suddenly having to take over command in an attack; even somehow jumping five levels of command and being in charge of a battalion. But being pinned down in a sandstone brick building on the edges of a city he'd never heard of, in charge of the bleeding remnants of a company, was not among those 3 A.M. nightmares.

Perhaps this was why Lieutenant Wilson was doing so well. As Mosby came down the steps to the first story, he heard Wilson on the horn with—Mosby recognized the voice—Shannon.

"Understood your last, Whirlaway. So what are your options?"

"We can either pull out when it gets quiet, or else break out toward the river. We'd have to abandon our WIAs then. Over."

Wilson saw Mosby and questioned silently. Anything else? Mosby shook his head.

"This is Citation. Can you hold out until first light? We have the bridge people here."

Again a questioning look. Mosby ran through his check. No way José. There were no more than two to three magazines left per man. The two M-60s, including Blind Pig's gun, had no more than a belt and a half per gun. Not a chance that the tatters of Charlie Company could hold out until dawn.

But pull back—Mosby knew that Wilson was right. Goddammit, there was no way he'd pull out on the wounded. And he knew by now his own capabilities. Maybe Rangers or Sneaky Petes could exfiltrate successfully. But not a bunch of grunts like Mosby. Fuck it, man. You might as well stand and die in place.

Blind Pig had other ideas. He'd dragged SFC Roger Blake away from his window and was questioning him.

"I be needin' some info, you chickenshit honkie motherfucker," he started diplomatically. "Now you gone tell me, an' quit curlin' like you be some worm, or I gone pitch you straight out that window."

Blake came back from where his mind was cowering, managing to nod dumbly.

"I be askin' about tanks. That gun be sittin' up there"—and Blind Pig waved at the window, its square sketched by the flames of the dying tank below—"when those motherfuckers want to be havin' that gun on the dirt, do they carry some kinda tripod or shit?"

Blake goggled, then understood.

"Yeah. Yeah. The tripod's kept in the turret."

"Fuck. Turret's crispy, man. That do no good whatsoever."

Blake remembered something.

"Wait a sec. I used to be in Germany . . . and when we went out, carrying a full load, we'd stick stuff like that in one of the track boxes."

"What the fuck are those?"

"Back of the turret. Long boxes on either side."

"Okay. I goin' out. Tell you what you be doin', Platoon Sergeant. You tell everybody Blind Pig's out the other side of the wire. So don't nobody be shootin'."

Do something? Blake curled again.

"Best you be movin'. 'Cause somebody shoots, I gone come back an' feed you your head like it be barbecue."

Somehow Blind Pig's threat sounded more immediate than any NVA death waiting outside. He did what he was told.

423

Mosby, on the first floor, maybe was too busy thinking of battle plans. Because he didn't see Blind Pig rumble down the stairs, crouch at the hall, and then flow over the overturned desks that now blocked the door from the stairs outside the tax building.

On the American side of the Song Nhanh, it was glaring lights and engines. Across the river, the city was silent, except for the occasional crash of a grenade or the spatter of tracer.

Dennis Shannon crouched behind a ruined wall, watching the engineer battalion unload the bridge sections from the five-ton trucks that had come up from Hue Duc. To either side, tanks growled into position.

Even though he still did not have clearance to fire into the city, Sinclair had bent the options—the tracks and the gunship flights orbiting overhead had orders to fire on any observed target. But there weren't any.

Shannon wanted to do something. Scream at the engineers who worked methodically, slowly, carefully. Have some amphib tanks to press across the river. Hell, be over there himself. Instead he waited for dawn, when the bridge would be done and the arrowhead of the division would cross. Knowing this time there was no way that the Seventh Cavalry wouldn't be a little late.

On the other side of the river an NVA soldier stared at a shadow. It had moved, had it not? He shook his head. He was behaving like a recruit. He was quite wrong.

The shadow was Blind Pig, now out of sight behind the burning tank, eyes glaring toward where the NVA must be, brown fingers opening that heavy box lid . . . touching across C-rat boxes, ponchos and poncho liners, hitting metal. Metal.

He lifted the tripod out of the track box onto the ground beside him. Then his fingers remembered to his brain. Cloth. Bandolier stuff. His hands went back into the track box and came out with the Claymore. Blind Pig formulated a plan. Of sorts, anyway. He screwed the detonator into the Claymore's top, and set the Claymore, face down, on top of the tank's boiling-hot rear engine deck. Then he became another shadow, moving back, trailing Claymore wire, with the tripod, plus two cans of ammo, into the tax building.

Now for the hardshit. Again, he crept out, and again made it, unnoticed, to the track. He heaved himself up onto the track, feeling the heat of the metal begin burning him through his fatigues. Blind Pig came up to his knees and oozed up on the turret.

The corpse of the track commander was, by now, a crumbling black ash effigy. Sorry to bother you, bro'—as his fingers seared themselves on the pin holding the .50 MG to the pintle and pulled—but I got my needs. Somehow, without being seen, Blind Pig lifted the 125 pounds of Ma Deuce gun off the pintle and, with hands burning and telling them I ain't got no time for your snivelin' shit, went back down the turret's side. Then he was off and lumbering back up the steps to the tax building.

At that point the NVA sentry decided he was not imagining attacking shadows and opened up. The rounds went high, into the doorway, as Blind Pig, chortling, rolled back over the blocking desk into the building.

Mosby, a day late and a dollar short, had just realized some shit was coming down and was waiting. Blind Pig was still laughing.

"Now, my man, we gone put these gooks in a world of hurt. Pull back them desks."

Outside, on the dead M-48, the plastic on the Claymore mine began melting . . .

Blind Pig's machinations might have saved Charlie Company—but its real salvation came from the North Vietnamese Army's tactics being a little bit too well planned.

The NVA held, watching the lights of the bridge builders move slowly across the river. So far, the battle was moving very much according to plan.

At 0430 hours, the finger of light was barely ten meters from the edge of the Song Nhanh. And at that point, according to plan, the NVA hit the tax building again.

According to the plan that the Sixty-seventh's commander—its ex-supply officer—had developed, with approval from Duan's headquarters, the surrounded infantry men would be hit just before the bridge was complete. It did not work out that way, for several reasons. Among them was that the surrounded imperialists in the tax building now had a heavy gun and Blind Pig had planted the Claymore. But the final flaw was the fact that the American soldiers, when the shit comes down, find their own set of orders to follow.

The first wave of NVA infantry came howling toward the tax building. A second wave came from the warehouses along the waterfront. The two waves should have joined forces—but their juncture was swept by First Platoon's sputtering fire.

The Sixty-seventh hesitated—and Blind Pig opened up. The big .50 caliber in the tax building's doorway chewed through men like a chainsaw through saplings. The Sixty-seventh lost its first wave, almost to a man. The next line rose from cover and came in. Blind Pig then fired the Claymore. The antipersonnel mine somehow hadn't cooked off in the night. The blast, fired straight down into the almost red-hot remnants of the tank engine, set the track and the diesel fuel in its tanks off.

Forty tons of steel blew up in the tiny square.

The ball of flame seared the Sixty-seventh, killing its last two remaining officers. The NVA troops scrambled back, blindly looking for cover.

Moments later, the bridge was finished and as the last engineer came off the structure onto the pontoons, an M-48A3, its headlights glaring, roared forward onto the bridge.

Then the next stage of the NVA trap was sprung, as Duan's second, held-in-concealment regiment came out of cover in its positions just below the bridges, and opened up on the turkey shoot of the pontoon bridge. Mosby, Wilson, Blind Pig, and the other men in the tax building were spectators of the battle, ignored as the stakes escalated.

Vo Le Duan had assumed that the imperialists would be slow to respond to a new, massive threat from an unexpected direction. He was wrong—Sinclair's forces, deployed along the west riverbank, had spent the night hoping for a target and imagining that one would materialize.

The spears of flame from the B-40s, the pack howitzers, the guns and the rifles lined out the bank. Across the river, the grunts got what they wanted: something to shoot at.

Violating orders again, Carruthers's orbiting gunship flights came in and the three F-4 fastmovers that Sinclair had managed to cozen out of MAC-V found targets.

The bombs from the jets and the cannon bursts from across the river exploded in the midst of the NVA. For the first time in its history, a unit of the 302d Division, People's Army of Vietnam, broke and ran—racing toward safety and the heart of the city.

The second tank across the river came halfway up the steps of the tax building. Behind it, at the head of a squad of infantry, doubled Major Shannon.

Expecting the worst, he came into the building.

The powder-masked face of Blind Pig, still behind his .50, glowered at him.

"Man . . . who the fuck you think you be? Miss Victory, 1968?"

CHAPTER SIXTY-THREE

DREW

IT WAS AN inopportune time when Captain Charles Drew dropped in on Duong Huong Ly and his family.

The house was in disarray, and Ly was arguing with his wife and her parents on exactly what belongings they should carry away on the family bicycle.

The amount had now reached the silliness stage: the bicycle would collapse under the weight. Ly argued loudly with his in-laws—hoping that over his reasoned arguments, they would not consider the most important thing of all: money.

In Ly's case, it was gold coins. He had an enormous cache buried out in the backyard under a small citrus tree that had not bloomed in fifteen years.

Everyone around him saw their current circumstances as a supreme emergency. Of course, they were right. It was time to leave. What they did not understand was that Ly had every intention of returning some day. He had not spent half a lifetime building up his business to abandon it.

Sooner or later, his logical merchant's mind told him, the current difficulties would be over. And then it would be morning tea and business as usual.

He would need the gold he had buried to take advantage of the aftermath. Duong Huong Ly had never been a man to rely on the present. He always prided himself on looking to the future. The gold was his future. It would not do to carry it with them.

Ultimately, Ly did not really care which side won. A practical man, he understood that gold was the only real passport no matter who reigned.

Therefore he was shouting loudly and with great fervor about things he had little interest in when Charles Drew kicked open the door.

The entire family turned with many screams of fright when the door smashed open. They all expected to die in that instant. They took no comfort from the fact that the man standing in the entryway, his gun moving snakelike back and forth, was an American.

"Settle down," Drew shouted.

Instant stillness, even though they didn't directly understand what he was saying. Drew looked at each of them until he spotted Ly.

This was the head of the family, he decided. He motioned at Ly with his weapon.

In Vietnamese, he told the man what he wanted and how quickly he wanted it.

Ly barked orders, and in a few moments, the American was squatting nervously on his heels, scooping down a bowl of rice and fish with one hand, his Thompson gun ready across one knee. Drew belched and a child squalled. Ly looked at the man, shrugging helplessly: Who could control a child? Drew just nodded back at him and kept eating.

Drew belched again. He wiped his fingers on his pants and took the gun in both hands. He pointed toward the back door with it. Fear clutched at Ly. He *knows* about the gold. Buried out back. Ly rose to his feet, his temples pounding. He would have to show him.

Drew grunted for him to stop. Ly sank back down again, bewildered. What did the man want? Drew explained. He was looking for a back way out. He was asking about certain interconnecting alleys. Also, he wanted to know what sounds they had heard. Was there anyone out there?

Ly assured him that it had been mostly quiet for some time now. He pointed to their heaped belongings and explained that he and his family had been about to take advantage of the quiet and flee.

Drew thought for a long time, then rose and walked to the back door. He cracked it open and peered out, listening more than looking. Then he closed it again and turned back to them. He brought the weapon up.

There would be no witnesses, Ly thought. He waited to die.

In fact, Drew was considering exactly this. If he left them behind, what if they stopped the first NVA patrol? Then he had a better idea.

To Ly's vast relief, he ordered the family to pack their belongings. They would leave with the American. He would move in their midst as a fellow refugee.

For the first time in many hours, Ly began to have hope. In a way, he would be traveling with an armed guard. The gold would be safe.

CHAPTER SIXTY-FOUR

LAU

It was a three-story hotel painted as blue as a bird's egg. It was a new hotel, constructed of stucco and wire. Not the nicest hotel in Song Nhanh, but certainly one of the more popular.

Sergeant Lau stood in the rear alleyway considering how it would fall. He had an interesting task in front of him, but he was almost too angry to enjoy it.

Lau had crews working inside and out. Normally, the job shouldn't have taken this long. A little digging here, a few cuts there, and some electrical lines laid to the det box across the alley.

Ngo Dinh Cuu came out the rear exit and walked toward him, grimacing in anger.

"They are moving," he said, "like rubber sap just before dawn."

Which meant moving hardly at all.

Lau cursed and started toward the door. Cuu laid a restraining hand on his arm.

"I wouldn't advise it, Sergeant," he said.

"What? Since when did you object to kicking a few pigs' asses?"

"They're not being pigs' asses," Cuu said. "They're frightened."

Lau cursed again, pulled out a hand-rolled cigarette, and lit it. He choked on the harsh smoke, looked at the thing in disgust, and threw it down. He ground it under his heel.

He was frightened himself, but not *for* himself, and certainly not of the advancing American force. Lau was scared for Duan. His general had personally ordered him to oversee this job.

Lau understood its importance and the lack of noncoms that forced Duan into giving him the order. But the assignment left Duan unprotected. Lau had nightmares of a lightning American attack on the general's headquarters. Who would be there to help him?

More important, Lau had a growing unease about the men under Duan's command. Green troops, many of them. Much worse, too many civilians. Lau had some of them in this particular detail. He'd practically had to threaten physical force with some of them.

This was a simple task that must be completed within the next few hours. But his workers were moving far too slowly. And from the looks some of them were giving him, Lau was sure they would turn on him if they had half a chance.

The Comrade General didn't realize, Lau was sure, that his greatest danger didn't necessarily come from the Americans.

"Try it this way," Lau suggested to Cuu. "Tell them . . . tell them if they are not done in half an hour, I shall personally turn their heads into pepper jelly."

Cuu laughed.

"You don't think they'll believe it?" Lau asked.

"They'd better, hadn't they?" Cuu said.

Lau nodded hard. They fucking well better believe it. He had to get back to Duan.

CHAPTER SIXTY-FIVE

DUAN

LAU COULD HAVE taken minor comfort in the fact that The Comrade General and Commissar Thuy had few illusions about the position they were in. Nor were the two men wasting any time in self-recrimination.

Duan fingered the map on his office wall, lightly tracing the newly drawn-in red lines of the advancing American forces.

"This General Sinclair," he said, "has a great deal of luck."

"That's all he has," Thuy scoffed. "Once the General Uprising comes . . ."

". . . If at all," Duan murmured.

Thuy was silent.

Like the general, he was coming to understand that something was quite wrong. He did not dare voice it—but in the back of his mind he was wondering: would there ever be . . . a General Uprising?

"Do you doubt?" he asked. He was immediately sorry that his voice came so harshly. What he wanted to say was that *he* had doubts.

"No," Duan said. "There have merely been delays. Our job now is to shift our plans to take these—uh—explainable, I'm sure—delays into account."

Like Thuy, he was very sorry he could not plainly speak his mind. Unlike Thuy, he knew that this fault in both of them could mean— No. That, too, had to remain unthinkable.

"Ours was the easy task," Duan said, as calmly as possible. "We only had to move our forces into a strategic position . . . and then wait for the correct moment."

Thuy was becoming enthused again. He nodded his head vigorously.

"Of course," he said. "The General Uprising—we've always understood—requires a nationwide effort. There have always been many things . . ."

That could go wrong, Duan wanted to complete for him. Instead he said:

". . . That require an overview beyond our present circumstances."

"So, what do you propose?"

Thuy hated saying that. He didn't want to place the entire burden on Duan. He should share it, shouldn't he? He had been in on this since the beginning, hadn't he? He was the division's commissar. Still . . . there was no place else to put it.

"What I propose," the Comrade General said, "is that we plan for the certainty of the General Uprising. In a day or so at the most it will come to fruition."

He said this hard. He said this as firmly as he could. Because this was what both of them *had* to believe.

Duan again traced the map—noting the increasingly smaller concentric circles of red.

"General Sinclair must be a very happy man, at this moment," he said. "We are fighting his war, for a change. I'm sure he has spent a lifetime preparing for this kind of battle. However. . ."

He paused at the map, hypnotized by his thoughts. Thuy straightened himself in the chair, sure that the silence meant the general had suddenly seen a plan that would . . . save them?

The silence grew longer.

"Yes?" Thuy said.

Duan was startled at his voice. He looked over and noticed that his commissar was still there. What had he been thinking about? No. Not thinking! Saying!

"Stalingrad is our answer," Duan said. "Do you remember Stalingrad?"

Thuy remembered. It was one of the most important battles of the Great Patriotic War. The Russians were faced with the overwhelming forces of the Fascist German Army. To win—or even to survive—they had to play for time. The Russians fought the Germans, inch by inch, house by house, until the time ran out—for the Fascists.

"Our solution," Duan said, smiling gently at his commissar, "is in using Stalingrad tactics. We must oppose Sinclair at every street corner. Every marketplace. Every . . ."

. . . Hole in the ground we can dig, he thought.

"When the General Uprising comes, we'll have caught him," Duan said. "He'll be pressed by our loyal forces from the rear . . ."

Yes. Yes, Thuy thought. That was the way. We only have to play for time until the General Uprising is truly under way.

As a political tactician, Thuy could almost feel sorry for Sinclair. His superiors would not be able to afford a major force so far away from the important scenes of battle. He would be forced to withdraw and shore up the Imperialists in more important places. Hadn't Thuy personally monitored the news from Saigon? The uprising was so close, they couldn't give up now. They merely had to give it time to gel.

That night, Thuy slept soundly.

The Comrade General paced.

CHAPTER SIXTY-SIX

THE SQUAD

IF THERE WAS any logic in war—which of course there isn't—the remnants of Charlie Company should have been pulled back across the river and seen no more of the battle for Song Nhanh.

And if there is any logic in infantrymen—which of course there also isn't—the grunts should have welcomed relief and wanted out of the battle.

Sergeant David Mosby knew he was a damned fool for standing there, eyes and mind glazed with only three hours of sleep, listening to Major Shannon announce Intentions. He should have been asking if his squad, his company, his platoon hadn't had enough. The last thing he wanted to do was to move into the heart of this evil city. But Mosby had crossed the line. Years later, he would remember looking at the other members of the squad, their eyes deepsunk and hollow, and wonder why the fuck he didn't see, right then, that they were all quite mad.

He should have broken into what Shannon was saying to them and said we've had enough of this war, Major. Why the fuck doesn't somebody else want to do this shit? Major, we've had our butts shot off. The Army never said you'd have to do this kind of thing. This isn't Bataan, Chosin or Bastogne. There's half a million grunts in-country who should be up here, and I don't give a damn about this Tet Offensive and who's busy down in Saigon. The only war I care about is the one affecting my own young ass.

Instead, Mosby leaned on his rifle and listened to Shannon explain to Wilson that Charlie Company would go into the city, on point for the rest of the battalion. With Edmunds dead, Shannon would be Company Commander for the day's movement.

Somehow, at that point in exhaustion, it sounded like exactly what Mosby wanted to hear. Lieutenant Wilson also looked grateful—he didn't even vaguely resent not getting the company commander's slot.

Charlie Company, with Company B behind them, started down the dirt-and-cobble street that pointed toward the heart of Song Nhanh. C Company would rather have a platoon of tanks—but clearance for them, as for artillery and air support, still hadn't been received.

Ngo Dinh Cuu crouched behind his RPD, watching the imperialists come up the street toward him.

He wished for a number of things. If the rest of the N-10 Battalion had positioned itself in the businesses to either side of this street, they would have destroyed the Americans in toto before they reached the hotel Cuu was in. He wished for the artillery that the NVA had promised for the General Offensive. Even more, he wished for the armor that somehow he had believed would be brought south for this battle.

But mostly he wanted more soldiers. He admired what Sergeant Lau had done, in spite of the reluctance of the lazy Song Nhanh volunteers, to the hotel. How much more could have been accomplished if there was a full company of willing volunteers to man this position? The blue hotel could be held for weeks.

Cuu concentrated on picking his line of fire. The battle would begin after the imperialists moved beyond that burned-out Citroën 2CV 200 meters away from the hotel.

Cuu saw the first American scouts move from door to door and find shelter behind the wreck. The street was peaceful in the late-morning sun. Cuu willed them to see nothing. The scouts moved on.

Cuu held his machine-gun sights on the blackened car. Yes. Five . . . ten . . . here is the command group. Cuu had wondered why the Americans had not, with all of their awesome technical ability, found a way to build radios without waving antennae.

He would have liked to have discussed this with an imperialist. What was the matter? Was it as the propaganda said and the workers of America opposed this colonial war? Or were these officers too dumb to realize why they were such instant targets?

There were four clangs from the roof two stories above him, and

Cuu had other things to consider. The 82mm mortars fired on the previously zeroed targets, dropped two more rounds down their tubes, and then the mortars were broken down and the crews were moving, down the stairs of the hotel, out the back, and to their next location.

Cuu saw the bombs explode in the street ahead of him, a killing blanket of shrapnel between the buildings.

Cuu cursed as all of the flattened green figures moved again. Mortars gave too much warning. These Americans were too experienced. No matter. They were still walking into an unescapable trap.

"Come on, men," Ramos shouted. "Let's take them."

Nobody in First Squad moved. Mosby and Fritsche were flat in a doorway, twenty meters in front of the burnt-out car.

"Whaddaya think?"

"That fuckin' hotel," Fritsche whispered—when grunts got hit, they stupidly whispered, regardless of how many ear-shattering bangs were going off around them—"that looks too fuckin' cute."

Shannon, too, was thinking the three-story building 150 meters away was too good a target. Of course the mortars came from there—but with no backing fire?

"Come on, Charlie Company! Let's get those bastids!" Ramos was in the open, headed toward the hotel. Some Charlie Company people were up and shooting. Ramos lived longer than most of them because he was the first to charge. The gunfire from the second story of the hotel spat toward the others, those men of Companies C and B who hadn't learned that a worm lives longer than a falcon in combat.

Ramos heard the fire above his head, but kept running. His M-16 slammed empty, and Ramos had a grenade off his webbing, the ring out, and the grenade ready to pitch through the blank window of the hotel in front of him.

Cuu lowered his aim and fired.

The burst caught Ramos in the chest, and he skidded forward onto the cobblestones. There was no pain. Ramos was fascinated, seeing the grenade drop from his numb hand, and roll against a brick just in front of him, its handle spinning away.

This is a very stupid way to die, he raged. The grenade went off and blew off most of First Sergeant Ramos's head. He died only ten meters in front of the hotel's door.

Above the body, on the second floor, Cuu swept his MG sights across the street, looking for targets. There were none, at least none sure to produce a dead imperialist.

These Americans were not so bad. Cuu wasn't worried. They would have to come out of their shelter in the building doorways and behind the debris. The killing would simply take a bit longer.

Shannon moved up the street like a brown rat in a dump, flickering from cover to cover. At each man, he pointed.

"See that window? No. That one. Yeah, you got it. When we move, you just shoot the shit out of that window. Don't fuckin' worry about anything else."

Wilson was huddled way behind him, wishing he knew what the hell Shannon intended, and wishing Shannon hadn't told him to keep his ass right where it was.

Shannon looked across the street and spotted Mosby and Fritsche. He breathed, then broke into the open, dove across the street and into their doorway. Too late, Viet Cong bullets sparked across the stones behind him.

Fritsche went down in squad history for coming up with a greeting.

"Howdy, General Custer. Who're all your Injun buddies?"

Mosby was too damned scared and too damned intent to come up with anything—as was Shannon. Shannon heaved air into his lungs.

"We're gonna take 'em," he finally said.

"What's this we shit? You got a mouse in your pocket?"

Fritsche, as much in terror as the other two, was wiseassing it.

"Shut the fuck up. Look. Here's what we got. The zips are set up. That fuckin' buildings's a deathtrap. The whole damned thing's rigged. Only way we got is to con 'em."

Shannon pulled two smoke grenades off his harness. He passed one to Fritsche.

"You peg that fucker as far as you can when I tell you."

"In which direction?"

"I want you to put it just as close to that door as you can."

Fritsche hefted the grenade, realized it was White Phosphorus, estimated the distance, and shook his head.

"You want Johnny Unitas, not me."

Shannon went on.

"I'm gonna toss smoke, and when I do, we're gonna do it . . . Okay, Hank!"

Fritsche pulled the pin from the Willy Peter grenade and threw. The phosphorus grenade hit, bounced and rolled, within twenty meters of the hotel, then exploded, and white, wavering feathers blew, two stories high. Shannon had the pin out of his conventional smoke grenade, and it went out into the middle of the street. Green

435

smoke billowed, and Shannon was up and firing. Mosby and Fritsche were somehow also running toward the hotel. Mosby saw, from the corner of his eye, the rest of the squad attacking. Somewhere there was machine-gun and rifle fire, but somehow none of the squad members were hit.

Mosby didn't know that Shannon had ordered B Company to charge when they saw green smoke.

Basic tactics dictate that when a unit is hit, the forward elements of that unit stay in place and shoot back. They are pinned down. Behind them should be the "maneuver elements" that perform the actual attack.

Shannon had out-tacticed the Viet Cong in the hotel.

Five B Company men were hit by the fire—but Mosby's squad, miraculously intact, found themselves nestled against the base of the hotel, in a dead zone. One Viet Cong did lean out the window and aim straight down—but Grubb, lying flat on his back, blew three rounds through the man's chest.

First Squad was safe—but the safety was very temporary, and only a grenade-drop away from being lethal. It was also very small.

"We be here like you say, Major," Blind Pig said, his head and the muzzle of his M-60 nestled against Shannon's stomach. "What you be wantin' next?"

"This building." The squad noticed that Shannon was dragging a satchel charge with a pull-fuse from his pack and about to toss it through the seemingly open doorway of the hotel two meters away from them. Mosby saved Shannon's ass—and very likely his own— seeing that the "open" doorway was actually blocked with a wooden wall just inside it. If Shannon had pitched the satchel charge, it would have bounced back out, and . . .

Shannon nodded his thanks and considered another way to go. Fritsche, however, had already figured it. The satchel charge was already out of Shannon's hands, fused and pitched, back and over, through the second-story window before Shannon was ready to move.

The explosion blew out most of the wall above them, and masonry cascaded down.

For the NVA and Viet Cong inside, the explosion signaled the time to move. They went down braced lumber toward the rear, retreating to their next fighting position.

Ngo Dinh Cuu may have been momentarily stunned by the explosion—or, more likely, he may have wanted to kill another imperialist. He was the only bo-doi who did not retreat. Below him, he could hear the smash as other grenades went off, and the imperialists were in the hotel, on the floor below him.

Cuu swung his RPD away from the window. The Americans would come up the stairs next. They did—but not as expected. Three grenades went up the stairwell. After the blast, Taliaferro and Godfrey doubled up the creaking stairs, with Blind Pig's M-60 chattering on the landing in front of them. Taliaferro spun into the upstairs landing to see Cuu lifting his machine gun. Taliaferro snap-fired.

The M-79 grenade does not arm itself until it's gone a few meters—but the grenade weighs almost a pound and travels faster than a baseball bat at full swing. Taliaferro's grenade buried itself in Cuu's chest, sending him stumbling back. That was probably lethal—but Godfrey sprayed ten rounds into the sapper as he fell to make sure.

They had the hotel.

One moment of triumph, before they realized that they were in a shooting gallery—the entire rear of the three-story building had been demolished by Lau and his men, and, instead of Charlie Company's having secured a temporary safety position, they were now targets more than ever.

Taliaferro and Godfrey tumbled back down the stairs as fire shattered at them from the bank building just behind the hotel. They found the squad in a tumble on the ground floor. The Viet Cong *had* opened up the rear of the hotel, but not quite that well. There was enough furniture, overturned desks, and rubble to provide a moment's shelter while they figured out what to do next.

One member of the squad was ahead of the others. Mosby watched in fascination as Arledge, lying on his belly, carefully removed his glasses, took his .45 from its holster and used its butt to shatter the lenses. He owl-eyed up, and said plaintively, "Sarge? Sergeant Mosby? My glasses got broke. I can't keep going!"

It was while Mosby was trying to figure out what to do next that he heard the sound of the tank, coming down the street from the NVA-held center of the city toward them.

Sergeant First Class Roger Blake was the first to hear—and mis-recognize—the sound. He was standing inside the doorway to the hotel, trying to remember what he'd felt like, years before, on the Naktong. And then he heard it.

The sound was actually that of an obsolete M-24 American light tank, given long ago to the ARVNs. The tank's maintenance had consisted of little more than keeping the track clean and painted and its engine running. Small things, like the rubber pads on the tracks, were let go.

One major thing separates early European and American tanks—Europeans did not use rubber cleats on the tracks, and so their armor sounds like so many caterpillar tractors. The M-24 coming toward the apartment building sounded exactly like those T-34 Russian tanks that Blake had shrunk from in terror years before. And so he moved.

Before he could think rationally, Blake had the LAW in his hands and was out the door, his fingers fumbling the tube open and extended, the pin pulled out, and he was aiming at the track grinding toward him.

The M-24 tank had been taken by the NVA along with the city, and three volunteers had become the tank's crew. As yet, the cannon's operation was beyond them—but the machine guns were well within their familiarity. As soon as the driver had figured out how to drive the track, the three men had moved the tank into combat.

Blake knelt in the middle of the street as the M-24 ground toward him. The tank was clear in his sights. He pressed the trigger down. Nothing happened. The M-72, as Fritsche had said, was truly unreliable.

Blake was standing—ready to run? ready to find another LAW?— when the machine-gun rounds spattered across him, and he slumped forward across a pile of cobbles.

Fritsche was on the second floor of the hotel, ignoring the fire coming into the building from the VC position in the bank to the rear. The track was only ten feet below, its tracks turning Blake's body into hamburger, when he sawed-off the VC in the gunner's position.

The M-24's driver, without commands from the turret above, stopped the tank. Fritsche needed nothing more. He was looking for—and realized that Shannon, reversing roles, was handing him— a smoke grenade. Pin out, it went down onto the greasy rear deck of the tank, where the engine's cooling vents showed. Flames showed, small flames. Fritsche stuck around long enough to dump two frag grenades out the window into the middle of the flames, then decided he had best go flat.

It was a wise decision. The M-24 blew seconds later. Smoke boiled and clouded the street, enough smoke to cover the hotel, enough smoke to save—at least momentarily—the lives of the trapped First Squad members.

CHAPTER SIXTY-SEVEN

SINCLAIR

SINCLAIR'S COMMAND POST track bristled with antennae. There were radio links to the battalions encircling Song Nhanh, to the gunships orbiting the city, to the Phantom flights circling high overhead—and, with the exception of the circuit to the engaged Fifteenth Infantry, all of them were waiting.

Two other radios—one to MAC-V, the other to Sinclair's headquarters south at Hue Duc—were very busy.

Sinclair was fighting to keep his temper. If a commander should never actually lose his temper, it would make even less sense to lose it into a radio handpiece.

There was still no permission for Sinclair to move his tanks into the city, to use any artillery bigger than the battalion mortars, and certainly no permission for any of the aviation elements to open up.

The late afternoon sun glared off the personnel carrier's lowered ramp. High overhead, there were flashes as yet another flight of F-4 jets ran low on gas, turned for home to be replaced by other planes.

Colonel Taylor sympathized with the general—this was really the first time Sinclair had been confronted with the nature of this war.

"What in the name of God is the matter with Saigon," Sinclair muttered. "We've got a whole damned division pinned in there, and we can't go get them?"

Taylor shook his head, although he could have offered a number of possible theories—that the palace was busy with its own problems since half of the capital was occupied by Viet Cong; that nobody was willing to tell Thieu that all previous reports from peaceful Song Nhanh were a tissue; or, Taylor's own theory, that somebody was trying to figure a way to build up his Swiss bank account by either giving or denying fire permission.

He wasn't about to offer any of these theories—Sinclair wouldn't be interested, and Colonel Taylor was being careful what he said with that idiot Ron Mead about, looking for some nice right-wing story that would give him headlines and the quoted officer a reassignment to Guam.

Sinclair looked up and gaped. Low—very low overhead—came a flight of four A-1E Skyraiders, the prop-driven, Korean War-vintage light bomber that could carry, under its wings, the bomb payload of *two* jets.

American pilots called the almost indestructible plane the Spad; Vietnamese pilots called it trau dien—the Crazed Water Buffalo.

The pilots driving the Spads were among the handful of South Vietnamese combat soldiers respected for having any balls at all by the Americans.

Colonel Taylor also had a personal fondness for the Water Buffalo pilots, since way back in 1962 one renegade pilot had thrown his own airstrike against Diem's palace before defecting to the North.

He added another plus, as the VNAF Skyraiders screamed over the command post at about thirty feet indicated, and Ron Mead splatted into the roiled-up muck beside the command track.

Taylor was about to ask Sinclair if he could get back to his battalion, but his attention was caught by the Spads as they went across the river, lifted slightly for the buildings, and nap-of-the-citied over Song Nhanh.

The four planes should have lifted over Song Nhanh's center, chandelled, and assumed an orbit between the gunships and the Phantom jets. But suddenly there was a burst of brown smoke around the lead A-1, just as the ship began its bank.

Even a Spad can be shot down—especially when it runs, engine-first, into a burst of 23mm cannon fire.

The Skyraider's bank became a climbing turn, then a tight spiral. The plane flattened, rolled onto its back, and the canopy opened. Taylor saw the pilot struggling away from his plane. A burst of white—the pilot must've yanked his ripcord—blossomed. The parachute whipped back and wrapped itself around the Skyraider's tailplane, just as the A-1's engine quit, and the huge fighter-bomber dropped, nose first, and dove.

Taylor, across the river, could hear the explosion. There are no old, bold pilots, he thought. Then he returned his attention to his current problems. There were many. His battalion was across the river, getting hit and hit hard. His place was with them.

Again, he was ready to ask Sinclair for permission to leave, when he noticed a livid Mead. The reporter was angrily digging through his asspack, which had been sitting, unnoticed, at the rear of the command APC.

"Something wrong?"

Mead started to snarl, then caught himself. Yes. There was something very wrong. He'd been planning to take out a carefully brought forward bottle of Jack Daniels to mourn the death of a young flier with General Sinclair. He could already see the lead he would write for the story.

But there was no bottle in the pack. Mead had been looted. It took him only a few moments to figure out who was the thief. Of course it could have been one of the radiomen or one of Sinclair's bodyguards—he realized they hated him. But they wouldn't be that stupid.

The thief must be that fucking Tarpy. He'd been sitting beside Mead's web gear on the flight north. And—of course it was Tarpy—he'd been most polite about helping Mead get his webbing on when the helicopter landed.

Jesus Christ, Mead thought. Things were different in the old days. What the hell ever happened to being a war correspondent?

America's changing, and I don't like the way it's going. They listen to . . . Christ, would Wally Cronkite or Ernie Pyle have stolen my whiskey? It was quite logical that Mead would not only call two journalists he'd never met by nicknames but also not realize the answer was hell yes . . .

Sinclair was still on the radio, trying to get fire permission. Within the hour, he would get it. Song Nhanh would be declared a free-fire zone.

Lee Sinclair assumed the reason he'd been given the okay to take Song Nhanh by any means necessary was that General Westmoreland and the government of South Vietnam realized what was going on. He was very wrong. The only reason the Twelfth Division was finally given carte blanche, and orders to take Song Nhanh as quickly as possible, was the crash of that VNAF Skyraider.

The pilot was the favored son of one of Thieu's most respected ministers, a young crazy who'd insisted on flying combat in spite of his father's cautions.

And because of his death, the Twelfth Division attacked at full strength.

CHAPTER SIXTY-EIGHT

TARPY

CLIFF TARPY, NOT knowing the password, announced himself to Charlie Company just at dusk.

The company had regrouped and attacked the bank building across clear ground. Now they were sitting on the bank's ground floor, staring numbly, thinking: yes we must get off our asses, yes we got to get ready for the night, yes we must wonder about food, and yes we must wonder about resupply.

Tarpy announced himself with a clang and a click. The clang was a big jerrycan of water. The click was Mead's bottle of Jack Daniels. Mosby almost kissed the reporter. He wasn't sure which he wanted more, the bourbon or the water. He did, however, first take the bottle from Tarpy and put it in his side pocket before he embraced the AP man.

"What the fuck are you doing here?"

"Shit, I dunno. Got tired of the REMFs, I guess. Fuck, I gotta tell ya. When this whole piss and padoodle is over, I'm gonna get myself a nice, safe job. Writing captions for *National Geographic*, or something."

Mosby managed to smile through his thousand-yard attitude. He let go of Tarpy and saw a somewhat puzzled Dennis Shannon beside him.

"Oh, yeah. Major, this is Cliff Tarpy. He's a reporter."

"No shit," Shannon said. He remembered him from the press conference when Tarpy had tried to toast Sinclair's balls.

"Welcome to the front lines, Cliff."

"I say again my last," Mosby broke in. "What're you doing up here?"

"Looking for a story. Heard you guys had a rough way to go."

"You don't even wanna know." Mosby sighed.

"Yeah. Talked to a guy from your squad. Said you'd stood off two, maybe three NVA companies today."

Mosby trusted Shannon enough to break in on this. "Whoinhell told you that?"

Tarpy took his notebook from his pocket and flipped pages. "A Private First Class Arledge . . . he said—"

Mosby was laughing and very grateful for that laughter. "That motherfucker? Cliff, that chickenshit asshole went and broke his glasses when we got hit so he could get dusted off."

Tarpy did not smile, but looked slightly relieved. "So, I guess I don't have any bad news."

Shannon and Mosby looked at each other, wondering if Tarpy had maybe nipped from the bottle on his hike.

"Bad news?"

"Yeah. This Arledge . . . he was on the first medevac ship out. The Huey took a B-40 round and went in. No survivors."

"Well, kiss my Irish ass," Shannon said, again believing for a moment in good old-fashioned Catholic Sin.

Mosby was also recovering and became aware of his Squad Leader Responsibilities. He was about to tell his troops to line up for water when he saw that the squad members were breaking away from their positions and filing their empty canteens from the jerrycan. Mosby decided to go explore the bank and try to figure out what night would bring.

But first, he pulled out the bottle. He planned to take a very healthy swig, then stopped. He dimly heard Casey's voice, wondering if there would be enough for everyone. Mosby, disgusted, touched enough bourbon on his tongue to feel the burn, then handed the bottle to Shannon and set out to look around the building.

He heard the sound of laughter before he reached the vault. Inside he found Fritsche, Taliaferro, Geiger, and Diaz. Geiger was posing, holding a bundle of paper in front of him. They were piaster notes.

"My dears," Geiger mocked, "couldn't I make a perfect coming-out gown from these silly slips of paper?"

Fritsche chortled. "Darling, you'd look fuckin' wondrous. I'd turn you out in a minute."

Mosby saw that in the middle of madness, his mad squad had found something to laugh about.

Geiger took out a cigarette. "If someone, dahling, would only send me a holder, I'd look like Franklin. Or Eleanor. Or Tallulah."

Fritsche lit Geiger's cigarette with a thousand-piaster note. Only Taliaferro didn't understand.

"What the fuck you guys doing? This zip dough's *money*, dammit."

"Sure it is," Fritsche said. "But there ain't none of us gonna live to spend it."

The wrong thing to say, as the realities of Song Nhanh came back to them. Mosby was glad to see Blind Pig come out of the vault's inner door, shaking his head.

"What's back there, babe?" Mosby asked.

"There be nothing but some dead gook clerk, stinkin' the whole scene up."

Mosby did not notice that Blind Pig was looking away from the others when he said it.

Later, Blind Pig was cuddled beside his M-60, Grubb catching zees behind him, as Lieutenant Wilson crawled up, checking posts.

"How's it going, Jefferson?"

"It be movin', Lieutenant. But, slow."

"Yeah."

Blind Pig handed his platoon leader the cigarette he had cupped. "Lieutenant," he started cautiously. "I be wantin' to ask you something."

Wilson choked on the smoke. The last thing he'd expected was Blind Pig wanting anything from him. "Uh . . . go ahead."

"Y'know," Blind Pig said, "I see you come in. An' I see you ain't got moves or nothin'. But the thing I be wantin' to ask is about what comes next?"

Wilson didn't have the vaguest idea what Blind Pig was talking about. But he had brains enough to stay silent.

"Sooner or later, this war be over. Maybe some of us live through it."

"I hope all of us."

"Good thought. But that don't be the way the world gone work. But I *think* some of us get back. Question be, if we don't want to be what we thought we gonna be, whatta we do?"

Jeff Wilson had about as much knowledge of street dialect as he did of Etruscan. But he sort of got the drift.

"There's the GI Bill."

"Yeah? What's that do?"

"You can go to college. Buy a house. Shit, I understand you can buy a farm."

"How much?"

"I don't know," Wilson confessed. "For college, I heard . . . maybe $400 a month."

"That don't be shit."

"I guess not. But it could help."

"Okay, Lieutenant," Blind Pig said. "Things don't be clear to me. I could go four hun a day I go back to the Deacon. But, say I go another way. Say I be you. You gone use this GI Bill?"

"I sure as hell am," Wilson said, surprising himself with the decision. Yeah, maybe some postgrad work would solve some of his problems.

"What you gone be?"

"A lawyer."

"I hear you got rich folks. What stopped you from not gettin' near this niggers' war and gettin' your three-piece?"

"My folks aren't rich. And"—Wilson never knew why he made the confession—"the girl I want to marry is white."

"Marry?"

"Yeah."

"Some chuck bitch?" Pause as Blind Pig thought about his words. "Sorry, sir."

Wilson also cut himself back. "Yeah."

"Real personal question," Blind Pig said. "Only white bi— women I gone with be spade freaks. How this woman be different? She back you? She write regular?"

Wilson could have answered. No, Marjorie did not write regularly. No, her letters weren't the sound of a person waiting lovingly. Instead they were full of the rock concerts she'd seen, the marches she'd carried signs in, and questions of how Wilson could support this imperalist war. Wilson could see that what he felt about Marjorie wasn't being reciprocated. In fact, Lieutenant Jeff Wilson was starting to wonder exactly what he felt about the woman.

Wilson chose to look out the loophole, in front of Blind Pig's MG.

"Never mind. Let's be watching out to see if they come in on us."

He crawled away. Blind Pig turned, watching his lieutenant. He had some answers—maybe some answers for questions he hadn't even thought of yet.

Shannon and Tarpy were ostensibly sharing the remains of the bottle—actually staring out the blown-open doors of the bank building at the night—and talking. Shannon's small picture had gotten somewhat larger. He'd learned from the reporter that the entire country was in flames.

He was wondering if he should tell Tarpy that none of this was surprising. He was feeling very much like he was fighting on the losing side—and beginning to see that he and the rest of the U.S. Army might even be fighting on the wrong side. That was a dumb, exhausted thought. He knew what would happen if the Communists did control the country. But, would it be that different than what Thieu's dictatorship already was doing? The only difference might be there wouldn't be as many rounds going off and killing people in the middle.

Shannon might have said this, in the heart of the night. But before he could speak, there was the clatter of cobblestones out to the front.

He was on his feet, his M-16 aimed out.

Toss a flare? Negative. There's nobody out there but zips.

Around the building, the rest of C Company had heard the sound. They were locked and loaded and ready for anything.

Anything, except the low voice:

"I got some friends here."

Shannon, his finger on the trigger, wondered. The voice was bass. The pronunciation was perfect.

Shannon—and he would get points with God for this—decided to answer back instead of shooting or throwing a grenade.

"Who the fuck are you?"

445

"Charles Drew. Captain. U.S. Infantry. 0257-985. West Point. Class of '64."

Shannon knew there were Viet Cong and NVA who spoke perfect English. But this was a little too much.

"What is a cow?"

"Uh . . . it's a lactose, load-bearing . . . for Chrissake, let us come in! We got gooks behind us!"

Shannon noticed that Blind Pig was beside him, M-60 at the hip. Okay. Keep making a fool of yourself, Major.

"One man. Forward."

Out of the shadows, hands held high, Thompson gun slung around his shoulders, came Charles Drew. Six feet away from the bank entrance, Shannon ID'd his height and the torn, filthy tigerstripes the adviser wore.

"What in the hell are—"

"Don't shit around," Drew said. "I got a whole bunch of people with me."

"Well, bring them in, dammit!"

Drew waved at the shadows behind him and a column of people came forward.

A whole bunch of people was a minor statement—Drew, in his flight toward American lines, had collected many more refugees beside the Ly family. His entourage consisted of eighty-six Vietnamese men, women and children.

Shannon and Drew shepherded them through the door to momentary safety. Cliff Tarpy stood to one side, marveling. He knew Special Forces could be good—but this was ridiculous. But it would also make a helluva story.

It was one of the two big stories that the AP man would not survive to file.

CHAPTER SIXTY-NINE

DUAN

DUAN LAY ON his cot, slowly forcing himself out of the dream. The thing kept scrabbling at him, pulling him back. Finally, he came fully awake. He lay there for a long time, shaking. Every joint in his body ached from the tension of the dream, and his skin was filmed with sweat.

Strangely, despite the power of the dream, he could not remember what it was about—only that it had occurred. He thought about going back to sleep—he'd had very little time over the past few days for rest. Duan decided against it; he was afraid of the dream.

The Comrade General sighed and sat up, swinging his feet over the side of the cot. He rubbed at the grit in his eyes.

Although he couldn't remember the exact content of the dream, he knew its theme: betrayal. And Duan was the traitor. Like most good ex-Catholics, the Comrade General believed that to think a sin was the same as committing it. He was ashamed that he had even imagined the idea. But he also knew that it was a decision that would have to be made within the next few hours.

Duan wondered how Thuy would react when he broached the subject. Would the man immediately order him relieved and then shot? Perhaps, he mused, he would have to kill Thuy first. A possibility. If this was so, he reminded himself, he would have to make sure Sergeant Lau was not involved.

There was a rapping at his door.

"In."

The man whose death he was considering entered.

Duan was shocked at Thuy's appearance. His uniform was filth. His eyes were tunnels of exhaustion. His face had sprouts of hair that he had missed in an obvious hurried shave.

"Yes, Comrade Colonel?" the general said gently.

Thuy was standing at perfect attention—his eyes piercing an area just above Duan's left shoulder. The Comrade General waited through a long struggle. He noted the quick rasping breathing, the sweat breaking, the pallor of the flesh.

At this moment Duan dismissed the idea of killing his commissar.

"Yes, Comrade?" he said again.

Thuy was a tension wire ready to break.

"Sir," Thuy said, "I am requesting that you relieve me of my duties. I have failed our . . . party . . . I have failed . . . our mission."

The man sagged slightly after this and then straightened in a quiver, waiting for the quizzing that would decide his fate.

Instead, Duan said: "We've lost."

He watched the bow that was Thuy's spine loosen for an instant, and then tighten again.

"The General Uprising, sir . . ." Thuy's voice slipped a note. "Any hour now, sir . . ."

". . . Is not going to happen," Duan said. His voice was rough with tears.

He motioned toward his cot.

"Sit down, young man," he said, "while I make us some tea."

Thuy hesitated and then walked the few steps to the cot. His knees buckled and he sat. Duan pretended not to notice and busied himself with firing up the Primus and loading the pot.

Hmmm. Luck was a strange thing. Thuy was now his potential ally. The only question that remained now was how he would put it.

The dream tugged at him again. As well as his guilt. Duan knew that he would be punished for what he was about to do. Yes, but how to do it . . . how to say it?

"I'm going to order a withdrawal," he said.

Duan purposely did not add "if you concur." He made an instant decision to remove Thuy from the line of fire. He was slightly amazed that Thuy did not stiffen, much less protest. The man was as beaten as he.

"There is not going to be a General Uprising," Duan said.

Thuy did not question his statement. Still, Duan felt it was his duty to go on.

"Comrade," he said. "Events have gone beyond our understanding. We had our instructions. We have fulfilled them. The rest . . ."

He waved his hand at empty air.

"The men who instructed us were in error," he said. He watched closely for Thuy's reaction. A long moment later, Thuy nodded.

"Do not blame yourself, Comrade," Duan said. "Work blame out later. We have more important things to deal with now than blame."

"If we remain in this city," Thuy blurted, "every one of our men will be dead."

Duan was mildly surprised. Through the long months of their journey down the Ho Chi Minh Trail, he was never convinced that Thuy cared about the young men. Perhaps he didn't at the beginning. But, after the many entertainments, the self-examination sessions . . . then Duan had a new realization. Thuy now had decided to die himself in their stead. What a fool! Then, secretly to himself: I am that same fool!

Duan knew that he could never survive his about-to-be-delivered orders. There was no language for retreat in the face of the enemy. And that is what he had to order if the South had any hope of becoming free. He had a thoroughly trained group of comrades who were quite capable of facing the imperialists under almost any circumstances and eventually defeating them.

But not under circumstances such as these. He tried to gentle it out to Thuy.

"If we can slip out of the city," he said, "and hide in the Octopus, our men will be available . . ."

"Instead of dead," Thuy broke in.

"Yes, instead of dead. Then when the General Uprising comes . . ."

Thuy looked up at him for help.

"Do you believe, Comrade General? Do you believe there really will be . . ."

Duan laughed.

"Of course, Comrade. As sure as I do in the will of our people."

It was a gentle lie, but a lie just the same.

"Then we should contact . . ."

"We will contact no one," Duan said—as firmly as possible under the circumstances.

"But . . ."

"If we do," Duan said, "we will be refused permission. Don't you understand, they cannot allow us to retreat under any circumstances."

Thuy accepted this.

"You and I . . ."

He left their individual fates unfinished.

"Let me concern myself with myself," Duan said. "As for you, I have a proposition."

What he gave Thuy was the commissar's dream—he was asking him to take over a line unit. For the first time Thuy would be able to oppose the Americans face to face. Duan laid out the plan for him quickly.

Thuy would command a group that would be one of the elements delaying the Americans. Duan had already sent out scouts to find the safest route to withdraw the division. Thuy agreed with him on almost every point—here and there adding some refinements that Duan just as quickly accepted.

Duan wondered if it would have been kinder just to have shot the man.

CHAPTER SEVENTY

CUNG

PHAN XUAN CUNG came out of the shadow of the city, running low. Around and behind him he could hear the rough breathing of his five companions. Their first terrible fear was nearly past: although the city was dark, the constant flashes of battle could have outlined a man against the marshes.

Sniper's meat.

The whole time they were moving, Cung kept thinking of the sniper. This was not a night to be out. First, they were ordered to strike east, toward the Octopus. On any night but tonight, their major danger would lie in the sudden illuminations of city fighting. But once out into the marshes, they should be safe.

Here the darkness of the presence they each filled could blend into the shadows and marsh brush. You only had to move slowly to blend in.

Tonight, however, was the worst possible night for a scouting party. The moon was brighter than the lantern used to illuminate a shadow show. And as they squelched into the beginning of the marsh, Cung knew that they were being outlined as clearly as any of the puppets he had ever seen play out their terrible fate in those village entertainments.

General Duan had overridden the scout's objections. There was no time to wait for a more appropriate night. They must instantly find what opposition they faced on the east. No one ever mentioned the word retreat to Cung and, to be truthful, it was not something he would have cared about if they had.

Cung had no pretensions about his role as a scout. He would seek and hope to hell he would not find.

Cung thought about the sniper.

He was not a superstitious man. But on a full moonlit night he knew there could be devils.

To move quickly, the six men had to slide across the well-mapped high ground of the marsh. Cung could see said map in his mind: forget the fucking north south and west, his job was to the east. The map was highlighted by many hand-drawn marsh symbols—three wavy lines resting on horizontal bars.

The team would push through the marsh and check the country-side immediately surrounding it. They would report back any enemy activity in and beyond the marsh.

He thought about the sniper.

Cung was point man in their run across the swamp. He took advantage of every speck of potential cover. Ducking . . . flattening . . . hiding . . . but always moving quickly.

Cung wished that he were alone.

They were two-thirds of the way across the second marsh when he heard the man to his right trip and fall. Cung cursed to himself at the man's clumsiness. Then he heard the sharp crack of the rifle and he realized the man had not stumbled.

The sniper had found them.

At that moment, Cung veered off the path and plunged neck deep into water. At any other time he would have felt like a fool. Instead, he turtled his head into the muck. There were more sounds of stumbling men followed by sharp cracks. Don't let him find me, Cung prayed.

Cung had grown to love his sniper. He knew the man like a member of his own family.

Cung's sniper was tall and dark—like most of the Americans he had studied from a distance. His sniper smoked tobacco that was so rich it made your head swim. He ate the best of food and drank whiskey so strong that it turned your quaking guts to a warm glow.

His sniper was never alone. He always had a minimum of two men with him: a spotter to find poor fool Cung, and a man to take out any equal fools Cung sent out to flank the sniper. The other two men were cross-trained, meaning each of them was capable of being the ghost that hunted Cung.

In his mind, Cung could see the weapon the man carried and how he looked through it. It was a 7.62mm M-14 rifle. With its silencer attached it stood just above Cung's eye level when balanced on its butt. When fired, it was so wonderfully suppressed that no one could ever see the flash of the explosion. The only sound from the supersonic bullet veed out to the front and rear, so that anyone not a target could never really tell where the sniper was positioned.

Most terrible of all was the starlight scope fixed to the rifle. Cung could almost see himself through the scope. He would be ghastly green picked out from shadows of black-black.

He heard another crack and another man die and knew that his sniper had still not found him.

Cung stayed there the rest of the night. In the morning he heard gunships—he dared not look—sweep the area. Miraculously, not one of the hundreds of bullets fired found him.

He waited longer. At dusk he slithered onward. Past his sniper.

Cung would never return to Song Nhanh to report to General Duan.

CHAPTER SEVENTY-ONE

SONG NHANH

THE WORD "SURROUNDED" suggests the Little Big Horn, with the enemy standing shoulder to shoulder and in serried backup ranks to the rear of the battlefield.

But not in modern combat. If an observer overlooked Song Nhanh and saw the NLF forces in black and the three battalions of the Twelfth Division in red, the area would show solid blocks of black and splotches of red. There were large areas, that observer would think, the trapped NVA could escape through.

But those open areas were either exposed to fire, covered by the orbiting helicopter gunships, or simply impassable. The 302d Division was well and truly trapped—and Sinclair was tightening the thuggee cord. The Twenty-ninth and Eleventh were closing in from the north and east, toward the city, and the Fifteenth was grimly pushing toward the city's heart.

The worst battlefield is the city. A unit committed to city fighting will, most likely, be destroyed, especially if opposed by a skilled and determined enemy. The skills of house-to-house combat are hard-learned and seldom trained. The United States Army, in 1968, had *no* schools teaching those skills. But Charlie Company learned them within twenty-four hours.

Their personal equipment had changed. Helmets were abandoned for scarves worn babushka-fashion around the head; other scarves were used as dust masks. They'd looted an optician's shop for clear glasses to protect their eyes from shrapnel. And they went loaded now. Their asspacks were now filled with grenades, spare magazines and blasting charges with detonators, a few inches of fuse, and pull fuse lighters already installed. Each of them carried at least two of the much despised M-72 LAWs on top of the asspack.

They'd learned new skills. Before they attacked a building, they shot it up with a basic load of ammo, plus a couple of LAWs just to make sure. Most of the ammo was wasted, firing into unoccupied buildings—but ammo was very cheap.

Now they had tanks, 106 recoilless rifles, and the battalion's mortars in close support. They'd learned to call in direct artillery support just meters ahead of their positions.

Sinclair had wanted an arena to mount his attack—and Tet had provided it. They destroyed the city as they attacked.

Mosby and Fritsche figured out that, when attacking a building next door to the one that had just been taken, there was no need to move into the open. Mosby specialized in finding long planks that would stretch from one second- or third-story window to another. Fritsche had independently invented what was known in WWII as mouseholing: A satchel charge was placed against your own wall and blown up. Through the hole, a second satchel charge would be tossed against the building you wanted to attack. When that wall blew down, a couple of LAWs and half a dozen grenades went into the hole. Then three men drove through the hole, their rifles on full auto.

It was expensive on real estate, ammunition, on the NVA, and on any poor civilians sheltering in those buildings. But it saved men's lives. Which was all that Shannon and his black-faced, catatonic-staring grunts gave a shit about.

Time—and perceptions—stopped. Mosby found himself stumbling down a half-blown-down set of steps, his rifle in one hand, Casey's bowie in the other. The knife ran red across the hilt—and Mosby had no idea what must have gone on at the top of those stairs. He numbly noted, however, that somehow he'd expanded all his grenades and hoped that resupply would be directly at hand. Also he wanted water—all of the line animals carried extra canteens, and found them emptied within minutes.

The Twelfth Division rolled on, directly toward General Duan and the center of Song Nhanh.

CHAPTER SEVENTY-TWO

DUAN

A SMALL PART of Vo Le Duan's mind found the circumstances amusing. He had spent many years rising through the ranks, from bo-doi through artillery captain to division commander. The imperialists had reduced him to the ranks in a few days.

His embattled division was fighting as independent units now—Duan's radios were only seldom able to operate. Most of his runners either failed to return from their missions or were killed as they went out. Duan's artillery was shattered—there were only a few 75mm recoilesses left. His 82mm and 120mm mortars were mostly destroyed.

Duan had been told that the Americans had counterbattery radar capabilities, but, like most experienced field soldiers, he had not believed that this magic could work.

He was quite wrong. The plotting tables on the other side of the Song Nhanh River quickly pinpointed the NVA artillery positions and brought in fire before the pieces could be moved.

The treasury building now resembled pictures that Duan had seen of Russian cities after the armies finished.

Duan had returned to basics.

He carefully examined each 7.62mm round, then wiped the oil off. Duan checked the spring tension of each of the curved magazines on the concrete floor beside him, then loaded those magazines. His AK was already spotless, lying on the floor in front of him.

Duan's Catholic past and Communist presence faultlessly combined—yes, he was going to die, and yes, his mission was a failure.

Somehow, there was some error in his past, in his thinking, that made this so. And of course Vo Nguyen Giap's natterings on the General Offensive were wrong—man proposes, but God and the progress of man disposes.

And so Vo Le Duan was left with nothing more than an AK-47 and a willingness to face death.

Plus, he suddenly realized, Sergeant Lau.

Duan, locked in his own mind, had not seen the sergeant enter the building and seat himself, cross-legged, across from his general.

"Do you remember that film you took me to see?" Lau started, irrelevantly.

"For . . . which one?"

"The very old one. The one where the film kept slipping off its sprockets, and it almost had to be shown by hand. The one with those two Americans—one was fat and sweaty, the other was skinny like you. He wore a trilby hat . . ."

Duan was grateful for the interruption.

"Laurel and Hardy. Yes. I remember."

"Do you remember what one of them said to the other, in the middle of some catastrophe," Lau said, almost smiling. "He said that this was another fine mess the other man had gotten him into."

Duan got it—and managed to find a remnant of laughter in his guts.

"You are blaming me for this?"

"Why not?"

Duan laughed aloud.

"Sergeant Lau," he said, most sincerely, "for that I would give you a medal. But Hanoi and your relatives would never hear of it."

"Do not be a defeatist, Comrade General," Lau said. "At our next kiem thao session, I shall expect you to devote some attention to your attitude at this moment."

"You think there's going to be another kiem thao for us?"

"Certainly."

"You are a dreamer."

"Wrong, Comrade General, and I say this with the greatest respect for your rank. You forget the elephants."

"What elephants?"

"The ones just before Dien Bien Phu."

Duan remembered how Lau had saved him after the French commando attack. He marveled at Lau.

"Do you really believe in elephants? Comrade Sergeant, you sell yourself very short. Do you believe *another* Sergeant Lau will appear?"

"Why not? I am but a peasant soldier, Uncle Ho has taught me, one among millions. Why shouldn't there appear another . . . and I am grateful for the compliment and you may buy me a drink when this is all over . . ."

Duan loaded a magazine in his AK, stuffed the others into his pockets, and stood up.

"Not a bad thought to die on," he observed.

"No. Not bad at all." And Sergeant Lau followed General Duan out of the building to the fighting positions.

CHAPTER SEVENTY-THREE

THE PARK

THE PARK WAS ringed by huge boulevards built in the French tradition. In normal times, the boulevards were beautiful, clean, and wide, with large traffic control corners. They perfectly sketched in the edges of the park.

From Shannon's point of view, the park was spooky. It was a bright shining day and the park was looking its best. This was a typical French-conceived park, with broad expanses of lawn, many clumps of carefully tended trees and hedges, and winding lanes inviting strolling families and Sunday couples. There was even, Shannon noted, a goddamned bandstand in the center.

There was also no one visible in the park. Not strange at all, considering the circumstances. Scary, with all that open lawn surrounded by hidey-holes, but not strange. What put his teeth on edge and his gut in knots was that the park was ringed with a recently built barbed-wire fence. Who the fuck would fence in a park? And why?

Mosby's squad took up covering positions while members of another squad snipped a gate through the wires. Moments later, Shannon was spearing men across the park. Mosby and his men took point, two other squads worked as wide wings. They had the entire park swept in a short period of time.

Nothing. Relief, at first. But Shannon still had a skin crawl. If he were VC he would've at least set up some nasty surprises, starting with a couple or three machine-gun ambushes. Quit being so fucking paranoid, Major. Take gifts from the gods when you can get them. Then he remembered that the only reason he had even a hope of reaching the ancient age of thirty was that he was a born paranoiac. In combat, believing that someone is hunting you with intent to kill is very, very sane.

Shannon got Taylor on the horn and filled him in. From Taylor's point of view the situation was perfect. He ordered Shannon and his men to dig in and wait while the rest of the troops caught up with them.

Most of the men were too tired to grumble when the order came to unlimber their entrenching tools and dig in. What the fuck, they were always digging in somewhere, weren't they? Taliaferro, on the other hand, was never too tired to bitch. He picked his entrenching tool into a section of the broad lawn.

The French have always been good at constructing parks to last. The mixture of grass seed they use produces a lawn that is rich, thick, and permanently green—no matter what the season. The roots also tend to net outward and downward two and a half to three feet deep. When Taliaferro dug in and pulled out, the grass pulled back. Taliaferro cursed, tried again. It was like trying to lift several tons. He realized he was facing many sore muscles and an ocean of sweat.

"Fuck this shit!" he said, throwing his entrenching tool down in disgust.

Diaz, meanwhile, had been expertly cutting through the lawn, gradually chopping through the tendrils of roots. He knew that, in the end, he would be able to dig down with relative ease.

"What's your problem?" Diaz wanted to know.

"This is stupid," Taliaferro said. "By the time we dig through this shit, we might as well be dead."

"Asshole," Diaz said. "I may be green but I ain't dead. I know too many cabrones that were too lazy to dig. My momma sent flowers to their mommas."

Taliaferro bristled at this. "I ain't lazy," he drawled. "I'm just particular."

"What's to be particular about? You never dug up a lawn? This is fuckin' duck soup. You oughta try digging some place real hard—places they give Mexicans to farm. That's a sonofabitch. This is chocolate layer cake."

Taliaferro grabbed his entrenching tool and stalked off to look for a better digging site. He was not about to get lessons from a flake-ass Californian. Especially if the Californian was suspiciously brownish.

As Taliaferro walked, searching the ground for something easier, he had many unkind thoughts about his colleague. He figured Diaz for a wetback; asshole probably joined the fucking Army so's he could sleaze a citizenship. Now, *that* was funny, from Taliaferro's point of view. Motherfucker'd probably be killed before he made American. This put Taliaferro in a much better mood. For this reason, he was able to really see the ground around him. He came to an abrupt halt.

"Jesus," he breathed, much in awe at his luck.

In front and around him were many trenches that had been dug out and then filled in again. It was a grunt's dream—many many yards of tough dirt ready for the next shoveler. It was the next best thing to not digging at all.

"Look what I found!" he shouted. Other members of the squad drifted over.

Taliaferro was already starting to dig into one of the trenches. The men stared at him in some fascination but for some reason didn't immediately join in and help.

"What the fuck's wrong with you guys?" Taliaferro yelled. He was spewing out dirt like a mole being pursued by things that considered moles as dinner.

"I don't think you ought to do that," Fritsche said.

"Why the fuck not?" Taliaferro shot this out as he kept swarming at the trench.

"Uh . . . grunts don't dig holes and then fill them back up again," Fritsche said.

Everyone else nodded in agreement. Taliaferro paused in his efforts to run this through. He liked to think of himself as a logical man. Finally: "Fuckin' slope sergeant probably made them do it."

He continued digging, satisfied with perfect logic. The trenches were all a little less than three feet deep. About a foot and a half down, Taliaferro found out why they'd been dug and filled in again.

"Madre mía," Diaz intoned.

"Jesus fucking Christ," Fritsche said.

Grubb vomited.

Masters turned away to shout: "Sar'nt Mosby!"

When the shout came, Mosby was in the middle of overseeing a discussion/interview between Geiger and Tarpy. He had introduced the two of them because he knew that Geiger was a phenomenon that Tarpy would find fascinating. At that time, homosexual was synonymous with coward. "Pansy" was worse than "pussy."

Geiger was neither. He was a definite male—and in the jargon, he possessed enormous balls. Mosby had seen him do things that Mosby wouldn't have the nerve to even consider. But it was obvious that he liked men. Not that Geiger propositioned the other young men in the platoon. As a matter of fact, he was very careful to stay a medic and not suggest playing doctor to anyone.

For a young man, Geiger pretty much had his act together. Mosby got the idea that Geiger—unlike most of them—had some thought of a future life. And it was a life to be envied. A structured life, filled with many interesting events and equally interesting work. What he could not know was that moments after Masters shouted, Geiger would become as much a casualty of the war as if he had been mortally wounded. Geiger was telling Tarpy about San Francisco.

"It's a city a man can really get his teeth into," Geiger was saying. "Not New York. Terrible empty scurrying-around city. We have *great* theater. Two hundred or three hundred theaters, last I was there. With *interesting* ideas. Not Off Broadway bullshit. If Eugene O'Neill were alive today, he'd be staging his performances in San Francisco."

He rattled on with much enthusiasm about restaurants, the Haight, street life, the Fillmore. People even read books in San Francisco.

"I gotta tell ya," Tarpy eventually said—waiting for the appropriate interviewer's moment to break in—"you're one hell of a great story. But there's not a desk in the world—much less AP—that would clear it!"

"Some one would in San Francisco," Geiger said.

While Tarpy was chewing on this, they heard the frightened shout from Masters: "Mosby! Sar'nt Mosby."

Mosby started running toward the group. Tarpy and Geiger sprinted after him.

Taliaferro was zombie-digging in awful fascination. At each shovel turn he was uncovering corpse after corpse after corpse. Mosby and the others were looking now at five almost completely uncovered bodies. They were all Vietnamese. Their hands were wired behind them. Their feet were bound. And many showed obvious signs of brutality—beyond the simple shot in the back of the head.

"Oh, Jesus," Geiger whispered.

He jumped in the trench beside Taliaferro and began examining each of the corpses—as if there were some hope that one of them could possibly be still alive.

Tarpy grabbed one of the two Nikons strung around his neck and began motor-driving pictures. He took a few broad views—the squad horrified, framing the gore before them. Then he moved in, snapping away at the bodies . . . Taliaferro digging . . . the medic feeling pulses that had turned to stone.

Ah, shit, Mosby thought. How was he going to stop this? He turned toward the clicking motor drive that was Tarpy. Mosby motioned to him.

Tarpy impatiently lowered his camera and turned to see what Mosby wanted.

The bullet came low and angled upward. It caught Cliff Tarpy in the mouth and exploded through the top of his head.

Mosby saw the thing that had been Tarpy fall . . .

As the American photographer fell, Thuy signaled his machine gunners on the outskirts of the park to open up. The adrenaline was pumping. Thuy had never felt so wonderful in his life.

Thuy had noted that Tarpy had become a threat almost more deadly than the American troops as he began snapping pictures of what Thuy knew to be legal atrocities. Thuy realized the pictures Tarpy was taking could seriously injure the Movement, so he had told the corporal beside him to kill the journalist. Thuy barely waited to see the results before he, too, was firing, his AK buried under the snarl of the RPD fire.

Charlie Company immediately took the attack in a V pattern with the men near the graves being at the apex of the V.

Mosby saw the lawn bursting around him and dove into the trench between Geiger and Taliaferro. He found himself staring directly into the eyes of a corpse. There was not time for any reaction. The bank above his head exploded and Mosby rolled off the man's body and dug himself in among the corpses.

Someone near him was cursing and weeping. It was Masters. The man's face was blood. Masters's scalp was hanging to one side. In a terrible focus, Mosby saw that the man's round-cherub face now drifted toward . . . his chest?

Master's hands fumbled with a new magazine. He kept dropping it, picking it up, and trying to reinsert it in his M-16. Mosby crawled forward and then he felt/saw Geiger swarm over him. Geiger pressed Masters back to the ground and then gently pulled the rifle from his hands.

He whispered to the man as he plunged in the morphine Syrette. Masters instantly relaxed.

Mosby always wondered what Geiger had said.

The rest of C Company fell back behind and around the band-shell, leaving Geiger, Masters, and Mosby trapped in the trench.

Blind Pig screamed obscenities at the world in general as he returned fire, hand-feeding new belts into the gun. Grubb was lying dead beside him, and Blind Pig was raging at a fate that would tease him with the prospect of having a full-time assistant gunner and then take him away.

Taliaferro pop-pop-popped away with an M-16, willing every shot into an RPD gunner. Then he saw Blind Pig's quandary, leap-rolled to his side, and began feeding the M-60.

Shannon shouted C Company under control and the men quickly settled into improvised positions and began pouring it back. The sudden return fire was so intense that there was a momentary pause from the opposing side.

Mosby and Geiger took the chance, and, dragging Masters between them, darted from the trench back to cover.

Mosby slumped down on the other side of Blind Pig just as Talia-ferro gave out another "Aw, shit!"

Taliaferro's right leg flooded red and he cursed and moaned and then rolled out of his sudden tight ball of pain to pick up his M-16 and snap off a few rounds before Geiger could get to him.

"Shit, shit, shit," Taliaferro wept. He didn't want Geiger to touch him.

He wanted to kill those little bastards.

Mosby grabbed the M-60 belt and took over for Taliaferro.

Blind Pig's burst slammed the corporal into Thuy. Thuy fell on his back, picked himself up, and then slid face down as his hands slipped in guts.

One of the machine guns next to Thuy went silent for a moment as the gunner went down. Thuy crawled across the body to join the team, and in a second the stutter of fire resumed.

Down the line, Private Vien Sang coldly fired at the Americans. He had just time to see the man next to the M-60 fall and then had to reload. He did this swiftly with sure hands. Sang could feel the luck in him. There was no fear. He had learned to calm himself to a near-machine, merely by thinking of the picture in his pocket—and then by projection almost seeing his young wife and child.

Then Lieutenant Lam was shouting as Sang raised his AK-47 again and pumped out rounds.

Across the park, Shannon bellowed out orders and C Company came alive.

Godfrey was the first up, charging, firing from the hip.

After him, Charlie Company came leapfrogging forward, keeping up a constant fire.

Blind Pig threw the M-60 belt over his shoulder and charged ahead a few yards, blazing as he went. Then he dropped to the ground and triggered off another burst to cover the men just ahead of him.

Mosby dropped behind a young tree, just as a hail of fire exploded it nearly in half. He fired back somewhat wildly and thought he saw someone fall.

Lam was hurled across Private Sang's body, pinning the young man to the ground. Sang struggled and fought and kicked his way out from under. As he came up, he just had time to see an American giant plunging toward him. The man looked like a cliff face. There was no way Sang could miss. He brought his weapon upwards . . .

Fritsche fired both barrels into Vien Sang. The rounds ground up an arm and shoulder and took away his face. Without pausing, Fritsche continued his run, breaking the shotgun and thumbing in new rounds.

For the Commissar, at that moment, there was barely time for thought, much less shock. The machine gun he had been helping with was as dead as the men around it.

He was popping away with his sidearm at any target he imagined he could see. Dimly, he could sense that the counterattack had come at them like an enormous unstoppable wave. It was something you could not stand against. He snapped off a puny round at something—knowing that he had missed.

Thuy wanted to lift all of his men up with him and hurl them at the Americans.

His left leg crumpled under him and he was lying on the ground. Thuy's body became very cold. Oddly, he could think now. There seemed to be plenty of time. He could smell the thick warmth of the uncut park lawn.

He felt an overwhelming sadness. Not for himself. No . . . no . . . not for me . . . for . . .

Blind Pig set up his M-60 just behind a man's body, chugging away as Charlie Company swept through the remnants of the enemy.

Many years later he would vaguely remember that moment. It

seemed to him he had partially rested his M-60 on someone wearing the uniform of an NVA officer. An officer?

Nice thought in any man's army.

Nice thought, but you're full of shit, Mr. Jefferson, he told himself.

CHAPTER SEVENTY-FOUR
DR. QUOT

DR. NGUYEN VAN QUOT was even more angry than usual. He was, for the second time in his life, trapped.

His field hospital was about a kilometer in front of Song Nhanh's city center—directly in the path of the advancing Americans. He cursed that northern general—Duan—for being so ignorant and putting him into a position of risk. He was also very aware that the General Uprising had not happened, and was not surprised. The Communists, he thought, could not even predict rainfall in the monsoon.

Quot saw, quite clearly, the defeat in Song Nhanh and was considering his options. He was not about to grab a rifle and do something terribly heroic and terribly stupid. On the other hand, he was not about to try a personal retreat—Dr. Quot assumed that the Americans must have encircled the city and would be killing anyone attempting to escape.

Quot had then considered surrender. But if he did so, wouldn't Thieu's government now exact their delayed revenge on him? Quot would rather die, if he must, from a bullet, than in a tiger cage from dehydration.

A new thought entered his mind—he was now a fairly high-ranking officer with the NLF. If he surrendered to the Americans and announced his intentions to recant publicly, might he not be a valuable propaganda tool? Valuable enough to be kept alive, to get access to one of his secret bank accounts and to get out of the country?

It was a possibility—but it was the only possibility of life Quot could think of, instead of the certainty of death.

Quot would never have admitted to it, but there was also the concern about his patients—the wounded men in the low building he'd chosen for his hospital. They desperately needed treatment, medical attention that only the despised Americans might provide. There were almost no medical supplies left—and even if, by a miracle, his wounded could be evacuated to the Octopus, most of them would still die.

Surrender. Yes. But how to surrender. Quot certainly did not want to walk out to meet the Americans—he could hear the gunfire closing toward him—and somehow get mistaken for a bo-doi and be shot down.

Quot's eyes hit on his surgical satchel. Of course, that kitbag would be known around the world, even to the stupid round-eyes. Quot was pleased with his thinking. He took his prized satchel and prepared himself. There was a grenade blast. The Americans could be only meters away. Hands held high, one hand dangling that satchel, Quot started toward the door.

Steve Geiger, still in shock from the park, was moving numbly forward. He'd determined, when the Army got him, that somehow his mind and his sensibilities would survive. But seeing the bodies, seeing the death of Tarpy, seeing the slaughter of people about him battered his determination. Geiger, not realizing he was as shell-shocked as any line animal, had decided that the only way to balance what had happened was to take revenge. Somewhere, he'd picked up a rifle and three grenades.

And revenge presented itself. A man stepped out of a building in front of him, holding a case in one hand. Geiger knew what the case was. A satchel charge.

His M-16 fired. The burst curled Dr. Nguyen Van Quot forward, his smile buried in blood.

Geiger spun to the building's wall, tugged a grenade from his harness, yanked the pin, and threw it into the building the "sapper" had come from. Explosion . . . and Geiger went in behind the blast. His grenade had killed most of the wounded in the building.

Geiger stumbled back, almost falling over the "sapper's" body. He looked down at the "satchel charge," and realized it was a surgeon's case—hemostats and scalpels were spilled across the cobblestones.

Geiger's eyes glazed, and his hands moved. Mosby got to him just before Geiger's rifle muzzle reached the medic's chin, and knocked Geiger flat.

Mosby saw the tools, saw the carnage inside the building, saw Geiger's face, and shouted to a radioman to get a dustoff.

CHAPTER SEVENTY-FIVE

THE SQUAD

BLIND PIG LOOKED around at his friends and spread a grin across his face.

"You realize, my men, that we all be the dudes our folks warned us against?"

Mosby managed a smile—Blind Pig was quite correct. After their days in the city the five men crouched behind the wall were uniformly blackened, uniformly staring, and uniformly smelling like a goat on Sunday.

"The Pig's got it nailed," Fritsche said after a pause. "I always was proud that my originals smelled worse'n I do. This fuckin' Army educates you to the higher shit, don't it?"

Mosby noted that not only did all five of them—himself, Blind Pig, Diaz, Shannon, and Fritsche—look and smell the same, but they also were starting to talk alike. Their eyes were always moving from side to side. Their thoughts came incoherently, and their speech very slowly, each man taking a beat before he spoke, but making not a great deal of sense.

To either side of the group were the remnants of C Company, backed up by two ranks. On the other side of the wall was the boulevard, which opened after twenty-five meters to the city center.

Lieutenant Wilson, down at the far end of the line, couldn't figure out if he was pissed at being excluded from the five-man group or pleased that he'd been put in charge of the line while they were conferring.

"Major Shannon," Diaz inquired, "I assume that tomorrow morning we will be attacking, correct?"

"Yeah."

"One question, sir. Why have we been on the point for so long? Are we the only grunts in Vietnam?"

Shannon didn't have an answer. He felt like he was a second john again, running A-team patrols.

But this was different—the entire country of Vietnam was a combat zone now, during Tet. Shannon, too, was wondering what the fuck he was doing here, having demoted himself to company commander, and why his people had spent too many days feeding themselves into the grinder.

Diaz was correct—there were thousands of Americans back of

the lines, running hotels, typewriters, officers's messes, and jeeps. Why did the command say that the American commitment in Vietnam was total, yet never sent any of their infantry-MOS'd waiters to the front lines?

Mosby, even though his mind was thousand-yarding, was also sensitive to everything around him. He caught the motion of Blind Pig's head and responded.

"Excuse me, sir. But I gotta check my line."

Shannon also'd seen Blind Pig's gesture, but ignored it. He was hoping that Blind Pig didn't want to tell Mosby that he'd had enough and wanted a Section Eight out. Shannon knew there was no way he could find, before tomorrow's assault, a machine gunner as good as Blind Pig. Christ, maybe he'd have to force Fritsche to take the gun.

His people were destroyed. There was no reason, except that America was trying to fight this war on the cheap, that Charlie Company and the entire Fifteenth Infantry battalion hadn't been pulled out of combat.

Shannon wondered why the fuck he'd ever taken John F. Kennedy seriously. If his father had taught him the old saw that wars are too important to be fought by generals, Shannon had learned that politicians could make it even worse. I wonder what, he thought after he made polite farewells and headed for the battalion CP, that cowlicked asshole'd think if he could see what he put us into.

Blind Pig did have a problem. Making sure that no one was watching, he opened his asspack and showed its contents to Mosby. Mosby goggled. The pack was almost full of large gold coins.

"Where the fuck . . . ?"

"Uh . . . 'member that bank we took? An' I come out of that back room sayin' there be nothin' there?"

Vaguely.

"Well, I be lyin'. There be a whole shitpot full of gold in bags there."

Mosby took one of the coins from the pack. It weighed about an ounce, he guessed, and was date-stamped 1915. The coin was a 100-korona coin from the Austro-Hungarian Empire.

"Reason I be asking," Blind Pig went on, "is I know shit about gold. What you be thinkin' this shit be worth?"

"Hell if I know," Mosby answered honestly. "But . . . Christ, man, you're rich."

"Yeah. If I get this shit back to the World. Other thing I be wondering, Mosby. How I gone move this gold?"

Mosby fingered the coin.

"If you're careful," he advised, "and don't want to dump it all at once, maybe coin dealers? Those fuckers look like they're rare."

"That's what I be thinking," Blind Pig said. "Maybe I don't need no Deacon no more."

Without thanks, of course, Blind Pig went back to his gun.

The exchange cheered Mosby up. Maybe Blind Pig'd live through tomorrow and go back to Detroit as a rich man.

Somebody ought to come out of this war on top.

CHAPTER SEVENTY-SIX

MEAD

FOR ONE OF the few times in his life, Ron Mead felt a bit of an asshole. He'd just been informed of what happened to Tarpy.

A fellow journalist had died bravely under the enemy guns.

Despite being only a tenuous member of the human race, this deeply affected Mead. And he was very sorry that the last thought he had had of the man was that the bastard had stolen his Jack Daniels.

It was especially unsettling because a little later Mead had found in his pack a hand-scrawled IOU from Tarpy, promising double the theft. Mead had called him every kind of a son-of-a-bitch again, when he read that.

Now he was close to tears. He kept that in mind, because Mead had always prided himself on his ability to write close to tears. Copley readers loved it.

Yes, a journalist—no, a *newsman*—had died in action. A member of the world press. The Fellowship. So he drank a bit. Lied a bit. Stole a bit. Tarpy was a man's man, wasn't he?

Mead would file the story. A story from the middle of the action. Then he made another, magnanimous decision. The story would not be exclusively for Copley. When a newsman dies in action, every wire service and newspaper in the Free World makes note of it. Mead could see his by-line now . . .

He felt better about that. Mead began planning his follow-ups. Ron Mead felt very warm about Tarpy now. It would be a feeling that would follow him the rest of his career.

The way he saw it, Mead had been chosen to carry on the banner. It was his duty to see that Tarpy did not fall in vain.

Sinclair was ready for his final move. In the morning the assault would be launched on the city center. And, Mead knew, every man jack involved—from Sinclair down to the lowliest doughboy—was spoiling for a fight.

Mead would see that their exploits were recounted: He would do it for Tarpy.

CHAPTER SEVENTY-SEVEN

SONG NHANH

MAPS AND BATTLE games ignore and destroy the reality of battle. A West Point wargame, covering the Twelfth Division's attack on Song Nhanh's city center and the 302d North Vietnamese Division, would be very clear.

Here, entrenched around the east and north side of the square, was the 302d's command center. Here, below the square, was Sinclair's command post.

From these two hearts, the battle would be fought.

Around these key points, the map would show the lesser units in semicircles. The NLF grouped in a C configuration to one side, with tactically placed combat elements in the square itself.

The American units would also be parenthesed around their own command element. Here were the grouped companies of the Fifteenth Infantry, there the tanks, and one street behind the command center, Sinclair's self-propelled artillery—8-inch and 105mm track-mounted cannons.

All these game pieces would be very visible on the map board. An amateur student of warfare might assume that a map board gives some simulacrum of the real battlefield, and that this student, given a god's eye point of view of the real battlefield, could see the positions.

Instead, the overhead observer would see, to the south and west, armored vehicles grouped into a parking lot. Knots of soldiers would gather, separate, then regather. On the other side, that overhead watcher would see no movement whatsoever—the National Liberation Front was invisible.

Add to that the drifting smoke from airstrikes, artillery and mortar explosions, and burning houses, and Song Nhanh looked less like an impending battle zone than a daguerreotype of San Francisco after the earthquake and fires of 1906.

The view was hardly dramatic. Nor was the order to begin the final attack.

Sinclair could hardly have screamed for a charge over the noise of the artillery rounds or posed nobly in front of his soldiers in silver helmet and armor without being instantly sniped. The word droned down the line on the voices of carefully monotoned enlisted radiomen.

"Splatter, we're moving forward . . . Bombard, stand by on fire missions . . . all Whirlaway elements, this is Citation . . . move out now . . ."

Sinclair's SP guns were set up, their barrels almost at full elevation. As one, they fired the first barrage—a Time On Target (all shells calculated to hit at the same time) barrage aimed across the city square, then shifted, ready for their preassigned barrages that the advancing grunts could call in.

The Fifteenth Infantry's mortars also began the hollow clang-whisperwhir-explosion, sending their lighter shells just in front of the attacking line companies.

In a war movie, General Sinclair, having ordered the attack, would have heroically mounted into his tank and ground forward.

That, in fact, would be the way Ron Mead wrote the story.

But what actually happened was that Lee Sinclair had one foot on the idler wheel of his M-48A3 when he noticed one strap on a tanker boot was loose. He bent to tighten it.

Also not in Mead's account of the moment was that Colonel Taylor, having gotten his orders and sent his troops forward, was taking a last moment to piss against the side of Sinclair's tank.

Just then the incoming rounds from the NVA 120mm mortars exploded around the two tracks. Taylor's head and chest disappeared, and his torso swayed forward and fell into the tank tracks.

The explosion blew General Sinclair back five feet, bits of shrapnel sharding in his side. As Sinclair slid on the cobblestones and fell, the weight of his head plus the weight of his helmet slammed him down into concussion and unconsciousness.

The shrapnel also shotgunned Mead. His face and the front half of his body welled blood. Mead looked at himself with slight surprise. This happened to me before. Yes. I was on the bridge of the *Bismarck Sea*. When the kamikaze hit. And then I had to behave like an officer. I had to tell people what to do.

Mead realized that now things were different. He had nobody to command and wondered why he was grateful. He found a pile of rubble to sit down on. It was quite relaxing. He knew he probably should be doing something, but found it much better to just sit where he was and listen to the shouting and watch the people running about. He was most likely not doing something he should have, but was not interested in remembering what it was at the moment.

The huts and bazaars of Song Nhanh's central square still stood, leaning and shell-shot ruins. Mosby could see, over them, the solid buildings the NVA still occupied. Big deal—first he had to get through this shit.

He waved the remnants of his squad forward, then remembered that he was now a platoon sergeant. The tank beside him ground forward, and the assault began.

The M-48 was called, by the grunts, a Zippo. This was not a hard-to-figure-out nickname—the tank, instead of having the usual cannon in its turret, mounted a flamethrower.

Mosby saw Blind Pig and Fritsche, plus other troops, move out. He went down, hearing bullets whipcrack around his head.

The track coughed, flame spat out the cannon mouth, and black-dripping fire incinerated the hut the NVA fire had come from.

Mosby had a chance to return the favor seconds later, as he saw an NVA soldier, kneeling beside an overturned cart, aim a B-40 at the tank. Mosby snapped three rounds, and the soldier fell forward. Mosby was coughing constantly—the smoke from the city center both screened and choked him.

The attack went on.

Sergeant Lau was envious of the Americans.

He could reassure his general all day long with talk of elephants. But that was a long time ago. He wished that, for ten minutes, he could have command of a pack of these fire-tanks the imperialists were sending forward.

You dream, you peasant? Didn't you also dream of having airplanes like the French as you led those stinking elephants toward Dien Bien Phu? True. Best to be content with what you have.

What Lau had, in his hand, was an American detonating box, its green wires leading forward through the ruined bazaar. He waited until the flame-tank, its nozzle drooling smoke and bits of fire, rolled forward to the right point, then twisted the box's handle.

The explosion was most unsatisfactory—evidently the charge in the mine was wet or old. The blast sounded like a wet fart on a muggy day, and its only result was that one of the flame-tank's tracks uncoiled, like a snake, toward him.

But that was still enough to immobilize one of the monsters. Lau signaled to his men, and they fell back, toward the next prepared position.

The radio screams had pulled Shannon back from Charlie Company to Division Forward.

He'd walked into blood and chaos. Taylor was dead. Sinclair, half his G-reps, that reporter, and seven radiomen were either being body-bagged or medevacked.

Major Dennis Shannon suddenly understood that, with one mortar attack, the NLF had beheaded the Twelfth Infantry Division. Under different circumstances, without the decimation the fight forward into the city had been, without the necessity to maintain that base back at Hue Duc, command replacement would have been possible.

After some hours to regroup, the command shock should have been tolerable, as officers would be flown in to replace the destroyed command group.

Major Dennis Shannon should have replaced Taylor, as temporary battalion commander of the Fifteenth. He might have continued the advance and, if he performed capably, been confirmed in his position by the new division commander.

But not now, not with an attack in progress.

Shannon, seeing the battle-shocked faces of the few remaining divisional staffers, took over the division. In a time of confusion, he thought, the man who sounds like he knows what he's doing is going to be listened to. And probably going to be shot at dawn for terminal stupidity.

What the fuck, Dennis. Sinclair busted you down because you were trying to behave like you were a division commander anyway, didn't he? And you were the clown who was always trying to second-guess him, weren't you?

Okay, Shannon. You got the title on the door. Let's see if you got the Bigelow on the floor.

Vo Le Duan, on the other hand, found himself fighting in a role he had not known for years. What was left of his division was battling around the city. His radios had failed or were jammed. His runners went out and did not come back. All that was left of the 302d Division directly under Duan's command were the men around the treasury building.

Duan was commanding them as if he were a battalion—battalion hell, a company—officer. And he found the rifle in his hand more than just an accessory. Duan had always thought that a combat soldier would never lose familiarity with his rifle—that it was like riding a bicycle. But Duan found himself awkward with the gun. He had seen targets and taken them under fire. He missed, to his enormous chagrin. The weapon felt uncomfortable in his hands.

But on the other hand, Duan was impressed with his men—and of course himself, since he had trained and led them. The Americans should have taken the city center by now. Instead, their advance was still creeping forward.

How very wonderful, he thought. You are becoming as much of an optimist as Sergeant Lau. Who is out there somewhere, and I hope is still alive.

Duan fell back into the sandbagged doorway to the treasury as yet another flight of Americans jets screamed down at the NVA positions.

"Citation Six, Citation Six, this is Whirlaway Six, over."

The voice on the other end of the radio was Wilson. Shannon was slightly impressed that Wilson must have taken over Charlie Company without being told.

"This is Citation Six," he said. "Go."

"Colonel . . . we're trying to go forward. But we're down to a couple of squads. We gotta have reinforcements. Over."

Shannon was about to get back on the PRC-25 and tell Wilson no way José, when he spotted about twenty-five men, prone along a building wall, who looked like they belonged together and weren't doing anything.

"This is Citation," he said. "I got some fresh blood headed yours. Out."

He doubled over to the men.

"Who're you guys?"

"Uh . . ." The speaker was a young captain. "We're the forward engineers, sir. We've got orders to report to the division commander."

"You've got him," and Shannon paid no attention to the captain's incredulous look at Shannon's blackened oak leaves.

"I want you to"—and Shannon held out his map—"take your men forward . . . here. Go forward. You're looking for a Lieutenant Wilson. Tell him you're the reinforcements I promised."

"But sir . . ."

"Move out, Captain!"

"Yessir."

Another radioman—this one the man on the all-important MAC-V link—was motioning, and Shannon ran back toward his command center. I tell one man come, and he cometh, I tell another man go, and he dies . . .

Tack . . . tack . . . tack . . . Mosby crawled toward the sound of the gun. Blind Pig was positioned behind a pile of melons.

Mosby was very glad to see that he was undamaged, even if a little melon-juice soggy. Mosby passed Blind Pig the two belts of M-60 ammo he'd brought up.

"Why ain't we be movin'?"

"Because there ain't nobody to fuckin' move with," Mosby snarled.

"Okay," Blind Pig accepted with equanimity. "Then we just stay where we be an' kill 'em."

"Where's Fritsche?"

"Over there." Blind Pig waved across the alley, to where an M-16 muzzle fingered out of a doorway.

Mosby went backward—he didn't know what the fuck was going on, but as long as his two main men were in place the zips weren't coming down this street. He stayed low until he hit an alleyway, then got up and ran back, looking for where he figured the company CP would be.

The CP was a string of bodies. Wilson must have been moving forward and gotten caught in the open. The RPG must have stitched right down the line.

A dead grunt—Mosby didn't recognize him—Wilson—and back of him Wilson's RTO.

The radio was crackling.

Mosby peered around cautiously. The NVA machine gunner must've moved on. He wasn't fired at as he dashed out, checked to make sure that Wilson was dead, and then grabbed the radio.

"Whirlaway Six, Whirlaway Six, do you receive this station, over?"

"This . . . is . . . Whirlaway," Mosby panted into the handpiece. "Six is dead. This is Whirlaway . . . fuck, I don't remember. This is Mosby. Over."

Mosby heard the shout—evidently the radioman had left his mike keyed open.

"Major. I have Whirlaway." Then Shannon's voice. "Wilson, this is Citation."

Mosby snarled without realizing it. Taylor must be dead too. Then he reported to Shannon. Wilson was dead, and whatever was left of the platoon was either killed, wounded, or pinned down. They were stuck where they were.

"Slow down, Mosby."

Slow down, you prick? You're back there playing god. Shut up. You can sound a lot stracker than he can. Mosby was framing his answer when he heard a shout.

He looked up, to see about twenty or so grunts in line. They looked scared, dusty but undamaged. Mosby didn't know any of them. At their front was a captain, beckoning to Mosby. Fuck him. One problem at a time.

"Citation Six, this is Whirlaway Six. Go ahead," Mosby said into the radio, hoping he sounded as emotionless as a good RTO should.

"Okay, Mosby. I got some people headed your way. About twenty-five engineers. There's a captain in charge. Do you know what your situation is?"

"Citation Six, this is Whirlaway," Mosby kept going. "As good as anybody does, yessir. Over."

"Okay, Whirlaway. You put those people where you want them. If that captain's got any problems, you put him on the line with me. I want you people moving again as soon as you get those engineers. This is Citation Six. Out."

Mosby, some time later, would tell the story of how he told a captain what to do, and how that captain did exactly that. He wouldn't spoil the story by explaining that the engineer officer'd overheard the radio broadcast or that he and his twenty-five men were more than willing to listen to anyone who sounded as if he knew what he was doing. Probably Mosby didn't instantly realize those things since he was concentrating on Shannon's orders to continue the attack.

Blind Pig found that he had an assistant gunner. The man feeding new M-60 belts to him wore tiger-stripe fatigues, a battered beanie that might have been green, and a glaring smile.

"Who the fuck you be?"

"What the fuck you care," Captain Charles Drew growled back. Good point, Blind Pig thought.

"Who's that ugly fucker over there?" Drew asked.

"That's my man. Fritsche."

"Okay. Here's what we're going to do."

He explained the plan to Blind Pig and then, before Blind Pig had a chance to say your ass, cowboy, darted across the alley to Fritsche, bullets spattering behind his heels.

Blind Pig wasn't about to move. But he saw Fritsche nodding in agreement. Aw fuck. That biker chuck's gone want to play hero on me. Gone get his silly fool ass killed listenin' to this dumbass sneakypete who come out of nowhere.

But Blind Pig, feeling like more than a fool, was already up and following when Drew and Fritsche, hollering like crazies, went down the alley, toward the NVA positions.

The NVA, even though they were trapped in an insane position, maintained their sanity and fell back.

Drew flopped on the other side of the abandoned NLF barricade, laughing loudly. He had his maneuver element.

Eventually the three of them hit fire intense enough to convince even Fritsche and Drew to hold in place until the rest of the unit caught up with them.

Ten minutes later, they saw Mosby, leading the remnants of the squad/platoon/company, plus the twenty-five engineers, forward.

They re-formed and attacked again. Attack gives the image of young heroes rising up as one and rushing forward. Those kinds of attacks make ten feet forward on the warmaps and six feet underground for the attackers.

Instead Mosby's ragtag ''company'' was scattered along a crossroads in the hoveled bazaar. The word came down to move forward.

Mosby crawled sideways and told the engineer captain that they were attacking, depending on him to pass the word down the line. He crawled back to the other side of the line, telling the grunts they were moving again. He took a moment to wonder why the fuck that Special Forces captain was at his right flank and behaving as if he were a PFC instead of giving Mosby a hand. Or better yet taking over.

Mosby went back to his radio and looked at the map. He got Bombard on the horn and called in three fire missions, trying, as exactly as he could, to specify the map coordinates. The American heavy artillery was firing very, very close to the attacking lines.

Finally he got Whirlaway mortars, told them where he was, and told them to roll the fire forward every four rounds. He at least trusted the Fifteenth's mortars—these big fuckers with Bombard he didn't know shit about.

There had to be a first man, and Mosby knew he had to be the man. He got to his feet and walked forward.

Mosby'd never realized that it was pretty easy to charge when somebody else gave the order. Heat of combat, and all that shit.

Mosby, the reluctant company commander, the equally reluctant shatter of Charlie Company/Twelfth Engineers, drove the attack forward.

And the NVA broke. First singly, then by squads and platoons, the National Liberation Forces fell back, away from their entrenched buildings, away from the treasury, toward the ruins of the palace near the swamp on the east.

The battle for Song Nhanh City and Province was over.

The General Offensive was a failure.

Forty percent of Song Nhanh City lay in ruins.

More than 10,000 civilians had died or disappeared.

Two elite fighting units, the 302d Division and the Phu Loi Battalion, were destroyed.

Over 5,000 National Liberation Front soldiers were dead, in a long scatter from the Three Sisters through the rubber plantation into the Octopus and in Song Nhanh itself.

Three hundred sixty-nine Americans were dead, and 932 were wounded.

But Song Nhanh was taken.

All that was left was the mopping up.

CHAPTER SEVENTY-EIGHT
DUAN

THE COMRADE GENERAL had set up his last command post in the shattered ruins of the ancient summer palace. He had taken refuge in a cave formed by two immense boulders and a toppled statue of the Smiling Buddha.

The huge stone head—severed from the body—was his only company in the cave.

The big guns thundered and rocked the earth outside, as the Americans rained artillery shells on the palace. The constant fire lit the Buddha's head in a flickering shadow show.

Duan stared at his smiling companion. If you stared at the face long enough, it appeared alive: the smile coming and going at the joke of each falling shell.

Look on my works, ye Mighty. Whose works? The Americans'? The National Liberation Front's? Uncle Ho's? General Giap's? or Vo Le Duan's?

The Comrade General had no doubt whom the Buddha was laughing at.

Duan considered his situation. There was no fear—he was looking at it from a great distance. Duan had no physical map, nor radios or runners to keep him constantly informed of the disposition of the enemy troops. He didn't need these things to imagine what was happening.

General Sinclair had not only ringed him in, but had drawn the noose so tight that Duan could feel the killing knot at his throat. Most of his men were either dead or attempting to flee. There were very few pockets of resistance left, Duan knew. He felt sorry for what was going to happen to them. Just as he felt sorry for the men attempting to flee. He doubted that the Americans would allow them to surrender.

So, General Sinclair, what will you do now? The answer was not difficult. All night long the artillery would pound in and the gunships keep up a constant rain of fire. It was a final softening up. In the morning, Sinclair would launch his final attack.

The Buddha smiled at him again, and Duan felt a strange urge to reassure Sinclair. He wanted to tell him that he had little to fear in the assault that must come at first light. Sinclair's casualties would be small.

"Ah, I see you've found a friend, Comrade General," came the voice. And Duan turned his attention from the Buddha to see Lau standing in the entrance of the cave.

Duan was very glad to see his batman. He hadn't been sure if Lau was still alive.

Lau walked inside, backlit by a sudden flare, and then squatted beside him. The sergeant placed an object in front of Duan. It clanked against the stone. The next flash showed what it was.

"Cognac," Lau said.

Duan remembered the promised bottle. He didn't say anything as Lau cracked the seal and passed the brandy to him. Duan took a small sip—this was not the time to overindulge—and passed it back. Lau took an equally small sip.

"Major Vinh is dead," Lau said.

"How?"

"Mortars. They're throwing them in like rain."

There was a long silence between the two. Both of them were thinking of the many years they had shared and of the last long march.

"At least we have the cognac," Duan said.

"What else could a man need, Comrade General?"

The entire sky turned blinding white, the ground shuddered, and the boulders creaked as artillery shells marched into the palace grounds.

The Buddha's head shifted and then slowly fell to one side.

Lau rose and walked over to it. He muscled it upright again and then gave it a pat.

"I hope you weren't too disturbed, my friend," he said. He came back to Duan. Lau took another sip from the cognac and handed it to his general. Duan toasted the smiling Buddha.

"Long life," he said.

And he drank, feeling the warmth spread in his stomach.

"Will there be anything else, Comrade General?"

Duan thought a moment.

476

"No," he finally said. "I don't think so."

"Alright then, I'll take first watch."

Lau took up position at the entrance. Duan settled back against the hard ground. The skies thundered again as the Comrade General curled up to sleep.

It wasn't the morning light that woke Duan up, but the smell of brewing tea.

He opened his eyes to see Lau holding a steaming cup in front of him. Where in God's grace did the man get . . . ?"

"Thank you, Sergeant," he told his batman.

Too bad it wasn't coffee, he thought, thick like the French liked it. Still, he smiled at Lau and forced a sip. His eyes widened as he tasted the cognac it was laced with.

"You never did like tea much, did you, Comrade General?"

So, Lau knew that.

"I like *this* fine," he said.

He sat full up and looked outside. Far in the distance he could hear the sounds of exploding shells and fighting. The artillery barrage, however, had stopped.

Sinclair would come soon.

Lau pressed something else in his face.

"What's this?"

"Breakfast, Comrade General."

And Duan saw that it was a bowl of rice. With the little fire-hot peppers from the Red River that Lau swore by.

He forced himself to swallow one pepper whole.

"You really should chew them, Comrade General," Lau said. "That's the only way to get the complete benefit. Never get a cold, my old mother always said, if you chew your peppers thoroughly."

Trying not to choke, Duan dutifully chewed the next pepper thoroughly.

There was a sudden rumble and clack.

Both men turned to look out the entrance of the cave. Duan carefully set the rice down and picked up his rifle. Without a word, both men slithered outside.

There was a huge grating shriek that cut down Duan's back and they saw a tank lumber into the courtyard.

It was firing round after round like an ancient battleship.

Duan and Lau ducked as a shell thundered overhead and then exploded behind them.

"Look," Lau shouted.

Duan saw one of his soldiers rise up and aim an RPG at the

oncoming tank. Duan prayed for him, but the tank's machine gun opened up and cut the man down. The RPG went tumbling away. The tank was within twenty meters of their position.

Duan saw Lau charge for the RPG.

Meters away Lau gave a great leap and then he had it. He rolled up and . . .

The tank fired its cannon point-blank.

Before the shock wave and shrapnel hit Duan, he saw Lau's body being lifted and hurled away.

It was the last time he would see Sergeant Lau.

CHAPTER SEVENTY-NINE

THE SQUAD

LATE AFTERNOON FOG drifted in from the marshes, across the doubly ruined palace, and into Song Nhanh.

Behind him Mosby could hear scattered pops as the last pockets of NVA resistance were silenced.

By rights, he should still be in that scatter of stone and blood. But David Mosby had decided he'd finished fighting this particular war. Let somebody else worry about the stray gooks in the ruins.

Fritsche slumped down nearby. Mosby looked at his point man.

He hoped that he didn't look as bad as the biker. The man's fatigues were ripped, caked canvaslike with sweat and dust, and pink knees showed through tears in the pants. His pants' legs hung below his bootheels.

Fritsche's eyes stared out of his burnt-powder-masked face.

Mosby found a little energy.

"How's it hangin', you defender of freedom's frontiers?"

"Not too shabby," Fritsche also managed. "How about you, capitalist babyraper?"

"I feel like I been shot at and missed and shit at and hit," Mosby confessed.

"Yeah." Fritsche scanned the ruins around them.

"Man, we sure liberated the shit out of this place, didn't we?"

"There be any more liberatin' done," Blind Pig put in from behind them, "this place be lookin' like Detroit."

"Where the fuck'd you get off to?"

"Just checkin' things out."

"Any good loot?"

"Nothin' worth stealin'. I already got me a pocketful of Ho stars."

Mosby spotted Shannon as he shambled away from the ruins. The major saw the three, redirected, and found himself a spot on the ground.

"You fuckers know better'n to bunch up like this," he said in greeting.

"Big deal. What're they gone do? Shoot us? Man, I could do with a little shooting."

"Thought you'd feel that way."

Shannon dug into his ruck and took out a half-empty bottle of cognac.

"Whyn't you start with this?"

Mosby didn't know he had any reactions left, but managed to grab the bottle before Fritsche or Blind Pig.

"Found this next to some mess gear," Shannon said. "Figured whoever left it'd want it to go to some deserving types like us."

Mosby pulled the cork with his teeth and spat it away.

He started to take a drink, then stopped.

"We ought to be drinking to something," he said.

"Can you think of anything on this fuckin' earth worth drinking to?" Fritsche asked.

Sergeant David Mosby honestly couldn't.

He and the other three just drank.

CHAPTER EIGHTY

DUAN

THE FOG BLANKETED Song Nhanh all that night, lifting early the next morning.

General Vo Le Duan had been moving for an hour by then. Wounded and still shocked, he'd stayed concealed in a swampy cluster of brush, letting the American patrols sweep past him, toward the city.

At false dawn, he was moving.

Slowly, very slowly.

His mouth was dry.

Duan scooped a palmful of water, then stumbled on through the mud of the swamps.

Somewhere ahead of him lay the Octopus.

Duan decided he could rest a few minutes and crouched. He noticed then that the fog was rising.

Looking behind and to either side of him, he could now see small clusters of NVA soldiers, all of them moving toward sanctuary.

The morning was very peaceful. Duan savored it.

Peace was intruded on and broken by the clatter overhead. The Comrade General got up.

A flight of three Huey Cobras crashed through the mist, their rotor blades drawing condensation circles behind them.

There was no cover.

Duan took the rifle from his shoulder as a gunship banked and dove forward.

As he fired at the Cobra, General Vo Le Duan was somehow quite grateful that he had been selected as its target.

EPILOGUE

All my brothers now are dead, yes dead.
I've come through alive, I don't know how.
In November I was Red, yes Red.
But it's January now.

> —Bertolt Brecht,
> *Drums in the Night,* Act IV

In my own country I am in a far-off land
I am strong but have no force or power
I win all yet remain a loser
At break of day I say good night
When I lie down, I have a great fear
of falling.

> —François Villon

THE AMERICANS

SHANNON:
Awarded the Distinguished Service Cross and other decorations for taking over command of the Twelfth Division. Sent through Command and General Staff School. Serves one more tour in Vietnam. Retires early as a lieutenant colonel. Now heads a crisis management firm, based in London.

MOSBY:
Recommended for the Congressional Medal of Honor by Shannon. Award downgraded to the DSC. Survives his tour. Now a professor of Contemporary American Folklore, Humboldt State College, California.

BLIND PIG:
Also completes his tour unscathed. Returns to Detroit to find Deacon Rayburn has been sentenced to Atlanta for twenty-to-life. Uses the gold coins and GI Bill to finance his way through college and law school. Currently an attorney in Detroit, specializing in consumer affairs.

CASEY:
MIA, declared officially Killed in Action, 1979.

TALIAFERRO:
His leg injury proves a glory wound in his hometown. Takes over the Ford agency from his father. Former American Legion post commander, former Chamber of Commerce president, former JayCee president, named one of his state's "Ten Outstanding Young Men," Junior Chamber of Commerce. Married. Wife notorious for extramarital affairs.

FRITSCHE:
His luck finally runs out on a sweep after the battle in Song Nhanh, and he hits a trip wire. Wounded superficially, he finished his tour as an instructor at the Twelfth Division's in-country training school, teaching new soldiers how to walk point.

Now owns a Harley-Davidson/Yamaha/Suzuki dealership in a large midwestern city. Rides a full-dresser instead of a chopper, but has pictures of a cobra painted on either side of the bike's gas tanks.

GEIGER:

Released from Letterman General Hospital's Psychiatric Division after a lengthy stay. Completes medical school, and is a practicing psychiatrist in San Francisco.

DIAZ:

Wounded later, he finishes his tour in Vietnam as Charlie Company's supply sergeant. He is now vice-president of his uncle's chain of independent insurance agencies. Married with six children.

MASTERS:

Recovers from his wounds. Career Army. Now a First Sergeant, Fort Polk, Louisiana.

CARRUTHERS:

Colonel Oreste Carruthers, CO, 7th Army Aviation, was killed in a routine training flight near Graz, Germany, 1980.

GODFREY:

Volunteers after Song Nhanh for Twelfth Infantry Division's LRRPs. Serves three tours. Discharged from the Army as a buck sergeant. Works transient jobs for several years. His family last hears from him in 1982, when he said he had a new job as pipeline security guard somewhere in the Mideast.

DREW:

Colonel Charles Drew now heads the U.S. Army's Escape and Evasion Schools.

DEEJAY:

During his convalescence, he falls in love with a nurse who is an evangelical Christian. He is now program director for a 50,000-watt religious station broadcasting from Texas.

FULLER:

Dies of wounds, Camp Zama, Japan, 1967.

BUELLTON:

Administers a new hospital in the Appalachians.

MEAD:

The best-selling author of *Tarpy: Death of a Newsman* is a senior consultant for a politically conservative think tank located outside Washington.

SINCLAIR:

Receives his third star in the course of his final assignment in the Pentagon. Retires. He is a candidate for the GOP nomination to the U.S. Senate. Defeated handily. Now divorced, he is writing his memoirs.

THE VIETNAMESE

LAU:
Was not killed by the cannon shell's explosion as Duan thought. He spends half a day buried in the rubble of the temple, then is rescued by a sympathizer and moved into the Octopus. Emergency surgery saves his life, but Lau loses an arm and a leg. Now he is chief of his native village, a village known for meeting all its quotas. He has never been investigated for his record-keeping. Twice married, seven children.

THO:
The village girl dies in Ubon Ratchathasni Refugee Camp, Thailand, of malnutrition, 1978.

NGHI:
Wounded and captured in the final hours of the battle, he is turned over to the RVN police. Dies "under interrogation."

THUY:
Despite his wounds, he manages to escape during the last stages of the battle. Now a high official in Hanoi. Is being treated for chronic insomnia.

LY:
Semiretired, he helps his two sons continue his successful business in Song Nhanh.

CUNG:
The scout guides NVA units into Saigon in 1975, flees Vietnam by boat in 1977. He now owns a small grocery store in Fresno, California.

TRAM:
Miss Tram returns underground and avoids the post-Tet purges by the South Vietnamese government. She is currently the province chief of Song Nhanh.

NOTES AND
ACKNOWLEDGMENTS

NOTES

There is, of course, no such place as the province or city of Song Nhanh.

Song Nhanh City was imagined as somewhat like Da Lat, with the city center being an enlarged version of Kontum's center.

There is also no Hue Duc, although many many villages were changed and corrupted by the American presence during the war.

Ba Rei is also fictional, although there were many hamlets such as Bau Bang or Ben Suc that were similarly obliterated.

The only real thing in Song Nhanh Province is Highway 13, as many Americans can unfortunately attest.

All of the South Vietnamese mentioned are wholly fictitious as well.

All NVA or Viet Cong in this book are fictional.

There is no 302d Division of the People's Army, and all other NVA or VC units mentioned are also creations of the authors, with two exceptions:

Sapper Unit N-10 existed, and was destroyed during the Tet Offensive, mostly operating around Saigon and to the immediate west.

The Phu Loi Battalion was also real, and was every bit as good as the book attempts to portray. It also was destroyed during Tet, although not under the circumstances we created.

All Americans, from generals to grunts, are fictional and have no real-life counterparts, again with two exceptions:

Major Archimedes Patti, the OSS officer, is real and was present with Ho Chi Minh and General Giap on Doc Lap in 1945.

Sergeant Casey also was evidently real—a member of the 504th Parachute Infantry during WWII. He was killed during the Ardennes offensive of 1944. He is described fully in the late Ross

491

Carter's brilliant and unfortunately out-of-print *Those Devils in Baggy Pants*.

We used the Casey character since *Devils* had a great deal to do with one of us deciding to fall out of airplanes and the other realizing it was total insanity. Also, we wanted a somewhat mysterious character as our way of dealing with the MIA issue.

There is no Twelfth Infantry Division. Subunits, however, may share a numerical identity with other units in the U.S. Army. We meant no comparison between our nonexistent battalions, etc., and any unit bearing the same number.

We made two deliberate cheats in *A Reckoning for Kings*:

In a real division, there would have been a commander of Second Brigade (a bird colonel), through whom Sinclair's orders would have passed. We ignored this to avoid further confusing the somewhat obscure (to nonmilitary people) pattern that's called chain of command.

For the same reason we cheated on our radio SOI (Signal Operating Instructions). In real life, the call signs of the various units would be changed regularly—probably several times in the course of a single operation.

For clarity (we hope), we left them alone.

All other errors or stupidities are the fault of the authors.

ACKNOWLEDGMENTS

Special thanks to Kathryn, Karen and Jason for their patience and support.

Lt. Col. Dennis Foley (U.S. Army—Ret.) for constantly saving our asses.

For their assistance, patience and encouragement: Russ Galen, Scott Meredith, Neil Nyren, Tom Stewart, and Lawrence McIntyre.

For invaluable technical advice and support: Lt. Col. Jim Channon (U.S. Army—Ret.), PFC Gaylord Courchesne (U.S. Army—Quit), Col. Rolf Schmitz and Sgt. Maj. Lucien Sias at U.S. Army Public Affairs, Mike Kerley, Brett Sadovnick at Robert Mandel, Danny and Ian at Martin B. Retting, Charles Cole, Bert Armus, Alex Kilgour, Bob Gaddes, Dave Klesura, the real Cliff Tarpy, U.S. Army Historical Center, and Lancer Militaria.

For making this book even vaguely possible: Arthur and Margaret Macrae, Owen Lock, Lee Dintsman, Al Godfrey, Jeff Freilich, Chris Trumbo, Nick Alexander, Frank Lupo, Stu Segall, Norman Spinrad, Jill Sherman, Phil Fehrle, Mark Pariser, Luz Tapia, Ken Kleinberg, Bob Urich, Jack Klugman, Jim Rush, Marshall Caskey, Genevieve Hinds, Stan Lee, Tony Pastour and the Gang at Marvel, Ron Taylor, Peter Thompson, the guys at Wolff's Liquors, Drew Cole, Philip Bunch, Mike Hodel, Chris and Liz Frye and the bookstores of Hay on Wye, and Dick Manetti and Clarence Moretti at the Far Western Steak House in Guadelupe, Ca.

Finally, we wish to thank three charitable institutions for their sponsorship: NBC, CBS, and ABC.

ABOUT THE AUTHORS

Chris Bunch and **Allan Cole** are free-lance writers who live in Los Angeles. They are former newsmen with nearly thirty years' experience between them. Friends since high school, they have been writing partners for ten years. One of them was in Vietnam. The other wasn't.